The Complete Works of Count Tolstoy, Volume 14

Leo Wiener, Leo Tolstoy

THE COMPLETE WORKS OF
COUNT TOLSTÓY
VOLUME XIV.

ЄVA∙Ѡ НОАНА∙ГЛА∙А҃

ⰎсконивЄслово
нсловоВЄѠтъ
Bа҃∙нЄѣѣ
словоѠсЄбЄ
нꙁконноу
Bа҃ нтѣмь ЄсаБꙑ
шаѕ҃нБеꙁнегонн
УьтоженеБꙑсть
кжеБꙑстьѣБꙑто
ꙁнжнвотъБѣ∙н

жнвотъБесвѣтъ
Улов҃коꙍ҃нсвѣ
тъБтьшесьвтн
тьса∙нтьманего
неоБатꙗ҃Бꙑсть
Ула҃вкъпосъланъ
отъБа҃∙ннакшоу
ноанꙋ҃тъпрнде
въсъвѣдетель
ствоꙁдасъвѣдѣтѣ

THE
FOUR GOSPELS
HARMONIZED

AND

TRANSLATED

VOLUME I.

BY

COUNT LEV N. TOLSTÓY

TRANSLATED FROM THE ORIGINAL RUSSIAN AND
EDITED BY

LEO WIENER

*Assistant Professor of Slavic Languages at
Harvard University*

COLONIAL PRESS CO.
NEW YORK AND BOSTON

CONTENTS

LIST OF ILLUSTRATIONS

---◆---

THE FOUR GOSPELS
HARMONIZED AND TRANSLATED

Volume I.

1881–1882

FROM THE AUTHOR

MY friends have proposed to print this Harmonization and Translation of the Gospel, composed by me ten years ago, and I have agreed to it, although the work is far from being finished, and there are many defects in it. I no longer feel the strength to correct and finish it, because that concentrated, ecstatic tension of my soul, which I constantly experienced during the whole time of this long work, can no longer be renewed.

But I think that even such as it is this work may be useful to some men, if to them will be communicated even a small part of that enlightenment which I experienced when I wrote it, and of that firm conviction of the truth of the path which has been revealed to me, and on which I travel with ever greater joy, the longer I live.

LEV TOLSTÓY.

Yásnaya Polyána, August 29, 1891.

PREFACE

HAVING been brought by reason without faith to despair and negation of life, I looked around at the living humanity and convinced myself that that despair was not the common lot of men, but that men have lived and still live by faith. I saw all about me men who had that faith and who deduced from it a meaning of life which gave them strength to live and die quietly and joyfully. I could not explain that meaning through reason. I tried to arrange my life like that of the believers; I tried to blend with them, and to do all that they did in life, even as to the external worship of God, thinking that in that way the meaning of life would be revealed to me. The more I cultivated the acquaintance of the masses, and lived as they did, and executed all the external rites of divine worship, the more I became conscious of two forces which had diametrically opposite effects upon me. On the one hand, there was revealed to me a meaning of life which more and more satisfied me, and which was not destroyed by death; on the other hand I saw that in that external confession of faith and worship there was much deception. I saw that the masses, because of their ignorance, lack of leisure, and unwillingness to think, failed to see the lie, but I could not help seeing it, and, having once beheld it, I could not shut my eyes to it, as educated people who were believers advised me to do. The longer I lived, fulfilling the obligations of a believer, the more did that lie startle me and demand an investigation of where that lie ended and truth began. I no longer doubted that in the Chris-

5

tian teaching was the truth of life. My internal discord
finally reached such a stage that I no longer could intentionally shut my eyes, as I had done before, and was
inevitably compelled to investigate the doctrine which I
wanted to make my own.

At first I asked for explanations from priests, monks,
bishops, metropolitans, learned theologians. There were
explained to me all the obscure passages, and these explanations were frequently unscrupulous, and more frequently contradictory: all of them referred to the holy
fathers, to catechisms, to theology. And I took the
theological books and began to study them, and that study
led me to the conviction that the faith which our hier-
archy confessed, and which it taught the masses, was not
only a lie, but also an immoral deception. In the Orthodox doctrine I found an exposition of the most unintelligible, blasphemous, and immoral propositions, which
were not only incompatible with reason, but were also
entirely incomprehensible and contrary to morality, and
not the slightest teaching about life, nor about its meaning. I could not help noticing that the exposition of
the theology was clearly directed, not to the explanation of the meaning of life and to the teaching about life,
but only to the confirmation of the most incomprehensible and useless of propositions, and to the refutal of all
those who did not recognize those propositions. That
exposition, which was directed to the refutal of other
teachings, involuntarily compelled me to turn my attention to those other creeds. These refuted creeds proved
to be of the same character as the Orthodox, which refuted them. Some are even more stupid, others are less
so, but all of them alike affirmed incomprehensible propositions which are useless for life, and in their name
deny each other and violate the union of men, — the
chief foundation of the Christian teaching.

I was brought to the conviction that there was no

church at all. All the differently believing Christians call themselves true Christians and deny each other. All these separate collections of Christians call themselves exclusively the church and assure us that their church is the true one, and that the others have departed from it, while it alone has remained intact. All the believers of whatsoever denomination entirely fail to see that the church is not true because their faith has remained such or such, but that they call it true because they were born in it or have chosen it, and that all the others say precisely the same about their own faith. Thus it is evident that there has never been one church, that the churches count by the thousand, and that they all deny each other and only assert that each one of them is the true and only church. They all say one and the same thing: Our church is the True, Holy, Catholic, Apostolic, Universal Church. Our Scripture is holy. Jesus Christ is the head of our church and the Holy Ghost guides it, and it alone comes by direct succession from Christ the God.

If we take a twig of a spreading bush, it will be quite correct to say that from twig to twig, from twig to branch, and from branch to root, every twig is derived from the trunk, but none of them is so exclusively. They are all alike. It will be absurd to say that every twig is the only true twig, but that is exactly what the churches say. Indeed, there are a thousand traditions, and each denies and curses all the others, and regards its own as the true one: Catholics, Lutherans, Protestants, Calvinists, Shakers, Mormons, Greek Orthodox, Old Believers, the Popish and the Popeless sects, Milkers, Mennonites, Baptists, Mutilators, Dukhobors, etc., etc., all of them equally assert about their own faith that it is the only true one, that in it alone is the Holy Ghost, that its head is Christ, and that all the others are in error. There are a thousand faiths, and each calmly considers itself to be holy; and all of them know that, and each man who confesses his faith as the only true faith knows that every other faith is just as much a stick with two ends, regarding itself as true and all the others as heresies. It will soon be eighteen hundred years that this self-deception has been going on.

In worldly matters men know how to discover the most cunning of traps and not to fall into them, but in this deception millions have been living for eighteen hundred years, shutting their eyes against it, both in our European world and in America, where everything is new. All, as though by plotting together, repeat one and the same stupid deception: they confess each his own truths of faith, regarding them as the only true ones, without noticing that all the others do precisely the same.

More than that. Long, very long ago freethinking men have cleverly and sharply ridiculed that human stupidity and showed to what extent it is stupid. They have clearly proved that that whole Christian teaching, with all its ramifications, has long ago outlived its day and that the time has come for a new faith, and some of them have even invented new faiths; but nobody listens to them or follows them, and all believe as of old, each in his own special Christian faith: the Catholics in their own, the Lutherans in their own, our Popish dissenters in their own, our Popeless dissenters in their own, the Mormons in their own, the Milkers in their own, and the Orthodox, those whom I wished to join, in their own. What does that mean? Why do men not give up that teaching? There is one answer to it, and in this all the freethinking people, who deny religion, and all men of other religions agree, and that is, that Christ's teaching is good, and so it is dear to people and they cannot live without it. But why have men, who believe in Christ's teaching, all divided into all kinds of creeds, and why do they keep dividing more and more, and denying and condemning each other, and why are they unable to agree on one confession of faith?

Again the answer is simple and obvious. The cause
of the division of the Christians is precisely this teaching about the church, a teaching which asserts that
Christ has established the one, true church, which, in its
essence, is holy and infallible, and can and must teach
others. If this conception about the church did not
exist, there could be no division among the Christians.
Each Christian church, that is, the creed, incontestably
rises from the teaching of Christ himself, but it is not the
only one to come from it : all the other doctrines come
just as much from it. They have all grown from one
seed, and what unites them, what is common among them
all, is that from which they have grown out, that is, the
seed. And so, in order properly to understand the teaching of Christ, we must not study it, as the only creed
does it, from the branches to the trunk ; nor must we, as
uselessly as science, the history of religion, does it, study
this teaching by starting from its foundation, by going
from the trunk to the branches. Neither the one nor the
other gives us the meaning of the teaching. The meaning is given only by the knowledge of the seed, of the
fruit, from which they have all come, and for which they
all live. They have all come from the life and works
of Christ, and all live only in order to reproduce the
works of Christ, that is, the works of good. And only
in these works will they all meet.

What brought me in particular to faith is the search
after a meaning of life, that is, the search after a path of
life, — how to live. When I saw the works of the life
of men who professed Christ's teaching, I clung to them.
Such men, who profess Christ's teaching by works, I meet
without distinction among the Orthodox, and among the
dissenters of all the sects, and among Catholics, and
among Lutherans, so that obviously the general meaning
of life, as given by Christ's teaching, is not received from
the creed, but from something else which is common to

all creeds. I have watched good people of more than one creed, and in all I saw the same meaning, which is based on the teaching of Christ. In all those different sects of Christians I saw a complete agreement in the conception of what is good, what evil, and of how one ought to live. All these men declared this conception of theirs through the teaching of Christ. The doctrines have multiplied, but their foundation is one; consequently, what is lying at the foundation of all faiths is the one truth. It is this truth that I am trying to find out now. The truth of faith is not to be found in the definite interpretations of Christ's revelation, those interpretations which have divided the Christians into a thousand sects, but is to be found in the very first revelation of Christ himself. And so I turned to the study of the gospels.

I know that according to the teaching of the church the meaning of the teaching is to be found not merely in the Gospel alone, but also in the whole Scripture and Tradition, which are guarded by the church. I assume that after everything said before, the sophistry, which consists in this, that the Scripture which serves as the foundation for my investigation is not subject to investigation, because the true and holy interpretation belongs exclusively to the church, that this sophistry cannot be repeated, the more so since every interpretation is destroyed by the contrary interpretation of another church, and because all holy churches reject one another. The prohibition to read and comprehend the Scripture is only a sign of those sins of interpretations, which the interpreting church is conscious of in its own case.

God has revealed the truth to men. I am a man, and so am not only entitled, but also compelled, to make use of it and stand face to face with it without any mediation. If God speaks in these books, he knows the weakness of my mind and will speak in such a way as not to lead me into deception. The argument of the church that the interpretation of the Scripture by individuals must not be permitted, lest those who interpret it be led astray and the interpretations multiply greatly, can have no meaning for me. It might have had a significance, if the interpretation of the church were intelligible, and if there were but one church and one interpretation; but now, since the interpretation of the church about the Son of God and about God, about God in three persons, about the virgin who bore a son without losing her virginity, and about the blood of God which is eaten in the form of bread, and so forth, can find no place in my sound mind, and since there are thousands of different interpretations, this argument, no matter how often repeated, can have no meaning whatever. Now, on the contrary, an interpretation is needed, and it has to be such that all could agree on it. But an agreement will only then be possible when the interpretation is rational. All of us agree on what is rational, in spite of our differences. If this revelation is the truth it cannot and must not fear the light of reason, if it wishes to be convincing, and is obliged to invoke this light. If the whole revelation will turn out to be absurd, so much the better, and God help it. God can do anything, but this: he cannot talk nonsense. And it would be stupid to write a revelation which cannot be understood.

I call revelation what is revealed to reason which has reached its highest limits, the contemplation of what is divine, that is, above the reason of the standing truth. I call revelation what gives an answer to the question, insoluble to reason, which has brought me to despair and suicide, the question as to what meaning life has. This answer must be intelligible and must not contradict the laws of reason, as would the assertion that an infinite quantity is even or odd. The answer must not contradict reason, for I will not believe a contradictory answer, and so it has to be not only intelligible and the contrary of wilful, but also inevitable to reason, as inevitable as is the assumption of infinity to him who can count.

The answer must reply to my question what meaning my life has. If it will not give this answer, it is useless for me. The answer must be such that, although its essence, in relation to God, may remain incomprehensible in itself, all the deductions of the consequences, derived from it, should correspond to all rational demands, and that the meaning ascribed to my life should solve all the questions of my life. The answer has to be not only rational and clear, but also true, that is, such as I can believe in with my whole soul, inevitably, as I believe in the existence of infinity.

Revelation cannot be based on faith, as the church understands it, as a trust in advance in what I shall be told. Faith is the consequence of the inevitableness and truth of the revelation, which fully satisfies reason.

Faith, according to the conception of the church, is an obligation which with threats and enticements is imposed on the soul of man.

According to my conception, faith is this, that the foundation on which every action of reason is reared is true. Faith is the knowledge of the revelation, without which it is impossible to live and think. Revelation is the knowledge of what man cannot attain by reason, but what is carried away by all humanity from what is hidden in the infinitude of the beginning of everything. Such, in my opinion, is to be the quality of the revelation which fosters faith, and such I seek in the Tradition about Christ, and so I turn to it with the sternest and most rational of demands.

I do not consider the Old Testament, because the question does not consist in this, what was the faith of the Jews, but what does the faith of Christ consist in, for there men find that meaning which makes it possible for them to live. The Jewish books may be interesting for us as an explanation of those forms in which Christianity has been expressed; but we cannot recognize any consecutiveness of faith from Adam to the present, for previous to Christ the faith of the Jews was local. The faith of the Jews is as foreign and as interesting to us as the faith of the Brahmins. But the faith of Christ is the one we live by. To study the faith of the Jews in order to understand the Christian religion is the same as studying a candle before lighting it in order to understand the significance of the light which proceeds from the burning candle. All that can be said is this, that the character and quality of the light may depend on the candle itself, just as the form of the expressions of the New Testament may depend on its relation to Judaism; but the light cannot be explained from the fact that it proceeds from this, rather than from that, candle. And so the blunder made by the church, in acknowledging the Old Testament as much a divinely inspired Scripture as the New Testament, is in the most obvious way reflected in this, that the church recognizes this in words, but not in fact, and so has fallen into contradictions from which it would never extricate itself, if sound reasoning were at all obligatory for it. And so I leave out the writings of the Old Testament, the revealed Scripture which, according to the expression of the church, is expressed in twenty-seven books. In reality, this tradition is not expressed in twenty-seven books, nor in five, nor in 138, just as the revelation of God cannot be expressed in a number of pages or letters.

To say that the revelation of God is expressed in 185 pages on paper, is the same as saying that the soul of such and such a man weighs fifteen hundredweights, or the light of the lamp measures seven bushels.

The revelation was expressed in the souls of men, and men transmitted it from one to another and wrote a few things down. From what has been noted down, it is

known that there existed more than one hundred gospels
and epistles, which were not accepted by the church.
The church selected twenty-seven books and called them
canonical. It is evident that some books expressed the
tradition better, some worse, and that there is no break
in the gradation. The church had to draw a line somewhere, in order to separate what it regarded as divinely
inspired. But it is evident that no such line could
sharply separate the full truth from the full lie. The
tradition is a shadow from the white to the black, or from
the truth to the lie, and no matter where the line may be
drawn, the shadows would inevitably be separated where
the black is. This is precisely what the church did,'
when it separated the tradition and called some canonical
and the rest apocryphal. This was done remarkably well.
The church chose so well that the newest investigations
have shown that nothing is to be added. From these investigations it became clear that what is best known and
is best has been included by the church in the canonical
books.

More than that: as though to correct the inevitable
error, which was due to the drawing of the line, the
church has accepted some of the traditions from the
apocryphal books.

Everything which could have been done was done
excellently. But in this separation the church erred in
this, that, wishing more emphatically to reject what was
not received by it, and to give more weight to what it did
receive, it put one general seal of infallibility on what it
accepted. Everything is from the Holy Ghost, and every
word is true. With this it ruined and harmed everything
which it received. By inevitably accepting in this strip
of the tradition the white, the bright, and the gray, that
is, the more or less pure teaching, and by imposing on
everything the seal of infallibility, it deprived itself of
the right to combine, exclude, elucidate what was ac-

cepted, which, indeed, was its duty to do, and which it
has never done. Everything is sacred: the miracles, the
Acts of the Apostles, Paul's advice concerning the wine,
and the delirium of the Apocalypse, and so forth, so that
after the eighteen hundred years of their existence these
books lie before us in the same coarse, clumsy, absurd,
contradictory form in which they have ever been. By
assuming that every word of the Scripture is sacred
truth, the church tried to combine, elucidate, solve the
contradictions, and understand, and did everything which
could be done in this sense, that is, gave the greatest
possible meaning to what is absurd. But the first mistake has been fatal.

By recognizing everything as sacred truth, it was
necessary to justify everything, shut the eyes, conceal,
make false deals, fall into contradictions, and, alas, frequently tell an untruth. While accepting everything in
words, the church has been compelled to reject certain
books in fact. Such are the whole of the Apocalypse
and parts of the Acts, which frequently not only fail
to be instructive, but are even offensive. It is evident
that Luke wrote about the miracles in order to strengthen
people in the faith, and no doubt there were some who
were confirmed in their faith by such reading, but now it
is not possible to find a more blasphemous book, one
which more undermines faith. Perhaps a candle is
needed where there is darkness. But if there is light,
there is no sense in illuminating it with a candle, for
it will be seen without it. Christ's miracles are the
candles which are brought into the light in order to
illuminate it. If there is light, it will be seen anyway; and if there is no light, then it is only the
candle which is shedding light.

And so it is impossible and unnecessary to read
the twenty-seven books in succession, recognizing each
word as holy, as the church reads them, for one would

only arrive at what the church has arrived at, namely, at the negation of self. In order to comprehend the contents of the Scripture which belongs to the Christian faith, it is necessary first to solve the question which of the twenty-seven books that are given out as constituting Holy Scripture are more or less essential and important, and then to begin with those that are most important. Such unquestionably are the four gospels. Everything which precedes them may, in a large measure, be only historical material for the comprehension of the Gospel, and everything subsequent only an elucidation of these books. And so it is not necessary, as the churches do, inevitably to harmonize all the books (we are convinced that that, more than anything else, has led the churches to preach unintelligible things), but in these four books, which, according to the teaching of the church, expound the most essential revelation, to find the most important bases of the teaching, without conforming with any teaching of the other books, not because I do not wish to do so, but because I am afraid of the errors of the other books, which offer such a bright and palpable example.

What I shall try to find in these books is this: (1) What is comprehensible to me, for no one can believe what is incomprehensible, and the knowledge of what is incomprehensible is equal to ignorance; (2) what answers my question as to what I am, what God is; and (3) what the one chief basis of every revelation is. And so I am not going to read the incomprehensible, obscure, half-intelligible passages as I want them to be, but so as to bring them most in agreement with entirely clear passages, with which they can be reduced to one basis. By reading in this manner, not once or twice, but many times, both the Scripture itself and what has been written about it, I came to the conclusion that the whole Christian tradition is contained in the four gospels; that the books of the Old Testament can serve only as an explanation of the form which Christ's teaching has chosen, and that they can only obscure, but in no way elucidate, the meaning of Christ's teaching; that the epistles of John and James are teachings which were called forth by the peculiar condition of the private elucidations, and that it is possible to find in them at times Christ's teaching expressed from a new side, and nothing more. Unfortunately, we frequently can find, especially in the epistles of Paul, an expression of the teaching which is liable to fill the reader with doubts, which obscure the teaching itself. But the Acts of the Apostles, like many of the epistles of Paul, not only have nothing in common with the Gospel and with the epistles of John, Peter, and James, but frequently contradict them. The Revelation absolutely reveals nothing. But the main thing is that, no matter at what different times they were written, the Gospel forms the exposition of the whole teaching, and everything else is only an interpretation of it.

I read the Gospel in Greek, in the language in which we possess it, and I translated as the sense and the dictionaries demanded, now and then departing from the translations which exist in the modern languages and which were made when the church had comprehended and defined the meaning of the tradition in its own way. Besides translating, I have inevitably been led to the necessity of harmonizing the four gospels, since they all expound, though variously, the same incidents and the same teaching. The new proposition of exegetics, that the Gospel of John, being exclusively theological, should be discussed separately, had no meaning for me, since my aim is not historical, nor philosophical, nor theological criticism, but the finding of the meaning of the teaching. The meaning of the teaching is expressed in the four gospels, and so, if all four are the exposition of one and the same revelation of truth, then one must confirm and elucidate the rest. And so I considered them by uniting them, without omitting the Gospel of John.

There have been many attempts made at combining the gospels, but all those which I know, Arnolde de Vence, Farrar, Reuss, Grechulévich, harmonize them on a historical basis, and are all equally unsuccessful. Not one of them is better than another in the historical sense, and all are equally satisfactory in the sense of the teaching. I leave the historical meaning entirely alone, and harmonize only in the sense of the teaching. The harmonization of the gospels on this basis has this advantage, that the true teaching represents, as it were, a circle, of which all the parts determine their mutual significance, and for the study of which it is immaterial from what place we begin. In studying in this manner the gospels, in which the historical events of Christ's life are so closely connected with the teaching, the historical consecutiveness appeared quite immaterial to me, and for the historical consecutiveness it made no difference to me which harmonization of the gospels I took as my basis. I selected two of the latest harmonizations, by authors who made use of the labours of all their predecessors, Grechulévich and Reuss, but since Reuss has separated John from the synoptics, Grechulévich's harmonization has been of greater use to me, and I took it for the basis of my work, collating it with Reuss and departing from both whenever the sense demanded it.

THE FOUR GOSPELS

HARMONIZED AND TRANSLATED

———

INTRODUCTION

ΕΥΑΓΓΕΛΙΟΝ ΚΑΤΑ ΜΑΤΘΑΙΟΝ, ΚΑΤΑ ΜΑΡΚΟΝ, ΚΑΤΑ ΛΟΥΚΑΝ, ΚΑΤΑ ΙΩΑΝΝΗΝ.	EVANGEL FROM MATTHEW, FROM MARK, FROM LUKE, FROM JOHN.	THE ANNOUNCE-MENT OF GOOD ACCORDING TO MATTHEW, MARK LUKE, JOHN.
1. Ἀρχὴ τοῦ εὐαγγελίου Ἰησοῦ Χριστοῦ υἱοῦ τοῦ Θεοῦ.	*Mark i.* 1. The beginning of the gospel of Jesus Christ, the Son of God.	1. The beginning of the announcement of good of Jesus Christ, the son of God.

(*a*) The word *Evangel* is generally not translated. Under this word are understood the books of the New Testament about Jesus Christ, and no other meaning is ascribed to it. However, this word has a definite meaning, which is connected with the contents of the books.

The literal translation of the word εὐαγγέλιον is in Russian *blagovyest'* (glad tidings). That translation is not correct: (1) because *blagovyest'* has in Russian a different meaning; (2) because it does not render the meaning of the two component parts εὖ and ἀγγέλιον. Εὖ means *good, well, true;* ἀγγέλιον means not so much *information given, news,* as the *very action of informing, imparting news,* and therefore the word is more exactly translated by the expression *announcement.* Consequently the compound word εὐαγγέλιον ought to be translated by *an-*

nouncement of good, or, more intelligibly in Russian, by *announcement about what is good*.

(*b*) The words κατὰ Ματθαῖον, and so forth, indicate that the announcement of good was made from stories, or notes, or indications, and, in general, from the information furnished about this announcement by Matthew, Mark, Luke, John, and, as it is not known in what manner the evangelists imparted their information, and as it is not mentioned that the evangelists wrote it themselves, the preposition κατά must be translated by *according to*, that is, that the information about the announcement, in whatever manner it may have been transmitted, was given by Matthew, Mark, Luke, John.

(*c*) The word Χριστός means *the anointed*.

The meaning of this word is connected with the traditions of the Jews. For the meaning of the contents of the announcement of good, this word offers nothing and may be indifferently rendered by *anointed* or *Christ*. I prefer the word *Christ*, as *anointed* has received a different meaning in Russian.

(*d*) The expression *son of God* is assumed by the church to be the exclusive appellation of Jesus Christ, but according to the gospel it has not this exclusive meaning: it refers equally to all men. This meaning is clearly expressed in many passages of the gospel.

Speaking to the people at large, Jesus Christ says:

Matt. v. 16. Let your light so shine before men, that they may see your good works, and glorify *your Father* which is in heaven.

In another place:

Matt. v. 45. That ye may be the children of *your Father* which is in heaven: for he maketh his sun to rise on the evil and on the good, and sendeth rain on the just and on the unjust.

Luke vi. 36. Be ye therefore merciful, as *your Father* also is merciful.

Matt. vi. 1. Take heed that ye do not your alms before men, to be seen of them : otherwise ye have no reward of *your Father* which is in heaven.

Matt. vi. 4. That thine alms may be in secret: and *thy Father* which seeth in secret, himself shall reward thee openly.

Matt. v. 48. Be ye therefore perfect, even as *your Father* which is in heaven is perfect.

Matt. vi. 6. But thou, when thou prayest, enter into thy closet, and when thou hast shut thy door, pray to *thy Father* which is in secret ; and *thy Father* which seeth in secret shall reward thee openly.

Matt. vi. 8. Be not ye therefore like unto them: for *your Father* knoweth what things ye have need of before ye ask him.

Matt. vi. 14. For if ye forgive men their trespasses, *your heavenly Father* will also forgive you.

And there are many other passages in the gospels where all men are called sons of God. More than that : In the Gospel of St. Luke there is a passage in which it says that by the word *son of God* is to be understood every man, and also that Jesus is called the son of God not in any exclusive sense, but because, like all men, he came from God and, therefore, was a son of God.

Setting forth the genealogy of Jesus, Luke, ascending from his mother to his grandfather, great-grandfather, and farther back, says : Which was the son of Enos, which was the son of Seth, which was the son of Adam, which was the son of God (Luke iii. 38).

Thus the words, Of Jesus Christ, the son of God, indicate the person by whom the announcement was made. This person is called Jesus, the name given him by men, and, besides, Christ, that is, God's chosen one, and, besides, the son of God.

The title defines the contents of the book. It says that in the book the good is announced to men. It is necessary to remember the meaning of this title in order to be able to pick out in the book the more essential from the less important passages ; since the contents of the book are the announcement of good to men, everything which defines this good to men is most essential, and everything which has not this aim of announcing the good is less essential.

Thus the full title will be:

The announcement of the true good, made by Jesus Christ, the son of God.

THE AIM OF THE BOOK

31. Ταῦτα δὲ γέγραπται, ἵνα πιστεύσητε ὅτι ὁ Ἰησοῦς ἐστιν ὁ Χριστὸς ὁ υἱὸς τοῦ Θεοῦ, καὶ ἵνα πιστεύοντες ζωὴν ἔχητε ἐν τῷ ὀνόματι αὐτοῦ.	*John xx.* 31. But these are written, that ye might believe that Jesus is the Christ, the Son of God; and that believing ye might have life in his name.[b]	31. This is written that men might believe that Jesus Christ is the son of God, and that believing they might receive life through what he has been.

(*a*) In many texts these words are differently placed, not ὅτι ὁ Ἰησοῦς ἐστιν ὁ Χριστὸς ὁ υἱὸς, but ὅτι ὁ Ἰησοῦς ὁ Χριστός ἐστιν ὁ υἱός.

I accept the second order, regarding it as clearer.

(*b*) The words ἐν τῷ ὀνόματι αὐτοῦ literally translated by *in his name* represent one of those expressions to which, through a verbal rendering, we ascribe an arbitrary and most frequently an indistinct meaning.

The Hebrew word which corresponds to the word ὄνομα designates not the name, but the person himself, that which he really is, and therefore the words *might have life in his name* must be understood as meaning that life is given by the very essence of that which is the *son of God*.

1. Ἐπειδήπερ πολλοὶ ἐπεχείρησαν ἀνατάξασθαι διήγησιν περὶ τῶν πεπληροφορημένων ἐν ἡμῖν πραγμάτων,	*Luke i.* 1. Forasmuch as many have taken in hand to set forth in order a declaration of those things which are most surely believed among us,	1. Since many have already begun to tell connectedly of the things which have happened among us,
2. Καθὼς παρέδοσαν ἡμῖν οἱ ἀπ᾽ ἀρχῆς αὐτόπται καὶ ὑπηρέται γενόμενοι τοῦ λόγου,	2. Even as they delivered them unto us, which from the beginning were eyewitnesses, and ministers of the word;[a]	2. As the eyewitnesses and executors of the teaching have transmitted to us;

| 3. Ἔδοξε κἀμοί, παρη-κολουθηκότι ἄνωθεν πᾶσιν ἀκριβῶς, καθεξῆς σοι γράψαι, κράτιστε Θεόφιλε, 4. Ἵνα ἐπιγνῷς περὶ ὧν κατηχήθης λόγων τὴν ἀσφάλειαν. | 3. It seemed good to me also, having had perfect understanding of all things from the very first, to write unto thee in order, most excellent Theophilus,[b] 4. That thou mightest know the certainty of that teaching, wherein thou hast been instructed. | 3. I, too, decided, having learned everything correctly from the very first, to write to you, in order, Mr. Theophilus, 4. That you might find out the real truth of those injunctions which you have been taught. |

(a) The words αὐτόπται καὶ ὑπηρέται τοῦ λόγου are incorrectly translated: in Slavic *witnesses or servants of the word*, and in German *Diener des Wortes*. Λόγος in this expression cannot mean *word*; one cannot be a witness of a word. The translation of the Vulgate *viderunt et ministri sermonis* is more correct. Here the word λόγος cannot signify anything else but the sermon of the teaching or wisdom.

(b) Luke's introduction is a private address to Theophilus, expository of the gospel, and does not touch the teaching.

In this preface it says that through faith in the fact that Jesus Christ was the son of God men will have life. Just as by the words *the announcement of good* is to be understood a certain special, more definite, more real good than that which men consider good, so by the word *life*, which men will have, apparently is meant a different life from what men regard as life. This other life is obtained through believing that there is a son of God, and it is pointed out that with this filial relation to God is connected the announcement of good itself. The verses, which say that these things had been written about before, and which tell what it is that has caused Luke to write out his exposition, do not touch the teaching and are, therefore, left out in my exposition, or ought to be printed in a smaller type, as an appendix.

Thus the meaning of Luke's verses is as follows:

The announcement of good is written in order that all men, having convinced themselves that Jesus Christ is the son of God, might receive life through believing that there is a son of God.

THE COMPREHENSION

1. 'Εν ἀρχῇ ἦν ὁ λόγος.	*John i.* 1. In the beginning was the Word.	1. The comprehension of life became the beginning of all.

In order to understand the necessity of elucidating the first verse and the following verses of the Introduction, it is necessary to have a clear account of the meaning of the existing translations.

The church translation of the first verse has no meaning whatever. The translation is: *In the beginning was the Word.* This is not a translation of a thought, but of words. No sense results from it, and each separate word is invested with a mystic and arbitrary gloss. In order to discover the meaning of these expressions, it is necessary to discard the church gloss, and to analyze each word.

(*a*) The preposition ἐν signifies sojourn in something; with a verb of motion it signifies transposition and sojourn in something.

(*b*) ἀρχή signifies not only temporal and fundamental beginning, but also beginning as the foundation of everything, and so I translate it by *beginning of all.*

(*c*) ἦν from the verb εἰμί signifies, in addition to existence, also change, and frequently may and must be translated by the words *become, turn.*

(*d*) λόγος has eleven chief meanings: (1) word, (2) speech, (3) conversation, (4) report, (5) eloquence, (6) reason, as distinguishing man from beast, (7) reflection, opinion, precept (it is the same which is rendered by *sermo* in the Vulgate), (8) cause, foundation of thought, (9) account, (10) esteem, (11) relation (λόγος ἐγένετο πρός) *to be in relation with some one.* Ask a pupil, who knows Greek, but who is not acquainted with the church teaching, to translate the first verse from John, and he will, to get any sensible translation of this passage, from the context immediately reject seven impossible meanings of λόγος from this sentence, namely, the meanings of word, speech, conversation, report, eloquence, account, and esteem, and will be choosing between the meanings of reason, cause, reflection, and correlation. All these four meanings, given to the word λόγος in translations, fit the sense of the clause, but each of them, taken separately, fits it only partially.

Reason is a man's capacity to think.

Reflection is only the action of this capacity.

Correlation is that which furnishes the material to the capacity to think.

Cause is one of the forms of thinking.

Each meaning, taken separately, defines one side of the activity of thought. Λόγος apparently has here a very broad and fundamental meaning. In order to render this word in Russian, I find most appropriate the word *comprehension* (*razumyenie*), because this word combines all the four possible meanings of λόγος.

Comprehension is not only reason, but also the action of reason leading to something; not only cause, but also the *seeking* of it; not only reflection, but also *reflection elucidating the cause;* and not only relation, but also *reasonable activity in relation to cause.* This translation is completely confirmed by the introduction to the teaching of the same writer, namely, in the first epistle of John. Thus, in the first verse the same expression is used: δ ἦν ἀπ' ἀρχῆς, δ ἀκηκόαμεν, and so forth, περὶ τοῦ λόγου τῆς ζωῆς. It is evident that it can be translated only by the words *comprehension of life.* By the addition of the word τῆς ζωῆς, which John makes in the epistle, the meaning becomes absolutely clear and defined — *comprehension of life.* Therefore, I translate the word λόγος by comprehension of life, because I find such translation clearer and more precise, though I do not refute any other translation. We may equally put down the word *reason*, and *all-wisdom*, and even the word *word*, by ascribing a broader meaning to it; we may even leave the word λόγος untranslated,— the meaning will always be one and the same.

Consequently I literally translate the first verse thus: In the beginning of all there grew to be the comprehension of life. This translation gives a clear sense, if the title is kept in view, that is, the announcement of good by Jesus Christ. In the beginning of all, or, *the* beginning of all grew to be the comprehension of life according to the announcement of Jesus Christ.

1. Καὶ ὁ λόγος ἦν πρὸς τὸν θεόν.	John i. 1. And the Word was God.[a]	1. And the comprehension of life stood for God.

(*a*) The second part of the verse is still more hopelessly incomprehensible in the church translation. In order to remove this perplexity, it is necessary first of all to direct our attention to the word *God*. The word *God* serves, as it were, as a definition of what λόγος is. Therefore we must above all else know what the author understands by the word God. There is an indication of it in the eighteenth verse of the same chapter, and in the first epistle of John (iv. 12) it says: No man hath seen God at any time. Therefore, in order that the reader may not unite with the word *God* a meaning which the author himself did not connect, it is necessary to remember how the author understood the word. Only through the indication that the word *God* must not and cannot be understood as something comprehensible and definite, does the meaning of the first verses become comprehensible.

(*b*) The preposition πρός with the accusative has eleven meanings: (1) to; (2) in the direction of; (3) the majority of meanings of the same preposition with the dative;

there are three such meanings: (*a*) near, (*β*) in, and, on, and (*γ*) besides, in addition to; (4) for, in view of; (5) in reference to; (6) against; (7) on an equality with, for somebody, for something; (8) in respect to something; (9) because of; (10) during the time of, and (11) almost, near something. The simplest and directest meaning is *to*.

(*c*) The words πρὸς τὸν θεόν in the literal translation, as given in the Slavic, are *was to God*. But the words *was to God* have no meaning. The translation of πρὸς τὸν θεόν by *with God, erat apud Deum, bei Gott*, has also no meaning, and has the further disadvantage that πρός with the accusative never means *apud*, and I have purposely written out all the meanings of πρός with the accusative in order that it may be clear to all that πρός with the accusative can never mean *with*. *Apud* means *before, near*, and nothing else. The only philological excuse for translating it so is that πρός with the accusative sometimes (very rarely) has the same meaning as with the dative, namely *near*, and *apud* also means *near*. Out of a thousand cases of πρός with the accusative there will, probably, be one when it has the meaning of *near;* admitting even that πρός means in this case *apud*, it will only give us that *the word was near God*, and not *with God*. For the church translation that was the only issue from a difficulty.

The church translation *with God* has received a mystic interpretation, and the church was satisfied with it, forgetting that this is not a translation, but an arbitrary interpretation. But since I am looking for sense in the book which I am reading, and do not allow myself to give arbitrary meanings to words, I was compelled either to reject these words as incomprehensible, or to find a meaning for them which would correspond to the laws of the language and of common sense. In order to ascribe some sense to this sentence, it is possible, by taking λόγος in the sense of *word* or *wisdom*, to give to the preposition πρός the meaning which it has in Greek, namely, *relative, in relation to something,* so that πρός may in this place be translated merely by the genitive, without any preposition, namely : *And the comprehension was,* or, *there grew to be a comprehension of God,* and then the translation will be like this : *In the beginning was the comprehension. And the comprehension was the comprehension of God.* But in this case the meaning of the preposition πρός will be stretched. It is also possible to give to the word λόγος the meaning of *comprehension, the activity of reason always directed toward something,* and then the preposition πρός may be translated in its direct and first meaning *to,* having in mind that the comprehension is directed to something, and that the translation will be : *The comprehension was,* or, *grew to be directed to God ;* but in that case the superfluous word *directed* must be added, or the translation will not be very clear. Then again, we may give to πρός the meaning of *equality, exchange of one thing for another.* This meaning is precisely covered by the popular *against (suprotiv).* Oxen will not work *against* horses. He respects him *against* his father, and so forth, and then the third translation will be : *Comprehension grew to be the beginning of everything. And the comprehension grew to be against God* (that is, the *comprehension took the place of God*).

The first two translations have almost the same meaning, but they are neither of them precise. In the first, the meaning of the words πρὸς τὸν θεόν (twice repeated and therefore obviously necessary for the expression of the thought) is entirely omitted ; in the second, it is necessary to add a new word *directed,* in order to give any meaning to this preposition.

The third translation expresses the same thought, and has this advantage : it renders πρός by a preposition, and adds nothing more.

In order to decide among these three translations, it is necessary to analyze all four sentences, which are connected with each other, where the preposition πρός is used.

The four sentences are these:

(1) In the beginning was the λόγος, or, the λόγος grew to be the beginning; (2) the λόγος was to God, or, the λόγος grew to be πρὸς τὸν θεόν; (3) the λόγος was, or, grew to be, God, and (4) in the beginning, or, as the beginning, the λόγος was, or grew to be, πρὸς τὸν θεόν.

In all three translations one part of the thought is equally clear, and the other part equally obscure. What is clear is the first sentence: The comprehension of God was, or grew to be, in the beginning, or, as the beginning, and the third: The comprehension was, or grew to be, God.

In the meaning of the first sentence, that in the beginning, or, as the beginning, grew to be comprehension, and of the third, that the comprehension was, or, grew to be, God, all three translations and the church translation agree.

In the beginning was the comprehension, or, comprehension grew to be the beginning, and, it was, or, grew to be, God, — that is the main idea. And one results from the other.

The second sentence explains this idea; it explains in what manner the comprehension grew to be, or, was, God, and the fourth sentence only repeats the first and the second. It says that it became God in that it was, or grew to be, πρὸς τὸν θεόν. Three meanings of πρός fit in here. The comprehension was, or, grew to be, the comprehension of God. It was, or, grew to be, turned to God, and it was, or, grew to be, *against*, in the place of, God.

The first two translations reduce themselves to one, namely, that the comprehension is that which expressed God. The comprehension was the comprehension of God means: the comprehension expressed God. The comprehension was turned to God, and grew to be God, also means: united with God, expressed God. The third translation expresses the same, namely: the comprehension grew to be *against*, that is, in the place of, God, expressed God. This translation includes the meaning of the other two. It is sufficient to put in the place of the awkward *against*, the preposition *for*, which expresses exchange, and we get the broadest and fullest, and literally most exact translation, which, for the Russian, preserves even the case of the original: *And the comprehension stood for God.*

	John 1.	
1. Καὶ Θεὸς ἦν ὁ λόγος.	1. And the word was God.	1. And the comprehension of life became God.
2. Οὗτος ἦν ἐν ἀρχῇ πρὸς τὸν Θεόν.	2. The same was in the beginning with God.	2. It grew to be the beginning of everything for God.

(*a*) In the first verse I transpose the words, and translate: *The comprehension became God.* I place the word *comprehension* before the word *God*, because, according to the spirit of the Russian language, the subject must precede the predicate, and λόγος is the subject, because it has the article, whereas the predicate is without the article.

(*b*) The verb εἰμί, in addition to meaning *to be, live, exist,* has also the meaning of *to become, grow, originate.* If it says that in the beginning was the *comprehension*, or *word*, and that the *word was to God*, or *with God*, or *for God*, it is impossible to go on and say that *it was God.* If it was God, it could stand in no relation to God. And so it is necessary in this place to translate ἦν by *became, grew to be*, and not by *it was.* The two verses translated accordingly receive a definite meaning.

The conception about God is assumed as known, and mention is made of the source from which this conception came. It says: According to the announcement of

Jesus Christ the beginning of everything was the comprehension of life. And the comprehension of life, according to Christ's teaching, took the place of the conception of God, or blended with it.

If it were necessary to get a confirmation of such an understanding of these two verses, the eighteenth verse, which includes the whole discussion and directly expresses the idea that no one has ever known God, but that the son has manifested him in the λόγος, and the whole discussion, which tells us the same, and the following verses, which tell us that by the λόγος everything is born, and without it nothing is born, and the whole subsequent teaching, which develops the same idea, everything confirms the same. The meaning of these verses is this : According to the announcement of good by Jesus Christ the comprehension of life became the foundation and beginning of everything. The comprehension of life stood in the place of God, — the comprehension of life became God.

It is this which according to the announcement of Jesus Christ became the foundation and beginning of . everything in the place of God.

| 3. Πάντα δι' αὐτοῦ ἐγένετο, καὶ χωρὶς αὐτοῦ ἐγένετο οὐδὲ ἕν, ὃ γέγονεν. | John i. 3. All things were made by him;⁵ and without⁶ him⁴ was not any thing made that⁶ was made.⁵ | 3. Everything was born through the comprehension, and without the comprehension is not anything born of that which is alive and lives. |

(a) The words δι' αὐτοῦ mean *by means of it, through it*, and cannot be rendered (in Russian) by the ablative case alone. Δι' αὐτοῦ does not mean ˙ *by him*, but *by its aid.* I translate *through the comprehension*, substituting the word which is meant by the pronoun.

(b) The word ἐγένετο means *was born*, in its first straight simple meaning. According to all the dictionaries this word has only five chief meanings : (1) *to be born ;* (2) *to become ;* (3) *to be, exist* (the first three meanings are all applicable in this sentence) ; (4) *to be frequently, to happen frequently ;* (5) *to be occupied with something* (the last two meanings are inapplicable). There are no other meanings. The meaning *facta sunt* (according to the Vulgate), *gemacht* (in Luther), cannot be applied to this verb, but in the Vulgate and in Luther these words are translated by *omnia per ipsum facta sunt, Dinge sind durch dasselbe gemacht.* In Church-Slavic it is translated by *byst'*, but from the explanations which are attached to this word, namely, that everything was created by him, this word *byst'* is taken in precisely the same sense as that in which it is translated in the Vulgate and by Luther; that is, as *made.* I translate the word in its first and simplest meaning, which includes the meanings of *become* and *be,* and so it is not for me to justify the departure from the customary translations, but for the previous translators to justify their own departures from the original. There can be no justification of the arbitrary translation of the word ἐγένετο by *facta sunt* and *gemacht.* The explanation why the word is so incorrectly translated may be found in the church interpretation of the whole passage. According to the church interpretation the λόγος is the second person of the Holy Trinity, and to it is ascribed the creation of the world. In translating into Latin *fio* was used, which does not correspond to γίγνομαι, but only to one of its meanings, *to become.* In Luther's translation the verb *gemacht* is used, though it answers but one of the meanings of *fio* in the active voice, and the word has entirely departed from its meaning.

Here is the interpretation of the church (Archimandrite Mikhaíl) :

Interpretation of St. John i 3. *All things were made by him :* all things received their existence, all things were created by him (Gen. i.; Heb. i. 2 ; Col. i. 16).

All things: St. Paul, in evolving the same idea about the creation of all things by the Word, explains *all things* in the following manner: All things that are in heaven, and that are in earth, visible and invisible, whether they be thrones, or dominions, or principalities, or powers: all things were created by him and for him (Col. i. 16). Consequently, in the sphere of all things created, whether in heaven, or in earth, whether in the spiritual, or in the material world, there is not a being, nor a thing, which has not received its existence through him. Consequently, the Word is the Creator of the world; consequently, it is God. The expression *by him* does not mean that that Word is a dependent Creator of the world, and not the prime moving cause of the creation of the world, or that God created the world by means of the Word, as an artist creates by means of a tool; such a turn of speech is used in Scripture whenever it speaks of the first cause, acting of its own force and independently (cf. 1 Cor. i. 9; xii. 8, 13; Chrys., and Theophilac.). Here it is so expressed in order to prevent one from imagining that the Son was not born (Chrys.).

By such a turn of speech our attention is directed to that relation of the Word to the Father, by which God the Father, who is invisible and abides in the inaccessible world, appears and always acts in his Son, who, therefore, is the image of the invisible God (Heb. i. 3). The Son never acts as though he fell away or separated from the Father, so that the creative activity of the Son is at the same time the activity of the Father, and the will of the Father is at the same time the will of the Son (John v. 19, 20).

Without him was not anything made that was made. Repetition, explanation, and intensification of the preceding expression and of the creative activity of the Word. In the created world everything is made by him, not excepting anything, but only in the created world (that was made). That no one might think that, if everything was made by him, so was also the Holy Ghost, the evangelist found it necessary to add *that was made,* that is, *that was created,* but the Holy Ghost is not a created being (cf. Chrys. and Theophilac.). "I shall not be frightened by what it says that all things received their being through the Son, as though in the words *all things* is also included the Holy Ghost; for it does not simply say all things, but all things that were made. The Father is not by the Son, nor is all that by the Son, which had no beginning of existence" (Greg. the Div. iii. 113).

(*c*) The simplest and most common meaning of the word χωρίς is *outside of*, and I leave it so.

(*d*) Instead of the pronoun, I for clearness' sake again put the word for which it stands.

(*e*) To δ I, in accordance with the demands of the Russian language, add *of that*. Any one who knows the Greek and the Russian languages knows that the relative pronoun is not translated literally into Russian, but always demands the addition of the word *that*.

(*f*) γέγονεν is a perfect, and so it is incorrectly translated by *byst'*; the perfect in Greek denotes what was and is, and so it has to be translated by *was born* and *lives*.

4. Ἐν αὐτῷ ζωὴ ἦν, καὶ ἡ ζωὴ ἦν τὸ φῶς τῶν ἀνθρώπων·	*John* 1.4. In him was life; and the life was the light of men.	4. In it there grew to be life, the same as, the light of men grew to be life.
5. Καὶ τὸ φῶς ἐν τῇ σκοτίᾳ φαίνει, καὶ ἡ σκοτία αὐτὸ οὐ κατέλαβεν.	5. And the light shineth in darkness; and the darkness comprehended it not.	5. Just as the light shines in the darkness, and the darkness does not swallow it.

(*a*) ἐν besides meaning *in* means also *in one's power*: ἐν σοί, ἐν ἐκγόνῳ, and so forth. It is used here in that sense. *In it is life* means *in it is the power over life, in it is the possibility of life.*

(*b*) From the construction of a sentence like καὶ ἡ ζωὴ ἦν τὸ φῶς and from the omission, in many texts, of the article before φῶς, *light* is the predicate.

John xii. 36. While ye have light, believe in the light, that ye may be the children of light.

(*c*) φῶς *light* from all the contexts signifies the true comprehension of life.

(*d*) καταλαμβάνω, to grasp, take, meet, understand, take in, accept, hold back, swallow. I translate it in the sense of *to swallow, put out, extinguish.*

Before that it said that the comprehension of life grew to be the beginning of everything. Now it says that only the comprehension gives life, and that without the comprehension there can be no life. Life consists only in its comprehension. The fourth verse confirms that, and says: Life is in the power of the comprehension. Only the comprehension gives the possibility of life. The true life is the one which is illuminated by the light of the comprehension. The light of men is the true life; light gives light, and there is no darkness in it. Even thus the comprehension gives life, in which there is no death.

Everything which became truly alive, is so only through the comprehension. The true life, according to the announcement of Jesus Christ, grew to be such only in the comprehension. Or, to say it differently: The light, the comprehension of men, became the true life for men, even as the light is that which truly exists, while the darkness is only the absence of light. And the darkness cannot destroy the light.

6. Ἐγένετο ἄνθρωπος ἀπεσταλμένος παρὰ Θεοῦ, ὄνομα αὐτῷ Ἰωάννης.	John i. 6. There was a man sent from God, whose name was John.	6. A man was sent from God, whose name was John.
7. Οὗτος ἦλθεν εἰς μαρτυρίαν, ἵνα μαρτυρήσῃ περὶ τοῦ φωτὸς, ἵνα πάντες πιστεύσωσι δι' αὐτοῦ.	7. The same came for a witness,[a] to bear witness of the Light, that all men through him might believe.	7. He came for the showing, to show the light of the comprehension, that all men might believe in the light of the comprehension.
8. Οὐκ ἦν ἐκεῖνος τὸ φῶς, ἀλλ' ἵνα μαρτυρήσῃ περὶ τοῦ φωτός.	8. He was not that Light, but was sent to bear witness of that Light.[b]	8. He himself was not the light, but came only to show the light of comprehension.

(a) μαρτυρία testimony, proof, showing.

(b) These verses sharply interrupt the train of thought and even the very discussion about the meaning of the light, by introducing details about John the Baptist. These verses by their contents do not confirm, nor contradict, the fundamental thought, and so do not enter into the exposition, but form only an addition.

9. Ἦν τὸ φῶς τὸ ἀληθινὸν, ὃ φωτίζει πάντα ἄνθρωπον ἐρχόμενον εἰς τὸν κόσμον.	John i. 9. That was the true[b] Light, which lighteth every man that cometh into the world.	9. It became the true light, such as lights up every man who comes into the world.

10. Ἐν τῷ κόσμῳ ἦν, καὶ ὁ κόσμος δι᾿ αὐτοῦ ἐγένετο, καὶ ὁ κόσμος αὐτὸν οὐκ ἔγνω.

11. Εἰς τὰ ἴδια ἦλθε, καὶ οἱ ἴδιοι αὐτὸν οὐ παρέλαβον.

12. Ὅσοι δὲ ἔλαβον αὐτὸν, ἔδωκεν αὐτοῖς ἐξουσίαν τέκνα Θεοῦ γενέσθαι, τοῖς πιστεύουσιν εἰς τὸ ὄνομα αὐτοῦ·

18. Οἳ οὐκ ἐξ αἱμάτων, οὐδὲ ἐκ θελήματος σαρκὸς, οὐδὲ ἐκ θελήματος ἀνδρὸς, ἀλλ᾿ ἐκ Θεοῦ ἐγεννήθησαν.

10. He was in the world, and the world was made by* him, and the world knew him not.

11. He came unto his own,ᵈ and his own received him not.ᵉ

12. But as many as receivedᶠ him, to them gave he powerᵍ to comeʰ the sons of God, even to them that believe on hisⁱ name.

13. Whichʲ were born,ᵏ not of blood, nor of the will of the flesh, nor of the will of man, but of God.

10. It appeared in the world, and the world was born through it, and the world did not know it.

11. It appeared in separate people, and the separate people did not receive it within them.

12. But to all those who understood it, it gave the possibility of becoming sons of God, through faith in its meaning;

13 They were generated not from blood, nor from the lust of flesh, nor from the lust of man, but from God.

(*a*) ἦν signifies, as in former passages, not only *was*, but also *became*.

(*b*) ἀληθινός does not mean *truthful*, but *real*.

(*c*) διά must again be translated by *through*, and has the same significance as before. ἐγένετο means *was born*.

(*d*) τὰ ἴδια means *separate, special*, and is obviously said in contradistinction to the world at large. The light was in the whole world and in separate men, and so to the word ἴδιος *separate*, which expresses that which in scientific language is expressed by the word *individual*, I add the word *people*.

(*e*) παραλαμβάνειν means *to receive within oneself*.

(*f*) λαμβάνειν *to receive* and more commonly *to understand*.

(*g*) ἐξουσία means *the permission, liberty, right, possibility to do something*. On the other hand, this word expresses what is expressed by the preposition ἐν in ἐν αὐτῷ ζωὴ ἦν. In it was the power to give life, and therefore, having been born in it, they received the possibility.

(*h*) Though γενέσθαι means also *to be born*, it can be translated here as *to be* or *to become*.

(*i*) ὄνομα αὐτοῦ occurs for the second time, and both times it is used after the word to *believe*. To believe in ὄνομα αὐτοῦ. In Russian ὄνομα means *name*, in Hebrew *the person itself*. To express both ideas, it is necessary to say: *in its essence, in its significance, in its meaning*, and that is the way I translate it.

(*j*) οἵ, which refers to τοῖς, has to be translated as *since they*.

(*k*) γεννάω means *to germinate* and then *to bear*.

It said before that the life of the world is like the light in the darkness. The light shines in the darkness, and the darkness does not detain it. Life lives in the world, but the world does not retain the life. Now, continuing the discussion about the comprehension, it says that it is that light which illuminates every living man, that real light of life which is known to every man, so that the comprehension is distributed throughout the world, which lives by it, but the whole world does not know it, does not know that in the comprehension alone is the power, foundation, strength of life. The comprehension was in separate people, and the separate people did not accept it within them, did not make it their own; they did not understand that life was only in it, or, the comprehension was in its own production, in the son, but the son did not recognize his Father.

Neither all humanity, nor the majority of men taken separately understood that they lived only through the comprehension, and their life was like a light that appears in the darkness, flickers up, and goes out.

There was a life which appeared amidst death and again was swallowed up by death. But to those who understood the comprehension it gave the possibility of becoming its sons through faith in their origin. The twelfth verse, which appears so incoherent and mixed up at its first reading, is so precise and clear when it is translated rigorously that it is impossible to add anything for its elucidation, except to repeat it with the substitution of a verbal noun in place of the participle πιστεύουσιν, as it expresses strictly the same idea. After it was said that the life of men was like the light in the darkness and that life appeared and was swallowed by death, we get: But, although it was so, the comprehension gave men a chance to become the sons of comprehension, and thus to free themselves from death. In the twelfth verse it says that the comprehension gave men the chance to become the sons of God. In order that we may understand what is meant by the expression *to become the sons of God*, which is expounded clearly and in detail in the discourse with Nicodemus (John iii. 3–21), it is necessary to recall what was said at first.

The comprehension is God, consequently, to become the son of God means to become the son of the comprehension.

What does *son* mean ? In the third verse it says that everything which was born, was born of the comprehension. What is born is the son, consequently, all of us are sons of the comprehension, so, then, what is meant by to become the sons of the comprehension ? To this question we find an answer in the fourth verse. It says that life is in the power of the comprehension. Thus there is a double sonhood of the comprehension : one, the natural, — all are sons of the comprehension ; the other, which depends on the will of men, on the recognition of the dependence of one's life on the comprehension. Even so carnal sonhood is always of two kinds. Every man is, whether he wants to be or not, of necessity the son of his father, and yet he may, or may not, acknowledge his father. Consequently, to become the son of the comprehension is the same as to acknowledge that life is all in the power of the comprehension. The same is expressed in verses 9–11. It says that men did not acknowledge that life was all in the comprehension, and in verse 12 it says that by believing in the significance of the comprehension they could become fully its sons, because all men were born not of the lust of man and the blood of woman, but of the comprehension.

It is necessary to acknowledge that, in order by origin and acknowledgment to be fully sons of the comprehension.

The meaning of the verses is as follows:

The comprehension was in all men. It was in that which it produced: all men are alive only because they are born of the comprehension. But men have not recognized their Father, the comprehension, and did not live by it, but assumed the source of their life to lie outside it (10, 11). But to every man, who understood that source of life, the comprehension gave the possibility through the faith in it to become a son of God — the comprehension (12), because all men are born and live not through the blood of woman and through the lust of man, but through God — the comprehension (13). In Jesus Christ appeared the full comprehension.

14. Καὶ ὁ λόγος σὰρξ ἐγένετο καὶ ἐσκήνωσεν ἐν ἡμῖν, (καὶ ἐθεασάμεθα τὴν δόξαν αὐτοῦ, δόξαν ὡς μονογενοῦς παρὰ πατρός·) πλήρης χάριτος καὶ ἀληθείας.	*John 1.* 14. And the Word was made flesh, and dwelt among us, (and we beheld his glory, the glory as of the only begotten of the Father,) full of grace and truth.	14. And the comprehension became flesh and took its abode among us, and we saw its teaching, as of him who is of the same origin with the Father, — the perfect teaching of godliness in fact.

(*a*) σκηνόω *to pitch a tent, make an abode, begin to live, settle.*

(*b*) δόξα from δοκέω means *Ansicht, conception, opinion, teaching.* Δόξα cannot here be translated by *rumour* or *glory.* The most correct would be *proposition, that which some one proposes,* but as the word is not used in this sense, I substitute for it *teaching.*

(*c*) μονογενής besides meaning *born alone, only begotten,* means also *of one origin, eines Geschlechts, of one kind, one essence, the same in essence with some one.* Μόνος in this

connection does not mean *only*, but *one*, or, as in μονόχρο-
νος *of the same sort of time*, and many other words. In
the Gospel of St. John the word is used but four times,
in the present case and in the following:

No man hath seen God at any time; the *one-born* Son, which
is in the bosom of the Father, he hath declared him (i. 18).

For God so loved the world, that he gave his *one-born* Son,
that whosoever believeth in him should not perish, but have
everlasting life (iii. 16).

He that believeth on him is not condemned: but he that believeth not is condemned already, because he hath not believed
in the name of the *one-born* Son of God (iii. 18).

(*d*) In many places in John prepositions are used for a
predicate. Thus πρός is used in the first verse, and thus
παρά is used here: it means *coming out of*, just as παρὰ
θεοῦ means *having come down from the Father*.

(*c*) ὡς has to be translated, not by *as*, but by *in that*.
Here the construction demands that it be translated by *as*,
but with the meaning *in that*.

(*f*) χάρις means: (1) charm, agreeableness, kindliness,
beauty; (2) favour; (3) gratitude; (4) everything which
produces gratitude, beneficence; (5) even sacrifice, offering,
godliness, *culte*. I translate it here by *godliness*, because in
the sixteenth verse it says that Christ gave us χάριν ἀντὶ
χάριτος, that is one χάρις for another. Now, χάρις is the
law of Moses, that is the law of godliness, consequently
its χάρις is godliness according to Christ's teaching.

(*g*) Instead of πλήρης many texts read πλήρη, that is
the accusative case, and that refers to δόξα, and not to
λόγος, and signifies *complete, full, accomplished*. The genitive case χάριτος and ἀληθείας may depend both on
πλήρη and on δόξα. In either case the meaning is one
and the same. Whether the comprehension was complete, as given to us by the teaching, or whether the
teaching of the comprehension was completely carried

out, I prefer to refer it to δόξα, and not to λόγος, because in the oldest variant, which I accept, δόξα stands later and seems to be intentionally repeated.

(*h*) ἀλήθεια means *truth, verity, reality, actuality.* In order to render the first two meanings, the word *truth* is proper, but in order properly to render the meaning of reality and actuality, it would be necessary to periphrase it and say *in fact,* and so I use that expression.

By accepting the canonical order of the words, namely, And the Word was made flesh, and dwelt among us, full of grace and truth, and we beheld his glory, the glory as of the only begotten of the Father, the translation will be: And the comprehension settled among us, the comprehension of perfect godliness in truth (or, in fact), and we understood its teaching, as the teaching of the one-born, coming from the Father.

	John i.	
15. Ἰωάννης μαρτυρεῖ περὶ αὐτοῦ, καὶ κέκραγε λέγων, Οὗτος ἦν ὃν εἶπον, Ὁ ὀπίσω μου ἐρχόμενος ἔμπροσθέν μου γέγονεν· ὅτι πρῶτός μου ἦν.	15. John bare witness of him, and cried, saying, This was he of whom I spake, He that cometh after me is preferred before me; for he was before me.	15. John shows about him, and cries, and says, This is he of whom I spoke, Who comes after me was born before me, for he was the first.

The fifteenth verse about John the Baptist is striking by its irrelevance, and by the violation of the sense, and even from philological considerations. In the fourteenth verse mention was made of perfect glory, or the teaching of grace, or the serving of God; in the sixteenth verse the same word πλήρης in the form of the noun πλήρωμα connects the further exposition about grace, and suddenly in the middle of it all there appears the verse about the witness of John the Baptist, which is in no way connected with the preceding, nor with what follows. This verse does not enter into the exposition, and may be printed as an addition.

| 16. Καὶ ἐκ τοῦ πλη-ρώματος αὐτοῦ ἡμεῖς πάν-τες ἐλάβομεν, καὶ χάριν ἀντὶ χάριτος· | John i. 16. And* of his fulness[b] have all we re-ceived,[c] and grace upon[d] grace. | 16. For from its fulfil-ment did we all get god-liness in place of godli-ness. |
| 17. Ὅτι ὁ νόμος διὰ Μωσέως ἐδόθη, ἡ χάρις καὶ ἡ ἀλήθεια διὰ Ἰησοῦ Χριστοῦ ἐγένετο. | 17. For the law was given by Moses, but grace and truth came by Jesus Christ. | 17. Because the law was given by Moses. Godliness in fact took place through Jesus Christ. |

(*a*) ὅτι is given in all the oldest texts and means *because*.

(*b*) πλήρωμα means *fulness, superabundance, comple-tion, fulfilment*. I translate it by *fulfilment*, because this whole passage in John, which speaks of the meaning of the teaching of Jesus Christ in relation to Moses' law, is apparently closely connected with and, as it were, eluci-dates the seventeenth verse of the fifth chapter of Mat-thew, where the verb πληρῶσαι is used in the sense of fulfilment: οὐκ ἦλθον καταλῦσαι, ἀλλὰ πληρῶσαι.

(*c*) λαμβάνω means *to accept, understand,* that is, *to take into one, ἐν σοὶ λαμβάνειν*. I use here *get* as having a broader meaning and embracing the majority of meanings of λαμβάνω *to comprehend*.

(*d*) ἀντί has precisely the meaning of the Latin *pro*, and of the Russian *in the place of*, and so it has to be trans-lated. The rendering of the preposition ἀντί by *vŭz* in Church-Slavic, *über* in German (*Gnade über Gnade*), in Russian *grace upon grace*, *sur* and *après* in French (*grace sur grace*, or *grace après grace*, as Reuss translates it), is not justified by anything. Only the English trans-lation, which uses the preposition *for* (for grace), comes near to using one of the meanings of *in the place of*.

In the translation of verses 16 and 17 I depart from the usual translation. The departures made by me are justified by the demands of language, by the clearness of the meaning thus obtained, by the connectedness of the whole discourse, and by the strict correspondence with what precedes. As in the translation of the words λόγος *word*, γίγνομαι *to be born*, even thus now the translation of the word δόξα *glory*, μονογενής *only begotten*, ἀντί *above*, *upon, quasi, als*, χάρις *grace*, and of the verb λαμβάνειν in this place as *receive*, demands explanations not from me, but from previous translators.

Only the desire to press the words into the service of a biassed opinion could have led the translators to such an obscure rendering of this passage, which is so out of keeping with the character of the language. Δόξα means *opinion, dogma, teaching, belief*, and only in rare cases does it mean *glory*, and then only in the sense which it has in popular Russian (*rumour, report*). The church translation gives in this place *gloria, glory*, for δόξα. But the meaning of these words is not applicable to comprehension, and so the church has given to the word *glory* the real meaning of *teaching of faith*, which it has, and says, We beheld his glory as of the only begotten Son, meaning by *glory* not exactly *gloria*, but something else. Frequently the church uses the word *glory* directly in the sense of *belief, teaching*, as for example, in the expression ὀρθὴ δόξα *right glory*, or, *right belief*. I use *teaching* instead of *glory*, as being a more exact word, but do not mind leaving the word *glory*, provided it has the meaning of *belief*.

The meaning of μονογενής *of the same origin* is confirmed by the version of this passage by Origen, where it says ἀληθῶς μονογενὴς ὡς παρὰ πατρός, that is, *truly one-born, as from the Father*. Παρὰ πατρός is only an explanation of what μονογενής signifies: precisely such as from the Father.

Χάρις is translated by the word *gracia, grace, Gnade, blagodat'*. The first two, *gracia* and *grace*, mean *charm*, but although the words are so translated, they are not used in that sense, but in the sense which they have acquired later. Just so the word *Gnade*, which signifies *mercy*, is not taken in the sense of *mercy*, but in another sense given to it later. Similarly *blagodat'* is not taken in the sense of *good gift*, as the composition demands, but in the sense which it received later. But if the word χάρις is to be taken in the sense of church grace, the seventeenth verse, where it says, *grace in place of*, or *for, grace*, does violence to this meaning. *Grace in place of grace* means that the former grace has given way to a new grace, but that meaning was contrary to the church interpretation, and so the translators had to change the meaning of the preposition ἀντί, on which the whole meaning is based, and quite arbitrarily rendered it by *vúz, na, sur, über, for*.

With this change the required meaning was obtained, namely, that from Christ we received an addition of grace. But with this arbitrary translation the explanation of the whole passage and especially of the sixteenth verse became harder still. It says, Of his fulness have we received grace upon grace, and these words are explained to mean that from Jesus Christ we received an addition to the grace which we had from Moses. But later it says that the law was given by Moses, while grace and truth were given by Jesus Christ, that is, grace and truth are opposed to the law of Moses.

The difficulty of the translation of this passage consists in this, that in the fourteenth verse it says that the comprehension became flesh, and we saw its teaching, or glory, as of one origin with the Father, filled (as the church understands it) with χάρις and truth. No matter how χάρις be understood, it is clear so far that the λόγος was full of χάρις and truth.

But in the sixteenth verse, which begins with ὅτι, it says: Because from the fulness of Jesus Christ have we received χάρις in the place of, or for, χάρις, and nothing is said about truth, whereas in the beginning it says that he, Christ, was full of χάρις and truth, and in the seventeenth verse it says again that χάρις and truth are from

Jesus Christ. If the sixteenth verse did not exist, we might be able to say that the λόγος was full of χάρις and truth (though, instead of, he taught us, gave us, χάρις and truth, it says very awkwardly, He was full of); but if he is full of χάρις and truth, then it is clear, as it says in the sixteenth verse, that the law was given by Moses, and χάρις and truth were given by Jesus Christ; but the fifteenth verse, which stands in the middle, and, as it were, explains the connection of the fourteenth with the seventeenth, completely upsets it. Even if we translate (which is impossible) ἀντί by *upon*, and χάριν ἀντὶ χάριτος by *grace upon grace*, and under the first grace understand the law of Moses, then it is hard to understand why it says in the seventeenth verse that grace and truth were given through Jesus Christ. It ought to have said that an addition to grace, and not grace and truth, was given. In order to give a meaning to this passage, χάρις has to be translated by *godliness*, and ἀλήθεια by *in fact, in reality*, which, indeed, we received from Jesus Christ, for from his perfection did we get a joyful, free, vital godliness, in the place of the external godliness. The law was given by Moses, but godliness, as performed in fact, was given us by Jesus Christ.

The previous verses spoke of the manner of the appearance of the comprehension in the world and in men. We were told that men could, by recognizing the comprehension as the foundation of their lives, become sons of God, — retain within them the comprehension. Now we hear of how that took place in the world. It says that the comprehension became flesh, appeared in the flesh, lived with us. Those words, in connection with the seventeenth verse, in which it says that the new teaching was given to us by Jesus Christ, cannot be understood otherwise than by referring them to Jesus Christ.

The teaching consists in that which, as said above, gives the true life, in the recognition of oneself as the son of God, as of one birth with him. These words, in accordance with the meaning of everything which precedes, signify that the basis of Jesus Christ was the fact that life originated from the comprehension and was of one birth with it. Farther on it says that this teaching is a full, complete teaching about godliness in fact. This teaching is full and complete even because to the teaching of godliness according to the law it adds the teaching about godliness in fact. All the consequent teaching, as in John, about the relations of the father to the son, and in Matthew and the other evangelists, about Christ's having come not to change the law, but to fulfil it, and many other things, clearly confirm the correctness of this meaning.

In the fourteenth verse it says that the teaching of Jesus Christ, as of the one-born Son of the Father, is the complete teaching of godliness in fact.

The meaning of the verses is as follows:

In Jesus Christ the comprehension blended with life and lived among us, and we understood his teaching, which was, that life originated from the comprehension and was of the same origin with it, as the son comes from the father and is of one birth with him; we have received the complete teaching of godliness in fact, because through the fulfilment by Jesus Christ we all comprehended the new teaching in place of the former, for the law was given by Moses, whereas godliness in fact originated through Jesus Christ.

WHEREIN THE COMPREHENSION OF JESUS CHRIST CONSISTED

18. Θεὸν οὐδεὶς ἑώρακε πώποτε· ὁ μονογενὴς υἱὸς, ὁ ὢν εἰς τὸν κόλπον τοῦ πατρὸς, ἐκεῖνος ἐξηγήσατο.

John 4. 18. No man hath seen God at any time; the only begotten Son, which is in the bosom of the Father, he hath declared.

18. No one has ever comprehended or will ever comprehend God; the one-born son, being in the heart of the Father, he has pointed out the path.

(a) ὁράω *to see, comprehend directly.* Here the perfect is used, and so it means *has not comprehended and will not comprehend.*

(b) ὤν is most correctly translated by an adverbial participle, which shows that, being in the heart of the Father, he only points out the path.

(c) εἰς denotes *motion into something;* εἰς and not ἐν is used here, because ὁ ὢν εἰς denotes not so much *being in the Father,* as *striving to be in the heart, the pith of the Father.*

(d) κόλπος *breast, bosom.* *To be in the breast, bosom, heart* denotes that one is included in the other, is embraced by it, exists in it. *To be in the heart* renders that meaning.

(e) ἐξηγέομαι has the meaning of *to tell, guide, point out the path.*

The words, No man hath seen God at any time, in addition to the general significance, have also this special meaning that they deny the Jewish conception of God, who was seen on Sinai and in the burning bush. If there could be the slightest doubt left about the direct and exact meaning of the words of the first verse about the comprehension having become God, this eighteenth verse, which does not permit any other interpretation, says that we cannot speak of God, whom we do not comprehend; that there is, and can be, no other God than the one who is revealed by the son of God in the comprehension of life, if the life is included in the comprehension: No one has ever seen or comprehended God, but the one-born son, being in the heart of the Father, has pointed out the path.

The *son* means *life, the living man,* as it says in the third verse, Everything which is born is born by the comprehension, and in the fourth verse, In him is life, and in the twelfth and thirteenth verses, The sons of God are those who have recognized that they are born through the comprehension.

The *one-born son* means *such as the Father*. *Being in the heart of the Father* means that life, the living man, being in the heart, that is, without coming out of the comprehension, blending with it, only points out the path to it, but does not declare it.

The meaning of the verse is as follows:

No one has ever seen or ever sees God, but the life in the comprehension has pointed out the path to him.

ANNOUNCEMENT OF GOOD OF JESUS CHRIST, THE SON OF GOD

INTRODUCTION

This announcement is written in order that men might believe that Jesus Christ is a son of God and that, by the very faith in the same which he was, they might receive life. No one has ever comprehended or ever will comprehend God. All we know about God, we know because we have the comprehension, and so the true beginning of everything is the comprehension. (What we call God is the comprehension. The comprehension is the beginning of everything, — it is the true God.)

Nothing can exist without the comprehension. Everything has originated through the comprehension. In the comprehension is the force of life. Even as the whole diversity of things exists for us only because there is light, so there exists for us the whole comprehension of life, life itself, only because there is the comprehension. The comprehension is the beginning of everything.

In the world, life does not embrace everything. In the world, life appears as the light amidst the darkness. The light shines so long as it shines, and the darkness does not retain the light and remains the darkness. Even thus in the world, life appears through death, and death does not retain life and remains death.

The source of life, the comprehension, was in the whole world and in each living man. But the living men, living only because the comprehension was in them, did not understand that they originated from the comprehension.

They did not understand that the comprehension gave them the possibility of blending with it, since they were not living from the flesh, but from the comprehension. By understanding this and believing in their sonhood to the comprehension, men could have the true life. But men did not understand that, and the life in the world was like the light in the darkness.   .

God, the beginning of all beginnings, no one has ever comprehended, or ever will comprehend, but the life in the comprehension has pointed out the path to him.

And so Jesus Christ, living among us, has declared the comprehension in the flesh, in as much as life originated from the comprehension and is of one birth with it, just as the son originates from the father and is of one birth with him.

And looking at his life, we comprehended the complete teaching of the godliness in fact, because, on account of his perfection, we comprehended the new godliness in the place of the old. The law was given by Moses, but the godliness in fact originated through Jesus Christ.

No one has ever seen, or ever can see, God, but the son of God in man has pointed out the path to him.

CHAPTER I.

THE INCARNATION OF THE COMPREHENSION. THE BIRTH AND CHILDHOOD OF JESUS CHRIST

LUKE i. 5–25. In these verses are told the miraculous occurrences in relation to the birth of John the Baptist.

These occurrences not only have nothing in common with the teaching of Jesus Christ and the announcement of good, but do not even touch on Jesus Christ himself, and so, no matter how these occurrences may be understood, they can change nothing in the meaning of the teaching of Jesus Christ.

Luke i. 26–79. These verses tell of the miraculous occurrences which preceded the birth of Jesus Christ, and are connected with just such miraculous occurrences, which are foreign to the teaching, at the birth of Jesus Christ.

Matt. i. 1–17 and Luke iii. 23–38. In these verses two genealogies of Jesus Christ are set forth. Even if the genealogies agreed with each other, they do not touch on the teaching and, no matter how they may be understood, can add nothing to, or take away from, or change in, the teaching, and so all these verses must be referred to an addition.

BIRTH

18. Τοῦ δὲ Ἰησοῦ Χριστοῦ ἡ γέννησις οὕτως ἦν. μνηστευθείσης γὰρ τῆς μητρὸς αὐτοῦ	*Matt.* i. 18. Now the birth of Jesus Christ was on this wise: When as his mother Mary was espoused to Joseph, be-	18. The birth of Jesus Christ was like this: when his mother was betrothed to Joseph before they came to-

Μαρίας τῷ Ἰωσήφ, πρὶν ἢ συνελθεῖν αὐτούς, εὑρέθη ἐν γαστρὶ ἔχουσα ἐκ Πνεύματος Ἁγίου.

19. Ἰωσὴφ δὲ ὁ ἀνὴρ αὐτῆς, δίκαιος ὢν, καὶ μὴ θέλων αὐτὴν παραδειγματίσαι, ἐβουλήθη λάθρα ἀπολῦσαι αὐτήν.

20. Ταῦτα δὲ αὐτοῦ ἐνθυμηθέντος, ἰδού, ἄγγελος Κυρίου κατ᾽ ὄναρ ἐφάνη αὐτῷ, λέγων, Ἰωσήφ, υἱὸς Δαβίδ, μὴ φοβηθῇς παραλαβεῖν Μαριάμ τὴν γυναῖκά σου· τὸ γὰρ ἐν αὐτῇ γεννηθὲν ἐκ Πνεύματός ἐστιν Ἁγίου.

21. Τέξεται δὲ υἱόν, καὶ καλέσεις τὸ ὄνομα αὐτοῦ ΙΗΣΟΥΝ· αὐτὸς γὰρ σώσει τὸν λαὸν αὐτοῦ ἀπὸ τῶν ἁμαρτιῶν αὐτῶν.

24. Διεγερθεὶς δὲ ὁ Ἰωσὴφ ἀπὸ τοῦ ὕπνου ἐποίησεν ὡς προσέταξεν αὐτῷ ὁ ἄγγελος Κυρίου. καὶ παρέλαβε τὴν γυναῖκα αὐτοῦ,

25. Καὶ οὐκ ἐγίνωσκεν αὐτήν, ἕως οὗ ἔτεκε τὸν υἱὸν αὐτῆς τὸν πρωτότοκον· καὶ ἐκάλεσε τὸ ὄνομα αὐτοῦ ΙΗΣΟΥΝ.

fore they came together, she was found with child of the Holy Ghost.[a]

19. Then Joseph her husband being a just man, and not willing to make her a public example, was minded to put her away privily.

20. But while he thought on these things, behold, the angel of the Lord appeared unto him in a dream, saying, Joseph, thou son of David, fear not to take unto thee Mary thy wife: for that which is conceived in her is of the Holy Ghost.

21. And she shall bring forth a son, and thou shalt call his name JESUS: for he shall save his people from their sins.

24. Then Joseph being raised from sleep did as the angel of the Lord had bidden him, and took unto him his wife:

25. And knew her not till she had brought forth her first-born son: and he called his name JESUS.

19. Joseph, her husband, was just: he did not wish to arraign her, and intended to send her away without public announcement.

20. But while he was thinking of this, he dreamed that a messenger from God had appeared to him and was saying, Fear not to receive Mary, thy wife, for what will be born of her will be born of the Holy Ghost.

21. And she will bring forth a son and will call him Jesus, which means the Saviour, for he will save people from their sins.

24. When Joseph awoke, he did as the angel of God had commanded him to do, and received her as his wife.

25. And had nothing to do with her till she had brought forth her first son, and he called him Jesus.

(a) The words of the Holy Ghost in this place designate birth from above, the same birth which in the discourse with Nicodemus is ascribed to all men.

Verses 22 and 23 affirm that the birth of Jesus fulfilled a prophecy. This prophecy is in the highest degree far-fetched and not only fails to confirm, but even subverts, the author's thesis.

The meaning of the verses is as follows:

There was a virgin Mary. This virgin became pregnant by some unknown person. Her husband, who was

betrothed to her, took pity on her and, concealing her
shame, received her.   From her and an unknown father
a boy was born.   The boy was named Jesus.   (And
this Jesus was the comprehension in the flesh.   He it
is who declared to the world God, whom no one has ever
known.)   This Jesus was the son of God who gave to the
world the teaching of which John speaks and which is
expounded in the gospels.

Luke i. 1–21; Matt. i. 1–12; Luke ii. 22–38; Matt. ii.
13–23; Luke ii. 39.   In these verses is described the
birth of Jesus Christ and his wandering with his mother,
which is accompanied by miraculous occurrences and
prophecies.   These verses contain nothing which refers
to the teaching of Jesus or even any occurrences which
might have had some influence upon him.   The only
explanation of these chapters is that they are legends
which were formed, even as they are formed now, about
the childhood of a person who after his death has become
of great importance.   The motive of these chapters is to
enhance as much as possible the importance of the person
by means of miracles and prophecies.   The invariable tone
of these descriptions, especially in Luke, reminding one of
many apocryphal accounts, is striking by its irrelevance
as compared with other places of the same books.   It is
impossible to imagine a man who should have completely
understood the teaching, as expressed in the introduction
of John, and yet should have accepted the legends of his
birth.   One excludes the other.   To him who has comprehended the meaning of the son of God as the son of
the comprehension, as it is explained in the introduction,
the stories about the occurrences which preceded the birth
of John and of Jesus and the story of the birth itself
and of the consequent occurrences cannot be intelligible,
and certainly not important; while he who ascribes a
meaning to the miraculous birth of Jesus from the virgin
and the Holy Ghost as her husband, and believes in the

possibility of it, has evidently not yet come to understand the significance of the son of the comprehension.

The meaning of the whole passage is to justify the disgraceful birth of Jesus Christ. It was said that Jesus Christ was the comprehension, — he alone declared God. And this Jesus Christ was born in what was considered to be the most disgraceful of circumstances, from a virgin. All these chapters are a justification, from the human point of view, of that disgraceful birth. The disgraceful birth and the ignorance of Jesus as to his father in the flesh are the only feature of these chapters, which is to have a meaning for the consequent teaching of Jesus Christ.

CHILDHOOD

Greek	Luke 44.	
40. Τὸ δὲ παιδίον ηὔξανε, καὶ ἐκραταιοῦτο πνεύματι, πληρούμενον σοφίας· καὶ χάρις Θεοῦ ἦν ἐπ' αὐτό.	40. And the child grew, and waxed strong in spirit, filled with wisdom; and the grace of God was upon him.	40. The boy grew and became manly in spirit, and his reason improved. And the love of God was upon him.
41. Καὶ ἐπορεύοντο οἱ γονεῖς αὐτοῦ κατ' ἔτος εἰς Ἰερουσαλὴμ τῇ ἑορτῇ τοῦ πάσχα.	41. Now his parents went to Jerusalem every year at the feast of the passover.	41. His parents went to Jerusalem every year for the feast of the passover.
42. Καὶ ὅτε ἐγένετο ἐτῶν δώδεκα ἀναβάντων αὐτῶν εἰς Ἰεροσόλυμα κατὰ τὸ ἔθος τῆς ἑορτῆς,	42. And when he was twelve years old, they went up to Jerusalem after the custom of the feast.	42. And when he was twelve years old, his parents went to attend the feast in Jerusalem, as was their custom.
43. Καὶ τελειωσάντων τὰς ἡμέρας, ἐν τῷ ὑποστρέφειν αὐτούς, ὑπέμεινεν Ἰησοῦς ὁ παῖς ἐν Ἰερουσαλήμ· καὶ οὐκ ἔγνω Ἰωσὴφ καὶ ἡ μήτηρ αὐτοῦ.	43. And when they had fulfilled the days as they returned, the child Jesus tarried behind in Jerusalem; and Joseph and his mother knew not of it.	43. When the feast was over and they started home, the boy Jesus tarried behind in Jerusalem; and Joseph and his mother did not notice it.
44. Νομίσαντες δὲ αὐτὸν ἐν τῇ συνοδίᾳ εἶναι, ἦλθον ἡμέρας ὁδόν, καὶ ἀνεζήτουν αὐτὸν ἐν τοῖς συγγενέσι καὶ ἐν τοῖς γνωστοῖς·	44. But they, supposing him to have been in the company, went a day's journey; and they sought him among their kinsfolk and acquaintance.	44. They thought that he was with his companions, and they went a day's journey, and they sought him among their kinsfolk and acquaintances.
45. Καὶ μὴ εὑρόντες αὐτόν, ὑπέστρεψαν εἰς Ἰερουσαλήμ, ζητοῦντες αὐτόν.	45. And when they found him not, they turned back again to Jerusalem, seeking him.	45. And they did not find him and returned to Jerusalem to find him.

46. Καὶ ἐγένετο μεθ' ἡμέρας τρεῖς, εὗρον αὐτὸν ἐν τῷ ἱερῷ, καθεζόμενον ἐν μέσῳ τῶν διδασκάλων, καὶ ἀκούοντα αὐτῶν, καὶ ἐπερωτῶντα αὐτούς.

47. Ἐξίσταντο δὲ πάντες οἱ ἀκούοντες αὐτοῦ ἐπὶ τῇ συνέσει καὶ ταῖς ἀποκρίσεσιν αὐτοῦ.

48. Καὶ ἰδόντες αὐτὸν ἐξεπλάγησαν· καὶ πρὸς αὐτὸν ἡ μήτηρ αὐτοῦ εἶπε, Τέκνον, τί ἐποίησας ἡμῖν οὕτως; ἰδού, ὁ πατήρ σου κἀγὼ ὀδυνώμενοι ἐζητοῦμέν σε.

49. Καὶ εἶπε πρὸς αὐτούς, Τί ὅτι ἐζητεῖτέ με; οὐκ ᾔδειτε ὅτι ἐν τοῖς τοῦ πατρός μου δεῖ εἶναί με;

50. Καὶ αὐτοὶ οὐ συνῆκαν τὸ ῥῆμα ὃ ἐλάλησεν αὐτοῖς.

51. Καὶ κατέβη μετ' αὐτῶν, καὶ ἦλθεν εἰς Ναζαρέτ· καὶ ἦν ὑποτασσόμενος αὐτοῖς. καὶ ἡ μήτηρ αὐτοῦ διετήρει πάντα τὰ ῥήματα ταῦτα ἐν τῇ καρδίᾳ αὐτῆς.

52. Καὶ Ἰησοῦς προέκοπτε σοφίᾳ καὶ ἡλικίᾳ, καὶ χάριτι παρὰ Θεῷ καὶ ἀνθρώποις.

---

46. And it came to pass, that after three days they found him in the temple sitting in the midst of the doctors, both hearing them, and asking them questions.

47. And all that heard him were astonished at his understanding and answers.

48. And when they saw him, they were amazed: and his mother said unto him, Son, why hast thou thus dealt with us? behold, thy father and I have sought thee sorrowing.

49. And he said unto them, How is it that ye sought me? wist ye not that I must be about my Father's business?

50. And they understood not the saying which he spake unto them.

51. And he went down with them, and came to Nazareth, and was subject unto them: but his mother kept all these sayings in her heart.

52. And Jesus increased in wisdom and stature, and in favour with God and man.

---

46. And they found him after awhile in the temple: he was sitting amidst the teachers, asking them questions, and listening to them.

47. And all that heard him were astonished at his understanding and at his speeches.

48. His parents saw him and were surprised, and his mother said to him, Son, what hast thou done to us? Thy father and I have been worrying and looking for thee.

49. And he said to them, Why are you looking for me? Do you not know that I must be in my Father's house?

50. But they did not understand what he was saying to them.

51. And he went up to them, and went with them to Nazareth, and obeyed them. And his mother took all his words to heart.

52. And Jesus increased in stature and understanding, and was in favour with God and man.

All these verses are translated without a change of meaning, and so do not demand any explanations.

---

23. Καὶ αὐτὸς ἦν ὁ Ἰησοῦς ὡσεὶ ἐτῶν τριάκοντα ἀρχόμενος, ὢν, ὡς ἐνομίζετο, υἱὸς Ἰωσήφ.

Luke iii. 23. And Jesus himself began to be about thirty years of age, being (as was supposed) the son of Joseph.[a]

23. And Jesus was about thirty years of age, and men thought that he was Joseph's son.

(*a*) The twenty-third verse of the third chapter is placed here for the sake of the consecutiveness of the exposition.

The verses about John the Baptist will be found in their proper place.

The meaning of the verses is as following:

About the childhood of Jesus Christ we are told in general only this, that without a father he grew, became manly, and increased in understanding beyond his years, so that it was evident that God loved him. From his whole childhood only one particular incident is mentioned, and that is how he was lost when Mary and Joseph were at the feast in Jerusalem, and how he was found in the temple with the teachers. He listened and asked questions, and all marvelled at his understanding. His mother began to rebuke him for having gone away from them and because they had been looking for him. But he said to her: Why did you look for me? Do you not know that you ought to look for each man in the house of his father? I have no man-father, consequently my Father is God. The temple is God's house. If you had been looking for me in the house of my Father, in the temple, you would have found me. This story, besides indicating an unusual intellect in the child Jesus, very clearly brings out the one train of thought, by which the clever, neglected child, seeing about him children who all of them had carnal fathers, and no father in the flesh of his own, recognized as his Father the beginning of all, God. The conception that God was the Father of all men was expressed in the Jewish books:

Mal. ii. 10. Have we not all one father? Hath not one God created us?

JOHN THE BAPTIST

4. 'Εγένετο 'Ιωάννης βαπτίζων ἐν τῇ ἐρήμῳ, καὶ κηρύσσων βάπτισμα μετανοίας εἰς ἄφεσιν ἁμαρτιῶν.	*Mark i.* 4. John did baptize in the wilderness, and preach the baptism of repentance[c] for the remission of sins.[d]	4. John the Baptist appeared in the prairie and preached bathing as a sign of the change of life, as a sign of the liberation from error.

(*a*) βαπτίζω means *to bathe, wash down.* I prefer the popular expression *to bathe* to the word *baptize*, because *baptize* has the ecclesiastic significance of a sacrament and does not express the action itself, which is expressed in the verb βαπτίζω.

(*b*) εἰς I translate by *in sign of*, as it is frequently translated, since the meaning *in* is not applicable here.

(*c*) μετάνοια is word for word *afterthought, change of mind.* *Repentance* would correctly render the meaning of the word, if repentance had not received a peculiar ecclesiastic significance. I prefer the word *renovation*, which in the popular language has the meaning of repentance, but not so much in the sense of *penitence*, as in the sense of *an inward change.*

(*d*) ἁμαρτία means *sin*, not in the sense of *a religious sin*, but in the sense of *mistake, oversight*, and so I translate it by *error.*

4. Αὐτὸς δὲ ὁ Ἰωάννης εἶχε τὸ ἔνδυμα αὐτοῦ ἀπὸ τριχῶν καμήλου, καὶ ζώνην δερματίνην περὶ τὴν ὀσφὺν αὐτοῦ· ἡ δὲ τροφὴ αὐτοῦ ἦν ἀκρίδες καὶ μέλι ἄγριον.	*Mark* iii. 4. And the same John had his raiment of camel's hair, and a leathern girdle about his loins; and his meat was locusts and wild honey.ᵉ	4. John's raiment was of camel's hair, and he was girded with a leathern girdle. He fed on locusts and herbs.
1. Ἀρχὴ τοῦ εὐαγγελίου Ἰησοῦ Χριστοῦ υἱοῦ τοῦ Θεοῦ·	*Mark* i. 1. The beginning of the gospel of Jesus Christ, the Son of God;	1. The beginning of the announcement of good of Jesus Christ the son of God was :ᵇ
2. Ὡς γέγραπται ἐν τοῖς προφήταις, ‘Ἰδού, ἐγὼ ἀποστέλλω τὸν ἄγγελόν μου πρὸ προσώπου σου, ὃς κατασκευάσει τὴν ὁδόν σου ἔμπροσθέν σου.’	2. As it is written in the prophets, Behold, I send my messenger before thy face, which shall prepare thy way before thee (Mal. iii. 1).	2. As it is written in the prophets, I send my messenger to prepare my way.
3. ‘Φωνὴ βοῶντος ἐν τῇ ἐρήμῳ, ‘Ετοιμάσατε τὴν ὁδὸν Κυρίου· εὐθείας ποιεῖτε τὰς τρίβους αὐτοῦ.’	3. The voice of one crying in the wilderness, Prepare ye the way of the Lord, make his paths straightᶜ (Is. xl. 3).	3. A voice calls to you. In the wilderness prepare ye the way of the Lord, make his paths easy.
5. Πᾶσα φάραγξ πληρωθήσεται, καὶ πᾶν ὄρος καὶ βουνὸς ταπεινωθήσεται· καὶ ἔσται τὰ σκολιὰ	*Luke* iii. 5. Every valley shall be filled, and every mountain and hill shall be brought low; and the crooked shall be	5. So that every hollow shall be made even, and every hill and mound shall be brought low; so that all the crooked

εἰς εὐθεῖαν, καὶ αἱ τρα- χεῖαι εἰς ὁδοὺς λείας.`	made straight, and the rough ways shall be made smooth;	places shall be made straight, and the mounds shall be made a smooth road.
6. Καὶ ὄψεται πᾶσα σὰρξ τὸ σωτήριον τοῦ Θεοῦ.'	6. And all flesh shall see the salvation of God (Is. xl. 3-5).	6. And the whole world shall see the salvation of God.

(a) Scholars think that by *wild honey* is to be understood *resin*. In order to be intelligible and express the same strictness of the fast, I use the word *herbs*.

(b) To connect the words, *The beginning of the announcement*, and, *as it is written*, it is necessary to add the word *was*, that is, that the beginning of the announcement was, that according to the words of certain prophecies there appeared John the Baptist.

(c) The change of punctuation, and therefore the change of the meaning of the passage, I take from Reuss's *Les Prophètes*, Vol. II. (1878).

This is the way it is translated there from the Hebrew:

> Une voix crie :
> Par le desert frayez le chemin de l'Eternel !
> Aplanassez, à travers la lande, une route pour notre Dieu !
> Que toute profondeur soit exhaussée,
> Que toute montagne, toute colline s'abaisse,
> Que ce qui est inégal se change en plaine,
> Et les crêtes escarpées en vallons,
> Pour que la gloire de l'Eternel apparaisse
> Et que tous les mortels ensemble l'aperçoivent !
> C'est la bouche de l'Eternel qui l'a dit.

Matt. iii. 1 ; Luke iii. 1. In these verses are set forth historical occurrences, which have no reference either to Christ, or to the contents of the teaching.

2. Καὶ λέγων, Μετα- νοεῖτε· ἤγγικε γὰρ ἡ βα- σιλεία τῶν οὐρανῶν.	*Matt. iii.* 2. And say- ing, Repent ye: for the kingdom of heaven' is at hand.	2. John said, Come to your senses, for the kingdom of heaven is here.

(a) ἤγγικε is a perfect and signifies what has taken place and is now taking place. The verb means *to approach.* In the perfect it signifies that the kingdom of heaven has approached in such a way that it cannot approach any nearer. Indeed, according to all the prophecies, the kingdom was in the future and still coming. Now it was already here. And so ἤγγικε must be translated in this place by *has come now, is here.*

(b) *The kingdom of heaven.* These words have received their church significance. They designate the kingdom which is formed of all the believers. Its king is Jesus Christ. Obviously John the Baptist could not have been speaking of that kingdom of heaven before Christ. In the mouth of John the Baptist and of Jesus Christ these words must receive a meaning which was intelligible to all the hearers of that time. The kingdom of heaven, for all the Jews who heard that, was the coming of God into the world and his enthronement over men, that with which are filled all the prophecies of Zechariah, Hosea, Malachi, Joel, Jeremiah. The peculiarity of the meaning of John the Baptist's words in distinction from the other prophets is this, that while the other prophets spoke indefinitely of the future enthronement of God, John the Baptist says that this kingdom has arrived and the enthronement is completed. Nearly all the prophets with this enthronement of God predicted external, miraculous, and terrible events; Jeremiah is the only one who predicted the enthronement of God among men not by external phenomena, but by an inward union of God with men, and so the assertion of John the Baptist that the kingdom of heaven has come, although no terrible event has taken place, is to be understood in this way, that what has arrived is the inward kingdom of God, which Jeremiah had predicted.

THE CONCOURSE OF PEOPLE TO BE BAPTIZED BY JOHN

5. Τότε ἐξεπορεύετο πρὸς αὐτὸν Ἱεροσόλυμα

Matt. iii. 5. Then went out to him Jerusalem, and all Judea, and all

5. And to John came the people from Jerusalem and from the vil-

καὶ πᾶσα ἡ Ἰουδαία καὶ πᾶσα ἡ περίχωρος τοῦ Ἰορδάνου·

6. Καὶ ἐβαπτίζοντο ἐν τῷ Ἰορδάνῃ ὑπ' αὐτοῦ, ἐξομολογούμενοι τὰς ἁμαρτίας αὐτῶν.

7. Ἔλεγεν οὖν τοῖς ἐκπορευομένοις ὄχλοις βαπτισθῆναι ὑπ' αὐτοῦ, Γεννήματα ἐχιδνῶν, τίς ὑπέδειξεν ὑμῖν φυγεῖν ἀπὸ τῆς μελλούσης ὀργῆς;

8. Ποιήσατε οὖν καρποὺς ἀξίους τῆς μετανοίας·

9. Ἤδη δὲ καὶ ἡ ἀξίνη πρὸς τὴν ῥίζαν τῶν δένδρων κεῖται· πᾶν οὖν δένδρον μὴ ποιοῦν καρπὸν καλὸν ἐκκόπτεται καὶ εἰς πῦρ βάλλεται.

10. Καὶ ἐπηρώτων αὐτὸν οἱ ὄχλοι, λέγοντες, Τί οὖν ποιήσομεν;

11. Ἀποκριθεὶς δὲ λέγει αὐτοῖς, Ὁ ἔχων δύο χιτῶνας μεταδότω τῷ μὴ ἔχοντι· καὶ ὁ ἔχων βρώματα ὁμοίως ποιείτω.

12. Ἦλθον δὲ καὶ τελῶναι βαπτισθῆναι, καὶ εἶπον πρὸ αὐτὸν, Διδάσκαλε, τί ποιήσομεν;

13. Ὁ δὲ εἶπε πρὸς αὐτούς, Μηδὲν πλέον παρὰ τὸ διατεταγμένον ὑμῖν πράσσετε.

14. Ἐπηρώτων δὲ αὐτὸν καὶ στρατευόμενοι, λέγοντες, Καὶ ἡμεῖς τί ποιήσομεν; καὶ εἶπε πρὸς αὐτούς, Μηδένα διασείσητε, μηδὲ συκοφαντήσητε· καὶ ἀρκεῖσθε τοῖς ὀψωνίοις ὑμῶν.

---

the region round about Jordan,

6. And were baptized of him in Jordan, confessing their sins.

Luke vii. 7. Then said he to the multitudes that came forth to be baptized of him, O generation of vipers,[b] who hath warned you to flee from the wrath[a] to come?

8. Bring forth therefore fruits worthy[d] of repentance.

9. And now also the axe is laid unto the root of the trees: every tree therefore which bringeth not forth good fruit is hewn down, and cast into the fire.

10. And the people asked him, saying, What shall we do then?

11. He answereth and saith unto them, He that hath two coats, let him impart to him that hath none; and he that hath meat, let him do likewise.

12. Then came also publicans[e] to be baptized, and said unto him, Master, what shall we do?

13. And he said unto them, Exact no more than that which is appointed you.

14. And the soldiers likewise demanded of him, saying, And what shall we do? And he said unto them, Do violence to no man, neither accuse any falsely; and be content with your wages.

---

lages along the Jordan, and from the whole country of Judea.

6. And he bathed in the Jordan all those who confessed their errors.

7. And he said to the people, O tribe of snakes! Who taught you to flee from the approaching will of God?

8. Bring fruits which are in conformity with the change.

9. The axe is already laid upon the root of the tree, and if a tree does not bring forth good fruit, it is cut down and burnt up.

10. And the people asked him, What shall we do?

11. He answered them, He that has two coats, let him give one to him who has none; and he that has bread, let him do likewise.

12. The farmers of taxes came to his bathing, and said to him, Teacher, what shall we do?

13. John said to them, Exact no more than is your right.

14. And the soldiers asked, What shall we do? And he said, Trouble no man, and accuse none falsely. Be content with your condition.

(*a*) In Matt. iii. 7 it says that the following words of John are addressed only to the Pharisees and the Sadducees, while in Luke it says that they are addressed to all. As there is nothing in the words which refers especially to the Pharisees and the Sadducees, Luke's version is preferable.

(*b*) There is a superstition that snakes have a presentiment of a fire and creep away from where one is to happen.

(*c*) ὀργή *natural disposition, expression of will.* I translate it by *will of God.*

(*d*) ἄξιος with the genitive, *worthy of something, as much as,* cannot be translated into Russian precisely, and is best rendered by *in conformity with.*

The words which serve as a continuation of the eighth verse, and which are that the Jews regard Abraham as their father, refer only to the Jews and contain no instruction and, besides, interrupt the speech about the fruits and the tree, and so are omitted here.

(*e*) τελώνης *tax-gatherer.* The taxes were farmed out, and so the tax-gatherers were farmers of taxes.

Verse 15 says, according to Luke, that the subsequent words about the one who is mightier who is coming into the world are spoken by John in reply to the supposition that he is Christ. But these words directly continue the speech about preparing the way for him who is coming, and do by no means answer a supposed question as to whether he is Christ or not. He does not say that he is Christ or not Christ, or that he who comes after him is Christ or not Christ, and so this verse is omitted.

18. Πολλὰ μὲν οὖν καὶ ἕτερα παρακαλῶν εὐηγγελίζετο τὸν λαόν.	*Luke* iii. 18. And many other things in his exhortation preached he unto the people.	18. And, calling up the people, he announced many other things about the true good.
11. Ἐγὼ μὲν βαπτίζω ὑμᾶς ἐν ὕδατι εἰς μετάνοιαν· ὁ δὲ ὀπίσω μου	*Matt.* iii. 11. I indeed baptize you with water unto repentance: but he that cometh after me is	11. And he called out to the people, and said, I bathe you in water in sign of the renovation,

ἐρχόμενος ἰσχυρότερός μου ἐστίν, οὗ οὐκ εἰμὶ ἱκανὸς τὰ ὑποδήματα βαστάσαι· αὐτὸς ὑμᾶς βαπτίσει ἐν Πνεύματι Ἁγίῳ καὶ πυρί.

mightier than I, whose shoes I am not worthy to bear: he shall baptize you with the Holy Ghost, and with fire.

but he is coming who is mightier than I and of whom I am not worthy.

8. Ἐγὼ μὲν ἐβάπτισα ὑμᾶς ἐν ὕδατι· αὐτὸς δὲ βαπτίσει ὑμᾶς ἐν Πνεύματι Ἁγίῳ

Mark 1. 8. I indeed have baptized you with water: but he shall baptize you with the Holy Ghost.[b]

8. I wash you in water, but he will purify you by the spirit (and fire).

12. Οὗ τὸ πτύον ἐν τῇ χειρὶ αὐτοῦ, καὶ διακαθαριεῖ τὴν ἅλωνα αὐτοῦ, καὶ συνάξει τὸν σῖτον αὐτοῦ εἰς τὴν ἀποθήκην, τὸ δὲ ἄχυρον κατακαύσει πυρὶ ἀσβέστῳ

Matt. 1:14. 12. Whose fan is in his hand, and he will thoroughly purge his floor, and gather his wheat into the garner; but he will burn up the chaff with unquenchable fire.

12. The fan is in his hand, and he will clean his floor. He will gather the wheat, and will burn the chaff.

13. Τότε παραγίνεται ὁ Ἰησοῦς ἀπὸ τῆς Γαλιλαίας ἐπὶ τὸν Ἰορδάνην πρὸς τὸν Ἰωάννην, τοῦ βαπτισθῆναι ὑπ᾽ αὐτοῦ.

13. Then cometh Jesus from Galilee to Jordan unto John, to be baptized of him.

13. And Jesus was purified by John.

16. Καὶ βαπτισθεὶς ὁ Ἰησοῦς ἀνέβη εὐθὺς ἀπὸ τοῦ ὕδατος.

16. And Jesus, when he was baptized, went up straightway out of the water.

(a) βαπτίζω not only means *to bathe*, but also *to purify*: the context demands the latter meaning here.

(b) *With the Holy Ghost and with fire.* The word *holy* is added later, as appears from many texts, and as it is always attached to the word Ghost. The word *fire* is not given in Mark, but is added in Luke and Matthew. The idea is that as the master purifies the threshing-floor with fire, so he will purify you who is mightier in spirit.

The fourteenth and fifteenth verses are not very intelligible and, in the sense in which they are taken, add nothing to our teaching.

The continuation of the sixteenth verse speaks of a miracle, an unnatural and unintelligible event. It adds nothing to the teaching, but, on the contrary, obscures it. How the miracles violate the sense of the teaching will be mentioned in its proper place.

THE GENERAL MEANING OF JOHN'S PREACHING

In what did John's teaching consist? It is generally said that we know nothing or very little about what John preached. Indeed, if we assume that John merely announced the coming of that kingdom of heaven of which Jesus taught, or preached, like the previous prophets, the coming of God, no contents will be left in John's preaching. But if we stop looking upon the written words as a magic fairy-tale, and trying to find in everything miracles and prophecies, John's preaching will become full of contents. Men of the church generally represent him as a forerunner of Christ; and freethinkers, as one of those liberal poets, called prophets, of whom there was never a lack among the Jews and who uttered moral commonplaces. But if we only give ourselves the trouble to understand the words which are before us in a simple manner and without any preconceived notion, the contents of John the Baptist's preaching, and the very important contents at that, will appear at once.

It says that the kingdom of heaven ἤγγικε, was already at hand. Not one of the prophets had said that. They had all said that God would come, would be king, would do this or that, but all that would be in the future. John said: The kingdom of heaven is already here. Nothing manifest has happened, but it is here. That the peculiarity of John's preaching consisted in the announcement that the kingdom of heaven was already at hand, or had come, or, at least, that Jesus Christ thus understood these words, is proved by this, that later on Jesus Christ said, The law and the prophets were until John: since that time the kingdom of God is preached, and every man presseth into it (Luke xvi. 16).

Consequently, that is the meaning of John's preaching. Not one prophet said that before. All the former prophets, with the exception of Jeremiah (xxxi. 31), predicted un-

usual external occurrences in connection with the coming
of God : executions, frosts, plagues, destructions, wars, and
carnal pleasures. John does not predict anything of the
kind. All he says is that no one can escape the will of
God, that what is not needed will be destroyed, and that
only that which is needed will be left. All he says is,
Be renovated! That is the chief characteristic of his
preaching, and the most important part of what he says
is: I purify you with water, but what will purify you
completely is the spirit, that is, something invisible, non-
carnal. John says, Heretofore you have been told that
the kingdom of heaven will come some day, but I say to
you that it is already here. In order to enter heaven it
is necessary to become renovated, to renounce error. I
can cleanse you externally, but only the spirit will purify
you. That is the teaching which Jesus Christ heard.
The kingdom is here, but in order to enter it, it is necessary to become purified by the spirit.

And thus Jesus Christ, full of the spirit, goes into the
wilderness to try his spirit.

CHRIST'S TEMPTATION IN THE WILDERNESS

1. Ἰησοῦς δὲ Πνεύματος Ἁγίου πλήρης ὑπέστρεψεν ἀπὸ τοῦ Ἰορδάνου· καὶ ἤγετο ἐν τῷ Πνεύματι εἰς τὴν ἔρημον	*Luke iv.* 1. And Jesus being full of the Holy Ghost returned from Jordan, and was led by the Spirit into the wilderness,[c]	1. Then Jesus being full of the spirit went from the Jordan into the wilderness,
2. Ἡμέρας τεσσαράκοντα, πειραζόμενος ὑπὸ τοῦ διαβόλου.	2. Being forty days tempted of the devil.[b]	2. And there the tempter tempted him.
18. Καὶ ἦν ἐκεῖ ἐν τῇ ἐρήμῳ ἡμέρας τεσσαράκοντα, πειραζόμενος ὑπὸ τοῦ Σατανᾶ, καὶ ἦν μετὰ τῶν θηρίων.	*Mark i.* 13. And he was there in the wilderness forty days tempted of Satan; and was with the wild beasts.	13. And Jesus was in that wilderness forty days, and ate nothing, and grew thin.
2. Καὶ οὐκ ἔφαγεν οὐδὲν ἐν ταῖς ἡμέραις ἐκείναις· καὶ συντελεσθεισῶν αὐτῶν, ὕστερον ἐπείνασε.	*Luke iv.* 2. And in those days he did eat nothing: and when they were ended, he afterward hungered.	

2. Καὶ νηστεύσας ἡμέρας τεσσαράκοντα καὶ νύκτας τεσσαράκοντα, ὕστερον ἐπείνασε.

Matt. iv. 2. And when he had fasted forty days and forty nights, he was afterward a hungered.

3. Καὶ προσελθὼν αὐτῷ ὁ πειράζων εἶπεν, Εἰ υἱὸς εἶ τοῦ Θεοῦ, εἰπὲ ἵνα οἱ λίθοι οὗτοι ἄρτοι γένωνται.

3. And when the tempter came to him, he said, If thou be the Son of God, command that these stones be made bread.

3. And the tempter came to him, and said, If thou art a son of God, command that these stones be changed into bread.

4. Ὁ δὲ ἀποκριθεὶς εἶπε, Γέγραπται, 'Οὐκ ἐπ' ἄρτῳ μόνῳ ζήσεται ἄνθρωπος, ἀλλ' ἐπὶ παντὶ ῥήματι ἐκπορευομένῳ διὰ στόματος Θεοῦ.'

4. But he answered and said, It is written, Man shall not live by bread alone, but by every word that proceedeth out of the mouth of God.

4. But Jesus answered, It is written, Man does not live by bread alone, but by everything which proceeds out of the mouth of God (by the spirit).

(*a*) In Luke it is written καὶ ἤγετο ἐν τῷ Πνεύματι εἰς τὴν ἔρημον, but in the older texts it is always written ἐν τῇ ἐρήμῳ, that is, it says simply and clearly that Jesus passed forty days in the wilderness, in the same spirit in which he went away from the Jordan. It is true in Matthew it says ἀνήχθη εἰς τὴν ἔρημον ὑπὸ τοῦ Πνεύματος and in Mark τὸ Πνεῦμα αὐτὸν ἐκβάλλει εἰς τὴν ἔρημον, that is, that he was carried by the spirit and that the spirit cast him away in the wilderness. Luke, apparently combining the two versions, says that he was full of the spirit, and in that spirit passed forty days in the wilderness.

(*b*) διάβολος I translate by *tempter*, in order to give the word its proper meaning, and not that of *devil*, which it now has.

(*c*) I omit the word ῥῆμα, because it is not found in the Hebrew text, Deut. viii. 3, from which these words are quoted. That passage determines the meaning of the words, and here is the translation of it.

Deut. viii. 2–5: 2. And thou shalt remember all the way which the Lord thy God led thee these forty years in the wilderness, to humble thee, and to prove thee, to know what was in thine heart, whether thou wouldest keep his commandments, or no.

3. And he humbled thee, and suffered thee to hunger, and fed thee with manna, which thou knewest not, neither did thy fathers know; that he might make thee know that man doth not live by bread only, but by every word that proceedeth out of the mouth of the Lord, doth man live.

4. Thy raiment waxed not old upon thee, neither did thy foot swell these forty years.

5. Thou shalt also consider in thine heart, that as a man chasteneth his son, so the Lord thy God chasteneth thee.

9. Καὶ ἤγαγεν αὐτὸν εἰς Ἰερουσαλήμ, καὶ ἔστησεν αὐτὸν ἐπὶ τὸ πτερύγιον τοῦ ἱεροῦ, καὶ εἶπεν αὐτῷ, Εἰ ὁ υἱὸς εἶ τοῦ Θεοῦ, βάλε σεαυτὸν ἐντεῦθεν κάτω·	*Luke iv.* 9. And he brought him to Jerusalem, and set him on a pinnacle of the temple, and said unto him, If thou be the Son of God, cast thyself down from hence:	9. The tempter brought Jesus Christ to Jerusalem, and set him on the roof of a church, and said to him, If thou art a son of God, cast thyself down from here:
10. Γέγραπται γάρ, ʼʼΟτι τοῖς ἀγγέλοις αὐτοῦ ἐντελεῖται περὶ σοῦ, τοῦ διαφυλάξαι σε·	10. For it is written, He shall give his angels charge over thee, to keep thee:	10. For it is written that he will charge his messengers in regard to thee, to keep thee:
11. Καὶ ὅτι ἐπὶ χειρῶν ἀροῦσί σε, μήποτε προσκόψῃς πρὸς λίθον τὸν πόδα σου.ʼ	11. And in their hands they shall bear thee up, lest at any time thou dash thy foot against a stone (Psalm xci. 11, 12).	11. And they shall catch thee in their arms, so that thy foot may not strike against a stone.
12. Καὶ ἀποκριθεὶς εἶπεν αὐτῷ ὁ Ἰησοῦς, ʼʼΟτι εἴρηται, ʻ Οὐκ ἐκπειράσεις Κύριον τὸν Θεόν σου.ʼ	12. And Jesus answering said unto him, It is said, Thou shalt not tempt the Lord thy God (Deut. vi. 16).	12. And Jesus answered him, and said, Because it is said, Thou shalt not tempt thy God.
5. Καὶ ἀναγαγὼν αὐτὸν ὁ διάβολος εἰς ὄρος ὑψηλὸν, ἔδειξεν αὐτῷ πάσας τὰς βασιλείας τῆς οἰκουμένης ἐν στιγμῇ χρόνου·	5. And the devil, taking him up into a high mountain, shewed unto him all the kingdoms of the world in a moment of time.	5. And again the tempter took him to a high mountain, and presented to him all the kingdoms of the earth in a twinkling of the eye.
6. Καὶ εἶπεν αὐτῷ ὁ διάβολος, Σοὶ δώσω τὴν ἐξουσίαν ταύτην ἅπασαν καὶ τὴν δόξαν αὐτῶν· ὅτι ἐμοὶ παραδέδοται, καὶ ᾧ ἐὰν θέλω δίδωμι αὐτήν·	6. And the devil said unto him, All this power will I give thee, and the glory of them: for that is delivered unto me; and to whomsoever I will, I give it.	6. And said to him, I will give thee all this power and their glory, for they are delivered to me, and to whomsoever I will, I give them.
7. Σὺ οὖν ἐὰν προσκυνήσῃς ἐνώπιόν μου, ἔσται σου πάντα.	7. If thou therefore wilt worship me, all shall be thine.	7. If thou wilt worship me, all shall be thine.
8. Καὶ ἀποκριθεὶς αὐτῷ εἶπεν ὁ Ἰησοῦς, Ὕπαγε ὀπίσω μου, Σα-	8. And Jesus answered and said unto him, Get thee behind me, Satan: for it is written, Thou	8. Then Jesus answered, and said, Go away (evil) foe! It is written, Thou shalt wor-

τανθ· γέγραπται γὰρ, 'Προσκυνήσεις Κύριον τὸν Θεόν σου, καὶ αὐτῷ μόνῳ λατρεύσεις.'

13. Καὶ συντελέσας πάντα πειρασμὸν ὁ διάβολος ἀπέστη ἀπ' αὐτοῦ ἄχρι καιροῦ.

11. Καὶ ἰδού, ἄγγελοι προσῆλθον καὶ διηκόνουν αὐτῷ.

14. Καὶ ὑπέστρεψεν ὁ 'Ιησοῦς ἐν τῇ δυνάμει τοῦ Πνεύματος εἰς τὴν Γαλιλαίαν.

shalt worship the Lord thy God, and him only shalt thou serve.*

13. And when the devil had ended all the temptation, he departed from him for a season.

Matt. iv. 11. And behold, angels/ came and ministered unto him.

Luke iv. 14. And Jesus returned in the power of the Spirit into Galilee.

ship the Lord, and for him alone shalt thou work.

13. Then the tempter departed from him for a time,

11. And God's power came and served him.

14. And Jesus returned in the power of the spirit to Galilee.

(*a*) In Luke ὅτι stands in this place, for Jesus says, I will not cast myself down, for it is written, Thou shalt not tempt.

(*b*) ἐκπειράζω means properly *to make a trial of;* but from the reference to the passage in Deuteronomy, from which it is quoted, it means *to doubt.*

Deut. vi. 16 is based on Exod. xvii. 1–7, where it says: The people began to murmur against Moses because there was no water. Moses turned to God. God told him to go up on the mountain and to strike it with the rod, and the water would come. And he called the name of the place Massah, and Meribah, because the Jews had murmured, and because they had despaired of the Eternal One, and had said, Is Jehovah among us, or not?

(*c*) οἰκούμενος *inhabited,* viz. the earth, and the translation is *of people living upon the earth.*

(*d*) Satan is a word that has no definite meaning. In Hebrew it means foe, and so I translate it.

(*e*) λατρεύω *to work for pay.* The significance of this word, which is rarely used and which is only once used in this sense, is very important. It does not mean *to serve,* not even *to work,* in the sense which it has in Russian, namely *to do a thing,* but *to work for a reward,* that is, unwillingly, with difficulty, not for the work itself, but for another purpose.

(*f*) Since ἄγγελοι is used in the sense of messengers of God, I translate it by *power of God*.

This passage about the temptation is particularly remarkable in that it forms a stumbling-block for the church interpretations, since the very idea of God being tempted by God himself forms an internal contradiction from which it is impossible to emerge.

This is the way the church interprets this passage (Archim. Mikh., Gos. of Matthew, p. 63):

Then : Immediately after the Holy Ghost at the baptism descended upon Jesus, and not at a later time, as some suppose.

Of the Spirit : By Spirit not the spirit of Jesus is to be understood here, nor the tempting spirit, but the Holy Ghost who descended upon Jesus. After the baptism Jesus gives himself up to the Holy Ghost and is led by him, whither he is commanded, and is brought into the wilderness for a struggle with the devil.

Into the wilderness : Tradition points out as the place of the Lord's temptation the so-called forty days' wilderness, which is to the west of Jericho, a wild and terrible place, where wild beasts and robbers sought shelter (it is also called the Desert of Jericho).

To be tempted : To tempt means in general to put to trial, to question. In a narrower sense to tempt means to seduce people, to turn them to something bad, pointing out the good side of that which is bad, by which the power of moral good in men or their impotence is made manifest. Here to tempt means to try whether Jesus is really Christ, to try him by means of enticements to commit sinful acts.

Of the devil : The devil is properly speaking a renegade, antagonist, enemy. In Scripture the devil is properly called a fallen angel, who did not persevere in the good, an enemy of everything good, an evil being, hostile to the good, hostile in particular to the salvation of man. The evangelists do not tell in what way he approached the Saviour. Perhaps not in a coarse sensuous form, with which his subsequent actions do not fully harmonize ; but, on the other hand, it is not to be doubted that he is not a personification of the seductive thoughts of the Lord himself, as some have assumed. He was the spirit of evil who in one form or another actually appeared to the Saviour.

When he had fasted: He entirely abstained from food (he ate nothing in those days) forty days or forty nights. Examples of such protracted fasts are known from the Old Testament. Thus Prophet Elijah fasted forty days, and so did Moses. Christ fasted not because he needed to fast, but in order to instruct us; he fasted forty days, and not more, in order that the excessive grandeur of the miracle might not make doubtful the very truth of his incarnation. If he had continued the fast much longer, that might have served for many as a cause for doubting the truth of the incarnation.

He was afterward a-hungered: After the lapse of forty days he felt the need of food, thus showing his humanity.

He came to him: When the Lord was a-hungered, the tempter for that very reason approached unto him.

The tempter: That is, the devil.

If thou be the Son of God: That is, the Messiah, whom God himself at the baptism solemnly called his beloved Son. Having heard the voice which had descended from heaven and had testified, This is my beloved Son, and having heard just as glorious a testimony from John, the tempter suddenly sees him hungry; that startles him: recalling what was said about Jesus, he cannot see how Jesus can be a simple man; on the other hand seeing him hungry, he cannot believe him to be the Son of God. While in this state of perplexity, he approaches him with ambiguous words.

These stones: They were, no doubt, in the wilderness, in the place of fasting and of temptation. The essence and strength of the temptation consists in this, that Christ is asked to perform a miracle without any cause, for the gratification of his sensuous needs, that is, to make a bad use of the miracle, which would display his pride and opposition to God's intentions. He has just been proclaimed the Son of God, and now he has a chance to show that to him. "He was a-hungered. If he is the Messiah, why should he be a-hungered, since one word of his is enough to turn stones into bread and satisfy his hunger with them? What sin was there in changing stones into bread? Know that it is a sin to obey the devil in anything." (Theophil.)

It is written, etc.: Christ repels this temptation as also the two next ones by the word of God. He points to the utterance from Deut. viii. 8. Moses says in that passage that God, humbling the nation of Israel, tormented it with hunger and fed it with manna, which neither it nor its fathers knew of, that he might make it know that man doth not live by bread only, that is, sustain his existence, that there are other objects which can support man's existence, for example, the manna and, in general, everything which the word of God, that proceedeth out of his mouth, may point out. And thus, the Saviour, pointing to this utterance, shows to the tempter that it is not necessary to do the miracle of turning the stones into bread, and that it is possible to satisfy the hunger with other objects than bread, according to God's indication, or word, or action. That is the nearest direct meaning of the utterance. But, without doubt, in this utterance is contained a hint at the spiritual food, on which the believer feeds, and with which he, as it were, for a time forgets about the bodily food and feels no need of it; this spiritual food is the word of God, the divine teaching, and the divine commandments and injunctions, the fulfilment of which forms the spiritual food, which is of greater use to the soul than bodily food. Every word of God to him who is a-hungered supports his life like food. God can feed him who is a-hungered with a word. And so the meaning of Christ's answer is this: My need of bread is at present not such as to compel me to do a miracle. Life depends on the will of God. God can support it, not with bread only, but with anything he may point out as food. Besides, the word of God, his commandments and injunctions, which man must carry out, are a spiritual food with which the hunger of the body is forgotten, and man, living by this word, as by food, does not seem to feel the need of bodily food.

Taketh him up and setteth him: That does not mean that the devil carried Jesus through the air, or that he compelled him to go against his will, or that he did anything miraculous for the purpose. There is nothing to prove that the devil had such power and force, and the meaning of the word *taketh* does not compel us to accept any of the propositions mentioned; the word designates *to lead* or *accompany*, and Satan led, or accompanied, Jesus, of course, not against his will, not by force, not by compulsion.

The devil, in tempting the Lord to cast himself down from the top of the building, refers to the text from the psalms, saying that if he is the Son of God, there can be no danger for him, for, if every one who puts his trust in God is promised his aid, so much the more will this aid be given to the Son of God, and the angels will keep him unharmed. The essence and strength of this temptation consists in inciting Jesus, so to speak, to exact a miracle on the part of God, which would manifest Christ's vanity, self-confidence, and spiritual pride. If thou be

the Son of God, says the devil, God will do everything for thee
and will do a miracle in response to thy mere wish.

And saith unto him, etc.: To these words the Lord again
answers with words from Deuteronomy vi. 16: Thou shalt not
tempt the Lord thy God. Moses says that to the Jews, forbidding them to tempt Jehovah, as they tempted him at Massah,
saying, Is the Lord among us, or not? when they asked him for
a miracle on account of the lack of water. Consequently the
meaning of Christ's answer is this: It is not right to demand a
miracle from God at will. It is true, God aids those who fear
him and promises them miracles, but only in order to free them
from danger, and not whenever they ask for them. Consequently the tempter, who was distorting the meaning of the
passage from Scripture, was rebuffed by another passage which
correctly interpreted the meaning of the utterance pointed out
by the tempter.

An exceeding high mountain: It is not known which. Apparently it is the summit of some mountain, from which a great
part of Palestine can be seen. Abbot Merit speaks of the top of
one such mountain: this summit commands the mountains
of Arabia, the land of Gilead, the land of the Amorites, the
valleys of Moab and of Jericho, the current of the Jordan and
all the country about the Dead Sea. It is that mountain which
even now is called the Mountain of Temptation. Even so Moses
before his death went up unto the mountain of Nebo, to the top
of Pisgah, and the Lord shewed him all the land, from Gilead to
Dan, and all the land of Ephraim and of Manasseh, and all the
land of Judah, up to the Western Sea, and the southern land,
and the plain of the valley of Jericho, the city of palm-trees,
unto Zoar. From this we see that there were mountains, from
which could be seen a great part of the land of Canaan and
of Palestine, and of their surroundings.

All the kingdoms of the world: It must be assumed that the
tempter showed them to Christ by some logical, incomprehensible action, and of this we find a confirmation in the words
of St. Luke concerning this: In a moment of time (iv. 5), "in a
vision" (Theophil.).

All these things will I give thee: The tempter appropriates to
himself the power over all these kingdoms, as though they
belonged to him and he had the right to transfer to whomsoever
he pleased the power and the right which belonged to God alone.
It is true, the pagans were for a time in the power of Satan, and
the inhabitants of Palestine, who were degraded in morals, were
under his rule; nevertheless, in these words of the devil is

expressed a proud and false enjoyment of power which belongs to God alone, as the Creator and Provider of the world, in whose power are all the kingdoms on earth.

If thou wilt fall down and worship me: In appropriating to himself the power and the right over the whole world, which belong to God, the tempter also asks to be worshipped like God, that is, he asks for religious worship, in which should be expressed complete humiliation, and the power of the temptation consists in this, that instead of the unusual work of the redemption of humanity by means of the death on the cross and the foundation in this manner of a universal, spiritual, and eternal kingdom, Christ is offered the external royal power over the world, that is, this temptation is a deviation from the whole great work of his ministration to the human race in the capacity of Messiah the Redeemer.

Then saith Jesus unto him, etc.: This is a bolder temptation than the first two. The Lord again repels him with words from Scripture, but before that he with his almighty word commands the tempter to stop his temptations : Get thee hence, Satan !

It is written: From Deut. vi. 13. In that passage Moses admonishes the Jews, when they come into possession of Palestine, not to follow the gods of those nations, who will be living around them, that is the pagan gods, for to Jehovah alone, the true God, does divine worship belong, and to no one else.

Reuss, the esteemed writer of the Tübingen school, explains the passage as follows (*La Bible, Nouveau Testament,* Vol. I., pp. 179–185):

Le récit de cette célèbre péricope, qui a exercé la sagacité des commentateurs plus qu'aucune autre, est connu sous le nom d'histoire de *la* tentation. Cette formule, cependant, n'exprime pas exactement la nature du fait relaté. Car tandis que le texte du second évangile ne parle que très-vaguement d'*une* tentation qui dura quarante jours, celui du premier se borne à raconter explicitement *trois* diverses tentations qui eurent lieu après ces quarante jours; enfin Luc combine ces deux versions et les adopte toutes les deux. Cette différence n'affecte pas le fond du récit. On peut en dire autant de quelques autres que nous voulons signaler en passant, sans y attacher de l'importance. Ainsi Matthieu seul dit que la tentation était le but de la retraite de Jésus au désert, l'Esprit voulant qu'il fût tenté. Les bêtes sauvages, mentionnées par Marc seul, servent simplement à exprimer d'une manière plus pittoresque l'idée de la solitude, rien ne nous obligeant de songer à des bêtes féroces. Des deux premiers textes nous recevons l'impression d'une retraite de Jésus en un lieu solitaire où il serait resté pendant quarante jours, pour s'y livrer (comme le veut l'explication populaire et usuelle) à des méditations sur son futur ministère. Le texte de Luc, corrigé d'après les anciens manuscrits, nous suggère au contraire l'idée d'un séjour sans repos, d'une course agitée et prolongée, et troublée en même temps par les assauts répétés du tentateur. Puis il y a cette différence assez notable que les trois scènes particulières ne se suivent pas dans le même ordre chez les deux évangélistes qui les racontent. Tous les commentateurs sont d'accord à donner à cet égard la préférence à Matthieu, et leurs raisons sont si évidemment fondées en logique et en psychologie que nous pouvons nous dispenser de les exposer au long. Nous ferons seulement observer qu'elles n'ont de valeur absolue qu'autant qu'on admet la réalité historique des faits eux-mêmes. Enfin les trois récits se terminent d'une manière différente. Matthieu donne à entendre que le tentateur, trois fois repoussé avec dédain, quitta la partie pour tout de bon ; Luc, au contraire, insinue qu'il revint à la charge plus tard. Cet auteur songeait sans doute, soit aux luttes que Jésus eut à soutenir pendant toute la durée de son ministère, soit à sa passion et à sa mort. Matthieu ajoute que le diable vaincu fut aussitôt remplacé auprès de Jésus par des anges serviteurs, envoyés, comme on peut le penser, soit pour pourvoir à ses besoins, soit pour rendre hommage à sa sainteté victorieuse. Marc aussi parle d'anges, mais il paraît vouloir dire qu'ils se trouvaient présents pendant tout le séjour au désert, lui tenant compagnie et le servant, ce qui exclurait encore l'idée du jeûne et de la faim dont parlent les autres textes.

Toutes ces différences, nous le répétons, ne portent que sur des détails accessoires. Nous avons maintenant à nous occuper du fond même de cette narration unique dans son genre, non-seulement dans les évangiles, mais dans la Bible tout entière. Avant tout rendons-nous bien compte du sens que nous devons attacher au mot *tenter*. Le langage biblique (Ancien et Nouveau Testament) emploie ce terme dans trois applications différentes : 1° on dit d'un homme qu'il tente Dieu, quand il prétend provoquer, par des sollicitations impatientes, une manifestation quelconque de sa puissance, par ex. un miracle ; comme une pareille sollicitation a toujours sa source dans un manque de confiance ou de résignation, l'Écriture déclare qu'elle est un péché ; 2° on dit de Dieu qu'il tente les hommes, quand il met leur foi à l'épreuve par des tribulations et des contrariétés de tout genre. Comme ici le but et les moyens sont également salutaires, les apôtres déjà ont compris que le terme était mal choisi (Jacq. i. 13) et le langage moderne l'abandonne de plus en plus, pour y substituer celui d'*éprouver*; 3° enfin un homme tente l'autre quand il cherche à l'entraîner au mal. Nul doute que les faits racontés dans notre péricope ne rentrent dans cette troisième catégorie et non dans la première. Le tentateur ne s'adresse pas à la *puissance* de Jésus pour lui extorquer des miracles à son propre profit; il y a plutôt un conflit *moral*, entre la sainte volonté de Christ et les tendances perverses du diable.

Ceci étant généralement reconnu, nous établirons avant toute autre chose que les trois narrateurs entendent bien raconter un fait objectif et matériel; des rencontres et des conversations entre deux personnages distincts, dont l'un était Satan lui-même, apparaissant d'une manière visible, à l'effet d'entraîner Jésus à des actes que celui-ci repoussa avec énergie. Et d'abord, lorsque, après avoir miraculeusement traversé une période de quarante jours sans prendre aucune nourriture, les besoins physiques se firent de nouveau sentir chez lui, le diable lui proposa de les satisfaire par l'opération d'un miracle. Jésus s'y refuse en alléguant un passage scripturaire (Deut. viii. 3), qui lui permet d'espérer ou de trouver des moyens de sustentation là même où les resources ordinaires lui faisaient défaut. Dieu, dit-il, peut me nourrir, de telle manière qu'il lui plaira; il n'a qu'à parler, qu'à commander, sans que j'aie besoin d'intervenir moi-même de manière à changer la nature des choses. (Il est également faux de traduire: l'homme peut vivre de toutes les *choses* [mangeables] créées par Dieu; ou: je puis me nourrir de *la* parole de Dieu, spirituellement, et n'ai point besoin de nourriture matérielle.) Le texte de Luc, rétabli d'après les plus anciens manuscrits, n'a pas cette phrase; celle qu'y ont insérée les copies vulgaires (*toute parole de Dieu*) ne donne point de sens plausible.

La seconde tentation consistait à inviter Jésus à s'exposer de gaîté de cœur à un danger imminent, en se précipitant du haut d'un édifice, dans la conviction ou dans l'espérance que Dieu le préserverait miraculeusement de tout accident. Nous ne savons pas quelle localité les évangélistes ont entendu désigner par le terme que nous avons traduit au hasard par le *faîte du temple*; il est douteux qu'il soit question du Sanctuaire lui-même, sur le toit duquel on ne montait pas. Peut-être s'agit-il d'un autre édifice compris dans l'enceinte sacrée, et placé du côté de l'est où le mont Moría dominait la profonde vallée de Qidron et présentait une paroi coupée à pic. Le tentateur prétend déterminer Jésus en lui rappelant les paroles du Psaume (xci. 12) interprétées au pied de la lettre. Jésus lui répond par un autre passage (Deut. vi. 16), qui condamne tout essai de *tenter* Dieu, dans le sens que nous avons indiqué plus haut.

Enfin le diable l'emmène sur une montagne du haut de laquelle il pouvait voir tous les royaumes de la terre, et contempler leur grandeur, leur puissance et leurs richesses. Tout cela lui est promis à condition qu'il serve les intérêts de celui qui s'en dit le maître. Jésus le repousse en invoquant simplement le principe fondamental de la religion révélée (Deut. vi. 13), lequel suffisait à lui seul pour écarter toute velléité ambitieuse. On pourrait presque dire à ce sujet que la tentation la plus séduisante des trois, est vaincue à la fois avec le moindre effort et avec le plus d'énergie.

La forme concrète de ces trois tentations a quelque chose de singulier, surtout la seconde, dont on a de la peine à entrevoir le motif. Mais pour le fond, elles ne sont point sans analogie dans l'histoire évangélique. Nous rappelons la scène de Gethsémané où Jésus disait : Si je le voulais, mon père m'enverrait douze légions d'anges ; ou celle de Golgotha où le peuple criait : S'il est le fils de Dieu, qu'il descende de la croix ; puis cette parole adressée aux Pharisiens : Cette génération demande un signe ; mais elle n'aura que celui donné par Jonas aux Ninévites ; enfin les occasions où la foule voulait le proclamer roi et sa déclaration solennelle : Mon royaume n'est pas de ce monde.

Tout de même le présent récit, tel qu'il est donné et compris par les évangélistes, présente des difficultés insurmontables, qu'il est de notre devoir de signaler. Nous ne nous arrêterons pas à celles qui ne tiennent qu'au cadre de l'histoire, par ex. à la question de savoir sous quelle forme le diable apparut ? comment Jésus fut transporté du désert au temple, du temple sur la montagne, et de là de nouveau au désert ? où doit être la montagne assez haute pour permettre à l'homme d'embrasser d'un seul coup d'œil tous les royaumes de la terre ? et autres questions semblables qui peuvent embarrasser l'exégèse littérale, mais qui sont des bagatelles à côté de celles qui se présentent à la méditation du théologien. Celui-ci est autorisé à demander d'abord si Jésus a reconnu le diable ? Quelle que soit la réponse qu'on voudra donner (le texte dit positivement *oui*), la notion de sa divinité se trouvera singulièrement amoindrie ; car, ou bien lui, Dieu, n'aurait pas connu celui qu'il était venu combattre et vaincre sur la terre, ou bien, tout en le connaissant, il se serait mis ou trouvé en son pouvoir. Or, il nous semble impossible que le diable ait eu prise sur le Fils de Dieu, dans le sens physique, et beaucoup moins possible encore que celui-ci ait consenti à suivre le diable, à entrer en quelque sorte, en le suivant, dans ses vues, à lui donner prise sur lui-même, dans le sens moral. En général, l'idée d'une *tentation de Dieu* dans ce sens, est une idée contraire aux notions les plus élémentaires d'une religion digne de ce nom; et cependant les textes eux-mêmes disent que la tentation était le but du séjour de Jésus au désert. Il s'ensuit de tout ce qui précède que la narration contenue dans notre péricope, *telle qu'elle est* sous nos yeux, est incompatible avec la formule ou conception consacrée officiellement, concernant la divinité du Christ. Ajoutons encore que cette conséquence résulte surtout de ce que le diable propose à Christ de l'adorer. D'après la théologie de l'Église, Christ, c'est-à-dire la seconde personne de la trinité, est le créateur du diable comme de tout ce qui existe. Le diable le sait mieux que personne. Sa prétention n'est donc pas seulement un blasphème, elle est la plus inconcevable sottise. Or, les évangélistes n'ont pas voulu raconter une absurdité: ils nous représentent Jésus, tenté comme un *homme*, mais triomphant sans hésitation, sans effort, d'une manière parfaite et décisive.

Mais encore à cet autre point de vue, qui, nous le répétons, est celui des évangélistes, il y a de graves difficultés qui arrêtent le lecteur. Car lors même que nous voudrions écarter toutes celles qui résultent de la présomption de la nature divine de Christ, notre sentiment religieux se refuse encore à admettre que la tentation, c'est-à-dire la provocation au mal, ait pu exercer sur lui une influence quelconque, ne fût-elle que passagère ou provisoire, ne se présentât-elle à son esprit que comme une question à résoudre, comme une hypothèse. En effet, si le mal a pu, nous ne disons pas obscurcir pour un instant la lucidité de son esprit, ou travailler fugitivement sa conscience morale, mais seulement glisser pour ainsi dire comme une ombre devant ses yeux de manière à attirer momentanément son attention, la notion de sa sainteté absolue, qui est un élément indispensable de la foi chrétienne, est nécessairement remise en question, ou plutôt elle est positivement compromise. Cela est si vrai que déjà quelques-uns des anciens pères de l'Église ont été d'avis que les scènes du temple et de la montagne n'ont pu être des faits réels, puisque autrement il faudrait admettre que Jésus a *cédé* jusqu'à un certain point à la tentation, sauf à s'arrêter au moment décisif. Des auteurs modernes ont été plus loin, et niant la réalité objective et extérieure de toute cette histoire, n'ont voulu y voir qu'un fait intérieur et subjectif, une évolution de la pensée de Jésus, une contemplation contradictoire de ses buts et moyens, un drame purement psychique. Mais il serait facile de prouver que cet expédient, dont le moindre tort est d'être contraire au texte, n'écarte pas la difficulté que nous venons de signaler ; tout au contraire, si nous mettons à la place du diable personnel, les propres pensées de Jésus, n'importe qu'elles aient surgi dans un songe, ou dans une vision, ou dans une lutte intérieure, nous ne faisons qu'affirmer la présence, dans sa nature morale, d'un élément de faiblesse qui est d'autant moins propre à nous rassurer, que l'objet de la tentation a été plus insolite. On pourrait même dire qu'à cet égard la ridicule explication des interprètes rationalistes, qui ont entrevu dans le diable un émissaire du Sanhédrin, ménageait beaucoup mieux l'intégrité du caractère de Jésus.

Un grand nombre de théologiens allemands de notre siècle, désespérant de faire accorder le récit des évangiles avec une saine appréciation de la personne et de la dignité de Jésus, et convaincus qu'aucune des transformations de l'histoire successivement essayées par les commentateurs n'efface complètement ce qui nous y arrête et nous choque, ont proposé l'explication très-spécieuse que voici : Ce que les évangélistes nous racontent comme un fait historique aurait été dans l'origine une parabole racontée par Jésus à ses disciples à l'effet de leur faire saisir la différence entre une conception fausse et mauvaise de l'œuvre messianique et des pouvoirs donnés à celui qui devait l'accomplir, et la conception vraie, qui était la sienne propre. Le diable, le désert, le temple et la montagne appartiendraient au cadre du récit figuré ; l'inévitable contradiction entre les *quarante* jours passés au désert, et les *deux* jours qui (d'après Jean) séparaient la noce de Cana du séjour sur les bords du Jourdain, disparaissait en même temps. On a objecté avec raison que ce serait le seul exemple d'une parabole dans laquelle Jésus se serait introduit lui-même nominativement, et de plus qu'elle aurait dû être bien mal comprise par les auditeurs pour finir par nous arriver dans la forme actuelle. Cela est très-vrai, cependant, de toute façon, à moins de dire que nous n'avons là qu'un pur mythe, il faudra admettre que la narration a été formulée primitivement par Jésus lui-même, qu'elle n'a pu être communiquée aux disciples que dans un but pédagogique, et qu'ainsi, parabole ou non, c'est le sens intime du récit, son élément moral et religieux, que nous avons à rechercher. Le jugement à porter sur les accessoires historiques est pour la chrétienté chose secondaire. Elle a un moindre intérêt à résoudre les questions que nous avons posées en commençant, qu'à savoir comment Jésus comprenait sa mission, ou plutôt quels moyens il entendait ne pas employer à l'appui de son ministère. Ses besoins personnels, dont la faim n'est ici que l'individualisation symbolique, ne devaient point être pour lui une préoccupation, un souci, un motif directeur de ses actes. Tout aussi peu la vaine gloire à obtenir auprès des hommes devait l'engager à faire parade de ce qui le distinguait du commun des mortels; il devait se défendre jusqu'au plaisir de constater pour lui-même, et sans utilité pour le monde, la puissance protectrice du rapport qui le rattachait à Dieu, et connaître la différence entre le dévouement salutaire qui sacrifie la vie parce qu'il en sait la valeur, et la folle témérité qui la risque parce qu'elle n'en a aucune. Enfin il ne pouvait se tromper sur la nature du royaume qu'il se proposait de fonder, ni ignorer que la direction mondaine, dans laquelle les espérances fantastiques et superstitieuses de son peuple auraient voulu l'entraîner, loin de servir son vrai but, lui ferait manquer sa vocation, et renier son Dieu par une idolâtrie aussi méprisable que blasphématoire.

Reuss assumes, like the church, that the author presented to himself a real person of Satan; but he does not explain why he assumes that. In this assumption, however, lies the whole mistake. From the meaning of the whole chapter it does not at all appear that the author imagined a real person under the name of Satan; on the contrary, the very opposite is quite obvious. If the author had imagined a person, he would have said something about him, about his appearance, about his actions, whereas not a word is said about the person itself. The personality of the tempter is mentioned just to the extent to which it is necessary, in order to express Christ's thoughts and feelings. Nothing is said as to how he approached him, nor how he carried him, nor how he disappeared. All that is mentioned is Jesus Christ and that foe, who is in every man, that principle of struggle without which the living man is unthinkable. It is evident that the author wants to express the ideas of Jesus Christ by simple methods. To express ideas, it is necessary to make him speak, but he is alone. So the author makes Christ speak with himself, and he calls one voice the voice of Jesus Christ, and the other now the devil, that is, the deceiver, and now the tempter.

In the church interpretation we are told directly that we must not and cannot (though, as always, it does not say why we must not and cannot) regard the devil as an idea, but must take him as a real person, and we are used to such an assumption, but why Reuss assumes the same demands an explanation. To any man who is free from the church interpretation it will be clear that the words which are ascribed to the tempter express only the voice of the flesh, which is contrary to the spirit of which Jesus Christ was possessed, after John's preaching. Such an acceptation of the meaning of the words " tempter, deceiver, Satan," which express the same thing, is confirmed by this: (1) that the personality of the tempter is introduced only to the extent to which it is needed to express the inward struggle; not a single feature is added about the tempter himself; (2) that the words of the tempter express only the voice of the flesh and nothing more, and (3) that all three temptations are the most common expressions of an inner struggle, which is repeated in the soul of every man.

Wherein does this inner struggle consist? Jesus is thirty years old. He regards himself as a son of God. That is all we know about him at the time that he is listening to John's sermon. John preaches that the kingdom of heaven has come upon earth, and that, in order to enter it, one needs a purification by the spirit, in addition to the purification by water. John does not promise any striking external condition. There will be no external sign of the approach of the kingdom of heaven. The only sign of its coming is a certain inward, non-carnal manifestation, the purification by the spirit. Filled with the idea about this spirit, Jesus Christ goes into the wilderness. His idea about his relation to God is expressed in what precedes. He regards God as his Father; he is a son of God, and, in order that his Father may be in the world and in himself, he has to find the spirit which is to purify the world, and with that spirit to purify himself.

In order to discover this spirit, he is subjected to temptation, departs from people, and goes into the wilderness. In the wilderness he suffers hunger. While he is conscious of his sonhood to God and of his spirituality, he wants to eat and suffers hunger. And the voice of the flesh says to him, If thou be the son of God, command that these stones be made bread. If we are to understand these words as the church understands them, namely, that the devil, tempting the son of God, wants of him proofs of his divinity, it is impossible to comprehend why Jesus Christ did not change the stones into bread, if he was able to accomplish that. That would have been the best and simplest and shortest answer, that would have attained its purpose. If the words, If thou be the son of God, command that these stones be made bread, are a provocation to perform a miracle, then it is necessary for Jesus to say in reply, I do not want to perform a miracle, or something to that effect, but Jesus Christ says nothing about being willing, or not willing, to do what the devil proposes to him, and answers something entirely different. He does not even mention anything about it, but replies, Man shall not live by bread alone, but by every word that proceedeth out of the mouth of God. These words not only are no reply to the devil's mention about the bread, but say something quite different. From the fact that Jesus not only fails to change the stones into bread, which is an obvious impossibility, but does not even answer this impossibility, but replies to the general meaning, it is evident that these words could not have the direct meaning, Command that these stones be made bread, but have that meaning which they have when they are directed to a man, and not to God. If they are directed simply to a man, their meaning is clear and simple. These words mean: Thou wantest bread, and so take care that thou hast the bread, for thou seest that thou canst not make bread with words. And Jesus does not reply to why he does not make bread out of stones, but to the meaning which lies in the words, Dost thou submit to the demands of the flesh? He says, Man does not live by bread, but by the spirit. The meaning of this separate utterance is very general. To understand it more definitely, it is necessary to recall the whole beginning of the chapter, and what these words refer to. In quoting the words from the book of Holy Scripture, Jesus Christ obviously has in mind the meaning which is to be found in that chapter.

In Deuteronomy, Chapter VIII., the fifth book of Moses, it is said:

1. All the commandments which I command thee this day shall ye observe to do, that ye may live, and multiply, and go in and possess the land which the Lord sware unto your fathers.

2. And thou shalt remember all the way which the Lord thy God led thee these forty years in the wilderness, to humble thee, and to prove thee, to know what was in thine heart, whether thou wouldest keep his commandments, or no.

3. And he humbled thee, and suffered thee to hunger, and fed thee with manna, which thou knewest not, neither did thy fathers know; that he might make thee know that man doth not live by bread only, but by every word that proceedeth out of the mouth of the Lord doth man live.

4. Thy raiment waxed not old upon thee, neither did thy foot swell, these forty years.

5. Thou shalt also consider in thine heart, that, as a man chasteneth his son, so the Lord thy God chasteneth thee.

6. Therefore thou shalt keep the commandments of the Lord thy God, to walk in his ways, and to fear him.

7. For the Lord thy God bringeth thee into a good land, a land of brooks of water, of fountains and depths that spring out of valleys and hills.

And so, to the devil's words about hunger, Jesus recalling Israel, who had lived for forty years in the wilderness without perishing, answers the tempter with the following words, Not by bread does man live, but by the will of God. And as Israel relied on God, and God brought the nation to Palestine, so I rely on God.

At these words of Jesus, the devil takes him and carries him to the top of a temple, again repeating, If thou be the son of God, cast thyself down.

These words have cost much labour to the church commentators; but no interpretation is wanted: the voice of the flesh, speaking in Jesus, is called the devil, and so these words mean simply that his imagination carried him to the top of the temple. Or: and he imagined that he was standing on an eminence, and the voice of the flesh said to him, repeating as before, If thou be a son of God, cast thyself down.

According to the interpretation of the church, these words are in no way connected with the first, and again have no other significance than that the devil is provoking Jesus Christ to perform an unnecessary miracle. The words of the devil from Psalm XCI. about the angels bearing him up, according to the church interpretation, are again not connected with what precedes, and the whole conversation is represented as aimless. The disconnectedness and senselessness of the church interpretation of the second temptation is due to the error in the comprehension of the meaning of the first words. The first words, Make bread out of stones, which are not understood as an expression of impossibility (to have bread when there is no supply of it), but as a· provocation to perform a miracle, have compelled the commentators to look also upon the subsequent words, Cast thyself down, as upon a provocation to perform a miracle; but evidently these words are connected with the first inward meaning. This connection is obvious, if from nothing else, from the fact that both the first and the second series of words begin with the same expression, If thou be the son of God.

Besides, the word ὅτι *because*, in the second answer, which is found in Luke, shows clearly that Jesus Christ is not answering to the words of the devil, Cast thyself down, but to his own refusal to cast himself down.   Neither in his first, nor in his third temptation, does Christ say, It is written, and so forth, but, Because it is written, that is, he says, I will not cast myself down, because it is written.

From the very start the voice of the flesh wants to show to Jesus the falseness of his convictions about being a spiritual being and a son of God.   Thou sayest that thou art a son of God, and wentest into the wilderness, and thinkest to free thyself from the craving of the flesh; but the craving of the flesh is tormenting thee.   Here thou wilt not gratify thy craving, thou wilt not change the stones into bread, so thou hadst better go where there is something to make bread of, and make it, or provide thyself with it and eat like all men.

That is what the voice of the flesh said in the first temptation.   To this Jesus Christ, recalling Israel in the wilderness, says, Israel lived forty years in the wilderness without bread, and found food, and remained alive, because God wanted it so.   Consequently man lives not by bread, but by the will of God.

Then the voice of the flesh, making him think that he is standing on an eminence, says to him: If that is so, and thou, as a son of God, dost not need to trouble thyself about the bread, prove it by casting thyself down. For didst thou not say thyself that everything is due, not to the care of man, but to the will of God?   That is an actual truth, and in David's psalm it is written, In their hands they shall bear thee up and keep thee from suffering harm.   So why dost thou suffer?   Cast thyself down! No harm will befall thee, for the angels shall bear thee up.

The moment the correct explanation is given to the first words, namely, that they are not a provocation to perform a miracle, but an indication of an impossibility, these

words, too, assume the same character and clear significance. In the words of the devil, Cast thyself down, is
to be found an objection to Jesus' reliance on God; but
in the subsequent words from the psalm there is expressed
this idea, that if one is to believe in God's will and live by
it alone, he cannot be subject to suffering, and the angels
will preserve him; and so the devil expresses his idea:
(1) that if a person believes that man lives by the will of
God, and not by his own care, he need not be heedful of
his life, and (2) that for the believer there can be no privations and sufferings, nor thirst, nor hunger, and all he
has to do is to cast himself down headlong and abandon
himself to the will of God, and the angels will bear him
up. That this second idea about Jesus Christ's ability to
free himself from hunger, if he really believes in the will
of God, by casting himself down from the temple, is contained in the words of the devil, is confirmed by Jesus
Christ's answer about not tempting God, as had happened
at Massah. The voice of the flesh with the words, Cast
thyself down, not only proves to Jesus the injustice of
his proof about life not being from human bread but from
God, but from the very fact that Jesus does not cast himself down we see that he does not believe in it. If he
believed in this, that life is not from human bread, not
from human cares, but from God, he would now not spare
himself in his hunger; but he suffers hunger and yet
does not fully abandon himself to the will of God. To
this Jesus answers with a refusal to cast himself down.
He says, I will not cast myself down, because it is
written, Do not tempt thy Lord.

Jesus Christ again answers with words from a book of
Moses, recalling the incident at Massah-Meribah. This
is what happened at Massah (Exod. xvii.):

2. Wherefore the people did chide with Moses, and said, Give
us water that we may drink. And Moses said unto them, Why
chide ye with me? wherefore do ye tempt the Lord?

3. And the people thirsted there for water; and the people murmured against Moses, and said, Wherefore is this that thou hast brought us up out of Egypt to kill us and our children and our cattle with thirst?

4. And Moses cried unto the Lord, saying, What shall I do unto this people? they be almost ready to stone me.

5. And the Lord said unto Moses, Go on before the people, and take with thee of the elders of Israel: and thy rod, wherewith thou smotest the river, take in thine hand, and go.

6. Behold, I will stand before thee there upon the rock in Horeb; and thou shalt smite the rock, and there shall come water out of it, that the people may drink. And Moses did so in the sight of the elders of Israel.

7. And he called the name of the place Massah, and Meribah, because of the chiding of the children of Israel, and because they tempted the Lord, saying, Is the Lord among us, or not?

With this reference Jesus Christ answers both considerations of the devil. To the statement made by the voice of the flesh that he does not believe in God, since he takes care of himself, he says, One must not tempt the Lord. To the suggestion of the voice of the flesh that, if he believed in God, he would cast himself down from the temple, in order to give himself into the charge of the angels and free himself from hunger, he replies by saying that he does not rebuke any one for his hunger, as the Israelites rebuked Moses at Massah. He does not lose his hope in God, and so he does not need to tempt God and finds it easy to bear his condition. The third temptation is a strict deduction from the first two. The first two begin with the words, If thou be the son of God, but the last has not that introduction. The voice of the flesh speaks directly to Jesus Christ, showing him all the kingdoms of the world, that is, how all men live, and says to him, If thou wilt worship me, I will give thee all these things. The absence of the introductory clause and the entirely new turn of speech, as though not addressing a man with whom one disputes, but a man who is vanquished, point to the connection of this passage with what precedes, if the preceding passages are understood in their real sense.

At first the voice of the flesh discusses, saying, If thou wert a son of God and a spirit, thou wouldst not suffer hunger, and if thou didst suffer hunger, thou wouldst be able by thy own will to make bread out of stones and gratify thy appetite. But if thou sufferest hunger and canst not make bread out of stones, thou art not a son of God and a spirit. But thou sayest that thou art a son of God in the sense of putting thy faith in God. That is not true, for, if thou didst rely upon God, as a son relies upon his father, thou wouldst not now suffer hunger, but wouldst at once abandon thyself to the power of God and wouldst not spare thy life, but no, thou wilt not cast thyself down from the roof.

To this Jesus Christ replies that he has no right to demand anything from God. What Jesus Christ meant by these words will be mentioned farther down, but the devil does not understand the argument.

The arguments of the devil are as follows:

Thou wantest to eat, so bestir thyself about the bread. If it be true that thou givest thyself over to the will of God, thou wouldst not try to save thyself; but thou dost save thyself, consequently thou art not right. And so the voice of the flesh says triumphantly, If thou dost not wish to think of food, do not spare thy life; but since thou art caring for thy life and dost not wish to cast thyself down from the roof, why dost thou not provide thyself with bread? The voice of the flesh seems to compel Jesus to recognize its might and the inevitableness of life of the flesh, and so it says, All this reliance of thine upon God and certainty concerning him are empty words, but in reality thou hast not gone away, and wilt not go away, from the flesh. Thou hast been and art just the same son of the flesh like all other men. And if thou art a son of the flesh, worship it and work for it.

I am the spirit of the flesh. And he shows the kingdoms of the world to Jesus. Thou seest what I give to those who serve me. Worship me, work for me, and thou wilt have the same.

To this Jesus again replies from a book of Moses (Deut. vi. 13): Thou shalt fear the Lord thy God, and serve him, and swear by his name.

This is not said simply in Deuteronomy, but is said to the Israelites, lest they should forget God and should forget to work for him alone, when they received all the benefits of the flesh.

The voice of the flesh grows silent, and the divine strength helps Jesus Christ to bear the temptation.

Everything which has to be said has been said. The church interpretations are wont to represent this passage as a victory of Jesus Christ over the devil. From no interpretation does a victory result: the devil may be regarded as much a victor as is Jesus Christ. There is no victory on either side: there is only an expression of two diametrically opposed principles of life, and both the one which Jesus Christ rejects and the one which he accepts are clearly expressed. Both trains of thought are striking in that all philosophic systems, the systems of morality, the religious sects, the different tendencies of life in this or that historical period have for their foundation nothing but the different sides of these two reflections. In every serious conversation about the meaning of life, or about religion, in every case of an inward struggle of each individual, there are always repeated the same discussions of this discourse of the devil with Jesus Christ, or of the voice of the flesh with the voice of the spirit.

What we call materialism is only an adherence to the whole discussion of the devil; what we call asceticism is only an adherence to Christ's first answer about man's not living by bread.

The suicidal sects, the philosophy of a Schopenhauer and of a Hartmann, are only the evolution of the devil's second reflection.

In the simplest form the discussion represents itself as follows :

Devil. Thou art a son of God, and yet hungry. With words thou canst not make bread. Talk what thou pleasest about God, but the belly craves for bread. If thou wantst to be alive, work, and provide thyself with bread.

Jesus. Man lives not by bread, but by God. What gives life to man is not the flesh, but the spirit.

Devil. If it is not the flesh that gives life, then man is free from the flesh and its demands. And if thou art free, cast thyself down from the roof, and the angels will bear thee up in their arms. Kill thy flesh, or kill thyself at once.

Jesus. The life in the body is from God, and so it is not right to murmur against it and doubt in it.

Devil. Thou sayest, What is the use of bread? and yet art suffering hunger. Thou sayest, Life is from God, in the spirit, and yet carest for thy flesh, consequently all that is nothing but talk. Not thou beginnest the world, and not with thee will it end. Look at people : they have lived and still live, providing bread for themselves and taking care of it. And they provide it not for a day, nor for one year, but for many years, and not bread only, but everything which man needs. And they take care of themselves and try not to fall, not to be killed by misery, and not to be offended by man : live likewise ! If thou wishest to eat, work ! If thou pitiest thy body, take care of thyself ! Worship thy flesh and work for it, and thou wilt live, and it will repay thee.

Jesus. Man lives not by the flesh, but by God. It is impossible to doubt the life from God, and in this life we must worship God alone and work for him alone.

The whole discussion of the devil, that is, of the flesh, is incontestable and invincible, if we place ourselves at his point of view.   Christ's contention is just as invincible, if we place ourselves at his point of view.   The only difference is that the contention of Jesus Christ includes the contention of the flesh.   Jesus Christ understands the discussion of the flesh and takes it for the basis of the whole discussion, but the discussion of the flesh does not include that of Jesus Christ and does not understand his point of view.   The devil's want of comprehension of Christ begins with the second question and answer. The devil says, If thou sayest that thou canst live without bread, which is necessary for life, then thou canst renounce thy whole carnal life, simply reject it, and cast thyself down from an eminence, in order to annihilate it.

Jesus replies, While refusing the bread I do not reject God, whereas by casting myself down from the temple I reject him.   But life is from God, and life is a manifestation of God within me, in my flesh.   Consequently, by renouncing life and doubting in it I doubt in God.   And thus, it is possible to reject everything in the name of God, but not life, because life is a manifestation of the Deity.

But the devil does not want to understand this.   He assumes that his contention is correct, and says, Why is it possible to reject the bread which is necessary for life, and not life itself?   That is not consistent.   And if it is not possible to reject life, it is not possible to reject anything which is necessary for it, and he makes the deduction, And if thou dost not cast thyself down from the roof and thinkest that thou art obliged to take care of thyself, thou art obliged to take care of everything and provide thyself with bread.

Jesus says that it is not possible to compare bread with life, that there is a difference there.   And the argument of Jesus leads him to an opposite conclusion.

The flesh says, I have placed within thee the necessity of caring for me. If thou thinkest that thou canst neglect any appetites of mine and go hungry, when thou wantest to eat, do not imagine that thou canst get away from me. If thou abstainest from them, thou dost so only because thou sacrificest some needs for other needs of mine; thou sacrificest them only for a short time and continuest to live for the gratification of my demands of the flesh. Thou sacrificest one set of needs for another, but the flesh itself thou wilt not sacrifice in any way. And so thou wilt not get away from me, and thou wilt always serve me alone, like all other men.

It is this one incontestable truth that Jesus Christ takes for the foundation of his discussion, and with the first word, while acknowledging the whole truthfulness of this discussion, transfers the question to another point of view. He asks himself, What is that demand to take care of the flesh, which I feel within me, those appetites and that inner struggle with those appetites? and he answers, It is the consciousness of life within me. What, then, is that consciousness of life? The flesh is not the life? What, then, is life? Life is something unknown, but something which does not resemble the flesh, something quite different from it. What is it, then? It is something from another source.

And so, recognizing the first proposition, that there is the flesh and that there is the necessity to preserve it, he says to himself that none the less everything which he knows about the flesh and its needs he knows only because there is life in him, and he says to himself that life is not from the flesh, but from something else, and this something else, which is the opposite of the flesh, he calls God, and says, Man lives not because he eats bread, but because life is within him; but that life comes from something else, from God.

To the second proposition of the flesh, that, after all, it is impossible to get away from the flesh, and that a man

lives only because he keeps it by a feeling of self-preser-
vation, Jesus Christ says, continuing the discussion from
his standpoint, that he is preserving his life not for the
sake of the flesh, but because it is from God, and because
life is a manifestation of God, and so, in the last conclusion about the necessity of working for the flesh, he
entirely departs from the tempter, and says, It is necessary to work for the spiritual principle of life, for God.
It is necessary to λατρεύειν not for the flesh, but for
God alone. The word λατρεύειν, which designates the
work of a hired labourer, compulsory work, for pay, is
not placed here by accident. It is important to keep in
mind the meaning which this word has.

Jesus says, It is true, I shall always be in the power of
the flesh; it will always urge its demands, but outside the
voice of the flesh I know also the voice of God, which is
independent of it. And thus, as in these temptations in
the wilderness, so also in my whole life, the voice of the
flesh and the voice of God will contend with each other,
and I shall have to work for the one or for the other, like
a labourer expecting to be paid. Two voices will be calling me and demanding my work for the one or for the
other. And I will make an effort for God in all such
controversies, and from him alone will expect my (reward)
pay, that is, in case of a struggle I will always choose the
effort for God.

And the spirit obtains a victory over the flesh, and
Jesus finds the spirit that is going to cleanse him, so that
the kingdom of heaven may come. In the consciousness
of this spirit Jesus Christ returns from the wilderness.

If we give the words *God* and *life* the meanings which
these words have in the Introduction, the words of Jesus
Christ became clearer still. In response to the devil's
first remark about the bread Christ says, Man lives not
by bread, but by the comprehension. To the devil's remark that Jesus should cast himself down from the roof,

he replies, I cannot doubt the comprehension; the comprehension is always with me. It gives me life, and life is the light of the comprehension, so how can I have any doubts about the comprehension and tempt it? And so I cannot work for anything else but that which is the source of my life, which is my life itself. The comprehension alone do I worship and it alone do I serve. Besides the inward meaning of this passage as regards the evolution of the teaching in Christ himself, it has the other meaning of the elucidation in the consciousness of Jesus Christ of God as the comprehension.

In the beginning of the temptation Jesus Christ speaks of the Jewish God, the Creator of everything, of God as a separate individual, distinct from man, of God who is pre-eminently carnal.

Thou canst make bread, says the tempter; and in reply, Christ says, though not clearly, that God is not an exclusively carnal God: Man lives not by bread alone, but by God. The words, Cast thyself down, or, If a man can deprive himself of bread, he can also deprive himself of life, express a doubt as to life being itself from God: Life is not from God, but in my power. And Christ says in reply, Everything is in my power but life, because life itself is from God. Life is a manifestation of God, life is in God.

Here we have a conclusion, from an entirely different side from what it was in the Introduction, that life is the light of men, and light is comprehension, and the comprehension is that which men call God, that is, the beginning of everything.

The third temptation transfers the whole discussion from the internal sphere to the external. It says, Thy judgment cannot be correct, since the whole world lives differently.

In replying to this, Christ repeats his conception about the inner, non-carnal God. He says, Amidst those benefits which I did not give to myself, I must worship none but my God and serve him alone. Besides, it is necessary to remember, in the evolution of the further teaching, that this idea of God and those relations of man to God, which are expressed in this passage, are worked out by Jesus Christ on the same path of thought. We must remember that in reply to the question as to what man lives by, bread or God, Jesus for the first time makes clear to himself his own teaching about the meaning of God and man, and for this reason he in very many places, whenever he wishes to express this relation of man to God, has recourse to the same train of thought and to the same comparison with the bread, through which this meaning had become clear to him.

Of the agreement of all the passages, where mention is made of the bread, food, and drink, with this passage we shall speak in another place.

THE MARRIAGE IN CANA

John ii. 1–11. This incident in Cana of Galilee, which is described with so much detail, is one of the most instructive passages in the gospels, instructive in so far as it shows how dangerous it is to accept the whole letter of the so-called canonical Gospel as something sacred. The event in Cana of Galilee does not present anything remarkable, nor anything instructive, nor anything important in any respect whatsoever. If it is a miracle, it is senseless; if it is a trick, it is offensive; but if it is a picture of life, it is unnecessary.

Matt. xiv. 3–5; Mark vi. 17–20; Luke iii. 19, 20; Matt. iv. 12; Mark i. 14; John iv. 1, 2; John iv. 44–54; Luke v. 1–10; Matt. iv. 19, 20; Mark i. 17, 18. In all these passages we have descriptions of events which do not give us the teaching.

BEGINNING OF CHRIST'S PREACHING

17. Ἀπὸ τότε ἤρξατο ὁ Ἰησοῦς κηρύσσειν

14. Τὸ εὐαγγέλιον τῆς βασιλείας τοῦ Θεοῦ.

15. Καὶ λέγων, Ὅτι πεπλήρωται ὁ καιρός, καὶ ἤγγικεν ἡ βασιλεία τοῦ Θεοῦ· μετανοεῖτε, καὶ πιστεύετε ἐν τῷ εὐαγγελίῳ.

Matt. iv. 17. From that time Jesus began to preach

Mark i. 14. The gospel of the kingdom of God,

15. And saying, The time is fulfilled, and the kingdom of God is at hand: repent ye, and believe the gospel.

17. From that time Jesus began to proclaim

14. The kingdom of God.

15. He said, The time has come, the kingdom of God is here. Renovate yourselves and believe in the announcement of the true good.

John i. 19–34. All it says is that upon seeing Jesus Christ John said, He comes after me, but was before me, but it does not say whether he was the Christ. And so, both in this place, and in the following ones, which have references to Jesus' being the Christ, it is necessary to separate the indications about his being the Messiah from the teaching, with which they are frequently blended. Whether Jesus, whose teaching has encompassed half of the world, was, from the point of view of the Jews, that Christ whom they had been expecting, or not, is a question which is quite foreign to the teaching.

For the Jews who became converted to Christianity it could have a meaning, and so it is easy to understand why the meaning of certain passages is obscured: this is done in order to prove that Jesus was the Christ, that is, the anointed one, and that, as David and Saul had been anointed, so Christ was anointed by John. But for people who were not followers of the Mosaic law and who were in no way convinced that Jesus was the true messenger of God, John's assertions about Jesus, even if they were made, are quite unnecessary.

John i. 19–34; Matt. iii. 16, 17; Mark i. 10, 11; Luke iii. 21, 22. These verses contain the assertion and proof that Jesus Christ is the son of God.

Whether Jesus Christ is the son of God according to the conceptions of the Jews is a matter of indifference for

us who are not Jews. If there were no other proofs
of his filial relation to God, than the voice which eighteen
hundred years ago was heard no one knows by whom, this
tradition about the voice from heaven would not convince
any one of his being chosen by God and being his son.
But for those who understand the reality of Jesus and his
filial relation to God as explained in Chapter I., the tradition
about the dove and the voice from heaven are, to say the
least, superfluous.

CHRIST'S FIRST DISCIPLES

35. Τῇ ἐπαύριον πάλιν εἱστήκει ὁ Ἰωάννης, καὶ ἐκ τῶν μαθητῶν αὐτοῦ δύο.	John i. 35. Again the next day after, John stood, and two of his disciples;	
36. Καὶ ἐμβλέψας τῷ Ἰησοῦ περιπατοῦντι, λέγει, Ἴδε ὁ ἀμνὸς τοῦ Θεοῦ.	36. And looking upon Jesus as he walked,ᵃ he saith, Behold the Lamb of God!	36. And John again came together with Jesus and said about him, This is the lamb of God.
37. Καὶ ἤκουσαν αὐτοῦ οἱ δύο μαθηταὶ λαλοῦντος, καὶ ἠκολούθησαν τῷ Ἰησοῦ.	37. And the two disciples heard him speak, and they followed Jesus.	37. Two of John's disciples, hearing these words, followed Jesus.
38. Στραφεὶς δὲ ὁ Ἰησοῦς, καὶ θεασάμενος αὐτοὺς ἀκολουθοῦντας, λέγει αὐτοῖς, Τί ζητεῖτε; οἱ δὲ εἶπον αὐτῷ, Ῥαββί, (ὃ λέγεται ἑρμηνευόμενον, Διδάσκαλε,) ποῦ μένεις;	38. Then Jesus turned, and saw them following, and saith unto them, What seek ye? They said unto him, Rabbi, (which is to say, being interpreted, Master,) where dwellest thou?ᵇ	38. Jesus turned around and, seeing that they followed him, said to them, What are you looking for? They said, Rabbi (which means Master), where dwellest thou?

(a) ἐμβλέψας τῷ περιπατοῦντι *seeing Jesus as he
walked*. Under these words is to be understood that
when Jesus went into Galilee, John saw him again.
The word πάλιν points to that. John the evangelist
tells the events in the curtest manner possible, but it
does not follow from that that nothing else happened.
It is as though a man, repeating a certain story about an
event, should mention only the prominent and memorable
points. Obviously Jesus saw John and spoke with him,
and after the conversation John said, He is the lamb

appointed by God, and these last words clearly defined what John had been talking about.

(b) *ποῦ μένεις where dwellest thou?* The words of the disciples and the answer of Jesus Christ, You shall see where I dwell, and the fact that the disciples see where he dwells, apparently mean more than what is said here. Apostle John mentions only the prominent words of the conversation, but the meaning of the whole passage obviously is this, that the disciples wish to be with him, to hear his teaching, and, perhaps, to see how he lives, and he invites them to come with him, and they see how he lives and hear his teaching, and are convinced of its truth.

---

39. Λέγει αὐτοῖς, Ἔρχεσθε καὶ ἴδετε. ἦλθον καὶ εἶδον τοῦ μένει· καὶ παρ᾽ αὐτῷ ἔμειναν τὴν ἡμέραν ἐκείνην· ὥρα δὲ ἦν ὡς δεκάτη.

40. Ἦν Ἀνδρέας, ὁ ἀδελφὸς Σίμωνος Πέτρου, εἷς ἐκ τῶν δύο τῶν ἀκουσάντων παρὰ Ἰωάννου, καὶ ἀκολουθησάντων αὐτῷ.

41. Εὑρίσκει οὗτος πρῶτος τὸν ἀδελφὸν τὸν ἴδιον Σίμωνα, καὶ λέγει αὐτῷ, Εὑρήκαμεν τὸν Μεσσίαν (ὅ ἐστι μεθερμηνευόμενον, ὁ Χριστός)·

42. Καὶ ἤγαγεν αὐτὸν πρὸς τὸν Ἰησοῦν. ἐμβλέψας δὲ αὐτῷ ὁ Ἰησοῦς εἶπε, Σὺ εἶ Σίμων ὁ υἱὸς Ἰωνᾶ· σὺ κληθήσῃ Κηφᾶς (ὃ ἑρμηνεύεται Πέτρος).

19. Καὶ προβὰς ἐκεῖθεν ὀλίγον, εἶδεν Ἰάκωβον τὸν τοῦ Ζεβεδαίου, καὶ Ἰωάννην τὸν ἀδελφὸν αὐτοῦ, καὶ αὐτοὺς ἐν τῷ πλοίῳ καταρτίζοντας τὰ δίκτυα.

John i. 39. He saith unto them, Come and see. They came and saw where he dwelt, and abode with him that day: for it was about the tenth hour.

40. One of the two which heard John speak, and followed him, was Andrew, Simon Peter's brother.

41. He first findeth his own brother Simon, and saith unto him, We have found the Messias, which is, being interpreted, the Christ.

42. And he brought him to Jesus. And when Jesus beheld him, he said, Thou art Simon the son of Jona: thou shalt be called Cephas, which is by interpretation, A stone.

Mark i. 19. And when he had gone a little further thence, he saw James the son of Zebedee, and John his brother, who also were in the ship mending their nets.

---

39. He said to them, Come and see. They came and saw where he dwelt, and they remained with him a day.

40. One of these two was Andrew, Simon Peter's brother.

41. He looked up his brother Simon, and said, We have found the Messiah, which means, the chosen one of God.

42. And he was brought to Jesus. Jesus looked at him, and said, Thou art Simon the son of John. Thou shalt be called Peter, which means, A stone.

19. And when he went a distance away from there, he saw James the son of Zebedee, and John his brother: they were in a ship mending their nets.

20. Καὶ εὐθέως ἐκάλεσεν αὐτούς· καὶ ἀφέντες τὸν πατέρα αὐτῶν Ζεβεδαῖον ἐν τῷ πλοίῳ μετὰ τῶν μισθωτῶν, ἀπῆλθον ὀπίσω αὐτοῦ.

43. Τῇ ἐπαύριον ἠθέλησεν ὁ Ἰησοῦς ἐξελθεῖν εἰς τὴν Γαλιλαίαν· καὶ εὑρίσκει Φίλιππον, καὶ λέγει αὐτῷ, Ἀκολούθει μοι.

44. Ἦν δὲ ὁ Φίλιππος ἀπὸ Βηθσαϊδά, ἐκ τῆς πόλεως Ἀνδρέου καὶ Πέτρου.

45. Εὑρίσκει Φίλιππος τὸν Ναθαναὴλ, καὶ λέγει αὐτῷ, Ὃν ἔγραψε Μωσῆς ἐν τῷ νόμῳ καὶ οἱ προφῆται, εὑρήκαμεν, Ἰησοῦν τὸν υἱὸν τοῦ Ἰωσὴφ τὸν ἀπὸ Ναζαρέτ.

46. Καὶ εἶπεν αὐτῷ Ναθαναὴλ, Ἐκ Ναζαρὲτ δύναταί τι ἀγαθὸν εἶναι; λέγει αὐτῷ Φίλιππος, Ἔρχου καὶ ἴδε.

47. Εἶδεν ὁ Ἰησοῦς τὸν Ναθαναὴλ ἐρχόμενον πρὸς αὐτὸν, καὶ λέγει περὶ αὐτοῦ, Ἴδε ἀληθῶς Ἰσραηλίτης, ἐν ᾧ δόλος οὐκ ἔστι.

49. Ἀπεκρίθη Ναθαναὴλ καὶ λέγει αὐτῷ, Ῥαββί, σὺ εἶ ὁ υἱὸς τοῦ Θεοῦ, σὺ εἶ ὁ βασιλεὺς τοῦ Ἰσραήλ.

51. Καὶ λέγει αὐτῷ, Ἀμὴν ἀμὴν λέγω ὑμῖν, Ἀπ᾽ ἄρτι ὄψεσθε τὸν οὐρανὸν ἀνεῳγότα, καὶ τοὺς ἀγγέλους τοῦ Θεοῦ ἀναβαίνοντας καὶ καταβαίνοντας ἐπὶ τὸν υἱὸν τοῦ ἀνθρώπου.

---

20. And straightway he called them: and they left their father Zebedee in the ship with the hired servants, and went after him.

John 1. 43. The day following Jesus would go forth into Galilee, and findeth Philip, and saith unto him, Follow me.

44. Now Philip was of Bethsaida, the city of Andrew and Peter.

45. Philip findeth Nathanael, and saith unto him, We have found him, of whom Moses in the law, and the prophets, did write, Jesus of Nazareth, the son of Joseph.

46. And Nathanael said unto him, Can there any good thing come out of Nazareth? Philip saith unto him, Come and see.

47. Jesus saw Nathanael coming to him, and saith of him, Behold an Israelite indeed, in whom is no guile!

49. Nathanael answered and saith unto him, Rabbi, thou art the Son of God; thou art the King of Israel.

51. And he saith unto him, Verily, verily, I say unto you, Hereafter ye shall see heaven open, and the angels of God ascending and descending upon the Son of man.

---

20. And he called them at once: and they left their father Zebedee in the ship with the hired servants.

43. Later, before going to Galilee, Jesus met also Philip, and said to him, Come with me.

44. Philip was of Bethsaida, of the same village with Peter and Andrew.

45. Philip found Nathanael, and said to him, We have found the one Moses wrote about in the law, — it is Jesus of Nazareth.

46. And Nathanael said to him, Can any good thing come out of Nazareth? Philip said to him, Go and see for thyself.

47. When Nathanael came and Jesus had a talk with him, he said to him, Now here is a man in whom there is no guile.

49. And Nathanael said to him, Thou art a son of God; thou art the King of Israel.

51. And he said, Thou wilt find out something more important than that, for I tell you the whole truth: You shall now find out that heaven is open and the powers of God will descend to the son of man and will ascend again to heaven.

(a) *Saw him* means here: had a conversation with him, followed him.

Verse 48 of the first chapter of John is a hint at something well known to the author, but it is entirely lost on us. What happened under the fig-tree and when Jesus saw him is unknown, and so the verse is omitted.

(*b*) Nathanael's assertion that Jesus is the son of God, that is, that Jesus thought of himself in the wilderness, and a King of Israel, that is, that with Christ the kingdom of God had come, precisely what John had been preaching about, shows that John talked a great deal with his first disciples, and interpreted things to them. When Nathanael understood the interpretation, he said, Yes, thou art a son of God, and thou art the King of Israel.

Verse 50 is a continuation of the conversation which took place under the fig-tree, during the event which is lost to us, and so it is omitted here.

(*c*) υἱὸς τοῦ ἀνθρώπου *the son of man*, both by its signification and by its use can mean nothing but *a man possessed of qualities common to all men*. In these words Jesus Christ says what he has come to understand in the wilderness.

According to the previous teaching God was a distinct being, separate from man. Heaven was the abode of God, and God himself was hidden from man. According to the teaching of Jesus Christ, heaven is open to man. The communion of God with man is established. The life of man is from God, and God is always with man, and so the power of God descends upon the son of man: man becomes conscious of it and ascends into heaven. Man recognizes God from within. In this consists the coming of the kingdom of God, which John preaches and Jesus confirms.

JESUS CHRIST PREACHING IN NAZARETH

16. Καὶ ἦλθεν εἰς τὴν Ναζαρέτ, οὗ ἦν τεθραμμένος· καὶ εἰσῆλθε κατὰ

Luke iv. 16. And he came to Nazareth, where he had been brought up: and, as his custom

16. And Jesus came to Nazareth, where he had been brought up. And, according to the custom

τὸ εἰωθὸς αὐτῷ, ἐν τῇ ἡμέρᾳ τῶν σαββάτων, εἰς τὴν συναγωγὴν, καὶ ἀνέστη ἀναγνῶναι.

17. Καὶ ἐπεδόθη αὐτῷ βιβλίον Ἡσαΐου τοῦ προφήτου· καὶ ἀναπτύξας τὸ βιβλίον, εὗρε τὸν τόπον οὗ ἦν γεγραμμένον,

18. 'Πνεῦμα Κυρίου ἐπ' ἐμέ· οὗ ἕνεκεν ἔχρισέ με· εὐαγγελίζεσθαι πτωχοῖς ἀπέσταλκέ με, ἰάσασθαι τοὺς συντετριμμένους τὴν καρδίαν, κηρύξαι αἰχμαλώτοις ἄφεσιν καὶ τυφλοῖς ἀνάβλεψιν, ἀποστεῖλαι τεθραυσμένους ἐν ἀφέσει,

19. Κηρύξαι ἐνιαυτὸν Κυρίου δεκτόν.'

20. Καὶ πτύξας τὸ βιβλίον, ἀποδοὺς τῷ ὑπηρέτῃ, ἐκάθισε· καὶ πάντων ἐν τῇ συναγωγῇ οἱ ὀφθαλμοὶ ἦσαν ἀτενίζοντες αὐτῷ.

21. Ἤρξατο δὲ λέγειν πρὸς αὐτούς, Ὅτι σήμερον πεπλήρωται ἡ γραφὴ αὕτη ἐν τοῖς ὠσὶν ὑμῶν.

22. Καὶ πάντες ἐμαρτύρουν αὐτῷ, καὶ ἐθαύμαζον ἐπὶ τοῖς λόγοις τῆς χάριτος, τοῖς ἐκπορευομένοις ἐκ τοῦ στόματος αὐτοῦ, καὶ ἔλεγον, Οὐχ οὗτός ἐστιν ὁ υἱὸς Ἰωσήφ;

3. Οὐχ οὗτός ἐστιν ὁ τέκτων;

55. Οὐχ οὗτός ἐστιν ὁ τοῦ τέκτονος υἱός; οὐχὶ ἡ μήτηρ αὐτοῦ λέγεται Μαριάμ, καὶ οἱ ἀδελφοὶ αὐτοῦ Ἰάκωβος καὶ Ἰωσῆς καὶ Σίμων καὶ Ἰούδας;

---

was, he went into the synagogue on the sabbath day, and stood up for to read.

17. And there was delivered unto him the book of the prophet Esaias. And when he had opened the book, he found the place where it was written,

18. The Spirit of the Lord is upon me, because he hath anointed me to preach the gospel to the poor; he hath sent me to heal the brokenhearted, to preach deliverance to the captives, and recovering of sight to the blind, to set at liberty them that are bruised,

19. To preach the acceptable year of the Lord (Isaiah lxi. 1, 2).ᵃ

20. And he closed the book, and he gave it again to the minister, and sat down. And the eyes of all them that were in the synagogue were fastened on him.

21. And he began to say unto them, This day is this Scripture fulfilled in your ears.

22. And all bare him witness, and wondered at the gracious words which proceeded out of his mouth. And they said, Is not this Joseph's son?

Mark vi. 3. Is not this the carpenter?

Matt. xiii. 55. Is not this the carpenter's son? is not his mother called Mary? and his brethren, James, and Joses, and Simon, and Judas?

---

of the holiday, he went into an assembly, and began to read.

17. And they gave him the book of the prophet Isaiah. And he opened it at the place where it was written,

18. The spirit of the Eternal One is upon me: he has ordained me to announce the good to the unfortunate, the broken-hearted, to proclaim freedom to those who are bound, and light to the blind, and salvation and rest to those who are weary.

19. To announce to all the time of God's mercy.

20. And closing the book and giving it back to the servant, he sat down. And the eyes of all were fastened on him.

21. And he began to speak to them, Now is the Scripture fulfilled in your eyes.

22. And all wondered at the graciousness of his words, and said, Is not this Joseph's son?

3. Is not this the carpenter?

55. And is not this the carpenter's son? Is not his mother called Mariam? and his brothers James, Joses, Simon, and Judas?

28. Καὶ εἶπε πρὸς αὐτούς, Πάντως ἐρεῖτέ μοι τὴν παραβολὴν ταύτην, Ἰατρέ, θεράπευσον σεαυτόν·	*Luke iv.* 28. And he said unto them, Ye will surely say unto me this proverb, Physician, heal thyself.	28. And he said to them, Of course, you say, Physician, heal thyself.
57. Οὐκ ἔστι προφήτης ἄτιμος, εἰ μὴ ἐν τῇ πατρίδι αὐτοῦ καὶ ἐν τῇ οἰκίᾳ αὐτοῦ.	*Matt.xiii.* 57. A prophet is not without honour, save in his own country, and in his own house.ᵇ	57. Because no prophet is understood in his own country.
13. Καὶ καταλιπὼν τὴν Ναζαρέτ, ἐλθὼν κατῴκησεν εἰς Καπερναοὺμ τὴν παραθαλασσίαν ἐν ὁρίοις Ζαβουλὼν καὶ Νεφθαλείμ.	*Matt. iv.* 13. And leaving Nazareth, he came and dwelt in Capernaum, which is upon the seacoast, in the borders of Zabulon and Nephthalim.	13. And from Nazareth he went to Capernaum.
21. Καὶ εὐθέως τοῖς σάββασιν εἰσελθὼν εἰς τὴν συναγωγὴν, ἐδίδασκε.	*Mark i.* 21. And straightway on the sabbath day he entered into the synagogue, and taught.	21. And straightway on the Sabbath he went into the assembly and began to teach.
22. Καὶ ἐξεπλήσσοντο ἐπὶ τῇ διδαχῇ αὐτοῦ· ἦν γὰρ διδάσκων αὐτοὺς ὡς ἐξουσίαν ἔχων, καὶ οὐχ ὡς οἱ γραμματεῖς.	22. And they were astonished at his doctrine: for he taught them as one that had authority,ᶜ and not as the scribes.	22. And they were delighted with his teaching, for he taught them freely, and not as the scribes.

(*a*) This passage from Isaiah breaks off where it begins to speak of the vengeance of God. In Isaiah it is thus: To proclaim the acceptable year of the Lord, and the day of vengeance of our God. I quote this, to show that the words cited from the book of Moses and the prophets have to be taken in the sense only which Jesus Christ gives to them. Apparently he selected those familiar words which expressed his idea, rejecting those which were opposed to it.

(*b*) The meaning of the verses about the prophet in his own country and about the physician is not clear to me. In any case, the meaning of this passage, as it is understood, has nothing in common with the teaching and so ought to be referred to the addition.

(*c*) ὡς ἐξουσίαν ἔχων means, *having freedom;* ἐξουσία has for its first meaning *freedom.* Here it inevitably means freedom, and not power, because it is opposed to the doctrine of the scribes. The scribes had power, and so it could not be said, Having power, but not as the scribes (who have power). The contradistinction consists here in this, that the scribes did not teach freely, for the very reason that they had power, that is, that the teaching of the scribes (as actually was the case) regarded men as the slaves of God and not free, while according to the teaching of Jesus Christ men were free. With such an explanation it becomes clear what the people were delighted with. If Jesus taught like one having power, that is, with boldness and impudence, the people would have nothing to be delighted with. But apparently there was something else in the teaching. And this other thing was that he taught ὡς ἐξουσίαν ἔχων, that is, freely, as being free from all bonds.

JESUS CHRIST'S BIRTH, CHILDHOOD, AND BEGINNING OF PREACHING

The comprehension was made incarnate in Jesus Christ. Jesus Christ announced the true good to men. But the birth of Jesus Christ was as follows. His mother Mary was betrothed to Joseph; but before they began to live together as husband and wife, Mary turned out to be with child. Joseph was a good man and did not wish to disgrace her, so he accepted her as his wife. And he had no relations with her until she bore her first son, whom she called Jesus. And the boy grew and became manly and was intelligent above his years.

Here is what happened with him in his childhood. Jesus was twelve years old, when Mary went with Joseph to Jerusalem to celebrate a holiday, and they took the boy with them. The holiday was over, and they went home and forgot about the boy. Then they thought of him, and it occurred to them that he might have walked off with some children, and they asked about him along the road. The boy could not be found, and they returned to Jerusalem after him. Not until two days later did they find him in a church, and he was sitting with the teachers and asking them questions and listening. And all marvelled at his intellect.

His mother saw him, and said, What hast thou done with us? Thy father and I have been worrying and looking for thee.

And he said to them, Where did you look for me? Do you not know that the son must be looked for in the house of his father?

And they did not understand his words. They did not understand that he, knowing that he had no carnal father, regarded God as his Father. After that Jesus lived with his mother and obeyed her in everything, and he increased in stature and understanding, and was in favour with God and man.

Thus he lived until he was thirty years of age. And all thought that Jesus was Joseph's son.

This is the way Jesus began to announce the good. The prophets had predicted that God was to come into the world. Prophet Malachi had said, My messenger will come before me to prepare the way for me.

Prophet Isaiah had said, A voice is calling to you: Prepare the way for the Lord in the wilderness, make his path even; let there be no hollows, nor mounds, nothing high, and nothing low. Then God will be among you and all will find their salvation.

In accordance with these words of the prophets, a new prophet, John, made his appearance in the time of Jesus Christ. John dwelt in the prairie of Judea on the Jordan. His raiment was of camel's hair, girded with a leathern girdle, and he fed on tree bark and on herbs. He called the people to a new life. And they confessed their errors to him, and he bathed them in the Jordan as a sign that their errors were corrected. He said to all, If you have observed that you shall not escape the will of God, be renovated. And if you wish to be renovated let it be seen from your works that you have changed. John said, Heretofore the prophets have said that God will come. I say to you that God has already come. He said, I purify you with water, but after me the one who is mightier than I will purify you with the spirit. When he comes he will purify you, as the master cleans his threshing-floor: the wheat he will gather, but the chaff he will burn. If a tree does not bring forth good fruit, it is cut down and burnt up. And the axe is already laid upon the root of the tree.

And the people asked him, What shall we do? He answered, He that has two coats, let him give one to him who has none; and he who has food, let him give it to him who has none.

Farmers of taxes came to him, and asked him, What shall we do? He said, Exact no more than is your right.

And the soldiers asked, What shall we do? He said, Offend no one. Do not cheat. Be satisfied with what is given you.

And many other things he proclaimed to the people about what is the present good.

Jesus was then thirty years old. He came to the Jordan to John, and heard his preaching about God's coming, about the necessity of being renovated, about people being purified by water, and about their future purification by the spirit, when God would come. Jesus did not know his carnal father and regarded God as his Father. He believed in John's preaching, and said to himself, If it is true that God is my Father, and I am a son of God, and if what John says is true, I need only to purify myself by the spirit that God may come to me.

And Jesus went into the wilderness to test the truth of his being a son of God, and of God's coming to him. He went into the wilderness and there lived for a long time without food and drink, and finally grew thin. And then doubt came over him, and he said to himself, Thou sayest that thou art a spirit, a son of God, and that God will come to thee, and yet thou art tormented because thou hast no bread, and God does not come to thee: consequently thou art no spirit, no son of God. But he said to himself, My flesh craves for bread, but not bread is needed for life: man lives not by bread, but by the spirit, by what is from God.

But hunger kept tormenting him. And he was overcome by another doubt, and he said to himself, Thou sayest that thou art a son of God, and that God will come to thee, and yet thou sufferest and canst not make an end to thy sufferings. And he imagined that he was standing on a roof of the temple, and the thought occurred to him, If I am a spirit, a son of God, I shall not be killed if I cast myself down from the temple, but an invisible power will preserve and sustain me, and will free me from all evil. Why should I not cast myself down, so as to cease suffering hunger?

But he said to himself, Why should I tempt God whether he is with me or not? If I tempt him, I do not believe in him and he is not with me. God the spirit gives me life, and so in life the spirit is always within me. And I cannot tempt him. I may stop eating, but I cannot kill myself, because I feel the spirit within me. But hunger continued to torment him. And it occurred to him, If I must not tempt God by casting myself down from the temple, I must not tempt him by starving when I want to eat. I must not deprive myself of all the appetites of the flesh. They are given to all men. And he imagined he saw all the kingdoms of earth and all men, as they lived and worked for the flesh, expecting a reward from it. And he thought, They work for the flesh, and the flesh gives them all which they have. If I shall work for it, the same will happen with me. But he said to himself, My God is not flesh, but spirit; by him I live, him I know always, him alone I worship, for him alone I work, and from him I expect my reward.

Then the temptation left him, and the spirit renovated him, and he knew that God had come to him and was always in him, and, having learned that, he returned to Galilee in the strength of the spirit. From that time on, having learned the power of the spirit, he began to announce the presence of God. He said, The time has come, renovate yourselves, believe in the announcement of the good.

From the wilderness Jesus went to John, and was with him.

When Jesus went away from John, John said of him, He is the true son of God (the chosen one). Two of John's disciples, hearing these words, left their old teacher and followed Jesus. Jesus saw that they were walking behind him, and so he stopped, and said, What do you want?

Teacher, we wish to be with thee and to learn thy teaching. He said, Come with me, and I will tell you everything. They went with him, and remained with him the whole day, staying until the tenth hour.

One of these disciples was called Andrew. And Andrew had a brother Simon. Having listened to Jesus, Andrew went to his brother Simon, and said to him, We have found the chosen one of God. Andrew took Simon with him, and brought him to Jesus. This brother of Andrew Jesus called Peter, which means a stone. And these two brothers became the disciples of Jesus.

And Jesus walked on with his two disciples. After they had gone a distance, Jesus saw some fishermen in a ship. Those were Zebedee the father with hired servants and with two sons, James and John. They were sitting and mending their nets. Jesus began to speak with

James and with John, and James and John left their
father with the hired servants in the ship and went with
Jesus and became his disciples.

Later, just before entering Galilee, Jesus met Philip,
and he called him. Philip was of Bethsaida, of the same
village with Peter and Andrew. When Philip recognized
Jesus, he went to find his brother Nathanael, to whom he
said, We have found the chosen one of God, of whom
Moses has written, He is Jesus, the son of Joseph, of
Nazareth. Nathanael was surprised to hear that the
chosen one was from a neighbouring village, and he said,
Brother, it is queer that a messenger of God should come
from Nazareth. Philip said, Come with me to him, and
thou shalt see and hear for thyself. Nathanael agreed to
it and went with his brother and met Jesus. When he
heard him, he said to him, Yes, now I see that it is true
that thou art the son of God and the King of Israel.

Jesus said to him, Thou wilt learn what is more important than this. Thou wilt learn that the kingdom of
God has come, and so I tell you truly that the divine
power will descend to all men, and from them will
emanate the divine power. From now on God will no
longer be separate from men, but men will blend with
God.

And from the wilderness Jesus went to his home in
Nazareth. And on a holiday he went, as usual, into an
assembly and began to read. And they gave him the
book of the prophet Isaiah. He unrolled it and began to
read. In the book it was written, The spirit of the Lord
is in me : he has chosen me to announce the good to the
unfortunate and the broken-hearted, to proclaim freedom,
light to the blind, and salvation and rest to the weary, to
announce to all the time of the salvation, of God's mercy.
He closed the book and gave it to the servant, and sat
down, and all waited to hear what he would say. And he
said, Now is the Scripture fulfilled in your eyes. God is

in the world. The kingdom of God has come, and all the unfortunate, the broken-hearted, the blind, the weary, — all shall receive salvation.

And many wondered at the goodness of his speech. And some said, But he is a carpenter and the son of a carpenter. And his mother is called Mariam, and his brothers, James, Simon, Judas, and Joses, and we know them all: they are as poor as we are. And he said to them, No doubt you think that because I say that there are no longer any unfortunate and weary, and I have a poor father and mother and brothers, I am telling an untruth, and that I ought to make them happy. If you think so, you do not understand what I am saying. And thus, a prophet is never understood in his own country.

And Jesus went to Capernaum, and on a Sabbath entered an assembly and began to teach. And all the people marvelled at his teaching, because his teaching was quite different from the teaching of the scribes. The scribes taught the law, which must be obeyed, and Jesus taught that all men were free.

CHAPTER II.

GENERAL REMARK. THE NEW WORSHIP IN THE SPIRIT BY WORKS. THE REJECTION OF THE JEWISH GOD

THIS second chapter contains a negative definition of God. John said, When you are purified by the spirit, God will be in the world. Jesus went into the wilderness, recognized the power of the spirit, returned to the world, and announced that God was in the world and his kingdom had come.

The meaning of the kingdom of God in the world Jesus expressed with the words of the prophet Isaiah. The kingdom of God is happiness for the unfortunate, salvation for the sufferers, light for the blind, freedom for those who are not free. Jesus told his disciples that the kingdom of God consisted in this, that henceforth God would no longer be that inaccessible God that he had been heretofore, but that he would be in the world and in communion with men; if God is in the world and in communion with men, what kind of a God is he? Is he God the Creator who sits in heaven, who had appeared to the patriarchs, and who had given the law to Moses, the revengeful, cruel, and terrible God whom men knew and worshipped, or another God?

In this chapter Jesus defines what God is not. In order that this may become clear, it is necessary to reëstablish the real significance of the discourses of Jesus Christ, a significance which all the churches have carefully obscured. The significance of the words and actions of Jesus Christ, as adduced in this chapter, is this, that Jesus Christ denies the whole, absolutely the whole Jewish faith. In reality this is so clear and unquestionable that one feels ashamed to have to prove it. It was necessary for our churches to succumb to that terrible historical fate, which contrary to common sense compelled them to combine into one the non-harmonizing, absolutely opposed teachings, the Christian and the Jewish, to permit them to affirm such an absurdity and to conceal what is manifest.

It is enough, not to read through, but only to run through the Pentateuch, in which all the actions of man are determined in tens of thousands of most varied circumstances, down to the minutest details, in order to see clearly that with such a detailed, petty definition of man's actions there can be no place for any continuation or completion of the teaching of the law, as the churches assert. There might be room left for some new law, if it were said that all the laws were human. But no, it says clearly and definitely that all this, as to how and when to cut off, or not to cut off, pimples of the extreme flesh, as to how and when to kill all the women and children, as to what people are to be reimbursed, and in what manner, for an ox accidentally killed, it says clearly that all these are the words of God himself. How can such a law be enlarged? Such a law can be enlarged only by new details about pimples of the extreme flesh, about who else may be killed, and so forth. But, by accepting this law as inspired by God, it is by that very fact impossible to preach the doctrine of Christ, or even any other teaching, however insignificant it may be. Everything is determined, and there is nothing to preach about.

For the first word of any sermon with the Pentateuch in view, it is necessary to destroy the Pentateuch, the law of the Pentateuch. And yet the church had to convince itself and others that the Pentateuch and the Gospel were both from God. What, then, could it do but close its eyes to what was manifest and strain all the powers of the glibness of mind in order to unite what cannot be united? That was done in consequence of Paul's false teaching, which preceded the knowledge of Christ's teaching, and by which the ill-understood teaching of Christ was represented as a continuation of the teaching of the Jews. But when this took place and the problem was no longer in the comprehension of the meaning of Christ's teaching, but in uniting what cannot be united, there was nothing left to do but look for subterfuges and utter those misty, incoherent, flowery discourses, such as Paul's Epistle to the Hebrews, and all that rigmarole of the same character which for eighteen hundred years has been preached by the so-called fathers of the church and the theologians. Indeed, we may as well imagine that men have proposed to themselves to harmonize Volume X. of the Code of laws and the works, say, of Proudhon, regarding both works as true to the very last line. I have selected Volume X. and Proudhon, but these works can much more easily be harmonized than the Pentateuch and the Gospel. Indeed, let us take anything we please:

In the Gospel we are prohibited not only from killing any one but even from bearing any one any ill-will; in the Pentateuch: Kill, kill, kill women, children, and cattle.

In the Gospel wealth is an evil; in the Pentateuch it is the highest good and a reward.

In the Gospel bodily purity consists in having but one wife; in the Pentateuch, Take as many wives as you please.

In the Gospel all men are brothers; in the Pentateuch, all are enemies, except the Jews.

In the Gospel there is no external divine worship; in the Pentateuch, the greater half of the books defines the details of the external ministration of God.

And this teaching of the Gospel, we are assured, is an enlargement and continuation of the Pentateuch.

In another place we shall speak of the lie and the inevitably false comprehension of Christ's teaching, which result from this absurd assertion in regard to other passages of the Gospel; now we are concerned with the external divine worship, against which Jesus contended.

According to the interpretations of the church all those passages which are put down in Chapter II., the rejection of the ablutions, of the non-communion with those who are not cleansed, of everything considered impure, the rejection of the fasts, the rejection of the most important covenant of the Jews with God, of the Sabbath, the rejection of all sacrifices, of the necessity of the hand-worked temple, the rejection even of the city most precious to the Jews, of Jerusalem, and finally the rejection of God himself as something external, and the recognition of God as a spirit, who must be served in the spirit, — all that, according to the interpretations of the church is some unnecessary, superfluous finesses invented by some Pharisees.

In the first place, if all that is merely a verbal contest with the Pharisees, it is superfluous; in the second, to every man who knows how to read and who reads the Pentateuch, and who can reason with his own mind, the assertion that Jesus contended with the Pharisees, and not with the law of Moses, becomes obviously false.

Jesus was contending against all the laws of the Pentateuch, with the exception, of course, of some truths, which could not help but be in that mass of monstrous and absurd things. Thus he understood the command to love one's father and mother, and one's neighbours. But the fact that the Pentateuch contained two or three sentences which Jesus could accept does not prove that he enlarged and continued it, just as nothing is proved by the fact that a man, in contending with another, uses a few of his antagonist's words in order to confirm his proofs. Jesus did not contend with the Pharisees, but with the whole law, and in his rejections of the external divine worship he took up everything which formed a dogma of faith of the external divine worship for every adult Jew.

This is the way the divine worship of the Jews was defined according to Deuteronomy:

On Purification. *Lev. xvii.* 7. And they shall no more offer their sacrifices unto devils, after whom they have gone a whoring: This shall be a statute for ever unto them throughout their generations.

8. And thou shalt say unto them, Whatsoever man there be of the house of Israel, or of the strangers which sojourn among you, that offereth a burnt-offering or sacrifice,

9. And bringeth it not unto the door of the tabernacle of the congregation, to offer it unto the Lord; even that man shall be cut off from among his people.

Num. xix. 13. Whosoever toucheth the dead body of any man that is dead, and purifieth not himself, defileth the tabernacle of the Lord; and that soul shall be cut off from Israel: because the water of separation was not sprinkled upon him, he shall be unclean; his uncleanness is yet upon him.

14. This is the law, when a man dieth in a tent: all that come into the tent, and all that is in the tent shall be unclean seven days.

15. And every open vessel which hath no covering bound upon it, is unclean.

16. And whosoever toucheth one that is slain with the sword in the open fields, or a dead body, or a bone of a man, or a grave, shall be unclean seven days.

17. And for an unclean person they shall take of the ashes of the burnt heifer of purification for sin, and running water shall be put thereto in a vessel:

18. And a clean person shall take hyssop, and dip it in the water, and sprinkle it upon the tent, and upon all the vessels, and upon the persons that were there, and upon him that touched a bone, or one slain, or one dead, or a grave:

19. And the clean person shall sprinkle upon the unclean on the third day, and on the seventh day: and on the seventh day he shall purify himself, and wash his clothes, and bathe himself in water, and shall be clean at even.

20. But the man that shall be unclean, and shall not purify himself, that soul shall be cut off from among the congregation, because he hath defiled the sanctuary of the Lord: the water of separation hath not been sprinkled upon him; he is unclean.

21. And it shall be a perpetual statute unto them, that he that sprinkleth the water of separation shall wash his clothes; and he that toucheth the water of separation shall be unclean until even.

22. And whatsoever the unclean person toucheth shall be unclean; and the soul that toucheth it shall be unclean until even.

On Fasting. *Lev. xvi.* 29. And this shall be a statute for ever unto you: that in the seventh month, on the tenth day of the month, ye shall afflict your souls, and do no work at all, whether it be one of your own country, or a stranger that sojourneth among you:

Lev. xxiii. 27. Also on the tenth day of this seventh month there shall be a day of atonement; it shall be an holy convocation unto you, and ye shall afflict your souls, and offer an offering made by fire unto the Lord.

On the Sabbath. *Exod. xxxi.* 13. Speak thou also unto the children of Israel, saying, Verily my sabbaths ye shall keep: for it is a sign between me and you throughout your generations; that ye may know that I am the Lord that doth sanctify you.

It is not worth while to quote passages in reference to the sacrifices, since a good part of the Pentateuch is filled with definite decrees by God himself as to what kind of sacrifices are to be brought to him.

The same may be said about Jerusalem. Jerusalem is a city of God. God lives there. That God is not a spirit, but an external being with arms, eyes, and legs, is to be seen from all passages where only God is mentioned. And so, rejecting the purification, and the fasts, and the Sabbath, and the sacrifices, and the temple, and the carnal God, Jesus did not continue the faith of Moses, but denied everything to the root.

THE ABOLITION OF THE LAW OF THE SABBATH

1. Ἐγένετο δὲ ἐν σαββάτῳ δευτεροπρώτῳ διαπορεύεσθαι αὐτὸν διὰ τῶν σπορίμων· καὶ ἔτιλλον οἱ μαθηταὶ αὐτοῦ τοὺς στάχυας, καὶ ἤσθιον, ψώχοντες ταῖς χερσί.

Luke vi. 1. And it came to pass on the second sabbath after the first, that he went through the corn fields; and his disciples plucked the ears of corn, and did eat, rubbing them in their hands.

1. He happened on a Sabbath to cross the corn fields; and his disciples plucked the ears of corn and rubbed them in their hands and ate them.

2. Τινὲς δὲ τῶν Φαρι-σαίων εἶπον αὐτοῖς, Τί ποιεῖτε ὃ οὐκ ἔξεστι ποιεῖν ἐν τοῖς σάββασι;	2. And certain of the Pharisees said unto them, Why do ye that which is not lawful to do on the sabbath days ?	2. And a few of the Orthodox saw that and said to them, Why do you do that which ought not to be done on a Sabbath ?

(*a*) The word Pharisee I translate by Orthodox, because from all investigations it appears that it means precisely the same as Orthodox. It comes from the Hebrew *parash*, and means *interpreter* ἐξηγέτης τοῦ νόμου κατ' ἐξοχὴν, which the Pharisees claimed to be, according to Josephus, or in the sense of *parush*, that is, he who separates himself from the crowd of unbelievers, and considers himself right, that is, *Orthodox*. The peculiarity of the Pharisees (according to all investigations, which agree among themselves) consisted in the following:

(1) Besides the Holy Scripture they recognized also the oral tradition, παράδοξις holy tradition, which demanded certain external rites, which they regarded as peculiarly important.

(2) They interpreted Holy Scripture literally, and regarded the fulfilment of the ceremonial as more important than the fulfilment of the moral law.

(3) They recognized the dependence of man on God, which, however, did not entirely exclude the freedom of the will. What, then, are they if not the same as our Orthodox? Of course, they were not exactly our Orthodox, but they occupied precisely the same place as our Orthodox.

Luke vi. 3, 4; Matt. xii. 5. These verses contain proofs of how David ate the shewbreads, and of how the priests defiled the Sabbath. These proofs were conclusive only for the Jews; for us they are the more superfluous since the last proof that God rejoices in love, and not in the sacrifices, excludes the necessity of the previous proofs. Of these verses the only important part is Christ's answer, which refers to us.

6. Λέγω δὲ ὑμῖν, ὅτι τοῦ ἱεροῦ μεῖζων ἐστὶν ὧδε.

7. Εἰ δὲ ἐγνώκειτε τί ἐστιν, ("Ἔλεον θέλω καὶ οὐ θυσίαν,") οὐκ ἂν κατεδικάσατε τοὺς ἀναιτίους.

27. Καὶ ἔλεγεν αὐτοῖς, Τὸ σάββατον διὰ τὸν ἄνθρωπον ἐγένετο, οὐχ ὁ ἄνθρωπος διὰ τὸ σάββατον.

28. Ὥστε κύριός ἐστιν ὁ υἱὸς τοῦ ἀνθρώπου καὶ τοῦ σαββάτου.

Matt. xii. 6. But I say unto you, That in this place is one greater than the temple.[a]

7. But if ye had known what this meaneth, I will have mercy, and not sacrifice, ye would not have condemned the guiltless.

Mark ii. 27. And he said unto them, The sabbath was made for man, and not man for the sabbath:

28. Therefore the Son of man[b] is Lord also of the sabbath.

6. I tell you, Here is something which is more important than external holiness.

7. If you knew what it means, I will have love for men, and not sacrifices, you would not be condemning the innocent.

27. And he said to them, The Sabbath was made for man, and not man for the Sabbath.

28. Therefore man is lord of the Sabbath.

(*a*) The words ὅτι τοῦ ἱεροῦ μεῖζων εστὶν ὧδε I translate by, Here is something which is more important than external holiness, because ἱερόν designates the abode of God upon earth, the holiness. Nothing was said here about a temple, and so these words refer in general to external holiness.

(*b*) *The son of man* can here in no way be taken in the sense of a divinity, for it was said that the Sabbath was made for man, and not man for the Sabbath, and so the conclusion can in no way refer to the new person, the son of man, to God. The son of man has here the same meaning as everywhere else, the meaning of man in general.

This whole discourse, which had an enormous importance when it was uttered, has also an enormous importance for us, if we wish to understand the teaching of Jesus. In consequence of the false representation of the interpreters that Jesus only continued the law of Moses, nothing is left of the discourse but a useless contention with some Pharisees.

For an unbiassed reader this passage has an enormous meaning, which is, that Jesus at his first conflict with the law of the external divine worship with all his might radically rejects it. The Sabbath is the chief covenant of God with his people. The non-observance of the Sabbath is punished by death. The Sabbath has been observed and still is observed, and half of the Talmud treats of it. The observance of the Sabbath is for the Jews what communion is for the Christians. Just as he who does not go to communion is not an Orthodox or a Catholic, so he who does not observe the Sabbath is not a Jew. To defile the Sabbath and to defile the communion are equally terrible.

And here Jesus says that this Sabbath is meaningless, a human invention; that man is more important than all external holiness; that, in order to understand that, it is necessary to understand what is meant by the words, I will have mercy, and not sacrifices; and that it is not necessary to observe the Sabbath, that is, that external divine worship which is regarded as most important. And this meaning is concealed by the interpreters. They say:

Moses commanded men to work on six days of the week, and forbade men on the seventh day (the Sabbath) to perform the customary work of every-day life, except what was most necessary (Exod. xx. 10; xxxv. 2, 3 ; Num. xv. 32–36). The traditions of the elders still more increased the severity of the Sabbath rest, so that even good works, works of godliness, were at times prohibited on the Sabbath. However, the Pharisees, who looked unfavourably on the Saviour, seem to have exaggerated the severity of the demands of the Sabbath rest toward him and his disciples; in respect to themselves and others they were, no doubt, more condescending. The plucking of the ears of corn by the disciples of Jesus, even in order to satisfy their hunger, consequently from necessity, they regarded as a violation of the Sabbath rest, as a defilement of the Sabbath, and they did not miss the opportunity of directing the Lord's attention to it, and of rebuking him for allowing his disciples to commit that which to them was such an obvious violation of the laws of the Sabbath, which was so offensive to others (Archim. Mikh., Gospel of Matthew, pp. 206 and 207).

Thus has the meaning of the passage been stealthily concealed. Nor could they help doing otherwise, for thieves give themselves away.

.

The words against the Sabbath refer only to the external divine worship, which was established by the church. But there are left the words, In this place is that which is greater than the temple. The church mutilates the text and says *one*, but that *one* still means *man*, as is evident from the meaning of what follows. But the commentators assure us that Jesus is speaking of himself as of God.

In this place is one greater than the temple: By these words the Lord speaks metaphorically of the grandeur of his person, as the Lord of his temple. The temple with all its arrangement, rites, ceremonies, sacrifices, was only an image of truth, but Christ is the truth itself, and so greater than the temple, as much as the truth is greater than an image. Thus, if the priests of the temple, the servants of the image, are permitted on a Sabbath day to perform their duties, and they are not to blame for violating in this manner the Sabbath rest as prescribed by the law, then how much less are to blame for the violation of the Sabbath the servants of that very truth which has the power to abolish the laws about the Sabbath, when they, those servants of truth, from necessity pluck the ears on the Sabbath day, in order to appease their hunger, and eat them for the glory of God. (*Ib.* p. 209.)

The meaning of the interpretation is that Jesus himself is a temple, and so his disciples may eat on the Sabbath. And such corrupt interpretations take the place of the profound and clear meaning of Christ's words.

But if ye had known, etc.: Having thus justified the action of his disciples by pointing to examples, the Saviour now discloses to the Pharisees that the source from which flowed their incorrect condemnation of his disciples is the non-comprehension of the character of the false prescriptions in their relation to the higher moral demands. They, the Pharisees, lack the merciful and compassionate love of their neighbours, such as, for example, God demands through his prophet Hosea (vi. 6); their whole attention is directed only to sacrifices, rites, ceremonies, and customs of tradition, which for them conceal the source of the pure love. If they understood that the compassionate love for the hungry man is higher than all tradition and ritualistic customs, even higher than sacrifices, they would not condemn the innocent, who to appease their hunger pluck some ears of corn.

Lord also of the sabbath: He who is higher than the temple is also higher than all law, which is centred on and in the temple, higher, also, than all statutes in regard to the Sabbath, is the Lord of the Sabbath itself. He who is to abolish the Sabbath of the Old Testament can even now command his disciples to renounce the protection of the Old Testament: "for the time has arrived for them to learn everything through most exalted subjects, and no longer is he to be bound by the law, who, having freed himself from malice, is tending toward all which is good." (Chrys.) (*Ib.* pp. 209 and 210.)

It turns out that the fact that the son of man is the lord of the Sabbath, and that the Sabbath is made for man, and not man for the Sabbath, as is said in Mark, —that the whole utterance is abolished and that the Sabbath is done away with, not by man, but by God.

10. Ἦν δὲ διδάσκων ἐν μιᾷ τῶν συναγωγῶν ἐν τοῖς σάββασι·

11. Καὶ ἰδού, γυνὴ ἦν πνεῦμα ἔχουσα ἀσθενείας ἔτη δέκα καὶ ὀκτὼ, καὶ ἦν συγκύπτουσα, καὶ μὴ δυναμένη ἀνακύψαι εἰς τὸ παντελές.

12. Ἰδὼν δὲ αὐτὴν ὁ Ἰησοῦς προσεφώνησε, καὶ εἶπεν αὐτῇ, Γύναι, ἀπολέλυσαι τῆς ἀσθενείας σου.

18. Καὶ ἐπέθηκεν αὐτῇ τὰς χεῖρας· καὶ παραχρῆμα ἀνωρθώθη, καὶ ἐδόξαζε τὸν Θεόν.

14. Ἀποκριθεὶς δὲ ὁ ἀρχισυνάγωγος, ἀγανακτῶν ὅτι τῷ σαββάτῳ ἐθεράπευσεν ὁ Ἰησοῦς, ἔλεγε τῷ ὄχλῳ, Ἓξ ἡμέραι εἰσὶν, ἐν αἷς δεῖ

Luke xiii. 10. And he was teaching in one of the synagogues on the sabbath.

11. And, behold, there was a woman which had a spirit of infirmity eighteen years, and was bowed together, and could in no wise lift up herself.

12. And when Jesus saw her, he called her to him, and said unto her, Woman, thou art loosed from thine infirmity.

13. And he laid his hands on her: and immediately she was made straight, and glorified God.

14. And the ruler of the synagogue answered with indignation, because that Jesus had healed on the sabbath day, and said unto the people, There are six days in which men

10. Jesus happened to be teaching in one of the assemblies, and it was a Sabbath.

11. And a woman was there, and a spirit of infirmity had been in her for eighteen years.

12. Jesus saw her, and called her, and said, Woman, thou art freed from thy infirmity.

14. The elder of the assembly grew angry because Jesus was practising on the Sabbath, and said to the people, There are six days in the week to work in, so practise in those six

ἐργάζεσθαι· ἐν ταύταις οὖν ἐρχόμενοι θεραπεύεσθε, καὶ μὴ τῇ ἡμέρᾳ τοῦ σαββάτου.

ought to work: in them therefore come and be healed, and not on the sabbath day.

days, and not on the Sabbath.

3. Καὶ ἀποκριθεὶς ὁ Ἰησοῦς εἶπε πρὸς τοὺς νομικοὺς καὶ Φαρισαίους, λέγων, Εἰ ἔξεστι τῷ σαββάτῳ θεραπεύειν;

Luke xiv. 3. And Jesus answering spake unto the lawyers and Pharisees, saying, Is it lawful to heal on the sabbath day?

3. And Jesus turned to the learned Orthodox, and asked, Is it not lawful to help people on the Sabbath?

4. Οἱ δὲ ἡσύχασαν.

4. And they held their peace.

4. And they did not know what to say.

15. Ἀπεκρίθη οὖν αὐτῷ ὁ Κύριος, καὶ εἶπεν, Ὑποκριτά, ἕκαστος ὑμῶν τῷ σαββάτῳ οὐ λύει τὸν βοῦν αὐτοῦ ἢ τὸν ὄνον ἀπὸ τῆς φάτνης, καὶ ἀπαγαγὼν ποτίζει.

Luke xiii. 15. The Lord then answered him, and said, Thou hypocrite, doth not each one of you on the sabbath loose his ox or his ass from the stall, and lead him away to watering?

15. And Jesus said to them, Hypocrites! Does not each one of you on the Sabbath untie his ox or his ass from the stall, and lead him away to be watered?

16. Ταύτην δέ, θυγατέρα Ἀβραὰμ οὖσαν, ἣν ἔδησεν ὁ Σατανᾶς, ἰδού, δέκα καὶ ὀκτὼ ἔτη, οὐκ ἔδει λυθῆναι ἀπὸ τοῦ δεσμοῦ τούτου τῇ ἡμέρᾳ τοῦ σαββάτου;

16. And ought not this woman, being a daughter of Abraham, whom Satan hath bound, lo, these eighteen years, be loosed from this bond on the sabbath day?

16. Why, then, is this woman not to be helped?

6. Καὶ οὐκ ἴσχυσαν ἀνταποκριθῆναι αὐτῷ πρὸς ταῦτα.

Luke xiv. 6. And they could not answer him again to these things.

6. And they could not answer him this.

5. Καὶ ἀποκριθεὶς πρὸς αὐτοὺς εἶπε, Τίνος ὑμῶν ὄνος ἢ βοῦς εἰς φρέαρ ἐμπεσεῖται, καὶ οὐκ εὐθέως ἀνασπάσει αὐτὸν ἐν τῇ ἡμέρᾳ τοῦ σαββάτου;

Luke xiv. 5. And answered them, saying, Which of you shall have an ass or an ox fallen into a pit, and will not straightway pull him out on the sabbath day?

5. And again he said, If a sheep of yours falls into a pit, will you not pull it out at once, even though it be a Sabbath?

12. Πόσῳ οὖν διαφέρει ἄνθρωπος προβάτου; ὥστε ἔξεστι τοῖς σάββασι καλῶς ποιεῖν.

Matt. xii. 12. How much then is a man better than a sheep? Wherefore it is lawful to do well on the sabbath days.

12. But a man is much better than a sheep. He said, For this reason it is necessary to do well on the Sabbath.

REMARK ON THE HEALING ON THE SABBATH

If there could be any doubt as to what the foundation is on which Christ rejects the observance of the Sabbath, this passage, it seems, would dispel it. Jesus rejects the Sabbath, that is, the external worship, not on the basis of his supposed Godhead, but on the basis of common sense, of that same comprehension which has come to be the foundation of everything. He says, A sheep may be pulled out from a pit, and a man may not be helped, — that is stupid. Most important are man and good works. All external worship can only be in the way of the performance of the work of life, and so it is not only unnecessary, but even harmful. And so he takes that which is regarded as the most important of all the works of the divine worship, adduces an example when it is diametrically opposed to good works, and rejects it. What is there here that cannot be understood? But no, the church has its own interpretation.

The Lord presents an objective rejection of the injustice of the imaginary tradition of the elders that it is not lawful to do even any works of mercy on the Sabbath. If somebody's only sheep (an only sheep would be so much dearer to him than to a man who has a whole flock) should fall into a pit, and he should thus be subject to the danger of losing it, would he not make an effort to get it out from there?

Of course he will pull it out, out of pity for the animal, and out of regard for his property. A man is more important than a sheep. If, then, you act with compassion on the Sabbath in relation to a speechless animal, you must act with so much more compassion and love in relation to man, the image and likeness of God, to man, for whose salvation and to give the everlasting life to whom the Saviour came.

It is lawful to do well on the sabbath days: The Pharisees could not help knowing that, but such is the power of preconceived notions, habits, and traditions, that what is clearly conceived to be true in the abstract is frequently subject to blame in practice. The Lord reproves such inconsistency. (*Ib.* p. 211.)

"The Lord reproves such inconsistency," — very well. But this does not refer to the Sabbath in particular, but to the external divine worship, the strongest example of which was then represented by the Sabbath. Jesus could not then have spoken in advance of our churches, masses, images, sacraments. These did not exist then, but of all of them he was speaking then.

Is not the same Sabbath represented by the Sunday, by the expenditure for candles and for the pay of the popes, by those riches of the churches, those cares about the external worship, which always are diametrically opposed to works of love toward man for the simple reason that the works of the worship are never directed toward man, but toward something dead, while the work of love can be directed only toward man. In no way can it be said, as I am always told, that masses, communion, prayers, do not keep people from doing good to men. Of course they keep one from doing good, since they are directed toward something else than men.

It must not be forgotten that the teaching of Jesus consists in directing every step toward doing good to men. How, then, can an activity which is directed away from men be useful for the fulfilment of this teaching? It is the same as though one were to assert that smoking a pipe is very useful for the ploughing of a field. It may be that it does not interfere with it much, and wastes little time, and even furnishes rest and pleasure, but this matter in itself does not help the ploughing of the field, and is opposed to it.

THE CALLING OF MATTHEW

9. Καὶ παράγων ὁ Ἰησοῦς ἐκεῖθεν, εἶδεν ἄνθρωπον καθήμενον ἐπὶ τὸ τελώνιον, Ματθαῖον λεγόμενον, καὶ λέγει αὐτῷ, Ἀκολούθει μοι. καὶ ἀναστὰς ἠκολούθησεν αὐτῷ.

10. Καὶ ἐγένετο αὐτοῦ ἀνακειμένου ἐν τῇ οἰκίᾳ, καὶ ἰδοὺ, πολλοὶ τελῶναι καὶ ἁμαρτωλοὶ ἐλθόντες συνανέκειντο τῷ Ἰησοῦ καὶ τοῖς μαθηταῖς αὐτοῦ·

Matt. ix. 9. And as Jesus passed forth from thence, he saw a man, named Matthew, sitting at the receipt of custom: and he saith unto him, Follow me. And he arose, and followed him.

10. And it came to pass, as Jesus sat at meat in the house, behold, many publicans and sinners came and sat down with him and his disciples.

9. One time Jesus saw a man sitting on the road and collecting taxes. That man's name was Matthew, and Jesus said to him, Follow me. And he got up, and followed him.

10. And Matthew entertained Jesus. And it happened that when Jesus was sitting in his house, there came other farmers of taxes and those who had gone astray, and they sat with Jesus and his disciples.

(a) ἁμαρτωλοί those who are mistaken. I translate it that way, and not *sinners*, because sinner has received a different meaning. Here ἁμαρτωλοί has the meaning of men opposed to the Pharisees, that is, to the Orthodox, who regarded themselves as in the right. And so I put down a word which corresponds to ἁμαρτωλοί and is the opposite of Orthodox, namely, those who have gone astray.

THE DESTRUCTION OF THE RITES

11. Καὶ ἰδόντες οἱ Φαρισαῖοι εἶπον τοῖς μαθηταῖς αὐτοῦ, Διατί μετὰ τῶν τελωνῶν καὶ ἁμαρτωλῶν ἐσθίει ὁ διδάσκαλος ὑμῶν;

17. Καὶ ἀκούσας ὁ Ἰησοῦς λέγει αὐτοῖς, Οὐ χρείαν ἔχουσιν οἱ ἰσχύοντες ἰατροῦ, ἀλλ᾽ οἱ κακῶς ἔχοντες, οὐκ ἦλθον καλέσαι δικαίους, ἀλλὰ ἁμαρτωλοὺς εἰς μετάνοιαν.

18. Πορευθέντες δὲ μάθετε τί ἐστιν, ''Ἔλεον θέλω, καὶ οὐ θυσίαν·'

1. Καὶ συνάγονται πρὸς αὐτὸν οἱ Φαρισαῖοι, καί τινες τῶν γραμματέων, ἐλθόντες ἀπὸ Ἱεροσολύμων·

2. Καὶ ἰδόντες τινὰς τῶν μαθητῶν αὐτοῦ κοιναῖς χερσί, τοῦτ᾽ ἐστιν ἀνίπτοις, ἐσθίοντας ἄρτους, ἐμέμψαντο·

3. (Οἱ γὰρ Φαρισαῖοι καὶ πάντες οἱ Ἰουδαῖοι, ἐὰν μὴ πυγμῇ νίψωνται τὰς χεῖρας, οὐκ ἐσθίουσι, κρατοῦντες τὴν παράδοσιν τῶν πρεσβυτέρων·

4. Καὶ ἀπὸ ἀγορᾶς, ἐὰν μὴ βαπτίσωνται, οὐκ

Matt. ix. 11. And when the Pharisees saw it, they said unto his disciples, Why eateth your master with publicans and sinners?

Mark ii. 17. When Jesus heard it, he saith unto them, They that are whole have no need of the physician, but they that are sick: I came not to call the righteous, but sinners to repentance.

Matt. ix. 13. But go ye and learn what that meaneth, I will have mercy, and not sacrifice.

Mark vii. 1. Then came together unto him the Pharisees, and certain of the scribes, which came from Jerusalem.

2. And when they saw some of his disciples eat bread with defiled, that is to say, with unwashen hands, they found fault.

3. For the Pharisees, and all the Jews, except they wash their hands oft, eat not, holding the tradition of the elders.

4. And when they come from the market, except they wash, they

11. And the learned Orthodox saw it, and said to his disciples, Why does your teacher eat with farmers of taxes and with those who have gone astray?

17. Jesus heard it, and said, Not those who are well, but those who are ill need a physician. I do not wish to call the Orthodox, but those who have gone astray to repentance.

13. Go and learn what is meant by, I want love toward men, and not sacrifices.

1. And there came together at his house Orthodox people, and some of them were learned, who came from Jerusalem.

2. And when they saw his disciples eat bread with unclean, that is, with unwashed hands, they began to curse.

3. For without washing their hands they do not eat with the hands, holding the tradition of the elders.

4. Nor do they eat when they come from the market, unless they

ἐσθίουσι· καὶ ἄλλα πολλά ἐστιν ἃ παρέλαβον κρατεῖν, βαπτισμοὺς ποτηρίων καὶ ξεστῶν καὶ χαλκίων καὶ κλινῶν·)

5. Ἔπειτα ἐπερωτῶσιν αὐτὸν οἱ Φαρισαῖοι καὶ οἱ γραμματεῖς, Διατί οἱ μαθηταί σου οὐ περιπατοῦσι κατὰ τὴν παράδοσιν τῶν πρεσβυτέρων ἀλλὰ ἀνίπτοις χερσὶν ἐσθίουσι τὸν ἄρτον;

6. Ὁ δὲ ἀποκριθεὶς εἶπεν αὐτοῖς, Ὅτι καλῶς προεφήτευσεν Ἡσαΐας περὶ ὑμῶν τῶν ὑποκριτῶν, ὡς γέγραπται, Οὗτος ὁ λαὸς τοῖς χείλεσί με τιμᾷ, ἡ δὲ καρδία αὐτῶν πόρρω ἀπέχει ἀπ' ἐμοῦ.

7. Μάτην δὲ σέβονταί με, διδάσκοντες διδασκαλίας, ἐντάλματα ἀνθρώπων.

8. Ἀφέντες γὰρ τὴν ἐντολὴν τοῦ Θεοῦ, κρατεῖτε τὴν παράδοσιν τῶν ἀνθρώπων, βαπτισμοὺς ξεστῶν καὶ ποτηρίων, καὶ ἄλλα παρόμοια τοιαῦτα πολλὰ ποιεῖτε.

9. Καὶ ἔλεγεν αὐτοῖς, Καλῶς ἀθετεῖτε τὴν ἐντολὴν τοῦ Θεοῦ ἵνα τὴν παράδοσιν ὑμῶν τηρήσητε.

10. Μωσῆς γὰρ εἶπε, Τίμα τὸν πατέρα σου καὶ τὴν μητέρα σου. καί, Ὁ κακολογῶν πατέρα ἢ μητέρα θανάτῳ τελευτάτω·

11. Ὑμεῖς δὲ λέγετε, Ἐὰν εἴπῃ ἄνθρωπος τῷ πατρὶ ἢ τῇ μητρί, Κορβᾶν, (ὅ ἐστι, Δῶρον,) ὃ ἐὰν ἐξ ἐμοῦ ὠφεληθῇς·

---

eat not. And many other things there be, which they have received to hold, as the washing of cups, and pots, brazen vessels, and of tables.

5. Then the Pharisees and scribes asked him, Why walk not thy disciples according to the tradition of the elders, but eat bread with unwashen hands?

6. He answered and said unto them, Well hath Esaias prophesied of you hypocrites, as it is written, This people honoureth me with their lips, but their heart is far from me.

7. Howbeit in vain do they worship me, teaching for doctrines the commandments of men (Isaiah xxix. 13).

8. For laying aside the commandment of God, ye hold the tradition of men, as the washing of pots and cups: and many other such like things ye do.

9. And he said unto them, Full well ye reject the commandment of God, that ye may keep your own tradition.

10. For Moses said, Honour thy father and thy mother; and, Whoso curseth father or mother, let him die the death:

11. But ye say, If a man shall say to his father or mother, It is Corban, that is to say, a gift, by whatsoever thou mightest be profited by me; he shall be free.

---

wash their hands. And they keep many other commandments, such as the washing of dishes, pots, and pans.

5. For that reason the learned Orthodox asked him, Why do not thy disciples hold to the tradition of the forefathers, but eat bread with unwashed hands?

6. And he said to them in reply, Well has Isaiah said of you hypocrites, as it is written, These people honour me with their mouths, but their hearts are far from me.

7. They worship me badly, teaching doctrines and commandments of men.

8. You lay aside the commandment of God, and hold the enactments of men, the washing of cups and glasses, and you do many other such things.

9. And Jesus said to them, You have readily rejected the commandment of God, that you may keep your own decree.

10. Moses has told you, Honour thy father and thy mother, and, Whoso curses father or mother, let him die.

11. But you think that if a man says, Corban (which means, a gift to God), that by which thou mightest profit by me,

12. Καὶ οὐκέτι ἀφίετε αὐτὸν οὐδὲν ποιῆσαι τῷ πατρὶ αὐτοῦ ἢ τῇ μητρὶ αὐτοῦ,

13. Ἀκυροῦντες τὸν λόγον τοῦ Θεοῦ τῇ παραδόσει ὑμῶν ᾗ παρεδώκατε· καὶ παρόμοια τοιαῦτα πολλὰ ποιεῖτε.

14. Καὶ προσκαλεσάμενος πάντα τὸν ὄχλον, ἔλεγεν αὐτοῖς, Ἀκούετέ μου πάντες, καὶ συνίετε.

15. Οὐδέν ἐστιν ἔξωθεν τοῦ ἀνθρώπου εἰσπορευόμενον εἰς αὐτὸν, ὃ δύναται αὐτὸν κοινῶσαι· ἀλλὰ τὰ ἐκπορευόμενα ἀπ' αὐτοῦ, ἐκεῖνά ἐστι τὰ κοινοῦντα τὸν ἄνθρωπον.

16. Εἴ τις ἔχει ὦτα ἀκούειν, ἀκουέτω.

17. Καὶ ὅτε εἰσῆλθεν εἰς οἶκον ἀπὸ τοῦ ὄχλου, ἐπηρώτων αὐτὸν οἱ μαθηταὶ αὐτοῦ περὶ τῆς παραβολῆς.

18. Καὶ λέγει αὐτοῖς, Οὕτω καὶ ὑμεῖς ἀσύνετοί ἐστε; οὐ νοεῖτε ὅτι πᾶν τὸ ἔξωθεν εἰσπορευόμενον εἰς τὸν ἄνθρωπον οὐ δύναται αὐτὸν κοινῶσαι;

19. Ὅτι οὐκ εἰσπορεύεται αὐτοῦ εἰς τὴν καρδίαν, ἀλλ' εἰς τὴν κοιλίαν· καὶ εἰς τὸν ἀφεδρῶνα ἐκπορεύεται, καθαρίζον πάντα τὰ βρώματα.

20. Ἔλεγε δὲ, Ὅτι τὸ ἐκ τοῦ ἀνθρώπου ἐκπορευόμενον, ἐκεῖνο κοινοῖ τὸν ἄνθρωπον.

21. Ἔσωθεν γὰρ ἐκ τῆς καρδίας τῶν ἀνθρώπων οἱ διαλογισμοὶ οἱ κακοὶ ἐκπορεύονται μοιχεῖαι, πορνεῖαι, φόνοι,

---

12. And ye suffer him no more to do aught for his father or his mother;

13. Making the word of God of none effect through your tradition, which ye have delivered: and many such like things do ye.

14. And when he had called all the people unto him, he said unto them, Hearken unto me every one of you, and understand:

15. There is nothing from without a man, that entering into him can defile him: but the things which come out of him, those are they that defile the man.

16. If any man have ears to hear, let him hear.

17. And when he was entered into the house from the people, his disciples asked him concerning the parable.

18. And he saith unto them, Are ye so without understanding also? Do ye not perceive, that whatsoever thing from without entereth into the man, it cannot defile him;

19. Because it entereth not into his heart, but into the belly, and goeth out into the draught, purging all meats?

20. And he said, That which cometh out of the man, that defileth the man.

21. For from within, out of the heart of men, proceed evil thoughts, adulteries, fornications, murders,

---

12. Him you no longer permit to do anything for his father or mother.

13. You destroy the word of God by that tradition of yours, which you have delivered. And you do many such things.

14. And he called together all the people, and said, Listen to me every one of you, and understand.

15. There is nothing which, entering man, can defile him; but what comes out of him will defile a man.

16. If you have ears to hear, then understand!

17. When he went away from the people into the house, the disciples asked him concerning the parable.

18. And he said to them, Have you not understood it? Do you not know that nothing that enters man from without can defile him?

19. Because it enters not his heart, but his belly, and goes out through the back, purging all food.

20. But that which comes out of man cannot help but defile him.

21. For from the heart of men proceed evil thoughts, fornication, lechery, murders,

22. Κλοπαί, πλεονεξίαι, πονηρίαι, δόλος, ἀσέλγεια, ὀφθαλμὸς πονηρὸς, βλασφημία, ὑπερηφανία, ἀφροσύνη.

23. Πάντα ταῦτα τὰ πονηρὰ ἔσωθεν ἐκπορεύεται, καὶ κοινοῖ τὸν ἄνθρωπον.

---

22. Thefts, covetousness, wickedness, deceit, lasciviousness, an evil eye, blasphemy, pride, foolishness:

23. All these evil things come from within, and defile the man.

---

22. Stealing, selfishness, deception, impudence, envious eyes, calumny, pride, foolishness.

23. All these evil things come from within, and defile the man.

(*a*) Having rejected the chief expression of the divine worship of the Jews, the Sabbath, and having shown that it is inapplicable, Jesus shows that it is also harmful in that people who perform external rites by this very performance consider themselves to be right. But, in regarding themselves as being right, they no longer seek deliverance from error. And he repeats once more that definite sacrifices are not necessary, but what is necessary is love for man.

THE DESTRUCTION OF THE EXTERNAL TEMPLE

13. Καὶ ἐγγὺς ἦν τὸ πάσχα τῶν Ἰουδαίων, καὶ ἀνέβη εἰς Ἱεροσόλυμα ὁ Ἰησοῦς.

14. Καὶ εὗρεν ἐν τῷ ἱερῷ τοὺς πωλοῦντας βόας καὶ πρόβατα καὶ περιστερὰς, καὶ τοὺς κερματιστὰς καθημένους.

15. Καὶ ποιήσας φραγέλλιον ἐκ σχοινίων, πάντας ἐξέβαλεν ἐκ τοῦ ἱεροῦ, τά τε πρόβατα καὶ τοὺς βόας. καὶ τῶν κολλυβιστῶν ἐξέχεε τὸ κέρμα, καὶ τὰς τραπέζας ἀνέστρεψε·

16. Καὶ τοῖς τὰς περιστερὰς πωλοῦσιν εἶπεν, Ἄρατε ταῦτα ἐντεῦθεν· μὴ ποιεῖτε τὸν οἶκον τοῦ πατρός μου οἶκον ἐμπορίου.

John ii. 13. And the Jews' passover was at hand, and Jesus went up to Jerusalem,

14. And found in the temple those that sold oxen and sheep and doves, and the changers of money sitting:

15. And when he had made a scourge of small cords, he drove them all out of the temple, and the sheep, and the oxen; and poured out the changers' money, and overthrew the tables;

16. And said unto them that sold doves,ᵃ Take these things hence; make not my Father's house a house of merchandise.

---

13. And the Jewish passover was at hand, and Jesus went to Jerusalem.

14. And he saw them sell oxen, sheep, and doves in the temple, and the changers were sitting there and changing money.

15. And he plaited a whip out of ropes, and drove out of the temple the sheep and the oxen, and scattered the changers' money, and threw down the tables of the dove sellers.

16. And he said, Take these things away from here, and do not imagine that a market can be a house of my Father

16. Καὶ οὐκ ἤφιεν ἵνα τις διενέγκῃ σκεῦος διὰ τοῦ ἱεροῦ.

17. Καὶ ἐδίδασκε, λέγων αὐτοῖς, Οὐ γέγραπται, ʽ῞Οτι ὁ οἶκός μου οἶκος προσευχῆς κληθήσεται πᾶσι τοῖς ἔθνεσιν;ʼ ὑμεῖς δὲ ἐποιήσατε αὐτὸν ʽσπήλαιον λῃστῶν.ʼ

18. Ἀπεκρίθησαν οὖν οἱ Ἰουδαῖοι καὶ εἶπον αὐτῷ, Τί σημεῖον δεικνύεις ἡμῖν, ὅτι ταῦτα ποιεῖς;

19. Ἀπεκρίθη ὁ Ἰησοῦς καὶ εἶπεν αὐτοῖς, Λύσατε τὸν ναὸν τοῦτον, καὶ ἐν τρισὶν ἡμέραις ἐγερῶ αὐτόν.

Mark xi. 16. And would not suffer that any man should carry any vessel through the temple.

17. And he taught, saying unto them, Is it not written, My house shall be called of all nations the house of prayer? but ye have made[a] it a den of thieves (Isaiah lvi. 7).[c]

John ii. 18. Then answered the Jews and said unto him, What sign[d] shewest thou unto us, seeing that thou doest these things?

19. Jesus answered and said unto them, Destroy this temple, and in three days I will raise[e] it up.

16. And he did not suffer any articles to be carried through the temple.

17. And he instructed them, and said, Do you not know that it is written, My house shall be called a house of prayer for all nations? But you consider a den of robbers to be my house.

18. And the Jews began to speak, and they said to him, What right wilt thou show us for doing these things?

19. And Jesus said to them, Destroy this temple, and in three days I will resuscitate it.

(*a*) There ought to be a period after πωλοῦσι, and then must be added καὶ εἶπεν. Otherwise it is incomprehensible why Jesus should say to the sellers of doves only, Take these things away. Evidently what he says has reference to all those whom he is driving out, and to everything that he is overturning.

(*b*) ἐποιήσατε has to be translated here not by *do*, but by "imagine, consider that a market can be the house of my Father." It is difficult to think that Jesus should in the same discourse, in which he says that a temple is not necessary, call the temple the house of his Father. He says, A market is not called a house of God.

(*c*) The words of the prophet Isaiah are used here in the same sense that the words to the Samaritan woman are used in the next chapter, Take all this away, for my house is not the one where sacrifices are brought, but the whole world, where men know the true God. The subsequent passage from Jeremiah, And not a den of robbers, confirms this meaning. Here is the passage from Jeremiah (vii. 4–11):

4. Trust ye not in lying words, saying, The temple of the Lord, The temple of the Lord, The temple of the Lord, are these.

5. For if ye thoroughly amend your ways and your doings; if ye thoroughly execute judgment between a man and his neighbour ;

6. If ye oppress not the stranger, the fatherless, and the widow, and shed not innocent blood in this place, neither walk after other gods to your hurt;

7. Then will I cause you to dwell in this place, in the land that I gave to your fathers, for ever and ever.

8. Behold, ye trust in lying words, that cannot profit.

9. Will ye steal, murder, and commit adultery, and swear falsely, and burn incense unto Baal, and walk after other gods whom ye know not;

10. And come and stand before me in this house, which is called by my name, and say, We are delivered to do all these abominations ?

11. Is this house, which is called by my name, become a den of robbers.

(*d*) σημεῖον *sign, symptom of justice.* I translate it by *right.*

(*e*) ἐγείρω never means, or can mean, *to build, raise,* but means *to waken,* and in this passage it means *to waken as something living,* and so it has to be translated by, " I will resuscitate the living temple."

The significance of this verse is explained in verses 21 and 22, where it is said that the temple means the body of Jesus Christ, and three days designate the time after which he shall rise from the dead. This explanation cannot satisfy me, who regard the resurrection as a most blasphemous invention, which lowered the teaching of Christ, of which mention will be made in its proper place. Jesus Christ could not have meant his resurrection in the body, for that would be a conception which destroys his whole teaching. This explanation has been invented later by those who believed or invented the story of the resurrection. But the words which gave rise to this explanation were said, and evidently had a definite meaning. This explanation is very unsatisfactory.

Why, speaking of his body, did Christ say a temple, and why did he speak of the resurrection after driving the sacrifices out of the temple? It is enough to forget the false church explanation in order that the meaning of the words should become not only clear, but even necessary as an explanation of what precedes. Jesus Christ drives out of the temple everything which is needed for the bringing of sacrifices, consequently for prayer, in accordance with the conceptions of the Jews, and, recalling the words of Jeremiah, he says that it is necessary to do good, and not to gather in the temple for the purpose of offering sacrifices. Thereupon he speaks not conditionally, as Jesus' words, Destroy the temple, are generally understood, but positively, I will make it alive, I will rear a new one. He quotes the words of Jeremiah, in which it is said that the house of God is the whole world of men, where all people recognize God, and not a den of robbers, and says, Destroy the temple, and I will make a new, a living temple for you, — I will show it to you and will teach you. And I will make this new temple quickly, because I do not have to build it with my hands. I will do in three days what you have made in forty-six years.

20. Εἶπον οὖν οἱ Ἰουδαῖοι, Τεσσαράκοντα καὶ ἓξ ἔτεσιν ᾠκοδομήθη ὁ ναὸς οὗτος, καὶ σὺ ἐν τρισὶν ἡμέραις ἐγερεῖς αὐτόν;	*John ii.* 20. Then said the Jews, Forty and six years was this temple in building, and wilt thou rear it up in three days?	20. The Jews said, This temple was forty-six years in building, and thou wilt resuscitate it in three days.
6. Λέγω δὲ ὑμῖν, ὅτι τοῦ ἱεροῦ μείζων ἐστὶν ὧδε.	*Matt. xii.* 6. But I say unto you, That in this place is one greater than the temple.ᵃ	6. And Jesus said to them, I tell you that more important than the temple is this,
7. Εἰ δὲ ἐγνώκειτε τί ἐστιν, ''Ἔλεον θέλω καὶ οὐ θυσίαν,' οὐκ ἂν κατεδικάσατε τοὺς ἀναιτίους.	7. But if ye had known what this meaneth, I will have mercy,ᵇ and not sacrifice, ye would not have condemned the guiltless.	7. That you should understand what is meant by, I want compassion toward men, and not church services.

(*a*) This verse, which is given in the chapter where the disciples are rebuked for plucking the ears of corn, is out of place there, since nothing is said there about the temple, but Jesus says, This is more important than the temple. In any case, the idea which is expressed in this verse and is repeated in Matt. ix. 13, answers directly the contentions of the Jews and expresses Jesus' view about the temple.

(*b*) ἔλεον *sympathy*. I translate it by *compassion for men*.

After that follow verses 21 and 22 of Chapter II. of John, which contain the author's imaginary explanation of these words.

23. Ὡς δὲ ἦν ἐν Ἱεροσολύμοις ἐν τῷ πάσχα, ἐν τῇ ἑορτῇ, πολλοὶ ἐπίστευσαν εἰς τὸ ὄνομα αὐτοῦ, θεωροῦντες αὐτοῦ τὰ σημεῖα ἃ ἐποίει.	*John ii.* 23. Now when he was in Jerusalem at the passover, in the feast day, many believed in his name, when they saw the miracles which he did.	23. And when he was in Jerusalem at the passover, many believed in his teaching, comprehending the proofs which he adduced.
24. Αὐτὸς δὲ ὁ Ἰησοῦς οὐκ ἐπίστευεν ἑαυτὸν αὐτοῖς, διὰ τὸ αὐτὸν γινώσκειν πάντας·	24. But Jesus did not commit himself unto them, because he knew all men.*e*	24. But Jesus himself did not commit himself to their faith, because he himself knew everything,
25. Καὶ ὅτι οὐ χρείαν εἶχεν ἵνα τις μαρτυρήσῃ περὶ τοῦ ἀνθρώπου· αὐτὸς γὰρ ἐγίνωσκε τί ἦν ἐν τῷ ἀνθρώπῳ.	25. And needed not that any should testify of man; for he knew what was in man.	25. And so he did not need to have any one point out about man to him; for he knew himself what was in man.
18. Καὶ ἤκουσαν οἱ γραμματεῖς καὶ οἱ ἀρχιερεῖς, καὶ ἐζήτουν πῶς αὐτὸν ἀπολέσουσιν· ἐφοβοῦντο γὰρ αὐτόν, ὅτι πᾶς ὁ ὄχλος ἐξεπλήσσετο ἐπὶ τῇ διδαχῇ αὐτοῦ.	*Mark xi.* 18. And the scribes and chief priests heard it, and sought how they might destroy him: for they feared him, because all the people was astonished at his doctrine.	18. And the scribes and the elders of the priests heard it. And they sought how they might destroy him: for they feared him, because all the people marvelled at his teaching.

(*a*) In many texts it reads πάντα.

Here are the explanations of the church about the expulsion from the temple.

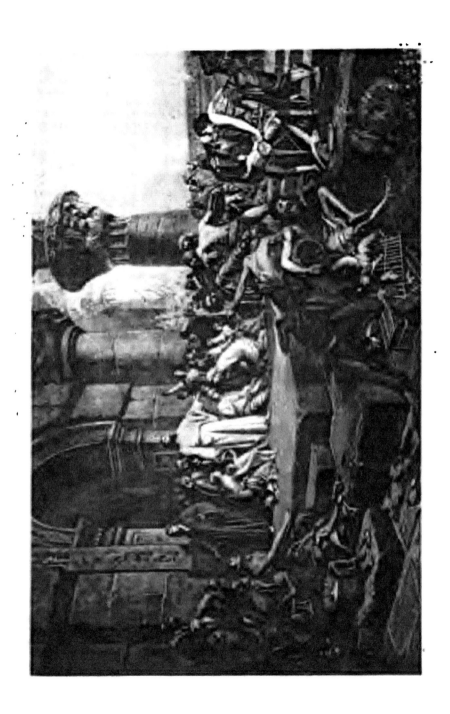

And found in the temple: That is, in the courtyard of the temple, called the yard of the pagans, they sold, etc.

A scourge of small cords: A symbol of the Lord's wrath against those who defile the sanctity of the temple, as also a symbol of the power of the Lord who is jealous of the purification of the house of his heavenly Father.

Take these things hence, etc.: The doves were in cages or baskets, and so the Lord, driving out the venders of animals with the latter, mentions especially that the venders should take them out.

Make not my Father's house a house of merchandise: When the Lord left the temple the last time, he called it not the house of his Father, but your house (Matt. xxiii. 38), meaning by it that the temple was left desolate by God; but now Christ calls it still the temple of my heavenly Father, for there has not yet been manifested the opposition of its devotees to Christ and to God, and he is expecting the repentance of the people in the person of their representatives.

A house of merchandise: A less strong expression than is used at the second purification of the temple, when the Lord said that the Jews had made the house of prayer into a den of thieves (Matt. xxi. 13). The first expresses that into the holy ministration of the church have entered highly impure worldly transactions, while the latter expresses a complete subversion of the character of the holy work, an iconoclastic fanaticism, to which the defilement of the whole worship had come and in which it found its expression. If one should ask how it happened that these venders submitted to the Lord's will and words, so that at his command they left their trade and went out of the temple with all their objects of trade, we should remark: (1) that their conscience naturally told them that they were, indeed, not doing a good work in a holy place, and so, when the Lord forcibly reminded them of it, their conscience spoke up more strongly still and caused them to carry out his command without gainsaying; (2) the fame about Jesus of Nazareth as a prophet or unusual man had by that time well spread among the people; pilgrims from Galilee naturally brought news to Jerusalem about the miracles wrought by him in Galilee, about the event at the Lord's baptism, and the testimonies of the prophet John in regard to him were, of course, fresh in the memory of the inhabitants of Jerusalem and its surroundings; (3) in any case the Lord manifested here his divine power, which nothing could oppose in the present case.

Then answered the Jews: Perhaps those were some of the

venders, who had been ordered to leave the temple with the objects of their trade ; more probably still those were the chiefs of the temple : the priests and the elders, who felt themselves offended in their power over the temple by such an unusual action of a Galilean who did not belong to it. With this action of his the Lord unquestionably appeared to them also in the capacity of a prophet, an extraordinary messenger of God ; but those who were more reasonable among them could have guessed from the words of the Lord, who called the temple the house of his Father, that he was more than a prophet. Since Moses, Elijah, and other extraordinary messengers of God now and then proved their extraordinary mission by means of unusual deeds and miracles, the Jews who now surrounded the Lord demanded of him some unusual action, a miracle, as a proof of his having the right to order them about in the temple like a prophet, like a son of God.

And said unto him: Assure us by some miracle that thou art the son of God, and that thou art sent by him, for how shall we know the Lord of this house is thy Father ? (Theophil.) They overlooked the sign shown them in the very act of clearing the temple, as an unusual act which had a powerful effect upon those who defiled the holy place by commerce, and demanded of the Lord a miracle which would be more striking to them in their spiritual blindness.

Destroy (the imperative has frequently the meaning of a future : ye shall destroy) *this temple,* etc.: The evangelist proceeds to explain what is meant by this utterance of the Lord when he says that he spake of the temple of his body (v. 21); it means that he spoke of his violent death. The words which correspond to this, In three days I will raise it up, hint at his resurrection, three days after his death, precisely as his disciples interpreted it after his resurrection (v. 22). Thus, in reply to the demand made by the Jews that he should work a miracle as a proof of his having the power to act so in the temple, he points to a very great miracle which bore testimony as to his being the Messiah, the miracle of his resurrection. Thus the Lord from the very beginning of his social service predicted his death and his resurrection.

I will raise it up : With these words the Lord proves his divine almightiness, for not one man who dies can by his power and force raise his body from the dead. He did not say, My Father will raise it, but, I will raise it, using my own power, without invoking any other power. (Theophil.) (Archim. Mikh., Gospel of John, pp. 72-75.)

This is what Reuss says (*Reuss, La Bible, Nouv. Test.*, Vol VI., pp. 137 and 138):

En face des disciples qui croient se trouvent (ici pour la première fois) les Juifs qui doutent, qui ne comprennent point, qui refusent de croire. Loin d'être convaincus par ce qu'ils viennent de voir, ils demandent un *signe*, c'est-à-dire un acte extraordinaire, un miracle, quelque chose enfin qui puisse prouver que Jésus était autorisé à agir comme il l'a fait. Son procédé avait bien en quelque chose d'imposant, de messianique même (Mal. iii. 1 suiv.), mais ils exigent une preuve plus palpable, une manifestation plus irrécusable. La réponse que Jésus leur fait a donné lieu à des discussions fort animées parmi les commentateurs. D'après l'auteur lui-même, voici ce qu'il a voulu dire : Tuez-moi, et en trois jours je reprendrai la vie. En d'autres termes : la résurrection de Jésus sera la preuve la plus éclatante de sa dignité supérieure. Elle l'a été en effet, et toujours, dans l'enseignement apostolique, au point de vue duquel ce discours se comprend parfaitement (comp. Matth. xii. 40). Si l'on objecte que Jésus n'a pas pu parler ainsi en ce moment, où aucun danger ne le menaçait où aucun conflit sérieux ne s'était encore élevé entre lui et le parti pharisaïque, on oublie complètement que dans notre livre il ne s'agit pas d'une évolution lente et successive des rapports ou des situations, mais que d'un bout à l'autre nous avons sous les yeux l'antagonisme du monde et de Christ, de la lumière et des ténèbres, et que Jésus n'est représenté nulle part comme ayant besoin d'apprendre peu à peu et par divers incidents qu'il a des adversaires, qu'il court des dangers, qu'il pourra éventuellement être mis à mort. Au contraire, il connaît dès le début tout ce qui arrivera, parce que cela ne dépend pas du caprice des hommes, mais de l'ordre providentiel établi d'avance. Ainsi rien n'est plus conforme à l'esprit de cet évangile que le discours mis ici dans sa bouche. Il y a plus ; ce discours est très-bien placé là où nous le lisons. Les scènes relatives aux disciples sont terminées, l'action du révélateur sur le monde doit maintenant commencer ; l'auteur indique ici d'avance quelles chances, pour un succès définitif, il a devant lui : le monde sera sollicité, mais non gagné ; il sera vaincu, non par une soumission volontaire, mais par la condamnation qu'il se sera attirée. C'est le programme de l'histoire que nous allons lire. Ces réflexions écarteront aussi l'objection que les paroles de Jésus, telles qu'elles sont relatées et expliquées ici, n'auraient pu être comprises par personne, par les disciples tout aussi peu que par les Juifs. A ce titre, on pourra faire ses réserves à l'égard de la presque totalité des paroles mises dans la bouche du Seigneur dans tout le cours du livre, car à la fin les disciples n'en comprennent pas plus qu'au commencement (chap. xiv. 9). Jésus parle et l'auteur écrit pour les intelligences chrétiennes, et pas le moins du monde pour la plèbe juive qui l'entoure. Enfin il ne faut pas perdre de vue cette circonstance que l'auteur dit lui-même que les Juifs se méprirent complètement sur le sens des paroles prononcées, en les appliquant au temple dont la construction avait été commencée sous Hérode. Mais c'est un phénomène qui se reproduira désormais dans chaque scène, nous aurions presque dit à chaque ligne. C'est l'expression vivante et concrète de ce fait fondamental de la théologie de notre évangile, que le monde est incapable de saisir le sens des révélations célestes qui lui sont faites (chap. iii. 12).

Everything is talked about, even what the whip was made for, but not a word about what is the meaning of the whole passage, which is repeated in all four gospels. From the interpretations of all the churches it follows that the whole meaning of this passage lies in the double repetition by Christ of the police duty in regard to the cleanliness of the temple, and in the two verses (21 and 22) which were said not by Christ, but by one of the writers of the gospels, the very verses which I omit. The meaning of it is that Christ will rise from the dead after three days. Very well, he rose from the dead and predicted his death. Was it really impossible to predict that more clearly and, above all, in a more appropriate place?

Something entirely different is meant. He came into the temple and threw out of it everything which was necessary for their prayers, just as a man would do who, going into our church, should throw out all the consecrated bread, the wine, the relics, the crosses, the corporals, and all those things which are considered necessary for the mass. He is asked what σημεῖον he will show of what he is doing. Σημεῖον never and according to no dictionary means *miracle*, but let us suppose that it does mean that. What, then, is the meaning of the question of the

Jews? The man throws everything out which is needed for the prayers, and they ask him, What miracle wilt thou show us that thou art doing all this? To say the least, such a question is unintelligible. The Jews can ask why he does that; they may ask what he will put in place of what he is destroying, or what right he has to do so. But why, instead of driving him out, do they ask him, Show us a miracle? Still more surprising is this, that to the request of the Jews to show them a miracle, he does not answer by, I will show you, or, I will not show you a miracle, but by, Abandon this temple, I will make you a new, a living temple in three days.

According to the interpretations of the church this means that the miracle which he will do he will perform after his death, a miracle which none of the Jews will believe in, even after his death. And these words of his convince all. And soon after, it says that his miracles, that is, what he promises to do after his death, convince all, and many people believe him. It is enough to take off the church spectacles in order to see that this is not mere talk, but the delirium of insane people. Jesus does a reckless thing, — he drives the cattle out of the temple. The Jews, instead of driving him out, for some reason say to him, Show us a miracle. He forgets that he for some reason has driven out everything necessary for the service, and says, I will show you a miracle when I am dead, and I will do that in such a way that you shall not see it, — and these words made all men believe in his teaching. And so the meaning of the whole passage is that Jesus shall rise from the dead in three days. And it is not Christ who says that, but the writer of the gospel, in parentheses. It is enough to keep the senses together and for a moment to refer to the words of the gospel, the divine revelation according to the doctrine of the church, with at least the respect and attention with which a farce is read, that is, without imagining in advance that we are going to hear the delirium of an insane man, so that we shall not understand a word, but supposing that what is written must have some meaning, and that it is not without interest for us to comprehend what is said, and everything will become clear to us.

According to the teaching of John the Baptist, it is necessary to be purified by the spirit in order to know God. Jesus is purified in the wilderness by the spirit and finds out the power of the spirit and announces the kingdom of God in men. He tells his disciples that God is in communion with men.

According to the evangelist John, the first work of Jesus is the so-called purging of the temple, in reality the destruction of the temple, and not any kind of a temple, but the temple in Jerusalem, the one that was regarded as the house of God, the holy of holies. Jesus comes into the temple and destroys everything needed for its ministration. In addition to what has been said in the Introduction about God, about no one having ever seen God, and about having received a new godliness through Jesus, Jesus repeats in the temple the words of the prophets, that the temple of God is the whole world of men, and not a den of robbers. To explain all this would be the same as trying to explain the incident if in our time Dukhobors should go to an Orthodox church and throw out all the corporals and say, God is spirit, and we must serve him in spirit and in deeds. The action and the words of the Scripture speak so plainly that there is nothing to add or interpret. The action and the words say clearly: Your worship is an abominable lie; you do not know the real God, and the deception of your worship is harmful, and it has to be destroyed. Precisely the same is expressed by the actions and words of Jesus in the temple.

He denies the worship and conception of the Jewish God. To these actions and words of his the Jews say,

What right hast thou to do this? And he replies, My right is this, that your service of God is a lie, and my living service is the truth. My service of God is a living service, by means of works. And many believe Jesus. The first act of his sermon is to reject the false, visible God of the Jews. In the next chapter he says that God is spirit, and he must be served by works. And it is evident that, in order that men may believe in God the spirit and serve him, it is necessary to destroy the false, invented God and the false worship of him, and that is precisely what Jesus does. It is impossible not to see this. If this passage is not understood by the churches, it is not through stupidity, but through too much understanding. We shall come across many such intentional insipid interpretations. Such interpretations occur every time when the church legalizes exactly what Jesus denies. Even so now Jesus denies God the Creator, the external God, and every divine worship, except the worship of God with works. But the church has legalized the external God the Trinity, and exists only by performing services and sacrifices. That will make a man stupid against his will.

But if one wants to understand the Gospel, it is necessary above all to remember that the first action of Jesus before preaching was to deny the external God and every kind of worship. The destruction of the temple, repeated by all the evangelists (which is very rare), is the purging of the soil for the sowing. Only after the destruction of the former God the teaching about the God of Jesus and about that service of God, which Jesus teaches, is made possible.

The whole passage is an elucidation of the verse. No one has ever seen God at any time.

CHRIST'S DISCOURSE WITH A WOMAN OF SAMARIA

8. 'Αφῆκε τὴν 'Ιουδαίαν, καὶ ἀπῆλθε πάλιν εἰς τὴν Γαλιλαίαν.	*John iv. 3.* He left Judea, and departed again into Galilee.	3. And Jesus went away from Judea, again into Galilee.

4. Ἔδει δὲ αὐτὸν διέρχεσθαι διὰ τῆς Σαμαρείας.

5. Ἔρχεται οὖν εἰς πόλιν τῆς Σαμαρείας λεγομένην Σιχάρ, πλησίον τοῦ χωρίου ὃ ἔδωκεν Ἰακὼβ Ἰωσὴφ τῷ υἱῷ αὐτοῦ.

6. Ἦν δὲ ἐκεῖ πηγὴ τοῦ Ἰακώβ. ὁ οὖν Ἰησοῦς κεκοπιακὼς ἐκ τῆς ὁδοιπορίας ἐκαθέζετο οὕτως ἐπὶ τῇ πηγῇ. ὥρα ἦν ὡσεὶ ἕκτη.

7. Ἔρχεται γυνὴ ἐκ τῆς Σαμαρείας ἀντλῆσαι ὕδωρ. λέγει αὐτῇ ὁ Ἰησοῦς, Δός μοι πιεῖν.

8. Οἱ γὰρ μαθηταὶ αὐτοῦ ἀπεληλύθεισαν εἰς τὴν πόλιν, ἵνα τροφὰς ἀγοράσωσι.

9. Λέγει οὖν αὐτῷ ἡ γυνὴ ἡ Σαμαρεῖτις, Πῶς σὺ Ἰουδαῖος ὢν παρ' ἐμοῦ πιεῖν αἰτεῖς, οὔσης γυναικὸς Σαμαρείτιδος; οὐ γὰρ συγχρῶνται Ἰουδαῖοι Σαμαρείταις.

10. Ἀπεκρίθη Ἰησοῦς καὶ εἶπεν αὐτῇ, Εἰ ᾔδεις τὴν δωρεὰν τοῦ Θεοῦ, καὶ τίς ἐστιν ὁ λέγων σοι, Δός μοι πιεῖν, σὺ ἂν ᾔτησας αὐτὸν, καὶ ἔδωκεν ἂν σοι ὕδωρ ζῶν.

11. Λέγει αὐτῷ ἡ γυνή, Κύριε, οὔτε ἄντλημα ἔχεις, καὶ τὸ φρέαρ ἐστὶ βαθύ· πόθεν οὖν ἔχεις τὸ ὕδωρ τὸ ζῶν;

12. Μὴ σὺ μείζων εἶ τοῦ πατρὸς ἡμῶν Ἰακώβ, ὃς ἔδωκεν ἡμῖν τὸ φρέαρ, καὶ αὐτὸς ἐξ αὐτοῦ ἔπιε, καὶ οἱ υἱοὶ αὐτοῦ, καὶ τὰ θρέμματα αὐτοῦ;

---

4. And he must needs go through Samaria.

5. Then cometh he to a city of Samaria, which is called Sychar, near to the parcel of ground that Jacob gave to his son Joseph.

6. Now Jacob's well was there. Jesus therefore, being wearied with his journey, sat thus on the well: and it was about the sixth hour.

7. There cometh a woman of Samaria to draw water: Jesus saith unto her, Give me to drink.

8. (For his disciples were gone away unto the city to buy meat.)

9. Then saith the woman of Samaria unto him, How is it that thou, being a Jew, askest drink of me, which am a woman of Samaria? for the Jews have no dealings with the Samaritans.

10. Jesus answered and said unto her, If thou knewest the gift of God, and who it is that saith to thee, Give me to drink; thou wouldest have asked of him, and he would have given thee living water.

11. The woman saith unto him, Sir, thou hast nothing to draw with, and the well is deep: from whence then hast thou that living water?

12. Art thou greater than our father Jacob, which gave us the well, and drank thereof himself, and his children, and his cattle?

---

4. And he had to go through Samaria.

5. One day he comes to a city of Samaria, Sychar by name, near to the place that Jacob gave to his son Joseph.

6. Jacob's well was there. Jesus was weary of his journey and sat down near the well.

7. There comes a woman of Samaria to draw water, and Jesus says to her, Woman, give me to drink.

8. For his disciples were gone to the city to buy food.

9. Then the woman of Samaria says to him, How is it that thou, a Jew, askest to drink of a Samaritan woman? for the Jews have no dealings with the Samaritans?

10. But Jesus, on the contrary, said to her, If thou knewest the gift of God, and who it is that says, Give me to drink, thou wouldst have asked of him, and he would have given thee spring water.

11. And the woman said to him, Thou hast no bucket, and the well is deep, from where, then, wilt thou get that spring water?

12. Art thou greater than our father Jacob? He gave us this well. He drank of it himself, and his children, and his cattle.

13. Ἀπεκρίθη ὁ Ἰησοῦς καὶ εἶπεν αὐτῇ, Πᾶς ὁ πίνων ἐκ τοῦ ὕδατος τούτου διψήσει πάλιν·

14. Ὃς δ' ἂν πίῃ ἐκ τοῦ ὕδατος οὗ ἐγὼ δώσω αὐτῷ, οὐ μὴ διψήσῃ εἰς τὸν αἰῶνα· ἀλλὰ τὸ ὕδωρ ὃ δώσω αὐτῷ, γενήσεται ἐν αὐτῷ πηγὴ ὕδατος ἀλλομένου εἰς ζωὴν αἰώνιον.

13. Jesus answered and said unto her, Whosoever drinketh of this water shall thirst again:

14. But whosoever drinketh of the water that I shall give him shall never thirst; but the water that I shall give him shall be in him a well of water springing up into everlasting life.

13. And Jesus said to her in reply, Whosoever drinks this water shall want to drink again:

14. But whosoever drinks of the water that I shall give, shall never thirst. But the water that I shall give him brings forth in him a spring of water which runs into everlasting, non-temporal life.

(*a*) The unnecessary details, such as the definition of the time when this happened, as also certain words of the woman of Samaria, which express nothing, may be transferred to the addition, so that the reader may not lose the essential meaning of this chapter.

(*b*) The words, If thou knewest, εἰ ᾔδεις τὴν δωρεὰν τοῦ θεοῦ I translate by, If thou knewest what the gift of God is and what God, and after ἐστιν I put a comma, because after that Jesus tells the Samaritan woman that there is a God.

Verses 15–18 have no meaning whatever. It says that Christ divined that a woman had five husbands, and that now she was not living with her husband. This unnecessary and annoying detail only impairs the exposition.

19. Λέγει αὐτῷ ἡ γυνή, Κύριε, θεωρῶ ὅτι προφήτης εἶ σύ.

20. Οἱ πατέρες ἡμῶν ἐν τούτῳ τῷ ὄρει προσεκύνησαν· καὶ ὑμεῖς λέγετε, ὅτι ἐν Ἱεροσολύμοις ἐστὶν ὁ τόπος, ὅπου δεῖ προσκυνεῖν.

21. Λέγει αὐτῇ ὁ Ἰησοῦς, Γύναι, πίστευσόν μοι, ὅτι ἔρχεται ὥρα, ὅτε οὔτε ἐν τῷ ὄρει τούτῳ οὔτε ἐν Ἱεροσολύμοις προσκυνήσετε τῷ πατρί.

John iv. 19. The woman saith unto him, Sir, I perceive that thou art a prophet.
20. Our fathers worshipped in this mountain; and ye say, that in Jerusalem is the place where men ought to worship.

21. Jesus saith unto her, Woman, believe me, the hour cometh, when ye shall neither in this mountain, nor yet at Jerusalem, worship the Father.

19. The woman says to him, Sir, I see that thou art a prophet.
20. Our fathers worshipped God in this mountain, and you say that in Jerusalem is the place where men ought to worship him.

21. And Jesus said to her, Woman, believe me, the time is near when you shall neither in this mountain, nor at Jerusalem, worship the Father.

22. Ὑμεῖς προσκυνεῖτε ὃ οὐκ οἴδατε· ἡμεῖς προσκυνοῦμεν ὃ οἴδαμεν· ὅτι ἡ σωτηρία ἐκ τῶν Ἰουδαίων ἐστίν.

23. Ἀλλ' ἔρχεται ὥρα, καὶ νῦν ἐστιν, ὅτε οἱ ἀληθινοὶ προσκυνηταὶ προσκυνήσουσι τῷ πατρὶ ἐν πνεύματι καὶ ἀληθείᾳ· καὶ γὰρ ὁ πατὴρ τοιούτους ζητεῖ τοὺς προσκυνοῦντας αὐτόν.

24. Πνεῦμα ὁ Θεός· καὶ τοὺς προσκυνοῦντας αὐτὸν ἐν πνεύματι καὶ ἀληθείᾳ δεῖ προσκυνεῖν.

25. Λέγει αὐτῷ ἡ γυνή, Οἶδα ὅτι Μεσσίας ἔρχεται (ὁ λεγόμενος Χριστός)· ὅταν ἔλθῃ ἐκεῖνος, ἀναγγελεῖ ἡμῖν πάντα.

26. Λέγει αὐτῇ ὁ Ἰησοῦς, Ἐγώ εἰμι, ὁ λαλῶν σοι.

22. Ye worship ye know not what: we know what we worship; for salvation is of the Jews.

23. But the hour cometh, and now is, when the true worshippers shall worship the Father in spirit and in truth: for the Father seeketh such to worship him.

24. God is a Spirit: and they that worship him must worship him in spirit and in truth.[a]

25. The woman saith unto him, I know that Messias cometh, which is called Christ: when he is come, he will tell us all things.

26. Jesus saith unto her, I that speak unto thee am he.

22. You worship you know not whom, but we worship whom we know.

23. But the time is coming, and is already here, when the true worshippers shall worship the Father in the spirit and in deeds, for the Father demands that such to worship him.

24. God is spirit, and he ought to be worshipped in spirit and in deeds.

25. And the woman said to him, I know that Messiah will come, who is called the chosen one of God. When he is come, he will tell us all things.

26. And Jesus said to her, I that speak to thee am he.

(a) ἀληθείᾳ I translate by *in deeds*, because in many passages in the New Testament it has this meaning, and here it seems to point to the contradistinction between external worship and works; besides, truth and spirit would be a pleonasm.

Verses 27–42, with the exception of 32–38, which will be translated elsewhere, contain particular and accidental details, which have no general meaning.

While preaching the kingdom of God, which consists in the love of men among themselves, Jesus goes from village to village, and once, upon entering the land of Samaria, which is hostile to the Jews, asks a Samaritan woman for a drink. Under the pretext that he is a Jew and she a Samaritan woman, she refuses him in the simplest act of love.

In explaining this passage, men generally forget this fea-. ture of the woman's refusal to give him to drink, and yet this is the key to the comprehension of the whole passage.

The woman says that the Jews may not have any dealings with the Samaritans, and so does not give him any water. To this he tells her that she thus deprives herself of the living water, the communion of love with men, of that which gives the true life. He tells her that he not only does not loathe receiving drink from her, but that he is prepared to teach her, like any other person, that renovation which will give her the true life.

To her remark that he cannot do that, because they, the Jews, have their own God, while the Samaritans have their own, or their own place of worship of God, he says to her, as though explaining the destruction of the temple, Now has come the time to worship God not here or there, but everywhere, because we ought to worship not the God whom we do not know, but the one whom we know as the son knows the father, that is, he repeats what was said in the Introduction, that no one knows God, but that the son has declared him, and what was said in the discourse with Nicodemus, namely, that we speak of what we know and see and that only the son who has come down from heaven has declared God. And speaking of God he calls him Father. And, expressing the idea of the Introduction, where it said that the teaching of Jesus was the teaching of what is good, he says that the Father is searching for worshippers everywhere, worshippers in deeds and in spirit, because God is spirit.

THE WITNESS OF JOHN CONCERNING CHRIST

22. Μετὰ ταῦτα ἦλθεν ὁ Ἰησοῦς καὶ οἱ μαθηταὶ αὐτοῦ εἰς τὴν Ἰουδαίαν γῆν. καὶ ἐκεῖ διέτριβε μετ' αὐτῶν καὶ ἐβάπτιζεν.	*John iii.* 22. After these things came Jesus and his disciples into the land of Judea; and there he tarried with them, and baptized.	22. After that Jesus and his disciples came into the land of Judea, and there lived with them, and purified.

28. Ἦν δὲ καὶ Ἰωάννης βαπτίζων ἐν Αἰνὼν ἐγγὺς τοῦ Σαλείμ, ὅτι ὕδατα πολλὰ ἦν ἐκεῖ· καὶ παρεγίνοντο καὶ ἐβαπτίζοντο.

24. Οὔπω γὰρ ἦν βεβλημένος εἰς τὴν φυλακὴν ὁ Ἰωάννης.

25. Ἐγένετο οὖν ζήτησις ἐκ τῶν μαθητῶν Ἰωάννου μετὰ Ἰουδαίων περὶ καθαρισμοῦ·

26. Καὶ ἦλθον πρὸς τὸν Ἰωάννην καὶ εἶπον αὐτῷ, Ῥαββί, ὃς ἦν μετὰ σοῦ πέραν τοῦ Ἰορδάνου, ᾧ σὺ μεμαρτύρηκας, ἴδε οὗτος βαπτίζει, καὶ πάντες ἔρχονται πρὸς αὐτόν.

27. Ἀπεκρίθη Ἰωάννης καὶ εἶπεν, Οὐ δύναται ἄνθρωπος λαμβάνειν οὐδὲν, ἐὰν μὴ ᾖ δεδομένον αὐτῷ ἐκ τοῦ οὐρανοῦ.

31. Ὁ ἄνωθεν ἐρχόμενος ἐπάνω πάντων ἐστίν. ὁ ὢν ἐκ τῆς γῆς ἐκ τῆς γῆς ἐστι, καὶ ἐκ τῆς γῆς λαλεῖ· ὁ ἐκ τοῦ οὐρανοῦ ἐρχόμενος ἐπάνω πάντων ἐστί.

34. Ὃν γὰρ ἀπέστειλεν ὁ Θεὸς, τὰ ῥήματα τοῦ Θεοῦ λαλεῖ·

32. Καὶ ὃ ἑώρακε καὶ ἤκουσε, τοῦτο μαρτυρεῖ· καὶ τὴν μαρτυρίαν αὐτοῦ οὐδεὶς λαμβάνει.

33. Ὁ λαβὼν αὐτοῦ τὴν μαρτυρίαν ἐσφράγισεν ὅτι ὁ Θεὸς ἀληθής ἐστιν.

34. Οὐ γὰρ ἐκ μέτρου δίδωσιν ὁ Θεὸς τὸ Πνεῦμα.

35. Ὁ πατὴρ ἀγαπᾷ τὸν υἱὸν, καὶ πάντα δέδωκεν ἐν τῇ χειρὶ αὐτοῦ.

---

23. And John also was baptizing in Enon near to Salim, because there was much water there: and they came, and were baptized.

24. For John was not yet cast into prison.

25. Then there arose a question between some of John's disciples and the Jews about purifying.

26. And they came unto John, and said unto him, Rabbi, he that was with thee beyond Jordan, to whom thou barest witness, behold, the same baptizeth, and all men come to him.

27. John answered and said, A man can receive nothing, except it be given from heaven.

31. He that cometh from above is above all: he that is of the earth is earthly, and speaketh of the earth: he that cometh from heaven is above all.

34. For he whom God hath sent speaketh the words of God:

32. And what he hath seen and heard, that he testifieth; and no man receiveth his testimony.

33. He that hath received his testimony hath set to his seal that God is true.

34. For God giveth not the Spirit by measure unto him.

35. The Father loveth the Son, and hath given all things into his hand.

---

23. And John was purifying in Enon near to Salim, because there was much water there, and they came and were purified.

24. For John was not yet cast into prison.

25. And there arose a contention between John's disciples with a Jew about the purifying.

26. And they came to John, and said to him, Sir, he who was with thee at the Jordan, and to whom thou borest witness, is purifying also, and all men come to him.

27. And John said, A man cannot take upon himself, if he is not instructed by God.

31. He who is above is higher than all, and he who is of earth will be of earth, and will speak of earth.

34. He whom God has instructed speaks the words of God.

32. And what he has comprehended, that he proves. No man receives his proof.

33. He who has received his proof has confirmed that God is true.

34. For it is impossible to measure the spirit of God.

35. For the Father loves the son, and has given all things into his power.

36. Ὁ πιστεύων εἰς τὸν υἱὸν ἔχει ζωὴν αἰώνιον· ὁ δὲ ἀπειθῶν τῷ υἱῷ οὐκ ὄψεται ζωήν, ἀλλ' ἡ ὀργὴ τοῦ Θεοῦ μένει ἐπ' αὐτόν.

36. He that believeth on the Son hath everlasting life: and he that believeth not the Son shall not see life; but the wrath of God abideth on him.

36. He who believes in the son lives for ever, and he who does not believe in the son is against God.

John declared before that the real purification is the purification by the spirit. Now Jesus has appeared and he destroys the external forms and purifies without the temple and even without the water. And the doubt arises as to which purification is the real one. And John's disciples contend with a Jew about the purification, and they go to John to ask him about it. John says in general words what he said before, that the chief purification is a purification by the spirit, and that this purification is not transmitted in words. As to whether Jesus really speaks the words of God, John says that no one can define that, and that there can be no proofs of what are the words of God. The one proof is that man accepts them, for it is impossible to measure the manifestation of the spirit.

JESUS DINING WITH SIMON. MARY MAGDALENE

14. Καὶ φήμη ἐξῆλθε καθ' ὅλης τῆς περιχώρου περὶ αὐτοῦ.

37. Ἐν δὲ τῷ λαλῆσαι, ἠρώτα αὐτὸν Φαρισαῖός τις ὅπως ἀριστήσῃ παρ' αὐτῷ· εἰσελθὼν δὲ ἀνέπεσεν.

38. Ὁ δὲ Φαρισαῖος ἰδὼν ἐθαύμασεν ὅτι οὐ πρῶτον ἐβαπτίσθη πρὸ τοῦ ἀρίστου.

39. Εἶπε δὲ ὁ Κύριος πρὸς αὐτόν, Νῦν ὑμεῖς οἱ Φαρισαῖοι τὸ ἔξωθεν τοῦ ποτηρίου καὶ τοῦ πίνακος καθαρίζετε· τὸ δὲ ἔσωθεν ὑμῶν γέμει ἁρπαγῆς καὶ πονηρίας.

Luke iv. 14. And there went out a fame of him through all the region round about.

Luke xi. 37. And as he spake, a certain Pharisee besought him to dine with him: and he went in, and sat down to meat.

38. And when the Pharisee saw it, he marvelled that he had not first washed before dinner.

39. And the Lord said unto him, Now do ye Pharisees make clean the outside of the cup and the platter; but your inward part is full of ravening and wickedness.

14. And there went out a fame of him in all the surrounding country.

37. After that a certain Orthodox came to him and asked him to lunch with him in his house.

38. And the Orthodox, seeing that Jesus did not wash before the lunch, was surprised.

39. And Jesus said to him, You Orthodox people wash the outside of the cup and the platter, but your inside is full of plunder and untruth.

40. Ἄφρονες, οὐχ ὁ ποιήσας τὸ ἔξωθεν καὶ τὸ ἔσωθεν ἐποίησε;

41. Πλὴν τὰ ἐνόντα δότε ἐλεημοσύνην· καὶ ἰδού, πάντα καθαρὰ ὑμῖν ἐστιν.

32. Οὐκ ἐλήλυθα καλέσαι δικαίους, ἀλλὰ ἁμαρτωλοὺς εἰς μετάνοιαν.

37. Καὶ ἰδού, γυνὴ ἐν τῇ πόλει, ἥτις ἦν ἁμαρτωλὸς, ἐπιγνοῦσα ὅτι ἀνάκειται ἐν τῇ οἰκίᾳ τοῦ Φαρισαίου, κομίσασα ἀλάβαστρον μύρου,

38. Καὶ στᾶσα παρὰ τοὺς πόδας αὐτοῦ ὀπίσω κλαίουσα, ἤρξατο βρέχειν τοὺς πόδας αὐτοῦ τοῖς δάκρυσι, καὶ ταῖς θριξὶ τῆς κεφαλῆς αὐτῆς ἐξέμασσε, καὶ κατεφίλει τοὺς πόδας αὐτοῦ, καὶ ἤλειφε τῷ μύρῳ.

39. Ἰδὼν δὲ ὁ Φαρισαῖος ὁ καλέσας αὐτὸν εἶπεν ἐν ἑαυτῷ, λέγων, Οὗτος εἰ ἦν προφήτης, ἐγίνωσκεν ἂν τίς καὶ ποταπὴ ἡ γυνὴ, ἥτις ἅπτεται αὐτοῦ· ὅτι ἁμαρτωλός ἐστι.

40. Καὶ ἀποκριθεὶς ὁ Ἰησοῦς εἶπε πρὸς αὐτὸν, Σίμων, ἔχω σοί τι εἰπεῖν. ὁ δέ φησι, Διδάσκαλε, εἰπέ.

41. Δύο χρεωφειλέται ἦσαν δανειστῇ τινι· ὁ εἷς ὤφειλε δηνάρια πεντακόσια, ὁ δὲ ἕτερος πεντήκοντα.

42. Μὴ ἐχόντων δὲ αὐτῶν ἀποδοῦναι, ἀμφοτέροις ἐχαρίσατο. τίς οὖν αὐτῶν, εἰπέ, πλεῖον αὐτὸν ἀγαπήσει;

---

40. Ye fools, did not he, that made that which is without, make that which is within also?

41. But rather give alms of such things as ye have; and, behold, all things are clean unto you.

Luke v. 32. I came not to call the righteous, but sinners to repentance.

Luke vii. 37. And, behold, a woman in the city, which was a sinner, when she knew that Jesus sat at meat in the Pharisee's house, brought an alabaster box of ointment,

38. And stood at his feet behind him weeping, and began to wash his feet with tears, and did wipe them with the hairs of her head, and kissed his feet, and anointed them with the ointment.

39. Now when the Pharisee which had bidden him saw it, he spake within himself, saying, This man, if he were a prophet, would have known who and what manner of woman this is that toucheth him; for she is a sinner.

40. And Jesus answering said unto him, Simon, I have somewhat to say unto thee. And he saith, Master, say on.

41. There was a certain creditor which had two debtors: the one owed five hundred pence, and the other fifty.

42. And when they had nothing to pay, he frankly forgave them both. Tell me therefore, which of them will love him most?

---

40. Fools, he who has made what is without has also made what is within.

41. Be merciful from within, and then you shall see that everything is clean.

32. For I have come here not to call the righteous to the renovation, but those who have erred.

37. And a woman of the city, who was an infidel, hearing that Jesus was sitting in the house of an Orthodox, went there and brought a pitcher of oil,

38. And standing at his feet behind, began to weep and to wash his feet with her tears, and to wipe them with the hair of her head, and to anoint him with the oil.

39. When the Orthodox host saw this, he thought, If he were a real teacher, he would know what manner of woman this is that is touching him.

40. And, turning around, Jesus said to him, Simon, I will tell thee a few words. And he said, Master, speak!

41. A certain master had two debtors; the one owed five hundred pence, and the other fifty.

42. And neither the one nor the other had anything to pay, and the master forgave them both. Tell me, which of them will be most obliged to the master?

43. Ἀποκριθεὶς δὲ ὁ Σίμων εἶπεν, Ὑπολαμβάνω ὅτι ᾧ τὸ πλεῖον ἐχαρίσατο. ὁ δὲ εἶπεν αὐτῷ, Ὀρθῶς ἔκρινας.

43. Simon answered and said, I suppose that he, to whom he forgave most. And he said unto him, Thou hast rightly judged.

43. Simon said, Certainly he to whom he forgave most. And Jesus said, Thou hast judged rightly.

44. Καὶ στραφεὶς πρὸς τὴν γυναῖκα, τῷ Σίμωνι ἔφη, Βλέπεις ταύτην τὴν γυναῖκα; εἰσῆλθόν σου εἰς τὴν οἰκίαν, ὕδωρ ἐπὶ τοὺς πόδας μου οὐκ ἔδωκας· αὕτη δὲ τοῖς δάκρυσιν ἔβρεξέ μου τοὺς πόδας, καὶ ταῖς θριξὶ τῆς κεφαλῆς αὐτῆς ἐξέμαξε.

44. And he turned to the woman, and said unto Simon, Seest thou this woman? I entered into thine house, thou gavest me no water for my feet: but she hath washed my feet with tears, and wiped them with the hairs of her head.

44. And he pointed to the woman, and said to Simon, Here I have come to thy house, and thou gavest me no water to wash my feet with; but she washes my feet with tears, and wipes them with the hair of her head.

45. Φίλημά μοι οὐκ ἔδωκας· αὕτη δὲ, ἀφ' ἧς εἰσῆλθον, οὐ διέλιπε καταφιλοῦσά μου τοὺς πόδας.

45. Thou gavest me no kiss: but this woman, since the time I came in, hath not ceased to kiss my feet.

45. Thou didst not embrace me when I entered; but she has not ceased kissing my feet.

46. Ἐλαίῳ τὴν κεφαλήν μου οὐκ ἤλειψας· αὕτη δὲ μύρῳ ἤλειψέ μου τοὺς πόδας.

46. My head with oil thou didst not anoint: but this woman hath anointed my feet with ointment.

46. Thou didst not give me oil to anoint my head with; but she anoints my feet with costly oil.

47. Οὗ χάριν λέγω σοι, Ἀφέωνται αἱ ἁμαρτίαι αὐτῆς αἱ πολλαί· ὅτι ἠγάπησε πολύ· ᾧ δὲ ὀλίγον ἀφίεται, ὀλίγον ἀγαπᾷ.

47. Wherefore I say unto thee, Her sins, which are many, are forgiven; for she loved much: but to whom little is forgiven, the same loveth little.[a]

47. For this very reason, I tell thee, she has been delivered from error and from great error, because she loves much. But he to whom little is to be forgiven loves little.

48. Εἶπε δὲ αὐτῇ, Ἀφέωνταί σου αἱ ἁμαρτίαι.

48. And he said unto her, Thy sins are forgiven.

48. And he said to her, Yes, all thy errors are corrected.

49. Καὶ ἤρξαντο οἱ συνανακείμενοι λέγειν ἐν ἑαυτοῖς, Τίς οὗτός ἐστιν ὃς καὶ ἁμαρτίας ἀφίησιν;

49. And they that sat at meat with him began to say within themselves, Who is this that forgiveth sins also?

49. And those that were sitting with him began to say to themselves, Who is he that he frees from error?

50. Εἶπε δὲ πρὸς τὴν γυναῖκα, Ἡ πίστις σου σέσωκέ σε· πορεύου εἰς εἰρήνην.

50. And he said to the woman, Thy faith hath saved thee; go in peace.

50. And he said to the woman, Thy faith has saved thee; go in peace.

(a) In my opinion verse 47 ought to read like this : ὅτι has to be transposed; instead of being before ἠγάπησε, it ought to stand before λέγω σοι. Then the translation will be as above.

The Pharisee is not pleased to see the sinner touch the teacher. Jesus says, A master had two debtors: he forgave one much, and the other little. How can he whom he forgave much help expressing his gratitude? These debtors before me and before all men and before God art thou and is this sinning woman. Thou imaginest that there is little to forgive thee, and thou hast not shown me any particular love; but she considers herself guilty before all, and before me, and before thee. Thou thoughtest thyself that she ought not to have been permitted to touch me. Well, I have not driven her away, and as I did not contemn thee, coming to thy house, so I do not contemn her, and for this she expresses her love for me. (She expresses her love for me, because I did not upbraid her for her sins.) She has many sins, and she expresses much love. Thou hast few sins, as thou thinkest, and thou expressest little love, and little will be forgiven thee. She believes that she is a sinner, and she is saved from her sins.

THE PARABLE OF THE PUBLICAN AND THE PHARISEE

10. Ἄνθρωποι δύο ἀνέβησαν εἰς τὸ ἱερὸν προσεύξασθαι· ὁ εἷς Φαρισαῖος, καὶ ὁ ἕτερος τελώνης.

11. Ὁ Φαρισαῖος σταθεὶς πρὸς ἑαυτὸν ταῦτα προσηύχετο· Ὁ Θεὸς, εὐχαριστῶ σοι, ὅτι οὐκ εἰμὶ ὥσπερ οἱ λοιποὶ τῶν ἀνθρώπων, ἅρπαγες, ἄδικοι, μοιχοὶ, ἢ καὶ ὡς οὗτος ὁ τελώνης.

12. Νηστεύω δὶς τοῦ σαββάτου, ἀποδεκατῶ πάντα ὅσα κτῶμαι.

13. Καὶ ὁ τελώνης μακρόθεν ἑστὼς οὐκ ἤθελεν οὐδὲ τοὺς ὀφθαλμοὺς εἰς τὸν οὐρανὸν ἐπᾶραι·

Luke xviii. 10. Two men went up into the temple to pray; the one a Pharisee, and the other a publican.

11. The Pharisee stood and prayed thus with himself, God, I thank thee, that I am not as other men are, extortioners, unjust, adulterers, or even as this publican.

12. I fast twice in the week, I give tithes of all that I possess.

13. And the publican, standing afar off, would not lift up so much as his eyes unto heaven, but smote upon his

10. And Jesus said to them, Two men went into the temple to pray; the one an Orthodox, and the other an infidel.

11. The Orthodox thought much of himself, and prayed as follows: I thank thee, O God, that I am not as other men are, selfish, unjust, adulterers, not as this infidel is.

12. I fast twice on the Sabbath, and give tithes of all I get.

13. And the infidel stood off and could not lift up his eyes to heaven, but struck his breast and kept saying,

ἀλλ' ἔτυπτεν εἰς τὸ στῆθος αὐτοῦ, λέγων, Ὁ Θεὸς, ἱλάσθητί μοι τῷ ἁμαρτωλῷ.

breast, saying, God be merciful to me a sinner.

God look at me erring one.

14. Λέγω ὑμῖν, Κατέβη οὗτος δεδικαιωμένος εἰς τὸν οἶκον αὐτοῦ, ἢ ἐκεῖνος. ὅτι πᾶς ὁ ὑψῶν ἑαυτὸν ταπεινωθήσεται· ὁ δὲ ταπεινῶν ἑαυτὸν ὑψωθήσεται.

14. I tell you, this man went down to his house justified rather than the other: for every one that exalteth himself shall be abased; and he that humbleth himself shall be exalted.

14. So I tell you, the infidel returned more delivered than the Orthodox; for he who exalts himself shall be abased, and he who humbles himself shall be exalted.

The Orthodox does not consider the deliverance necessary for himself and could not be freed from anything. The infidel wished to be freed from error and confessed it, and so was freed from it.

14. Τότε προσέρχονται αὐτῷ οἱ μαθηταὶ Ἰωάννου, λέγοντες, Διατί ἡμεῖς καὶ οἱ Φαρισαῖοι νηστεύομεν πολλά, οἱ δὲ μαθηταί σου οὐ νηστεύουσι;

Matt. ix. 14. Then came to him the disciples of John, saying, Why do we and the Pharisees fast oft, but thy disciples fast not?

14. Then the disciples of John walked up to him and said, Why do we and the Orthodox fast oft, but thy disciples do not fast?

15. Καὶ εἶπεν αὐτοῖς ὁ Ἰησοῦς, Μὴ δύνανται οἱ υἱοὶ τοῦ νυμφῶνος πενθεῖν, ἐφ' ὅσον μετ' αὐτῶν ἐστιν ὁ νυμφίος; ἐλεύσονται δὲ ἡμέραι ὅταν ἀπαρθῇ ἀπ' αὐτῶν ὁ νυμφίος, καὶ τότε νηστεύσουσιν.

15. And Jesus said unto them, Can the children of the bridechamber mourn, as long as the bridegroom is with them? but the days will come, when the bridegroom shall be taken from them, and then shall they fast.

15. And Jesus said to them, The guests cannot mourn at the wedding, as long as the bridegroom is with them. When the bridegroom is not there, they mourn.

The words about the bridegroom are obscure, for there is no explanation of what is to be understood by the bridegroom. In the parable of the ten virgins life is to be understood by the bridegroom, and then, by giving the same meaning of life to the word bridegroom, the meaning of the utterance will be this, that there is no cause for mourning as long as there is life in man; one ought to mourn and fast only when life is gone.

THE PARABLE OF THE GARMENTS AND THE WINE

36. Ἔλεγε δὲ καὶ παραβολὴν πρὸς αὐτούς, Ὅτι οὐδεὶς ἐπίβλημα ἱματίου καινοῦ ἐπιβάλλει ἐπὶ ἱμάτιον παλαιόν· εἰ δὲ μήγε, καὶ τὸ καινὸν σχίζει, καὶ τῷ παλαιῷ οὐ συμφωνεῖ ἐπίβλημα τὸ ἀπὸ τοῦ καινοῦ.

37. Καὶ οὐδεὶς βάλλει οἶνον νέον εἰς ἀσκοὺς παλαιούς· εἰ δὲ μήγε, ῥήξει ὁ νέος οἶνος τοὺς ἀσκούς, καὶ αὐτὸς ἐκχυθήσεται, καὶ οἱ ἀσκοὶ ἀπολοῦνται·

38. Ἀλλὰ οἶνον νέον εἰς ἀσκοὺς καινοὺς βλητέον, καὶ ἀμφότεροι συντηροῦνται.

Luke v. 36. And he spake also a parable unto them; No man putteth a piece of a new garment upon an old; if otherwise, then both the new maketh a rent, and the piece that was taken out of the new agreeth not with the old.

37. And no man putteth new wine into old bottles; else the new wine will burst the bottles, and be spilled, and the bottles shall perish.

38. But new wine must be put into new bottles; and both are preserved.

36. No man tears a new garment, in order to put a new patch on an old garment, for it will tear the new, and the old will be of no use.

37. And no man puts new wine into old bottles; else the wine will burst, and the wine will run out, and the bottles will be lost.

38. But new wine must be put into new bottles; and both are preserved.

Luke v. 39 is not clear.

Luke iv. 33–37. These verses may be printed in the addition. The prediction and expulsion of the unclean spirit and the repetition of what Christ has been teaching, and that the fame of him has spread, have no significance. The same is true of the following verses: Luke iv. 38–41; Mark i. 35–39; Matt. viii. 18; Luke viii. 26–40; Luke v. 17–26; Mark v. 22–43; Matt. ix. 27–34.

CHRIST'S PREACHING

15. Καὶ αὐτὸς ἐδίδασκεν ἐν ταῖς συναγωγαῖς αὐτῶν, δοξαζόμενος ὑπὸ πάντων.

42. Καὶ ἦλθον ἕως αὐτοῦ, καὶ κατεῖχον αὐτὸν τοῦ μὴ πορεύεσθαι ἀπ' αὐτῶν.

43. Ὁ δὲ εἶπε πρὸς αὐτούς, Ὅτι καὶ ταῖς

Luke iv. 15. And he taught in their synagogues, being glorified of all.

42. And came unto him, and stayed him, that he should not depart from them.

43. And he said unto them, I must preach the kingdom of God to other

15. And he taught in the assemblies and was respected by all.

42. The people held him back, that he should not depart from them.

43. But he said to them, I must preach the true good to others also,

ἐτέραις πόλεσιν εὐαγγε-
λίσασθαί με δεῖ τὴν
βασιλείαν τοῦ Θεοῦ· ὅτι
εἰς τοῦτο ἀπέσταλμαι.

14. Ἵνα πληρωθῇ τὸ
ῥηθὲν διὰ Ἠσαΐου τοῦ
προφήτου, λέγοντος,

15. Γῆ Ζαβουλὼν καὶ
γῆ Νεφθαλείμ, ὁδὸν θα-
λάσσης πέραν τοῦ Ἰορ-
δάνου, Γαλιλαία τῶν
ἐθνῶν,

16. Ὁ λαὸς ὁ καθήμε-
νος ἐν σκότει εἶδε φῶς
μέγα, καὶ τοῖς καθημένοις
ἐν χώρᾳ καὶ σκιᾷ θανά-
του, φῶς ἀνέτειλεν
αὐτοῖς.

17. Ὅπως πληρωθῇ
τὸ ῥηθὲν διὰ Ἠσαΐου
τοῦ προφήτου, λέγοντος,

18. Ἰδοὺ ὁ παῖς μου,
ὃν ᾑρέτισα· ὁ ἀγαπητός
μου, εἰς ὃν εὐδόκησεν ἡ
ψυχή μου· θήσω τὸ
πνεῦμά μου ἐπ' αὐτόν,
καὶ κρίσιν τοῖς ἔθνεσιν
ἀπαγγελεῖ·

19. Οὐκ ἐρίσει, οὐδὲ
κραυγάσει· οὐδὲ ἀκούσει
τις ἐν ταῖς πλατείαις τὴν
φωνὴν αὐτοῦ.

20. Κάλαμον συντε-
τριμμένον οὐ κατεάξει,
καὶ λίνον τυφόμενον οὐ
σβέσει, ἕως ἂν ἐκβάλῃ
εἰς νῖκος τὴν κρίσιν.

21. Καὶ ἐν τῷ ὀνό-
ματι αὐτοῦ ἔθνη ἐλ-
πιοῦσι.

7. Καὶ ὁ Ἰησοῦς ἀνε-
χώρησε μετὰ τῶν μαθη-
τῶν αὐτοῦ πρὸς τὴν θά-
λασσαν· καὶ πολὺ πλῆθος
ἀπὸ τῆς Γαλιλαίας ἠκο-
λούθησαν αὐτῷ, καὶ ἀπὸ
τῆς Ἰουδαίας,

8. Καὶ ἀπὸ Ἱεροσο-
λύμων, καὶ ἀπὸ τῆς

cities also: for therefore am I sent.

Matt. iv. 14. That it might be fulfilled which was spoken by Esaias the prophet, saying,

15. The land of Zabulon, and the land of Nephthalim, by the way of the sea, beyond Jordan, Galilee of the Gentiles;

16. The people which sat in darkness saw great light; and to them which sat in the region and shadow of death light is sprung up. (Isaiah ix. 1, 2.)

Matt. xii. 17. That it might be fulfilled which was spoken by Esaias the prophet, saying,

18. Behold my servant, whom I have chosen; my beloved, in whom my soul is well pleased: I will put my Spirit upon him, and he shall shew judgment to the Gentiles.

19. He shall not strive, nor cry; neither shall any man hear his voice in the streets.

20. A bruised reed shall he not break, and smoking flax shall he not quench, till he send forth judgment unto victory.

21. And in his name shall the Gentiles trust. (Isaiah xlii. 1–3.)

Mark iii. 7. But Jesus withdrew himself with his disciples to the sea: and a great multitude from Galilee followed him, and from Judea,

8. And from Jerusalem, and from Idumea, and from beyond Jor-

for I am intended for that.

14. And the word of the prophet Isaiah was fulfilled.

16. In the pagan countries the people walked in darkness and saw a great light; to them who had lived in the darkness of death, a new light sprung up.

17. So that also another prophecy of the prophet Isaiah was fulfilled.

18. Here is my child whom I love, my beloved one, in whom my soul is pleased. I have put my spirit in him, that he may show the truth to the nations.

19. He does not quarrel, nor cry; and his voice is not heard in the streets.

20. He will not break a bruised reed, and will not put out the light when it goes out, so that the truth may vanquish the lie.

21. In him is all the hope of men.

7. Then Jesus went to the sea.

8. And a great multitude followed him from Galilee, and from Judea

'Ιδουμαίας, καὶ πέραν τοῦ Ἰορδάνου· καὶ οἱ περὶ Τύρον καὶ Σιδῶνα, πλῆθος πολὺ, ἀκούσαντες ὅσα ἐποίει, ἦλθον πρὸς αὐτόν.

35. Καὶ περιῆγεν ὁ Ἰησοῦς τὰς πόλεις πάσας καὶ τὰς κώμας, διδάσκων ἐν ταῖς συναγωγαῖς αὐτῶν, καὶ κηρύσσων τὸ εὐαγγέλιον τῆς βασιλείας.

dan; and they about Tyre and Sidon, a great multitude, when they had heard what great things he did, came unto him.

Matt. ix. 35. And Jesus went about all the cities and villages, teaching in their synagogues, and preaching the gospel of the kingdom.

and from Idumea, and from Jerusalem, and from beyond the Jordan, and people from Tyre and Sidon.

35. And he went about the cities and villages proclaiming in the assemblies the announcement about the true good of the kingdom of heaven.

THE NEW WORSHIP IN THE SPIRIT BY WORKS. THE REJECTION OF THE JEWISH GOD

And Jesus showed to all people that the former worship was a lie, and that God ought to be served by works and by compassion toward men.

He happened on a Sabbath to walk with his disciples across a field. On their way the disciples plucked some ears of corn, and rubbed them in their hands, and ate them.

The Pharisees, the Orthodox, saw that, and said, It is not proper to do that on a Sabbath. It is not lawful to work on a Sabbath, but you rub the ears. Jesus heard that, and said to them, If you understood what is meant by the words said by God to the prophet, I rejoice in the love of men among themselves, and not in the sacrifices which they bring me, you would not be condemning the innocent. The Sabbath has not been established by God, but by man, consequently man is more important than the Sabbath.

It happened another time on a Sabbath that, as Jesus was teaching in an assembly, a sick woman went up to him and asked him to help her.

And Jesus began to treat her. Then a lawyer, an elder of the assembly, grew angry at Jesus for it and said to the people, In the law of God it is written, Six days in the week are for work, but on the Sabbath God has not permitted men to work. Thereupon Jesus asked the lawyers and the Pharisees, Is it according to you not permitted to aid a man on a Sabbath?

And they did not know what to say.

Then Jesus said, Does not each one of you untie the cattle from the stall and take them to drink on a Sabbath? Or if one of your sheep should fall into a well, would you not run quickly to pull it out on a Sabbath? And is not a man much better than a sheep? What, then, according to you, is a man to do on a Sabbath, good or evil? To save the soul or to let it perish? One must always do good, even on a Sabbath.

Pharisees and lawyers came to Jesus from Jerusalem. And they saw that his disciples and he himself were eating bread together, with unwashed hands. And the scribes began to condemn them, because they themselves lived strictly as of old, washing their vessels, and without washing them they would not eat. Nor would they eat upon returning from the market, unless they first washed their hands.

And the lawyers asked him, Why do you not live according to the old customs, and why do you take and eat bread with unwashed hands? And he said to them, Well has the prophet Isaiah said of you. God had said to him, Because these people cling to me only with words, and worship me only with their mouths, while their hearts are far from me, and because their fear of me is only a human command, which they have learned by heart, I will make a wonderful, unusual work over this people. The wisdom of their wise men shall disappear, and the reason of their thinking men shall be obscured. Woe to them who bestir themselves to conceal their desires from the Eternal One, and who do their works in the dark. Even so you omit that which is important in the law, that which is the commandment of God, and observe your own commandments, which is, to wash the cups. Moses said to you, Honour your father and your mother, and who will not honour his father or mother shall be put to death, but you have invented what any one may say, I give to God what my parents have given, and fail to provide for your father or mother. Thus you destroy the commandments of God by human enactments. You do many such things.

And Jesus called all the people, and said, Listen all, and understand, There is nothing in the world which, going into man, can defile him, but that which comes out of him will defile a man. Let there be love and mercy in thy heart, and then all will be pure. Try to understand that.

And when he returned home, his disciples asked him what those words meant. And he said, Have you really not comprehended them? Do you not understand that nothing external and carnal can defile a man, because it enters not his soul, but his belly. It enters the belly, and with the excrements comes out of the back. Only that can defile a man which comes out of his soul, for from a man's soul come: fornication, lust, murder, theft, selfishness, malice, cheating, impudence, envy, pride, and every foolishness. All that evil comes out of the soul, and this alone can defile a man.

Jesus teaches the people that a new life has begun and that God is in the world upon earth, and this he tells everybody, and he tells his disciples that between man and God there is always a communion. This he teaches to all. And all are delighted with his teaching, because he teaches differently from the lawyers. The lawyers teach men that they must obey the laws of God, but he teaches them that they are free.

After that the passover came, and Jesus went to Jerusalem, where he entered the temple.

In the hall of the temple there were cattle, cows, oxen, and sheep, and baskets with doves, and behind counters sat changers with money. All that was necessary for the offerings to God. The animals were killed and sacrificed in the temple, and the money was offered there. In that consisted the prayers of the Jews.

Jesus entered the temple, plaited a whip, and drove all the cattle out of the hall, and let out all the doves, and scattered all the money.

And he commanded that no one should carry those things into the temple. He said, the prophet Isaiah has said, the house of God is not the temple in Jerusalem, but the whole world of God's people. And the prophet Jeremiah has also said to you, Do not believe the lying words that here is the house of the Eternal One, the house of the Eternal One, the house of the Eternal One. Do not believe that, but mend your life, do not judge falsely, do not oppress the stranger, the widow, and the orphan, do not spill innocent blood, and do not come into the house of the name of God, and do not say, Now we can calmly commit evil things. Do not make of my house a den of robbers.

And the Jews began to dispute, and they said to him, If thou prohibitest our prayer and our image of God, what kind of prayer wilt thou give?

And turning to them, Jesus said, Abandon this temple, and in three days I will call to life a new, a living temple to God.

And the Jews said, How canst thou make at once a new temple, since it took forty-six years to build this one?

And Jesus said, I am speaking to you about what is more important than the temple. You would not be speaking thus, if you understood the words of the prophet, I, God, do not rejoice in your sacrifices, but in your love among yourselves. The living temple is the whole world of the men of God, when they love each other.

And then many people in Jerusalem believed in what he spoke.

But he himself did not believe in anything external, because he knew everything which was in man.

He did not need to have any one to teach him about man, for he knew that the spirit of God was in man.

And the lawyers and the elders heard all that and sought how they might work his ruin, but they were afraid of him because all the people marvelled at his teaching.

And Jesus went again from Judea to Galilee. And it happened that he had to pass through Samaria. He was going past a Samaritan village, Sychar by name, near the place which Jacob had given to his son Joseph. Jacob's well was there. Jesus was tired from his journey, and he sat down near the well; but his disciples went to the town to buy bread.

And there comes a woman from Sychar to fetch water. Jesus asks her to give him to drink.

She says to him, How is it thou askest me to give thee to drink? You Jews do not have dealings with us Samaritans.

And he says to her, If thou knewest me and knewest what it is I teach, thou wouldst not say that, but wouldst give me to drink, and I, too, would give thee living water. He who drinks of this water will want to drink again, but he who drinks of my water will be satisfied for ever, and this water of mine will lead him to life eternal.

The woman understood that he was speaking of divine things, and said to him, I saw that thou art a prophet and want to teach me; but how canst thou teach me divine things since thou art a Jew, and I a Samaritan? Our people pray to God in this mountain, and you Jews say that it is necessary to pray in Jerusalem. Thou canst not teach me divine things, because you have one God, and we another.

Then Jesus said to her, Believe me, woman, the time is near when neither in this mountain nor at Jerusalem will they pray to the Father. You pray to him whom you do not know, but we pray to the Father whom it is impossible not to know.

And the time has arrived and is already here when the true worshippers of God will worship the Father in the spirit and with deeds. The Father needs such worshippers. God is spirit, and he ought to be worshipped in spirit and with deeds.

The woman did not make out what he was telling her, and she said, I have heard that a messenger of God will come, the one who is called the anointed. He will tell everything.

And Jesus said to her, I who am talking with thee am he. Wait for nothing else.

After that Jesus came into the land of Judea, and there he lived with his disciples, and purified.

At that time John purified men near Salim in the river Enon, for John had not yet been cast into prison.

And there arose a dispute between the disciples of John and those of Jesus as to which was better, John's purification in water, or the teaching of Jesus.

And they came to John, and said to him, Now thou purifiest with water, but Jesus teaches only, and all men go to him. What dost thou say about it?

And John said, A man cannot teach of himself, if God does not instruct him. Whoever speaks of earth is earthly; and whoever speaks from God, is from God.

It is impossible to prove in any way whether words that are spoken are from God or not from God. God is spirit. He cannot be measured nor proved. He who understands the words of God by that proves that he has comprehended God.

At one time Jesus saw a farmer of taxes collecting taxes. His name was Matthew. Jesus spoke with him, and Matthew understood him and liked his teaching and invited him to his house, and entertained him.

When Jesus came to Matthew, there came also Matthew's friends, tax-collectors and corrupt people. Jesus did not loathe them, but sat down himself with his disciples. And the lawyers and Pharisees saw that and said to the disciples of Jesus, How is it your teacher is feasting with tax-collectors and corrupt men? Jesus heard that, and said, He who boasts of being well does not need a physician, but he who is sick needs one. For this reason I do not wish to convert those who regard themselves as just, thinking that they are living in the truth, but teach those who think that they are living in sin.

While he was sitting in Matthew's house, there came a city woman, who was a whore. She had heard that Jesus was in Matthew's house, and came thither, and brought a vial with perfume. And she knelt down at his feet, and wept, and washed his feet with her tears, and wiped them with her hair, and poured the perfume out of the vial upon them.

Matthew saw that, and thought, He is hardly a prophet; if he were really a prophet, he would know what manner of woman is washing his feet; he would know that she is a whore, and would not permit her to touch him.

Jesus divined it, and turned around to Matthew, and said, Matthew, shall I tell thee what I think?

Tell me, he said.

And Jesus said, Listen. Two men considered themselves debtors of the same master: one to the amount of five hundred pence, and the other of fifty. And neither the one nor the other had any money to pay his debt. The master forgave both. Well, according to thy judgment, which of them will love the master and tend on him?

And Matthew said, of course, the one who owes most.

Jesus pointed to the woman, and said, Even thus it is with this woman. Thou considerest thyself a small debtor. I came to thy house, and thou didst not give me water with which to wash my feet, while she washes them with her tears and dries them with her hair.

Thou didst not kiss me, but she kisses my feet. Thou didst not give me oil with which to anoint my head, but she is rubbing costly ointments on my feet. He who thinks that he has nothing to be forgiven does not love. He who thinks that he is very guilty loves much. But for love everything is forgiven.

And he said to her, Thy sins are forgiven thee. And Jesus said, the whole thing is what each considers himself to be. He who considers himself to be good will not be good, and who considers himself bad is good.

Two men once came to the temple to pray, one of them a Pharisee, the other an infidel.

The Pharisee prayed like this, I thank thee, O Lord, that I am not as other men are, neither stingy, nor a cheat, nor a debauchee, nor such a worthless man as this tax-collector. I fast twice a week, and of my possessions I give away a tithe.

But the infidel stood at a distance and did not dare to look up to heaven, and only struck his breast with his hands, and kept saying, O Lord, look down upon me, worthless man!

Well? The infidel was forgiven more than the Pharisee, because whoever exalts himself shall be humbled, and whoever humbles himself shall be exalted.

After that John's disciples came to Jesus, and said, Why do we and the lawyers fast much, while thou and thy disciples do not fast? And Jesus said to them, As long as the bridegroom is at the wedding no man mourns. Only when the bridegroom is not there do they mourn. If there is life there is no need of mourning.

And Jesus said also this, No one tears off a piece of a new garment to sew it on an old garment, for the new garment will be torn and the old one will not be mended. So we cannot accept your fasts. And we cannot pour new wine into old bottles, for the bottles will be torn, and the wine will run out. New wine has to be put in new bottles, and then both will be preserved.

And after that a Pharisee came to him, and called him to lunch at his house. He went in and sat down at the table. The Pharisee observed that he did not wash before lunch, and was surprised. Jesus said to him, Pharisees, you wash all the time from without, but are you clean from within? Be merciful to men, and everything will be clean.

And the fame spread about Jesus, and he was respected by all, so that the people kept him that he might not go away from them. But he said that he came to announce the good not only to one city, but to all men. And he went on to the sea.

And a large multitude followed him from various cities. And he helped all. And he walked through cities and villages, everywhere announcing the kingdom of heaven and freeing men from all sufferings and vices.

Thus in Jesus Christ were fulfilled the prophecies of Isaiah, namely, that the people who had lived in darkness, in the darkness of death, saw the light; that he who received this light of truth will do no violence and no harm to men; that he is meek and humble; that, in order to bring truth to men in the world, he does not dispute and cry; that his loud voice is not heard; that he will not break a straw and will not blow out a night candle, and that the whole hope of men is in him.

CHAPTER III.

2. Ὁ δὲ Ἰωάννης ἀκούσας ἐν τῷ δεσμωτηρίῳ τὰ ἔργα τοῦ Χριστοῦ, πέμψας δύο τῶν μαθητῶν αὐτοῦ,

Matt. xi. 2. Now when John had heard in the prison the works of Christ,ᵃ he sent twoᵇ of his disciples,

2. John heard in the prison about the works of Jesus, and through his disciples he said to him,

3. Εἶπεν αὐτῷ, Σὺ εἶ ὁ ἐρχόμενος, ἢ ἕτερον προσδοκῶμεν;

3. And said unto him, Art thou he that should come, or do we look for another?

3. Art thou he that should come, or shall we look for another?

(*a*) Many texts read *of Jesus.*

(*b*) Many texts have διὰ instead of δύο. Διὰ is better, because the number of disciples is unnecessary.

John in the wilderness preached the kingdom of God, and said after him would come the one who was mightier than he, and would renovate by the spirit. Hearing of Jesus' works, John sends to find out whether he was that person, or whether another would come, that is, whether Jesus is fulfilling his two predictions, the announcement of the establishment of the kingdom and of the renovation by the spirit.

4. Καὶ ἀποκριθεὶς ὁ Ἰησοῦς εἶπεν αὐτοῖς, Πορευθέντες ἀπαγγείλατε Ἰωάννῃ ἃ ἀκούετε καὶ βλέπετε·

Matt. xi. 4. Jesus answered and said unto them, Go and shew John again those things which ye do hear and see:

4. And in reply Jesus said to them, Go and tell John those things which you hear and see.

5. Τυφλοὶ ἀναβλέπουσι, καὶ χωλοὶ περιπατοῦσι· λεπροὶ καθαρί-

5. The blind receive their sight, and the lame walk, the lepers are cleansed, and the deaf

5. The blind see, the lame walk, the deaf hear, the impure are cleansed, the dead wake up, and

157

ζονται, καὶ κωφοὶ ἀκού-
ουσι· νεκροὶ ἐγείρονται,
καὶ πτωχοὶ εὐαγγελίζον-
ται·

hear, the dead are raised up, and the poor have the gospel preached[a] to them.

the poor learn of their good.

6. Καὶ μακάριός ἐσ-
τιν, ὃς ἐὰν μὴ σκανδαλι-
σθῇ ἐν ἐμοί.

6. And blessed is he, whosoever shall not be offended[a] in me.

6. And happy is he who will not renounce me.

(a) σκανδαλίζειν ἔν τινι means *to be offended by one*, and *to renounce one.* Matt. xiii. 57; xvii. 27; xxvi. 31. In reply to John's question, Art thou he who will come and reveal the kingdom of heaven, he says, Tell them that happy are all those who do not turn away from me.

(b) πτωχοὶ εὐαγγελίζονται. In Luke and Matthew these words stand last. Everywhere this is translated by *the good is announced to the poor.* The meaning of the translation is almost correct, but the translation itself is not quite correct. In Luke xvi. 16 it says ἡ βασιλεία τοῦ θεοῦ εὐαγγελίζεται and that is not translated by *the gospel is preached to the kingdom*, but by *the kingdom of God is preached.* Thus here it ought to be translated by *the poor are evangelized*, that is, the poor receive the announcement of the good, or the poor learn of their good. On the other hand, these words express the same as what is said in the words, Blessed are the poor; in Matthew and in Luke these words stand last, showing thus that the whole essence of the matter is in them. And it must not be forgotten that all the subsequent discourse only develops and explains this idea about the blessedness of the poor in contradistinction to the rich Pharisees and lawyers.

The words from Luke vii. 21 are evidently put in as an explanation of the intelligible words about the blind seeing, etc.

John asks, Dost thou announce the kingdom which was preached by the prophet Isaiah (xxv. 5; lxi. 1), and of which I said that it is at hand, and that for its attainment nothing but the purification by the spirit is needed? And Jesus replies, Go and tell him what you see, namely, that men are now blessed in the spirit. What Isaiah has prophesied is fulfilled: all men are blessed in the spirit. The poor have learned of blessedness.

7. Τούτων δὲ πορευομένων, ἤρξατο ὁ Ἰησοῦς λέγειν τοῖς ὄχλοις περὶ Ἰωάννου, Τί ἐξήλθετε εἰς τὴν ἔρημον θεάσασθαι; κάλαμον ὑπὸ ἀνέμου σαλευόμενον;

Matt. xi. 7. And as they departed, Jesus began to say unto the multitudes concerning John, What went ye out into the wilderness to see? A reed shaken with the wind?

7. When they went away, Jesus began to talk to the multitudes concerning John, What did you go to see in the wilderness? A reed shaken in the wind?

8. Ἀλλὰ τί ἐξήλθετε ἰδεῖν; ἄνθρωπον ἐν μαλακοῖς ἱματίοις ἠμφιεσμένον; ἰδού, οἱ τὰ μαλακὰ φοροῦντες ἐν τοῖς οἴκοις τῶν βασιλέων εἰσίν.

8. But what went ye out for to see? A man clothed in soft raiment? behold, they that wear soft clothing are in kings' houses.

8. Or what else did you go out to see? A man clothed in rich raiment? Here they are before you, those who wear rich raiment and live in ease, — they live in palaces.

9. Ἀλλὰ τί ἐξήλθετε ἰδεῖν; προφήτην; ναί, λέγω ὑμῖν, καὶ περισσότερον προφήτου·

9. But what went ye out for to see? A prophet? yea, I say unto you, and more than a prophet.ᵃ

9. So what did you go out to see? A prophet? Verily, I shall tell you about what is greater than a prophet.

10. Οὗτος γάρ ἐστι περὶ οὗ γέγραπται, ʻἸδού, ἐγὼ ἀποστέλλω τὸν ἄγγελόν μου πρὸ προσώπου σου, ὃς κατασκευάσει τὴν ὁδόν σου ἔμπροσθέν σου·ʼ

10. For this is he, of whom it is written, Behold, I send my messenger before thy face, which shall prepare thy way before thee. (Mal. iii. 1.)

10. This is he, of whom it is written, I send a messenger before thy face; he shall prepare the way before thee.

11. Ἀμὴν λέγω ὑμῖν, Οὐκ ἐγήγερται ἐν γεννητοῖς γυναικῶν μείζων Ἰωάννου τοῦ βαπτιστοῦ· ὁ δὲ μικρότερος ἐν τῇ βασιλείᾳ τῶν οὐρανῶν μείζων αὐτοῦ ἐστιν.

11. Verily I say unto you, Among them that are born of women there hath not risen a greater than John the Baptist: notwithstanding, he that is least in the kingdom of heaven is greater than he.ᵇ

11. Verily I tell you, No greater man has been born of a woman than John the Baptist. The least here is there, in the kingdom of God, greater than all.

(*a*) λέγω ὑμῖν, καὶ περισσότερον προφήτου *I will tell you what is greater than a prophet.*

(*b*) Generally the words ὁ δὲ μικρότερος ἐν τῇ βασιλείᾳ τῶν οὐρανῶν μείζων αὐτοῦ ἐστιν are translated by *the least in the kingdom of God is greater than he.* This translation is incorrect, because the least in the kingdom of God is opposed to the greatest in something else. It ought to be: the least in the kingdom of heaven is greater than he who is not in the kingdom. This translation is incorrect chiefly because it violates the meaning of everything which precedes and which follows. It has just been said that John is greater than all men, and suddenly he is less than the least in the kingdom of heaven, whereas Jesus preaches only the kingdom of heaven for all; αὐτοῦ is here an adverb and means *there*, and then the meaning is connected with the rest of the discourse.

John is less, more insignificant than all, according to the judgment of men; he is a beggar. But it says that the most insignificant is the greatest in the kingdom of God; the same is many times repeated in the gospels, beginning with the sermon where it says that blessed are the poor, and not the rich. Besides, the words μικρός, μέγας, as used in the gospels, have to be translated not by *small* and *great*, but by *insignificant, low,* and *important, high.*

16. Ὁ νόμος καὶ οἱ προφῆται ἕως Ἰωάννου· ἀπὸ τότε ἡ βασιλεία τοῦ Θεοῦ εὐαγγελίζεται, καὶ πᾶς εἰς αὐτὴν βιάζεται.	*Luke xvi.* 16. The law and the prophets were until John: since that time the kingdom of God is preached, and every man presseth into it.	16. The law and the prophets were before John. Since that time the kingdom of God has been preached and every man passes into it according to his strength.
13. Πάντες γὰρ οἱ προφῆται καὶ ὁ νόμος ἕως Ἰωάννου προεφήτευσαν·	*Matt. xi.* 13. For all the prophets and the law prophesied[b] until John.	13. For all the prophets and the law before John expressed the will of God.
14. Καὶ εἰ θέλετε δέξασθαι, αὐτός ἐστιν Ἠλίας ὁ μέλλων ἔρχεσθαι.	14. And if ye will receive it, this is Elias, which was for to come.	14. If you will, receive him as Elijah, who was to come.

(*a*) In Matthew xi. 12 it says, From the days of John the Baptist until now the kingdom of heaven suffereth violence, and the violent take it by force. In Luke it says, καὶ πᾶς εἰς αὐτὴν βιάζεται, that is, pushes his way in as if by force in a crowd. Therefore, choosing Luke's version, which is more exact, I render the word βιάζομαι by *to enter according to his power.*

(*b*) προφητεύω means *to have the power of prophecy, to express the will of God.*

What is said is that the law and all the prophets expressed the will of God before John. All that came to an end with John. From his time on the kingdom of God is taken by internal effort, and so everything which was said before the coming of Elijah has to be abandoned. If you think that Elijah must come before the coming of God, you may regard John as having come in the place of Elijah.

15. Ὁ ἔχων ὦτα ἀκούειν ἀκουέτω.	*Matt. xi.* 15. He that hath ears to hear, let him hear.	15. He who wants to understand will understand.

This expression is three times repeated in Matthew, and each time in those passages where the words may have a double meaning. This expression is a warning that the words are not to be taken coarsely, but in a transferred sense.

29. Καὶ πᾶς ὁ λαὸς ἀκούσας καὶ οἱ τελῶναι ἐδικαίωσαν τὸν Θεόν, βαπτισθέντες τὸ βάπτισμα Ἰωάννου·	*Luke vii.* 29. And all the people that heard him, and the publicans, justified God, being baptized with the baptism of John.	29. And all the rabble heard him and the tax-collectors justified God, having been purified by John's purification.
30. Οἱ δὲ Φαρισαῖοι καὶ οἱ νομικοὶ τὴν βουλὴν τοῦ Θεοῦ ἠθέτησαν εἰς ἑαυτούς, μὴ βαπτισθέντες ὑπ' αὐτοῦ.	30. But the Pharisees and lawyers rejected the counsel of God against themselves, being not baptized of him.	30. But the Pharisees and lawyers rejected the counsel of God, not being purified by John.
31. Εἶπε δὲ ὁ Κύριος, Τίνι οὖν ὁμοιώσω τοὺς ἀνθρώπους τῆς γενεᾶς ταύτης; καὶ τίνι εἰσὶν ὅμοιοι;	31. And the Lord said, Whereunto then shall I liken the men of this generation? and to what are they like?	31. And Jesus said, To whom are the men of this tribe to be likened?
32. Ὅμοιοί εἰσι παιδίοις τοῖς ἐν ἀγορᾷ καθημένοις, καὶ προσφωνοῦσιν ἀλλήλοις, καὶ λέγουσιν,	32. They are like unto children sitting in the market-place, and calling one to another, and saying, We have piped	32. They are like little children. The children sit in the street and prattle with one another. They say, We are play-

Ἠὐλήσαμεν ὑμῖν, καὶ οὐκ ὠρχήσασθε· ἐθρηνήσαμεν ὑμῖν, καὶ οὐκ ἐκλαύσατε.

unto you, and ye have not danced; we have mourned to you, and ye have not wept.

ing, and you do not dance; we mourn, and you do not weep.

33. Ἐλήλυθε γὰρ Ἰωάννης ὁ βαπτιστὴς μήτε ἄρτον ἐσθίων μήτε οἶνον πίνων, καὶ λέγετε, Δαιμόνιον ἔχει·

33. For John the Baptist came neither eating bread nor drinking wine; and ye say, He hath a devil.

33. John came, and he does not eat, nor drink, and you say, The devil is in him.

34. Ἐλήλυθεν ὁ υἱὸς τοῦ ἀνθρώπου ἐσθίων καὶ πίνων, καὶ λέγετε, Ἰδοὺ ἄνθρωπος φάγος καὶ οἰνοπότης, τελωνῶν φίλος καὶ ἁμαρτωλῶν.

34. The Son of man is come eating and drinking; and ye say, Behold a gluttonous man, and a winebibber, a friend of publicans and sinners!

34. The son of man comes and eats and drinks, and you say, He is an eating man and a drunkard, a friend of tax-collectors and of people who err.

35. Καὶ ἐδικαιώθη ἡ σοφία ἀπὸ τῶν τέκνων αὐτῆς πάντων.

35. But wisdom is justified of all her children.[b]

35. And wisdom is justified by its works.

(a) *Men of this tribe* evidently refers to the Pharisees.

(b) In many texts it reads ἔργον; the meaning is the same, but clearer, and so I choose ἔργον.

The obscure place about the children becomes clear when it is referred to the Pharisees and lawyers, that is, to the rich proprietors in distinction from the rabble and despised tax-collectors. The idea is that, in order to find out God, the Pharisees and lawyers accept the teaching from one another.

John v. 43. I am come in my Father's name, and ye receive me not: if another shall come in his own name, him ye will receive.

44. How can ye believe, which receive honour one of another, and seek not the honour that cometh from God only?

They prattle like children in the street, and so marvel why they are not listened to and why they do not understand. But how are they to understand since they hear only themselves? They want to make merry, and John demands repentance and the rejection of wealth. They want fasts, the observance of the Sabbath, the rejection of the sinners, — while Jesus orders neither fasts, nor the observance of the Sabbath, nor the rejection of the sinners.

THE UPBRAIDING OF THE CITIES

20. Τότε ἤρξατο ὀνειδίζειν τὰς πόλεις, ἐν αἷς ἐγένοντο αἱ πλεῖσται δυνάμεις αὐτοῦ, ὅτι οὐ μετενόησαν·

21. Οὐαί σοι, Χοραζίν, οὐαί σοι, Βηθσαϊδάν· ὅτι εἰ ἐν Τύρῳ καὶ Σιδῶνι ἐγένοντο αἱ δυνάμεις αἱ γενόμεναι ἐν ὑμῖν, πάλαι ἂν ἐν σάκκῳ καὶ σποδῷ μετενόησαν.

22. Πλὴν λέγω ὑμῖν, Τύρῳ καὶ Σιδῶνι ἀνεκτότερον ἔσται ἐν ἡμέρᾳ κρίσεως, ἢ ὑμῖν.

23. Καὶ σύ, Καπερναούμ, ἡ ἕως τοῦ οὐρανοῦ ὑψωθεῖσα, ἕως ᾄδου καταβιβασθήσῃ· ὅτι εἰ ἐν Σοδόμοις ἐγένοντο αἱ δυνάμεις αἱ γενόμεναι ἐν σοί, ἔμειναν ἂν μέχρι τῆς σήμερον.

24. Πλὴν λέγω ὑμῖν, ὅτι γῇ Σοδόμων ἀνεκτότερον ἔσται ἐν ἡμέρᾳ κρίσεως, ἢ σοί.

Matt. xi. 20. Then began he to upbraid the cities wherein most of his mighty works* were done, because they repented not:

21. Woe unto thee, Chorazin! woe unto thee, Bethsaida! for if the mighty works, which were done in you, had been done in Tyre and Sidon, they would have repented long ago in sackcloth and ashes.

22. But I say unto you, It shall be more tolerable for Tyre and Sidon at the day of judgment, than for you.

23. And thou, Capernaum, which art exalted unto heaven, shalt be brought down to hell: for if the mighty works, which have been done in thee, had been done in Sodom, it would have remained* until this day.

24. But I say unto you, That it shall be more tolerable for the land of Sodom in the day of judgment, than for thee.

(*a*) δυνάμεις is translated by *miracle*, a meaning which it never had.

(*b*) ἔμειναν refers to Sodom, though it stands in the plural and in context with δυνάμεις. Just so μετενόησαν in the 20th verse refers to some unknown persons, though in context with δυνάμεις.

These verses, translated as they are, not only fail to be instructive, but even make no sense. Why does he upbraid the cities? If they did not believe his miracles, there evidently was no need of performing them, or he did not perform enough and did them badly. But even if he upbraids them for their unbelief of the miracles, what is meant by the words that if the same miracles were performed in Tyre and in Sidon as in Chorazin and Capernaum, they would have repented in sackcloth and ashes, and if the same were performed in Sodom as in Capernaum, it would have remained until this day?

Besides, this translation does not connect with what precedes, nor with what follows. Suddenly, on the occasion of the explanation of John's meaning and of the kingdom of heaven there begins a vituperation of the cities. Such is the meaning, or, rather, the absence of meaning. The translation is quite arbitrary, and nothing but an absurdity results from it.

I have tried to translate differently, but I must confess even my translations do not remove all the difficulties, and so this passage, obscure as it is and containing neither a negation of what precedes or follows, nor any new meaning, must remain unintelligible.

THE COMING OF THE KINGDOM OF GOD

20. Ἐπερωτηθεὶς δὲ ὑπὸ τῶν Φαρισαίων, πότε ἔρχεται ἡ βασιλεία τοῦ Θεοῦ, ἀπεκρίθη αὐτοῖς, καὶ εἶπεν, Οὐκ ἔρχεται ἡ βασιλεία τοῦ Θεοῦ μετὰ παρατηρήσεως·

21. Οὐδὲ ἐροῦσιν, Ἰδοὺ ὧδε, ἤ, Ἰδοὺ ἐκεῖ. ἰδοὺ γὰρ, ἡ βασιλεία τοῦ Θεοῦ ἐντὸς ὑμῶν ἐστιν.

23. Καὶ ἐροῦσιν ὑμῖν, Ἰδοῦ ὧδε, ἤ, Ἰδοῦ ἐκεῖ· μὴ ἀπέλθητε, μηδὲ διώξητε.

24. Ὥσπερ γὰρ ἡ ἀστραπὴ ἡ ἀστράπτουσα ἐκ τῆς ὑπ᾽ οὐρανὸν εἰς τὴν ὑπ᾽ οὐρανὸν λάμπει, οὕτως ἔσται καὶ ὁ υἱὸς τοῦ ἀνθρώπου ἐν τῇ ἡμέρᾳ αὐτοῦ.

Luke xvii. 20. And when he was demanded of the Pharisees, when the kingdom of God should come, he answered them and said, The kingdom of God cometh not with observation:

21. Neither shall they say, Lo here! or, lo there! for, behold, the kingdom of God is within you.

23. And they shall say to you, See here; or, see there: go not after them, nor follow them.

24. For as the lightning, that lighteneth out of the one part under heaven, shineth unto the other part under heaven; so shall also the Son of man be in his day.

20. And the Pharisees asked Jesus, When and how does the kingdom of God come? And he answered them, The kingdom of God does not come in such a way that it can be seen.

21. And it cannot be said about it, Here it is, or, There it is, for the kingdom of God is within you.

23. And they shall say to you, Here it has come, or, Here it is; do not go, do not run after it.

24. For it shines suddenly, like sheet lightning in the sky; and so shall also be the son of man in his time.

THE DISCOURSE WITH NICODEMUS

1. Ἦν δὲ ἄνθρωπος ἐκ τῶν Φαρισαίων, Νικόδημος ὄνομα αὐτῷ, ἄρχων τῶν Ἰουδαίων.

John iii. 1. There was a man of the Pharisees, named Nicodemus, a ruler of the Jews:

1. There was a man, a Pharisee, named Nicodemus, a Jewish elder.

2. Οὗτος ἦλθε πρὸς τὸν Ἰησοῦν νυκτὸς, καὶ εἶπεν αὐτῷ, Ῥαββὶ, οἴδαμεν ὅτι ἀπὸ Θεοῦ ἐλήλυθας διδάσκαλος· οὐδεὶς γὰρ ταῦτα τὰ σημεῖα δύναται ποιεῖν ἃ σὺ ποιεῖς, ἐὰν μὴ ᾖ ὁ Θεὸς μετ᾽ αὐτοῦ.

3. Ἀπεκρίθη ὁ Ἰησοῦς καὶ εἶπεν αὐτῷ, Ἀμὴν ἀμὴν λέγω σοι, Ἐὰν μή τις γεννηθῇ ἄνωθεν, οὐ δύναται ἰδεῖν τὴν βασιλείαν τοῦ Θεοῦ.

2. The same came to Jesus by night, and said unto him, Rabbi, we know that thou art a teacher come from God: for no man can do these miracles* that thou doest,⁵ except God be with him.

3. Jesus answered and said unto him, Verily, verily, I say unto thee, Except a man be born⁰ again,⁴ he cannot see the kingdom of God.

2. He came to Jesus at night, and said to him, Sir, we know that thou comest from God to teach, for no man would be able to prove it in such a way, if God were not with him.

3. And Jesus replied to him, Verily, I tell thee, Only he who is not begotten by God from above can fail to understand what the kingdom of God is.

(a) σημεῖον means *a sign by which something is recognized.*

(b) ποιεῖν besides meaning *to do,* in connection with a noun expressing action loses its meaning and acquires the meaning of the action of the noun, for example, πρόθεσιν ποιεῖν to make up the mind (Eph. iii. 11), ὁ ποιήσας τὸ ἔλεος *to be merciful* (Luke x. 37), and so forth. σημεῖα ποιεῖν has to be translated by *to prove.*

(c) γεννάομαι *to be begotten, to be born of the Father.* The expression, To be born from above, means *to be begotten by God the Father.*

(d) ἄνωθεν *from above, from him who is in heaven, from God,* because later this word is exchanged for "from God." To avoid obscurity, I translate it from heaven, that is, from the Eternal One.

To the words of Nicodemus, We know that thou art from God, and so forth, Jesus replies by speaking of the kingdom of God. The absence of any connection in Jesus' answer and the words of Nicodemus has been noticed by all. But it seems to me that if the discourse with Nicodemus is to be understood as it is always understood, there is not only no connection between the words of Nicodemus and those of Jesus, but the words of Nicodemus have absolutely no meaning, ask for no answer, and ought to be omitted as superfluous.

The words of Nicodemus acquire a meaning only when we recall that to the words of Nicodemus ought to be added the following : How then sayest thou that no worship and no temple is needed, and yet thou speakest of the kingdom of God ?

Nicodemus sees that the teaching is just and important, but from everything which Jesus has said heretofore, he sees that he rejects the divine worship, and he fails to see how there can be a kingdom of God without the Jewish God who is worshipped in the temple. He does not comprehend that, and in the night he comes all alone to Jesus and asks him, How is it thou teachest about the kingdom of God, and yet destroyest every relation to God ? This meaning results from the preceding, the destruction of the temple, and from the following, the answer of Jesus, who speaks of what his God is, and what he understands by the words, " the kingdom of God."

It is evident that if the words which connected the remark of Nicodemus with Jesus' answer, in relation to the Jewish God, ever existed, they were thrown out or changed by the copyists, who believed in the Jewish God. But even without these words the connection of the words is evident, if they are understood in the sense of what precedes.

The teaching of Christ is expressed in his preaching of the kingdom of God; at the same time he rejects every execution of the law and the worship of the external God.

The idea of Nicodemus is as follows : Thou preachest the kingdom of God, and yet deniest the Jewish God. What, then, is thy kingdom of God and thy God ? And with the very first words Jesus says to Nicodemus, as it is written (Luke xvii. 23), that the kingdom of God is always here, that it is within us, that it is impossible not to see the kingdom of God, that a man could only then fail to see the kingdom of God, if he were not begotten by God. The conventional form of the third and fifth verses does not signify that it is to begin from God and that man must try and be reborn from above and from the spirit, as the church understands it and as it has no sense, but that every man, for the very reason that he is a man, is inevitably begotten from above and from the spirit.

4. Λέγει πρὸς αὐτὸν ὁ Νικόδημος, Πῶς δύναται ἄνθρωπος γεννηθῆναι γέρων ὤν; μὴ δύναται εἰς τὴν κοιλίαν τῆς μητρὸς αὐτοῦ δεύτερον εἰσελθεῖν καὶ γεννηθῆναι;

John iii. 4. Nicodemus saith unto him, How can a man be born when he is old? can he enter the second time into his mother's womb, and be born?

4. And Nicodemus said, How can a man be begotten when he is old? He cannot enter a second time into his mother's womb, and be born.

(a) The meaning of γεννάομαι as *to be begotten by the father* is confirmed by these words of Nicodemus. Nicodemus says, Man was begotten before he was born, by the flesh from the father, how can he be begotten once more?

It is necessary to be destroyed and again to be begotten by God.

Nicodemus, in his lack of comprehension, repeats word for word what the church says of Jesus' procreation from Mary by the Holy Ghost in the sense of a carnal father.

5. Ἀπεκρίθη ὁ Ἰησοῦς, Ἀμὴν ἀμὴν λέγω σοι, Ἐὰν μή τις γεννηθῇ ἐξ ὕδατος καὶ Πνεύματος, οὐ δύναται εἰσελθεῖν εἰς τὴν βασιλείαν τοῦ Θεοῦ.

6. Τὸ γεγεννημένον ἐκ τῆς σαρκὸς σάρξ ἐστι· καὶ τὸ γεγεννημένον ἐκ τοῦ Πνεύματος πνεῦμά ἐστι.

John iii. 5. Jesus answered, Verily, verily, I say unto thee, Except a man be born of water and of the Spirit, he cannot enter into the kingdom of God.

6. That which is born of the flesh is flesh; and that which is born of the Spirit is spirit.

5. And Jesus answered him, Verily, I tell thee, He who is not begotten by the flesh and also by the spirit cannot enter the kingdom of God.

6. That which is begotten by the flesh is flesh, and that which is begotten by the spirit is spirit.

8. Τὸ πνεῦμα ὅπου θέλει πνεῖ, καὶ τὴν φωνὴν αὐτοῦ ἀκούεις, ἀλλ οὐκ οἶδας πόθεν ἔρχεται καὶ τοῦ ὑπάγει. οὕτως ἐστὶ πᾶς ὁ γεγεννημένος ἐκ τοῦ Πνεύματος.

8. The wind bloweth where it listeth, and thou hearest the sound thereof, but canst not tell whence it cometh, and whither it goeth: so is every one that is born of the Spirit.

8. The spirit blows wherever and whenever it pleases, and thou understandest its voice, but canst not tell whence it comes, and whither it goes. So is every one that is begotten by the spirit.

(*a*) ὕδωρ not only means *water,* but also *the liquid part of the human body, liquid flesh.* John xix. 34: And forthwith came there out blood and water.

(*b*) ὅπου means indiscriminately *where* and *when.*

I transpose verses eight and seven, because according to our manner of thought and of language it is more natural first to give the explanation and then to add, And so do not wonder, than to say, as is said in John, That thou mightest not wonder at what I tell thee, and then give the explanation.

7. Μὴ θαυμάσῃς ὅτι εἶπόν σοι, Δεῖ ὑμᾶς γεννηθῆναι ἄνωθεν.

7. Marvel not that I said unto thee, ye must be born again.

7. And so do not marvel, because I have told thee that we must be begotten by God.

The eighth verse has an important and profound meaning. And so has every word of this verse an important and profound meaning, and this meaning is not at all mysterious and mystical, but exceedingly clear, though profound.

First it was said, in the third verse, that man must be begotten from heaven, that is, by God. When Nicodemus understood this procreation in a carnal sense, Jesus said that besides the carnal procreation there is also a procreation by something else than the flesh. In order to express what this something other is, the word spirit is used.

Now we get the explanation that in man there is flesh of flesh, and spirit of spirit; in the eighth verse he defines what is the principle of the carnal life, and says, The spirit, that is, that which is not flesh; blows, that is, moves and lives where and when it pleases, that is, freely, independently of everything, by itself; and thou understandest its voice, that is, rationally; but canst not tell whence it comes, and whither it goes, that is, outside cause and outside result, outside the law of causality.

It is necessary to say, The spiritual principle lives freely, rationally, and outside of cause and purpose. Let them say it so that every man may understand it, and it is not possible to say it in any other way than it is said.

	John iii.	
9. Ἀπεκρίθη Νικόδημος καὶ εἶπεν αὐτῷ, Πῶς δύναται ταῦτα γενέσθαι;	9. Nicodemus answered and said unto him, How can these things be?	9. And Nicodemus said in reply, How can that be?
10. Ἀπεκρίθη ὁ Ἰησοῦς καὶ εἶπεν αὐτῷ, Σὺ εἶ ὁ διδάσκαλος τοῦ Ἰσραὴλ, καὶ ταῦτα οὐ γινώσκεις;	10. Jesus answered and said unto him, Art thou a master of Israel, and knowest not these things?ᵃ	10. And Jesus answered him, Thou art a teacher and dost not understand these things.
11. Ἀμὴν ἀμὴν λέγω σοι, ὅτι ὃ οἴδαμεν λαλοῦμεν, καὶ ὃ ἑωράκαμεν μαρτυροῦμεν· καὶ τὴν μαρτυρίαν ἡμῶν οὐ λαμβάνετε.	11. Verily, verily, I say unto thee, We speak that we do know, and testify that we have seen; and ye receive not our witness.	11. Verily, I tell thee, We speak of what we know, and show what we have seen, but you do not receive the proofs of our testimony.
12. Εἰ τὰ ἐπίγεια εἶπον ὑμῖν, καὶ οὐ πιστεύετε, πῶς, ἐὰν εἴπω ὑμῖν τὰ ἐπουράνια, πιστεύσετε;	12. If I have told you earthly things, and ye believe not, how shall ye believe, if I tell you of heavenly things?ᵇ	12. I have told you of what is upon earth, and you do not believe; how, then, shall you believe, if I tell you of what is in heaven?
13. Καὶ οὐδεὶς ἀναβέβηκεν εἰς τὸν οὐρανὸν, εἰ μὴ ὁ ἐκ τοῦ οὐρανοῦ καταβὰς, ὁ υἱὸς τοῦ ἀνθρώπου ὁ ὢν ἐν τῷ οὐρανῷ. ·	13. And no manᶜ hath ascended up to heaven, but he that came down from heaven, even the Son of manᵈ which is in heaven.ᵉ	13. Forᶜ no man has ascended heaven, but he that came down from heaven, the son of man, the one who is in heaven.

(a) The question mark is unnecessary here. Jesus says, Thou, as a teacher of Israel, of course, canst not know that.

(b) τὰ ἐπίγεια and τὰ ἐπουράνια are incorrectly translated by *earthly* and *heavenly things*; they mean *that which is on earth and in heaven.*

(c) In many texts it is οὐδεὶς δή.

(d) Here we, for the first time, come across the expression *son of man*. In the verse about the Sabbath, where it said, The Sabbath was made by the son of man, this expression had the meaning simply of man. In the verse, The angels will ascend and descend, this expression may be taken simply in the sense of man, in the particular sense which Jesus ascribes to it. But here the meaning is clearly defined in a particular sense.

Before this it was said that in man there is present a spirit begotten from heaven by God, begotten by the spirit; but now it says that no man has ever been in heaven with God, no man has ascended to God, and so we cannot speak about God; but from God in heaven came down, was begotten, the son of the spirit, the spirit of man, the one which always remains in heaven with God. And so the son of man means spirit, the son of the spirit in man.

For him who knows the Gospel, it is superfluous to quote the passages in which the expression son of man and son of God are used, when applied to men. In all the passages they have the same meaning.

John vi. 27. The son of man, for whom God the Father hath sealed.

Matt. v. 45. That ye may be the children of your Father which is in heaven.

Luke vi. 35. Ye shall be the children of the Highest, and so forth.

(e) ὁ ὢν ἐν τῷ οὐρανῷ word for word *he who is in heaven*. *To be in heaven* means *to be God;* the heavenly and the divine are the same. And so he who is in heaven means he who is God.

14. Καὶ καθὼς Μωσῆς ὕψωσε τὸν ὄφιν ἐν τῷ ἐρήμῳ, οὕτως ὑψωθῆναι δεῖ τὸν υἱὸν τοῦ ἀνθρώπου·	*John iii.* 14. And as Moses lifted up the serpent in the wilderness, even so must the Son of man be lifted up:	14. And as Moses exalted the serpent in the wilderness (that men should not perish) even so the son of man must be exalted.

(a) ὑψόω means *to raise up, exalt, lift oneself,* in the spiritual sense, in pride (Luke i. 25; Acts xiii. 17; 2 Cor. xi. 7, and in many other places). From the context, where mention is made of the serpent which Moses commanded the Jews to worship, and the worship of which saved them, the word must be taken in the sense of "deifying." In order fully to understand the expression, To lift up like a serpent in the wilderness, we must understand what was said about the serpent in the wilderness.

Numbers xxi. 5. And the people spake against God, and against Moses, Wherefore have ye brought us up out of Egypt to die in the wilderness? for there is no bread, neither is there any water; and our soul loatheth this light bread.

6. And the Lord sent fiery serpents among the people, and they bit the people; and much people of Israel died.

7. Therefore the people came to Moses, and said, We have sinned, for we have spoken against the Lord, and against thee; pray unto the Lord, that he take away the serpents from us. And Moses prayed for the people.

8. And the Lord said unto Moses, Make thee a fiery serpent, and set it upon a pole: and it shall come to pass, that every one that is bitten, when he looketh upon it, shall live.

9. And Moses made a serpent of brass, and put it upon a pole; and it came to pass, that if a serpent had bitten any man, when he beheld the serpent of brass, he lived.

That is what is said about the serpent in the Book of Numbers. *To exalt the son of man as Moses exalted the serpent* means *to treat the son of man as the Jews treated the serpent in the wilderness,* that is, that men should rely upon him and should look to him for their salvation and life.

In the Book of the Wisdom of Solomon, XVI., it says about the same:

And they (the Jews) were perishing by the bites of crooked serpents, thy wrath continued not to the uttermost; but for admonition were they troubled for a short space, having a token of salvation, to put them in remembrance of the commandments of thy law: for he that turned toward it was not saved because of that which was beheld, but because of thee, the Saviour of all.

And so, *to exalt the son of God in man*, as Moses exalted the serpent, means *to give a picture of salvation.*

15. Ἵνα πᾶς ὁ πιστεύων εἰς αὐτὸν μὴ ἀπόληται, ἀλλ' ἔχῃ ζωὴν αἰώνιον.	*John iii.* 15. That whosoever believeth in him should not perish,a but have eternalb life.	15. That whosoever believed in him should not perish, but should have non-temporal life.
16. Οὕτω γὰρ ἠγάπησεν ὁ Θεὸς τὸν κόσμον, ὥστε τὸν υἱὸν αὐτοῦ τὸν μονογενῆ ἔδωκεν, ἵνα πᾶς ὁ πιστεύων εἰς αὐτὸν μὴ ἀπόληται, ἀλλ' ἔχῃ ζωὴν αἰώνιον.	16. For God soc loved the world, that he gave his only begotten Son, that whosoever believeth in him should not perish, but have everlasting life.	16. For God so loved the world of men, and gave his son, just such as he is, that all relying on him should not perish, but have non-temporal life.

(*a*) ἀπόλλυμι means *to kill, destroy, perish.* Since it is here put in contradistinction to the eternal life, its meaning obviously is *to perish, be destroyed, die.*

(*b*) αἰώνιον means *being outside of time.*

(*c*) οὕτω does not refer to ὥστε, in the first place, because in the whole Gospel there is no such correlation of the two particles, and it is not peculiar to the language of the Gospel; in the second place and chiefly, because such a correlation gives a most perverted meaning which is not in keeping with the whole sentence.

God so loved that he gave his son,—as the church understands it,—is an impossible conception in relation to God. We can say of a man that he so loved that he gave away his last dollar, but of the infinite beginning, of God, we cannot speak of sacrifices of God.

Οὕτω γάρ only connects what precedes with what follows. It was said that as Moses exalted the serpent, so it is necessary to exalt the son of man, so that men should not die, but should have eternal life.

Now it says that, as Moses, loving his people, made a serpent that men should be saved, so God gave a son to the world that men might be saved. This verse and the next one answer the idea which Nicodemus must have had and which lives in all men when they think of the meaning of their life. Why did some one create me that I might die? It is to this feeling of each man that Jesus makes a reply. He said before that man may keep from perishing, from being destroyed; now he confirms this and says, God could not have given them his son, — life, — for their perdition, but that he loved the world and for its good gave it life, not that it might perish, but that it might be eternal. We must also understand that by the word *God* we must not understand in this place any particular God, our God, or the Jewish God, — not at all any definite being.

It was said before that no one has ever known God, and it was said that no man has ever been in heaven, but that there is he who has come down from heaven; and it was said that man is born of the spirit, for here we must understand by God only the source, the beginning of the spirit in man.

Of this beginning it was said that it loved the world, that is, that all we know of it is that it is subjectively love, objectively the good.

	John iii. 17. For God	17. For God sent his
17. Οὐ γὰρ ἀπέστειλεν ὁ θεὸς τὸν υἱὸν αὐτοῦ εἰς τὸν κόσμον ἵνα κρίνῃ τὸν κόσμον, ἀλλ' ἵνα σωθῇ ὁ κόσμος δι' αὐτοῦ.	sent* not his Son into the world* to condemn* the world; but that the world through him might be saved.	son into the world not to punish the world, but that the world might live through him.

(*a*) *To come into the world*, according to the Hebrew manner of expression, means *to be born*, and so *sent into the world* ought to be translated by *bore for the world*.

(*b*) κόσμος means *world*, in the popular sense, that is, all men.

(c) κρίνειν means *to divide, weed out, separate, select, judge;* but in the gospels, the epistles, and in the Acts, and especially in John, it has more frequently one meaning, that of *to punish,* which fits all the cases.

John vii. 24. Judge not according to the appearance, but judge righteous judgment.

John viii. 50. And I seek not mine own glory: there is one that seeketh and judgeth.

John xviii. 31. Then said Pilate unto them, Take ye him, and judge him according to your law. The Jews therefore said unto him, It is not lawful for us to put any man to death:

Acts xxiii. 3. Then said Paul unto him, God shall smite thee, thou whited wall: for sittest thou to judge me after the law, and commandest me to be smitten contrary to the law?

Acts xxiv. 6. Who also hath gone about to profane the temple: whom we took, and would have judged according to our law.

And many other passages. In these historical passages the word has unquestionably that meaning. In the didactic parts, wherever the words κρίνειν and κρίσις occur, nothing but *punish* and *penalty* fit all the passages without exception. Such passages as —

John v. 24. Verily, verily, I say unto you, He that heareth my word, and believeth on him that sent me, hath everlasting life, and shall not come into condemnation; but is passed from death unto life.

John xii. 47. And if any man hear my words, and believe not, I judge him not: for I came not to judge the world, but to save the world.

John xii. 31. Now is the judgment of this world: now shall the prince of this world be cast out.

John iii. 17. For God sent not his Son into the world to condemn the world; but that the world through him might be saved —

show at once, since it is opposed to *life,* that by κρίνειν a mortal condition is meant.

God sent, gave his son to the world, bore a son for the world. No man has entered heaven, except the son of man who came down. Every man is born of God. Consequently the spirit, which is in man and which is born of God, and the son of man, who came down from heaven, and the son of God, who was given to the world, and the light which came into the world, — are one and the same.

But the light is what in the Introduction was called the comprehension λόγος. That the light means the same as the son of God and the son of man and spirit is confirmed by what follows.

And so we must keep in mind that all these appellations, (1) God, (2) spirit, (3) the son of God, (4) the son of man, (5) the light, and (6) the comprehension, have one and the same meaning and are used according to the relation that they bear to the subjects under discussion.

When mention is made of its being the beginning of everything, it is called God; when it says that it is opposed to the flesh, it is called spirit; when it is used in relation to its source, it is called the son of God; when reference is made to its manifestation, it is called the son of man; when it is mentioned in its correlation to reason, it is called light and comprehension.

18. Ὁ πιστεύων εἰς αὐτὸν οὐ κρίνεται· ὁ δὲ μὴ πιστεύων ἤδη κέκριται, ὅτι μὴ πεπίστευκεν εἰς τὸ ὄνομα τοῦ μονογενοῦς υἱοῦ τοῦ Θεοῦ.

19. Αὕτη δέ ἐστιν ἡ κρίσις, ὅτι τὸ φῶς ἐλήλυθεν εἰς τὸν κόσμον, καὶ ἠγάπησαν οἱ ἄνθρωποι μᾶλλον τὸ σκότος, ἢ τὸ φῶς· ἦν γὰρ πονηρὰ αὐτῶν τὰ ἔργα.

20. Πᾶς γὰρ ὁ φαῦλα πράσσων μισεῖ τὸ φῶς,

John iii. 18. He that believeth on him is not condemned : but he that believeth not is condemned already, because he hath not believed in the name of the only begotten Son of God.

19. And this is the condemnation, that light is come into the world, and men loved darkness rather than light, because their deeds were evil.

20. For every one that doeth evil hateth the

18. He who believes in the son, will not be punished; but he who does not believe is already punished, because he does not believe that the son is just such as God.

19. And this punishment is that the light is come into the world, and men preferred darkness to light, because their deeds were evil.

20. For whoever does evil spurns the light. so

καὶ οὐκ ἔρχεται πρὸς τὸ φῶς, ἵνα μὴ ἐλεγχθῇ τὰ ἔργα αὐτοῦ·

21. Ὁ δὲ ποιῶν τὴν ἀλήθειαν ἔρχεται πρὸς τὸ φῶς, ἵνα φανερωθῇ αὐτοῦ τὰ ἔργα, ὅτι ἐν Θεῷ ἐστιν εἰργασμένα.

light, neither cometh to the light, lest his deeds should be reproved.ᵈ

21. But he that doeth truth cometh to the light, that his deeds may be made manifest, that they are wrought in God.

that his deeds do not appear.

21. But who lives in truth goes toward the light, so that his deeds are made manifest.

(a) μονογενής means *one-born, the same in substance.*

(b) φαῦλος means *bad, insignificant, empty.*

(c) ἵνα in the language of the Gospel, especially in John, has the meaning of ὥστε *so that*, and it has this meaning here (*cf.* John ix. 2, 39; xii. 38, 40; xviii. 9, 32; xix. 24; Rev. xiii. 13).

(d) Many texts have φανεροί.

The discourse with Nicodemus is a full exposition of all the principles of the teaching about the kingdom of God upon earth. This discourse is an explanation of what man is, what God, what life, and what the kingdom of God. This discourse is, on the one hand, a development of the main ideas expressed in the temptation in the wilderness, and, on the other, an exposition, in the name of Jesus, of those principles of the teaching which are expressed in the Introduction in the name of the evangelist John.

In the subsequent chapters of the Gospel of John, except the farewell discourse, in which is expressed what has not been fully evolved here, the same thing is explained from various sides, but the fundamental ideas are all expressed here.

Chapter V., concerning the healing on the Sabbath, and Chapter VI., concerning the heavenly bread and the discourse in the temple, and the words uttered on the occasion of the healing of the man born blind, elucidate, illuminate, confirm many things, but all of them are said for certain occasions and are fragmentary, repeat what has been said before, are not complete, and at times appear obscure, if we do not keep in mind the exposition of the discourse with Nicodemus, which elucidates the ideas expressed in the temptation and repeats the ideas of the Introduction.

For a full comprehension of all the subsequent discourses we need a clear comprehension of these ideas.

WHAT IS SAID IN THE DISCOURSE WITH NICODEMUS

(1) In verses 1–5 it says: Besides the cause of life which one can see in the fetation of the child in the mother's womb from a carnal father, there is also another cause of life, a non-carnal one.

Jesus calls this non-carnal principle of life Father, spirit. It is that idea which was expressed by Jesus in his infancy in the temple, when he called God his Father, the same idea with which the temptation begins, If thou art the son of God, and which is also expressed in the answer, Man lives not by bread, but by what proceeds from the mouth of God, by the spirit. The same idea is expressed in the Introduction, In the beginning was the comprehension, Everything is born by him and without him.

(2) Verses 7–9 express the idea that every man knows in himself the rational, free, non-carnal principle of life, and that he understands it, though he does not know its source.

In the Introduction the same idea was expressed in verses 4 and 5:

John i. 4. In him was life; and the life was the light of men.
5. And the light shineth in darkness; and the darkness comprehended it not.

(3) In verses 11–13 it says that we cannot comprehend what is in heaven, and that this non-carnal,

infinite principle is within us, but that we know this infinite principle, because in us, in men, is to be found this spirit, which came out of the infinite and itself is infinite, and that this spirit in man is that which we must regard as the beginning of all beginnings.

The same idea is expressed in the Introduction:

John i. 18. No man has seen God at any time; the only begotten Son, which is in the bosom of the Father, he hath declared him.

1. In the beginning was the Word, and the Word was with God, and the Word was God.

2. The same was in the beginning with God.

(4) In the fourteenth verse it says that this spirit in man, which comes out of the infinite and is related to him as the son is to the father, this infinite principle in man is that which shall deify, that is, take the place of the invented God, as a real and only God.

The same is said in the words of John the Baptist, When the spirit shall purify men; the same is said to Nathanael, when it says, Heaven is open, and man is in communion with God. The same is said to the woman of Samaria, God is spirit and we must serve him in the spirit, with deeds.

(5) In verse 15 it says that the belief in this only, true God frees men from perdition and gives them non-temporal life.

The same thought is expressed in the Introduction:

John i. 10. He was in the world, and the world was made by him, and the world knew him not.

11. He came unto his own, and his own received him not.

12. But as many as received him, to them gave he power to become the sons of God.

John xx. 31. But these are written, that ye might believe that Jesus is the Christ, the Son of God; and that believing ye might have life through his name.

In verse 15 of the discourse with Nicodemus it says that faith in the son of man gives indestructible life. In the Introduction it was said that faith will make men sons of God. To believe in the son and have non-temporal life is one and the same. In the temptation it said the same when it said that Jesus after the temptation came to know the mighty spirit.

(6) In verses 16 and 17 it says that if we have the highest good, life, then that which gave us that good must have wished our good, that is loved us, and so, though we cannot know the infinite principle itself, we know this much of it, that it is good (loves us), and its relation to us is love, and our life is good.

But if God, loving us, gave us life, as a good, then he does not punish and destroy us, but gives us the real non-temporal life, without any evil. As is said in the epistle of John, God is light, and there is not the slightest darkness in him. And this life we have, reposing our life in that spirit, the light, God, who is the source of our life.

The idea that the source of our life is love is expressed clearly and in detail in the parable about the vineyard and in the farewell discourse.

(7) In verse 18 it says that non-temporal life is given us in our spirit, and that only by departing from the source of life we are destroyed temporally, and by not departing from it we have non-temporal life.

The same idea is expressed in the temptation when, after Jesus has decided to serve God alone, the power of God came to serve him.

(8) In verses 19–21 it says that what appears to us as punishment, death, annihilation, is not the consequence of some will without us, of God, as we imagine him to be, but the consequence of our will.

In order clearly to understand this thought it is necessary to understand that Jesus has at no time said anything about the life after death; denying it, he said directly, Let the dead bury the dead; God is the God of the living, and not of the dead. All he said was that life had a temporal source, the flesh, and another, non-temporal, the spirit, the son of God.

By relying on the source of temporal life, believing in it, man is destroyed, dies; but by relying only on the source of life, of the spirit, believing only in it, the son of God, he has non-temporal, indestructible life.

The manifestation of the comprehension in the world of life is like the manifestation of light amidst darkness. And the relation of men to life is just such as the relation of men to light. Just as it is in the power of each man to walk to the light or to depart from it, so it is in the power of each man to walk to the comprehension and life, or to depart from it. Perdition, the annihilation of men, is only an arbitrary departure from the comprehension and life, just as darkness is only an arbitrary departure of men from light.

The punishment consists in this, that men who do evil themselves depart from the comprehension and life. And here the comparison is made only as an identity: just as men who commit evil deeds do not like the light and do not walk to it, so that their deeds might not be seen, for they are bad, even so men who do wrong do not like the comprehension and do not walk toward it, that it may not be seen that their deeds are bad.

To be in the light means to live in the comprehension, non-temporally; to be in the darkness means to live outside the comprehension, to perish.

The same is expressed in the Introduction in verses 4, 5, and 10:

John i. 4. In him was life; and the life was the light of men.

5. And the light shineth in darkness; and the darkness comprehended it not.

10. He was in the world, and the world was made by him, and the world knew him not.

The same is said in the temptation, when Jesus says that he is working for God only, that he has completely vanquished the devil.

(9) All these ideas express what Jesus understands by the words *kingdom of God,* which John preached before him and preaches now.

The discourse began by Jesus' saying that every man from the time he is begotten by God is found in the kingdom of God, and the whole discourse expounds what it is necessary to understand by the kingdom of God and how to enter it.

To exalt the son of God in man, to depend upon him, to live in the truth, means to be in the kingdom of God. To do the opposite means to destroy oneself and not be in the kingdom of God. The discourse with Nicodemus ends with the following words, God sent his son into the world, such as he himself is, the life of the comprehension, and thus accomplished this, that every man may save himself from perdition and live non-temporally, be the son of the kingdom of God.

The aim of God is not the death of men, but their life. Life, the light of the comprehension, is not given them for death, but for life.

Those men who believe in the spirit, the son, live in the world of the comprehension, do not die, and remain in the kingdom of God; but those who do not believe in the light of the spirit, in the son, do not live, but die.

Death consists only in this, that the light of life is given them, and they do evil and thus deprive themselves of life.

Every man who does wrong goes out of the light of the comprehension and is destroyed, but he who lives in the truth and remains in the light of the comprehension lives in the kingdom of God.

The parable of the sower illuminates the thought of these words: the sower is God, the seed — the comprehension.

Men keep this comprehension as the wayside, the stones, the thorns, and the good ground retain the seed. Thus all understand it, and thus I, too, understand it.

The difference between my understanding of it and that of the church consists in this, that I understand by the word God what Jesus has defined in his temptation, in the discourse with Nicodemus, in his talk with the woman of Samaria, and not God the Creator of the Jews, whom Jesus denied, and whom the church accepts.

If God is an almighty, good, and omniscient God, as the church understands him, then there arises the question, Why, if he is good, has he created man such that he can be bad and perish? Why death?

Almighty and omniscient God might have abstained from creating evil and might have stopped evil, and yet he admitted its continuation and increase. Why has he sent to ruin men whom he could have freed from sin and death? Why did he make the devil and allow him to fall?

In admitting God as the creator of everything, it is necessary, for the elucidation of this contradiction, to invent the devil, the fall of Adam, redemption, and grace.

The lack of comprehension of the teaching of Christ concerning the rejection of the Jewish God, the Creator, and the substitution for this God of the one God the spirit, the Father of the son of man, the comprehension, inevitably led to the invention of meaningless, offensive, and immoral dogmas about the creation of evil spirits by God, about the redemption, and about everlasting torments. It suffices to understand directly what has been said in the preceding chapters and in the whole Gospel about the son of man, the one-born Father, whom Jesus recognizes, in order that these contradictions should not exist.

The parables concerning the sower and others, as it were, present the question as to what that is which men call evil, and answer that question.

Jesus has declared that no one has ever known God the creator, lawgiver, and judge, and that there is only a spirit in man, which has come out of the infinite principle, the son of the spirit, the light of the comprehension, and in it is life.

In the discourse with Nicodemus it says that the source of life, God, gave life to the world, by loving it. It does not say that God loved each man, nor does it say so elsewhere; but it does say that God loved the world, that is, men in general, and wanted to give them life, and so he gave the son to the world, and thus gave to the world, that is, to men in general, life and the possibility of entering the kingdom of God. And with this verse are connected the parables of the sower.

PARABLE OF THE SOWER

The first parable of the sower is an extreme representation of what that God is who gave life to the world, and why and how he gave life to the world. This extreme representation about God, the beginning of everything, can be expressed only by a simile.

The simile is as follows: The sower who likes the wheat and takes care of the wheat expresses God who loves the world and takes care of the world, and as the sower does not take care of each separate seed, so God does not take care of each separate man. As the sower takes care of the crop, knowing that, in spite of the loss of many seeds, there will be a crop, and sows the seed everywhere, so also God sows everywhere, knowing that in spite of the loss of many there will be a crop.

And God does not any further enter into the affairs of the world, as that is expressed in the parable (Matt. iv. 26-29).

If we comprehend God as Jesus defines him, the accusation against God, that he has created the evil,

death, and therefore loves evil and death, is done away
with. As a rule it becomes a personal question which is
irregularly transferred to the general phenomenon. The
accusation preferred by man against God for having
admitted death is like the accusation of the desire of
its death which a birch seed, one out of a million, might
prefer, because others are growing, while it falls into the
river and perishes. He who has made millions of seeds
has not made millions that they might perish, but, on the
contrary, that they might not perish, and so his aim is
life, and not death.

From the general standpoint, from the point of view of
God, the beginning of everything, it is rational.

But if you ask why death is in you, there is an internal
answer to it (and this answer is given in the parable and
in all the didactic passages in the Gospel). Because you
want it. Each seed has the possibility of growing and
bearing fruit, and each man has the possibility of becoming a son of God and of not knowing death.

To the inexactness of the comparison in the explanation of the parable Jesus directs his attention, when he
says in Luke, See how you understand it. Thus the
parable answers the question from two sides, from the external and from the internal side, and makes a clear
division between the internal comprehension of the kingdom of God, — the aims and ways of God, and the internal comprehension of the kingdom of God, the possibility
which each has of entering into it.

1. Ἐν δὲ τῇ ἡμέρᾳ ἐκείνῃ, ἐξελθὼν ὁ Ἰησοῦς ἀπὸ τῆς οἰκίας ἐκάθητο παρὰ τὴν θάλασσαν·	*Matt. xiii.* 1. The same day went Jesus out of the house, and sat by the sea side.	1. Jesus went out of the house, and sat down by the sea.
2. Καὶ συνήχθησαν πρὸς αὐτὸν ὄχλοι πολλοί, ὥστε αὐτὸν εἰς τὸ πλοῖον ἐμβάντα καθῆσθαι· καὶ πᾶς ὁ ὄχλος ἐπὶ τὸν αἰγιαλὸν εἰστήκει.	2. And great multi- tudes were gathered to- gether unto him, so that he went into a ship, and sat; and the whole mul- titude stood on the shore.	2. And such a multi- tude gathered around him that he left the shore and went into a ship; and the multitude stood on the shore.

8. Καὶ ἐλάλησεν αὐτοῖς πολλὰ ἐν παραβολαῖς, λέγων, Ἰδοὺ, ἐξῆλθεν ὁ σπείρων τοῦ σπείρειν.

4. Καὶ ἐγένετο ἐν τῷ σπείρειν, ὃ μὲν ἔπεσε παρὰ τὴν ὁδὸν, καὶ ἦλθε τὰ πετεινὰ τοῦ οὐρανοῦ καὶ κατέφαγεν αὐτό.

5. Ἄλλο δὲ ἔπεσεν ἐπὶ τὸ πετρῶδες, ὅπου οὐκ εἶχε γῆν πολλὴν· καὶ εὐθέως ἐξανέτειλε, διὰ τὸ μὴ ἔχειν βάθος γῆς·

6. Ἡλίου δὲ ἀνατείλαντος ἐκαυματίσθη, καὶ διὰ τὸ μὴ ἔχειν ῥίζαν ἐξηράνθη.

7. Καὶ ἄλλο ἔπεσεν εἰς τὰς ἀκάνθας· καὶ ἀνέβησαν αἱ ἄκανθαι, καὶ συνέπνιξαν αὐτὸ, καὶ καρπὸν οὐκ ἔδωκε.

8. Καὶ ἄλλο ἔπεσεν εἰς τὴν γῆν τὴν καλήν· καὶ ἐδίδου καρπὸν ἀναβαίνοντα καὶ αὐξάνοντα, καὶ ἔφερεν ἐν τριάκοντα, καὶ ἐν ἑξήκοντα, καὶ ἐν ἑκατόν.

9. Καὶ ἔλεγεν αὐτοῖς, Ὁ ἔχων ὦτα ἀκούειν ἀκουέτω.

---

8. And he spake many things unto them in parables, saying, Behold, a sower went forth to sow;

Mark iv. 4. And it came to pass, as he sowed, some fell by the way side, and the fowls of the air came and devoured it up.

5. And some fell on stony ground, where it had not much earth; and immediately it sprang up, because it had no depth of earth:

6. But when the sun was up, it was scorched; and because it had no root, it withered away.

7. And some fell among thorns, and the thorns grew up, and choked it, and it yielded no fruit.

8. And other fell on good ground, and did yield fruit that sprang up and increased, and brought forth, some thirty, and some sixty, and some a hundred.

9. And he said unto them, He that hath ears to hear, let him hear.

---

3. And he said, A farmer went out to sow.

4. And some seeds fell on the road, and the birds picked them up.

5. And others fell on a stone, and immediately sprang up and grew.

6. And when the sun grew warm, they wilted, for there was no soil under them to take root in, and they withered.

7. Some fell among thorns and grew up, but the thorns choked them (and they yielded no seed).

8. And still others fell on good ground, and the ears grew out and filled up, and they brought forth, some a hundred, some fifty, and some thirty.

9. He who has understanding will understand.

Into the infinite, incomprehensible world of men there was sent the comprehension by some one, and it made its appearance. The comprehension is scattered among all men, just as an endless number of seeds is scattered by the sower over the whole field, and over the wayside, and over stones, and over the thorns.

Just as the sower knows that there are roads, stones, and thorns in his field and that many seeds will perish, so he knows that it is none the less more advantageous to sow over the whole field, and that, in spite of the loss of many seeds, they will grow up, and there will be a crop, so the life of the comprehension is scattered among men, and there will be a loss. Innumerable seeds give uneven returns; a small part perishes,— they are not needed; another part yield some one hundred, some fifty, and some thirty. Even so the life of the comprehension is scattered among men; some lose this life, others return it a hundredfold.

The sower has sowed the seed and he needs only seeds, and will garner nothing but seeds.

The mysterious sower sows the life of the comprehension, and he will garner only the life of the comprehension. Those men who have the life of the comprehension are wanted by the sower; those who have lost it are useless to him. They were all seeds, and some perished in the seed, others in the sprouts, and others again in the blades.

Even so it is with men. Some lose the life of the comprehension earlier, some later. Only those who preserve within them the comprehension, so that they may not cease being life, being that from which they have come, live, and all the rest perish.

Such is the external meaning. Some men, like the seed which fall on bad ground, are predestined, as it were, for perdition, others are predestined for a life with a superabundance. But, having uttered these words, Jesus immediately adds, He who has ears, let him hear. He uses those words which he adds every time when his words may be understood wrongly, when there can be a double meaning to them.

The same idea as to how we may understand God's aim and manner of participation in the life of the world is expressed also by another parable about the sower.

26. Καὶ ἔλεγεν, Οὕτως ἐστὶν ἡ βασιλεία τοῦ Θεοῦ, ὡς ἐὰν ἄνθρωπος βάλῃ τὸν σπόρον ἐπὶ τῆς γῆς,

Mark iv. 26. And he said, So is the kingdom of God, as if a man should cast seed into the ground;

26. And he said, So is the kingdom of God, as if a farmer cast seed into the ground;

27. Καὶ καθεύδῃ καὶ ἐγείρηται νύκτα καὶ ἡμέραν, καὶ ὁ σπόρος βλαστάνῃ καὶ μηκύνηται ὡς οὐκ οἶδεν αὐτός.

28. Αὐτομάτη γὰρ ἡ γῆ καρποφορεῖ, πρῶτον χόρτον, εἶτα στάχυν, εἶτα πλήρη σῖτον ἐν τῷ στάχυΐ.

29. Ὅταν δὲ παραδῷ ὁ καρπός, εὐθέως ἀποστέλλει τὸ δρέπανον, ὅτι παρέστηκεν ὁ θερισμός.

27. And should sleep, and rise night and day, and the seed should spring and grow up, he knoweth not how.

28. For the earth bringeth forth fruit of herself; first the blade, then the ear, after that the full corn in the ear.

29. But when the fruit is brought forth, immediately he putteth in the sickle, because the harvest is come.

27. He sleeps himself at night and gets up in the daytime, and the seed springs up and swells, and he does not know how.

28. The earth brings forth fruit of itself, first the blade, then the ear, and then fills the ear with seeds.

29. But when the seed dries up, he immediately sends the reapers, because the time of the harvest has come.

The comprehension gives life to men, but the source of the comprehension, God, that God whom no one has ever known, does not rule men like that peasant who has sown the seed and has forgotten about it; he knows only of his own, and receives it, — that comprehension: just as the peasant reaps from the field the seed which he has sown, so the comprehension in men is united with the source of the comprehension.

The same meaning is expressed in the parable of the leaven.

THE PARABLE OF THE LEAVEN

33. Ἄλλην παραβολὴν ἐλάλησεν αὐτοῖς· Ὁμοία ἐστὶν ἡ βασιλεία τῶν οὐρανῶν ζύμῃ, ἣν λαβοῦσα γυνὴ ἐνέκρυψεν εἰς ἀλεύρου σάτα τρία, ἕως οὗ ἐζυμώθη ὅλον.

Matt. xiii. 33. Another parable spake he unto them; The kingdom of heaven is like unto leaven, which a woman took, and hid in three measures of meal, till the whole was leavened.

33. The kingdom of heaven is like a leaven. A woman took it and put it into a measure of flour, till the whole was leavened.

The woman put in the leaven and allowed the whole to leaven, until the dough was formed.

The woman did not have anything else to do. What she did was enough, in order to get what she wanted.

As the earth brings forth of its own account and as the leaven rises of itself, so the life of the comprehension lives of itself and is not cut short.

And again the same idea is expressed by the parable of the sower and the tares, but with a new and profound meaning, which gives a direct answer to the question of men as to what is evil and how man must understand the evil and bear himself toward it.

THE PARABLE OF THE WHEAT AND THE TARES

24. Ἄλλην παραβολὴν παρέθηκεν αὐτοῖς, λέγων, Ὡμοιώθη ἡ βασιλεία τῶν οὐρανῶν ἀνθρώπῳ σπείροντι καλὸν σπέρμα ἐν τῷ ἀγρῷ αὐτοῦ·

Matt. xiii. 24. Another parable put he forth unto them, saying, The kingdom of heaven is likened unto a man which sowed good seed in his field:

24. And Jesus said, The kingdom of heaven may be likened to this: A farmer sowed good seed in his field:

25. Ἐν δὲ τῷ καθεύδειν τοὺς ἀνθρώπους, ἦλθεν αὐτοῦ ὁ ἐχθρὸς καὶ ἔσπειρε ζιζάνια ἀνὰ μέσον τοῦ σίτου, καὶ ἀπῆλθεν.

25. But while men slept, his enemy came and sowed tares among the wheat, and went his way.

25. In the night his enemy came and sowed tares among the wheat, and went away.

26. Ὅτε δὲ ἐβλάστησεν ὁ χόρτος, καὶ καρπὸν ἐποίησε, τότε ἐφάνη καὶ τὰ ζιζάνια.

26. But when the blade was sprung up, and brought forth fruit, then appeared the tares also.

26. When the wheat was in the ear and began to fill up, then also appeared the tares.

27. Προσελθόντες δὲ οἱ δοῦλοι τοῦ οἰκοδεσπότου εἶπον αὐτῷ, Κύριε, οὐχὶ καλὸν σπέρμα ἔσπειρας ἐν τῷ σῷ ἀγρῷ; πόθεν οὖν ἔχει τὰ ζιζάνια;

27. So the servants of the householder came and said unto him, Sir, didst not thou sow good seed in thy field? from whence then hath it tares?

27. The servants came to the master and said, Didst thou sow impure seed in thy field? There are many tares there.

28. Ὁ δὲ ἔφη αὐτοῖς, Ἐχθρὸς ἄνθρωπος τοῦτο ἐποίησεν. οἱ δὲ δοῦλοι εἶπον αὐτῷ, Θέλεις οὖν ἀπελθόντες συλλέξωμεν αὐτά;

28. He said unto them, An enemy hath done this. The servants said unto him, Wilt thou then that we go and gather them up?

28. The master said, Not I, but another man, has done that. The servants said, Command us, and we will weed out the tares.

29. Ὁ δὲ ἔφη, Οὔ· μήποτε, συλλέγοντες τὰ ζιζάνια, ἐκριζώσητε ἅμα αὐτοῖς τὸν σῖτον.

29. But he said, Nay; lest while ye gather up the tares, ye root up also the wheat with them.

29. But the master said, It is not necessary to weed them out, for when you weed out the tares you will ruin the wheat.

30. Ἄφετε συναυξάνεσθαι ἀμφότερα μέχρι τοῦ θερισμοῦ· καὶ ἐν τῷ

30. Let both grow together until the harvest; and in the time of harvest I will say to the

30. Let the wheat grow with the tares until harvest time; and in the time of harvest I will

καιρῷ τοῦ θερισμοῦ ἐρῶ τοῖς θερισταῖς, Συλλέ-ξατε πρῶτον τὰ ζιζάνια, καὶ δήσατε αὐτὰ εἰς δέ-σμας πρὸς τὸ κατακαῦσαι αὐτά· τὸν δὲ σῖτον συνα-γάγετε εἰς τὴν ἀποθήκην μου.

reapers, Gather ye to-gether first the tares, and bind them in bun-dles to burn them: but gather the wheat into my barn.

tell the reapers to pick out the tares and burn them, and then I will harvest the wheat and take it to the barn.

· (a) ζιζάνια is a plant which exactly resembles wheat before it is in the ear.

The words about the master's burning the useless, and taking the useful, the wheat, to the barn, repeats what is said in Matt. iii. 12 : Whose fan is in his hand, and he will thoroughly purge his floor, and gather his wheat into the garner ; but he will burn up the chaff with unquench-able fire.

Here is defined who will destroy what is useless and will collect what is useful, — he who will purify with the spirit. Here it says that it is the son of man.

36. Τότε ἀφεὶς τοὺς ὄχλους, ἦλθεν εἰς τὴν οἰκίαν ὁ Ἰησοῦς. καὶ προσ-ῆλθον αὐτῷ οἱ μαθηταὶ αὐτοῦ, λέγοντες, Φράσον ἡμῖν τὴν παραβολὴν τῶν ζιζανίων τοῦ ἀγροῦ.

Matt. xiii. 36. Then Jesus sent the multitude away, and went into the house: and his disciples came unto him, saying, Declare unto us the par-able of the tares of the field.

36. And the disciples began to ask Jesus, Ex-plain to us the parable about the tares of the field.

37. Ὁ δὲ ἀποκριθεὶς εἶπεν αὐτοῖς, Ὁ σπείρων τὸ καλὸν σπέρμα ἐστὶν ὁ υἱὸς τοῦ ἀνθρώπου·

37. He answered and said unto them, He that soweth the good seed is the Son of man;

37. And Jesus said to them, The farmer who is sowing the good seed is the son of man.

38. Ὁ δὲ ἀγρός ἐστιν ὁ κόσμος· τὸ δὲ καλὸν σπέρμα, οὗτοί εἰσιν οἱ υἱοὶ τῆς βασιλείας· τὰ δὲ ζιζάνιά εἰσιν οἱ υἱοὶ τοῦ πονηροῦ.

38. The field is the world; the good seed are the children of the kingdom; but the tares are the children of the wicked one;

38. The field is the world of men; the good seed are the children of the kingdom of God; the tares are the evil men.

39. Ὁ δὲ ἐχθρὸς ὁ σπείρας αὐτά ἐστιν ὁ διά-βολος· ὁ δὲ θερισμὸς συν-τέλεια τοῦ αἰῶνός ἐστιν· οἱ δὲ θερισταὶ ἄγγελοί εἰσιν.

39. The enemy that sowed them is the devil; the harvest is the end of the world; and the reapers are the angels.

39. The stranger is temptation. The har-vest is the end of the life on earth; and the reapers are the power of God.

40. Ὥσπερ οὖν συλλέγεται τὰ ζιζάνια, καὶ πυρὶ κατακαίεται, οὕτως ἔσται ἐν τῇ συντελείᾳ τοῦ αἰῶνος τούτου.

41. Ἀποστελεῖ ὁ υἱὸς τοῦ ἀνθρώπου τοὺς ἀγγέλους αὐτοῦ, καὶ συλλέξουσιν ἐκ τῆς βασιλείας αὐτοῦ πάντα τὰ σκάνδαλα καὶ τοὺς ποιοῦντας τὴν ἀνομίαν,

42. Καὶ βαλοῦσιν αὐτοὺς εἰς τὴν κάμινον τοῦ πυρός· ἐκεῖ ἔσται ὁ κλαυθμὸς καὶ ὁ βρυγμὸς τῶν ὀδόντων.

43. Τότε οἱ δίκαιοι ἐκλάμψουσιν ὡς ὁ ἥλιος, ἐν τῇ βασιλείᾳ τοῦ πατρὸς αὐτῶν. Ὁ ἔχων ὦτα ἀκούειν ἀκουέτω.

40. As therefore the tares are gathered and burned in the fire; so shall it be in the end of this world.

41. The Son of man shall send forth his angels, and they shall gather out of his kingdom all things that offend, and them which do iniquity;

42. And shall cast them into a furnace of fire: there shall be wailing and gnashing of teeth.

43. Then shall the righteous shine forth as the sun in the kingdom of their Father. Who hath ears to hear, let him hear.

40. As the tares are gathered and burned, so will it be at the end of the life upon earth.

41. The son of man will send his servants, and they will take away from among the people of his kingdom all the deceptions and all those who do wrong.

42. And will cast them into the fire, and there will be wailing and gnashing of teeth.

43. Then will the righteous shine as the sun in the kingdom of their Father. He who has reason will understand.

(a) The present tense must be noticed here; it does not say that those who did wrong will be taken away, as ought to have been said, if the judgment at the end of the world were meant, according to the church interpretation, but who do wrong, that is, that those who do wrong will take themselves away, as is said in the discourse with Nicodemus.

(b) ἐκεῖ means *there* and *then;* here it has the latter meaning, as in Luke xiii. 28, where ἐκεῖ means *then*, in the same expression. It means that then men might, though too late, weep and in anger gnash their teeth because they had not lived in the comprehension.

The spirit of God in man, the son of man, all that we know of God, gives the life of the comprehension to men, just as a peasant sows good seed in his field, and it grows.

Amidst the life of the comprehension there appears something resembling life, which ends in death.

In Luke viii. 18 it says, And that will be taken from him which he thinks he has. What, then, is this likeness of life? Whence does it come?

This question does not refer to God the spirit, but only to men. God the spirit, the source of life, sows the life and harvests it. Only foolish servants may counsel the stamping out of life. Life alone is needed; it alone remains, and nothing else exists for God the spirit.

The temporal life ends, everything temporal vanishes, perishes; what does not end and perish is the life of the comprehension, that alone which is spirit, which is from God.

In this parable there are two main thoughts, two answers to the questions which are propounded.

1. What is evil in relation to God? and

2. What is evil in relation to man?

The answer to the first question is that there is no evil for God, the son of man. He is the God of life and of good, and does not know the evil. Since he is the God of life and of good, there is no evil for him, and he cannot wish to destroy it. The desire to destroy evil is evil and can be only in men, and not in him.

This deduction from the second thought, which is expressed here only from one side, will be developed later in the teaching of the non-resistance to evil.

The son of man gives life and knows life only in the comprehension, and so every man, transferring his life to the son, to the spirit, is unable to know evil and so unable to resist it.

The second thought and the answer to the question as to what that is which we men call evil consists in this, that what we call evil is a free departure from the light, and perdition, which is mentioned in the discourse with Nicodemus; it is this, that the light came into the world, and men went away from it.

The idea that there can be no evil for God, and that
for men it is a departure from the comprehension is expounded in the parable of the drawnet.

THE PARABLE OF THE DRAWNET

47. Πάλιν ὁμοία ἐστὶν ἡ βασιλεία τῶν οὐρανῶν σαγήνῃ βληθείσῃ εἰς τὴν θάλασσαν, καὶ ἐκ παντὸς γένους συναγαγούσῃ·	*Matt. xiii.* 47. Again, the kingdom of heaven is like unto a net, that was cast into the sea, and gathered of every kind:	47. Again, the king-dom of God is like a drawnet: it was cast into the sea and gath-ered fish of every kind.
48. Ἦν, ὅτε ἐπληρώ-θη, ἀναβιβάσαντες ἐπὶ τὸν αἰγιαλὸν, καὶ καθί-σαντες, συνέλεξαν τὰ καλὰ εἰς ἀγγεῖα, τὰ δὲ σαπρὰ ἔξω ἔβαλον.	48. Which, when it was full, they drew to shore, and sat down, and gathered the good into vessels, but cast the bad away.	48. The net was full; they drew it out to the shore and sat down, and gathered the good fish into pails, and the worthless were thrown away.

God does what the fishermen do: the worthless fish
they throw away, and leave only what is of some use.
The fishermen select such fish as they can use, and the
rest they throw into the sea, as they are useless.   There
is no question as to whether it will be better or worse for
the fish.   Such of the fish as are in the sea do not exist
for the fishermen, just as for God are not those men who
are not his sons, whose life is not in the light of the
comprehension.   For God there is no evil, but for man
there is.   The evil for him is the life outside of the
comprehension.

And so it is necessary to differentiate our conceptions
about evil in general — the objective, the external evil,
as the philosophers call it, and the evil of each man —
the subjective, internal evil.   There is no objective evil.
The subjective evil is the departure from the comprehension, otherwise, death.

This differentiation of the concepts is expounded in
the interpretation of the parable of the sower and of the
seeds that fell into different soils.

EXPLANATION OF THE PARABLE OF THE SOWER

10. Καὶ προσελθόντες οἱ μαθηταὶ εἶπον αὐτῷ, Διατί ἐν παραβολαῖς λαλεῖς αὐτοῖς;

9. Τίς εἴη ἡ παραβολὴ αὕτη;

10. Ἠρώτησαν αὐτὸν τὴν παραβολήν.

Matt. xiii. 10. And the disciples came, and said unto him, Why speakest thou unto them in parables?

Luke viii. 9. What might this parable be?

Mark. iv. 10. Asked of him the parable.

10. And his disciples came to him and said,

9. Why dost thou speak in parables?

According to Mark and Luke the disciples ask, What does a parable mean? According to Matthew they ask, For what purpose dost thou speak in parables?

I think that according to Mark and Luke it means that the disciples ask both what a parable means and for what purpose he speaks in it. According to Matthew it also means, Why dost thou speak in parables, and what do they mean? And the words of Jesus reply to both questions. He elucidates the meaning of the parable, and from its meaning it follows that those who do not know the secrets of the kingdom of God cannot speak otherwise than in parables. Only the external meaning presents itself to them, and they do not know the internal meaning.

In Matthew it says, διατὶ ἐν παραβολαῖς λαλεῖς αὐτοῖς. The word αὐτοῖς is omitted in many texts, for the noun to which it might refer is lacking. It is apparently added, because the question διατί refers both to the speaking in parables and to the parables themselves. Διατί means here the German *warum*, wherefore.

The disciples ask, Why dost thou speak in parables? Thus Mark and Luke report the questions to us, and so αὐτοῖς is superfluous, and verses 11–23 are not accidental utterances, but an explanation of the parable. And so, combining the meaning of the question and answer from the three gospels, I translate it, Why speak in parables? which question refers both to the

meaning of the parable and to the reason why he speaks
in parables to the multitude.

11. 'Ο δὲ ἀποκριθεὶς εἶπεν αὐτοῖς, 'Ότι ὑμῖν δέδοται γνῶναι τὰ μυστήρια τῆς βασιλείας τῶν οὐρανῶν, ἐκείνοις δὲ οὐ δέδοται.	*Matt. xiii.* 11. He answered and said unto them, Because it is given unto you to know the mysteries of the kingdom of heaven, but to them it is not given.	11. He replied to them Because it is given to you to know the inward meaning of the kingdom of God.
11. 'Εκείνοις δὲ τοῖς ἔξω ἐν παραβολαῖς τὰ πάντα γίνεται·	*Mark iv.* 11. But unto them that are without, all these things are done in parables:	11. But those who are without receive it in parables.

It is given to you to know the inward meaning of the
kingdom of God, — you are the good ground which brings
forth a hundredfold, and fifty, and thirty.

But to the others it is not given, — they are the
wayside, stones, and thorns.

And the meaning of the parable is that to some the
meaning is revealed, and to others not. He says, The
reason why I speak to them in parables is that they
cannot understand otherwise, for they do not understand
the inward meaning. In Luke it says, It is given to you
to know the inward meaning of the kingdom of God, but
to others only in examples.

13. Διὰ τοῦτο ἐν παραβολαῖς αὐτοῖς λαλῶ.	*Matt. xiii.* 13. Therefore speak I to them in parables.	13. For this reason I speak to them in parables.

(a) λαλέω *to speak, communicate.* It would be more
correct to say here *to commune,* for this passage corresponds to the same passages in Mark and Luke, where
it says, But to them everything is manifested in parables.
The idea is not this: I speak to them in parables, but,
They cannot understand otherwise than in parables, and
that is explained farther down.

Διὰ τοῦτο shows that what is being said is in reply to
διατί. After the word λαλῶ there ought to be a period
or semicolon. We then do not get that offensive mean-

ing which we had before, namely, that Jesus speaks to them in parables because they do not understand, that is, he does not speak directly to them, but speaks in similes, for the purpose that they may not understand, but we get, on the contrary, the opposite, clear meaning, namely, that, as they do not know the inward meaning of the kingdom of God, they cannot understand it in any other way than in an external manner, that is, in parables.

And so I take the first part of the verse from Matt. xiii. 11, and the second half from Mark iv. 11.

	Matt. xiii.	
9. Ὁ ἔχων ὦτα ἀκούειν ἀκουέτω.	9. Who hath ears to hear, let him hear.	9. He who has reason will understand.
14. Καὶ ἀναπληροῦται ἐπ' αὐτοῖς ἡ προφητεία Ἡσαίου, ἡ λέγουσα, ''Ακοῇ ἀκούσετε, καὶ οὐ μὴ συνῆτε· καὶ βλέποντες βλέψετε, καὶ οὐ μὴ ἴδητε.	14. And in them is fulfilled the prophecy of Esaias, which saith, By hearing ye shall hear, and shall not understand; and seeing ye shall see, and shall not perceive:	14. And in them is fulfilled the prophecy of Isaiah. By hearing you will hear, and will not understand; and you will look with your eyes, and will not see.
15. Ἐπαχύνθη γὰρ ἡ καρδία τοῦ λαοῦ τούτου, καὶ τοῖς ὠσὶ βαρέως ἤκουσαν, καὶ τοὺς ὀφθαλμοὺς αὐτῶν ἐκάμμυσαν· μήποτε ἴδωσι τοῖς ὀφθαλμοῖς, καὶ τοῖς ὠσὶν ἀκούσωσι, καὶ τῇ καρδίᾳ συνῶσι, καὶ ἐπιστρέψωσι, καὶ ἰάσωμαι αὐτούς.'	15. For this people's heart is waxed gross, and their ears are dull of hearing, and their eyes they have closed; lest at any time they should see with their eyes, and hear with their ears, and should understand with their heart, and should be converted, and I should heal them (Isaiah vi. 9, 10).	15. For the people's heart has grown fat, and they have closed their eyes so that they do not see, and with their ears they do not hear; and into their heart they do not receive, lest they be converted and I heal them.
16. Ὑμῶν δὲ μακάριοι οἱ ὀφθαλμοί, ὅτι βλέπουσι· καὶ τὰ ὦτα ὑμῶν, ὅτι ἀκούει.	16. But blessed are your eyes, for they see: and your ears, for they hear.	16. But your eyes are blessed, for they see; and your ears, for they hear.
17. Ἀμὴν γὰρ λέγω ὑμῖν, ὅτι πολλοὶ προφῆται καὶ δίκαιοι ἐπεθύμησαν ἰδεῖν ἃ βλέπετε, καὶ οὐκ εἶδον· καὶ ἀκοῦσαι ἃ ἀκούετε, καὶ οὐκ ἤκουσαν.	17. For verily I say unto you, That many prophets and righteous men have desired to see those things which ye see, and have not seen them; and to hear those things which ye hear, and have not heard them.	17. Verily I tell you that the prophets and saints have desired to see what you see, and could not perceive and hear what you have comprehended.
18. Ὑμεῖς οὖν ἀκούσατε τὴν παραβολὴν τοῦ σπείροντος.	18. Hear ye therefore the parable of the sower.	18. Now you will understand the parable of the sower.

11. Ὁ σπόρος ἐστὶν ὁ λόγος τοῦ Θεοῦ·

19. Παντὸς ἀκούοντος τὸν λόγον τῆς βασιλείας καὶ μὴ συνιέντος, ἔρχεται ὁ πονηρὸς καὶ ἁρπάζει τὸ ἐσπαρμένον ἐν τῇ καρδίᾳ αὐτοῦ· οὗτός ἐστιν ὁ παρὰ τὴν ὁδὸν σπαρείς.

20. Ὁ δὲ ἐπὶ τὰ πετρώδη σπαρείς, οὗτός ἐστιν ὁ τὸν λόγον ἀκούων, καὶ εὐθὺς μετὰ χαρᾶς λαμβάνων αὐτόν·

21. Οὐκ ἔχει δὲ ῥίζαν ἐν ἑαυτῷ, ἀλλὰ πρόσκαιρός ἐστι· γενομένης δὲ θλίψεως ἢ διωγμοῦ διὰ τὸν λόγον, εὐθὺς σκανδαλίζεται.

22. Ὁ δὲ εἰς τὰς ἀκάνθας σπαρείς, οὗτός ἐστιν ὁ τὸν λόγον ἀκούων, καὶ ἡ μέριμνα τοῦ αἰῶνος τούτου καὶ ἡ ἀπάτη τοῦ πλούτου συμπνίγει τὸν λόγον, καὶ ἄκαρπος γίνεται.

23. Ὁ δὲ ἐπὶ τὴν γῆν τὴν καλὴν σπαρείς, οὗτός ἐστιν ὁ τὸν λόγον ἀκούων καὶ συνιῶν· ὃς δὴ καρποφορεῖ, καὶ ποιεῖ ὁ μὲν ἑκατόν, ὁ δὲ ἑξήκοντα, ὁ δὲ τριάκοντα.

18. Βλέπετε οὖν πῶς ἀκούετε· ὃς γὰρ ἂν ἔχῃ, δοθήσεται αὐτῷ· καὶ ὃς ἂν μὴ ἔχῃ, καὶ ὃ δοκεῖ ἔχειν ἀρθήσεται ἀπ' αὐτοῦ.

Luke viii. 11. The seed is the word of God.

Matt. xiii. 19. When any one heareth the word of the kingdom, and understandeth it not, then cometh the wicked one, and catcheth away that which was sown in his heart. This is he which received seed by the way side.

20. But he that received the seed into stony places, the same is he that heareth the word, and anon with joy receiveth it;

21. Yet hath he not root in himself, but dureth for a while: for when tribulation or persecution ariseth because of the word, by and by he is offended.

22. He also that received seed among the thorns is he that heareth the word; and the care of this world, and the deceitfulness[b] of riches, choke the word, and he becometh unfruitful.

23. But he that received seed into the good ground is he that heareth the word, and understandeth it; which also beareth fruit, and bringeth forth, some a hundredfold, some sixty, some thirty.

Luke viii. 18. Take heed therefore how ye hear: for whosoever hath,[a] to him shall be given; and whosoever hath not, from him shall be taken even that which he seemeth to have.[d]

---

11. The seed is the comprehension of God.

19. When any one hears the teaching about the kingdom of God and does not take it to his heart, there comes the enemy and takes away what was sown in his heart. That is the seed which is sown by the wayside.

20. What is sown on the stone is he who hears the teaching of the kingdom of God and understands the teaching, and then receives it with joy in his heart;

21. And does not hold the root in himself, but for a while only. And when pressure and persecution for the teaching comes, he at once submits to deception.

22. And what is sown among the thorns is he who understands the teaching; and worldly cares and love of riches choke the teaching, and it brings no fruit.

23. But what has fallen on good ground is he who has understood the teaching and receives it into his heart; that bears some a hundredfold, some fifty, and some thirty.

18. See to it how you understand. He who holds on gets it, and he who does not hold on has even that taken from him which he thinks he has.

(*a*) οὖν is translated by *now*, which meaning it has here.

(*b*) In many texts stands ἀγαπή, which is simpler and clearer and more correct.

(c) ἔχω means *to hold*. This expression sounds like a proverb and may refer to a pail or bag: A strong bag will hold all, but a poor bag will lose the last.

(d) I take this verse from Matthew and Luke, as it is the same in both.

The disciples ask why he speaks in parables and what he means by them. And Jesus answers, Only to you is it given to understand the kingdom of God, like the seed that has fallen on good ground. But to the others, like the seed that perishes, it is not given. And it is given to you to increase, like the good seed in the ground, but from the others even that life will be taken which, it seemed, was in them, just as the seed is destroyed by the wayside, on the stone, and in the thorns. It is this that I say in the parables, for they do not see, do not comprehend the whole good. They are like those men of whom Isaiah says that God punished them, because looking on they did not see and listening they did not hear. The heart of these men has grown fat, and so they do not understand what is before them.

You are happy in that you understand. Such is the meaning of the parable from the external side; but the internal meaning is quite different.

And Jesus explains the internal meaning.

The external meaning of the parable is this, that some people are predetermined for death, and others for life. The internal meaning is this, that there is no predetermination, but that each can retain the comprehension and acquire it with a surplus.

What has fallen by the wayside is the indifference, the neglect in respect to the comprehension, and so Jesus cautions men against indifference and neglect, and says that they must make an effort, in order to receive the comprehension into their hearts.

What has fallen on the stones is weakness, and so

Jesus cautions against it, and shows that man must make an effort, in order not to waver during offences and persecutions.

The thorns are the worldly cares, and Jesus cautions against them and points out that man must make an effort in order to reject them.

The good ground is the comprehension and fulfilment, in spite of offences and cares.

And Jesus shows that he who will make this effort and will fulfil it will receive life with a surplus.

PARABLE OF THE HIDDEN TREASURE

44. Πάλιν ὁμοία ἐστὶν ἡ βασιλεία τῶν οὐρανῶν θησαυρῷ κεκρυμμένῳ ἐν τῷ ἀγρῷ, ὃν εὑρὼν ἄνθρωπος ἔκρυψε· καὶ ἀπὸ τῆς χαρᾶς αὐτοῦ ὑπάγει, καὶ πάντα ὅσα ἔχει πωλεῖ, καὶ ἀγοράζει τὸν ἀγρὸν ἐκεῖνον.

Matt. xiii. 44. Again, the kingdom of heaven is like unto treasure hid in a field, the which when a man hath found, he hideth, and for joy thereof goeth and selleth all that he hath, and buyeth that field.

44. The kingdom of God is like a treasure hidden in a field. A man has found the treasure and has hidden it (again). And for the joy of having found it he goes and sells all that he has, and buys that field.

45. Πάλιν ὁμοία ἐστὶν ἡ βασιλεία τῶν οὐρανῶν ἀνθρώπῳ ἐμπόρῳ ζητοῦντι καλοὺς μαργαρίτας·

45. Again, the kingdom of heaven is like unto a merchantman, seeking goodly pearls:

45. Again, the kingdom of heaven is as when a merchant is buying up precious stones;

46. Ὃς εὑρὼν ἕνα πολύτιμον μαργαρίτην, ἀπελθὼν πέπρακε πάντα ὅσα εἶχε, καὶ ἠγόρασεν αὐτόν.

46. Who, when he had found one pearl of great price, went and sold all that he had, and bought it.

46. And having found a precious stone, he goes and sells all (the former) that he had, and buys that one.

The kingdom of God is like the one who wants to have a pearl or treasure, which he knows is buried in the field. And having learned of it, he sells everything, in order to acquire the pearl and the field.

PARABLE OF THE MUSTARD SEED

31. Ὁμοία ἐστὶν ἡ βασιλεία τῶν οὐρανῶν κόκκῳ σινάπεως, ὃν λαβὼν ἄνθρωπος ἔσπειρεν ἐν τῷ ἀγρῷ αὐτοῦ·

Matt. xiii. 31. The kingdom of heaven is like to a grain of mustard seed, which a man took, and sowed in his field:

31. The kingdom of heaven is like a birch seed, which a man took, and sowed in his field.

32. Ὁ μικρότερον μέν ἐστι πάντων τῶν σπερμάτων· ὅταν δὲ αὐξηθῇ μεῖζον τῶν λαχάνων ἐστί, καὶ γίνεται δένδρον, ὥστε ἐλθεῖν τὰ πετεινὰ τοῦ οὐρανοῦ, καὶ κατασκηνοῦν ἐν τοῖς κλάδοις αὐτοῦ.

32. Which indeed is the least of all seeds: but when it is grown, it is the greatest among herbs, and becometh a tree, so that the birds of the air come and lodge in the branches thereof.

32. Though it is the least of all seeds, it will be greater than any grass when it is grown, and will become a tree, and the feathered birds will make nests in its branches.

THE KINGDOM OF GOD

Jesus announces that the kingdom of God has come, and yet no visible change has taken place. He announces to his disciples that from now on heaven is open, and between heaven and men there is a constant communion. He announces that it is not necessary to separate ourselves from corrupt people, that they are not guilty, and that those only are guilty who think that they are good because they execute the law of God.

He announces that no external purification is needed, that only that which comes from within can defile, and that only the spirit purifies.

He announces that it is not necessary to observe the Sabbath, that this observance is foolish and false, and that the Sabbath is a human institution.

He announces that not only are fasts useless, but that all the old external rites are harmful for his teaching.

Finally, he announces that it is not right to serve God with sacrifices. We do not need oxen, nor sheep, nor doves, nor money, not even the temple itself; that there is a spirit; that the spirit does not want sacrifices, but love; and that the spirit is to be served — by all, always, at all times — in the spirit and with deeds.

When the Pharisees saw and heard all that, they came to Jesus and began to ask him how he preached the kingdom of God, since he rejected God. And he answered them, The kingdom of God, as I preach it, is not the same as what the former prophets preached about. They said that God will come with all kinds of manifestations, but I say that the kingdom of God is such that its coming cannot be seen.

And if you are told that it has come or is coming, or that it is here, you do not believe. The kingdom of God is not in time and not in any place; it is like lightning, — here and there and everywhere, and it has no time and no place, because here it is, within you.

After that a Pharisee, a Jewish elder, Nicodemus, came to Jesus in secret, and said to him, Thou teachest that the kingdom of God has come, and that it is within us, and yet thou dost not order men to fast and to offer sacrifices, but destroyest the temple; so what kind of a kingdom of God is yours, and where is it?

And Jesus answered him, Thou must understand that if a man is begotten by God the Father, he sees the kingdom of God. Nicodemus did not understand what Jesus told him, that every man was already begotten by God, and said, How can a man, if he is begotten from the flesh of the father and has grown old, again creep into the womb of his mother and again be begotten by the flesh by God?

And Jesus answered him, Understand what I say, I say that man, besides the flesh, is begotten by the spirit, and so each man is of flesh and of the spirit, and so each man can enter the kingdom of God. Of the flesh is flesh. Of the flesh can not the spirit be born; only of the spirit can there be the spirit. The spirit is that which lives in thee, and it lives freely and rationally, and it is that for which thou knowest neither beginning nor end. And every man feels it in himself. And so why dost thou wonder when I tell thee that we must be begotten from heaven by God, by the spirit?

Nicodemus said, Still I do not believe that that could be possible.

Then Jesus said to him, What teacher art thou if thou dost not understand that? Thou must understand that

I am not talking of any recondite things; I am talking of what we all know; I assure men of what we all see. How wilt thou believe in what is in heaven, if thou dost not believe in what is on earth, in thyself? No one has been in heaven, but there is on earth in man the son of God, the spirit, the one which is God.

The very son of God in man must be worshipped, as you worshipped God, when Moses in the wilderness exalted not the flesh of the serpent, but its image, and that image became the salvation of men. Even so we must exalt the son of God in man, not the flesh of man, but the son of God in man, in order that men, relying upon it, may not know death, but shall have non-temporal life in the kingdom of God.

Not for the ruin, but for the good of the world has God given his son, who is like himself. He gave him for this, that every man, relying upon him, might not perish, but might have non-temporal life. He did not bring his son, life, into the world of men, in order to destroy men, but that the world of men might live by it and be in the kingdom of God.

And he who relies on God is in the kingdom of God, in the power of God; and he who does not depend on him destroys himself, by not relying on that which is life. Destruction consists in this, that life came into the world, but men themselves walk away from life. Life is the light of men. The light came into the world, but men prefer darkness to light, and do not walk toward the light. The light is the comprehension, and so he who does evil evades the light, the comprehension, that his deeds may not be seen, and remains in the power of God.

In his remarks to the Pharisees and discourse with Nicodemus Jesus explains what he means by the kingdom of God and by God.

God and the kingdom of God are in men. God is the non-carnal principle which gives life to man. This non-

carnal principle he calls the son of God in man, the son
of man. The son of man is the comprehension. It
has to be exalted and deified, and by it we must live.
He who lives in the comprehension lives non-temporally;
he who does not live in it does not live, — he perishes.

What, then, is this God the Father, who is not the
creator of everything and not separate from the world, as
the Jews understood him to be? How are we to understand this Father, whose son is in man, and how are we
to understand his relation to men?

To this Jesus replies in parables.

The kingdom of God is not to be understood as you
think, namely, that for all men the kingdom of God will
come in some one place and at some certain time, but
that in the whole world there are always some people
who rely upon God, who become the sons of the kingdom, and others, who do not rely upon him, who are
destroyed.

God the spirit, the Father of that spirit which is in
man, is God and the Father of those only who recognize
themselves as his sons. And so only those exist for
God who have retained within them what he has given
them.

And Jesus began to talk to them about the kingdom of
God, and he explained it by examples. He said, God the
Father sows in the world the life of the comprehension,
just as the farmer sows his seeds in his field. He sows
in the whole field, without paying any attention to where
each seed will fall.

And some seeds fall by the wayside and the birds
come and pick them. And other seeds fall on the stones,
where they grow indeed, but soon wither, because they
cannot take root. And others again fall into the thorns,
and the thorns choke the wheat, and the ears will grow,
but will not fill up. And others again fall in good
ground, and these spring up and make up for the lost

seeds and grow full in the ears, and some ears give a hundredfold, and some sixty and some thirty.

Just so God has scattered the comprehension among men. In some it is lost, and in others it bears a hundredfold, and they form the kingdom of God.

Thus the kingdom of God is not such as you imagine it to be, namely, that God is ruling over you. God is only the comprehension, and the kingdom of God will be in those who will take it. But God does not govern men.

As the farmer casts the seeds into the ground and does not think of them, but the seeds swell and sprout themselves, and grow into blades and ears, and fill up, and the master sends the reapers to cut them down, when they are ripe; so also has God given his son, the comprehension, to the world, and the comprehension grows of itself in the world, and the sons of the comprehension form the kingdom of God.

As a woman puts the leaven into the trough and mixes it with the flour, and does not mix it any more, but waits for it to leaven of itself and rise; so God does not enter into the life of men, as long as they live. God gave the comprehension to the world, and the comprehension lives itself among men and forms the kingdom of God. God the spirit is the God of life and good, and so there are no death and no evil for him. Death and evil are for men, and not for God.

The kingdom of heaven may be compared with this: a farmer has sowed good seed in his field. The farmer is the spirit of God; the field is the world; and the seeds are the sons of the kingdom of God.

The farmer lies down to sleep, and the enemy comes and sows tares. The enemy is temptation; the tares are the sons of the temptation. And now the servants come to the farmer and say, Hast thou sowed bad seed? Many tares have sprung up in thy field. Send us to weed them out. But the farmer says, It is not necessary, for when you weed out the tares you will tramp down the wheat. Let them grow together; when the harvest comes, I will tell the reapers to pick out the tares and will have them burned, and the wheat I will gather in my barn.

The harvest is the end of human life, and the reapers are the power of God. And as the tares will be burned and the wheat will be cleaned and garnered, even so at the end of life everything will perish which was the deception of time, and there will be left only the true life in the spirit. For God there is no evil. God preserves that which he needs, which is his own; and what is not his does not exist for him.

The kingdom of heaven is like a drawnet. The net is cast out in the sea and brings up all kinds of fish. Then, when the drawnet is pulled out, the spoiled fish are taken out and cast into the sea. Even so it will be at the end of time. The power of God will pick out the good, and the bad will be rejected.

And when he finished speaking, his disciples began to ask him how these parables were to be understood.

And he said to them, These parables have to be understood in two ways. All these parables I speak because there are some, like you, my disciples, who understand what the kingdom of God consists in, who understand that the kingdom of God is within us, and who know how to enter it, but others do not understand that. Others look and do not see, and listen and do not understand, because their hearts have grown fat.

And so I speak in parables for two purposes; I speak to both. To some I say what the kingdom is to God, and I tell them that some enter the kingdom, and others do not, and they can understand me. But to you I tell how to enter the kingdom of God. And look and understand the parable of the sower as is proper. For you the parable means this:

Every man who hears the teaching of the kingdom of God, but does not take it to his heart, is overcome by deceit, and he destroys the teaching in his heart, — it is the seed sown by the wayside. What is sown on the stones is he who hears the teaching and accepts it with joy. But there is no root in him, and he receives it only for a while, and when pressure is brought to bear and offence is offered him for his teaching, he himself takes offence. What is sown among the worm-wood is he who hears the teaching, but the cares of the world and his eagerness for wealth chokes the teaching and it gives forth no fruit. And what is sown on the good ground is he who hears the teaching and understands and brings forth fruit, some a hundredfold, and some sixty, and some thirty.

For he who holds on will get much, and he who does not hold will be deprived of the last.

And so see to it how you understand the parables. Understand them in such a way that you do not submit to deception, offences, cares, but bring forth fruit a hundredfold and enter the kingdom of God.

The kingdom of God grows large in the soul from nothing, but gives everything. It is like a birch seed, which is the smallest of seeds; when it grows up it is greater than all the trees, and the birds of heaven make their nests in it.

. After that there came the disciples of John to ask Jesus whether he was the one of whom he had said that he opened the kingdom of God and renovated men by the spirit.

Jesus replied, and said, Look and listen, and tell John whether the kingdom of God has come and whether men are renovated by the spirit. Tell him how I preach the kingdom of God. In the prophecies it says that when the kingdom of God comes, all men will be blessed; tell him, then, that my kingdom of God is such that the poor are blessed, and that every man who hears me becomes blessed.

Having dismissed the disciples of John, Jesus began to explain to the people what kingdom of God John had announced.

He said, When you went to be baptized by John in the wilderness, what did you go to see? If you wanted to see a man dressed in rich raiment, such men live here in palaces. What, then, is it that you saw in the wilderness? Do you think that you went because John was a prophet? Do not think so. John was not a prophet, but the one of whom the prophets have written. He is the one who has announced the coming of the kingdom of God.

Verily I tell you, No greater man has been born than John. He was in the kingdom of God, and so he was greater than all.

The law and the prophets were needed before John; but since John, and even now, the kingdom of God upon earth is announced, and he who makes an effort enters into it.

The lawyers and the Pharisees did not understand what it was John was announcing, and they had no regard for him. This tribe, the lawyers and the Pharisees, regard as truth only what they themselves invent. They learn their law by rote and listen to each other. But what John has said and what I say they do not hear, nor understand. Of all that John has said they understood only so much, that he fasted in the wilderness, and they say, The devil is in him. Of what I say they have understood only this much, that I do not fast, and they say, He eats and drinks with the tax-collectors, and is a friend of corrupt people.

They are like children in the street, who prattle with one another and wonder why no one listens to them. Their wisdom is seen by their works.

Everything which I teach men to do is easy and simple, for the kingdom of God is announced as bliss.

CHAPTER IV.

THE LAW (THE SERMON ON THE MOUNT). THE RICH AND THE POOR

85. Καὶ περιῆγεν ὁ Ἰησοῦς τὰς πόλεις πάσας καὶ τὰς κώμας, διδάσκων ἐν ταῖς συναγωγαῖς αὐτῶν, καὶ κηρύσσων τὸ εὐαγγέλιον τῆς βασιλείας, καὶ θεραπεύων πᾶσαν νόσον καὶ πᾶσαν μαλακίαν ἐν τῷ λαῷ.

Matt. ix. 35. And Jesus went about all the cities and villages, teaching in their synagogues, and preaching the gospel of the kingdom, and healing every sickness and every disease among the people.

35. And Jesus went about all the cities and villages, teaching in the assemblies, and, preaching, announced the presence of God.

36. Ἰδὼν δὲ τοὺς ὄχλους, ἐσπλαγχνίσθη περὶ αὐτῶν, ὅτι ἦσαν ἐκλελυμένοι καὶ ἐρριμμένοι ὡσεὶ πρόβατα μὴ ἔχοντα ποιμένα.

36. But when he saw the multitudes, he was moved with compassion on them, because they fainted, and were scattered abroad, as sheep having no shepherd.

36. Looking at the multitudes, Jesus was moved with compassion for them, for they were like mangy sheep without a shepherd.

37. Τότε λέγει τοῖς μαθηταῖς αὐτοῦ, Ὁ μὲν θερισμὸς πολύς, οἱ δὲ ἐργάται ὀλίγοι·

37. Then saith he unto his disciples, The harvest truly is plenteous, but the labourers are few;

38. Δεήθητε οὖν τοῦ κυρίου τοῦ θερισμοῦ, ὅπως ἐκβάλῃ ἐργάτας εἰς τὸν θερισμὸν αὐτοῦ.

38. Pray ye therefore the Lord of the harvest, that he will send forth labourers into his harvest.

1. Ἰδὼν δὲ τοὺς ὄχλους ἀνέβη εἰς τὸ ὄρος· καὶ καθίσαντος αὐτοῦ, προσῆλθον αὐτῷ οἱ μαθηταὶ αὐτοῦ·

Matt. v. 1. And seeing the multitudes, he went up into a mountain: and when he was set, his disciples came unto him:

1. And seeing the multitudes, Jesus went up into a mountain and sat down there, and his disciples came to him.

20. Καὶ αὐτὸς ἐπάρας τοὺς ὀφθαλμοὺς αὐτοῦ εἰς τοὺς μαθητὰς αὐτοῦ ἔλεγε, Μακάριοι οἱ πτωχοί, ὅτι ὑμετέρα ἐστὶν ἡ βασιλεία τοῦ Θεοῦ.

Luke vi. 20. And he lifted up his eyes on his disciples and said, Blessed be ye poor: for yours is the kingdom of God.

20. And lifting his eyes to his disciples he said, Blessed are you mendicants, for yours is the kingdom of God.

21. Μακάριοι οἱ πεινῶντες νῦν, ὅτι χορτασθήσεσθε.

21. Blessed are ye that hunger now: for ye shall be filled.

21. Blessed are those of you who hunger now, for you shall be filled.

(*a*) I leave out *healing every sickness*, as un necessary and referring to the miracles, the proofs of the truth of the teaching.

(*b*) We must not forget that both according to Matthew, where it says that the disciples went up to Jesus before he began to speak, and according to Luke, where it says that, raising his eyes to his disciples, he began to speak, Jesus was speaking to the multitudes, though he directed his remarks to his disciples, and, according to Luke, he said to them, Blessed are you, the poor, meaning them as much as himself, the poor, the vagrants.

(*c*) In Matthew it says πτωχοὶ τῷ πνεύματι; in Luke it is simply πτωχοί. Is τῷ πνεύματι omitted in Luke, or is it added in Matthew?

In order to solve this, it is necessary first to understand what πνεύματι means in this passage.

This is what the church interpretations say to the word *in spirit*:

Blessed: What blessedness is meant here, is shown by the explanations which follow after each blessed, — namely, the blessedness of the kingdom of Messiah.

The poor in spirit: To be poor in spirit means to have an humble conception of one's spiritual qualities, to destroy oneself, consider oneself a sinner; in general, a poor man in spirit is an humble man, whose quality is opposed to that of pride, ambition, or selfishness. Since Adam fell from pride, having presumed to be God, Christ regenerates us by means of humility. He added *in the spirit* that thou mightest understand humility and not poverty. Why, then, did he not say *humble* instead of *poor?* Because the latter is more striking than the first. To them belongs the kingdom of heaven, that is, they are capable and worthy of receiving blessedness in the kingdom of heaven; for the humble man, recognizing his sinfulness and unworthiness, completely surrenders himself to the guidance of divine grace, not in the least relying on his spiritual powers, and grace takes him to the kingdom. Humility is the door to the kingdom of heaven. (Archim. Mikh., Gospel of Matt., p. 66.)

This is what Reuss says (*Nouv. Test.*, Vol. I., pp. 195 and 196).

En général, ces macarismes exaltent la condition de ceux qui préfèrent aux jouissances de ce monde la vie en Dieu et la paix avec le ciel. L'expérience prouve que ce choix est douloureux et difficile, parce que la faiblesse humaine se heurte contre deux écueils également formidables et dangereux. D'un côté on se trouve en face de l'antipathie du monde qui n'a que le mépris ou la haine pour tout ce qui lui est étranger ; de l'autre côté il y a l'orgueil naturel de l'esprit et les mauvais penchants du cœur, qui nous sollicitent incessamment et nous écartent de la voie du salut. Voilà pour quoi Jésus appelle heureux ceux qui savent éviter ces écueils, vaincre leurs affections vicieuses, reconnaître leur imperfection naturelle, braver les séductions et les menaces d'un monde pervers et hostile, et accepter ce que cette résolution courageusement prise et exécutée peut leur valoir d'épreuves et de tribulations.

All that may be profound, but all those utterances are merely the ideas of a Theophilactes, a St. Jerome, a Reuss, and not of Christ. For if Christ wanted in this passage to speak of humility, he would have said so clearly, as he has said so in many, many places. Here, apparently, Jesus did not wish to speak of humility, in the first place, because poverty of spirit, that is the combination of words πτωχοὶ τῷ πνεύματι makes no sense whatever. Πτωχός means *a mendicant, homeless man, vagrant*, without that contemptuous meaning which is ascribed to the word, and so it is impossible to say *vagrants in spirit ;* in the second place, because the whole Gospel teaches that it is necessary to elevate the spirit, live by the spirit, so how can Jesus say that those are blessed who are poor in the spirit? In the third place, it says in Matthew that blessed are in general those who are poor in spirit, and then, among the number of blessed people, are counted out other cases of blessedness which result from this condition. However, "which hunger after righteousness," in no way harmonizes with the idea of humility. Even though the conception of hungering after righteousness is not opposed to the idea of humility, it in no way follows from humility.

In the fourth place, all the subsequent beatitudes, from the fact that only to the first is attached the clause, For theirs is the kingdom of heaven, apparently ought to explain the first. But the idea of hungering after righteousness, of being merciful and pure of heart, does not follow from the idea of humility.

In the fifth place, the rewards promised for the qualities counted out are opposed to the idea of humility: Shall see God, inherit the earth, be called the children of God.

From all that we see that the translation of πτωχοὶ τῷ πνεύματι by *humble* is quite irregular and impossible, and that these two words have no meaning in this context.

What meaning can πτωχοί have without πνεύματι?

According to Luke, Jesus says, Blessed are you vagrants, because you are in the kingdom of God.

(1) The meaning of these words may be quite out of harmony with the judgments of St. Jerome and of a rich youth and of all the present and former rich men, who call themselves Christians and bearers of Christian truths, but it is philologically none the less quite correct. Jesus says that according to his teaching the vagrants are blessed, precisely what he had them tell to John, when he was asked what his teaching consisted in.

(2) This meaning is entirely in accord with the meaning of the teaching after and before the sermon on the mount.

John was a mendicant, a vagrant. Jesus was a vagrant all his life. Jesus taught that the rich could not enter the kingdom of heaven and that one must renounce everything, and so forth, and nearly the whole sermon on the mount speaks of nothing else. The sermon of the mount begins by saying that the vagrants are blessed, and ends by saying that we must not collect, but live as the birds and field flowers live.

From all this it is clear that the word $\tau\hat{\varphi}$ $\pi\nu\epsilon\acute{\nu}\mu\alpha\tau\iota$ is not omitted in Luke, but is added in Matthew. But why and how was it added?

It may be that in some version it said, Blessed in the spirit are the poor $\mu\alpha\kappa\acute{\alpha}\rho\iota o\iota$ $o\acute{\iota}$ $\pi\tau\omega\chi o\grave{\iota}$ $\tau\hat{\varphi}$ $\pi\nu\epsilon\acute{\nu}\mu\alpha\tau\iota$, that is, that the mendicants, the vagrants, are still blessed in the spirit. This would explain the appearance in this passage of the unexpected word $\tau\hat{\varphi}$ $\pi\nu\epsilon\acute{\nu}\mu\alpha\tau\iota$. In copying and orally repeating the passage, it was natural for men who were guided by the same feeling which took possession of the rich youth, when he heard that the kingdom of God belonged to the homeless men, to transfer this $\tau\hat{\varphi}$ $\pi\nu\epsilon\acute{\nu}\mu\alpha\tau\iota$ to $\pi\tau\omega\chi o\acute{\iota}$, and, as St. Jerome did, to explain that Jesus purposely added *in the spirit*, that we might understand that the humble, and not the poor, were meant. The obscured meaning of these first words of Matthew had this effect, that in copying there entered into these first verses of Matthew the utterances which have nothing at all in common with the first beatitude, namely, verses 5–9:

5. Blessed are the meek: for they shall inherit the earth.
6. Blessed are they which do hunger and thirst after righteousness: for they shall be filled.
7. Blessed are the merciful: for they shall obtain mercy.
8. Blessed are the pure in heart: for they shall see God.
9. Blessed are the peacemakers: for they shall be called the children of God.

The ideas expressed in these verses, outside of the obscurity of some of them, and of the fact that these utterances are repetitions of utterances in the Old Testament, really express nothing which is not expressed more appropriately and more strongly in other passages of the Gospel; here they are obviously out of place and accidental.

With the obscure meaning which is gotten from the third verse by the addition of the word *spirit*, they may have been added; but with the clear meaning which Luke's version gives, they are evidently out of place and impair the sense. And so I omit $\tau\hat{\omega}$ $\pi\nu\epsilon\acute{\upsilon}\mu\alpha\tau\iota$ as an unintelligible word, as also the interpolated verses. In order that it may be clear that this omission changes nothing in the meaning of the sermon and introduces no new ideas, I copy here the interpretations of the church and of Reuss. From either it is apparent that the interpreters invent a meaning, which could be attached to any most obscure and unimportant words.

Meek: Meekness is expressed mainly in the patient endurance of offences offered by others. It is not a weakness of character, not a neglect of one's legal rights, not cowardice, but a quality which is opposed to anger, malice, and revengefulness. The meek man, in bearing an insult, is convinced that God in his justice will himself avenge his insult, if that is necessary (Rom. xii. 19). Meekness brings forth peace and subdues wrath and wrangling.

Inherit the earth: A metaphorical expression borrowed, no doubt, from the inheritance of the promised land by the Jews. The promise of inheriting the land of Canaan was an expression of good-will, of the highest good. Thus this expression in the passage under discussion does not signify that the meek will get the possession of the land, but that they will receive the highest blessings, the highest good, especially in the life to come. However, the sensuous goods in this life are not excluded here.

Since a meek man may think that he is losing his property, Christ promises the opposite, saying that the meek man safely holds his possessions, — he is not impudent, or ambitious; but he who, on the contrary, will be such, will lose even the inherited possessions, and will even cause the ruin of his soul. Consequently the promises of the Saviour signify that the meek in his kingdom will receive the benefits which he brings with him, both here, upon earth, and above, in the kingdom of heaven.

Which do hunger and thirst after righteousness: Hunger and thirst serve as a picture of a strong desire to receive this or that spiritual good. Righteousness is truth before God, or the justification before the judgment of God's truth, brought forward by our Lord Jesus and appropriated by man by his faith in its redeeming action.

To hunger and thirst after righteousness thus signifies a strong desire, like physical hunger and thirst, to be righteous before God by faith in the Lord Christ as the redeemer of the world.

They shall be filled: That is, with this righteousness; the justification will be given to them in the kingdom of Messiah, they will obtain it, will be brought to it. If we understand here righteousness in the narrower sense of the word, as that species of righteousness which is the opposite to the love of litigation, we may by *being filled* understand a sensuous reward, for he who loves justice possesses everything with security. They shall be filled even here, because they are satisfied with little, and still more in the world to come.

The merciful: Those who will be touched by the misfortunes and in general by the sufferings of others, and help them in whatever way they can, with their efforts or counsels, or condescensions to their foibles, or in general with what their neighbours may have a need of. For this they shall themselves be dealt with mercifully. The Lord himself will be merciful to them for their mercy. He will receive them into his kingdom, which in itself serves as a sign of God's mercy toward man.

However, they shall obtain mercy even here from men, for he who yesterday has shown mercy and to-day has fallen into misfortune will obtain mercy from all.

The pure in heart: Those whose actions, thoughts, intentions, and moral rules of activity are pure, unselfish, and truthful, — in general men who preserve their spiritual purity, who have obtained absolute purity and are not conscious of any cunning, or who pass their lives in chastity, for, in order to see God, we have no other need than this virtue.

Shall see God: Not only in spiritual contemplation, but also with their physical eyes, in his manifestations, and not only in the world to come, when with all the saints they will enjoy the contemplation of God, but also in this world, when in the purity of their hearts they will be more able than any one else to see God in his proper beauty and to enter into communion with him. As a mirror reflects the pictures when it is pure, thus only a pure heart can contemplate God and comprehend the Scripture. This promise does not contradict those passages of Scripture where mention is made of the impossibility of seeing God, for in those latter passages reference is had to the full vision or comprehension of God in his essence, which is really impossible;

Scripture frequently speaks of seeing God, in so far as that is possible for man, for God reveals himself to man in accessible images, though in himself he is purest spirit.

Peacemakers: Those who, living in the world with all, use their means, their influence, for making peace among men in any relation whatever, who avert contentions and discord, who make peace among antagonists, and so forth.

Children of God: All the believers are children of one heavenly Father, but especially the peacemakers.

God is a God of peace: Those who make peace among men are like to God particularly in this, and are especially worthy to be called the children of God. They are particularly like the God-man, who came upon earth for the especial reason that he might reconcile God and men, and in this case they are indeed the children of the God-man.

Shall be called: That is, shall actually be such.

Reuss (p. 196):

Nous pensons qu'on peut facilement ramener toutes les qualités du vrai disciple de Christ, énumérées dans notre texte, à cette idée fondamentale et simple. La *pauvreté* en esprit n'est donc ni la misère matérielle supportée pieusement, ni le manque de capacités intellectuelles. Elle est opposée à la richesse imaginaire, qui est essentiellement celle de l'homme qui prétend être moralement parfait ou quitte envers Dieu; et de même qu'elle a la conscience de ce qui lui manque à cet égard, elle s'empresse aussi d'aller à la véritable source du bien et de la vérité. (Le terme est fréquemment employé dans les Psaumes dans un sens analogue.) Les autres qualifications n'ont pas besoin d'explication; nous aurons seulement à justifier l'emploi du mot *résigné*, que nos prédécesseurs remplacent par *doux* et *débonnaire*. Cette dernière version est acceptable, et semble bien s'accorder avec la *miséricorde* et l'esprit *pacifique*. Mais comme dans les premières phrases il s'agit plutôt de rapports religieux que sociaux, et qu'à vrai dire tout se concentre dans l'idée qu'il faut agir de manière à être bien avec Dieu, la *douceur* d'humeur s'exprimera dans la soumission à la volonté suprême, l'amour de la *paix* se révélera dans l'abnégation, dans la patience, dans le renoncement à la lutte aggressive ou rémunératrice avec le monde (v. 38 suiv.). Et la *miséricorde* même (dont le nom en hébreu est identique avec celui de la charité) peut rentrer dans le même cercle d'idées. La *pureté* du cœur est naturellement opposée à la pureté légale, à une pratique réglementaire des devoirs civils ou rituels. Enfin la *justice*, qui dans le sens judaïque est l'exact accomplissement des prescriptions positives, sera dans le sens évangélique (v. 20) la perfection intérieure, telle que la suite du discours la décrira par une série d'exemples.

(d) ὅτι ὑμετέρα ἐστὶν means *is accessible to you*, you are already in the kingdom of God, because you are vagrants. The kingdom of God is open and accessible to vagrants and closed against rich men.

	Luke vi.	
21. Μακάριοι οἱ κλαίοντες νῦν, ὅτι γελάσετε.	21. Blessed are ye that weep now: for ye shall laugh.	21. Happy are those who weep now, for you will laugh.
22. Μακάριοί ἐστε, ὅταν μισήσωσιν ὑμᾶς οἱ ἄνθρωποι, καὶ ὅταν ἀφορίσωσιν ὑμᾶς, καὶ ὀνειδίσωσι, καὶ ἐκβάλωσι τὸ ὄνομα ὑμῶν ὡς πονηρὸν, ἕνεκα τοῦ υἱοῦ τοῦ ἀνθρώπου.	22. Blessed are ye, when men shall hate you, and when they shall separate you from their company, and shall reproach you, and cast out your name as evil, for the Son of man's sake.	22. Happy are you, when men will account you for nothing and will renounce you, and reproach you, and condemn your work, and call it bad for the sake of the son of man.
23. Χαίρετε ἐν ἐκείνῃ τῇ ἡμέρᾳ καὶ σκιρτήσατε· ἰδοὺ γὰρ, ὁ μισθὸς ὑμῶν πολὺς ἐν τῷ οὐρανῷ· κατὰ ταῦτα γὰρ ἐποίουν τοῖς προφήταις οἱ πατέρες αὐτῶν.	23. Rejoice ye in that day, and leap for joy: for, behold, your reward is great in heaven: for in the like manner did their fathers unto the prophets.	23. Rejoice then and dance, for your reward is great with God. Their fathers did the same with the prophets.
24. Πλὴν οὐαὶ ὑμῖν τοῖς πλουσίοις, ὅτι ἀπέχετε τὴν παράκλησιν ὑμῶν.	24. But* woe unto you, that are rich! for ye have received your consolation.*	24. But pitiable are you who are rich! You are pitiable, because you remove consolation from yourselves.
25. Οὐαὶ ὑμῖν, οἱ ἐμπεπλησμένοι, ὅτι πεινάσετε. οὐαὶ ὑμῖν, οἱ γελῶντες νῦν, ὅτι πενθήσετε καὶ κλαύσετε.	25. Woe unto you that are full! for ye shall hunger. Woe unto you that laugh now! for ye shall mourn and weep.	25. Pitiable are you that are full! for you will be suffering. Pitiable are you who laugh now! for you will mourn and weep.
26. Οὐαὶ ὑμῖν, ὅταν καλῶς ὑμᾶς εἴπωσι πάντες οἱ ἄνθρωποι· κατὰ ταῦτα γὰρ ἐποίουν τοῖς ψευδοπροφήταις οἱ πατέρες αὐτῶν.	26. Woe unto you, when all men shall speak well of you! for so did their fathers to the false prophets.	26. Pitiable you are, when all men praise you! for so did their fathers praise the false prophets.

(a) οὐαί with the dative cannot be translated otherwise than by the adjective *pitiable*.

(b) πλήν, which points to contradistinction, shows that οὐαί with the dative is opposed to μακάριος.

(c) The words ὅτι ἀπέχετε τὴν παράκλησιν ὑμῶν is generally translated in the most incorrect manner possible, *received consolation.* ἀπέχω means *to remove from one*, that is, not to enter the kingdom of God. This expression corresponds to the expression, Because yours is the kingdom of God. As the subsequent beatitudes are the result of poverty, so here the subsequent misfortunes are the consequences of the rejection of the consolation of the kingdom of God.

From the whole teaching and example of Jesus it follows that, in order to obtain the kingdom of God, it is necessary not to care for the carnal life. John, who was the first to proclaim the kingdom of God, lived in the wilderness. Jesus, too, went into the wilderness, and after the wilderness lived without a home and without possessions. The chief idea of the temptation is the renunciation of worldly goods.

The discourse with Simon and with the whore, the parable of the Pharisee and the tax-collector, the instruction as to what defiles man, the conversation with the woman of Samaria, the discourse with the Pharisees and with Nicodemus, express the uselessness of everything earthly and carnal for the human good and for life. The parable of the sprouting seeds, where it says that the two chief obstacles for entering the kingdom of God are the fear of persecutions and the love of riches, everything speaks of the renunciation of earthly cares. A man who has renounced all earthly cares is a mendicant.

And so Jesus names directly that external condition which is necessary in order to enter the kingdom of God. He says, Blessed are the poor, for theirs is the kingdom of God.

In the discourse concerning John, Jesus said that the teaching consisted in this, that the mendicants, the vagrants, were blessed.

Before this the proposition that for one's good one must not care for earthly things resulted from other propositions, but now Jesus, in expounding the essence of his teaching, says, as he turns to the multitude and expresses his idea in intelligible words, that only the mendicant and vagrant can enter the kingdom of God; and that the rich, those who are filled and praised, will not enter it, because riches, overfeeding, and fame remove the kingdom of God, and the rest of the sermon is only a proof of this proposition.

THE SALT OF THE EARTH, THE LIGHT OF THE WORLD

13. 'Υμεῖς ἐστε τὸ ἅλας τῆς γῆς· ἐὰν δὲ τὸ ἅλας μωρανθῇ, ἐν τίνι ἁλισθήσεται; εἰς οὐδὲν ἰσχύει ἔτι, εἰ μὴ βληθῆναι ἔξω, καὶ καταπατεῖσθαι ὑπὸ τῶν ἀνθρώπων.	*Matt. v.* 13. Ye are the salt of the earth : but if the salt have lost his savour, wherewith shall it be salted? it is thenceforth good for nothing, but to be cast out, and to be trodden under foot of men.	13. You are the salt of the world. If the salt is not salted, with what shall we salt? It is not good for anything, but to be thrown under people's feet.

(*a*) γῆ *the inhabited earth, the world,* and so I translate it by *the whole world.*

(*b*) μωρανθῇ means *will grow bad,* but it cannot be translated otherwise than by *lose its saltiness.* The salt in Palestine was not like ours, which is evaporated or mined, and easily lost its saltiness.

The meaning is that you serve as the salt for the world, that is, make it good; but if the salt is no longer salt, what will season the world of men, what will make them good ?

14. 'Υμεῖς ἐστε τὸ φῶς τοῦ κόσμου· οὐ δύναται πόλις κρυβῆναι ἐπάνω ὄρους κειμένη·	*Matt. v.* 14. Ye are the light of the world. A city that is set on a hill cannot be hid.	14. A city that is set on a hill cannot be hid.

15. Οὐδὲ καίουσι λύχνον καὶ τιθέασιν αὐτὸν ὑπὸ τὸν μόδιον, ἀλλ' ἐπὶ τὴν λυχνίαν, καὶ λάμπει πᾶσι τοῖς ἐν τῇ οἰκίᾳ.

16. Οὕτω λαμψάτω τὸ φῶς ὑμῶν ἔμπροσθεν τῶν ἀνθρώπων, ὅπως ἴδωσιν ὑμῶν τὰ καλὰ ἔργα, καὶ δοξάσωσι τὸν πατέρα ὑμῶν τὸν ἐν τοῖς οὐρανοῖς.

15. Neither do men light a candle, and put it under a bushel, but on a candlestick; and it giveth light unto all that are in the house.

16. Let your light so shine before men, that they may see your good works, and glorify* your Father which is in heaven.

15. And he who lights a candle does not put it under a bushel, but on a candlestick, that it may light all in the room.

16. Let your light so shine before men, that they may see your good works and understand God your Father.

(a) δοξάζω to think, understand, assume. "Glorify" is a metaphorical meaning, which is not applicable here.

This is the way the passage is explained by the church:

Ye: Refers both to the nearest disciples of the Lord, who heard him directly, and to all other disciples of Christ, to true Christians.

The salt of the earth: An allegorical expression. Salt preserves eatables against corruption and makes food wholesome and agreeable. Similarly Christians must by their activity, their conduct, and their example preserve the world against moral corruption and decay, and succour its moral health. By attracting divine blessing with their prayers and having a moral influence on their surroundings by the purity of their lives, they must avert the complete fall of the world into vices and crimes, develop and strengthen in it healthy ideas and conceptions and healthy principles for moral activity.

But if the salt have lost its savour, etc.: Will become unsalted; that, of course, is impossible, but the Saviour only assumes the case: if it happened that the salt became unsalted. Still, travellers have observed that in those countries there is a kind of salt which entirely loses its power and is good for nothing except to be thrown out into the road, to be tramped upon by men.

" I broke off a piece of such salt," says one of the travellers (Mondrel, *Nach Palestina*, p. 162), "and put it out in the rain, the sun, and the air, and though some crystals of salt could be seen, it had entirely lost its power. But within the power was preserved, as an experiment taught me."

This metaphorical expression means: If you, my disciples and teachers of the universe, should lose your inner, moral worth and influence on the world, what could give it power and influence? Nothing. Even if you should prove impotent to renovate the world, having preserved it against further corruption and morally strengthened it, what will become of it and what will strengthen you and make you capable of renovating the world? Nothing, and you yourselves will perish, like salt which has lost its power and is thrown out to be trodden upon. Especially, if a teacher loses his mind, that is, does not teach, arraign, and correct, and grows lazy, how will he mend? He must be deprived of his vocation and be subject to contempt.

Ye are the light of the world: Again an allegorical expression. By the light, or rather the luminary, of the world the sun is meant. The sun makes objects visible, shows their form, beauty, or monstrousness, and revives.

The word *light* is used in speech concerning mental and moral enlightenment. The light is the source and image of enlightenment. In this sense the appellation of light refers more particularly to our Lord Jesus, for he is the light which enlightens the world, the source of light of every vision. The apostles, Christ's disciples, and all true Christian believers are the rays of the sun of righteousness and the candlesticks of the world to the extent to which they by their lives and teaching enlighten that which God himself announces to us about himself: they must enlighten the blind mentally and vivify those who are like the dead.

Of the world: Again not the world (as in v. 13) of one nation, but of the whole universe.

A city cannot be hid, etc.: Many cities of Judea, as of other countries, were situated on tops of mountains or hills, so that they could be seen from afar. Mondrel says that near the place where (presumably) the Lord delivered this sermon, there is still a little town called Safat (ancient discourse), which is seen from afar, and it may be that the Saviour, pronouncing these words, pointed to this town, comparing it with his disciples. They are visible from a distance and must be seen; their actions cannot be concealed: the eyes of the world must be and will be turned toward them. If they were of little spirit and wished to conceal themselves, that would be as unnatural as it would be for a city that stands on a hill to be invisible or hid.

Put it under a bushel: Which would conceal the light; but in that case there would be no reason for lighting the candle. The same is true in relation to the Christian faith and to all Christians. They have to be the light of the faith and with a life that is in conformity with the faith they must enlighten the whole world and extend its benefits upon all. The Christians must not hide it, but must confess and disseminate it everywhere, otherwise Christ's high aim will not be fully attained.

Let your light so shine, etc. : Let your faith, your virtuous life, and your pure confession of faith be visible and known to all and everywhere, in every social condition, in all your public duties, at home and outside your home, in happiness and in misfortune, in wealth and in poverty.

Glorify your Father, etc. : The impelling cause why the Christians must appear so to the world is not that they might be seen by the world, which would be boasting, but only the glory of the heavenly Father. He did not say, Show your virtue, for that is not good, but, Let your light shine by itself in such a way that your enemies even may wonder and glorify, not you, but your heavenly Father. The Pharisees showed their virtues to the world, that they might be seen by men; a Christian must not care for that, but that through him men may glorify God, seeing their high life and purity of faith ; not ambition, which is strictly prohibited by the Saviour, but the glory of God is the aim of a Christian's conduct in relation to others. (Archim. Mikh., Gospel of Matt. pp. 71–74.)

From these interpretations it follows again that these words have really no meaning, no connection with what precedes and what follows, and are said merely that the church might interpret them to us in its own manner.

From Reuss follows the same. Reuss says directly that these words are out of place, and that it is possible to find a meaning for them, and he finds it (Reuss, pp. 198–200):

Ce second morceau non-seulement se détache de ce qui précède et de ce qui suit, de sorte qu'on aurait tort de rechercher péniblement une liaison plus intime des divers éléments, mais les passages parallèles des autres évangiles, que nous avons dû emprunter à quatre contextes absolument différents, peuvent faire naître des doutes au sujet de la place qui est assignée ici aux sentences alléguées. Néanmoins il y aura moyen de leur trouver un sens parfaitement approprié à la tendance de tout ce discours, celui-là même que le rédacteur a dû avoir en vue en les plaçant ici.

Il s'agit encore des disciples de Jésus, mais pas le moins du monde exclusivement de ceux qu'il a appelés ses premiers apôtres. Tout à l'heure il leur a été dit qu'ils avaient à s'attendre à des conflits avec le monde, et à une séparation d'avec lui, laquelle à plusieurs égards serait même un devoir pour eux. Maintenant, au contraire, il leur est parlé de devoirs qui les rapprocheront du monde, qui les mettront avec lui dans des relations directes et suivies. Cela est exprimé d'une manière figurée ou allégorique.

1. *Vous êtes le sel de la terre.* Le sel sert à assaisonner la nourriture, mais surtout à la préserver de la corruption ou décomposition. Jésus se servait de cette image avec l'application spéciale à la fabrication du pain (Matth. xiii. 33), et de manière que sa pensée ne présente pas d'obscurité. Sur la *terre*, c'est-à-dire dans la grande masse de l'humanité, ses disciples sont et doivent être un élément salutaire, destiné à la pénétrer et à lui communiquer une vertu ou qualité indispensable pour sa santé, comme le levain est pour la pâte de farine une condition de saveur et de salubrité. Il importe donc que ce principe de santé, cette puissance de régénération active, soit réellement en eux d'abord, car si elle faisait défaut, il n'y aurait pas moyen de la remplacer. Le sel qui a perdu sa force, sa nature, ne peut plus la recouvrer, litt.: ne peut plus être *salé* de nouveau, il n'existe pas d'autre matière qui puisse lui donner ce qu'il possédait et ce qu'il aurait perdu. Il convient de se placer au point de vue d'une époque où Jésus lui-même n'y serait plus, et où, par conséquent, il ne susciterait plus d'autres disciples à la place de ceux qui auraient manqué à leur vocation. Il parle ici à la totalité et n'a pas égard à la distinction à faire éventuellement entre ceux qui resteraient fidèles et ceux qui feraient défaut.

2. *Vous êtes la lumière du monde.* Cette seconde image est si populaire qu'il suffira de rappeler qu'elle ne doit pas être restreinte au progrès de l'intelligence. Le Nouveau Testament ne sépare pas dans l'homme la nature spirituelle et la nature morale. Dans le ménage, quand on allume un flambeau, c'est pour éclairer la chambre ; il serait absurde d'aller cacher sous un meuble ce qui doit répandre la clarté. C'est ainsi que ceux qui ont eux-mêmes reçu communication de la lumière que Jésus est venu apporter au monde, doivent à leur tour la faire servir à d'autres. Il ne suffit pas de la posséder soi-même, on ne doit pas s'en contenter comme d'un bien à mettre à profit individuellement: le grand devoir, c'est l'activité au dehors, c'est le travail pour le bien général, ce que l'apôtre plus tard, en se servant d'une autre image, a appelé l'édification. Voilà les *bonnes œuvres* dont parle le texte. S'il s'agissait d'œuvres de bienfaisance, Jésus ne parlerait pas de la nécessité de les faire voir (chap. vi.). *Glorifier Dieu* veut dire, en style biblique, se ranger de son côté, se convertir à lui.

La phrase incidente qui parle de la *ville* bâtie sur la montagne
et qu'on voit de loin, dérange la simplicité de la comparaison, et
pourrait bien avoir été primitivement étrangère à ce contexte.
Elle ne saurait se rapporter au *devoir* dont il vient d'être question, elle constate plutôt un fait. Appliqué aux disciples de
Christ, ce fait, c'est qu'ils se trouveront placés en évidence, que
tous les regards se porteront sur eux ; il en résultera également
des devoirs particuliers qu'il est facile d'entrevoir, mais auxquels
notre texte ne s'arrête pas ; ce serait une exégèse bien singulière
et bien froide qui ferait dire au Seigneur : De même qu'une
ville bâtie sur le haut d'une montagne ne *peut* pas être invisible,
de même vous *devez* vous faire voir.

It is evident that not only by failing to understand
the words, Blessed are the mendicants and vagrants, with
which the discourse begins, but also by intentionally
ascribing to these words another, obscure meaning, the
subsequent elucidation of a falsely understood thought
must have appeared out of place and obscure. But we
need only keep in mind the words and thoughts of Jesus,
and the words about the salt and the light are by no
means obscure, and without them what precedes and
follows would remain obscure.

The words, We the mendicants, the vagrants, are
blessed, because ours is the kingdom of God, are not
flowers of sentimental eloquence, such as the words,
Blessed are the poor in spirit, appear to be, but a terrible,
awful idea for those men who regard as good that position
in society, which they have created for themselves, and a
truth full of joy for all those who are unhappy.

And these words, comprehended in all their significance, demand elucidation, and everything which follows
gives this elucidation. The elucidation is this, that you,
the mendicants, are the salt of the earth, and you are
blessed, because yours is the kingdom of God, but it is
yours only when you are the salty salt, when you know
that blessedness consists in poverty, when you wish it.
Then you are the salt of the earth. You are the adorn-

ment, the meaning of the world. But if you are accidentally vagrants and wish to be something else than
vagrants, you are good for nothing, like unsalted salt, —
then you are the outcasts of the human race. Vagrants,
mendicants, who are not satisfied with their condition,
are good for nothing, and men properly tread them underfoot. By having understood that you are blessed in your
poverty, you are the light of the world, and as the light
is not hid, but put out, so you must not deny your poverty, not hide it, but put it out, like the light. And this
light will shine for other men, and other men, looking at
your voluntary and blessed life of mendicants, will understand the life of the spirit of your Father.

THE ETERNAL LAW

17. Μὴ νομίσητε ὅτι ἦλθον καταλῦσαι τὸν νόμον ἢ τοὺς προφήτας· οὐκ ἦλθον καταλῦσαι, ἀλλὰ πληρῶσαι.

18. Ἀμὴν γὰρ λέγω ὑμῖν, Ἕως ἂν παρέλθῃ ὁ οὐρανὸς καὶ ἡ γῆ ἰῶτα ἓν ἢ μία κεραία οὐ μὴ παρέλθῃ ἀπὸ τοῦ νόμου, ἕως ἂν πάντα γένηται.

19. Ὃς ἐὰν οὖν λύσῃ μίαν τῶν ἐντολῶν τούτων τῶν ἐλαχίστων, καὶ διδάξῃ οὕτω τοὺς ἀνθρώπους, ἐλάχιστος κληθήσεται ἐν τῇ βασιλείᾳ τῶν οὐρανῶν· ὃς δ᾽ ἂν ποιήσῃ καὶ διδάξῃ, οὗτος μέγας κληθήσεται ἐν τῇ βασιλείᾳ τῶν οὐρανῶν.

20. Λέγω γὰρ ὑμῖν, ὅτι ἐὰν μὴ περισσεύσῃ ἡ δικαιοσύνη ὑμῶν πλεῖον τῶν γραμματέων καὶ Φαρισαίων, οὐ μὴ εἰσέλθητε εἰς τὴν βασιλείαν τῶν οὐρανῶν.

Matt. v. 17. Think not that I am come to destroy the law,[b] or the prophets:[c] I am not come to destroy, but to fulfil.

18. For verily I say unto you, Till heaven and earth pass, one jot or one tittle shall in no wise pass from the law, till all be fulfilled.[d]

19. Whosoever therefore shall break[e] one of these[f] least commandments[g] and shall teach men so, he shall be called the least in the kingdom of heaven: but whosoever shall do and teach them, the same shall be called great in the kingdom of heaven.

20. For I say unto you, That except your righteousness shall exceed the righteousness of the scribes and Pharisees, ye shall in no case enter into the kingdom of heaven.

17. Do not think that I am teaching how to destroy the law. I am not teaching to destroy, but to fulfil.

18. Verily I tell you, As long as heaven and earth stand, so long will every statute of the law stand before you, until it is fulfilled.

19. So that if any one will regard as unnecessary even one of these few rules and will teach men so, he will be the least in the kingdom of God. But he who will do and teach will be the greatest in the kingdom of God.

20. I tell you in advance that if your fulfilment will be such as is the fulfilment of the scribes and the Pharisees, you will in no case enter into the kingdom of God.

(*a*) ἔρχομαι has in all places, where it has for a modifier a verb or a verbal noun, to be translated by *to come, to disclose, show, teach*, or simply by *to show, teach*.

(*b*) καταλῦσαι means *to destroy*, and νόμος with the article means in the whole Gospel *the law of God*, in distinction from the law of Moses, which was always expressed by the same word, but without the article. Examples of the use of the law in general with the article is to be found in the Gospel:

Matt. xxii. 36. Διδάσκαλε, ποία ἐντολὴ μεγάλη ἐν τῷ νόμῳ;

Matt. xxiii. 23. Οὐαὶ ὑμῖν, γραμματεῖς καὶ Φαρισαῖοι, ὑποκριταί, ὅτι ἀποδεκατοῦτε τὸ ἡδύοσμον καὶ τὸ ἄνηθον καὶ τὸ κύμινον, καὶ ἀφήκατε τὰ βαρύτερα τοῦ νόμου, τὴν κρίσιν. . . .

Examples of the use of the law of Moses without the article:

Luke ii. 23 and 24. Παραστῆσαι τῷ Κυρίῳ, καθὼς γέγραπται ἐν νόμῳ Κυρίου, . . . καὶ τοῦ δοῦναι θυσίαν, κατὰ τὸ εἰρημένον ἐν νόμῳ Κυρίου, 'Ζεῦγος τρυγόνων ἢ δύο νεοσσοὺς περιστερῶν,' but especially there are examples of both in the epistles.

(*c*) In many texts the words ἢ τοὺς προφήτας are omitted.

The law and the prophets was a customary expression, and so it was easy to attach προφῆται to the word νόμος; but this addition breaks the sense, for there is no reference here to the law and the prophets, but to the law in general.

Jesus says, From everything which you have heard and seen of me, — the rejection of ceremonies, of the temple, and now, my saying that blessed are the vagrants and admonishing all to become vagrants, — you may think that I loose people's hands and say, Do as you please, there is neither good, nor bad, nor law. Do not think so: I do not teach that at all, — I do not teach lawlessness, but the fulfilment of the law, namely, of this, — and he goes on to speak of the short rules which he gives : He who will do so, that is, as I am going to tell you, will be in the kingdom of God.

More than that. In some of the quotations of the Fathers the whole passage reads as follows : τὶ δοκεῖτε; ὅτι ἦλθον πληρῶσαι τὸν νόμον ἢ τοὺς προφήτας; οὐκ ἦλθον πληρῶσαι, ἀλλὰ καταλῦσαι. Word for word, What do you think? That I have come to fulfil the law or the prophets? I did not come to fulfil, but to destroy. Only in this context are the words or the prophets intelligible. Apparently this whole turn of speech was not accepted in the canon, but the words *or the prophets* were taken and transferred into the sentence where they are unintelligible.

(*d*) This whole eighteenth verse has served up to the present as a stumbling-block for the theologians.

This is what Reuss says (pp. 202 and 203):

A première vue on dirait que l'intention du Seigneur est de déclarer, de la manière la plus positive et la plus énergique, qu'il entend maintenir l'autorité absolue de la Loi jusque dans ses moindres parties. (*La loi et les Prophètes*, c'est la formule consacrée dans la synagogue pour désigner les livres saints dont on faisait lecture à la communauté assemblée. Voyez notre histoire du Canon, chap I.) Mais en y réfléchissant, on est d'abord arrêté par le fait que l'Église chrétienne a mis de côté une bonne partie de la Loi, celle-là même à laquelle les contemporains de Jésus attachaient le plus d'importance; ensuite on se souvient que l'apôtre Paul a proclamé très-hautement la déchéance de la Loi, pour y substituer un principe régulateur tout différent. Enfin on se représente nécessairement les nombreuses occasions où Jésus lui-même, ou bien se met au-dessus de la Loi (Marc ii. 27. Matth. xii. 6, etc.), ou bien en proclame la fin (Marc xiv. 58. Jean iv. 24), ou la réduit à l'un de ses éléments de manière à écarter les autres ou du moins à les refouler sur l'arrière-plan (Matth. xxiii. 23 ; vii. 12 ; xxii. 40 ; ix. 13, etc.), ou enfin la condamne directement comme imparfaite (Matth. xix. 8, comp. xv. 11 suiv.). A moins de supposer un changement survenu dans ses idées, ou une contradiction flagrante dans les traditions relatives à son enseignement, on se trouve donc dans une grande perplexité en face des versets 18 et 19 de notre texte, et beaucoup d'interprètes n'ont cru pouvoir se tirer d'embarras qu'en accusant les judéo-chrétiens d'avoir coloré à leur gré les paroles du Maître, si tant est qu'ils ne l'aient pas fait parler tout à fait gratuitement dans leur sens. D'autres encore, fermant les yeux sur tout le reste, se sont arrêtés à ces déclarations pour en conclure que Jésus ne s'est point élevé, pour sa part, au-dessus du niveau de la conception de ses disciples galiléens. Nous ne parlons pas d'une troisième supposition, absolument inadmissible, qui consiste à dire que Jésus n'a eu en vue ici que la loi morale.

Ces suppositions sont infirmées d'un côté déjà par le fait que Luc, l'évangéliste dit paulinien et universaliste, reproduit la même assertion, de l'autre par celui que notre texte même contient des éléments très-caractéristiques dans le sens évangélique et anti-légal. Il ne peut donc être question, ni de rejeter les déclarations des versets 18 et 19 comme purement et simplement inauthentiques, ni de les accepter dans un sens qui serait absolument incompatible avec ce dernier point de vue.

All that is quite true, except the last frivolous and entirely unjustifiable conclusion that it is inadmissible to assume that Jesus has in view only the moral law. This bold denial is surprising.

Still more surprising is the mention of Luke's text as overthrowing all the assumed explanations. Such a bold denial of the only clear and simple meaning which this verse has would be absolutely inexplicable if we did not see that the meaning of the discourse was unintelligible from the very beginning. The failure to understand the simple meaning, and the substitution of an artificial one, has taken place here also for the same reason that this has happened in verses 14–16.

To the first verses of the beatitudes, which is the thesis of the whole discourse, a false meaning has been given, so how could they help but blunder in the explanation of what follows?

For Reuss (just as for the church) the verses about the salt and the light are an interpolation which is not connected with what precedes, and the whole discourse, from the seventeenth to the forty-eighth verse of Chapter V. of Matthew is an obtrusive interpolation. Reuss says directly (p. 202):

Ce morceau qui ne se trouve dans aucune liaison d'idées avec celui qui précède et dont il ne se rencontre que quelques fragments dans la rédaction de Luc, forme un tout, et doit être étudié dans son ensemble, quoique l'évangéliste y ait inséré par ci par là des éléments qui, tout en présentant quelque analogie avec le texte principal, lui ont été primitivement étrangers. Cette circonstance nous explique pourquoi cette page, l'une des plus belles et des plus importantes dans les Évangiles, offre maintenant quelques difficultés et a pu donner lieu à des méprises. Il est facile de voir que Jésus parle ici de sa position à l'égard de la Loi. La question est de savoir au juste ce qu'il en dit.

This is what the church says:

Verily I say unto you: An assertion of the indubitableness of what is said.

Till heaven and earth pass, etc.: As long as this world stands, that is, to the end of time, or, Sooner will heaven and earth pass, sooner will there be an end to the world than that the law will remain unfulfilled in its spirit and its essence.

Jot: A letter of the Hebrew alphabet, a line, a small turn, by which one letter differs from another, which it resembles in form; these words state that the least and apparently most insignificant part of the law will not pass, will not remain without fulfilment, as the immutable word of God, which cannot be void and remain without fulfilment.

Till all be fulfilled: That is, in the spirit and in the essence, and not according to the letter. The whole law was a shadow of the future; when the body itself appeared, the shadow lost its significance, but at the same time there was fulfilled what the shadow pointed to. The obsolete Old Testament was obliterated; it gave way to a most perfect one, of which it was only the shadow. He who fulfils the New Testament at the same time fulfils the Old, not according to the dead letter, but in the highest perfection, as, for example, he who is not angry with his brother fulfils in the highest degree the commandment, Thou shalt not kill, for he who is not angry cannot kill, and so forth.

This explanation, like all church explanations, explains nothing as to what is to be understood by the word of God, and in what relation Christ's teaching stands to the law of Moses, and what is to be understood by the law.

All we have to do is not to disrupt the teaching and to view it in connection with what precedes and follows, and again the meaning is not only clear, but also conclusive. Jesus says, One has to be a mendicant, a vagrant, in order to enter the kingdom of God, that is, to renounce all the forms of life. The vagrant has always been a detested being, to whom, as it were, everything is permitted, who is outside of the law. In verses 15 and 16 Jesus said, One must be a voluntary vagrant and not against one's will; in these two verses he again says that one has to be a vagrant, not one who is outside of the law, for whom there is no law, and to whom everything is permitted, but a vagrant who fulfils the law, that is, certain rules.

The word νόμος with the article is to be understood as the *loi morale*.

The context in Luke, which Reuss adduces so frivolously in confirmation of his discussion, shows as clearly as possible, from the very passage where it is found, what is to be understood by νόμος and by the phrase, Not one jot of the law shall pass.

Luke xvi. 16. The law and the prophets were until John: since that time the kingdom of God is preached, and every man presseth into it.

It says, The law and the prophets, that is, the written, Jewish law was needed before John, but now, The kingdom of God is announced, and so forth, and soon after, It is easier for heaven and earth to pass, than one tittle of the law to fail. Either Luke purposely put together two verses that contradict each other, or he understood by, The law and the prophets, what was destroyed since the time of John, or by the law, without the addition of the prophets, he meant that other thing which can never be destroyed as long as there are men.

The understanding of the law as the *loi morale*, and the writing it without the article, are particularly clear in the following passages from Paul's epistles to the Romans:

Rom. iii. 27. Where is boasting then? It is excluded. By what law? of works? Nay; but by the law of faith.

28. Therefore we conclude that a man is justified by faith without the deeds of the law.

31. Do we then make void the law through faith? God forbid: yea, we establish the law.

Here reference is made to the law and the prophets, to the written law, then again:

Rom. vii. 16. If then I do that which I would not, I consent unto the law that it is good.

21. I find then a law, that, when I would do good, evil is present with me.

23. But I see another law in my members, warring against the law of my mind, and bringing me into captivity to the law of sin which is in my members.

Here reference is made to the *loi morale*. That the moral law is meant is also evident from this, that at the end of the sermon, after counting out everything which ought to be done, Jesus says, In this, that is, in these small rules, lies the whole law and the prophets, that is, these few rules take the place of the whole written law. Jesus says, I do not destroy the law; on the contrary, I fulfil it, because the law exists for man more unchangeably than heaven and earth, — until all be done.

In Luke we must understand it: Until all shall be done according to the law.

The idea is that the law, the indication of what must be done, existed, and will exist, as long as the world exists and until all shall be fulfilled, that is, the law can fail to exist only in two cases: (1) if the world came to an end, (2) if men always executed the law, since the law is only an indication of what is not executed, an indication of the deviation.

(ε) λυειν cannot be translated otherwise than by *to regard as unnecessary*.

John v. 18.   Therefore the Jews sought the more to kill him, because he not only had broken the sabbath, but said also that God was his Father, making himself equal with God.

John vii. 23.   If a man on the sabbath day receive circumcision, that the law of Moses should not be broken ; are ye angry at me, because I have made a man every whit whole on the sabbath day ?

(ƒ) ἐντολή *command*.   I do not translate it by *commandment*, because with this word we are wont in Russian to connect the idea of the commandments of Moses.

(g) τούτων refers to the commandments, commands, rules.

If we do not keep in mind the fact that the meaning of the discourse was distorted in the beginning, it will be difficult to understand why this word τούτων is, as it were, omitted and referred to the commandments of the law of Moses.   If the reference were to the commandments of Moses, why would it be said, These commandments ?   What these ?   All ?   If so, it would not be necessary to say these, which will be mentioned only to be destroyed.   How, then, does it say that not one letter of the law will be lost ?   And yet the church and Reuss take the eighteenth and nineteenth verses to refer to the commandments of Moses.

Reuss says (p. 203):

Nous pourrions encore demander la permission de regarder les deux versets suivants comme n'étant pas ici à leur vraie place, et le 20ᵐᵉ comme se rattachant directement au 17ᵐᵉ, mais nous n'insistons pas sur cette simplification.

The church says (Archim. Mikh., Gospel of Matt., p. 76):

Break: Transgress, do what is contrary to the commandment, or by a distorted interpretation to take away the obligatory force of the commandment, for example, by representing the commandment as of little importance and its violation as not a sinful matter and the guilty person as not subject to responsibility or subject to small responsibility.

One of these least commandments: The Pharisees divided the commandments of the law into two classes, into large and small ones, and of the latter they said that it is no sin to break them, though among them they placed the commandments which have reference to the very essence of the law, to love, charity, justice. It is of these that the Lord is speaking, calling them the least according to the false conception of the Pharisees.

After that it says:

St. Chrysostom and Theophilactes, on the other hand, interpret this differently: they say that the Lord does not call the least the commandments of the law of the Old Testament, but those which he intended to give, and that he calls them so from humility; as he has humbled himself and in many places speaks modestly of himself, so he also speaks of his law.

And after all we do not find out how it is to be understood.

Jesus says, You shall be vagrants, but there is and must be a law for every man, and I will give you a few rules; but if you observe these few rules, you will be in the kingdom of heaven, and, elucidating this, he says, In order to enter the kingdom of God it is necessary to be better than the Pharisees; to enter the kingdom of heaven it is necessary that your righteousness in relation to the law should be greater than the righteousness of the Pharisees, who do not fulfil the law.

FIRST COMMANDMENT: THOU SHALT NOT BE ANGRY

21. Ἠκούσατε ὅτι ἐββέθη τοῖς ἀρχαίοις, Οὐ φονεύσεις· ὃς δ' ἂν φονεύσῃ, ἔνοχος ἔσται τῇ κρίσει.

22. Ἐγὼ δὲ λέγω ὑμῖν, ὅτι πᾶς ὁ ὀργιζόμενος τῷ ἀδελφῷ αὐτοῦ εἰκῆ, ἔνοχος ἔσται τῇ κρίσει· ὃς δ' ἂν εἴπῃ τῷ ἀδελφῷ αὐτοῦ, Ῥακὰ, ἔνοχος ἔσται τῷ συνεδρίῳ· ὃς δ' ἂν εἴπῃ, Μωρὲ, ἔνοχος ἔσται εἰς τὴν γέενναν τοῦ πυρός.

Matt. v. 21. Ye have heard that it was said by them of old time, Thou shalt not kill; and whosoever shall kill shall be in danger of the judgment (Ex. xx. 13):

22. But I say unto you, That whosoever is angry with his brother without a cause[b] shall be in danger of the judgment: and whosoever shall say to his brother, Raca,[c] shall be in danger of the council:[d] but whosoever shall say, Thou fool, shall be in danger of hell fire.[e]

21. You have heard that it was said to those of old time, Thou shalt not kill; he who kills is subject to judgment.

22. But I tell you, He who is angry with his brother is already subject to judgment. And he who says to his brother, Rascal, is subject to criminal prosecution. And he who says to his brother, Crazy, is subject to fire.

(*a*) Book of Numbers xxv. 1–28.

(*b*) In many texts the word εἰκῆ is wanting; it is not in Luther, nor in the Vulgate, nor in Tischendorf's edition, and this word has been acknowledged to be an interpolation. It is superfluous to prove the obviousness of this interpolation. Everybody knows how rudely it contradicts the meaning of the whole teaching, how simply stupid it is. If it is only without a cause that it is not good to be angry, then it is permitted to be angry with a cause. And who will be the judge what is a cause, and what not?

Here is the reflection made upon this occasion by the church (Gospel of Matt., p. 79):

But I say unto you: Christ as the plenipotentiary lawgiver speaks here, as in other passages, as one who hath power, and not as the scribes and Pharisees.

Dost thou see the complete power? Dost thou see the manner of action proper to a lawgiver? Who of the prophets spoke that way? Who of the righteous? Who of the patriarchs? Nobody. Such words spake the Lord, they said, but not so speaketh the son. They gave a law to slaves like themselves, but this one gives it to his slaves.

Angry without a cause: There is an anger which, so to speak, is legitimate, just, when it is directed against sin, against lawlessness, against crime, and grows out of jealousy for the glory of God and salvation of one's neighbour. God himself is angry with the sinners. Christ looked in anger upon the hypocritical Pharisees (Mark iii. 5). Not of such anger is mention made here, but of anger without cause, for nothing, out of selfishness, of the anger which is not based on the love of truth and virtue. If one is angry justly, for the sake of correction through spiritual jealousy, he will not be condemned.

This interpolation is remarkable as an example of those intentional corruptions to which the Gospel was subjected. A tiny word, but how it ruins the whole meaning, and how many other such interpretations there are!

(c) Raca, a Chaldee word which means *contempt;* it may be translated by *apostate* or *rascal.*

(d) Sanhedrim, a special court which for the most part condemned to death.

(e) Gehenna of fire was a valley where men were burnt as sacrifices to Molech. *To give into Gehenna* means *to burn.*

The whole discourse, which is begun with the example of the law of Moses, that one has to be judged for murder, is carried on in accordance with the assumed comparison. According to the law of Moses it is necessary to judge, that is, the highest penalty is to be meted out for murder.

Jesus says, As you have been forbidden to kill, so I with the same severity forbid you to harbour anger in your heart against your brother. Still more severely do I forbid the manifestation of this anger in the expression of contempt for a man, and more severely still a greater manifestation of contempt (crazy, that is a man who cannot be treated rationally).

The degree of the severity of the prohibition is expressed in the punishment, and so Jesus expresses it.

But evidently Jesus prescribes neither the sanhedrim, nor Gehenna. If we are to understand it in that way, the sanhedrim ought to be introduced. If we are to understand it that it is going to be so in the world to come, then it is not clear what that sanhedrim will be.

For that reason it is evident that neither the sanhedrim nor the Gehenna is meant as something which is to be in the next world. The whole significance is only in the greater degree of criminality.

23. Ἐὰν οὖν προσφέρῃς τὸ δῶρόν σου ἐπὶ τὸ θυσιαστήριον, κἀκεῖ μνησθῇς ὅτι ὁ ἀδελφός σου ἔχει τι κατὰ σοῦ,

24. Ἄφες ἐκεῖ τὸ δῶρόν σου ἔμπροσθεν τοῦ θυσιαστηρίου, καὶ ὕπαγε, πρῶτον διαλλάγηθι τῷ ἀδελφῷ σου, καὶ τότε ἐλθὼν πρόσφερε τὸ δῶρόν σου.

Matt. v. 23. Therefore if thou bring thy gift to the altar, and there rememberest that thy brother hath aught against thee;

24. Leave there thy gift before the altar, and go thy way; first be reconciled to thy brother, and then come and offer thy gift.ᵃ

23. So that if thou bringest thy gift to the altar, and there rememberest that thou hast a brother and that he has something against thee;

24. Leave there thy gift before the altar, and go, first make thy peace with thy brother, and then come and offer the gift.

(*a*) Then come and offer thy gift. Before that it was said that God needs no gift. Everything which served for the offering of gifts was driven out of the temple and it was forbidden to carry anything in, and so Jesus could not contradict himself and order a gift to be brought. The last words would be clearer thus: Then, when thou goest and makest thy peace with thy brother, thou by that very fact bringest a gift to God.

That it is necessary thus to understand the words follows from the Lord's prayer, in which all the relation to God is expressed in forgiving those who are indebted to us.

To this verse the church gives the following interpretation (Gospel of Matt., p. 82):
It is more important and necessary to have a right heart than only to fulfil external ceremonies; the latter

without the first have no meaning in the eyes of God, and are important and have power only before God in connection with peace and love of our neighbours. Of course, if there is for some reason no possibility of becoming personally reconciled with our neighbours, we ought to make peace at least in our heart.

Reuss, who has got off the track and is convinced that Jesus is talking only of the commandment of Moses, speaks like this of this passage and of the following verse (p. 207): ⸰

A ce premier exemple le rédacteur rattache deux autres sentences qui lui semblaient appartenir au même ordre d'idées. 1° En opposition avec la colère doit se trouver l'esprit de conciliation. C'est une très-belle pensée, que le rétablissement de l'accord fraternel entre des hommes mal disposés l'un contre l'autre doit primer même ce qu'on appelle le devoir religieux et que Dieu agréera mieux les offrandes qui sont présentées avec de pareils gages de sincérité. Mais cette sentence n'est pas à sa place dans ce contexte, elle n'a rien à faire avec l'explication évangélique du 6° commandement. L'analogie est tout juste assez grande pour nous faire comprendre le procédé du rédacteur. 2° Mais cette analogie n'existe plus du tout et la combinaison devient incompréhensible à l'égard de la seconde sentence que Luc nous a conservée aussi dans un tout autre contexte. En effet, l'adversaire dont il y est question ne peut être qu'un créancier qui emmène son débiteur devant le juge pour le faire condamner à la prison. Le débiteur doit se hâter de s'arranger à l'amiable avec le créancier avant que l'arrêt ne soit prononcé. On dit que par cet exemple de prudence Jésus a voulu faire comprendre l'importance de la réconciliation. Il est possible que l'évangéliste l'ait compris ainsi ; mais outre que l'application est abandonnée à la sagacité des lecteurs, toute cette parabole nous mène bien loin du sujet essentiel du discours.

25. Ἴσθι εὐνοῶν τῷ ἀντιδίκῳ σου ταχύ, ἕως ὅτου εἶ ἐν τῇ ὁδῷ μετ᾽ αὐτοῦ· μήποτέ σε παραδῷ ὁ ἀντίδικος τῷ κριτῇ, καὶ ὁ κριτής σε παραδῷ τῷ ὑπηρέτῃ, καὶ εἰς φυλακὴν βληθήσῃ.

Matt. v. 25. Agree with thine adversary quickly,ᵃ while thou art in the way with him ; lest at any time the adversary deliver thee to the judge, and the judge deliver thee to the officer, and thou be cast into prison.

25. Show thy good-will to thy adversary, while he is still on the way with thee; lest he deliver thee to the judge, and the judge deliver thee to the officer, and thou find thy way into prison.

26. Ἀμὴν λέγω σοι, Οὐ μὴ ἐξέλθῃς ἐκεῖθεν, ἕως ἂν ἀποδῷς τὸν ἔσχατον κοδράντην.

26. Verily I say unto thee, Thou shalt by no means come out thence, till thou hast paid the uttermost farthing.

26. Then, thou know-est thyself, thou wilt not get out of it until thou hast paid the last cent.

(a) The word ταχύ is omitted in many texts, and is unnecessary. The words *on the way* express the same idea, that it is necessary to make peace as soon as possible.

(b) ἀμήν or ἀμὴν λέγω σοι are every time used in those passages where Jesus asserts that which is known to everybody, and so the best translation is, *Thou knowest thyself.*

According to Reuss this sermon is out of place. But according to its real meaning it directly continues the idea as begun.

In regard to anger it says that the inner meaning of restraint from anger lies in this, that it is impossible to think of God, to turn to God, having anger against men. Now reference is made to the external, practical meaning of anger.

Anger is thy enemy, the adversary of truth, ἀντίδικος, and so thou must as quickly as possible get rid of him, as thou knowest that it is more profitable to settle with thy adversary before the trial.

In the same sense this sermon is used in Luke, as will be explained in its place.

In nearly all the explanations of the rules which are given by Jesus, two proofs are adduced why it is neces-sary to do what he commands: one proof is an internal one, why it is good, another an external one, why it is advantageous. And here the example of the reconcilia-tion with the adversary before the trial is an example of the statement that abstinence from anger is not only good, but also profitable.

The same will be true in the next example.

SECOND COMMANDMENT: THOU SHALT NOT COMMIT ADULTERY

27. Ἠκούσατε ὅτι ἐρρέθη τοῖς ἀρχαίοις, Οὐ μοιχεύσεις.

31. Ἐρρέθη δὲ, ὅτι ὃς ἂν ἀπολύσῃ τὴν γυναῖκα αὐτοῦ, δότω αὐτῇ ἀποστάσιον.

32. Ἐγὼ δὲ λέγω ὑμῖν, ὅτι ὃς ἂν ἀπολύσῃ τὴν γυναῖκα αὐτοῦ, παρεκτὸς λόγου πορνείας, ποιεῖ αὐτὴν μοιχᾶσθαι· καὶ ὃς ἐὰν ἀπολελυμένην γαμήσῃ, μοιχᾶται.

28. Ἐγὼ δὲ λέγω ὑμῖν, ὅτι πᾶς ὁ βλέπων γυναῖκα πρὸς τὸ ἐπιθυμῆσαι αὐτῆς ἤδη ἐμοίχευσεν αὐτὴν ἐν τῇ καρδίᾳ αὐτοῦ.

29. Εἰ δὲ ὁ ὀφθαλμὸς σου ὁ δεξιὸς σκανδαλίζει σε, ἔξελε αὐτὸν καὶ βάλε ἀπὸ σοῦ· συμφέρει γάρ σοι ἵνα ἀπόληται ἓν τῶν μελῶν σου, καὶ μὴ ὅλον τὸ σῶμά σου βληθῇ εἰς γέενναν.

30. Καὶ εἰ ἡ δεξιά σου χείρ σκανδαλίζει σε, ἔκκοψον αὐτὴν καὶ βάλε ἀπὸ σοῦ. συμφέρει γάρ σοι ἵνα ἀπόληται ἓν τῶν μελῶν σου, καὶ μὴ ὅλον τὸ σῶμά σου βληθῇ εἰς γέενναν.

Matt. v. 27. Ye have heard that it was said by them of old time, Thou shalt not commit adultery[a] (Isaiah xx. 14).

31. It hath been said, Whosoever shall put away his wife, let him give her a writing of divorcement (Deut. xxiv. 1).

32. But I say unto you, That whosoever shall put away his wife, saving for the cause of fornication, causeth her to commit adultery: and whosoever shall marry her that is divorced committeth adultery.

28. But I say unto you, That whosoever looketh on a woman to lust after her hath committed adultery with her already in his heart.[b]

29. And if thy right eye offend[c] thee, pluck it out, and cast it from thee: for it is profitable for thee that one of thy members[d] should perish, and not that thy whole body should be cast into hell.

30. And if thy right hand offend thee, cut it off, and cast it from thee: for it is profitable for thee that one of thy members should perish, and not that thy whole body should be cast into hell.

27. You have heard that it is said, Thou shalt not commit adultery.

31. And it is said, Whoever will separate from his wife, let him give her a discharge.

32. But I tell you, That whoever separates from his wife, not only commits debauchery, but also causes her to commit adultery. And he who marries a divorced woman also commits adultery.

28. And whoever looks on a woman to lust after her is really committing adultery.

29. If thy eye catches thee, pluck it out, and cast it away from thee, for it is more profitable for thee that one eye should perish, than that thy whole body should burn.

30. If thy right hand catches thee, cut it off, and cast it from thee. It is more profitable for thee that one of thy hands should perish, than that the whole body should burn.

(a) In the Book of Leviticus it says, If a man commits adultery with a married woman or with the wife of his compatriot, both the man and the woman are to be put to death, etc. The words evidently refer to the commandment what to do with the adulterer.

For the clearness of the idea and expression verses thirty-one and thirty-two must follow verse twenty-seven, and then come verses twenty-eight and twenty-nine.

(b) In many texts the words *in his heart* are wanting. It is better to omit these words, because they obscure the meaning.

(c) σκανδαλίζω comes from σκάνδαλον *a trap.*

Here, as everywhere in the gospels, it is used in its direct sense. As a bird which is caught in a net would gladly give up its eyes which have enticed it, that it might not perish altogether, and a fox would give up its paw, only not to be caught in the trap, as it frequently does, by wrenching off its paw, so thou shouldst know that deep is the narrow ditch of a whore, and he who falls into it perishes (Solomon). Thou hadst better tear off all that which entices, catches thee, than that thou shouldst perish all of thee.

(d) The word δεξιός has no meaning whatever here, and nothing is added to the meaning about the adultery, while it only burdens the discourse. Evidently the statement that the right hand which offends thee should be torn off became a proverb first, since it is used by Mark and by Matthew in another place, and then the word δεξιός was also added to ὀφθαλμός.

(e) Instead of the word *member*, I repeat *eye*, as we cannot speak in Russian of the eye as a member.

The words παρεκτὸς λόγου πορνείας (v. 32) seem to me to be incorrectly translated. The detail of the condition when a wife may be sent away is contrary to the whole composition of the teaching.

Either the words have to be omitted, or the comma has to be left out, and the introductory clause must not be referred to the predicate *separates*, but to the predicate *causes her to commit adultery.* Then the meaning will be, A husband by casting off his wife not only commits debauchery, but is also guilty of this, that by abandoning

her he causes both her and him with whom she comes
together to commit adultery.

As with the explanation as to why a man must have
no anger against his brother Jesus gave an internal reason,
— one must not think of God, harbouring resentment, —
and an external reason, — it is worse for the man himself, — so even in this case Jesus says that the internal
reason is this, that a man who abandons himself to lust
causes his soul to perish, and that it is better, as in the
case of the hand, to cut off that which draws him into
ruin, and he says further that the external reason is this,
that every lust, like every anger, grows and spreads of its
own accord.

He says, Every married man ought not to have any
other women and abandon his wife, for, if he abandons
her, she will be incited to commit debauchery, both she
and he who comes together with her, and that there is
then no limit to debauchery.

Reuss again finds that these verses are out of place,
and says (p. 208):

Ici encore le rédacteur intercale quelques sentences intimement liées entre elles, que l'on retrouve ailleurs dans d'autres
contextes, et dont la première pouvait paraître à sa place après
ce qui venait d'être dit du péché commis, ou se manifestant par
un simple regard. La combinaison se fait facilement dans ce
sens : Il vaudrait mieux être aveugle que de se laisser entraîner
à des pensées, éventuellement à des actes, coupables et condui-
sant à la perdition éternelle. Cependant nous concevons des
doutes très-sérieux au sujet de ces sentences qui ne nous parais-
sent pas du tout être à leur place ici. D'abord on ne voit réellement pas ce que la seconde formule (qui parle de la *main* droite)
doit apporter de lumière à la pensée principale. En second lieu,
la mention expresse de l'œil *droit*, écarte complètement la seule
association possible des idées, un homme borgne étant absolument dans la même position qu'un homme qui a ses deux yeux,
dans les circonstances mentionnées ; enfin il est de fait que le
manque de l'un de ces membres ne change pas les instincts
vicieux de l'homme. Il y a même à objecter que le parallélisme

du langage figuré compromet l'idée morale elle-même : Plutôt
perdre un *membre* que le *corps* entier, plutôt renoncer à quelque
chose de moins grand, moins nécessaire, que de perdre le tout.
Avec ce parallélisme le péché serait, à vrai dire, représenté comme
quelque chose de *relativement* inférieur, tandis qu'il est *absolument*
mauvais.   Nous verrons que toutes ces difficultés disparaissent
quand nous retrouverons ces textes dans un autre entourage.

This is what Theophilactes says (Gospel of Matt.,
p. 87):

The Lord does not break the law of Moses, but corrects it, and
forbids the husband to despise his wife without any cause. If he
leaves her for good cause, that is, for adultery, he is not subject
to judgment; but if he leaves her for some other reason than
adultery, he is subject to judgment, because he thus causes her
to commit adultery. But even he who takes her becomes an
adulterer, for if no one took her she might return to her former
husband and submit to him (Cf. Chrys.).

From the interpretations of the church and of Reuss
it follows that Jesus, according to Reuss, gives an example of how to fulfil the law of Moses; according to
Theophilactes, of how to correct the law, that is, that
he merely defines what is to be called an adultery,
whereas Jesus does not define anything, but, as he shows
in the first example of anger why the sons of the kingdom
of God can have no anger, so he shows here why the
children of the kingdom of God must not be adulterers.

He says, If a man will wish to have a woman, he will
thereby cause his soul to perish, and, yielding to this and
changing wives, he will spread debauchery both in women
and in men.   He shows the harm of debauchery in itself,
and does not define what may be done and what not,
what may be called adultery and what may not be called
so.   He gives his second little rule.

The first rule was that thou shalt never be angry.
After he said this little rule, he showed why it is necessary and sensible.

Now he enunciated the second rule, Never regard as good the feeling of love of woman, that which in our Christian society is regarded as a most beautiful thing and is exalted in every manner possible in millions of books. Having said this, Jesus pointed out why this second little rule is necessary and sensible.

THIRD COMMANDMENT: THOU SHALT NOT SWEAR

33. Πάλιν ἠκούσατε ὅτι ἐρρέθη τοῖς ἀρχαίοις, Οὐκ ἐπιορκήσεις, ἀποδώσεις δὲ τῷ Κυρίῳ τοὺς ὅρκους σου.

34. Ἐγὼ δὲ λέγω ὑμῖν μὴ ὀμόσαι ὅλως· μήτε ἐν τῷ οὐρανῷ ὅτι θρόνος ἐστὶ τοῦ Θεοῦ·

35. Μήτε ἐν τῇ γῇ, ὅτι ὑποπόδιόν ἐστι τῶν ποδῶν αὐτοῦ· μήτε εἰς Ἱεροσόλυμα, ὅτι πόλις ἐστὶ τοῦ μεγάλου βασιλέως·

36. Μήτε ἐν τῇ κεφαλῇ σου ὀμόσῃς, ὅτι οὐ δύνασαι μίαν τρίχα λευκὴν ἢ μέλαιναν ποιῆσαι.

37. Ἔστω δὲ ὁ λόγος ὑμῶν, Ναὶ ναί, Οὔ οὔ· τὸ δὲ περισσὸν τούτων ἐκ τοῦ πονηροῦ ἐστιν.

Matt. v. 33. Again, ye have heard that it hath been said by them of old time, Thou shalt not forswear thyself, but shalt perform unto the Lord thine oaths :[a]

34. But I say unto you, Swear not at all;[b] neither by heaven; for it is God's throne :

35. Nor by the earth; for it is his footstool: neither by Jerusalem;[c] for it is the city of the great King.

36. Neither shalt thou swear by thy head, because thou canst not make one hair white or black.

37. But let your communication be, Yea, yea; Nay, nay: for whatsoever is more than[d] these cometh of[e] evil.

33. You have also heard that it has been said to those of old time, Keep thy oath, perform what thou hast sworn before God;

34. But I tell you, Do not swear at all; do not swear by heaven, — God is there;

35. Nor by the earth, — it is God's; nor by the church, — it is also God's.

36. Nor swear by thy head, because thou canst not make one hair of thy head white or black.

37. And so let your words be, Yes, yes; No, no; and what is superfluous in respect to these words is begotten by the devil (deception).

(a) *Lev. xix.* 12. And ye shall not swear by my name falsely, neither shalt thou profane the name of thy God: I am the Lord.

Ex. xx. 7. Thou shalt not take the name of the Lord thy God in vain: for the Lord will not hold him guiltless that taketh his name in vain.

Those are the two passages to which the church points. There are no others. Both passages express the oath differently from what it is expressed here. The idea of the Old Testament is to fulfil the oath.

(*b*) *Do not swear at all*, is given in many texts, and so it ought to be, for the whole strength of this proposition is in the word ὅλως.

(*c*) I say *church* instead of *Jerusalem*, in order to make the expression comprehensible, without changing the meaning.

(*d*) I put in the words *in respect to these words*, more clearly to render the meaning of περισσόν.

(*e*) I put in *begotten*, because that is the meaning of ἐκ.

This is what Reuss has to say about this brief passage, which is remarkable for the prophetic significance which it has for us (pp. 209 and 210):

Le *quatrième exemple* est celui du serment. Le décalogue, au 3e commandement, et la loi en général (Lév. xix. 12), se contentait de défendre le parjure, soit dans le sens propre de ce mot, d'après lequel il signifie un mensonge placé sous le patronage de Dieu invoqué comme témoin, et où il est par conséquent un crime de lèse-majesté divine, soit dans le sens de la rupture d'une promesse faite sous la foi du serment (il ne s'agit pas spécialement dans notre texte de ce qu'on appelle des *vœux*). Jésus va beaucoup plus loin ; il *accomplit* la loi, comme il l'a déjà fait dans l'exemple précédent, de manière à la contredire en quelque sorte, du moins à la représenter comme imparfaite, comme restant au-dessous du niveau auquel doivent se placer les membres du royaume des cieux (Matth. xix. 8). Il interdit le serment péremptoirement. L'usage de cette forme particulière de l'assertion est la conséquence du manque de véracité parmi les hommes, qui ont ainsi voulu se prémunir contre les chances de fraude dont ils auraient pu devenir les victimes. Ce fait seul fait reconnaître le serment comme indigne d'une *société* comme doit l'être celle du royaume des cieux. Là, on se bornera à dire *oui* ou *non*, selon le cas. Cette seule parole doit être une garantie suffisante. Tout ce qu'on y ajouterait, dans le but d'écarter toute méfiance, prouverait plutôt que celle-ci a sa raison d'être et que, par conséquent, le *Malin*, le diable, l'instigateur de tout mal, y a sa main de manière ou d'autre, ne serait-ce que parce que celui qui jure justifie par cela même les soupçons de celui qui demande le serment.

Reuss evidently does not understand the meaning of this passage. The church understands it, but intentionally conceals what it understands, purposely debases the teaching, distorts it, and makes it the servant of its abominable purposes.

This is what the church has to say:

Thou shalt not forswear thyself, etc.: That is not a literal repetition of the law of Moses, as contained in Lev. xix. 12 and Deut. xxiii. 21-23: Ye shall not swear by my name falsely. If thou vowest a vow unto Jehovah thy God, perform it at once. Christ's words apparently express the same as the letter of the law: Thou shalt not swear except for the assertion of a truth, and if thou hast sworn, do not transgress thy oath.

But shalt perform: That is, in thy oath thou must tell the truth, and perform what thou hast promised with an oath. An oath is a solemn assertion in the name of God as to the truth of what is said; whereat it is self-understood that God will make him who swears responsible, if he swears in order to assert an untruth, because by an oath of lying the name of God is desecrated. In the course of time the Jews became accustomed to avoid an oath in the name of God and to swear by different objects, such as heaven, earth, Jerusalem, the temple, and these oaths they did not consider immutable and obligatory, that is, they allowed themselves to swear falsely by them, without apparently breaking the letter of the law.

Swear not at all: By none of the manners of oaths pointed out as being in use, for all was created by God and was created holy, consequently to swear by any creation of his would be the same as swearing by him who created, and to swear falsely by him would impair the sacredness of the oath itself.

Neither by heaven: Heaven is the place of God's especial presence, for which reason it is said to be God's throne. To swear by heaven is also the same as swearing by him who sits on the heavenly throne, that is, by God himself.

Nor by the earth: The earth is called God's footstool, consequently to swear by it would be the same as swearing by God himself.

Neither by Jerusalem: Jerusalem is called the city of the great King, that is, of God, who is the true King, both of every country and more particularly of the Jewish kingdom, the chief city of which was Jerusalem, where was the temple, the only one in the world where God the King could be worshipped.

Neither by the head: The oath by the head was very customary in every-day life, just as among our common people improper oaths of every kind are used. To swear by the head means also the same as swearing by one's life, that is, I give my life, or, Let my life be taken from me, May I die, if what I say is not true. God is the creator of life and it is in his power to take or prolong life; consequently those who swear by it swear by what does not belong to them, but to God, consequently they swear by God himself.

Not one hair: So small is our power to change our life that we cannot even change the colour of our hair; consequently we must not swear by what is not ours.

Yea, yea; Nay, nay: That does not mean that a Christian is always to use these words in place of an oath, but that he must simply and directly assert a truth or deny a lie, tell the truth, and not tell a lie. Besides, everything strengthened by an oath, an asseveration, is from the evil, from the wicked, from untruth, hence from the devil, since he is the cause of every evil.

The prohibition of all swearing at all evidently does not include the legal oath, — which is necessary in social and private life, — the oath by the name of God. He himself confirmed the oath in the court, when to the words of the high priest, I entreat thee by the living God, he replied, Thou hast said, since with the Jews the judge generally pronounced an oath formula, which the defendant applied to himself with the words, Amen, be it as thou hast said.

Apostle Paul invoked God as a witness to the truth of his words, which is evidently the same oath (Rom. i. 9; ix. 1.; 2 Cor. i. 23; ii. 27; Gal. i. 20; Phil. i. 8; 1 Thes. ii. 5; Heb. vi. 16).

Oaths were prescribed by the law of Moses, and the Lord did not do away with these oaths (Ex. xxii. 11; Lev. v. 1; Num. v. 19; Deut. xxix. 12–14).

What is abolished is the empty, hypocritical oaths of the Pharisees.

Here is the third of the rules given by Jesus for the purpose of entering the kingdom of God, and the church assumes the same attitude to all three of them: it simply rejects them.

In the first it was said, Thou shalt not be angry. The church interpolates the word *εἰκῆ* and explains that it is permissible to be angry, and Jesus' words are made to mean nothing. If thou wantest to pray, Go and be reconciled with thy brother. The church says, That may be inconvenient, and so a man may pray even if he does not go to make his peace, even if millions of men suffer from him, if millions are in want, in prisons, being murdered, and he is to blame for it; a man may pray, and all he has to say is that he has made peace in his heart, and the words of Jesus have no meaning.

It is said, Thou shalt commit no adultery, and as an example of it it says that he who is divorced from his wife is himself an adulterer and causes his wife to commit adultery, and also him who marries a divorced woman.

The church takes this to mean that Jesus has given rules of what is regarded as lawful and what as unlawful. Well? The church sanctifies divorces.

In respect to the third rule the same is done, but in a still more striking manner. The third rule is expressed so briefly and so clearly, that one would think that no place was left for interpretations, except for the useless verses about what word one must not swear by. All the whole third rule says is, Anciently they said, Keep an oath, and I say, Swear neither by God, nor by thy head, because everything is in the power of God, even thy head, and so say, Yes, yes, No, no, and what is above these words is evil. It is impossible to fail to understand this meaning. If the church lies in such a manner, it knows why; it knows that the structure of society and its own institution are based on the oath, and so it cannot help but lie. Jesus is speaking about that very oath which the church wants to justify.

The real meaning of these words is what is said in them. It says, Do not swear. The connection with the whole teaching is as follows: When an agreement is confirmed by this, that both parties vow themselves to God, when they say, May God kill me, if I do not do so and so, God becomes the pledge of it, and that is an oath. In explaining the reason why a man should not swear, Jesus says that a man should not make such agreements, because there is nothing to give as a pledge. If he pledges heaven, he makes God a pledge of his agreement; but God does not go bail for him, so all these oaths are senseless.

If a man pledges his head, he can do so only if he is not in the kingdom of God. In the kingdom of God every man knows that he is entirely in the power of God and himself can do nothing, not even change a hair on his head. Every oath is a promise that a man will do this or that in any case; but how can a man who recognizes the kingdom of God, that is, God's power over himself, promise an earthly thing? One and the same earthly thing may be good or bad, in agreement with or opposed to the will of God. I will come to such and such a place on the Sabbath, and to that I will swear, but on the Sabbath my friend, my father, my wife will die, and I shall be asked to stay with them. I swear that I will give three dollars on such and such a day, but one who is starving will ask me for these three dollars, and how can I refuse him?

I swear that I will obey Iván Ivánovich, and he commands me to kill men, which is forbidden by God. It was possible to do so, when the will of God was not known, when there was a law and the teachers (the prophets), but not when the kingdom of God has come. Man is entirely in the power of God, and he obeys nobody else. His whole business is to do the will of God. So to whom is he going to swear? And why? And in what? And so you must not swear at all; Say Yes, if you have to say Yes, and No, if you have to say No; and know that every promise, no matter what it be, which is affirmed by an oath, is an evil deed, a deed which originates from evil, a deed under which an evil purpose is hidden.

FOURTH COMMANDMENT: RESIST NOT EVIL

38. Ἠκούσατε ὅτι ἐῤῥέθη, Ὀφθαλμὸν ἀντὶ ὀφθαλμοῦ, καὶ ὀδόντα ἀντὶ ὀδόντος.

39. Ἐγὼ δὲ λέγω ὑμῖν μὴ ἀντιστῆναι τῷ πονηρῷ· ἀλλ᾽ ὅστις σε ῥαπίσει ἐπὶ τὴν δεξιάν σου σιαγόνα, στρέψον αὐτῷ καὶ τὴν ἄλλην·

41. Καὶ ὅστις σε ἀγγαρεύσει μίλιον ἕν, ὕπαγε μετ᾽ αὐτοῦ δύο.

42. Τῷ αἰτοῦντί σε δίδου· καὶ τὸν θέλοντα ἀπὸ σοῦ δανείσασθαι μὴ ἀποστραφῇς.

40. Καὶ τῷ θέλοντί σοι κριθῆναι καὶ τὸν χιτῶνά σου λαβεῖν, ἄφες αὐτῷ καὶ τὸ ἱμάτιον·

37. Καὶ μὴ κρίνετε, καὶ οὐ μὴ κριθῆτε. μὴ καταδικάζετε, καὶ οὐ μὴ καταδικασθῆτε. ἀπολύετε, καὶ ἀπολυθήσεσθε·

2. Ἐν ᾧ γὰρ κρίματι κρίνετε, κριθήσεσθε· καὶ ἐν ᾧ μέτρῳ μετρεῖτε, ἀντιμετρηθήσεται ὑμῖν.

3. Τί δὲ βλέπεις τὸ κάρφος τὸ ἐν τῷ ὀφθαλμῷ τοῦ ἀδελφοῦ σου, τὴν δὲ ἐν τῷ σῷ ὀφθαλμῷ δοκὸν οὐ κατανοεῖς;

4. Ἢ πῶς ἐρεῖς τῷ ἀδελφῷ σου, Ἄφες, ἐκβάλω τὸ κάρφος ἀπὸ τοῦ ὀφθαλμοῦ σου· καὶ ἰδοὺ ἡ δοκὸς ἐν τῷ ὀφθαλμῷ σου;

5. Ὑποκριτά, ἔκβαλε πρῶτον τὴν δοκὸν ἐκ

Matt. v. 38. Ye have heard that it hath been said, An eye for an eye, and a tooth for a tooth. (Ex. xxi. 24):

39. But I say unto you, That ye resist not evil: but whosoever shall smite thee on thy right cheek, turn to him the other also.

41. And whosoever shall compel thee to go a mile, go with him twain.

42. Give to him that asketh thee, and from him that would borrow of thee turn not thou away.

40. And if any man will sue thee at the law, and take away thy coat, let him have thy cloak also.

Luke vi. 37. Judge not, and ye shall not be judged: condemn not, and ye shall not be condemned: forgive, and ye shall be forgiven:

Matt. vii. 2. For with what judgment ye judge, ye shall be judged: and with what measure ye mete, it shall be measured to you again.

3. And why beholdest thou the mote that is in thy brother's eye, but considerest not the beam that is in thine own eye?

4. Or how wilt thou say to thy brother, Let me pull out the mote out of thine eye; and, behold, a beam is in thine own eye?

5. Thou hypocrite, first cast out the beam out of thine own eye;

---

38. You have heard that it has been said, An eye for an eye, and a tooth for a tooth:

39. But I say, Do not struggle against evil; if one strike thee on thy right cheek, turn to him the left also.

41. And if one compels thee to walk a mile with him, walk two.

42. Give to each man who asks thee. Do not run away from him who wants to borrow from thee, and do not ask back thy own, which another has taken from thee.

40. And so, if a man wants to sue thee to take thy coat away, give him also thy cloak.

37. And do not sue, that you may not be sued, and do not judge any one, that you may not be judged: forgive, and you shall be forgiven.

2. For in what way you judge, you shall be judged; and with what measure you measure, it shall be measured to you.

3. Why dost thou look for the mote in thy brother's eye? Thou dost not see that there is a whole chip in thy own eye.

4. How wilt thou say to thy brother, Brother, I will take the mote out of thy eye, since thou dost not feel the chip in thy own eye?

5. Deceiver! First pull the chip out of thy own eye, then thou wilt see

τοῦ ὀφθαλμοῦ σου, καὶ τότε διαβλέψεις ἐκβαλεῖν τὸ κάρφος ἐκ τοῦ ὀφθαλμοῦ τοῦ ἀδελφοῦ σου.

and then shalt thou see clearly to cast out the mote out of thy brother's eye.

how to take the mote out of thy brother's eye.

39. Εἶπε δὲ παραβολὴν αὐτοῖς, Μήτι δύναται τυφλὸς τυφλὸν ὁδηγεῖν; οὐχὶ ἀμφότεροι εἰς βόθυνον πεσοῦνται;

Luke vi. 39. And he spake a parable unto them; Can the blind lead the blind? shall they not both fall into the ditch?

39. Can the blind lead the blind? They will both fall into a ditch.

40. Οὐκ ἔστι μαθητὴς ὑπὲρ τὸν διδάσκαλον αὐτοῦ· κατηρτισμένος δὲ πᾶς ἔσται ὡς ὁ διδάσκαλος αὐτοῦ.

40. The disciple is not above his master: but every one that is perfect shall be as his master.

40. The disciple is not above his teacher. Even if he has learned everything he will be as his teacher.

43. Οὐ γάρ ἐστι δένδρον καλὸν, ποιοῦν καρπὸν σατρόν· οὐδὲ δένδρον σατρὸν, ποιοῦν καρπὸν καλόν.

43. For a good tree bringeth not forth corrupt fruit; neither doth a corrupt tree bring forth good fruit.

43. For no bad fruit can come from a good tree; no good tree brings forth bad fruit.

44. Ἕκαστον γὰρ δένδρον ἐκ τοῦ ἰδίου καρποῦ γινώσκεται·

44. For every tree is known by his own fruit.

44. Every tree is known by its fruit.

35. Ὁ ἀγαθὸς ἄνθρωπος ἐκ τοῦ ἀγαθοῦ θησαυροῦ τῆς καρδίας ἐκβάλλει τὰ ἀγαθά· καὶ ὁ πονηρὸς ἄνθρωπος ἐκ τοῦ πονηροῦ θησαυροῦ ἐκβάλλει πονηρά.

Matt. xii. 35. A good man out of the good treasure of the heart bringeth forth good things: and an evil man out of the evil treasure bringeth forth evil things.

35. A good man out of the good treasure in his heart brings forth good things; and an evil man out of the evil treasure in his heart brings forth evil things.

6. Μὴ δῶτε τὸ ἅγιον τοῖς κυσὶ· μηδὲ βάλητε τοὺς μαργαρίτας ὑμῶν ἔμπροσθεν τῶν χοίρων, μήποτε καταπατήσωσιν αὐτοὺς ἐν τοῖς ποσὶν αὐτῶν, καὶ στραφέντες ῥήξωσιν ὑμᾶς.

Matt. vii. 6. Give not that which is holy unto the dogs, neither cast ye your pearls before swine, lest they trample them under their feet, and turn again and rend you.

6. Do not give what is holy to the dogs, and do not cast what is most precious before the swine, lest they trample them under their feet, and then turn against you and tear you up.

15. Προσέχετε δὲ ἀπὸ τῶν ψευδοπροφητῶν, οἵτινες ἔρχονται πρὸς ὑμᾶς ἐν ἐνδύμασι προβάτων, ἔσωθεν δέ εἰσι λύκοι ἅρπαγες.

15. Beware of false prophets, which come to you in sheep's clothing, but inwardly they are ravening wolves.

15. Keep away from the false teachers, who come to you in sheep's clothing, but inwardly are ravening wolves.

34. Γεννήματα ἐχιδνῶν, πῶς δύνασθε ἀγαθὰ λαλεῖν, πονηροὶ ὄντες; ἐκ γὰρ τοῦ περισσεύματος τῆς καρδίας τὸ στόμα λαλεῖ.

Matt. xii. 34. O generation of vipers, how can ye, being evil, speak good things? for out of the abundance of the heart the mouth speaketh.

34. Brood of monsters! How can you speak good things, since you are evil?

36. Λέγω δὲ ὑμῖν, ὅτι πᾶν ῥῆμα ἀργὸν, ὃ ἐὰν λαλήσωσιν οἱ ἄνθρωποι, ἀποδώσουσι περὶ αὐτοῦ λόγον ἐν ἡμέρᾳ κρίσεως.

37. Ἐκ γὰρ τῶν λόγων σου δικαιωθήσῃ, καὶ ἐκ τῶν λόγων σου καταδικασθήσῃ.

36. But I say unto you, That every idle word that men shall speak, they shall give account thereof in the day of judgment.

37. For by thy words thou shalt be justified, and by thy words thou shalt be condemned.

36. I tell you that every idle word that men speak, they will pay for when the accounting comes.

37. For by words thou shalt be justified, and by words thou shalt be condemned.

(a) An eye for an eye, and a tooth for a tooth, is an extract from the following passage from Exodus.

Ex. xxi. 1. Now these are the judgments which thou shalt set before them.

2. If thou buy a Hebrew servant, six years he shall serve : and in the seventh he shall go out free for nothing.

8. If he came in by himself, he shall go out by himself : if he were married, then his wife shall go out with him.

4. If his master have given him a wife, and she have borne him sons or daughters ; the wife and her children shall be her masters, and he shall go out by himself.

5. And if the servant shall plainly say, I love my master, my wife, and my children ; I will not go out free :

6. Then his master shall bring him unto the judges ; he shall also bring him to the door, or unto the door post ; and his master shall bore his ear through with an awl ; and he shall serve him for ever.

7. And if a man sell his daughter to be a maidservant, she shall not go out as the menservants do.

8. If she please not her master, who hath betrothed her to himself, then shall he let her be redeemed : to sell her unto a strange nation he shall have no power, seeing he hath dealt deceitfully with her.

9. And if he have betrothed her unto his son, he shall deal with her after the manner of daughters.

10. If he take him another wife, her food, her raiment, and her duty of marriage, shall he not diminish.

11. And if he do not these three unto her, then shall she go out free without money.

12. He that smiteth a man, so that he die, shall be surely put to death.

13. And if a man lie not in wait, but God deliver him into his hand ; then I will appoint thee a place whither he shall flee.

14. But if a man come presumptuously upon his neighbour, to slay him with guile; thou shalt take him from mine altar, that he may die.

15. And he that smiteth his father, or his mother, shall be surely put to death.

16. And he that stealeth a man, and selleth him, or if he be found in his hand, he shall surely be put to death.

17. And he that curseth his father, or his mother, shall surely be put to death.

18. And if men strive together, and one smite another with a stone, or with his fist, and he die not, but keepeth his bed:

19. If he rise again, and walk abroad upon his staff, then shall he that smote him be quit: only he shall pay for the loss of his time, and shall cause him to be thoroughly healed.

20. And if a man smite his servant, or his maid, with a rod, and he die under his hand; he shall be surely punished.

21. Notwithstanding, if he continue a day or two, he shall not be punished: for he is his money.

22. If men strive, and hurt a woman with child, so that her fruit depart from her, and yet no mischief follow: he shall be surely punished, according as the woman's husband will lay upon him; and he shall pay as the judges determine.

23. And if any mischief follow, then thou shalt give life for life,

24. Eye for eye, tooth for tooth, hand for hand, foot for foot,

25. Burning for burning, wound for wound, stripe for stripe.

26. And if a man smite the eye of his servant, or the eye of his maid, that it perish; he shall let him go free for his eye's sake.

27. And if he smite out his manservant's tooth, or his maid-servant's tooth; he shall let him go free for his tooth's sake.

28. If an ox gore a man or woman, that they die: then the ox shall be surely stoned, and his flesh shall not be eaten; but the owner of the ox shall be quit.

29. But if the ox were wont to push with his horn in time past, and it hath been testified to his owner, and he hath not kept him in, but that he hath killed a man or a woman; the ox shall be stoned, and his owner also shall be put to death.

30. If there be laid on him a sum of money, then he shall give for the ransom of his life whatsoever is laid upon him.

31. Whether he have gored a son, or have gored a daughter, according to this judgment shall it be done unto him.

32. If the ox shall push a manservant or a maidservant; he shall give unto their master thirty shekels of silver, and the ox shall be stoned.

33. And if a man shall open a pit, or if a man shall dig a pit, and not cover it, and an ox or an ass fall therein;

34. The owner of the pit shall make it good, and give money unto the owner of them; and the dead beast shall be his.

35. And if one man's ox hurt another's, that he die; then they shall sell the live ox, and divide the money of it; and the dead ox also they shall divide.

36. Or if it be known that the ox hath used to push in time past, and his owner hath not kept him in; he shall surely pay ox for ox; and the dead shall be his own.

xxii. 1. If a man shall steal an ox, or a sheep, and kill it, or sell it; he shall restore five oxen for an ox, and four sheep for a sheep.

2. If a thief be found breaking up, and be smitten that he die, there shall no blood be shed for him.

3. If the sun be risen upon him, there shall be blood shed for him; for he should make full restitution: if he have nothing, then he shall be sold for his theft.

4. If the theft be certainly found in his hand alive, whether it be ox, or ass, or sheep; he shall restore double.

5. If a man shall cause a field or vineyard to be eaten, and shall put in his beast, and shall feed in another man's field; of the best of his own field, and of the best of his own vineyard, shall he make restitution.

6. If fire break out, and catch in thorns, so that the stacks of corn, or the standing corn, or the field, be consumed therewith; he that kindled the fire shall surely make restitution.

7. If a man shall deliver unto his neighbour money or stuff to keep, and it be stolen out of the man's house; if the thief be found, let him pay double.

8. If the thief be not found, then the master of the house shall be brought unto the judges, to see whether he hath put his hand unto his neighbour's goods.

9. For all manner of trespass, whether it be for ox, for ass, for sheep, for raiment, or for any manner of lost thing, which another challengeth to be his, the cause of both parties shall come before the judges; and whom the judges shall condemn, he shall pay double unto his neighbour.

10. If a man deliver unto his neighbour an ass, or an ox, or a sheep, or any beast, to keep; and it die, or be hurt, or driven away, no man seeing it:

11. Then shall an oath of the Lord be between them both, that he hath not put his hand unto his neighbour's goods; and the owner of it shall accept thereof, and he shall not make it good.

12. And if it be stolen from him, he shall make restitution unto the owner thereof.

13. If it be torn in pieces, then let him bring it for witness, and he shall not make good that which was torn.

14. And if a man borrow aught of his neighbour, and it be hurt, or die, the owner thereof being not with it, he shall surely make it good.

15. But if the owner thereof be with it, he shall not make it good : if it be a hired thing, it came for his hire.

16. And if a man entice a maid that is not betrothed, and lie with her, he shall surely endow her to be his wife.

17. If her father utterly refuse to give her unto him, he shall pay money according to the dowry of virgins.

18. Thou shalt not suffer a witch to live.

19. Whosoever lieth with a beast shall surely be put to death.

20. He that sacrificeth unto any god, save unto the Lord only, he shall be utterly destroyed.

That is the whole thing that the Jews had in view when Christ said, You have been told, An eye for an eye, etc. In adducing the words, An eye for an eye, and a tooth for a tooth, which refer to the injured woman, Jesus apparently does not speak of this one case, but in general of trials and punishments, which form the contents of these chapters. He speaks of the ancient means of defence against evil, of trials and punishments, and soon after he says, But I tell you, Do not struggle against evil, or, more correctly, do not defend thyself against evil in that manner, but do the opposite, and he goes on to show what the opposite actions are.

For that reason the verses of man's judgment, which in Matthew are given in the seventh chapter, and in Luke follow the passage where it says that one should give to those who ask, and that one should be merciful, are transferred by me into this chapter, where they directly follow from the passage in the Old Testament, where reference is had to the criminal procedure. The transference of these verses to the seventh chapter, where they stand out of connection with what follows and what precedes, is quite clearly explained by the fact that the words about the criminal procedure are understood as words which refer only to the condemnation by words. In consequence of these considerations I transpose also Verse 40 of Chapter V. of Matthew after Verses 41 and 42, since Verse 40 speaks of the judgment. After that verse naturally follow Verses 37 from Matthew and 37, Chapter VI., from Luke.

(b) καὶ τὸν χιτῶνά σου λαβεῖν *and to take thy coat.*

Here, in the sermon on the mount, the word κρίνειν is used for the first time, and its meaning is itself defined by the context. If there did not exist a false interpretation of the words κρίνω and κρίνομαι, in the sense of speaking ill, it would never have occurred to any one to interpret the clear meaning of the passage, *To sue and take away the coat.* To say that in the sermon, where Jesus is expounding before the vagrants the essence of his teaching, he is saying that the vagrants ought not to be given to speaking ill would appear as a senseless joke, if we were not used to the blasphemous interpretations of the church. Fortunately the word stands here in such a context that it is impossible to give it another interpretation, but the church continues even here to blaspheme.

This is what it says (Gospel of Matt., p. 91):

Will sue : That we must yield to the oppressor who wants to take something away from us by a case at law is, even more than the preceding one, a commandment which ought to be taken in a general sense. The Saviour wants us to show a similar absence of malice, not only when we are beaten, but also when people want to deprive us of our possessions. However, the legal defence of property is not excluded by it, nor the just litigation. When Paul heard that lawsuits were instituted in the church at Corinth, he did not definitely exclude them from the Christian society, but only said, Why do you not rather take wrong than do wrong? (1 Cor. vi. 7.)

This is what Reuss says (pp. 211 and 212):

C'est encore la recommandation de la patience et de la résignation en face de l'injustice, considérée comme préférable à des procédés, légaux à la vérité, mais étrangers au sentiment fraternel qui doit rapprocher les hommes, durs, violents, agressifs. Mais dans ces nouveaux cas il ne s'agit plus de rendre la pareille, seulement de repousser une attaque contre la personne ou la propriété. Nous devons donc les étudier à part. Quant à la forme de la pensée, nous voulons dire quant aux exemples choisis pour l'exposer populairement, voici ce qu'il y a à dire. On remarquera la différence entre les deux rédactions dans ce qui est dit du manteau et de la tunique. On sera porté à dire que la version de Luc est la meilleure, parce que celui qui dépouille l'autre, commence par le vêtement qui recouvre les autres. Cependant l'autre version nous paraît de beaucoup préférable. Il s'agit d'un procès injuste, par lequel un homme est méchamment dépouillé de son bien. Or, il faut se rappeler que le manteau est considéré comme l'objet le plus indispensable du pauvre homme, parce qu'il lui sert de lit, et que la loi mosaïque déjà (Exod. xxii. 25. Deut. xxiv. 13) contient des dispositions protectrices à cet égard. Le sens est donc : Si quelque adversaire méchant veut, par des intrigues judiciaires, vous enlever une partie de votre bien, plutôt que de faire des efforts pour vous défendre énergiquement, laissez-lui prendre le tout. Le mot grec, d'origine persane, que nous avons rendu par *corvée*, se rapporte proprement à des services publics pour lesquels on met un homme en réquisition (Matth. xxvii. 32). La recommandation porte donc qu'il faut plutôt faire plus qu'il n'est exigé que de refuser tout à fait.

Il se présente ici une difficulté en vue de laquelle on a souvent reproché à la morale de Jésus d'être simplement inapplicable, parce qu'aucune société ne saurait subsister là où les honnêtes gens laisseraient ainsi patiemment le champ libre aux méchants. Pour écarter cette objection, il ne suffit pas de dire qu'il ne s'agit pas ici de lois sociales, mais de devoirs privés, ni de rappeler que d'autres passages de l'Écriture sauvegardent l'ordre public. Il faut admettre que la recommandation de Jésus, bien que *figurée dans sa forme*, est sérieuse et réellement practicable. Or, on trouvera sans peine qu'il y a des coups, plus durs et plus irritants que des soufflets, que le chrétien peut être dans le cas de supporter et de pardonner : des attaques contre le fruit de son travail, plus méchantes que ne le sont d'injustes procès; des charges plus lourdes que de brutales extorsions, qu'on peut lui imposer sans qu'il regimbe. Nous parlons de cas où aucune loi positive n'est violée, mais où un sentiment plus délicat du devoir nous engage à subir les effets de l'égoïsme d'autrui sans nous opposer à ses exigences ; où il nous serait même aisé de dire : non, en nous prévalant du droit strict, et où l'esprit de Jésus nous fait dire : oui, en nous guidant par son exemple.

Le v. 42 est plus étranger au contexte, en ce qu'il n'y a plus là aucune liaison quelconque avec la loi du talion. Pour le fond, même observation que tout à l'heure. Prise à la lettre et dans son acception la plus illimitée, cette règle ferait plus de mal que de bien. Mais il restera toujours le principe que la rédaction de Luc insère en cet endroit même et que notre évangéliste ne mentionne que plus bas (vii. 12) : ce n'est pas mon intérêt, mais celui de mon prochain, qui doit régler mes actes.

To a man who is searching after a meaning of the teaching and who does not regard the present order of things as the realization of a Christian organization of society, this passage points incontestably to this, that the words μὴ κρίνετε καὶ οὐ μὴ κριθῆτε must be translated by *to judge in court and be judged*, and that the same is true of κριθῆτε, the passive voice of this verb, and that Jesus forbids judging and litigating.

(c) In Matthew vii. 1: μὴ κρίνετε, ἵνα μὴ κριθῆτε *Judge not, that ye be not judged*. Many texts have, as in Luke, μὴ καταδικάζετε, that is, *Do not condemn by a trial*.

(d) Such is the context of these verses in Luke. That these words are here in place, there can be no doubt to him who by the words κρίνω and καταδικάζω understands what they mean, and not what we want them to mean. The courts and the judges are the men with the chips in their eyes who are trying to find the motes in others, they are the blind who are leading the blind, the teachers of revenge and malice, who can teach nothing but revenge and malice.

(e) This verse is placed in Luke after the verse about the beam in the eye, and evidently refers to the judges. Courts cannot be good if they lead to punishment and evil, and those who judge and pronounce sentence cause their sentences to come from evil.

(*f*) This verse is found only in Matthew, where it stands immediately after the verse about the beam in the eye. Both the church and Reuss give to this verse a meaning which is independent of the discourse.

Here is the interpretation of the church (pp. 120 and 121):

Give not that which is holy unto the dogs: Again an allegorical discourse. What is holy unto the dogs: the picture is borrowed from what one might do who should throw what is holy, that is, consecrated, offered to God as a sacrifice, to the dogs to desecrate it. What is holy here signifies everything which has reference to the Christian faith: the whole gospel truth, the commandments, rules, teaching, and also all sacred objects.

Pearls: A precious object of adornment. It serves as a picture of high spiritual subjects, and here signifies also high subjects of Christian faith and evangelical truth (Athanasius the Great understands by them in particular the mysteries of Christ's body and blood).

Dogs and swine: These unclean animals designate those who are morally corrupt and incapable of receiving the evangelical truth of men, to whom what is holy and spiritual is foreign and even annoying, since they cannot understand its value.

They trample under their feet: As a swine, which does not know the high value of a costly pearl, tramples it underfoot, so also corrupt people, who do not comprehend the high value of evangelical truths, mix them with unclean subjects, contort them, and frequently even scoff at them. In many passages he makes the corruption of life the cause why the most perfect teaching is not accepted, for which reason he commands that the doors be not opened to them, for when they have learned they become bolder still.

And turn again and rend you: Wild dogs, whose hunger has been irritated, but not satisfied, and voracious swine, which instead of food receive that which they cannot devour, being irritated, may throw themselves on those who have irritated their hunger without satisfying it, and tear them to pieces. Even so corrupt people, incapable of understanding and receiving the evangelical truth, may in their rage turn on the very preachers of the truth and cause them all kinds of calamities, even death.

The sense of the discourse, divested of its allegory, is thus: Do not offer the evangelical truths and everything holy to men who are morally corrupt, ungodly, and evil, lest they, not understanding what is holy and most precious, should defile it, mingle it with human sophistries, distort it, and scoff at it, and you yourselves should not escape being ruthlessly destroyed by them. How often the apostles during their preaching had occasion to convince themselves of that, when they had to suffer all kinds of calamities from evil, senseless, immoral men.

Similarly the Lord has here forbidden that ungodliness which we practise on the Lord's holy words by transgressing them.

The consequence of such a transgression is this, that those who are outside the faith similarly regard the injunctions of the Lord as worthy of neglect, and for that reason rise with greater boldness against us, and, as it were, tear the transgressor to pieces with their rebukes and arraignments.

The same in Reuss.

It seems to me that the significance of the verse flows from what precedes, and is much simpler than the meaning attached to it by the church.

The whole point is that men should not litigate. If a man litigates and expects justice from the judges, who judge tooth for tooth, he gives that which is holiest and most precious in him — his desire to have justice — to the dogs, throws it under the feet of the swine. The dogs and swine will trample underfoot his feeling of justice and will tear him to pieces, that is, they will condemn him, or will cause another man to be condemned.

So here is the fourth of those small rules of Jesus, which are to teach us how to fulfil the law. Both this rule and the preceding one show that Jesus, speaking of the law, never had in mind the law of Moses, but the general and eternal moral law of men. Jesus does not teach how to fulfil the injunctions of the book of oaths of Moses, but teaches us how to fulfil the eternal law, which forbids all oaths.

Similarly in respect to justice Jesus does not teach us to fulfil the law of Moses, but says outright that human justice is an evil, and teaches us to fulfil the eternal law, — the non-resistance to evil. He retains one thing, the aim of the law, as a reason for expressing his rules. The aim of the law of human justice is the good of men. And he says, In order that you may obtain this good, you are told in the law, Put out an eye of him who has put out an eye, knock out a tooth of him who has knocked out a tooth, cut off his hand and kill him who has killed; but I tell you, in order to obtain the good, do not defend yourselves against evil men. Do not defend yourselves at all. If a man strike thee on a cheek, offer him the other. If he wants thee to work for him, work for him twice as much. If thou knowest that he wants to borrow of thee, do not run away from him, but give him; and if thou givest him, do not ask back; if he wants to take thee to court and take away thy coat, give him thy cloak also.

Christ dwells in detail upon this and counts out the cases in which an evil man may offend one who is not evil, and in all cases he says directly and clearly what one ought to do, and what not; he says that one must give everything up and not have recourse to human justice, the courts, and not take part in them.

The aim of the law is that no one should lay his hand on another, on his liberty, his security, his life, and so the law cannot lay its hands on the liberty, security, and life of another. And there cannot be a law, Thou shalt not kill, and another law, Thou shalt kill such and such a man.

This rule follows naturally from the first rule, Be not angry, and make thy peace with thy brother. Its chief meaning is only a rejection of the human judgment, which is confirmed by a false law.

Jesus says, Do not judge and be not judged, but forgive, forgive everything. If you will forgive, you will be forgiven. And if you will judge, you will be judged, and the evil will never end.

And as with the former rules, Jesus, having given the rule, explains it from two sides, from the internal side, for each man, and from the external side, for all men. For each man he says, How can a man judge others? He who judges ought to see what is good and what bad, but how is he to see that, since he judges himself, that is, wants to avenge and punish? By his very judging he confirms the evil, and so, if he judges, he is himself a blind man who wants to lead a blind man. So it turns out for each man.

For all men it turns out that, in the first place, if he judges, he will be judged himself, and, in the second place, though he intends to correct and teach, he only spoils and corrupts. Very well, he teaches and punishes. But the pupil can learn only what the teacher knows. The teacher teaches that vengeance should be wrought on men. It is this that the pupil will learn. Thus men teach others to punish, and thus they go farther and farther into the darkness. They say that they are doing this for the good. They kill! Murder cannot come from a good desire, just as bad fruit cannot grow on a good tree, and as good fruit is got from a good tree, so vengeance and punishment cannot come from a good man. And so, if they punish, do not believe them that they are good. Such is the meaning of this passage.

This is the way the church interprets it:

Resist not evil: An evil action caused by a bad or evil man; and since the devil is the cause of evil, we may understand by the evil the devil who acts through the man who offers the offence. Does it really mean that the devil is not to be resisted? He is to be, but as the Saviour has commanded it, that is, the evil is to be borne with patience.

Whosoever shall smite thee: The feeling of love and meekness, which to an offence answers with a readiness to receive a new offence, which twice satisfies an unjust pretension, and which is prepared to give to him who asks, is the distinctive feature of those who have become perfected in the spirit of the Christian law.

But it is self-evident that all these commandments about long-suffering, about rejecting retribution, being directed only against the Jewish love of revenge, do not exclude the public measures for the suppression of evil and for the punishment of those who do wrong, and also the private personal efforts and cares of each man to preserve the inviolability of righteousness, to bring the offenders to justice, to put a stop to the attempts of the evil-minded to harm others, for otherwise the very spiritual laws of the Saviour would in Jewish fashion turn only into a letter, which might serve for the success of evil and the suppression of virtue. Christian love must be like divine love, but divine love limits and punishes evil, and the love of a Christian must endure the evil only to the extent to which it is regarded more or less as harmless for the glory of God and for the salvation of our neighbours; in the contrary case it should limit and punish the evil, which is especially the duty of the authorities.

The Lord himself, when he was smitten on his cheek, said to the offender, Why dost thou smite me? and commanded his disciples to save themselves from oppressions and persecutions by flight. Apostle Paul, in a case of an injustice shown to him, instead of suffering without murmuring, turns to the authorities for justice and replies reproachfully to the high priest who has commanded that he be beaten.

Judge not: What is prohibited is not a simple judgment or well-intentioned estimation of the actions of other men, which is in any case necessary in life, especially in public life, but the condemnation of the mode of action of one's neighbour, and withal the condemnation by an illegal judgment, which is common in every society, and the personal condemnation, in private relations and in private intercourse, — so to speak, private, personal faultfinding, in which cases the condemnation generally takes place from some selfish and impure purposes, from ambition, pride, and so forth. Judgments concerning the quality of this or that action of our neighbours, even the action provoked by such a judgment, is permissible, if it is based on a true understanding of the matter and on a godly jealousy for the glory of God. Christ himself and the apostles and all their true followers have always condemned actions which were contrary to faith and godliness, and took certain measures against everything which in their opinion was evil. Not of such judgment does the Lord speak, but of the unfair, selfish, egotistical judgment, which at that is expressed without any need, from personal, selfish impulses, and especially by people who themselves are more at fault than those whom they judge. Evidently the Lord had in view the Pharisees who, priding themselves on their supposed righteousness and purity in their external conduct, severely judged the actions of other men, with-out knowing their circumstances, nor their impelling causes, and did not try to mend themselves.

The Lord said this not that we should act or do anything without judgment, but having in view the Pharisees and scribes, who judged each other, but did not mend their own ways.

This is what Reuss says (p. 288):

Ces maximes se rattachent de plus près à ce qui a déjà été dit plus haut, chap. v. 25 ; vi. 12, 14, 15. Car il est impossible de méconnaître que c'est le jugement de Dieu qui est ici mis en parallèle avec celui des homme set qu'il ne s'agit pas de la réci-procité entre ceux-ci. En apparence il y a là une conception anthropopathique du jugement de Dieu, en ce qu'il est dit que celui-ci jugera les hommes comme ils auront jugé leurs sembla-bles, comme si les passions, les antipathies, les préventions, qui nous dictent si souvent nos jugements, pouvaient se retrouver dans les motifs du juge suprême. Le point de comparaison ne porte pas sur les *défauts* comme tels, mais sur la présence ou l'absence de cet amour fraternel qui doit primer le droit strict. Il ne faut pas oublier que Dieu, le Saint et le Juste par excel-lence, serait autorisé à nous mettre en jugement pour chaque faute ou transgression et à nous appliquer la peine méritée, tandis que nous, qui sommes tous pécheurs, nous avons bien tort d'être rigoureux envers les autres. Nous avons tous grandi-ment besoin de la grâce de Dieu, donc avant tout il convient que nous soyons animés, nous aussi, les uns envers les autres, d'un sentiment analogue.

Κριθῆναι is used in the fortieth verse in the sense of litigating, as which it is translated by all ; κρίνω alone might, by stretching the point, be translated by *to judge, pass judgment*, though in the direct sense it means *to weed out, separate the bad from the good* ; it does not mean *to judge with the tongue*, but *to sentence* or *separate* ; but in connection with καταδικάζω, which seems to be put in on purpose that the word κρίνω might not be interpreted wrongly, its rendering by *to judge* is quite impossible. The word καταδικάζω means, from its derivation from δικάζω, and according to all the dictionaries, *to condemn to punishment after a trial.*

More than that. These words are said after speaking of the necessity of offering the other cheek, giving away the coat, and so forth, but in Luke, immediately after it has been explained that according to the law of Moses justice was obtained by trial and by punishments. But I tell you, says Jesus, Do not defend yourselves against evil, and then you will obtain justice. It seems to be self-evident that we must not sit in judgment and sentence to punishments. Even if it were not said after that, Judge not and do not sentence to punishment, it would be clear that it is self-understood, because Jesus Christ teaches all to forgive. Who is going to punish, if he teaches all, Resist not evil, and Wreak no vengeance? Even in the first interpretation of the law, Thou shalt not kill, it said, Be not angry with thy brother. Besides, does not the whole teaching of forgiveness, all the parables, of the forgiven whore, of the debtor, the prayer itself which teaches us to forgive those who are indebted to us, do not all those things tell the same? But here it says directly, in two or three words, such as can under no condition have any other meaning, Judge not in courts, sentence not to punishments. What happens? All the churches, all the interpreters say that that means *évitez la médisance, do not gossip,* and that is all. Not to gossip and not to speak ill of people is not bad; but first of all they are not to be judged in courts, not punished, not corrected, not to have vengeance wrought upon them, — and that is the main thing which is said.

Again the fourth rule given by Jesus, like the three former ones, is rejected, so that if all the passage, all the fuur rules, were omitted, the teaching of the church would not be changed in the least, and would even be clearer than before.

The same will be true of the fifth rule.

FIFTH COMMANDMENT: WAGE NO WAR

48. Ἠκούσατε ὅτι ἐρ-ρέθη, Ἀγαπήσεις τὸν πλησίον σου, καὶ μισή-σεις τὸν ἐχθρόν σου.

44. Ἐγὼ δὲ λέγω ὑμῖν, Ἀγαπᾶτε τοὺς ἐχθροὺς ὑμῶν, εὐλογεῖτε τοὺς κα-ταρωμένους ὑμᾶς, καλῶς ποιεῖτε τοὺς μισοῦντας ὑμᾶς, καὶ προσεύχεσθε ὑπὲρ τῶν ἐπηρεαζόντων ὑμᾶς καὶ διωκόντων ὑμᾶς·

45. Ὅπως γένησθε υἱοὶ τοῦ πατρὸς ὑμῶν τοῦ ἐν οὐρανοῖς, ὅτι τὸν ἥλιον αὐτοῦ ἀνατέλλει ἐπὶ πο-νηροὺς καὶ ἀγαθοὺς, καὶ βρέχει ἐπὶ δικαίους καὶ ἀδίκους.

33. Καὶ ἐὰν ἀγαθο-ποιῆτε τοὺς ἀγαθοποιοῦν-τας ὑμᾶς, ποία ὑμῖν χάρις ἐστί; καὶ γὰρ οἱ ἁμαρ-τωλοὶ τὸ αὐτὸ ποιοῦσι.

32. Καὶ εἰ ἀγαπᾶτε τοὺς ἀγαπῶντας ὑμᾶς, ποία ὑμῖν χάρις ἐστί; καὶ γὰρ οἱ ἁμαρτωλοὶ τοὺς ἀγαπῶντας αὐτοὺς ἀγαπῶσι.

48. Ἔσεσθε οὖν ὑμεῖς τέλειοι, ὥσπερ ὁ πατὴρ ὑμῶν ὁ ἐν τοῖς οὐρανοῖς τέλειός ἐστι.

Matt. v. 43. Ye have heard that it hath been said,[e] Thou shalt love thy neighbour, and hate thine enemy[b] (Lev. xix. 17, 18).

44. But I say unto you, Love your enemies, bless them that curse you,[e] do good to them that hate you, and pray for them which despitefully use you, and persecute you;

45. That ye may be the children[d] of your Father which is in heaven: for he maketh his sun to rise on the evil and on the good, and sendeth rain on the just and on the unjust.

Luke vi. 33. And if ye do good to them which do good to you, what thank have ye? for sin-ners[e] also do even the same.

32. For if ye love them which love you, what thank have ye? for sin-ners[f] also love those that love them.

Matt. v. 48. Be ye therefore perfect, even as your Father which is in heaven is perfect.[g]

43. You have heard that it has been said, Do good to thy neighbour, and count thy enemy as nothing.

44. But I tell you, Do good to your enemies, do good to those who account you as nothing; do good to those who threaten you, and pray for those who attack you;

45. That you may be-come the equal chil-dren of your Father in heaven. He makes the sun rise on the evil and on the good, and sends the rain on the just and on the unjust.

33. And if you do good to those who do good to you, what desert is there in that? For all nations do the same.

32. And if you do good to your brothers only, what additional thing do you do toward the other nations? Every nation does the same.

48. Be therefore good to all men, as your Father in heaven is good to all.

(*a*) *Lev. xix.* 17. Thou shalt not hate thy brother in thine heart: thou shalt in any wise rebuke thy neighbour, and not suffer sin upon him.

And, besides, those passages where it says, Love God and thy neighbour, which have all reference to the love of the neighbour. The following passages refer to the hatred of the enemy :

Ex. xxxiv. 12. Take heed to thyself, lest thou make a covenant with the inhabitants of the land whither thou goest, lest it be for a snare in the midst of thee :

13. But ye shall destroy their altars, break their images, and cut down their groves :

Deut. xx. 1. When thou goest out to battle against thine enemies, and seest horses, and chariots, and a people more than thou, be not afraid of them : for the Lord thy God is with thee, which brought thee up out of the land of Egypt.

2. And it shall be when ye are come nigh unto the battle, that the priest shall approach and speak unto the people,

3. And shall say unto them, Hear, O Israel, ye approach this day unto battle against your enemies : let not your hearts faint, fear not, and do not tremble, neither be ye terrified because of them ;

4. For the Lord your God is he that goeth with you, to fight for you against your enemies, to save you.

5. And the officers shall speak unto the people, saying, What man is there that hath built a new house, and hath not dedicated it ? let him go and return unto his house, lest he die in the battle, and another man dedicate it.

6. And what man is he that hath planted a vineyard, and hath not yet eaten of it? let him also go and return unto his house, lest he die in the battle, and another man eat of it.

7. And what man is there that hath betrothed a wife, and hath not taken her? let him go and return unto his house, lest he die in the battle, and another man take her.

8. And the officers shall speak further unto the people, and they shall say, What man is there that is fearful and faint-hearted? let him go and return unto his house, lest his brethren's heart faint as well as his heart.

9. And it shall be, when the officers have made an end of speaking unto the people, that they shall make captains of the armies to lead the people.

10. When thou comest nigh unto a city to fight against it, then proclaim peace unto it.

11. And it shall be, if it make thee answer of peace, and open unto thee, then it shall be, that all the people that is found

therein, shall be tributaries unto thee, and they shall serve thee.

12. And if it will make no peace with thee, but will make war against thee, then thou shalt besiege it:

13. And when the Lord thy God hath delivered it into thine hands, thou shalt smite every male thereof with the edge of the sword:

14. But the women, and the little ones, and the cattle, and all that is in the city, even all the spoil thereof, shalt thou take unto thyself: and thou shalt eat the spoil of thine enemies, which the Lord thy God hath given thee.

15. Thus shalt thou do unto all the cities which are very far off from thee, which are not of the cities of these nations.

16. But of the cities of these people which the Lord thy God doth give thee for an inheritance, thou shalt save alive nothing that breatheth:

17. But thou shalt utterly destroy them, namely, the Hittites, and the Amorites, the Canaanites, and the Perizzites, the Hivites, and the Jebusites, as the Lord thy God hath commanded thee:

18. That they teach you not to do after all their abominations which they have done unto their gods; so should ye sin against the Lord your God.

19. When thou shalt besiege a city a long time in making war against it to take it, thou shalt not destroy the trees thereof by forcing an axe against them; for thou mayest eat of them: and thou shalt not cut them down (for the tree of the field is man's life) to employ them in the siege.

(b) ἐχθρός means *enemy, foe*. The word is used here in the sense in which it is employed in Matthew.

In the time of Moses Hebrew *oyev* εχθρός signified a man of another nationality, a Philistine, and so forth. Every non-Jew was an *oyev*, ἐχθρός. In this passage the significance as of a man of another nationality is incontestable, if for no other reason than because it is opposed to πλησίος, which in the language of the gospels means *compatriot*. The question is who is a πλησίος, and it turns out that a πλησίος is a man of another nation, a Samaritan (Parable of the Samaritan, Luke x. 29–37).

This is what Reuss has to say about this place (pp. 212 and 213):

La *dernière* antithèse entre le point de vue légal et celui de la morale évangélique est en quelque sorte le résumé de celles qui ont précédé et en tout cas elle en est le couronnement. La loi (Lev. xix. 18) disait : tu aimeras ton prochain ; elle n'a dit nulle part explicitement : tu haïras ton ennemi. Mais le *prochain*, c'était l'Israélite, d'après les Pharisiens c'était même seulement l'ami. La haine de l'étranger, et l'identification de l'étranger avec l'ennemi, étaient les conséquences naturelles, inévitables du point de vue particulariste de l'ancienne constitution religieuse. Jésus n'est donc pas injuste envers la loi en formulant son assertion comme il le fait. Ses contemporains du moins n'avaient aucun motif de le contredire à cet égard. Son *accomplissement* de la loi, en la ramenant à l'intention non méconnaissable du créateur, père commun de tous les hommes, établissait donc un universalisme des sentiments de fraternité tel que le monde ne l'avait point encore connu. Heureusement la formule du devoir, à cet égard, n'a pas besoin ici de commentaire, tout imparfaite qu'est toujours encore la réalisation de l'idéal. Nous nous bornerons à quelques observations de détail. Le texte de Matthieu (v. 44) a été complété dans les copies et dans les éditions vulgaires au moyen de celui de Luc, qui est plus riche d'amplifications sans rien ajouter à la pensée essentielle. L'effet de cet amour, qui ne se circonscrit pas dans les bornes tracées par les imperfections du prochain, mais qui aspire à la ressemblance de l'immensité des perfections de Dieu, c'est que le chrétien devient l'enfant de celui-ci, un fils digne de son père. Car il va sans dire que la *perfection* de Dieu qui nous est proposée ici comme un but idéal à poursuivre, ne peut s'entendre que de ce que nous appelons ses attributs moraux. Le fait même de l'impossibilité de jamais atteindre ce but, fait évident pour la raison et la conscience, ne doit pas être un obstacle pour la volonté ; et le texte affirme cela au point de se servir du futur et non de l'impératif pour nous faire marcher dans cette direction. Ce qui est dit du soleil qui luit pour tous indistinctement, et de la pluie qui féconde tous les champs, ne doit pas servir de *preuve* matérielle et directe de l'amour universel de Dieu. Car il y a aussi des fléaux dans la nature qui frappent également, sans distinction, les hommes de toutes les conditions morales. Mais c'est une *image* de la grâce offerte à tous, de la longanimité qui les supporte tous, par conséquent du sentiment qui doit nous animer à l'égard de tous à notre tour. Tant que l'amour, la charité, la bienfaisance et les autres sentiments et actes sociaux se règlent sur le principe de la réciprocité, ils n'ont aucune valeur ; l'intérêt n'est pas un élément moral. On trouve cela chez les plus méchants, les plus vils, les plus étrangers à la connaissance du vrai Dieu. L'amour du chrétien doit être complétement dégagé de tout élément d'intérêt.

Quelle idée Jésus a-t-il dû se faire, ou vouloir que nous nous fissions de la nature humaine, pour lui proposer un pareil but? Serait-ce bien celle à laquelle s'est arrêtée la théologie? Et s'il est vrai qu'ici-bas personne n'atteint ce but, a-t-il peut-être supposé ou insinué que nous l'atteindrons le lendemain de notre mort, par l'effet d'un acte de gracieuse donation?

It is strange that Reuss, who understands what Jesus is saying concerning men of other nations, should invent a mysterious meaning for the words and should not see what is most simple and clear, that simple, intelligible purpose which the societies of the world now pursue with so little success. He seems to be afraid to attach the simple, intelligible, profound meaning to the words of Jesus.

This is what the church says (p. 93):

Love your enemies: An enemy is he who does wrong in one way or another. There are two kinds of love for men: the first is a favourable disposition toward a man, whose life and actions we approve of, whom we like; the second is a favourable disposition and wishing well to those whose life and action we do not approve of, whose bad actions toward us or toward others we counteract. This latter feeling is the love which we ought to show our enemies.

It is impossible to love the actions of a man who offends and harms us, and who violates divine and human laws; but we can, by turning away from his actions, wish him well personally, not pay him with evil for evil, help him in his needs and difficulties, offer him our services, and wish him eternal good. This love of our enemies testifies to a high degree of perfection in those who have this virtue. They have attained the highest virtue, for what is higher than this?

Bless them that curse you, etc.: A more particular development of the general idea of the love of our enemies, an indication in what manner this love for those who variously manifest their enmity may be expressed. To bless really does not mean merely not to speak evil of our enemy, but to speak well of him, not to minimize his good qualities, but to praise them, point them out, then bless them and wish them well. To use despitefully means

unjustly to prosecute, to accuse unjustly, to offend, to insult by
words or acts.   It is evident that with the commandment to love
our enemies would not at all agree a love of our enemies which
would include a sympathy for their actions; on the contrary,
true love now and then demands arraignments and rebukes, when
the hostile action offends the glory of God, or men are enticed
away from the path of salvation.   For that reason the Lord himself and his apostles frequently turned to their enemies with
menacing and arraigning words.   Do you see what steps he has
ascended, and how he has placed us on the very top of virtue?
Look and count them out, beginning with the first.

(1) The first step : not to begin an offence ; (2) when it has
been given, not to repay the offender with equal evil ; (3) not
only not to do to him who has offended you what you have suffered from him, but also to remain calm ; (4) to offer yourself to
suffering ; (5) to give up more than the offender wants to take
from you ; (6) not to hate him ; (7) even to love him ; (8) to do
him good; (9) to pray to God for him.   Do you see what height
of merciful love ?

The church fails to understand this rule, just as it has
misunderstood all the previous ones : it speaks of something else and tries to destroy the chief meaning of the
teaching.   It says, Bless thy enemies, and the church says,
It is permissible to curse them.   The discourse of Jesus
says only that we must not defend ourselves against our
enemies, that under no conditions ought we to wage war ;
but the church has for fifteen hundred years been preaching the very opposite and has been blessing the warriors.

And yet this fifth, the last little rule is expressed, even
in the form in which it has reached us, with so much
clearness that it would seem there could be no doubt of
its meaning.

You are told, Love thy Russian, and hate a Jew, a German, a Frenchman ; but I say, Love the men of other
nations, even when they attack thee, do them good.
Germans and Russians have the same God, and he loves
them all, and do you be his equal children, be as good to
all as he is.

What can be more explicit, more simple and clear? And if we consider for what purpose this discourse was held, who delivered it, it will become more evident still that it can have no other meaning.

For what purpose is this discourse delivered?

Jesus teaches the true good to men, so how can he pass in silence that phenomenon which then, even as now, presented itself as the greatest evil, — the enmity of nations and wars? Is it possible that we only are so intelligent and that he overlooked that evil and that inexhaustible source of evil, and spoke only of communing with bread and wine, and spoke nothing of the societies of the millions and of wars? And could we believe that of Jesus, who recognizes no mother, no brothers, no family, no ancient faith, and speaks to such vagrants as he himself is?

Is it possible that he recognizes the state and does not speak of the relations of the nations, because he finds that these relations and wars are very good, because wars, which cause millions to suffer and other millions to be the cause of suffering, have nothing to do with his teaching?

In the beginning of his discourse Jesus says that not only must we not kill, but that we must not be angry with a man, so how could he help mentioning that eternal phenomenon of the wars, when not only anger is expressed toward people, but people are even killed?

This lack of comprehension is due to the fact that the teaching of Christ is not taken to be a teaching of what the life of men ought to be, but as a certain complement and adornment of the existing life, which is supposed to be the real one. If Christ's teaching does not agree with life, it has to be interpreted differently. Jesus forbids all hatred of foreigners, forbids defence, and commands us to submit to the enemy, but we have governments, rights, etc. The teaching does not fit in, and it becomes necessary to interpret it differently, and the teaching is transformed. And kingdoms and wars are continued. And if the question is put, How can there be wars in Christian countries? the answer is, Jesus says nothing of kingdoms and wars. And so it turns out that Jesus, who forbids the application of a coarse word to a man, who forbids the having of even one offended person, without peace being made with him, permits violence and murders on an enormous scale. He forgot to say anything about it, or that does not concern the teaching about the good. But if you read as it is written, this is what results:

The first little rule of Jesus is the law about man in himself, in his heart: taking the commandment, Thou shalt not kill, the purpose of which is that men in their badness should not harm each other, Jesus says, Not only shalt thou not kill, but thou shalt have no anger against thy brother, and if thy brother be angry with thee, make thy peace with him.

The second little rule is about man and woman, about the family: taking the commandment, Thou shalt not commit adultery, the purpose of which is that men should not harm each other in their sexual relations, Jesus says, Do not regard carnal lust as a good deed.

The third little rule is about man in his private worldly relations with others: taking the commandment about the oaths, the purpose of which is the correctness of relations, Jesus says that the sources of evil are the obligations which man takes upon himself. We cannot promise anything: swear no oaths about anything.

The fourth little rule is about the relations of man to his state and to the laws of the state: taking a statute out of the laws of his nation, Christ teaches that it is impossible to correct by punishment, and that it is necessary to give up everything which they take from you, to forgive everything, and never to go to law.

The fifth and last little rule of the teaching, which began with the life of a single man, embraces more

and more men, and here refers to all humanity, to all
men whom we call enemies, when our nation is at war
with them, to other nations, to all of humanity : hostile
nations, enemies, should not exist for you. If they make
war on you, submit, do good, and wage no war. Do as
God does, for whom there is no distinction between the
good and the bad. Be good to all men, no matter of
what nation they may be, — make no distinction.

(*c*) The words *bless them that curse you* are not found
in many texts ; they are not in the Vulgate, nor in
Luther, nor in Tischendorf's edition. It was evidently
added later, and here breaks the sense, since the discourse is not about personal enemies, but about enemies
of state, about wars.

(*d*) In many texts it is written ὅμοιος υἱός, which
again confirms the meaning of the whole discourse as
being not about personal enemies, but enemies of state.

(*e*) In many texts it reads ἐθνικός, which means *a
Gentile, not a Jew*. This variant again confirms the
assumption that the whole discourse does not refer to
personal enemies, but to enemies of state.

(*f*) The whole context in Luke in this passage has
evidently reference to a personal enemy and may be
referred to the rule of non-resistance to evil. Its connection with the same place in Matthew only impairs
the separate meaning of Matthew's text, which defines the
relation to ἐθνικοί, ἐχθροί, to foreign nations.

(*g*) τέλειος means *perfect*, but in Russian this word has
to be complemented, perfect in something. Here the perfection obviously means *goodness which is not limited to
certain people*. And so I translate it by *good*.

12. Πάντα οὖν ὅσα ἂν θέλητε ἵνα ποιῶσιν ὑμῖν οἱ ἄνθρωποι, οὕτω καὶ ὑμεῖς ποιεῖτε αὐτοῖς· οὗτος γάρ ἐστιν ὁ νόμος καὶ οἱ προφῆται.	*Matt. vii.* 12. There-fore all things whatso-ever ye would that men should do to you, do ye even so to them: for this is the law and the prophets.ᵃ	12. Therefore all things which you would that men should do to you, do you to them; for this is the law and the proph-ets.

(*a*) This verse, which in Matthew is placed in Chapter V. after the discourse about the judgment, I transfer here to the conclusion of the fifth rule.

Having warned his hearers that he did not destroy the law, but only gave a few additional little rules, the fulfilment of which gives the kingdom of God, Jesus expresses these five rules, namely: Be not angry; commit no adultery; swear not; go not to law; war not.

Jesus says, Here are five rules, but they all come down to one. This rule is, What you would that others should do to you, do you to others. This rule takes the place of all the former law.

OF ALMS, FASTING, AND PRAYER

1. Προσέχετε τὴν ἐλεημοσύνην ὑμῶν μὴ ποιεῖν ἔμπροσθεν τῶν ἀνθρώπων, πρὸς τὸ θεαθῆναι αὐτοῖς· εἰ δὲ μήγε, μισθὸν οὐκ ἔχετε παρὰ τῷ πατρὶ ὑμῶν ἐν τοῖς οὐρανοῖς.

2. Ὅταν οὖν ποιῇς ἐλεημοσύνην, μὴ σαλπίσῃς ἔμπροσθέν σου, ὥσπερ οἱ ὑποκριταὶ ποιοῦσιν ἐν ταῖς συναγωγαῖς καὶ ἐν ταῖς ῥύμαις, ὅπως δοξασθῶσιν ὑπὸ τῶν ἀνθρώπων· ἀμὴν λέγω ὑμῖν, Ἀπέχουσι τὸν μισθὸν αὐτῶν.

3. Σοῦ δὲ ποιοῦντος ἐλεημοσύνην, μὴ γνώτω ἡ ἀριστερά σου τί ποιεῖ ἡ δεξιά σου,

4. Ὅπως ᾖ σου ἡ ἐλεημοσύνη ἐν τῷ κρυπτῷ· καὶ ὁ πατήρ σου ὁ βλέπων ἐν τῷ κρυπτῷ, αὐτὸς ἀποδώσει σοι ἐν τῷ φανερῷ.

Matt. vi. 1. Take heed that ye do not your alms before men, to be seen of them: otherwise ye have no reward of your Father which is in heaven.

2. Therefore when thou doest thine alms, do not sound a trumpet before thee, as the hypocrites do in the synagogues and in the streets, that they may have glory of men. Verily I say unto you, They have their reward.

3. But when thou doest alms, let not thy left hand know what thy right hand doeth:

4. That thine alms may be in secret: and thy Father which seeth in secret himself shall reward thee openly.

1. Take heed that you do not do the truth for men, to be seen of them. If you do so, there is no desert in your truth before your Father in heaven.

2. So when thou art compassionate to men, do not sound a trumpet before thee, as the comedians do in the gatherings, in the streets, that men may praise them. You see yourselves that they have received their reward.

3. But when thou art compassionate, do it so as not to know whether it is thy right hand, or thy left, which is doing it,

4. So that thy pity for men may be in the secret of thy heart; thy Father sees in the secret of thy heart and will repay thee.

16. Ὅταν δὲ νη-
στεύητε, μὴ γίνεσθε
ὥσπερ οἱ ὑποκριταὶ σκυ-
θρωποί· ἀφανίζουσι γὰρ
τὰ πρόσωπα αὐτῶν, ὅπως
φανῶσι τοῖς ἀνθρώποις
νηστεύοντες· ἀμὴν λέγω
ὑμῖν, ὅτι ἀπέχουσι τὸν
μισθὸν αὐτῶν·

17. Σὺ δὲ νηστεύων
ἄλειψαί σου τὴν κε-
φαλὴν, καὶ τὸ πρόσωπόν
σου νίψαι·

18. Ὅπως μὴ φανῇς
τοῖς ἀνθρώποις νηστεύων,
ἀλλὰ τῷ πατρί σου τῷ
ἐν τῷ κρυπτῷ· καὶ ὁ
πατήρ σου ὁ βλέπων ἐν
τῷ κρυπτῷ ἀποδώσει σοι
ἐν τῷ φανερῷ.

5. Καὶ ὅταν προσεύχῃ,
οὐκ ἔσῃ ὥσπερ οἱ ὑποκρι-
ταί, ὅτι φιλοῦσιν ἐν ταῖς
συναγωγαῖς καὶ ἐν ταῖς
γωνίαις τῶν πλατειῶν
ἑστῶτες προσεύχεσθαι,
ὅπως ἂν φανῶσι τοῖς
ἀνθρώποις· ἀμὴν λέγω
ὑμῖν, ὅτι ἀπέχουσι τὸν
μισθὸν αὐτῶν.

6. Σὺ δὲ, ὅταν προ-
σεύχῃ, εἴσελθε εἰς τὸ
ταμεῖόν σου, καὶ, κλεί-
σας τὴν θύραν σου, πρό-
σευξαι τῷ πατρί σου τῷ
ἐν τῷ κρυπτῷ· καὶ ὁ
πατήρ σου ὁ βλέπων ἐν
τῷ κρυπτῷ ἀποδώσει σοι
ἐν τῷ φανερῷ.

7. Προσευχόμενοι δὲ
μὴ βαττολογήσητε,
ὥσπερ οἱ ἐθνικοί· δοκοῦσι
γὰρ ὅτι ἐν τῇ πολυλογίᾳ
αὐτῶν εἰσακουσθήσονται.

8. Μὴ οὖν ὁμοιωθῆτε
αὐτοῖς· οἶδε γὰρ ὁ πατὴρ
ὑμῶν ὧν χρείαν ἔχετε,
πρὸ τοῦ ὑμᾶς αἰτῆσαι
αὐτόν.

16. Moreover when ye fast,*/ be not, as the hypocrites, of a sad countenance: for they disfigure their faces, that they may appear unto men to fast. Verily I say unto you, They have their reward.

17. But thou, when thou fastest, anoint thine head, and wash thy face;

18. That thou appear not unto men to fast, but unto thy Father which is in secret: and thy Father which seeth in secret shall reward thee openly.*

5. And when thou prayest, thou shalt not be as the hypocrites are: for they love to pray standing in the synagogues and in the corners of the streets, that they may be seen of men. Verily I say unto you, They have their reward.

6. But thou, when thou prayest, enter into thy closet, and when thou hast shut thy door, pray to thy Father which is in secret; and thy Father which seeth in secret shall reward thee openly.*

7. But when ye pray, use not vain repetitions,* as the heathen do: for they think that they shall be heard for their much speaking.

8. Be not ye therefore like unto them: for your Father knoweth what things ye have need of, before ye ask him.*

16. When thou deprivest thyself of anything, be not morose, like comedians, for they purposely sadden their faces that men may see that they fast. Thou knowest thyself, they receive their reward for it.

17. When thou restrainest thyself from anything, perfume thy head and wash thy face;

18. That men may not see that thou art fasting, but that thy Father may see in thy heart. And thy Father, seeing in thy heart, will reward thee.

5. And when thou prayest, be not as the liars: they always pray in the assemblies, stopping in the corners of the streets, that they may be seen by men. Thou seest thyself, they receive their reward.

6. But thou, when thou prayest, enter into thy closet, shut the door, and pray to thy Father. And thy Father will see in thy soul and will repay thee.

7. When you pray, do not wag your tongues, as the comedians do. They think that their prattling will be heard.

8. Be not like them, for your Father knows what you need, before you open your mouths.

9. Οὕτως οὖν προσ-εύχεσθε ὑμεῖς· Πάτερ ἡμῶν ὁ ἐν τοῖς οὐρανοῖς, ἁγιασθήτω τὸ ὄνομά σου·

9. After this manner therefore pray ye: Our Father which art in heaven, Hallowed be thy name.[a]

9. Pray like this: Father!

10. Ἐλθέτω ἡ βασι-λεία σου· γενηθήτω τὸ θέλημά σου, ὡς ἐν οὐρα-νῷ, καὶ ἐπὶ τῆς γῆς·

10. Thy kingdom come. Thy will be done in earth, as it is in heaven.[a]

10. Let thy kingdom be. Let thy will be in thee and in me.

11. Τὸν ἄρτον ἡμῶν τὸν ἐπιούσιον δὸς ἡμῖν σήμερον·

11. Give us this day our daily[a] bread.

11. Give us our daily food which we need.

12. Καὶ ἄφες ἡμῖν τὰ ὀφειλήματα ἡμῶν, ὡς καὶ ἡμεῖς ἀφίεμεν τοῖς ὀφειλέταις ἡμῶν·

12. And forgive us our debts as we forgive our debtors.

12. And forgive us our guilt, because we forgive all who are guilty toward us.

13. Καὶ μὴ εἰσενέγκῃς ἡμᾶς εἰς πειρασμόν, ἀλλὰ ῥῦσαι ἡμᾶς ἀπὸ τοῦ πονηροῦ. ὅτι σοῦ ἐστιν ἡ βασιλεία καὶ ἡ δύναμις καὶ ἡ δόξα εἰς τοὺς αἰῶνας· ἀμήν.

13. And lead us not into temptation, but de-liver us from evil.[a] For thine is the kingdom, and the power, and the glory, for ever. Amen.

25. Καὶ ὅταν στήκητε προσευχόμενοι, ἀφίετε εἴ τι ἔχετε κατά τινος· ἵνα καὶ ὁ πατὴρ ὑμῶν ὁ ἐν τοῖς οὐρανοῖς ἀφῇ ὑμῖν τὰ παραπτώματα ὑμῶν.

Mark xi. 25. And when ye stand praying, for-give, if ye have aught against any; that your Father also which is in heaven may forgive you your trespasses.

25. When you begin to pray, forgive, if you have anything against any, so that your Father in heaven may forgive you your trespasses.

26. Εἰ δὲ ὑμεῖς οὐκ ἀφίετε, οὐδὲ ὁ πατὴρ ὑμῶν ὁ ἐν τοῖς οὐρανοῖς ἀφήσει τὰ παραπτώματα ὑμῶν.

26. But if ye do not forgive, neither will your Father which is in heaven forgive your trespasses.

26. If you do not for-give, your Father in heaven will not forgive your trespasses.

(a) ἔμπροσθεν has here a meaning which is defined by what follows: *for, only for men.*

(b) Many texts have here δικαιοσύνην instead of ἐλεημοσύνην. It is self-evident that it ought to be δικαιοσύνην, since the verse refers to the fulfilment of everything prescribed by Jesus. What has misled the copyists is that in counting up what forms virtue, Jesus in the second verse calls ἐλεημοσύνη, *compassion,* one of the first, but this compassion is not to be taken in the sense of an act, but of sympathy for men. Δικαιοσύνη means *the execution of the truth, justice*, but the latter word has received with us a meaning which is so far removed from truth, that *truth* has to be substituted for it; ποιεῖν δικαιοσύνην must be translated by *to do the truth*; ποιεῖν ἐλεημοσύνην *to be merciful, compassionate*.

(c) Again the word ἀμήν is used in the sense of what is clear to everybody, namely, that they have received their reward by being praised, so what other reward do they want?

(d) That is, Do so as to abandon thyself with thy whole soul to the work, so that thou hast no time to find out whether thy right or thy left hand has done the work.

(e) κρυπτός means *hidden*; ἐν τῷ κρυπτῷ in the language of the gospels means more than *in secret*; it means *in the invisible secrecy of thy heart*: In the day when God shall judge the secrets of men by Jesus Christ according to my gospel (Rom. ii. 16).

(f) ἐν τῷ φανερῷ is not found in many texts and was apparently added, because the expression ἐν τῷ κρυπτῷ was not understood. These words are not in Tischendorf.

(g) νηστεύω means *to deprive oneself of something, to restrain oneself*.

(h) I translate this passage before the discourse about prayer, as being less important.

(i) φιλοῦσι stands here in the sense of *do always* and in Russian has to be translated by the one word *always*.

(j) ἐν τῷ φανερῷ is again wanting in the majority of texts.

(k) It does not say ὅταν προσεύχη, as before, but προσευχόμενοι δὲ μὴ βαττολογήσητε *while praying do not wag your tongues*, that is, prayer does not consist in the wagging of the tongue, in the speaking of words.

(l) Many texts have ὑποκριταί and not ἐθνικοί.

(m) In many texts we find ἀνοῖξαι τὸ στόμα, *before you open your mouth*.

(*n*) In many texts the words *hallowed be thy name* are omitted and instead words are given about the coming of the kingdom. In spite of all the attempts at interpretation, these words remain in the existing interpretations the same πολυλογία which Jesus forbids. For the same reason I omit the words *our . . . in heaven,* which are not in Luke.

(*o*) *In earth as it is in heaven,* again a wordiness without any contents ; these words are not in Luke.

(*p*) The word ἐπιούσιος is incorrectly translated by *daily :* it means *necessary.*

(*q*) In Matthew it says, Lead us not into temptation, but deliver us from evil; in Luke the last words, But deliver us from evil, are wanting. The latter words are evidently an addition to Luke's text. Neither phrase contains any idea, and they even impair the connection with what follows and what precedes. The preceding verse of Matthew says, There is no need of speaking much and the Father knows what you want before you open your mouth. And mention is made of that one thing which may be wished for and asked of God. This one thing consists in recognizing him as the Father, wishing for his kingdom and will, and therefore forgiving everybody. And immediately after that it says, If you do not forgive, the Father will not forgive you.

This is what is to take the place of the prayer with you. These words can have no other meaning; but as has happened with many, many things in the teaching of Jesus, even so here, the very words which he used in order to reject all external prayer, those very words with some misty additions are taken as a sample of a precative prayer. How much clearer could he have said that there is no need of praying ? The temple of the sacrifice is destroyed; it says, What is needed is not sacrifices, but your love among yourselves. It says, God is spirit, and for him one must work in the spirit and with works. More than that: as though foreseeing the stubbornness of the people, who would want to retain the prayers, he says directly, Do not pray in words. The whole prayer is to consist in the desire of the kingdom of God and in the execution of its rules, and all the rules consist in not regarding any one as guilty, but loving and forgiving all. And what happens? These very words, by which prayers are denied, are received as the words of a prayer.

Here is what the church says:

After this manner therefore pray ye: The Lord proposes only a sample of a Christian prayer, and so it does not mean that a Christian must always pray with the words of this prayer, and must not use any other form of prayer. In it is contained the essence of the Christian prayer, and the further details may evidently form the subjects of a mass of other prayers, which have actually been composed in the church of Christ, and which are used in one form or another by all the Christian nations and creeds.

Reuss is nearer to the truth, but he, too, does not want to see the simple, clear meaning of the words, because in the beginning he has incorrectly understood the whole sermon; he, too, sees a prayer in these words.

Here is what Reuss has to say (pp. 216–221):

1° La prière ne doit pas consister en formules vides de sens ou tellement nombreuses qu'elles servent plutôt à donner de la distraction à celui qui les récite, qu'à concentrer ses pensées sur ce qui élève l'âme à Dieu. Celui-ci n'a pas besoin d'une longue prière, parce que, à vrai dire, il n'a pas besoin de prière du tout : il sait ce qu'il nous faut, ce que nous pouvons désirer, ce qu'il veut nous octroyer. C'est pour nous-mêmes que nous prions, c'est-à-dire pour nous rapprocher de Dieu, pour nous laisser pénétrer et diriger par son esprit, pour amener notre volonté à se soumettre avec confiance à la sienne. La prière a rempli son but dès qu'elle aboutit à nous faire répéter de bon cœur ce que Jésus a dit à Gethsémané. Une prière courte, simple, mais riche et profonde d'idées suffit pleinement, bien entendu si elle part du cœur et n'est pas simplement un acte de la mémoire.

2° Jésus paraît avoir un jour saisi l'occasion de donner à ses disciples, et peut-être sur leur demande même (sect. 62), la formule d'une pareille prière. Ce n'a pas été certes avec l'intention de la faire réciter officiellement par eux dans n'importe quelle occasion, mais pour préciser en quelques mots la nature des choses qui pouvaient devenir le sujet de la prière. L'Église n'a pas eu tort de faire de cette formule sa nourriture journalière : l'expérience des siècles en a constaté l'inépuisable richesse. Mais en comparant le texte conservé dans la rédaction de Luc, on voit que les premiers chrétiens n'en avaient point encore fait une formule officielle et invariable, comme cela a dû être le cas à l'époque où les copistes ont cru devoir rendre le texte moins complet conforme à celui qui, à cause de son étendue même, avait passé en usage.

Il suffira de peu de mots pour diriger l'étude de ces quelques lignes qui sont un sujet de méditation incessante pour tous les chrétiens. On serait d'autant plus sûr de se fourvoyer dans l'interprétation de l'Oraison dominicale qu'on y rechercherait des choses étrangères aux besoins et aux aspirations d'une piété simple et naïve, et accessibles seulement à l'esprit scolastique. Ainsi rien n'est moins bien placé ici que la controverse sur le nombre des prières particulières comprises dans cette oraison, ou les prétendues découvertes relatives à leur disposition symétrique et au rapport du prologue à l'épilogue ou de l'ensemble avec le dogme de la trinité, qu'on y a cherché d'autant plus avidement que le texte s'y prêtait moins. Supposer ici des arrière-pensées dogmatiques, ou des préoccupations de forme, c'est méconnaître étrangement et l'esprit du Seigneur et le but qu'il avait en vue en formulant cette prière.

Dans l'allocution qui est mise en tête, on remarque immédiatement le nom de *Père*, si rarement employé dans l'Ancien Testament, si caractéristique pour la religion de l'Évangile. Le sens de ce terme n'est pas épuisé tant qu'on songe seulement à la bonté du Créateur ; il rappelle de préférence que Jésus veut faire des hommes les enfants de Dieu, et c'est cet élément à la fois pratique et mystique, le souvenir du devoir et le sentiment de l'union spirituelle, qui doit dès l'abord mettre celui qui prie dans la vraie disposition d'esprit. Il dira : *Notre* père, bien qu'il puisse aussi dire : *Mon* père, parce qu'il aimera à se rappeler la solidarité fraternelle qui l'unit à ses semblables. Et il continuera, même au dix-neuvième siècle, à parler des *Cieux*, comme de la résidence du Très-Haut, sans se préoccuper de questions de cosmologie, parce que cette expression est le symbole de la grandeur, de la puissance et de la providence de Dieu, par conséquent pour lui-même à la fois une constatation de sa dépendance, et le gage d'une foi confiante et assurée.

La première prière se présente d'abord comme une simple formule d'adoration, comme un acte d'humilité de la créature en face du Créateur. La sanctification peut être comprise comme une manifestation du respect. Mais dans ce cas même, il conviendra de substituer au *nom* la personne, en nous rappelant l'usage constant du langage biblique. Cependant on aurait tort de s'arrêter là. Une vraie sanctification de Dieu, dans le sens indiqué, n'étant possible que de la part de celui qui se sera sanctifié d'abord lui-même, c'est-à-dire qui se sera rendu digne d'approcher le Très-Saint, la première prière (qui ne peut même être une prière qu'à cette condition) implique donc en même temps un engagement moral, et une demande en assistance à l'effet de pouvoir s'en acquitter.

La seconde prière demande la venue, c'est-à-dire la réalisation du royaume de Dieu. C'est du moins là l'expression française dont nous nous sommes servi partout jusqu'ici pour rendre le terme grec que nous avons devant nous. Ici, cependant, nous avons cru devoir nous conformer à l'usage, en y substituant le mot de *règne*. Quoique cela ne doive rien changer au sens, il faut pourtant convenir que ce dernier mot écarte plus facilement toute conception judaïque, ou du moins se prête plus directement à celle que l'esprit de l'Évangile veut faire prévaloir. En effet, il ne s'agit pas de demander l'accomplissement d'un fait concret, visible, spécial, d'une révolution enfin qui changerait la face du monde, subitement et avec éclat, comme l'espéraient les Juifs ; mais d'exprimer le désir de voir s'établir un ordre de choses où la sainte volonté de Dieu prévaudra seul dans toutes les relations et sera l'unique règle du gouvernement des affaires d'ici-bas, une phase du développement progressif de l'humanité où l'idéal de la théocratie, tel que les prophètes l'avaient entrevu, sera devenu une réalité. Comme il est évident que ce n'est pas Dieu qui mettra obstacle à cette transformation, cette prière aussi, comme la précédente, implique la promesse, de la part de l'homme, de prêter son concours actif à une œuvre si désirable. Cela nous fait voir aussi que Luc a pu omettre la troisième prière, qui n'est que l'explication ou, si l'on veut, la traduction subjective de la seconde, sans qu'il manquât rien d'essentiel à la formule entière. D'un autre côté, pour faire voir que la rédaction plus complète ne renferme pas de redites, on peut faire remarquer que la seconde prière, en mentionnant le règne, relève plus particulièrement l'idée de la solidarité entre les hommes, de la communauté du but et du travail qui les doit unir ; tandis que la troisième insiste plus explicitement sur l'activité même de l'homme qui n'avait été que sous-entendue dan les deux précédentes. Car la *volontè*, dont il est question ici, est bien celle qui s'adresse à l'être libre, et non celle qui régit la nature. Mais toutes les trois prières concernent des faits qui réclament la coopération des hommes ; c'est une preuve de plus que la prière est essentiellement faite pour l'homme et non pour Dieu.

Quant à la quatrième prière, nous ne nous arrêterons pas à réfuter ceux qui l'interprètent allégoriquement, de manière à voir dans le *pain quotidien* autre chose que la nourriture et en général la satisfaction des besoins de la nature physique et de la condition terrestre : nous n'avons rien à objecter si l'on veut appeler la méditation de la parole de Dieu le pain quotidien du chrétien ; nous affirmons seulement que Jésus n'a pas voulu parler de cela ici. L'allégorie, le sens caché, sont choses étrangères à l'Oraison dominicale ; et loin de dire que le Seigneur aurait dérogé à la dignité de l'ensemble en descendant jusque dans la région matérielle, nous trouvons plutôt admirable qu'il ait su rattacher la matière même, c'est-à-dire les nécessités physiques de notre existence, à un ordre d'idées plus élevé et nous montrer ainsi le devoir et les moyens de les sanctifier. Il y a une immense consolation pour le mortel à se pénétrer de la conviction que Dieu ne l'abandonne pas à lui seul, même dans les affaires les plus ordinaires, et la recherche de l'assistance céleste vivifie et ennoblit son travail. Quant à la formule usuelle dont nous venons de nous servir également en passant, il est positif qu'elle est inacceptable, bien qu'elle ne contienne rien qui soit déplacé dans un pareil texte. Philologiquement parlant, le terme grec, employé par les deux évangélistes, mais qui ne se rencontre chez aucun autre auteur, ne peut être ramené qu'à deux combinaisons étymologiques. Ou bien le mot doit être dérivé d'un verbe qui signifie *aller*, et ce sera le *jour survenant*, le lendemain. C'est le sens que Jérôme dit avoir trouvé exprimé dans l'évangile hébreu, le pain du lendemain. Ou bien il vient d'un nom qui signifie la substance : alors l'adjectif du texte parle de ce qui est dans la proportion de la substance, c'est-à-dire *suffisant*, en opposition avec ce qui est au-delà de la substance ou superflu. Nous préférons cette dernière interprétation. Elle fait valoir un élément de réserve et de modération à l'égard des biens de cette terre, qui certes ne déparera pas l'ensemble.

En employant dans la cinquième prière le terme d'*offense* et *offensé*, nous nous sommes encore conformé à l'usage. Mais il importe de constater que ce terme affaiblit beaucoup le sens de l'original. A la lettre il faudrait dire : Remets-nous nos dettes comme nous les avons remises à nos débiteurs. Cette formule reçoit son explication la plus simple et la plus juste par la parabole des deux serviteurs, sect. 56. Tout manquement au devoir, soit envers Dieu, soit envers le prochain, est comparé à une dette contractée, dont le créancier peut, s'il le veut bien, nous faire grâce sans paiement. Cette comparaison est usitée également dans le langage rabbinique et la langue allemande l'a conservée purement et simplement. Pour le fond, on peut observer que l'humble aveu de la dette (de la culpabilité, du péché) doit rendre le pécheur plus disposé à faire aux autres ce qu'il réclame pour lui-même, ou plutôt (d'après chap. v. 23 suiv.) il ne doit se présenter devant Dieu pour lui demander la remise de la grande dette, qu'autant qu'il a déjà *préalablement* remis la petite à son frère. C'est là ce qu'exprime le texte tel qu'il a été rétabli par la critique, ainsi que celui de Luc, bien qu'il ne soit pas exactement le même. Le texte vulgaire paraît être dû à une certaine faiblesse du sentiment moral, car il exprime plutôt une promesse qu'un fait accompli, et a de plus le grand inconvénient d'introduire l'idée d'une mesure proportionnelle, qui serait à la fois à notre désavantage, et contraire à la réalité.

Dans la sixième prière aussi l'usage a introduit des corrections arbitraires. On dit fréquemment en chaire : Ne nous laisse pas succomber à la tentation, parce qu'on se trouve choqué de l'idée d'attribuer la tentation à Dieu même (Jacq. i. 13). Mais cette difficulté n'est qu'apparente. Un seul et même mot grec servant à désigner les épreuves auxquelles Dieu soumet les hommes, dans un but pédagogique et salutaire, et les sollicitations venant de la part des mauvais instincts, à la suite desquelles notre faiblesse nous fait commettre des péchés, l'assertion de Jacques, confirmée par une saine intelligence de la nature de Dieu, et la prière de Jésus, qui se fonde sur la connaissance de la nature humaine, sont également dans le vrai. Le chrétien, se méfiant de lui-même, peut demander comme une grâce que Dieu veuille lui épargner les épreuves, absolument comme Jésus l'a demandé lui-même à Gethsémané, mais, comme pour lui aussi, cette prière elle-même doit être un moyen d'affermissement de la volonté, une source de force et de courage, et partant un gage de la victoire, ce que Paul exprime très-bien, 1 Cor. x. 13. La dernière phrase, qu'on a tort de compter comme une septième prière, et que Luc a pu omettre sans tronquer le texte, n'est à vrai dire que le complément de ce qui précède. En effet, si l'on traduit, comme nous avons fait, le *Malin*, au masculin, elle nous remet sous les yeux le fait que l'épreuve envoyée par Dieu peut devenir une véritable tentation, une occasion de chute, à cause de notre faiblesse sur laquelle agit le démon du mal. Si l'on préfère mettre le *mal*, au neutre, le sens revient au même, seulement la puissance du mal n'est plus personnifiée. En aucun cas il ne saurait être question de mettre : préserve-nous du malheur.

Nous avons supprimé la doxologie que l'Église grecque, dans sa liturgie, a ajoutée à l'Oraison dominicale, et qui, par cette raison même, a fini par pénétrer dans les manuscrits de l'Évangile. L'Église latine ne la connaît pas, elle manque donc aussi dans la Vulgate et dans toutes les bibles catholiques. Elle paraît dater du quatrième siècle. Il importe peu de préciser le sens de pareilles formules. Elles servent à la glorification de Dieu et emploient généralement des locutions bibliques; ici on pourrait à la rigueur y voir une espèce de confirmation de l'Oraison : Dieu veut et peut accorder ce qu'on lui demande, et nous l'en remercions d'avance. Observons en passant que c'est à la présence ou à l'absence de cette formule qu'on peut reconnaître le plus facilement si une traduction du Nouveau Testament est d'origine catholique ou protestante.

3° Les v. 14 et 15 ne font pas partie intégrante de l'Oraison dominicale, comme il est aisé de le voir. Peut-être est-ce un fragment d'une explication que Jésus en aurait donnée, car ils se rapportent directement à la cinquième prière. Il sera plus sûr de dire que c'est une pensée très-fréquemment reproduite dans l'enseignement de Jésus, voy. Marc xi. 25 ss. (sect. 92). Matth. xviii. 35 (sect. 56), etc. L'empressement de se réconcilier avec le prochain est la condition du pardon de la part de Dieu. Sans elle, la confiance dans sa grâce céleste serait illusoire.

OF LAYING UP TREASURE

19. Μὴ θησαυρίζετε ὑμῖν θησαυροὺς ἐπὶ τῆς γῆς, ὅπου σὴς καὶ βρῶσις ἀφανίζει, καὶ ὅπου κλέπται διορύσσουσι καὶ κλέπτουσι·

20. Θησαυρίζετε δὲ ὑμῖν θησαυροὺς ἐν οὐρανῷ, ὅπου οὔτε σὴς οὔτε βρῶσις ἀφανίζει, καὶ ὅπου κλέπται οὐ διορύσσουσιν οὐδὲ κλέπτουσιν.

21. Ὅπου γάρ ἐστιν ὁ θησαυρὸς ὑμῶν, ἐκεῖ ἔσται καὶ ἡ καρδία ὑμῶν.

Matt. vi. 19. Lay not up for yourselves treasures upon earth, where moth and rust doth corrupt, and where thieves break through and steal:

20. But lay up for yourselves treasures in heaven, where neither moth nor rust doth corrupt, and where thieves do not break through nor steal:

21. For where your treasure is, there will your heart be also.

19. And do not increase your livings upon earth; here moths and rust corrupt all, and thieves dig under and steal.

20. But lay up for yourselves livings in heaven; there moths and rust do not corrupt things, and thieves do not dig under and steal.

21. For where your living is, there will also your heart be.

22. Ὁ λύχνος τοῦ σώματός ἐστιν ὁ ὀφθαλμὸς· ἐὰν οὖν ὁ ὀφθαλμός σου ἁπλοῦς ᾖ, ὅλον τὸ σῶμά σου φωτεινὸν ἔσται·

22. The light of the body is the eye : if therefore thine eye be single, thy whole body shall be full of light.

22. The eyes are the light of the body. If thy eyes are not dim, the whole body will be full of light.

23. Ἐὰν δὲ ὁ ὀφθαλμός σου πονηρὸς ᾖ, ὅλον τὸ σῶμά σου σκοτεινὸν ἔσται. εἰ οὖν τὸ φῶς τὸ ἐν σοὶ σκότος ἐστί, τὸ σκότος πόσον;

23. But if thine eye be evil, thy whole body shall be full of darkness. If therefore the light that is in thee be darkness, how great is that darkness!

23. But if thy eyes are dim, thy whole body will be full of darkness. If therefore thy light is darkness, how great is that darkness!

24. Οὐδεὶς δύναται δυσὶ κυρίοις δουλεύειν· ἢ γὰρ τὸν ἕνα μισήσει, καὶ τὸν ἕτερον ἀγαπήσει· ἢ ἑνὸς ἀνθέξεται, καὶ τοῦ ἑτέρου καταφρονήσει. οὐ δύνασθε Θεῷ δουλεύειν καὶ μαμμωνᾷ.

24. No man can serve two masters : for either he will hate the one, and love the other; or else he will hold to the one, and despise the other. Ye cannot serve God and mammon.

24. No man can work for two masters, for he will esteem one little, and will respect the other; he will do one's will, and will forget the other. You cannot work for God and for mammon.

15. Ὁρᾶτε καὶ φυλάσσεσθε ἀπὸ τῆς πλεονεξίας· ὅτι οὐκ ἐν τῷ περισσεύειν τινὶ ἡ ζωὴ αὐτοῦ ἐστιν ἐκ τῶν ὑπαρχόντων αὐτοῦ.

Luke xii. 15. Take heed, and beware of covetousness: for a man's life consisteth not in the abundance of the things which he possesseth.

15. Take heed, and beware of every selfishness, for a man's life does not consist in having more than he needs.

26. Τί γὰρ ὠφελεῖται ἄνθρωπος, ἐὰν τὸν κόσμον ὅλον κερδήσῃ, τὴν δὲ ψυχὴν αὐτοῦ ζημιωθῇ; ἢ τί δώσει ἄνθρωπος ἀντάλλαγμα τῆς ψυχῆς αὐτοῦ;

Matt. xvi. 26. For what is a man profited, if he shall gain the whole world, and lose his own soul? or what shall a man give in exchange for his soul?

26. What profit is it to a man, if he gains the whole world, and loses his soul? You cannot redeem the soul with riches.

25. Διὰ τοῦτο λέγω ὑμῖν, Μὴ μεριμνᾶτε τῇ ψυχῇ ὑμῶν, τί φάγητε καὶ τί πίητε· μηδὲ τῷ σώματι ὑμῶν, τί ἐνδύσησθε. οὐχὶ ἡ ψυχὴ πλεῖόν ἐστι τῆς τροφῆς, καὶ τὸ σῶμα τοῦ ἐνδύματος;

Matt. vi. 25. Therefore I say unto you, Take no thought for your life, what ye shall eat, or what ye shall drink; nor yet for your body, what ye shall put on. Is not the life more than meat, and the body than raiment?

25. Therefore I tell you, Do not trouble yourselves about what you are going to eat and drink; nor trouble yourselves about your body, what you will put on. Is not the life more than food, and the body more than raiment?

26. Ἐμβλέψατε εἰς τὰ πετεινὰ τοῦ οὐρανοῦ, ὅτι οὐ σπείρουσιν, οὐδὲ θερίζουσιν, οὐδὲ συνάγουσιν εἰς ἀποθήκας, καὶ ὁ πατὴρ ὑμῶν ὁ οὐράνιος τρέφει αὐτά· οὐχ ὑμεῖς μᾶλλον διαφέρετε αὐτῶν;

26. Behold the fowls of the air : for they sow not, neither do they reap, nor gather into barns; yet your heavenly Father feedeth them. Are ye not much better than they?

26. Look at the birds of the air: they do not sow, nor reap, nor gather into barns; but the Father feeds them. Is not man more precious than the birds?

27. Τίς δὲ ἐξ ὑμῶν μεριμνῶν δύναται προσθεῖναι ἐπὶ τὴν ἡλικίαν αὐτοῦ πῆχυν ἕνα;

28. Καὶ περὶ ἐνδύματος τί μεριμνᾶτε; καταμάθετε τὰ κρίνα τοῦ ἀγροῦ πῶς αὐξάνει· οὐ κοπιᾷ, οὐδὲ νήθει·

29. Λέγω δὲ ὑμῖν, ὅτι οὐδὲ Σολομὼν ἐν πάσῃ τῇ δόξῃ αὐτοῦ περιεβάλετο ὡς ἓν τούτων.

30. Εἰ δὲ τὸν χόρτον τοῦ ἀγροῦ, σήμερον ὄντα, καὶ αὔριον εἰς κλίβανον βαλλόμενον, ὁ Θεὸς οὕτως ἀμφιέννυσιν, οὐ πολλῷ μᾶλλον ὑμᾶς, ὀλιγόπιστοι;

31. Μὴ οὖν μεριμνήσητε, λέγοντες, Τί φάγωμεν, ἢ τί πίωμεν, ἢ τί περιβαλώμεθα;

32. Πάντα γὰρ ταῦτα τὰ ἔθνη ἐπιζητεῖ· οἶδε γὰρ ὁ πατὴρ ὑμῶν ὁ οὐράνιος ὅτι χρῄζετε τούτων ἁπάντων·

34. Μὴ οὖν μεριμνήσητε εἰς τὴν αὔριον· ἡ γὰρ αὔριον μεριμνήσει τὰ ἑαυτῆς. ἀρκετὸν τῇ ἡμέρᾳ ἡ κακία αὐτῆς.

33. Ζητεῖτε δὲ πρῶτον τὴν βασιλείαν τοῦ Θεοῦ καὶ τὴν δικαιοσύνην αὐτοῦ, καὶ ταῦτα πάντα προστεθήσεται ὑμῖν.

7. Αἰτεῖτε, καὶ δοθήσεται ὑμῖν· ζητεῖτε, καὶ εὑρήσετε· κρούετε, καὶ ἀνοιγήσεται ὑμῖν.

8. Πᾶς γὰρ ὁ αἰτῶν λαμβάνει, καὶ ὁ ζητῶν εὑρίσκει, καὶ τῷ κρούοντι ἀνοιγήσεται.

---

27. Which of you by taking thought can add one cubit unto his stature?

28. And why take ye thought for raiment? Consider the lilies* of the field, how they grow; they toil not, neither do they spin:

29. And yet I say unto you, That even Solomon in all his glory was not arrayed like one of these.

30. Wherefore, if God so clothe the grass of the field, which to-day is, and to-morrow is cast into the oven, shall he not much more clothe you, O ye of little faith?

31. Therefore take no thought, saying, What shall we eat? or, What shall we drink? or, Wherewithal shall we be clothed?

32. (For after all these things do the Gentiles* seek :*) for your heavenly Father knoweth that ye have need of all these things.

34.ᵖ Take therefore no thought for the morrow: for the morrow shall take thought for the things of itself. ‖Sufficient unto the day is the evil thereof.

33. But seek* ye first the kingdom of God, and his righteousness; and all these things shall be added unto you.ʳ

Matt. vii. 7. Ask,ˢ and it shall be given you; seek, and ye shall find; knock, and it shall be opened unto you:

8. For every one that asketh receiveth; and he that seeketh findeth; and to him that knocketh it shall be opened.

---

27. Try as you may, you cannot add the least bit to your life.

28. And why do you trouble yourselves about raiment? Look at the flowers of the field, how they bloom; they do not work, nor spin.

29. And Solomon in all his glory was not better dressed than one of the flowers of the field.

30. If God can clothe so the grass of the field, which lives to-day, and to-morrow is burned up, why should he not clothe you? You do not believe well!

31. Therefore do not trouble yourselves; do not consider what you are going to eat and what to drink, and how you will be clothed.

32. All these things all the nations need, and your Father in heaven knows that you need all that.

34. So do not trouble yourselves about what will be to-morrow. To-morrow will have its own care. Sufficient are the cares for one day.

33. First of all seek to be in the will of God and to entrust yourselves to the will of God; ask for the chief thing, and the insignificant will come itself.

7. Ask, and it shall be given you; seek, and you shall find; knock, and it shall be opened to you.

8. For every one who wishes receives; and he who seeks finds; and to him who knocks it shall be opened.

9. Ἡ τίς ἐστιν ἐξ ὑμῶν ἄνθρωπος, ὃν ἐὰν αἰτήσῃ ὁ υἱὸς αὐτοῦ ἄρτον, μὴ λίθον ἐπιδώσει αὐτῷ;

10. Καὶ ἐὰν ἰχθὺν αἰτήσῃ, μὴ ὄφιν ἐπιδώσει αὐτῷ;

11. Εἰ οὖν ὑμεῖς, πονηροὶ ὄντες, οἴδατε δόματα ἀγαθὰ διδόναι τοῖς τέκνοις ὑμῶν, πόσῳ μᾶλλον ὁ πατὴρ ὑμῶν ὁ ἐν τοῖς οὐρανοῖς δώσει ἀγαθὰ τοῖς αἰτοῦσιν αὐτόν;

9. Or what man is there of you, whom if his son ask bread, will give him a stone?

10. Or if he ask a fish, will he give him a serpent?

11. If ye then, being evil, know how to give good gifts* unto your children, how much more shall your Father which is in heaven give good things* to them that ask him?*

9. Is there a man among you who, if his son asks bread, will give him a stone?

10. Or, if his son asks him for a fish, will give him a snake?

11. If you, evil people, know what is good and give it to your children, how then will your Father in heaven not give the good spirit to him who asks him for it?

(*a*) θησαυρός ought to be translated by *treasure*, but the word has a different meaning. A treasure has too special a meaning as of something particularly precious. *Property* has not that meaning of preciousness which θησαυρός has. The popular word *a living* fully expresses the idea.

(*b*) λύχνος is generally translated by *luminary*, but ought to be here *light*.

(*c*) I say *eyes*, in the plural, as the organ of vision is meant.

(*d*) μισεῖν has everywhere to be translated by *to neglect, despise*; I choose the periphrase to *esteem little*, as more Russian and exact.

(*e*) I render it by *please, forget*.

(*f*) καταφρονεῖν not to *pay any attention, forget*.

(*g*) Since δουλεύειν means *to be a labourer*, I translate it by *to work for*, in order to retain the same meaning.

(*h*) I put here Luke xii. 15, which expresses the same idea from another side.

(*i*) Many texts, so also the Sinaitic, have πάσης πλεονεξίας.

(*j*) Matt. xvi. 26 again expresses the same idea from another side.

(*k*) ψυχή, as in the majority of the places of the synoptics, has to be translated by *life*.

(*l*) ἡλικία never means *stature*, and the translation as *stature*, which is found in the Vulgate and in Luther, is one of the bad blunders which are met with so frequently. Ἡλικία means *time of life*, that is, *length of life*.

(*m*) κρίνα I render simply by *flowers*.

(*n*) ἐπιζητέω means *to be in need of*, and is irregularly translated as *to search*. If ἐπιζητέω means *to search*, then ζητεῖν (Matt. vi. 33) must mean something different.

(*o*) τὰ ἔθνη is irregularly translated by *Gentiles, païens*. Where reference is had to the pagans, ἐθνικοί is used. Ἔθνη means here *all the nations*. In confirmation of such a translation many texts have in this place τὰ ἔθνη τοῦ κόσμου. This whole passage is everywhere incorrectly translated, even in Reuss, namely, that only the Gentiles have a thought for their body and their raiment, but you are mine, and need not worry about them. That is incorrect on account of the meaning of ἐπιζητέω and of ἔθνη, and on account of the variant τοῦ κόσμου, but more especially because it makes Jesus say that the Gentiles are apostates, which he never says, and because he would be contradicting himself. He says, You have a thought, and then he says, Only the Gentiles have a thought.

(*p*) I transpose Verses 33 and 34, because Verse 33 concludes the idea.

(*q*) ζητέω means *to seek, try to obtain*.

(*r*) Many texts read: αἰτεῖτε τὰ μεγάλα καὶ τὰ ὑμῖν προστεθήσεται, καὶ αἰτεῖτε τὰ ἐπουράνια καὶ τὰ ἐπιγεία προστεθήσεται ὑμῖν.

(*s*) αἰτέω without a modification does not mean *to ask*, but *to wish, tend toward something*.

(*t*) δόματα *gifts, that which is given*. Οἴδατε δόματα ἀγαθά *you know how to give good, useful gifts*, that is, you know what is good.

(*u*) In this passage from Luke, there are different variants; we find here: ἀγαθὸν δόμα, δόματα ἀγαθά, πνεῦμα ἀγαθόν, χάριν πνευματικήν (spiritum, bonum, donum, spiritus sancti). All these variants and the accepted text of Luke, in which it says, He will give the Holy Ghost, are important, for it is evident that the majority understood these words not in relation to earthly possessions, but in relation to the spirit, which is needed for the participation in the kingdom of God.

(v) This whole passage follows immediately after the verse about the judgment and is there not connected with what precedes, but is here directly connected both by the unity of idea and even by the very form of the expression ζητεῖτε.

Be not angry at anything, no matter how much men may offend thee; seek no carnal solaces; if thou hast a wife, live with her alone; make no promises of any kind; in no way defend thy labour, nor thy leisure; without going to law, give everything to those who want to take it away from thee; do not consider thyself a member of any nation, recognize no distinction of nationalities, and make no war on account of such distinctions, neither by attacking, nor by defending thyself. Be vagrants, — this and nothing else is said in Christ's little rules. In them and in doing to others what thou wantest that others should do to thee is the whole law and the prophets.

Such as men now are, such as the organization of life now is, so it was even then. And what men have said, say, and will say about this teaching, men thought and spoke of then. Now they say and then they said, But if we are not to resist evil and will give everything away which is taken from us, then the whole meaning of our life is destroyed. There is no state, no property, no family. I have prepared, collected, treasured up for myself, my family, my nation, and any bad man will come, will extort from me, and I must give him. The

Germans, the French, the Turks will come and take away what I have stored up, and I must submit. And Jesus Christ gives a direct answer to this. He speaks neither of the family, nor of society, nor of the state; he speaks only of what forms the subject of his teaching, of what is the light of men, of the divine essence of man, of his soul. But he gives a direct answer to the natural question of what will become of the fruit of my labours, of the treasure, of the capital, which I have collected. He answers, Man may in life acquire two kinds of riches: one kind is the spirit in God, and the other is what you call riches. Your wealth perishes, you know that; if not to-day, it will perish to-morrow, in a hundred years, and nothing will be left of it.

The wealth in God, the life of the spirit, is the only one which will not perish and is not subject to earthly changes. Treasure up what will not perish. If that which thou wishest for, that which thou strivest after, — the wealth which thou treasurest up, is evil, what will thy life be, which is all directed toward evil? If thy eyes see well, they will take the body where it will be well off; but if thy eyes are blind, they will take the whole body to where evil is. Thy desires and strivings are thy eyes which lead thee. What will become of thee, if thy eyes are directed toward evil?

And so it is impossible to work at the same time for mammon, that is, for the perishing riches, and for God, for the imperishable spirit.

The love of wealth is a deception. One needs only to think of it in order to understand it. What is it for? We are in the habit of saying, How can I help troubling myself about what I am going to eat? But who is it that wants to eat? The soul, life. Where does it come from? It did not grow out of the bread; first it is born, and then only do we sustain it with bread. Where does it come from? From God. Consequently God has made both life and bread. What is more precious for God, life or bread? Certainly life. Then it is about the life, which is from God, that we must trouble ourselves. And if God has made life, he has made also what will sustain it. For does not God feed the birds, and they do not sow, nor reap; so he will feed you, too. The same is true of raiment and of everything which each man needs. So do not trouble yourselves about your food, or about anything else. Your Father, God, knows what you need; do not trouble yourselves in advance; sufficient evil there is in the care of one day, from which you . will not escape. Why add more evil by caring for the morrow? Hold only to the present moment, trying only at this moment to fulfil the will of God, and you will enter into the life. Seek only in order that you may be in the kingdom of God, to fulfil the will of the Father, and everything else will come of itself. Wish for, search after this alone, and God will give you this life, not the bodily, but the spiritual life. He knows what is good for you, and that he gives you. That seems hard for you, because you do not see the path. You think that the path is everywhere. There is only one path, the one which I am showing you, — the path of these rules, and upon it will you enter the kingdom of God. Be not afraid, you will enter, for God himself wants it.

Here is the way the church and Reuss judge this part. The church says:

The passion for the acquisition of earthly goods is not compatible with the service of God; however, riches, as a divine blessing, in its proper relation to man, do not hinder one in his service of God. Examples: Abraham, Job, and other righteous men.

"Do not mention to me wealth, but those who were slaves to wealth. Job was rich, but did not serve mammon; he had riches and possessed them, was the master of them, and not their slave. He made use of his wealth as a distributer of somebody else's

possessions and did not indulge in what he had with him."
(Chrys.)

Within certain limits it is necessary to have a thought for
worldly cares; the Saviour himself and the apostles command us
to work for their gratification, while heedlessness is always
blamed. The Lord does not teach us to be heedless: he only
forbids too great anxiety.

Reuss says (pp. 224 and 225):

Ici il importe beaucoup qu'on ne se méprenne pas sur la portée
des paroles de Jésus. Il n'a pas pu vouloir recommander la négli-
gence et l'oisiveté, ni inspirer à qui que ce soit l'indifférence pour
le travail, ou enlever à celui-ci l'honneur qui lui revient (comp.
1 Cor. iv. 12, Eph. iv. 28, 1 Thess. iv. 11, 2 Thess. iii. 8 suiv.,
etc.). Mais on connaît la méthode du Seigneur d'exprimer ses
principes d'une manière absolue, de donner à ses maximes les
formes du paradoxe, pour faire ressortir ce que les hommes
ordinairement ne prennent pas le plus en considération, tandis
qu'il affecte de laisser de côté ce qui s'entend de soi-même et n'a
pas besoin d'être prêché avec une égale insistance. Il est de fait
que les nécessités de la vie matérielle s'imposent au père de
famille, et en général à l'immense majorité des hommes, avec
une force telle qu'il ne risque guère de les perdre de vue. Il
risque bien plus de se laisser complètement absorber par elles,
non-seulement dans ce sens qu'il détournerait son attention de
toute autre chose et notamment de ses intérêts spirituels, mais
encore de manière à oublier qu'il n'est pas seul à veiller à ses
besoins de tous les jours, mais que Dieu y veille tout autant que
lui, ou plutôt d'une façon beaucoup plus efficace et plus prévo-
yante. Le discours est donc adressé à la fois à ceux qui se rép-
occuperaient exclusivement de leurs devoirs matériels, et à ceux
qui le feraient avec un certain manque de confiance dans le gouvernement providentiel du monde, aux gens de petite foi. Le
souci est donc ici autre chose que le soin légitime qu'on aurait
pour les siens ou pour soi-même : c'est ce qui entrave la liberté
de l'esprit et trouble sa sérénité, ce qui naît de l'absence ou de la
faiblesse de la foi en Dieu.

Every one of the five rules has been rejected or misin-
terpreted singly, and so it is only natural to reject the
deduction. What is remarkable is that the deduction is
rejected and considered paradoxical, not on the basis of

the falseness of the deduction itself, but because it does not fit in with the existing order of things, just as it did not fit in at the time when it was preached. More than that: the deduction is taken to be false, not because nothing fits into its definition (many mendicant Christians fully fit in with the definition), but because we with our circle of men, whom we call the church, do not fit with it. But there it says that not many, only a little flock, enter by the narrow way. No, we will not recognize the deduction and be a little flock.

THE NARROW WAY

18. Εἰσέλθετε διὰ τῆς στενῆς πύλης. ὅτι πλατεῖα ἡ πύλη, καὶ εὐρύχωρος ἡ ὁδὸς ἡ ἀπάγουσα εἰς τὴν ἀπώλειαν, καὶ πολλοί εἰσιν οἱ εἰσερχόμενοι δι᾽ αὐτῆς·

14. Ὅτι στενὴ ἡ πύλη, καὶ τεθλιμμένη ἡ ὁδὸς ἡ ἀπάγουσα εἰς τὴν ζωήν, καὶ ὀλίγοι εἰσὶν οἱ εὑρίσκοντες αὐτήν.

32. Μὴ φοβοῦ, τὸ μικρὸν ποίμνιον· ὅτι εὐδόκησεν ὁ πατὴρ ὑμῶν δοῦναι ὑμῖν τὴν βασιλείαν.

Matt. vii. 13. Enter ye in at the strait gate: for wide is the gate, and broad is the way, that leadeth to destruction, and many there be which go in thereat:

14. Because strait is the gate, and narrow is the way, which leadeth unto life, and few there be that find it.

Luke xii. 32. Fear not, little flock; for it is your Father's good pleasure to give you the kingdom.

13. Enter by the narrow entrance, for an even entrance and a broad way lead to destruction, and many enter that way.

14. And a narrow entrance and a narrow way lead into life, and not many find it.

32. Fear not, little flock, for the Father has wished to teach us his will.

PARABLE OF THE HOUSE BUILT UPON A ROCK

22. Πολλοὶ ἐροῦσί μοι ἐν ἐκείνῃ τῇ ἡμέρᾳ, Κύριε, Κύριε, οὐ τῷ σῷ ὀνόματι προεφητεύσαμεν, καὶ τῷ σῷ ὀνόματι δαιμόνια ἐξεβάλομεν, καὶ τῷ σῷ ὀνόματι δυνάμεις πολλὰς ἐποιήσαμεν;

23. Καὶ τότε ὁμολογήσω αὐτοῖς, Ὅτι οὐδέποτε ἔγνων ὑμᾶς· ἀποχωρεῖτε ἀπ᾽ ἐμοῦ οἱ ἐργαζόμενοι τὴν ἀνομίαν.

Matt. vii. 22. Many will say to me in that day, Lord, Lord, have we not prophesied in thy name? and in thy name have cast out devils? and in thy name done many wonderful works?

23. And then will I profess unto them, I never knew you: depart from me, ye that work iniquity.

22. Many will tell me on that day, Lord, Lord, have we not taught and driven out the evil for thy sake? and have we not established the power for thy sake?

23. And then will I tell them, I never knew you: go away from me, you that have committed lawlessness.

24. Πᾶς οὖν ὅστις ἀκούει μου τοὺς λόγους τούτους, καὶ ποιεῖ αὐτούς, ὁμοιώσω αὐτὸν ἀνδρὶ φρονίμῳ, ὅστις ᾠκοδόμησε τὴν οἰκίαν αὐτοῦ ἐπὶ τὴν πέτραν·

24. Therefore whosoever heareth these sayings of mine, and doeth them, I will liken him unto a wise man, which built his house upon a rock:

24. Therefore whosoever hears these words and fulfils them is like a wise man who built his house upon a rock.

25. Καὶ κατέβη ἡ βροχὴ καὶ ἦλθον οἱ ποταμοὶ καὶ ἔπνευσαν οἱ ἄνεμοι, καὶ προσέπεσον τῇ οἰκίᾳ ἐκείνῃ, καὶ οὐκ ἔπεσε· τεθεμελίωτο γὰρ ἐπὶ τὴν πέτραν.

25. And the rain descended, and the floods came, and the winds blew, and beat upon that house; and it fell not: for it was founded upon a rock.

25. And the rain came down, and the brooks began to flow, and the winds blew, and pressed against the house, and it did not fall: for it was founded on a rock.

26. Καὶ πᾶς ὁ ἀκούων μου τοὺς λόγους τούτους, καὶ μὴ ποιῶν αὐτούς, ὁμοιωθήσεται ἀνδρὶ μωρῷ, ὅστις ᾠκοδόμησε τὴν οἰκίαν αὐτοῦ ἐπὶ τὴν ἄμμον·

26. And every one that heareth these sayings of mine, and doeth them not, shall be likened unto a foolish man, which built his house upon the sand:

26. And every one that understands these words and does not do what I tell him is like a foolish man who built his house upon the sand.

27. Καὶ κατέβη ἡ βροχὴ καὶ ἦλθον οἱ ποταμοὶ καὶ ἔπνευσαν οἱ ἄνεμοι, καὶ προσέκοψαν τῇ οἰκίᾳ ἐκείνῃ, καὶ ἔπεσε· καὶ ἦν ἡ πτῶσις αὐτῆς μεγάλη.

27. And the rain descended, and the floods came, and the winds blew, and beat upon that house; and it fell: and great was the fall of it:

27. And the rain came, and the brooks began to flow, and the wind blew and struck the house, and it fell, and there was a great noise;

28. Καὶ ἐγένετο ὅτε συνετέλεσεν ὁ Ἰησοῦς τοὺς λόγους τούτους, ἐξεπλήσσοντο οἱ ὄχλοι ἐπὶ τῇ διδαχῇ αὐτοῦ·

28. And it came to pass, when Jesus had ended these sayings, the people were astonished at his doctrine:

28. And it happened that when Jesus finished his discourse, the people were delighted with his teaching:

29. Ἦν γὰρ διδάσκων αὐτοὺς ὡς ἐξουσίαν ἔχων, καὶ οὐχ ὡς οἱ γραμματεῖς.

29. For he taught them as one having authority, and not as the scribes.

29. For he taught them as a free man, and not as the scribes taught.

THE CHOOSING OF THE TWELVE APOSTLES

12. Ἐγένετο δὲ ἐν ταῖς ἡμέραις ταύταις, ἐξῆλθεν εἰς τὸ ὄρος προσεύξασθαι· καὶ ἦν διανυκτερεύων ἐν τῇ προσευχῇ τοῦ Θεοῦ.

Luke vi. 12. And it came to pass in those days, that he went out into a mountain to pray, and continued all night in prayer to God.

12. At that time Jesus went into the mountains to pray, and he prayed all night to God.

13. Καὶ ὅτε ἐγένετο ἡμέρα, προσεφώνησε τοὺς

13. And when it was day, he called unto him his disciples: and of

13. And when it was day, he called his disciples, and chose of them

μαθητὰς αὐτοῦ· καὶ ἐκλε-
ξάμενος ἀπ' αὐτῶν δώ-
δεκα, οὓς καὶ ἀποστόλους
ὠνόμασε,

14. Σίμωνα ὃν καὶ
ὠνόμασε Πέτρον, ·καὶ
'Ανδρέαν τὸν ἀδελφὸν
αὐτοῦ, 'Ιάκωβον καὶ
'Ιωάννην, Φίλιππον καὶ
Βαρθολομαῖον,

15. Ματθαῖον καὶ
Θωμᾶν, 'Ιάκωβον τὸν τοῦ
'Αλφαίου καὶ Σίμωνα τὸν
καλούμενον Ζηλωτὴν,

16. 'Ιούδαν 'Ιακώβου,
καὶ 'Ιούδαν 'Ισκαριώτην,
ὃς καὶ ἐγένετο προδότης·

17. Καὶ καταβὰς μετ'
αὐτῶν, ἔστη ἐπὶ τόπου
πεδινοῦ, καὶ ὄχλος μαθη-
τῶν αὐτοῦ, καὶ πλῆθος
πολὺ τοῦ λαοῦ ἀπὸ πάσης
τῆς 'Ιουδαίας καὶ 'Ιερου-
σαλήμ, καὶ τῆς παραλίου
Τύρου καὶ Σιδῶνος, οἳ
ἦλθον ἀκοῦσαι αὐτοῦ.

them he chose twelve, whom also he named apostles:

14. Simon, (whom he also named Peter,) and Andrew his brother, James and John, Philip and Bartholomew,

15. Matthew and Thomas, James the son of Alpheus, and Simon called Zelotes,

16. And Judas the brother of James, and Judas Iscariot, which also was the traitor.

17. And he came down with them, and stood in the plain, and the company of his disciples, and a great multitude of people out of all Judea and Jerusalem, and from the sea coast of Tyre and Sidon, which came to hear him.

twelve and called them his messengers:

14. Simon (whom he had named a Rock), and Andrew his brother, and James, and John, Philip and Bartholomew,

15. Matthew and Thomas, James the son of Alpheus, and Simon called Zelotes,

16. And Judas the brother of James, and Judas Iscariot, the one who became the traitor.

17. And he came down with them, and stopped in the plain; and his disciples and a great multitude from Judea and from Jerusalem, and from the sea coast of Tyre and Sidon. They all came to hear him.

(a) δύναμις means *power*. If we are not going to give to this passage a mystical significance, that is, to destroy its meaning, we shall get that men who profess the civil and church laws will say, We have established all that and the governmental powers for the good and to the glory of God, — precisely what they say.

THE LAW

John announced the coming of God into the world. He said that men must be purified in the spirit in order that they may know the kingdom of God.

Jesus, who did not know his carnal father and who recognized God as his Father, heard John's sermon and asked himself what this God was, how he came into the world, and where he was. And, departing into the wilderness, Jesus learned that the life of man was in the spirit, and having convinced himself of this, that man always lives through God, that God is always in men, and that the kingdom of God has always been and is always, and that men need only recognize that, Jesus left the wilderness and began to prophesy to men that God has always been and is always in the world, and that to know him we need be purified or regenerated in the spirit.

He announced that God wants no prayers, sacrifices, or temples, but that what he wants is serving him in the spirit, doing good; he announced that the kingdom of God must not be understood in this way, that God will come at some particular time and in some particular place, but that in the whole world and at all times all men, having purified themselves in the spirit, may live in the power of God. He announced that the kingdom of God does not come in a visible manner, but that it is within men. To be a participant in the kingdom one must be purified in the spirit, that is, exalt the spirit within oneself, and serve it. He who exalts his spirit enters the kingdom of God and receives non-temporal life. The possibility of exalting the spirit and becoming a participant in the kingdom of God lies in every man, and ever since John announced the kingdom of God, the Jewish law has become unnecessary. Every man who understands the kingdom of God, by his own efforts, having exalted the spirit in himself and working for God, enters into the power of God.

To work for God and live in the kingdom, that is, to submit to him and fulfil his will, it is necessary to know the law of this kingdom. And so Jesus announces wherein the exaltation of the spirit and the work for God must consist, what is the law of the kingdom of God.

Jesus prays all night long, and choosing twelve men, who understand him completely, goes out to the people with them, and tells them what the exaltation of the spirit and the service of God consists in, what the law of the kingdom of God is.

The law of God's power consists above all in this, that the whole man should give himself over into the power of God, and Jesus, casting a glance at the people and pointing to the disciples, says:

Happy are you, vagrants, you are in the power of God. You are happy. What of it if you are hungry now? After you have been hungry, you will eat. You are happy. Even though you are mourning and weeping now, you will have your consolation later. You are happy. Let men esteem you little and drive you away from everywhere. Be glad of it, for thus did they drive all those men who announced the will of God.

But unfortunate are you, rich men, for you have received everything which you have wished for, and shall receive nothing more. If you are filled now, you will be hungry. If you are merry now, you shall be sad. Unfortunate you are, if all praise you, for all men praise only liars.

Happy are you, vagrants, for you are in the power of God; you are happy only when you are vagrants not only in appearance, but with your soul; just as the salt is good only when it is salt not merely in appearance, but is salty in itself. You know yourselves that true happiness lies in being a vagrant. But if you are vagrants only in appearance, you are like unsalted salt, and are good for nothing. If you understand this, then show by your deeds that you want to be vagrants, and be not like others.

If you are the light of men, show your light, and do not hide it, so that men may see indeed that you know the truth, and, looking at your deeds, may understand that you are the children of the Father your God.

Do not think that being a vagrant means being lawless. I do not teach in order to loosen your hands from the divine law; on the contrary, I teach you to fulfil the divine law. As long as there are men under heaven, the law as to what may be done, and what not, exists for men. There will be no law when men will naturally do everything according to the law. Here I give you some rules for the fulfilment of the law.

If a man shall not fulfil a single one of them and shall teach you that it may be left unfulfilled, he will be farthest away from God; but he who fulfils them all and teaches you to do so, will be nearest to God. For, if in the fulfilment of the law by you there will not be more truth than in the fulfilment of the law of the Pharisees and the scribes, you will not unite with God.

Here are the rules:

First rule: The justice of the scribes and the Pharisees consists in this, that if a man kills another, he must be tried and sentenced to punishment.

But my rule is that it is as bad to grow angry with your brother as it is to kill. I forbid anger against a brother with the same threat with which the Pharisees and scribes forbid murder. Still more severely and with a greater threat do I forbid you cursing a brother, and still more severely and with a still greater threat do I forbid your insulting a brother.

I forbid this, because you consider it necessary to go to the temple, to offer sacrifices, and you go and offer sacrifices and regard the sacrifices as important; still more important are peace, concord, and love among yourselves for the sake of God, and you cannot pray or think of God if there is even one man with whom you are not at peace.

Second rule:

The Pharisees and scribes say, If thou committest adultery, thou and the woman are to be killed together, and if thou wantest to commit adultery, give thy wife a writ of divorcement.

But I say, If thou leavest thy wife, thou art not only a debauchee, thou also causest her to commit debauchery, and him also who takes her up. If thou livest with thy wife and takest it into thy head to fall in love with another woman, thou art already an adulterer, and art worthy of having that done to thee which is done with an adulterer. And I forbid this with the same threat with which the Pharisees and scribes forbid committing fornication with another woman, because every debauchery causes the soul to perish, and it is better for thee to renounce carnal pleasure than to cause the ruin of thy life.

And so the second rule is: Satisfy thy lust with thy wife and do not think that love of woman is good.

The third rule is this:

The Pharisees and scribes say, Do not pronounce in vain the name of the Lord thy God, for God will not let go unpunished the man who uses his name in vain, that is, Do not invoke God in a lie, and again, Do not swear in my name in a lie, and do not dishonour the name of thy God. I am the Lord (your God), that is, do not swear by me in untruth, so as to defile your God.

But I say that every oath is a defilement of God, and so do not swear at all. Thou canst not promise anything, for thou art entirely in the power of God. Thou canst not make a single gray hair black, how then canst thou swear in advance that thou wilt do so and so, and how canst thou swear by God? Every oath of thine is a defilement of God, for if thou hast to carry out an oath which is contrary to the will of God, it will turn out that thou hast promised to act against his will, and so every oath is an evil. Besides, an oath is foolish and meaningless.

So here is the third rule: Never swear to any one about anything. Say, Yes, when it is, Yes, and, No, when it is, No, and know that if thou art required to swear, it is evil.

Fourth rule:

You have heard that it has been said of old time, An eye for an eye, and a tooth for a tooth. The Pharisees and scribes teach you to do everything which is written in the old books as to how you are to punish for all kinds of crimes. It says there that he who destroys life must give his life, an eye for an eye, a tooth for a tooth, a hand for a hand, an ox for an ox, a slave for a slave, and so forth.

But I tell you, Do not struggle against evil with evil, and not only do not demand an ox for an ox, a slave for a slave, life for life, but do not even resist evil. If a man wants to get thy ox by a lawsuit, give him two; if a man wants to get thy coat away, give him also thy cloak; if a man knocks a tooth out of one jaw, offer him also the other jaw. If they compel thee to do a certain amount of work, work twice as much. If they take thy property from thee, give it to them. If they do not return thy money to thee, do not ask for it, and so, do not judge and do not litigate, and do not punish, and you will not be judged and punished. Forgive everybody and you will be forgiven, for if you are going to judge men, they will judge you. Besides, you must not judge, because all of us men are blind and do not see the truth. How can I with dust-filled eyes see the dust in my brother's eye? First I must clean my own eyes, and whose eyes are clean? If we judge, we are ourselves blind. If we are going to judge others and punish them, we are like the blind guiding the blind.

Besides, says Jesus, What do we teach? We punish by force, with wounds, maiming, and death, that is, with malice, precisely what is forbidden in the commandment, Thou shalt not kill. And what comes of it? We want to teach men, and we corrupt them. What else can there be but that the pupil will learn from the teacher and be exactly like him? What will he do after he has learned everything? The same that the teacher does: he will commit violence, and will kill.

And do not think that you will find justice in the courts. To turn the love of justice over to the courts is the same as throwing precious pearls before the swine, for they will tread them underfoot and will break them.

And so the fourth rule is: No matter how much they may offend thee, do not put out the evil by evil, do not sit in judgment or go to court, do not punish, and do not complain.

Fifth rule:

The Pharisees and scribes say, Make no war on thy brother in thy heart; arraign thy neighbour, and thou wilt not bear his sins; kill all the men, and take all the wives and the cattle from thy enemy, that is, Respect thy countrymen and have no regard for strangers.

But I tell you, Do good not only to thy countrymen, but also to strangers. Let strangers esteem you little, let them attack and offend you, respect them, and do them good. Only then will you be true children of your Father. To him all are alike. If you are good to your countrymen alone, you are doing what all nations are doing, and that leads to wars. But be the same to all nations, and you will be the children of God. All men are his children, consequently all are your brothers.

And so the fifth rule is: Observe toward foreign nations what I have told you to observe among yourselves. There are no hostile nations, no different kingdoms and kings. All are brothers, all are children of the same Father. Make no distinction among people according to nations and kingdoms.

So: (1) Do not be angry; (2) do not amuse yourself with the lust of fornication; (3) do not swear to any one about anything; (4) do not sit in judgment and do not litigate; and (5) make no distinction between the different nations; know no kings and no kingdoms.

And here is another instruction, which includes all these rules: *Everything which you wish that men should do to you, do you to them.* When you will execute this, it is clear that your life will be changed. You will have no property, and that is not necessary. Do not build up your life upon earth, but build it in God. The life on earth will perish, and the life in God will not perish. And do not think of the life upon earth, for if you will think of it, you will not be able to think of the life in God. Where the soul is, there is the heart also.

And if there is no light in your eyes, you are all in darkness. So if you wish and look for the darkness, you will enter the darkness. It is impossible to look with one eye upon heaven and with the other upon earth; it is impossible to repose your heart in an earthly life and to think of God. You will work either for the earthly life, or for God. And so: Beware of every selfishness. Man's life is not from what he has, but from God, so that if a man should take the whole world, there would be no profit to his soul from it. And foolishly will act the man who will cause his life to perish in order to obtain as many possessions as possible.

Consequently, do not trouble yourselves as to what you are going to eat and drink, and how you are going to clothe yourselves. Life is more important than food and raiment, and God has given it to you.

Look at God's creatures, at the birds. They do not sow, nor reap, nor collect the grain, but God feeds them. And is not man as much as the birds before God? If God has given life to man, he will be able to feed him also. And you know yourselves that no matter how much you trouble yourselves, you are not able to do anything for yourselves. You cannot lengthen your life for one little hour. (The thought is beyond the mountains, but death is behind the shoulders.)

And do not trouble yourselves so much about your

raiment. The flowers of the field do not work, nor spin, and yet they are adorned as Solomon never adorned himself. If God has so adorned the grass, which grows to-day and to-morrow will be mowed down, will he not clothe you ?

Do not have any care and trouble yourselves; do not say that you must think of what you are going to eat and what you will wear. All men need that, and God knows the need of every one.

Even so do not trouble yourselves as to what will be, as to the future. Live for the present day. Take heed that you are in the will of God. Desire only the one thing which is important, and the rest will come to you itself. Try only to be in the will of God, and you will be in it. He who knocks, to him it will be opened; who asks, to him it will be given. If you will ask for what is present, what you need, it will be given to you.

Is there a father who would give his son a stone instead of bread, or a snake instead of a fish ? How, then, will your Father refuse to give you what you really need, if you ask him for it ? But what you really need is the life of the spirit, so ask for that alone.

To pray does not mean to do what the hypocrites are doing in the churches, or in the sight of men. They do so for men, and from them they receive their praise, and not from God. But if thou wishest to enter into the will of thy Father, go there where no one can see thee and pray to thy Father the spirit, and the Father will see what there is in thy soul, and will give thee the true spirit. And do not uselessly wag thy tongue, as the hypocrites do. Thy father knows what thou needest, before thou openest thy mouth.

This is the way you ought to pray : Our Father! Let me be in thy kingdom, that is, let thy will be in me. Give me such food as I need. And forgive me my faults, as I forgive them in others.

If you ask God for the spirit, find no fault with men, and God will forgive you your faults. And if you do not forgive men, God will not forgive you.

Do nothing to be praised by men. If you do so for men, you will receive your reward from men.

So if thou art compassionate toward men, do not sound thy trumpet about it before men, for the hypocrites do so, that men may praise them. They receive what they wish. But thou, if thou art compassionate to men, do good in such a way that no one may see it. And thy Father will see it, and will give thee what thou needest.

And if thou sufferest oppression for the sake of God, do not weep and complain before men, as the hypocrites do, that men may see and praise them, for they receive what they want. But do differently: if thou sufferest for the sake of God, go about with a happy face, that men may not see, but thy Father will see, and will give thee what thou needest.

Such is the entrance into the kingdom of God. There is but one entrance to the will of God, and it is narrow. There is always but one entrance, and all around is a large and broad field, and if you walk over it you will not come to the haven. Only a narrow path leads into life, and only a few walk over it.

Do not lose your courage, though a little flock you be. You will enter into it, because the Father will teach you his will.

CHAPTER V.

THE FULFILMENT OF THE LAW GIVES THE TRUE LIFE. THE NEW TEACHING ABOUT GOD

THE prophets promised the coming of God into the world. After the prophets John announced that God was already in the world, and that in order to know him it was only necessary to be reborn in the spirit. Where is God? And going into the wilderness, Jesus learned that there was a life of the flesh, which was incomprehensible to him, and at the same time a manifestation of God, which was comprehensible to him (Chap. I.).

Having comprehended that, Jesus went away from the wilderness and announced that God was in the world, among men, but not the God imagined by the men of the world, but the God who is expressed by the life of men, God the spirit (Chap. II.).

The spirit of God is in every man. Every man, besides his carnal origin, besides his dependence on the flesh, knows in his freedom another origin and dependence on the spirit. This consciousness is God in the world. God, the beginning of everything, gave men this consciousness of himself and no longer takes part in the affairs of the world. Men may find God in themselves. He is in their soul. And so the coming of God depends on the will of men, on their making an effort to fulfil the will of the carnal life, or of the will of the spirit of God (Chap. III.).

The will of the spirit of God is good. And for the fulfilment of this good there is the law. This law consists of five rules: not to be angry, not to commit adultery, not to promise anything, not to struggle against evil, not to wage war (Chap. IV.).

From these rules follows the renunciation of wealth, of all property, of all honours, of violence against other men, — the renunciation of everything which has formed the aim of all carnal desires. Mendicancy and vagrancy is the only path for obtaining the true life.

36. Ἰδὼν δὲ τοὺς ὄχλους, ἐσπλαγχνίσθη περὶ αὐτῶν, ὅτι ἦσαν ἐκλελυμένοι καὶ ἐῤῥιμμένοι ὡσεὶ πρόβατα μὴ ἔχοντα ποιμένα.

28. Δεῦτε πρὸς μὲ, πάντες οἱ κοπιῶντες καὶ πεφορτισμένοι, κἀγὼ ἀναπαύσω ὑμᾶς,

29. Ἄρατε τὸν ζυγόν μου ἐφ᾽ ὑμᾶς, καὶ μάθετε ἀπ᾽ ἐμοῦ, ὅτι πρᾷός εἰμι καὶ ταπεινὸς τῇ καρδίᾳ· καὶ εὑρήσετε ἀνάπαυσιν ταῖς ψυχαῖς ὑμῶν.

30. Ὁ γὰρ ζυγός μου χρηστὸς, καὶ τὸ φορτίον μου ἐλαφρόν ἐστιν.

Matt. ix. 36. But when he saw the multitudes, he was moved with compassion on them, because they fainted, and were scattered abroad, as sheep having no shepherd.

Matt. xi. 28. Come unto me, all ye that labour and are heavy laden, and I will give you rest.

29. Take my yoke upon you, and learn of me; for I am meek and lowly in heart: and ye shall find rest unto your souls.

30. For my yoke is easy, and my burden is light.

36. Jesus was sorry for the people, because they did not understand what the true life consisted in, and were tormented without knowing why, like sheep without a shepherd.

28. And he said, Give yourselves to me, all you who are in labour, who are laden above your strength, and I will give you rest.

29. Take my yoke upon you, and learn of me; for I am meek and lowly in heart, and you will find rest in life.

30. For my yoke is easy, and my wagon is light.

Men put on a yoke which is not made for them and hitch themselves to a wagon which is not according to their strength. Men live for the carnal life and want to find calm and rest. Only in spiritual life is there rest and joy. Only this yoke is made according to the strength of men, and it is this that Jesus teaches. Try it, and see how easy and light it is.

John viii. He who wants to know whether I am speaking the truth, let him do what I say.

1. Μετὰ δὲ ταῦτα ἀνέδειξεν ὁ Κύριος καὶ ἑτέρους ἑβδομήκοντα, καὶ ἀπέστειλεν αὐτοὺς ἀνὰ δύο πρὸ προσώπ·ου αὐτοῦ, εἰς πᾶσαν πόλιν καὶ τόπον οὗ ἔμελλεν αὐτὸς ἔρχεσθαι.

2. Ἔλεγεν οὖν πρὸς αὐτούς, Ὁ μὲν θερισμὸς πολύς, οἱ δὲ ἐργάται ὀλίγοι· δεήθητε οὖν τοῦ κυρίου τοῦ θερισμοῦ, ὅπως ἐκβάλλῃ ἐργάτας εἰς τὸν θερισμὸν αὐτοῦ.

7. Πορευόμενοι δὲ κηρύσσετε, λέγοντες, Ὅτι ἤγγικεν ἡ βασιλεία τῶν οὐρανῶν.

8. Καὶ παρήγγειλεν αὐτοῖς, ἵνα μηδὲν αἴρωσιν εἰς ὁδόν, εἰ μὴ ῥάβδον μόνον· μὴ πήραν, μὴ ἄρτον, μὴ εἰς τὴν ζώνην χαλκόν·

9. Ἀλλ' ὑποδεδεμένους σανδάλια· καὶ μὴ ἐνδύσασθαι δύο χιτῶνας.

10. Ἄξιος γὰρ ὁ ἐργάτης τῆς τροφῆς αὐτοῦ ἐστιν.

10. Ὅπου ἐὰν εἰσέλθητε εἰς οἰκίαν, ἐκεῖ μένετε ἕως ἂν ἐξέλθητε ἐκεῖθεν.

12. Εἰσερχόμενοι δὲ εἰς τὴν οἰκίαν, ἀσπάσασθε αὐτήν.

13. Καὶ ἐὰν μὲν ᾖ ἡ οἰκία ἀξία, ἐλθέτω ἡ εἰρήνη ὑμῶν ἐπ' αὐτήν· ἐὰν δὲ μὴ ᾖ ἀξία, ἡ εἰρήνη ὑμῶν πρὸς ὑμᾶς ἐπιστραφήτω.

11. Καὶ ὅσοι ἂν μὴ δέξωνται ὑμᾶς, μηδὲ

Luke x. 1. After these things the Lord appointed other seventy also, and sent them two and two before his face into every city and place, whither he himself would come.

2. Therefore said he unto them, The harvest truly is great, but the labourers are few: pray ye therefore the Lord of the harvest, that he would send forth labourers into his harvest.

Matt. x. 7. And as ye go, preach, saying, The kingdom of heaven is at hand.*

Mark vi. 8. And commanded them that they should take nothing for their journey, save a staff only; no scrip, no bread, no money in their purse:

9. But be shod with sandals; and not put on two coats.

Matt. x. 10. For the workman is worthy* of his meat.

Mark vi. 10. In what place soever ye enter into a house, there abide till ye depart from that place.*

12. And when ye come into a house, salute it.

13. And if the house be worthy,* let your peace come upon it: but if it be not worthy, let your peace return to you.

Mark vi. 11. And whosoever shall not receive you, nor hear you, when

1. After that Jesus appointed other seventy men, and sent them two and two in his place into every city and place, where he himself had to be.

2. And he said to them, The field is great, but the labourers are few. The master must send the labourers into the field.

7. Go and proclaim, saying, The kingdom of God has come.

8. And commanded them that they should take nothing on their journey, save a staff; no scrip, no bread, no money in their purse.

9. And put on bast-shoes and one coat,

10. For he who works is worthy of his coat.

10. And whatever house you enter, stay there till you leave that place.

12. When you enter a house, greet the host, saying, Peace be to your house.

13. If the hosts agree, peace will be in that house, and if they do not agree, your peace will remain with you.

11. And if they do not receive you, nor listen to you, go away from

ἀκούσωσιν ὑμῶν, ἐκπορευόμενοι ἐκεῖθεν ἐκτινάξατε τὸν χοῦν τὸν ὑποκάτω τῶν ποδῶν ὑμῶν, εἰς μαρτύριον αὐτοῖς.

22. Καὶ ἔσεσθε μισούμενοι ὑπὸ πάντων διὰ τὸ ὄνομά μου· ὁ δὲ ὑπομείνας εἰς τέλος, οὗτος σωθήσεται.

23. Ὅταν δὲ διώκωσιν ὑμᾶς ἐν τῇ πόλει ταύτῃ, φεύγετε εἰς τὴν ἄλλην.

16. Ἰδού, ἐγὼ ἀποστέλλω ὑμας ὡς πρόβατα ἐν μέσῳ λύκων· γίνεσθε οὖν φρόνιμοι ὡς οἱ ὄφεις, καὶ ἀκέραιοι ὡς αἱ περιστεραί.

9. Βλέπετε δὲ ὑμεῖς ἑαυτούς. παραδώσουσι γὰρ ὑμᾶς εἰς συνέδρια, καὶ εἰς συναγωγὰς δαρήσεσθε, καὶ ἐπὶ ἡγεμόνων καὶ βασιλέων σταθήσεσθε ἕνεκεν ἐμοῦ, εἰς μαρτύριον αὐτοῖς·

19. Ὅταν δὲ παραδιδῶσιν ὑμᾶς, μὴ μεριμνήσητε πῶς ἢ τί λαλήσητε· δοθήσεται γὰρ ὑμῖν ἐν ἐκείνῃ τῇ ὥρᾳ τί λαλήσετε·

20. Οὐ γὰρ ὑμεῖς ἐστε οἱ λαλοῦντες, ἀλλὰ τὸ Πνεῦμα τοῦ πατρὸς ὑμῶν τὸ λαλοῦν ἐν ὑμῖν.

23. Οὐ μὴ τελέσητε τὰς πόλεις τοῦ Ἰσραὴλ, ἕως ἂν ἔλθῃ ὁ υἱὸς τοῦ ἀνθρώπου.

26. Μὴ οὖν φοβηθῆτε αὐτούς·

22. Οὐ γάρ ἐστί τι κρυπτὸν, ὃ ἐὰν μὴ φανερωθῇ· οὐδὲ ἐγένετο ἀπόκρυφον, ἀλλ' ἵνα εἰς φανερὸν ἔλθῃ.

---

ye depart thence, shake off the dust under your feet for a testimony against them.

Matt. x. 22. And ye shall be hated of all men for my name's sake: but he that endureth to the end shall be saved.

23. But when they persecute you in this city, flee ye into another.

16. Behold, I send you forth as sheep in the midst of wolves: be ye therefore wise as serpents, and harmless as doves.

Mark xiii. 9. But take heed to yourselves: for they shall deliver you up to councils; and in the synagogues ye shall be beaten: and ye shall be brought before rulers and kings for my sake, for a testimony against them.

Matt. x. 19. But when they deliver you up, take no thought how or what ye shall speak: for it shall be given you in that same hour what ye shall speak.

20. For it is not ye that speak, but the Spirit of your Father which speaketh in you.

23. Ye shall not have gone over the cities of Israel, till the Son of man be come.

26. Fear them not therefore:

Mark iv. 22. For there is nothing hid, which shall not be manifested; neither was any thing kept secret, but that it should come abroad.

---

there, shake off the dust under your feet as a sign that you do not want anything from them.

22. And they will hate you for my teaching, but he who will be firm to the end will be safe.

23. And if they attack you in one city, flee to another.

16. And so I send you like sheep into the midst of wolves: be therefore as wise as serpents, and simple as doves.

9. But take heed: for they will deliver you to the courts; and they will flog you in the assemblies, and will bring you to the rulers and kings for my sake, to show before them.

19. But when they deliver you to the courts, take no thought how and what you will speak; for you will be taught at that hour what you shall speak.

20. Not you yourselves will speak, but the spirit of the Father will speak in you.

23. You will not have gone over the cities of Judea, when the son of man will appear.

26. Therefore do not fear them.

22. For in the soul is hid what will be manifested; everything which is kept, is kept in order that it may become manifest in the world.

3. Ἀνθ' ὧν ὅσα ἐν τῇ σκοτίᾳ εἴπατε, ἐν τῷ φωτὶ ἀκουσθήσεται· καὶ ὃ πρὸς τὸ οὖς ἐλαλήσατε ἐν τοῖς ταμείοις, κηρυχθήσεται ἐπὶ τῶν δωμάτων.

4. Λέγω δὲ ὑμῖν τοῖς φίλοις μου, Μὴ φοβηθῆτε ἀπὸ τῶν ἀποκτεινόντων τὸ σῶμα, καὶ μετὰ ταῦτα μὴ ἐχόντων περισσότερόν τι ποιῆσαι.

5. Ὑποδείξω δὲ ὑμῖν τίνα φοβηθῆτε· φοβήθητε τὸν μετὰ τὸ ἀποκτεῖναι ἐξουσίαν ἔχοντα ἐμβαλεῖν εἰς τὴν γέενναν· ναί, λέγω ὑμῖν, τοῦτον φοβήθητε.

6. Οὐχὶ πέντε στρουθία πωλεῖται ἀσσαρίων δύο; καὶ ἐν ἐξ αὐτῶν οὐκ ἔστιν ἐπιλελησμένον ἐνώπιον τοῦ Θεοῦ·

7. Ἀλλὰ καὶ αἱ τρίχες τῆς κεφαλῆς ὑμῶν πᾶσαι ἠρίθμηνται. μὴ οὖν φοβεῖσθε· πολλῶν στρουθίων διαφέρετε.

8. Λέγω δὲ ὑμῖν, Πᾶς ὃς ἂν ὁμολογήσῃ ἐν ἐμοὶ ἔμπροσθεν τῶν ἀνθρώπων, καὶ ὁ υἱὸς τοῦ ἀνθρώπου ὁμολογήσει ἐν αὐτῷ ἔμπροσθεν τῶν ἀγγέλων τοῦ Θεοῦ·

34. Μὴ νομίσητε ὅτι ἦλθον βαλεῖν εἰρήνην ἐπὶ τὴν γῆν· οὐκ ἦλθον βαλεῖν εἰρήνην, ἀλλὰ μάχαιραν.

49. Πῦρ ἦλθον βαλεῖν εἰς τὴν γῆν, καὶ τί θέλω εἰ ἤδη ἀνήφθη;

50. Βάπτισμα δὲ ἔχω βαπτισθῆναι, καὶ πῶς συνέχομαι ἕως οὗ τελεσθῇ;

Luke xii. 3. Therefore, whatsoever ye have spoken in darkness shall be heard in the light; and that which ye have spoken in the ear in closets shall be proclaimed upon the housetops.

4. And I say unto you my friends, Be not afraid of them that kill the body, and after that have no more that they can do.

5. But I will forewarn you whom ye shall fear: Fear him, which after he hath killed hath power to cast into hell;[a] yea, I say unto you, Fear him.

6. Are not five sparrows sold for two farthings, and not one of them is forgotten before God?

7. But even the very hairs of your head are all numbered. Fear not therefore; ye are of more value than many sparrows.

8. Also I say unto you, Whosoever shall confess me before men, him shall the Son of man also confess before the angels of God:

Matt. x. 34. Think not that I am come to send peace on earth: I came not to send peace, but a sword.[b]

Luke xii. 49. I am come to send fire on the earth; and what will I, if it be already kindled?

50. But I have a baptism to be baptized with; and how am I straitened till it be accomplished!

---

3. And everything which you have spoken in secret will be heard in the light; what you have spoken in the ear in closets will be proclaimed from the housetops.

4. I tell you, my friends, Be not afraid of those who kill the body, and beyond that can do nothing to you.

5. I will show you whom you shall fear. Fear him who kills and destroys the soul. Verily I tell you, Fear him.

6. Are not five sparrows sold for a cent? and they are not forgotten by God, and not one will die without your Father.

7. Even the hairs of your head are all numbered. Therefore be not afraid: you are of more value than sparrows.

8. I tell you, Whoever will be with me before men, with him the son of man will be before the powers of God.

34. Do not think that I have brought peace upon earth: I have not brought peace, but discord.

49. I have come to send fire on earth; how anxious I am that it should burn up!

50. There is a regeneration through which I must pass, and I languish till it be accomplished.

9. Ὁ δὲ ἀρνησάμενός με ἐνώπιον τῶν ἀνθρώπων ἀπαρνηθήσεται ἐνώπιον τῶν ἀγγέλων τοῦ Θεοῦ.

9. But he that denieth me before men shall be denied before the angels of God.

9. And whoever will deny me before men will be denied before the powers of God.

51. Δοκεῖτε ὅτι εἰρήνην παρεγενόμην δοῦναι ἐν τῇ γῇ; οὐχί, λέγω ὑμῖν, ἀλλ᾽ ἢ διαμερισμόν.

51. Suppose ye that I am come to give peace on earth? I tell you, Nay; but rather division:ʲ

51. Or do you think that I teach peace upon earth? No, not peace, but discord:

52. Ἔσονται γὰρ ἀπὸ τοῦ νῦν πέντε ἐν οἴκῳ ἑνὶ διαμεμερισμένοι, τρεῖς ἐπὶ δυσί, καὶ δύο ἐπὶ τρισί.

52. For from henceforth there shall be five in one house divided, three against two, and two against three.

52. For from now on five in one house will be divided, three from two, and two from three.

53. Διαμερισθήσεται πατὴρ ἐφ᾽ υἱῷ, καὶ υἱὸς ἐπὶ πατρί· μήτηρ ἐπὶ θυγατρί, καὶ θυγάτηρ ἐπὶ μητρί· πενθερὰ ἐπὶ τὴν νύμφην αὐτῆς, καὶ νύμφη ἐπὶ τὴν πενθερὰν αὐτῆς.

53. The father shall be divided against the son, and the son against the father; the mother against the daughter, and the daughter against the mother; the mother in law against her daughter in law, and the daughter in law against her mother in law.

53. The father will be divided from his son, and the son from his father; and the mother from the daughter, and the daughter from the mother; and the mother-in-law from the daughter-in-law, and the daughter-in-law from the mother-in-law.

36. Καὶ ἐχθροὶ τοῦ ἀνθρώπου οἱ οἰκιακοὶ αὐτοῦ.

Matt. x. 36. And a man's foes shall be they of his own household.

36. And a man's foes will be his own household.

21. Παραδώσει δὲ ἀδελφὸς ἀδελφὸν εἰς θάνατον, καὶ πατὴρ τέκνον· καὶ ἐπαναστήσονται τέκνα ἐπὶ γονεῖς, καὶ θανατώσουσιν αὐτούς.

21. And the brother shall deliver up the brother to death, and the father the child: and the children shall rise up against their parents, and cause them to be put to death.

21. And the brother will deliver the brother up to death, and the father the child; and the children will rise up against their parents, and will deliver them up to death.

26. Εἴ τις ἔρχεται πρός με, καὶ οὐ μισεῖ τὸν πατέρα ἑαυτοῦ καὶ τὴν μητέρα, καὶ τὴν γυναῖκα καὶ τὰ τέκνα, καὶ τοὺς ἀδελφοὺς καὶ τὰς ἀδελφάς, ἔτι δὲ καὶ τὴν ἑαυτοῦ ψυχὴν, οὐ δύναταί μου μαθητὴς εἶναι.

Luke xiv. 26. If any man come to me, and hate not his father, and mother, and wife, and children, and brethren, and sisters, yea, and his own life also, he cannot be my disciple.

26. If a man wants to be with me, and will not esteem little his father, and mother, and wife, and children, and brothers, and sisters, and his own life, he cannot be my disciple.

37. Ὁ φιλῶν πατέρα ἢ μητέρα ὑπὲρ ἐμὲ, οὐκ ἔστι μου ἄξιος· καὶ ὁ φιλῶν υἱὸν ἢ θυγατέρα ὑπὲρ ἐμὲ, οὐκ ἔστι μου ἄξιος·

Matt. x. 37. He that loveth father or mother more than me is not worthy of me: and he that loveth son or daughter more than me is not worthy of me.

37. He who loves his father and mother more than me does not agree with me; and he who loves his son or daughter more than me does not agree with me.

23. Ἔλεγε δὲ πρὸς πάντας, Εἴ τις θέλει ὀπίσω μου ἐλθεῖν, ἀπαρ-

Luke ix. 23. And he said to them all, If any man will come after me, let him deny himself,

23. And he said to all, If any man wants to be my disciple, let him deny his desires, and let

ησάσθω ἑαυτὸν, καὶ ἀράτω τὸν σταυρὸν αὐτοῦ καθ᾽ ἡμέραν, καὶ ἀκολουθείτω μοι.	and take up his cross daily, and follow me.	him at any hour be ready for the gallows, and then only will he be my disciple.
39. Ὁ εὑρὼν τὴν ψυχὴν αὐτοῦ ἀπολέσει αὐτήν· καὶ ὁ ἀπολέσας τὴν ψυχὴν αὐτοῦ ἕνεκεν ἐμοῦ εὑρήσει αὐτήν.	*Matt. x. 39.* He that findeth his life shall lose it: and he that loseth his life for my sake shall find it.	39. He who takes care of his life will cause his life to perish, and he who ruins his life for my sake will save it.

(*a*) I exclude the sixth verse from Matthew, which is wanting in Luke and which puts into the mouth of Jesus a thought which is foreign to his teaching.

The words *heal the sick*, etc. (Verse 8) are omitted, as external proofs of the truth, which are unnecessary for the teaching.

(*b*) ἄξιος means *of equal weight, that which will equalize the scales*. Here it means *in conformity*. In this passage the words mean this: a man who works cannot help but receive what he needs for his sustenance; and so a man who wants and is ready to work is in no need of a supply of money and garments.

(*c*) Do not seek a place where it is better, but stay where you happen to be.

(*d*) ἄξιος here again means *in conformity*, but I translate it by *agreeing* in this sense, that if the hosts will receive you in conformity with your view, that is, if they will agree.

(*e*) εἰς μαρτύριον αὐτοῖς *as a proof to them*. A proof of what? To shake off the dust under the feet as one comes out of a house one can do only as a proof that nothing belonging to the house is to be taken away.

(*f*) ἀκέραιος means *simple, unmixed*.

(*g*) ἕως ἂν ἔλθῃ can mean here nothing but *to be exalted*, what Jesus told Nicodemus, and said also in other places. Here is understood εἰς φανερὸν ἔλθῃ, as in Mark iv. 22, οὐ γάρ ἐστί τι κρυπτὸν, ὃ ἐὰν μὴ φανερωθῇ· οὐδὲ ἐγένετο ἀπόκρυφον, ἀλλ᾽ ἵνα εἰς φανερὸν ἔλθῃ, and elsewhere. In any case, ἔλθῃ cannot be rendered, as

in many other passages, by *to come*. The verb *to come*
can be used only when somebody comes from somewhere.
But here it says neither whence nor whither, and he who
comes, the son of man, is an abstract principle, to which
walking is not proper.

Verse 25 is omitted. The words about Beelzebub refer
to the passage of the accusations of the Pharisees. The
verse is wanting in Mark and in Luke.

(*h*) The expression *to throw into Gehenna* was met
with in the parables. Its meaning is definite there.
It is not only a carnal death, but a complete destruction,
to which the tares were subject.

(*i*) In Luke we have in this passage διαμερισμόν *division*, and so μάχαιρα has to be translated by *discord*, in
which sense it is used in Rom. vii. 35.

(*j*) The sentence is without a verb, and so the verb
must be in the same future in which the whole discourse
is carried on. By these words a mysterious meaning is
ascribed to the fact that a man's household are always his
foes. This verse has not this meaning; in this sentence
is expressed what was said before: They will divide and
be as enemies.

(*k*) The words about the cross, which had no meaning
before the crucifixion of Jesus, have to be omitted.

Nothing more clearly than this discourse of Jesus
to his disciples before sending them out to preach,
which is repeated in all three gospels, defines the actual
significance of Jesus. If the significance of his preaching
were only what the church acknowledges it to be, the
whole discourse would be unintelligible. Why, indeed,
are the disciples to be beaten and killed, if the preaching
which they are to carry abroad is only a preaching about
making peace with the brother, about bodily purity, about
not sitting in judgment over a neighbour, about forgiving
the enemies, and about God's sending his son down upon

earth ? It is impossible to imagine sufficiently stupid and idle men who would take the trouble for this to drive away and beat people. It is impossible to imagine the causes which the oppressors could invent in order to torment, strike, and kill harmless preachers of good moral rules and of the invention about the son of God. Whom could they offend ? Those who wanted, listened to them; who did not want, did not listen to them. Why, then, were they to be hated ? If it had been a good, but paradoxical, moral teaching, such as the freethinking historians represent it to have been, there would still be no cause for persecuting them. If this teaching was about God's having sent his son down on the earth to redeem the human race, there were still fewer causes for being angry at men, who imagined that and found pleasure in it. If it was a rejection of the Jewish law, there was still no reason for persecuting them, especially no reason for the Gentiles to do so, and then, as now, it was the Gentiles who persecuted them. If it had been a political doctrine, an opposition to the rich and the mighty, such opposition would have been suppressed by the rich and the mighty then and there, as such oppositions have been suppressed before and since. It was something else.

Only when we fully understand the teaching, as it is expressed in the sermon on the mount and in the whole Gospel; if we understand that Jesus forbids directly every kind of murder and even resistance to evil; forbids oaths (that apparently unimportant affair which leads to most terrible violence); forbids courts, that is, punishments, every counteraction to violence and rapine, and so forbids property, as his first disciples understood it; forbids the aloofness of the nations, the famous love of country, — we shall be able to understand those persecutions to which Jesus and his first and subsequent disciples were subjected, and we can understand the anticipation of Jesus as to the persecutions, an anticipation which was evidently shared also by his disciples, and we comprehend also the division which was to take place.

Naturally, if one man in the family, having grasped the teaching, refuses to make a promise under oath, or to be a judge, or to go to court, or to coöperate with the authorities, or to take part in war, or to collect taxes, or to carry out punishments, or neglects wealth, naturally a division must arise in the family, if the other members have not comprehended the teaching.

Jesus obviously knew that; he knew that it would be so and could not be otherwise; he knew that his teaching was not a teaching, but a spark, which kindled the consciousness of God in the hearts of men, and that, burning up, it could not be put out. It is for this reason that Jesus Christ knew that in each house five would be divided, and some of them would be against the rest. Some would be kindled, and the others would be putting out those who were burning up. And he was anxious to see the flame as quickly as possible. And the flame was kindled and burned later, and burns even now, and will always burn, as long as there are men.

If it were only a moral teaching about conduct in the existing order of things, it is evident that the preachers would not be in anybody's way, and it would not be a flame which embraces everything, but a candle which would light up those who are near to it.

If it had been only a church teaching about God's having come down into the world to save people, no one would have known the teaching, as we do not know the beliefs of the Zulus or of the Chuvashes, and nobody would have given it any thought. It would not only have gone out, but would never have been kindled.

If it had been a social-revolutionary teaching, it would have burned up and gone out long ago, as such teachings burned up and went out in China, in every place where there are men: the poor would have taken the property away from the rich and mighty and would themselves have become rich and mighty, or the rich and mighty would have crushed the poor, and the flame would have been extinguished. But the flame did not go out and will not go out, because Jesus does not speak of rules about how a man may live in society in the best manner possible with the existing order of things, nor of the manner of praying to God, nor what God is, nor of the reorganization of society. He tells the truth about what man is, and what his life consists in. And a man who comprehends what his life is will live that life. A man who understands the meaning of life can no longer see any meaning in anything else. When he has come to understand what is life and what death, he cannot help walking toward the life and running away from death. And no matter what may stand on the path toward life, — moral rules, God, beliefs of men, the social order, — a man who has come to understand life will walk toward it without paying any attention to anything, and in his forward movement will include all the phenomena of life: morality, and divine worship, and the social structure.

Jesus Christ has revealed his teaching not to inform men that he was God, not to improve the life of men upon earth, not in order to overthrow the authorities, but because in his soul, as in the soul of every man who comes into the world, he knew, lay the consciousness of God, which is life, and to which every evil is opposed. Jesus Christ knew and kept repeating that he was saying what he was saying, and what was speaking in him was God, who is in the soul of every man. And, sending out his disciples, Jesus Christ says, Fear nobody; pity nobody, and do not worry in advance what you are going to say. Live the true life, — it is the comprehension of God, and when you will need to speak, have no care, the spirit of

God will speak for you. And your words, spoken to a few, will be borne everywhere, because they are the truth.

	Luke x.	
17. Ὑπέστρεψαν δὲ οἱ ἑβδομήκοντα μετὰ χαρᾶς, λέγοντες, Κύριε, καὶ τὰ δαιμόνια ὑποτάσσεται ἡμῖν ἐν τῷ ὀνόματί σου.	17. And the seventy returned again with joy, saying, Lord, even the devils are subject unto us through thy name.	17. And the seventy whom he sent out returned with joy, and said, Sir, the evil is vanquished by us through thy power.
18. Εἶπε δὲ αὐτοῖς,	18. And he said unto them,	18. And he said to them,
20. Πλὴν ἐν τούτῳ μὴ χαίρετε, ὅτι τὰ πνεύματα ὑμῖν ὑποτάσσεται· χαίρετε δὲ μᾶλλον, ὅτι τὰ ὀνόματα ὑμῶν ἐγράφη ἐν τοῖς οὐρανοῖς·	20. Notwithstanding, in this rejoice not, that the spirits are subject unto you; but rather rejoice, because your names are written in heaven.[c]	20. But do not rejoice that the evil is vanquished by you; rather rejoice, because you are in the kingdom of heaven.
21. Ἐν αὐτῇ τῇ ὥρᾳ ἠγαλλιάσατο τῷ πνεύματι ὁ Ἰησοῦς, καὶ εἶπεν, Ἐξομολογοῦμαί σοι, πάτερ, κύριε τοῦ οὐρανοῦ καὶ τῆς γῆς, ὅτι ἀπέκρυψας ταῦτα ἀπὸ σοφῶν καὶ συνετῶν, καὶ ἀπεκάλυψας αὐτὰ νηπίοις· ναί, ὁ πατήρ, ὅτι οὕτως ἐγένετο εὐδοκία ἔμπροσθέν σου.	21. In that hour Jesus rejoiced in spirit, and said, I thank thee, O Father, Lord of heaven and earth,[d] that thou hast hid these things from the wise and prudent, and hast revealed them unto babes: even so, Father,[e] for so it seemed good[f] in thy sight.[g]	21. Then Jesus rejoiced in his spirit, and said, I recognise thee, my Father, lord of heaven and earth, because thou hast hid this from the wise and prudent, and hast revealed it to children. Thou art truly the Father! In this has thy love been expressed.
	Matt. xi.	
27. Πάντα μοι παρεδόθη ὑπὸ τοῦ πατρός μου· καὶ οὐδεὶς ἐπιγινώσκει τὸν υἱόν, εἰ μὴ ὁ πατήρ· οὐδὲ τὸν πατέρα τις ἐπιγινώσκει, εἰ μὴ ὁ υἱός, καὶ ᾧ ἐὰν βούληται ὁ υἱὸς ἀποκαλύψαι.	27. All things are delivered unto me of my Father: and no man knoweth the Son, but the Father; neither knoweth any man the Father, save the Son, and he to whomsoever the Son will[h] reveal him.	27. Everything has been delivered to me by my Father, and no man recognises the son, but the Father; neither does a man know who the Father is, but the son, and he to whom the son will reveal him.

(a) In Verse 17 it says τὰ δαιμόνια; in Verse 20 the same is called τὰ πνεύματα. If the unintelligible Verses 18 and 19 did not exist, no one would think of translating δαιμόνια and πνεύματα by *devil*, but in the plural, that is, *souls of men*, that is, the meaning is that evil men, the evil itself, is being vanquished by his teaching.

Verses 18 and 19 are excluded, not because they express anything which does not agree with the teaching, but because in the form in which they have reached us they are unintelligible.

(b) What are these spirits, πνεύματα? This word is found in the gospels, in the epistles, and in the Acts, and always in the same sense, as immaterial powers, spirit, not the divine spirit, but false spirit. Thus the word is used in 1 Tim. iv. 1, and in many other places. It is very easy to translate it by *devil*, and to say that those who wrote it believed in the devil. But the trouble is that, if we translate it so, we must throw out this passage, because devil means nothing to us. The meaning of the word is, however, clearly defined in all the passages, and especially in the one under discussion: πνεύματα means *false spirit*. The spirit is the comprehension, and so it means *false comprehension, deception, false teaching, debauchery*, in the general sense, *evil*.

(c) Names are written in heaven, can mean nothing but, Participation in the kingdom of heaven.

(d) There ought to be a period here, since what follows is an explanation why Jesus recognizes his Father to be the Lord of everything. He recognizes him as the Father, because he has revealed the secret of the kingdom of God not to the wise and the prudent, but to all unthinking children.

(e) ὁ πατήρ is here by no means the vocative, either grammatically, or by the sense. It is the continuation of the discourse. There is a comma here, and for clearness' sake I add *thou*.

(f) εὐδοκία *good will, love*.

(g) ἔμπροσθέν σου means *before thee*. According to the Hebrew meaning anything done before one is agreeable. The idea ἐγένετο εὐδοκία ἔμπροσθέν σου has to be translated by *love loved by thee*.

The general meaning is that not wisdom and learning, but the direct relation of the son to the Father, which is revealed to all, gave that love for the spirit which is the foundation of everything, and revealed the truth through this love, this turning of the son to the Father.

(*h*) *Will* is omitted in many texts.

No man can know the son, but the Father, and no man can know the Father, but the son. These words mean, what was said in the discourse of Nicodemus, that in man there is a spirit, which is incomprehensible to him, and that this spirit is the son of the spirit, and that is the last meaning of God. Here Jesus for the first time identifies himself with the son of man and, saying *I*, means not himself, Jesus of Galilee, but the spirit which dwells in man.

EVIL IS NOT DESTROYED BY EVIL

20. Καὶ ἔρχονται εἰς οἶκον· καὶ συνέρχεται πάλιν ὄχλος, ὥστε μὴ δύνασθαι αὐτοὺς μήτε ἄρτον φαγεῖν.

21. Καὶ ἀκούσαντες οἱ παρ' αὐτοῦ ἐξῆλθον κρατῆσαι αὐτόν· ἔλεγον γὰρ, Ὅτι ἐξέστη.

22. Καὶ οἱ γραμματεῖς οἱ ἀπὸ Ἱεροσολύμων καταβάντες ἔλεγον, Ὅτι Βεελζεβοὺλ ἔχει, καὶ, Ὅτι ἐν τῷ ἄρχοντι τῶν δαιμονίων ἐκβάλλει τὰ δαιμόνια.

23. Καὶ προσκαλεσάμενος αὐτοὺς, ἐν παραβολαῖς ἔλεγεν αὐτοῖς, Πῶς δύναται Σατανᾶς Σατανᾶν ἐκβάλλειν;

24. Καὶ ἐὰν βασιλεία ἐφ' ἑαυτὴν μερισθῇ, οὐ δύναται σταθῆναι ἡ βασιλεία ἐκείνη·

26. Καὶ εἰ ὁ Σατανᾶς ἀνέστη ἐφ' ἑαυτὸν καὶ μεμέρισται, οὐ δύναται σταθῆναι, ἀλλὰ τέλος ἔχει.

Mark iii. 20. And they went into a house, and the multitude cometh together again, so that they could not so much as eat bread.

21. And when his friends heard of it, they went out to lay hold on him: for they said, He is beside himself.

22. And the scribes which came down from Jerusalem said, He hath Beelzebub,[c] and by the prince of the devils casteth he out devils.

23. And he called them unto him, and said unto them in parables, How can Satan[b] cast out Satan?

24. And if a kingdom[c] be divided[d] against itself, that kingdom cannot stand.

26. And if Satan rise up against himself, and be divided, he cannot stand, but hath an end.[e]

20. And they came home, and again there was gathered a multitude, so that they could not dine.

21. And when his household heard of it, they went to seize him, for they said, He is beside himself.

22. And the scribes came from Jerusalem and said that he was an evil spirit, and that he destroyed evil by evil.

23. And calling them up, he said to them in parables, How can evil be cast out by evil?

24. And if a power rises against itself, that power cannot stand.

26. And if evil will go against itself, it cannot stand, but has an end.

19. Εἰ δὲ ἐγὼ ἐν Βεελζεβοὺλ ἐκβάλλω τὰ δαιμόνια, οἱ υἱοὶ ὑμῶν ἐν τίνι ἐκβάλλουσι; διὰ τοῦτο κριταὶ ὑμῶν αὐτοὶ ἔσονται.

20. Εἰ δὲ ἐν δακτύλῳ Θεοῦ ἐκβάλλω τὰ δαιμόνια, ἄρα ἔφθασεν ἐφ' ὑμᾶς ἡ βασιλεία τοῦ Θεοῦ.

29. Ἤ πῶς δύναταί τις εἰσελθεῖν εἰς τὴν οἰκίαν τοῦ ἰσχυροῦ καὶ τὰ σκεύη αὐτοῦ διαρπάσαι, ἐὰν μὴ πρῶτον δήσῃ τὸν ἰσχυρόν, καὶ τότε τὴν οἰκίαν αὐτοῦ διαρπάσαι;

30. Ὁ μὴ ὢν μετ' ἐμοῦ, κατ' ἐμοῦ ἐστι· καὶ ὁ μὴ συνάγων μετ' ἐμοῦ, σκορπίζει.

31. Διὰ τοῦτο λέγω ὑμῖν, Πᾶσα ἁμαρτία καὶ βλασφημία ἀφεθήσεται τοῖς ἀνθρώποις·

32. Καὶ ὃς ἂν εἴπῃ λόγον κατὰ τοῦ υἱοῦ τοῦ ἀνθρώπου, ἀφεθήσεται αὐτῷ· ὃς δ' ἂν εἴπῃ κατὰ τοῦ Πνεύματος τοῦ Ἁγίου, οὐκ ἀφεθήσεται αὐτῷ, οὔτε ἐν τούτῳ τῷ αἰῶνι οὔτε ἐν τῷ μέλλοντι.

Luke xi. 19. And if I by Beelzebub cast out devils, by whom do your sons cast them out? therefore shall they be your judges.

20. But if I with the finger of God cast out devils, no doubt the kingdom of God is come upon you.

Matt. xii. 29. Or else, how can one enter into a strong man's house, and spoil his goods, except he first bind the strong man? and then he will spoil his house.

30. He that is not with me is against me; and he that gathereth not with me scattereth abroad.

31. Wherefore I say unto you, All manner of sin and blasphemy shall be forgiven unto men:

32. And whosoever speaketh a word against the Son of man, it shall be forgiven him: but whosoever speaketh against the Holy Ghost, it shall not be forgiven him, neither in this world, neither in the world to come.

19. If I cast out evil with evil, how do you cast it out? Be therefore your own judges.

20. But if I cast out the evil with the spirit of God, then the kingdom of God was before.

29. Or else, how can one enter into a strong man's house and ruin him? First the strong man has to be bound and then only can his house be ruined.

30. He who is not with me is against me. He who does not gather, scatters.

31. Therefore I tell you, Every error, every false word is left to men;

32. And if a man says a false word against the son of man, it will be forgiven him: but if a man says something against the spirit of God, it will not be forgiven him, neither in this world, nor in the world to come.

(*a*) In John δαιμόνιον ἔχει. Βεελζεβοὺλ ἔχει means the same as δαιμόνιον ἔχει, as can be seen from the continuation of the discourse.

(*b*) Σατανᾶς again means the same as πνεῦμα δαιμονίων.

(*c*) βασιλεία means here *every power.*

(*d*) μερίζομαι not only means *to divide,* but also *to turn.*

In Mark it reads, And if an house be divided against itself, the house cannot stand (Mark iii. 25); in Matthew: Every kingdom and every city divided against itself,

shall not stand (Matt. xii. 25). This verse has no sense
in either gospel. There is no simile. In Luke the word
οἶκος stands in a different sense, ἐρημοῦται καὶ οἶκος
πίπτει. The same we find in one Latin variant, so that
οἶκος is not a new comparison, but a strengthening of the
first: the power will not stand and will fall, as a house
from a house. Apparently the meaning of the verse is
lost. In the form in which it is rendered it adds nothing and only confuses, and so has to be omitted.

(e) That is, if evil went against itself, there would be
no evil, and yet it exists.

(f) If you acknowledge that I expel evil, I certainly
cannot do so with evil, for then there would be no evil.
If you expel evil, you certainly do not do so with evil,
but with something else, with good. Therefore, if I
expel evil, I do so not with evil, but with good.

(g) If there were only Σατανᾶς and δαιμόνια, that is,
deception and evil, deception would destroy deception,
evil would destroy evil, and there would be no evil. But
you yourselves expel evil with good. And if I expel evil
with the spirit of God, that means that the spirit of God
was in men, and even before me the divine will was in men.

(h) If I expel evil with the spirit of God, the spirit of
God was already in men; or else I should not be able to
expel evil, just as a man cannot enter the house of a
strong man and rob it, unless he first binds that man.
But man is already bound by the spirit of God and by
the consciousness of its power.

(i) The false interpretation of what is the son of man
can do no harm, but the false interpretation of what is
the spirit of God cannot pass by unpunished. A man
who does not recognize the spirit of God, by that very
fact is deprived of life.

The meaning of the whole place is this, that the learned,
the lawyers, rebuked Christ that his teaching would lead

to even greater evil than what he wanted to correct.
Jesus says that it is not he who corrects the world with
evil, but they, and that the world stands not through
evil, but through something else. I, he says of himself,
do not correct the world with evil, but with the divine
spirit, that divine spirit which lives in you. If I corrected by means of evil, I should have no power; but I
correct with the divine spirit, and that has power. Follow my teaching, and all the evil will be vanquished in
the world, all the evil will be destroyed. The spirit of
God is the only life. He who does not live in the spirit
of God is against it, in that he causes his life to perish, as
a man causes his wheat to perish, when he does not gather
it from the field, and thus the most important mistake for
life is the false comprehension of the spirit of God. Those
men who falsely interpret the divine spirit deceive men,
and cause their own ruin and that of others. They are
those through whom evil is disseminated in the world.

33. ῾Η ποιήσατε τὸ δένδρον καλὸν, καὶ τὸν καρπὸν, αὐτοῦ καλὸν, ἢ ποιήσατε τὸ δένδρον σαπρὸν, καὶ τὸν καρπὸν αὐτοῦ σαπρόν· ἐκ γὰρ τοῦ καρποῦ τὸ δένδρον γινώσκεται.	*Matt. xii.* 33. Either make the tree good, and his fruit good; or else make the tree corrupt, and his fruit corrupt: for the tree is known by his fruit.	33. Either make the tree good, then its fruit will be good: or make the tree bad, and then the fruit will be bad: for the tree is known by its fruit.
34. Γεννήματα ἐχιδνῶν, πῶς δύνασθε ἀγαθὰ λαλεῖν, πονηροὶ ὄντες; ἐκ γὰρ τοῦ περισσεύματος τῆς καρδίας τὸ στόμα λαλεῖ.	34. O generation of vipers, how can ye, being evil, speak good things? for out of the abundance of the heart the mouth speaketh.	34. Tribe of snakes, you cannot speak good things, because you are evil. The mouth speaks what the heart wants to utter.
35 ῾Ο ἀγαθὸς ἄνθρωπος ἐκ τοῦ ἀγαθοῦ θησαυροῦ τῆς καρδίας ἐκβάλλει τὰ ἀγαθά· καὶ ὁ πονηρὸς ἄνθρωπος ἐκ τοῦ πονηροῦ θησαυροῦ ἐκβάλλει πονηρά.	35. A good man out of the good treasure of the heart bringeth forth good things: and an evil man out of the evil treasure bringeth forth evil things.	35. A good man lets out of his heart whatever good he has treasured in it; and an evil man lets out whatever evil he has gathered in his heart.
36. Λέγω δὲ ὑμῖν, ὅτι πᾶν ῥῆμα ἀργὸν, ὃ	36. But I say unto you, That every idle word	36. And I tell you, Every idle word which

ἐὰν λαλήσωσιν οἱ ἄνθρωποι, ἀποδώσουσι περὶ αὐτοῦ λόγον ἐν ἡμέρᾳ κρίσεως.

that men shall speak, they shall give account thereof in the day of judgment.ᵃ

a man speaks will be looked into, to see why it has been said, in the day of the accounting.

49. Ἀποκριθεὶς δὲ ὁ Ἰωάννης εἶπεν, Ἐπιστάτα, εἴδομέν τινα ἐπὶ τῷ ὀνόματί σου ἐκβάλλοντα τὰ δαιμόνια· καὶ ἐκωλύσαμεν αὐτὸν, ὅτι οὐκ ἀκολουθεῖ μεθ᾿ ἡμῶν.

Luke ix. 49. And John answered and said, Master, we saw one casting out devils in thy name; and we forbade him, because he followeth not with us.

49. And John said to him, Teacher, we saw a man casting out evil like thee, and we forbade him, because he does not go with us.

50. Καὶ εἶπε πρὸς αὐτὸν ὁ Ἰησοῦς, Μὴ κωλύετε· ὃς γὰρ οὐκ ἔστι καθ᾿ ἡμῶν, ὑπὲρ ἡμῶν ἐστιν.

50. And Jesus said unto him, Forbid him not: for he that is not against us is for us.ᵇ

50. Jesus said to them, Do not forbid him: he who is not against us is with us.

(*a*) Verse 37, according to the received translations, means that Jesus says that with words one is justified, and with words condemned. Such a meaning of the verse is immoral and directly opposed to the whole teaching.

Jesus continually says, Work, and do not speak. This verse has to be excluded, as an interpolation, or has to be translated differently. I translate λόγος in this place in the sense of the cause which impels a man to say a word. Such an interpretation is in harmony with what precedes.

(*b*) The disciples of Jesus think that there is a special teaching of Jesus, and that it is necessary to follow him exclusively, and that he who does not follow him is in error. Jesus says, You have no reason to think so: he who expels evil does not act against us, but does what we are doing, and is for us.

THE IMPOTENT MAN HEALED

1. Μετὰ ταῦτα ἦν ἑορτὴ τῶν Ἰουδαίων, καὶ ἀνέβη ὁ Ἰησοῦς εἰς Ἱεροσόλυμα.

John v. 1. After this there was a feast of the Jews; and Jesus went up to Jerusalem.

1. After this there was a feast of the Jews; and Jesus went to Jerusalem.

2. Ἔστι δὲ ἐν τοῖς Ἱεροσολύμοις ἐπὶ τῇ προβατικῇ κολυμβήθρα, ἡ ἐπιλεγομένη Ἑβραϊστὶ Βηθεσδὰ, πέντε στοὰς ἔχουσα.

3. Ἐν ταύταις κατέκειτο πλῆθος πολὺ τῶν ἀσθενούντων, τυφλῶν, χωλῶν, ξηρῶν, ἐκδεχομένων τὴν τοῦ ὕδατος κίνησιν.

4. Ἄγγελος γὰρ κατὰ καιρὸν κατέβαινεν ἐν τῇ κολυμβήθρα, καὶ ἐτάρασσε τὸ ὕδωρ· ὁ οὖν πρῶτος ἐμβὰς μετὰ τὴν ταραχὴν τοῦ ὕδατος ὑγιὴς ἐγίνετο, ᾧ δήποτε κατείχετο νοσήματι.

5. Ἦν δέ τις ἄνθρωπος ἐκεῖ τριάκοντα ὀκτὰ ἔτη ἔχων ἐν τῇ ἀσθενείᾳ.

6. Τοῦτον ἰδὼν ὁ Ἰησοῦς κατακείμενον, καὶ γνοὺς ὅτι πολὺν ἤδη χρόνον ἔχει, λέγει αὐτῷ, Θέλεις ὑγιὴς γενέσθαι ;

7. Ἀπεκρίθη αὐτῷ ὁ ἀσθενῶν, Κύριε, ἄνθρωπον οὐκ ἔχω, ἵνα, ὅταν ταραχθῇ τὸ ὕδωρ, βάλλῃ με εἰς τὴν κολυμβήθραν· ἐν ᾧ δὲ ἔρχομαι ἐγὼ, ἄλλος πρὸ ἐμοῦ καταβαίνει.

8. Λέγει αὐτῷ ὁ Ἰησοῦς, Ἔγειραι, ἆρον τὸν κράββατόν σου, καὶ περιπάτει.

9. Καὶ εὐθέως ἐγένετο ὑγιὴς ὁ ἄνθρωπος, καὶ ἦρε τὸν κράββατον αὐτοῦ, καὶ περιεπάτει.

---

2. Now there is at Jerusalem by the sheep gate a pool, which is called in the Hebrew tongue Bethesda, having five porches.

3. In these lay a great multitude of impotent folk, of blind, halt, withered, waiting for the moving of the water.[a]

4. For an angel went down at a certain season into the pool, and troubled the water: whosoever then first after the troubling of the water stepped in was made whole of whatsoever disease he had.

5. And a certain man was there, which had an infirmity thirty and eight years.

6. When Jesus saw him lie, and knew that he had been now a long time in that case, he saith unto him, Wilt thou be made whole ?

7. The impotent man answered him, Sir, I have no man, when the water is troubled, to put me into the pool: but while I am coming, another steppeth down before me.

8. Jesus saith unto him, Rise, take up thy bed, and walk.

9. And immediately the man was made whole, and took up his bed, and walked.

---

2. There is in Jerusalem at the sheep market a pool, which is called in Hebrew Bethesda, with five porches.

3. On these lay a great multitude of sick people: of blind, impotent, and lame. They were all waiting for the motion of the water.

4. For they supposed that an angel went down at certain times into the pool, and stirred the water, and that if one was the first after the stirring of the water to enter the pool, he would be made well, no matter what disease he had.

5. And there was there a certain man, who had been infirm for thirty-eight years.

6. Jesus saw him lie, and learned that he had been so for a long time, and said to him, Dost thou wish to be made well ?

7. The feeble man said, Why should I not want it, sir ? But I have no man, when the water is stirred, to put me in the pool; I am always too late. When I rush in, another has leaped in before me.

8. And Jesus said to him, Wake up, take thy bed, and walk.

9. And the man awoke immediately, and took up his bed, and walked.

(a) ἐκδεχομένων means *who were waiting*. The next sentence, An angel went down to stir the water, must be referred to ἐκδεχομένων, that is, they waited for an

angel to come down and stir the water, and then, and
so forth; and so I translate, They waited for the water
to be moved, supposing that an angel, and so forth,
and to this sentence I add *as if* (they supposed that).

This is what the church says about it (Interpretation
of the Gospel of John, p. 174):

Now at Jerusalem: Josephus, the Jewish historian, does not
mention this pool, but that does not weaken the authenticity
of John's narration about this pool; Josephus does not mention
many important things and circumstances.

There is: Either John in his vivid imagination transfers
himself to the time when Jerusalem was not yet destroyed, and
so says *there is*, as though he had the pool before his eyes; or at
the destruction of Jerusalem by Titus this pool with its build-
ings was spared, as a public charitable institution, and was still
standing during the writing of the gospel, though it may have
been in a different form from what it was in the lifetime of
Jesus.

By the sheep gate: This is mentioned in the book of Nehemiah;
it was at the northeast of the city wall, on the road across the
brook Cedron into Gethsemane and the Mount of Olives (now
the gate of St. Stephen). It was called Sheep Gate, no doubt,
because through it the sacrificial animals were driven to the
temple, or because near it there was a market where these sacrificial animals were brought and sold, and whence they were
driven to the temple to be sacrificed.

Pool: A small basin in which people washed or bathed. No
doubt there was here a spring which formed this pool, from
which the water again flowed into the ground. In Hebrew
Bethesda means the house of pity or mercy, that is, God's house,
since the spring had a curative power, which God, in his mercy,
had given to his nation.

Five porches: Galleries, on which the sick, protected against
the inclemencies of the weather and against the heat of the sun,
could walk, sit, and lie. "Bithasa (Bithesda) it is called even
at this day" (Eusebius), and in the fifth century they still
pointed out the five porticoes of the pool.

In these lay, and so forth: This medicinal spring attracted
a great multitude of the sick of every kind (a diversity of diseases is indicated: blindness, lameness, consumption), who were
placed in galleries built for the purpose. Maybe they came

or were led or carried there only at certain times, when they expected the troubling of the water; maybe some remained there for a long time in this expectation.

For an angel, etc.: The spring had curative properties not at all times, but only at certain seasons, namely, when an angel of the Lord went down into it and troubled the water, and was not useful for all people, but only for those who immediately after the troubling of the water stepped into it, consequently only for a short time, but then it cured all diseases. From the narration it does not appear that the angel came down in visible form into the pool and troubled the water; it was not visible for others, but it was an action which was contemplated with the spiritual eye of the apostle; the sick people and others knew only by the troubling of the water that it was time to step into it in order to be cured. The holy writers and the Jews in general ascribed especial visible benefactions of God, which appeared in certain powers and actions of Nature, to an especial ministration and action of angels, whom God has appointed as governors of such or such elements of Nature. What for others are the actions of the elements of Nature are for their enlightened vision actions of the angels who are in charge of the elements of Nature. The spring, like many mineral springs, cured all kinds of diseases which did not yield to the action of other customary means, and, like some of these springs, acted with particular force at certain times, periodically. It seems that at certain times the water in this spring welled up with especial force and in great abundance, and so was troubled, became turbid (or red, — bloody), as Eusebius says, and at that time became particularly powerful to cure all kinds of diseases. This welling up in especial abundance was the invisible action of the angel of God, which the apostle, the seer of secrets, interpreted in such a manner; but for others it was a usual action of the elements of Nature, as which, it seems, it appeared to the sick man who was here cured by Christ.

Whosoever first stepped in: The expression does not seem to indicate that only one was cured, the first who stepped in after its troubling; but that in general, the water immediately after the troubling exerted a special, unusual, curative power, and then lost its energetic action, and only those who managed to get in immediately after the troubling were cured; then the water lost its power and did not exert such an unusual action.

Was made whole: From the account of the narrator it does not appear that the cure took place at once, suddenly, miraculously, as in the case of the healing of the sick by Christ;

perhaps it was gradual, receiving only the first impulse from the curative spring. In the latter case, the sudden cure of the impotent man who was lying there was the more striking.

Which had an infirmity: It does not appear which; as can be seen from what follows, he could not walk freely, was infirm in his legs, and had been lying thirty-eight years, that is, had been sick for thirty-eight years, but was himself older. The long duration and apparent incurability of the disease made exceedingly striking the miracle of healing which was performed on him.

Knew that he had been now a long time in that case: He learned it from others who were there, or directly through his divine omniscience; *had been*, that is, in that disease.

Wilt thou be made whole? A question which has for its purpose to rouse the energy of the sick man's faith. The very necessity of the question compelled the sick man to concentrate his thoughts and to turn them to the face of him who was asking, and to expect succour from him. But, evidently, the sick man did not understand to what the speech of his interlocutor was tending; he turned in thought to the medicinal spring and seemed to be complaining because he could not make use of its curative power.

Sir: That is, I want to be well, but have no man who could help me to be healed in this pool, when the water is troubled.

While I am coming: The sick man could walk, but only slowly, and was not able to anticipate the others, while the others got ahead of him and snapped their cure away from him. He answers very meekly, without expressing any blasphemy, does not deny Christ, who seems to have proposed an irrelevant question, does not curse the day of his birth, as we of little faith do, even in the slightest indisposition, and. answers meekly and timidly.

Rise, etc.: The Lord took pity on him who had suffered so long and, seeing the possibility of faith in him, cured him with his mighty word.

Take up thy bed: See note to Matt. ix. 6-7.

This is what Reuss says (Vol. VI., pp. 166–168):

Comme l'auteur ne précise pas l'époque de l'année où ce fait a dû se passer, il est inutile de se livrer à des conjectures pour déterminer la fête en question. Les copistes, qui ont biffé l'article, ont sans doute été du même avis (*une* fête quelconque). *La* fête, dans la pensée du rédacteur, pouvait être celle où les Juifs se rendaient à Jérusalem de préférence, une Pâque. Mais cela n'est pas absolument nécessaire ; c'était toujours celle qui amena Jésus, et les récits de ce livre nous représentent Jésus comme ayant la coutume de se rendre assez régulièrement aux fêtes. On comprend que cet article gênait les lecteurs ; mais on ne voit pas pourquoi on l'aurait ajouté, s'il n'était pas authentique. La principale raison qu'on sait alléguer contre la Pâque, c'est qu'alors il y en aurait une de plus, et l'on a pourtant souverainement décidé que Jésus n'a pu vivre et voyager aussi longtemps. Par ce motif, on se rabat ici sur la fête de Purim (les Saturnales des Juifs), célébrée en Février ou Mars.

Rien de certain sur l'emplacement et sur la construction du bassin de *Béthesda*. Le lieu qu'on nomme ainsi de nos jours ne porte plus de traces des anciens portiques et il n'y a plus d'eau. La porte du bétail a été probablement au nord-est, dans le voisinage du temple.

Quant au phénomène physique qui se produisait dans le bassin (ébullition locale intermittente de la source), il paraît qu'anciennement déjà l'explication que l'auteur en donne a soulevé des doutes. Il y a des manuscrits et autres témoins anciens qui omettent soit les derniers mots du v. 3 (*qui attendaient*, etc.), soit tout le v. 4, soit toutes ces parties du texte. Des critiques modernes, en grand nombre, ont jugé que ces témoingages étaient assez décisifs pour condamner les quatre lignes en question comme étrangères à la rédaction primitive. On suppose alors qu'il y a là une légende judaïque ou chrétienne qui aurait fini par trouver place dans le récit pour expliquer ce que dit le malade au v. 7, et qui, à tout prendre, serait indigne de l'apôtre.

A première vue, cette manière de voir est assez plausible. Comme les Juifs et les chrétiens ne marchandaient nulle part l'intervention des anges dans les affaires de ce monde, on ne voit pas pourquoi elle aurait été effacée ici, si l'auteur en avait réellement parlé dans sa narration. Cependant il y a aussi des arguments à faire valoir dans le sens opposé. La question n'est pas de savoir s'il y a moyen de donner une explication naturelle du phénomène, ou si Jean a pu partager une opinion populaire ; il faut voir si l'ensemble de son texte demande que les phrases suspectes y soient comprises, ou si l'on peut les omettre sans déranger le reste. Or, on voit plus loin que l'auteur parle de l'agitation de l'eau comme d'une chose connue de ses lecteurs ; il met dans la bouche du malade des paroles qui supposent que le lecteur sait déjà de quelle condition tout exceptionnelle dépendait la guérison. Nous demanderons donc si l'auteur, qui ailleurs explique à ses lecteurs des détails que tous les Juifs, et surtout ceux de Jéru-

salem, pouvaient savoir, et cela par la simple raison qu'il n'écri-
vait pas pour les Juifs, si l'auteur, disons-nous, a pu supposer que
des étrangers connaîtraient la nature particulière de la source de
Béthesda, si différente pourtant, par les phénomènes qu'elle présentait, de toutes les autres qui servaient alors à des bains
hygiéniques? Évidemment non! Il a dû donner des explica-
tions préalables, et le v. 7 reste inintelligible si l'on efface le
4, et la moitié du 3e. Nous admettons donc que ce retranche-
ment s'est fait après coup, comme celui, non moins remarquable,
des v. 43 et 44 du 22e chapitre du Luc. Le phénomène en lui-
même, tel que le passage suspect le décrit, n'a rien d'étrange;
l'action de l'eau jaillissante peut parfaitement avoir été plus
forte dans l'espace restreint de l'embouchure. On nous a reproché de vouloir maintenir la leçon vulgaire, uniquement pour
le plaisir d'attribuer à l'apôtre une superstition. Mais si les
apôtres, d'après ce point de vue, font preuve de superstition en
croyant à l'intervention des anges dans le monde physique, il
faut biffer bien d'autres passages encore pour leur épargner ce
reproche.

Quoi qu'il en soit, le fait est raconté dans un tout autre but.
Il s'agit de caractériser l'action bienfaisante de Christ dans le
monde, action sans doute essentiellement spirituelle, mais sym-
bolisée par des guérisons du corps; et action permanente, non
soumise à des conditions de temps et de circonstances extérieures,
telles que seraient l'assistance de quelque autre force, naturelle ou
surnaturelle, en dehors de lui, ou bien encore une règle légale qui
eût pu le gêner. C'est par cette dernière considération que le
récit continue, ou plutôt qu'il passe de la narration d'un fait à
l'exposition des vérités absolues, de l'histoire à la théologie.
Jésus a voulu guérir un homme malade de paralysie depuis un
temps immémorial; voici la légalité traditionnelle qui se met en
travers. Il n'est pas difficile de saisir le sens profond du récit
qui nous est offert.

Le terme, dont l'auteur se sert pour motiver l'intervention de
Jésus, a été traduit par le mot: *sachant*, et non: *ayant appris*.
De fait, la première de ces expressions n'implique pas nécessairement l'idée du miracle, mais elle ne l'exclut pas non plus, et nous
croyons devoir la maintenir précisément par cette raison. Il ne
s'agit pas seulement de compassion et de miséricorde, mais de la
manifestation d'une puissance supérieure.

To my way of thinking, the peculiarity of this miracle
as distinguished from the others, is this, that in the other

the miracle appears amidst what is natural, as a proof of the divinity of Christ; but here, on the contrary, the natural appears amidst what is miraculous, as a proof of the divinity of Christ. A sick man has been waiting for twenty years for a miracle to happen, and Jesus says to him, Do not wait for anything; what is in thee, that will be. Wake up. If thou hast the power to get up and walk, walk. He tried, got up, and walked.

All this passage, which is taken as a miracle, is an indication of the fact that there can be no miracles, and that the man who is waiting for a miracle to happen is sick. That life itself is the greatest miracle, while the event itself is very simple, can frequently be seen in our midst. I know a lady who lay in bed for twenty years and got up only when morphine injections were administered to her; after twenty years the doctor who administered the injections confessed to her that he injected water only, and when the lady heard that she took up her bed, and walked.

The story about the pool is the same: it is narrated simply and clearly. Its significance is this, that men wait for miracles, for God's interference, but God is in them, God is life: so abandon thyself to it, believe it, and thou art alive. The whole subsequent discourse, save the interpolated ridicule of the belief in the Sabbath, which strengthens the meaning of the story about the pool, is only an elucidation of the idea that the one miracle, the one truth, the one power, is life, that life which is in every man and on which we ought to rely.

9. Ἦν δὲ σάββατον ἐν ἐκείνῃ τῇ ἡμέρᾳ.	*John v.* 9. And on the same day was the sabbath.	9. That happened on a Sabbath.
10. Ἔλεγον οὖν οἱ Ἰουδαῖοι τῷ τεθεραπευμένῳ, Σάββατόν ἐστιν· οὐκ ἔξεστί σοι ἆραι τὸν κράββατον.	10. The Jews therefore said unto him that was cured, It is the sabbath day; it is not lawful for thee to carry thy bed.	10. And the Jews said to the man, To-day is the Sabbath: thou shouldst not take up thy bed.

11. Ἀπεκρίθη αὐτοῖς, Ὁ ποιήσας με ὑγιῆ, ἐκεῖνός μοι εἶπεν, Ἆρον τὸν κράββατόν σου, καὶ περιπάτει.

12. Ἠρώτησαν οὖν αὐτόν, Τίς ἐστιν ὁ ἄνθρωπος ὁ εἰπών σοι, Ἆρον τὸν κράββατόν σου, καὶ περιπάτει;

13. Ὁ δὲ ἰαθεὶς οὐκ ᾔδει τίς ἐστιν· ὁ γὰρ Ἰησοῦς ἐξένευσεν, ὄχλου ὄντος ἐν τῷ τόπῳ.

14. Μετὰ ταῦτα εὑρίσκει αὐτὸν ὁ Ἰησοῦς ἐν τῷ ἱερῷ, καὶ εἶπεν αὐτῷ, Ἴδε, ὑγιὴς γέγονας· μηκέτι ἁμάρτανε, ἵνα μὴ χεῖρόν τί σοι γένηται.

15. Ἀπῆλθεν ὁ ἄνθρωπος, καὶ ἀνήγγειλε τοῖς Ἰουδαίοις, ὅτι Ἰησοῦς ἐστιν ὁ ποιήσας αὐτὸν ὑγιῆ.

16. Καὶ διὰ τοῦτο ἐδίωκον τὸν Ἰησοῦν οἱ Ἰουδαῖοι, καὶ ἐζήτουν αὐτὸν ἀποκτεῖναι, ὅτι ταῦτα ἐποίει ἐν σαββάτῳ.

17. Ὁ δὲ Ἰησοῦς ἀπεκρίνατο αὐτοῖς, Ὁ πατήρ μου ἕως ἄρτι ἐργάζεται, κἀγὼ ἐργάζομαι.

18. Διὰ τοῦτο οὖν μᾶλλον ἐζήτουν αὐτὸν οἱ Ἰουδαῖοι ἀποκτεῖναι, ὅτι οὐ μόνον ἔλυε τὸ σάββατον, ἀλλὰ καὶ πατέρα ἴδιον ἔλεγε τὸν Θεόν, ἴσον ἑαυτὸν ποιῶν τῷ Θεῷ.

19. Ἀπεκρίνατο οὖν ὁ Ἰησοῦς καὶ εἶπεν αὐτοῖς, Ἀμὴν ἀμὴν λέγω ὑμῖν, οὐ δύναται ὁ υἱὸς ποιεῖν ἀφ' ἑαυτοῦ οὐδέν, ἐὰν μή

---

11. He answered them, He that made me whole, the same said unto me, Take up thy bed, and walk.

12. Then asked they him, What man is that which said unto thee, Take up thy bed, and walk?

13. And he that was healed[c] wist not who it was: for Jesus had conveyed himself away, a multitude being in that place.

14. Afterward Jesus findeth him in the temple, and said unto him, Behold, thou art made whole: sin no more, lest a worse thing come unto thee.

15. The man departed, and told the Jews that it was Jesus, which had made him whole.

16. And therefore did the Jews persecute Jesus, and sought to slay him, because he had done these things on the sabbath day.[b]

17. But Jesus answered them, My Father worketh hitherto, and I work.

18. Therefore the Jews sought the more to kill him, because he not only had broken the sabbath, but said also that God was his Father, making himself equal with God.

19. Then answered Jesus and said unto them, Verily, verily, I say unto you, The Son can do nothing of himself, but what he seeth

---

11. And he answered them, The man who raised me told me, Take up thy bed and walk.

12. And they asked him, What man is it who told thee, Take up thy bed, and walk?

13. And the weak man did not know who he was, for Jesus had secretly mingled with the people.

14. Afterward Jesus met him in the temple, and said to him, Now thou art well; see to it that thou makest no new mistakes, or thou wilt fare worse.

15. And the man went and told the Jews that it was Jesus who had raised him.

16. And the Jews attacked Jesus, for what he had done on the Sabbath.

17. Jesus answered them, My Father works without cessation, and so do I.

18. And the Jews tried the more to kill him, because he not only had broken the Sabbath, but also called God his Father, and made himself equal with God.

19. And Jesus said, Do you not understand that the son of man can do nothing of himself, if he did not know what the Father is doing?

τι βλέπη τὸν πατέρα ποιοῦντα· ἃ γὰρ ἂν ἐκεῖνος ποιῇ, ταῦτα καὶ ὁ υἱὸς ὁμοίως ποιεῖ.

20. Ὁ γὰρ πατὴρ φιλεῖ τὸν υἱόν, καὶ πάντα δείκνυσιν αὐτῷ ἃ αὐτὸς ποιεῖ· καὶ μείζονα τούτων δείξει αὐτῷ ἔργα, ἵνα ὑμεῖς θαυμάζητε.

21. Ὥσπερ γὰρ ὁ πατὴρ ἐγείρει τοὺς νεκροὺς καὶ ζωοποιεῖ, οὕτω καὶ ὁ υἱὸς οὓς θέλει ζωοποιεῖ.

22. Οὐδὲ γὰρ ὁ πατὴρ κρίνει οὐδένα, ἀλλὰ τὴν κρίσιν πᾶσαν δέδωκε τῷ υἱῷ·

23. Ἵνα πάντες τιμῶσι τὸν υἱὸν καθὼς τιμῶσι τὸν πατέρα. ὁ μὴ τιμῶν τὸν υἱόν, οὐ τιμᾷ τὸν πατέρα τὸν πέμψαντα αὐτόν.

24. Ἀμὴν ἀμὴν λέγω ὑμῖν, ὅτι ὁ τὸν λόγον μου ἀκούων, καὶ πιστεύων τῷ πέμψαντί με, ἔχει ζωὴν αἰώνιον· καὶ εἰς κρίσιν οὐκ ἔρχεται, ἀλλὰ μεταβέβηκεν ἐκ τοῦ θανάτου εἰς τὴν ζωήν.

25. Ἀμὴν ἀμὴν λέγω ὑμῖν, ὅτι ἔρχεται ὥρα καὶ νῦν ἐστιν, ὅτε οἱ νεκροὶ ἀκούσονται τῆς φωνῆς τοῦ υἱοῦ τοῦ Θεοῦ, καὶ οἱ ἀκούσαντες ζήσονται.

26. Ὥσπερ γὰρ ὁ πατὴρ ἔχει ζωὴν ἐν ἑαυτῷ, οὕτως ἔδωκε καὶ τῷ υἱῷ ζωὴν ἔχειν ἐν ἑαυτῷ·

27. Καὶ ἐξουσίαν ἔδωκεν αὐτῷ καὶ κρίσιν ποιεῖν, ὅτι υἱὸς ἀνθρώπου ἐστί.

---

the Father do: for what things soever he doeth, these also doeth the Son likewise.

20. For the Father loveth the Son, and sheweth him all things that himself doeth: and he will shew him greater works[d] than these, that ye may marvel.

21. For as the Father raiseth up the dead,[e] and quickeneth them; even so the Son quickeneth whom he will.

22. For the Father judgeth no man:[f] but hath committed all judgment[g] unto the Son:

23. That all men should honour the Son, even as they honour the Father. He that honoureth not the Son honoureth not the Father which hath sent him.

24. Verily, verily,[h] I say unto you, He that heareth[i] my word, and believeth on him that sent me, hath everlasting life, and shall not come into condemnation[j] but is passed from death unto life.

25. Verily, verily, I say unto you, The hour is coming, and now is, when the dead shall hear the voice of the Son of God: and they that hear shall live.

26. For as the Father hath life in himself: so hath he given to the Son to have life in himself;[k]

27. And hath given him authority to execute judgment also; because he is the Son of man.

What the Father is doing, the son does also.

20. The Father loves the son, and has shown him everything. And he will show him greater things, so that you will marvel.

21. For as the Father rouses the mortals and vivifies them, even so the son vivifies whom he will.

22. For the Father does not choose, but has committed the choice to the son.

23. That all men should honour the son, as they honour the Father. He who does not honour the son does not honour the Father, who has sent him.

24. You understand that he who understands my comprehension and relies upon him who has sent me has non-temporal life, and for him there is no death, but he has already passed from death to life.

25. Truly I tell you, The hour has come, when the mortals will understand the voice of the son of God, and, having understood, will live.

26. For as the Father lives in himself, so has he given to the son life in him;

27. And has given him freedom to make a choice, and even by this he is a man.

28. Μὴ θαυμάζετε τοῦτο· ὅτι ἔρχεται ὥρα, ἐν ᾖ πάντες οἱ ἐν τοῖς μνημείοις ἀκούσονται τῆς φωνῆς αὐτοῦ,

29. Καὶ ἐκπορεύσονται, οἱ τὰ ἀγαθὰ ποιήσαντες εἰς ἀνάστασιν ζωῆς, οἱ δὲ τὰ φαῦλα πράξαντες εἰς ἀνάστασιν κρίσεως.

30. Οὐ δύναμαι ἐγὼ ποιεῖν ἀπ᾽ ἐμαυτοῦ οὐδέν. καθὼς ἀκούω, κρίνω· καὶ ἡ κρίσις ἡ ἐμὴ δικαία ἐστίν· ὅτι οὐ ζητῶ τὸ θέλημα τὸ ἐμὸν, ἀλλὰ τὸ θέλημα τοῦ πέμψαντός με πατρός.

31. Ἐὰν ἐγὼ μαρτυρῶ περὶ ἐμαυτοῦ, ἡ μαρτυρία μου οὐκ ἔστιν ἀληθής.

32. Ἄλλος ἐστὶν ὁ μαρτυρῶν περὶ ἐμοῦ, καὶ οἶδα ὅτι ἀληθής ἐστιν ἡ μαρτυρία ἣν μαρτυρεῖ περὶ ἐμοῦ.

36. Τὰ γὰρ ἔργα ἃ ἔδωκέ μοι ὁ πατὴρ ἵνα τελειώσω αὐτά, αὐτὰ τὰ ἔργα ἃ ἐγὼ ποιῶ μαρτυρεῖ περὶ ἐμοῦ, ὅτι ὁ πατήρ με ἀπέσταλκε·

37. Καὶ ὁ πέμψας με πατήρ, αὐτὸς μεμαρτύρηκε περὶ ἐμοῦ. οὔτε φωνὴν αὐτοῦ ἀκηκόατε πώποτε, οὔτε εἶδος αὐτοῦ ἑωράκατε.

38. Καὶ τὸν λόγον αὐτοῦ οὐκ ἔχετε μένοντα ἐν ὑμῖν, ὅτι ὃν ἀπέστειλεν ἐκεῖνος, τούτῳ ὑμεῖς οὐ πιστεύετε.

39. Ἐρευνᾶτε τὰς γραφάς, ὅτι ὑμεῖς δοκεῖτε ἐν αὐταῖς ζωὴν αἰώνιον ἔχειν. καὶ ἐκεῖναί εἰσιν αἱ μαρτυροῦσαι περὶ ἐμοῦ·

---

28. Marvel not at this: for the hour is coming, in the which all that are in the graves shall hear his voice,

29. And shall come forth; they that have done good, unto the resurrection of life; and they that have done evil, unto the resurrection of damnation.

30. I can of mine own self do nothing: as I hear, I judge: and my judgment is just; because I seek not mine own will, but the will of the Father which hath sent me.

31. If I bear witness of myself, my witness is not true.

32. There is another that beareth witness of me; and I know that the witness which he witnesseth of me is true.

36. For the works which the Father hath given me to finish, the same works that I do, bear witness of me, that the Father hath sent me.

37. And the Father himself, which hath sent me, hath borne witness of me. Ye have neither heard his voice at any time, nor seen his shape.

38. And ye have not his word abiding in you: for whom he hath sent, him ye believe not.

39. Search the Scriptures; for in them ye think ye have eternal life: and they are they which testify of me.

---

28. Do not marvel at this: for the hour has come, when all the mortals will understand the voice of the son of God.

29. And those who have done good will enter into the awakening of life; and those who have done evil will enter into the exile of death.

30. I can do nothing of my own self: as I understand, so I choose. My choice is correct, for I do not seek my will, but the will of the Father who has sent me.

31. If I were the only one to give assurance of myself, my assurance would be false;

32. But there is another who assures concerning me that I am doing the truth. And you know that his assurance is correct as to my doing the truth.

36. For the works which my Father has taught me to fulfil, the same works that I do witness of me that the Father has sent me.

37. And the Father who has sent me, he shows and has shown concerning me. But you have in no way understood his voice, and you have not known who he is.

38. And you have not within you the comprehension, such as would abide in you, for you do not believe him whom he has sent.

39. Read carefully the Scriptures: By them you think you have eternal life; and they assure concerning me.

40. Καὶ οὐ θέλετε ἐλθεῖν πρός με, ἵνα ζωὴν ἔχητε.	40. And ye will not come to me, that ye might have life.	40. You will not believe me that you will have life.
41. Δόξαν παρὰ ἀνθρώπων οὐ λαμβάνω·	41. I receive not honour from men.	41. Human judgments I do not receive.
42. Ἀλλ ἔγνωκα ὑμᾶς, ὅτι τὴν ἀγάπην τοῦ Θεοῦ οὐκ ἔχετε ἐν ἑαυτοῖς.	42. But I know you, that ye have not the love of God in you.	42. But I have learned that in you there is no truth and no love of God.
43. Ἐγὼ ἐλήλυθα ἐν τῷ ὀνόματι τοῦ πατρός μου, καὶ οὐ λαμβάνετέ με· ἐὰν ἄλλος ἔλθῃ ἐν τῷ ὀνόματι τῷ ἰδίῳ, ἐκεῖνον λήψεσθε.	43. I am come in my Father's name, and ye receive me not: if another shall come in his own name, him ye will receive.	43. I teach you in the name of my Father, and you do not receive my teaching. And if another will teach you in his own name, his teaching you will receive.
44. Πῶς δύνασθε ὑμεῖς πιστεῦσαι, δόξαν παρὰ ἀλλήλων λαμβάνοντες, καὶ τὴν δόξαν τὴν παρὰ τοῦ μόνου Θεοῦ οὐ ζητεῖτε ;	44. How can ye believe, which receive honour one of another, and seek not the honour that cometh from God only?	44. What can you rely upon, since you receive your teaching from men, and do not seek the teaching that comes from the only son, who is of the same birth with the Father.
45. Μὴ δοκεῖτε ὅτι ἐγὼ κατηγορήσω ὑμῶν πρὸς τὸν πατέρα· ἔστιν ὁ κατηγορῶν ὑμῶν, Μωσῆς, εἰς ὃν ὑμεῖς ἠλπίκατε.	45. Do not think that I will accuse you to the Father: there is one that accuseth you, even Moses, in whom ye trust.	45. I do not accuse you before the Father, but Moses, in whom you trust, accuses you.
46. Εἰ γὰρ ἐπιστεύετε Μωσῇ, ἐπιστεύετε ἂν ἐμοί· περὶ γὰρ ἐμοῦ ἐκεῖνος ἔγραψεν.	46. For had ye believed Moses, ye would have believed me: for he wrote of me.	46. If you had believed Moses, you would believe me too, for he wrote of me.
47. Εἰ δὲ τοῖς ἐκείνου γράμμασιν οὐ πιστεύετε, πῶς τοῖς ἐμοῖς ῥήμασι πιστεύσετε ;	47. But if ye believe not his writings, how shall ye believe my words?	47. If you do not believe his writings, how can you believe my words?

(*a*) A very important variation, accepted by Griesbach, reads, instead of ἰαθείς *healed*, ἀσθενῶν *weak*, as it stands everywhere.

(*b*) The man was as one dead because he believed in all the nonsense invented by the Jews, and was waiting for a miracle from without, and did not believe the life, which was in him. Jesus showed him that all the stories about the pool were nonsense and a mere invention, and that the only miracle was one's own life. The man believed him and became alive. The superstition is proved, the truth is proved, and the man is alive and walks. It seems there is no room for disputes here. No, men have some arguments to adduce. Why did he make a man alive on the Sabbath? On a Friday it was all right to be alive, but on a Sabbath it was not.

(c) In many texts μᾶλλον is wanting.

(d) Greater than the work of carnal healing.

(e) There does not seem to be any need of proving to any one who has read the gospels in Greek that νεκρός in the gospel language does not always mean *dead*. It is enough to remember Matt. vii. 22, Let the dead bury the dead, and Verse 24 of the chapter under discussion, where it seems to be defined what is to be understood by νεκρός.

(f) οὐδενά is wanting in many texts.

(g) κρίσις is in this discourse used in two meanings: in the sense of *choice* and of *sentence of death*. Such a use of synonyms is peculiar to the language of the gospel of John. Such synonymous uses are found here with the words χάρις, ἀνάστασις, and now with κρίσις. Here it is used in the sense of *choice*.

(h) In many texts the word ἀμήν is wanting.

(i) ἀκούω *to hear, to understand*, in the popular language.

(j) Here κρίσις is used in the sense of *sentence of death*.

(k) Many texts have ἐν αὐτῷ instead of ἐν ἑαυτῷ.

(l) ἀνάστασις has the meaning of *arousal, expulsion, destruction*. In John these plays on words are common: χάρις ἀντὶ χάριτος, where χάρις is used once in the sense of *love*, and the other time in the sense of *worship*. Here, too, ἀνάστασις *arousal* is opposed to ἀνάστασις *expulsion*.

Only with such an interpretation do we get any sense at all. Ἀνάστασις κρίσεως has no meaning, if ἀνάστασις means *arousal, regeneration, resurrection*; the only possibility of explaining it is to give to ἀνάστασις ζωῆς the meaning of *arousal*, and to ἀνάστασις κρίσεως the meaning of *expulsion, destruction*.

(*m*) Many texts have οἴδατε.

Verses 33–35 and the beginning of 36 about John add nothing to the teaching and break the sense, Not only I am a witness, but also my works.

(*n*) I translate ἐωράκατε by *you did not know him*.

THE PARABLE OF THE INHERITANCE (THE TALENTS)

11. Ἀκουόντων δὲ αὐτῶν ταῦτα, προσθεὶς εἶπε παραβολὴν, διὰ τὸ ἐγγὺς αὐτὸν εἶναι Ἱερουσαλὴμ, καὶ δοκεῖν αὐτοὺς ὅτι παραχρῆμα μέλλει ἡ βασιλεία τοῦ Θεοῦ ἀναφαίνεσθαι·

Luke xix. 11. And as they heard these things, he added and spake a parable, because he was nigh to Jerusalem, and because they thought that the kingdom of God should immediately appear.

11. When they heard this, Jesus added and spoke a parable, that they might not think that the kingdom of God would come without an effort.

12. Εἶπεν οὖν, Ἄνθρωπός τις εὐγενὴς ἐπορεύθη εἰς χώραν μακρὰν λαβεῖν ἑαυτῷ βασιλείαν, καὶ ὑποστρέψαι.

12. He said therefore, A certain nobleman went into a far country to receive for himself a kingdom, and to return.

12. He said, A certain nobleman received an inheritance and had to go to a distant kingdom to get it, and to return.

13. Καλέσας δὲ δέκα δούλους ἑαυτοῦ, ἔδωκεν αὐτοῖς δέκα μνᾶς,

13. And he called his ten servants, and delivered them ten pounds.

13. So he called his ten servants, and gave them his property.

15. Καὶ ᾧ μὲν ἔδωκε πέντε τάλαντα, ᾧ δὲ δύο, ᾧ δὲ ἕν, ἑκάστῳ κατὰ τὴν ἰδίαν δύναμιν·

Matt. xxv. 15. And unto one he gave five talents, to another two, and to another one; to every man according to his several ability.

15. To one he gave five talents, to another two, and to another one; to every man according to his ability.

13. Καὶ εἶπε πρὸς αὐτοὺς, Πραγματεύσασθε ἕως ἔρχομαι.

Luke xix. 13. And said unto them, Occupy till I come.

13. And said to them, Turn it to account.

15. Καὶ ἀπεδήμησεν εὐθέως.

Matt. xxv. 15. And straightway took his journey.

15. And himself went away.

16. Πορευθεὶς δὲ ὁ τὰ πέντε τάλαντα λαβὼν, εἰργάσατο ἐν αὐτοῖς, καὶ ἐποίησεν ἄλλα πέντε τάλαντα.

16. Then he that had received the five talents went and traded with the same, and made them other five talents.

16. Then the man who had received the five talents went and traded with them, and made other five talents.

17. Ὡσαύτως καὶ ὁ τὰ δύο, ἐκέρδησε καὶ αὐτὸς ἄλλα δύο.

17. And likewise he that had received two, he also gained other two.

17. And likewise did he who had two talents.

14. Οἱ δὲ πολῖται αὐτοῦ ἐμίσουν αὐτὸν, καὶ

Luke xix. 14. But his citizens hated him, and sent a message after

14. But the countrymen of the man had no use for him, and an-

ἀπέστειλαν πρεσβείαν ὀπίσω αὐτοῦ, λέγοντες, Οὐ θέλομεν τοῦτον βασιλεῦσαι ἐφ᾽ ἡμᾶς.

him, saying, We will not have this man to reign over us.

nounced to him, We will not have thee as a king.

15. Καὶ ἐγένετο ἐν τῷ ἐπανελθεῖν αὐτὸν λαβόντα τὴν βασιλείαν, καὶ εἶπε φωνηθῆναι αὐτῷ τοὺς δούλους τούτους οἷς ἔδωκε τὸ ἀργύριον, ἵνα γνῷ τίς τί διεπραγματεύσατο.

15. And it came to pass, that when he was returned, having received the kingdom, then he commanded these servants to be called unto him, to whom he had given the money, that he might know how much every man had gained by trading.

15. And it came to pass, that that man received the kingdom and returned home and sent for the servants, to whom he had given the money, that he might know how much each had gained.

19. Καὶ συναίρει μετ᾽ αὐτῶν λόγον.

Matt. xxv. 19. And reckoneth with them.

19. And he asked for their accounts.

20. Καὶ προσελθὼν ὁ τὰ πέντε τάλαντα λαβὼν, προσήνεγκεν ἄλλα πέντε τάλαντα, λέγων, Κύριε, πέντε τάλαντά μοι παρέδωκας· ἴδε, ἄλλα πέντε τάλαντα ἐκέρδησα ἐπ᾽ αὐτοῖς.

20. And so he that had received five talents came and brought other five talents, saying, Lord, thou deliveredst unto me five talents: behold, I have gained beside them five talents more.

20. And he who had received five talents came and brought other five talents, and said, Master, thou gavest me five talents: I have gained five talents more with them.

21. Ἔφη δὲ αὐτῷ ὁ κύριος αὐτοῦ, Εὖ, δοῦλε ἀγαθὲ καὶ πιστέ, ἐπὶ ὀλίγα ἦς πιστός, ἐπὶ πολλῶν σε καταστήσω· εἴσελθε εἰς τὴν χαρὰν τοῦ κυρίου σου.

21. His lord said unto him, Well done, thou good and faithful servant: thou hast been faithful over a few things, I will make thee ruler over many things: enter thou into the joy of thy lord.

21. And his master said to him, Well done! Thou art a good and faithful servant: thou hast been faithful in little things, I will put thee in charge of greater things. Rejoice with thy master.

22. Προσελθὼν δὲ καὶ ὁ τὰ δύο τάλαντα λαβὼν εἶπε, Κύριε δύο τάλαντά μοι παρέδωκας· ἴδε, ἄλλα δύο τάλαντα ἐκέρδησα ἐπ᾽ αὐτοῖς.

22. He also that had received two talents came and said, Lord, thou deliveredst unto me two talents: behold, I have gained two other talents beside them.

22. Then came another, to whom two talents had been given, and said, Master, thou gavest me two talents, and I have gained two more with them.

17. Καὶ εἶπεν αὐτῷ, Εὖ, ἀγαθὲ δοῦλε· ὅτι ἐν ἐλαχίστῳ πιστὸς ἐγένου, ἴσθι ἐξουσίαν ἔχων ἐπάνω δέκα πόλεων.

Luke xix. 17. And he said unto him, Well, thou good servant: because thou hast been faithful in a very little, have thou authority over ten cities.

17. And the master said to both, Well done! You are good and faithful servants. You have been faithful in small things, and so I will put you in charge of greater things: Rejoice with the master.

18. Καὶ ἦλθεν ὁ δεύτερος, λέγων, Κύριε, ἡ μνᾶ σου ἐποίησε πέντε μνᾶς.

18. And the second came, saying, Lord, thy pound hath gained five pounds.

18. And another to whom one talent had been given came, and said, Master, with thy talent I have gained five more.

23. Ἔφη αὐτῷ ὁ κύριος αὐτοῦ, Εὖ, δοῦλε

Matt. xxv. 23. His lord said unto him, Well done, good and ἀγαθὲ καὶ πιστὲ, ἐπὶ ὀλίγα ἦς πιστὸς, ἐπὶ πολλῶν σε καταστήσω· ἄσελθε εἰς τὴν χαρὰν τοῦ κυρίου σου.

24. Προσελθὼν δὲ καὶ ὁ τὸ ἓν τάλαντον εἰληφὼς εἶτε, Κύριε, ἔγνων σε ὅτι σκληρὸς εἶ ἄνθρωπος, θερίζων ὅπου οὐκ ἔσπειρας, καὶ συνάγων ὅθεν οὐ διεσκόρπισας·

25. Καὶ φοβηθεὶς, ἀπελθὼν ἔκρυψα τὸ τάλαντόν σου ἐν τῇ γῇ· ἴδε, ἔχεις τὸ σόν.

26. Ἀποκριθεὶς δὲ ὁ κύριος αὐτοῦ εἶπεν αὐτῷ, Πονηρὲ δοῦλε καὶ ὀκνηρὲ, ᾔδεις ὅτι θερίζω ὅπου οὐκ ἔσπειρα, καὶ συνάγω ὅθεν οὐ διεσκόρπισα·

23. Καὶ διατί οὐκ ἔδωκας τὸ ἀργύριόν μου ἐπὶ τὴν τράπεζαν, καὶ ἐγὼ ἐλθὼν σὺν τόκῳ ἂν ἔπραξα αὐτό;

24. Καὶ τοῖς παρεστῶσιν εἶπεν, Ἄρατε ἀπ' αὐτοῦ τὴν μνᾶν, καὶ δότε τῷ τὰς δέκα μνᾶς ἔχοντι.

25. (Καὶ εἶπον αὐτῷ, Κύριε, ἔχει δέκα μνᾶς.)

26. Λέγω γὰρ ὑμῖν, ὅτι παντὶ τῷ ἔχοντι δοθήσεται· ἀπὸ δὲ τοῦ μὴ ἔχοντος, καὶ ὃ ἔχει ἀρθήσεται ἀπ' αὐτοῦ.

30. Καὶ τὸν ἀχρεῖον δοῦλον ἐκβάλλετε εἰς τὸ σκότος τὸ ἐξώτερον.

27. Πλὴν τοὺς ἐχθρούς μου ἐκείνους, τοὺς μὴ θελήσαντάς με βασιλεῦσαι ἐπ' αὐτοὺς, ἀγάγετε ὧδε, καὶ κατασφάξατε ἔμπροσθέν μου.

faithful servant; thou hast been faithful over a few things, I will make thee ruler over many things: enter thou into the joy of thy lord.

24. Then he which had received the one talent came and said, Lord, I knew thee that thou art a hard man, reaping where thou hast not sown, and gathering where thou hast not strewed:

25. And I was afraid, and went and hid thy talent in the earth: lo, there thou hast that is thine.

26. His lord answered and said unto him, Thou wicked and slothful servant, thou knewest that I reap where I sowed not, and gather where I have not strewed:

Luke xix. 23. Wherefore then gavest not thou my money into the bank, that at my coming I might have required mine own with usury?

24. And he said unto them that stood by, Take from him the pound, and give it to him that hath ten pounds.

25. (And they said unto him, Lord, he hath ten pounds.)

26. For I say unto you, That unto every one which hath shall be given; and from him that hath not, even that he hath shall be taken away from him.

Matt. xxv. 30. And cast ye the unprofitable servant into outer darkness.

Luke xix. 27. But those mine enemies, which would not that I should reign over them, bring hither, and slay them before me.

24. And he to whom one talent had been given, came, and said, Master, here is thy talent. I knew that thou art a hard man, taking where thou hast not placed, and reaping where thou hast not sown.

25. And I was afraid of thee, and wrapped it in a cloth, and hid it in the earth. Here it is, take it.

26. And his master said to him, Thou art a bad and lazy servant. According to thy speech will I judge thee. Thou knewest that I am a hard man, taking where I do not place, and reaping where I do not sow:

23. Why, then, didst thou not turn my money to account? Then I should have received it with usury at my coming.

24. And the master said to his servants. Take from him the talent, and give it to him who has ten.

25. And they said, Master, he has already ten.

26. I tell you, A surplus will be given to him who saves; and from him who does not save, even what he has will be taken from him.

30. And take the useless servant and throw him out.

27. But my enemies, who did not want me to be their king, shall not exist for me.

(*a*) I omit the words, Because he was nigh to Jerusalem, as in no way connected with the meaning of the parable. If they are to be understood as they are generally understood, that Jesus is denying the opinion of his disciples, that the kingdom of God will soon be made manifest in Jerusalem, the whole parable becomes senseless. Therefore I prefer to throw out the above words, and to retain the profound meaning of the parable, which is directly connected with the preceding parables. That this parable is accidentally and arbitrarily referred by Luke to the expectation of the accusation of the king is proved by the fact that by Matthew this parable is referred to the elucidation of the idea that we must always be prepared for the coming of the son of man.

I choose the parable according to Luke, because it includes the parable according to Matthew.

(*b*) παραχρῆμα I translate by *without effort.*

(*c*) I combine the parable of Matthew and of Luke into one, since they complement one another, and have the same significance, except that something is omitted in one, and something in the other.

The nobleman who departs from his house to become a king is God, the comprehension, the spirit. His departure from the world, which at the same time is his house, expresses the same idea which is expressed in Mark's parable of the sower who until the harvest does not trouble himself about the seeds, and the parable of the leaven. Having endowed men with the comprehension, God leaves them to live alone. The possessions which he distributes to his servants are the comprehension. The varying quantities of the talents given to each are the different degrees of the comprehension, — a repetition of the parable of the seeds which fell by the wayside, on the stones, and in the thorns. Here there can no longer be any doubt as to the increase depending on God, on external causes. Here it says outright that the entrance into the kingdom of God depends directly on the effort exerted by each person; only the degree of the comprehension depends on external causes. The countrymen of the nobleman, who do not wish to acknowledge him as their king, are the men who have not the comprehension, the men of darkness, of that which does not exist for God. It is that which is expressed by the tares in the parable of the sower and the tares. The return of the nobleman is the completion of the whole life, what is expressed in the parable of the tares, their burning; the same that is expressed in the parable of the drawnet; the same that is expressed in John by the word *death*.

The accounts of the servants are the condition of those who have had the comprehension, as a seed. The accounts of the first two servants are the condition of those who have retained the comprehension, as the seeds on the good ground; their reward is the union with the master. The account of the last servant is the condition of him who, having the comprehension, has not retained it, like the seeds by the wayside, on the stones, and in the thorns. He is a useless servant, he does not exist for the comprehension. The countrymen who have not acknowledged the king are the men outside the comprehension, — they, too, do not exist for the comprehension.

The talent is the comprehension in man. The servant who worked with it gained something and fulfilled the will of his master. The master received him as his companion, — he united with his master.

The comprehension and life remained comprehension and life. But the bad servant hid his talent; he said to himself, I do not want to know the master, I want to work for myself; but the master's talent accused him, and so he buried the talent, so as not to think of the master. The life of the comprehension is given to the servant, but he does not want to work for it; he thinks that it is foreign and useless to him, and he hides it from himself, so that he may work for the flesh, for bodily food, and not for the fulfilment of the master's will. The bad servant did not understand that the life of the comprehension is not given for the master, but for himself. He said to himself, The master wants to take from me what he has not given me, my carnal pleasures; but I will not give them to him, — I will live for them. But the life of the comprehension will be such as it is. And the master came and, seeing that the life of the comprehension did not grow in this man, took it away.

The seed of the divine spirit is planted in all hearts alike, and every man may increase in himself this seed of the spirit. God has given to each the spirit. Some, having received this spirit, took a liking for it, made it grow, doubled it, and brought forth fruit, each according to his ability; but the others, like those who informed the lord that they would not be under his power, like that last servant, said to themselves, Why shall I give up the life of the flesh, the carnal pleasures, for the sake of the spirit, which is not mine? He wants me, for the sake of the spirit, to give up to him what he has not given me, — my carnal life. I shall do better to hide as far as possible from me this germ of the spirit, which is given to me, and I will live the life of the flesh. But he lost even the last germ of the divine spirit, and his carnal life ended in death.

Life is abroad in all men. He who recognizes in himself the son of man will live the true life, will acquire the true life. The true life can be neither more nor less. If in the earthly life some men appear to us to have more, and others less, some five talents, and others two or one, they are all alike for the true life, they all exist for the master's joy. Only he who has hid this life away deprives himself of his own accord of life, and passes out of the sphere of life into the darkness.

This parable expresses also this, that the human conceptions about justice are inapplicable to the question of life and death.

The conception of the Old Testament, that God rewards for such and such works, and punishes for such other, is false. There are no rewards, no punishments. He who holds on to life gets even more; he who does not hold on to life has life taken from him. As in the beginning of the Gospel, so also in the discourse with Nicodemus, and so in all the parables and discourses, Jesus says the same, that life is only the comprehension. Life is only life to the extent to which it is the comprehension. The animal life Jesus calls death, and he calls it so since it is indeed but a moment which ends in eternal death. And so we must not think that man with his feet and hands is all alive. Alive is only that which recognizes its divinity. Men must not look upon themselves as living beings only because they move, eat, breathe, but because they acknowledge themselves to be the children of God. We do not know and cannot know where the beginning of all this terrestrial world is. All that we know is the comprehension which is given to us, and by it alone can we live. The Lord gave his talents to men and left them in their possession, and went away. God has implanted his comprehension in men and left them in the world of death. Even if men do not feel the power of the Lord over them, they none the less have those talents of the Lord, which have been given to them, and they have to do something with them. The comprehension is given to men. It is given in varying degrees, but it is given to all, and they have to do something with it. And every man does with this comprehension what he pleases. One works much, another less, a third does nothing, a fourth does not recognize it at all. But the question is not as to what he has worked, but as to whether he has comprehended that within him is life and whether he has worked over that which is life, has striven to increase life.

And with men does not take place what we are accustomed to regard as just, that is, that for great work there should be a corresponding reward, that a man who has done nothing harmful should not suffer, that a man should be responsible for what he is guilty of.

All that is so when we represent to ourselves some human power which punishes for what we consider bad, and rewards for what we consider good; but that is not so when we contemplate the essence of life itself.

From the very beginning to the end Jesus says that there can be no rewards and no punishments, either from men, or from God. The comprehension is in itself the true good, and the aim, and the means, and the life. Consequently, he who has the comprehension and has transferred his life into it has life. He who has it not and does not place his efforts in it has no life.

From a general point of view: Though many seeds will fall on the stones and by the wayside, the other seeds which fall on the good ground will make up for them, and there will be a harvest. The seeds which have fallen on the stones and by the wayside are not guilty and are not punished, and those that have fallen on the good ground are not rewarded; but in order that there should be a harvest, the seeds that have fallen on the good ground must bring forth fifty-fold and more. The comprehension in the world in general returns to God, though many human beings live without this comprehension; many bear this comprehension and increase it.

From the personal point of view: To each a talent is given, and it is not possible to forget it. If thou forgettest it, thou showest that thou dost not need it, and it will be taken from thee. If thou forgettest like that servant, and wilt assert thy justice, thou wilt accuse thyself. What good will it do thee, if thou hidest it in the ground? It must be given to him who has gained something by his. The comprehension is in all men, it is life.

If thou dost not wish to go toward life, life will get away from thee. There are no rewards and no punishments for men. Men do not live for themselves. If they did, there would be rewards and punishments for them. Men do not live for themselves, but God in men lives for himself.

If a man lives for God, he lives. If he lives for himself without God, he does not live, and as it is impossible to live more or less, it is impossible not to live more or less, — man lives, or does not live. There is no punishment, no reward, but there is life and death.

Christ's teaching is only a teaching of what life and what death is. Life is comprehension, everything else is death.

OF THE BREAD OF LIFE

31. Ἐν δὲ τῷ μεταξὺ ἠρώτων αὐτὸν οἱ μαθηταί, λέγοντες, Ῥαββί, φάγε.

32. Ὁ δὲ εἶπεν αὐτοῖς, Ἐγὼ βρῶσιν ἔχω φαγεῖν ἣν ὑμεῖς οὐκ οἴδατε.

33. Ἔλεγον οὖν οἱ μαθηταὶ πρὸς ἀλλήλους, Μήτις ἤνεγκεν αὐτῷ φαγεῖν;

34. Λέγει αὐτοῖς ὁ Ἰησοῦς, Ἐμὸν βρῶμά ἐστιν, ἵνα ποιῶ τὸ θέλημα τοῦ πέμψαντός με, καὶ τελειώσω αὐτοῦ τὸ ἔργον.

35. Οὐχ ὑμεῖς λέγετε, ὅτι ἔτι τετράμηνόν ἐστι, καὶ ὁ θερισμὸς ἔρχεται; ἰδού, λέγω ὑμῖν, ἐπάρατε τοὺς ὀφθαλμοὺς ὑμῶν, καὶ θεάσασθε τὰς χώρας, ὅτι λευκαί εἰσι πρὸς θερισμὸν ἤδη.

John iv. 31. In the meanwhile his disciples prayed him, saying, Master, eat.

32. But he said unto them, I have meat to eat that ye know not of.

33. Therefore said the disciples one to another, Hath any man brought him aught to eat?

34. Jesus saith unto them, My meat is to do the will of him that sent me, and to finish his work.

35. Say not ye, There are yet four months, and then cometh harvest? behold, I say unto you, Lift up your eyes, and look on the fields; for they are white already to harvest.

31. Once his disciples asked him, Teacher, hast thou eaten?

32. And he said to them, I have food that you know not of.

33. And the disciples said to one another, Has any one brought him something to eat?

34. And Jesus said to them, My food is this, that I do the will of him who has sent me, and fulfil his works.

35. Do not say, There are four months yet, and then comes the harvest. I tell you, Lift up your eyes and look on the fields: they are white already for the harvest.

36. Καὶ ὁ θερίζων μισθὸν λαμβάνει, καὶ συνάγει καρπὸν εἰς ζωὴν αἰώνιον· ἵνα καὶ ὁ σπείρων ὁμοῦ χαίρῃ καὶ ὁ θερίζων.

37. Ἐν γὰρ τούτῳ ὁ λόγος ἐστὶν ὁ ἀληθινὸς, ὅτι ἄλλος ἐστὶν ὁ σπείρων, καὶ ἄλλος ὁ θερίζων.

38. Ἐγὼ ἀπέστειλα ὑμᾶς θερίζειν ὃ οὐχ ὑμεῖς κεκοπιάκατε· ἄλλοι κεκοπιάκασι, καὶ ὑμεῖς εἰς τὸν κόπον αὐτῶν εἰσεληλύθατε.

36. And he that reapeth receiveth wages, and gathereth fruit unto life eternal: that both he that soweth and he that reapeth may rejoice together.

37. And herein is that saying true, One soweth, and another reapeth.

38. I sent you to reap that whereon ye bestowed no labour:[b] other men laboured, and ye are entered into their labours.

36. And he who reaps is paid, and he gathers fruit for the non-temporal life, so that he who has sowed rejoices with him who reaps.

37. For the proverb is true, One sows, and another reaps.

38. I teach you to reap where you did not labour. Others laboured, but you participate in the labour of others.

(a) ἵνα is used here in the sense of ὥστε.
(b) Your carnal life.

These verses are not clear. By the church they are explained more obscurely still. The church understands this to be said of the Samaritans who are roused to the teaching. In my opinion the meaning of this passage is this: having told his disciples that his food is the fulfilment of the divine will, the same that he told himself in the wilderness, the same that he told the woman of Samaria, Jesus says, The fulfilment of God's will must not be put off, as one puts off the harvest to the time when it is ripe. This harvest is always ripe, that is, the execution of God's will is always possible, when the food of this execution is your carnal life, and there is always something to reap, to offer as a sacrifice to the spirit. He who reaps receives his reward, — non-temporal life. And this is an equal joy to him who reaps and to him who sows, that is, the man who reaps is he who lives in the spirit, and God the Father is he who has implanted his spirit in men. And so the proverb is correct, What one sows, another reaps. God sows, and man reaps. I teach you to reap, to cut down what you have

not laboured on, for God has made for you your carnal
life.

Verses 39–42 have no meaning, and so I omit them.
They tell about how the Samaritans believed him.

27. Ἐργάζεσθε μὴ τὴν βρῶσιν τὴν ἀπολλυμένην, ἀλλὰ τὴν βρῶσιν τὴν μένουσαν εἰς ζωὴν αἰώνιον, ἣν ὁ υἱὸς τοῦ ἀνθρώπου ὑμῖν δώσει· τοῦτον γὰρ ὁ πατὴρ ἐσφράγισεν ὁ Θεός.	*John vi.* 27. Labour not for the meat which perisheth, but for that meat which endureth unto everlasting life, which the Son of man shall give unto you: for him hath God the Father sealed.	27. And Jesus said to the multitude, You are caring for your earthly food, but I tell you, Earn not the perishable food, but the one which will endure into everlasting life, which the son of man will give you: on him is God's seal.
28. Εἶπον οὖν πρὸς αὐτὸν, Τί ποιῶμεν, ἵνα ἐργαζώμεθα τὰ ἔργα τοῦ Θεοῦ;	28. Then said they unto him, What shall we do, that we might work the works of God?	28. And they said to him, What must we do that we may do the works of God?
29. Ἀπεκρίθη ὁ Ἰησοῦς καὶ εἶπεν αὐτοῖς, Τοῦτό ἐστι τὸ ἔργον τοῦ Θεοῦ, ἵνα πιστεύσητε εἰς ὃν ἀπέστειλεν ἐκεῖνος.	29. Jesus answered and said unto them, This is the work of God, that ye believe on him whom he hath sent.	29. And Jesus replied to them, This is the work of God, that you trust him whom he has sent.
30. Εἶπον οὖν αὐτῷ, Τί οὖν ποιεῖς σὺ σημεῖον, ἵνα ἴδωμεν καὶ πιστεύσωμέν σοι; τί ἐργάζῃ;	30. They said therefore unto him, What sign shewest thou then, that we may see, and believe thee? what dost thou work?	30. What example will thou give us that we may believe thee? What art thou doing?

(a) ἐργάζω with the accusative means *to earn, lay by.*
(b) βρῶσις *food,* in either sense.

The church understands these words of Jesus to mean
that Jesus commands them to believe in himself. Jesus
says nothing of the kind; he exhorts them to believe in
what he says, and the answer of the Jews shows that
they do not even mean to understand him in such a way.
Thou commandest us to believe in him whom he has
sent.   Well, what art thou doing?

31. Οἱ πατέρες ἡμῶν τὸ μάννα ἔφαγον ἐν τῇ ἐρήμῳ, καθώς ἐστι γεγραμμένον, "Ἄρτον ἐκ τοῦ οὐρανοῦ ἔδωκεν αὐτοῖς φαγεῖν.'	*John vi.* 31. Our fathers did eat manna in the desert; as it is written, He gave them bread from heaven to eat.	31. Our fathers ate manna in the desert, as it is written, He gave them bread from heaven to eat.

In order not to get mixed in the comprehension of the
subsequent words about the eating of the body and blood
of the son of man, which have called forth so many idolatrous explanations, we must not lose sight of the sense of
the whole discourse, and must remember that the first
idea of Christ's teaching during the temptation in the
wilderness presented itself to him in the comparison of
the earthly food with the divine food, and that ἄρτος is
not exactly *food*, but *eating*, and so has the meaning both
of *food* and of *rearing*. In response to the temptation
with food, he replied to himself that man is not satisfied
with bread, but with the divine spirit which proceeds
from the mouth, that is, not with the flesh. In his conversation with the woman of Samaria he expressed in the
same way the essence of his teaching (John iv. 14): If
thou knewest the gift of God, thou wouldst thyself ask
me to drink not the water of the earth, after which one
wants to drink again, but such as satisfies one completely,
after which there is no more thirst. In the sermon on
the mount he again expresses the same in the form of
food, when he says that the soul is more than food.

To his disciples he says, My food does the will of him
who has sent me, and his works.

Here the discourse begins with the same: Jesus says,
Have no care for the perishable food, that is, do not think
that the bread which you put into your belly gives you
life, but have a care for the food which does not perish,
for the comprehension. Our life is the comprehension,
and the comprehension is more than food, — it alone is
life. This real life is given to you by the son of man,
with God's seal on him, that is, the son of man who lives
according to the law of God.

The people ask him, What must one do in order to
work for the true life, for this comprehension? Jesus
replies that for this one has only to believe, to be fully
convinced that life is comprehension, to live by that com-

prehension, and to rely on the life in the comprehension. To this the Jews adduce Verse 24 of Psalm lxxviii.: And had rained down manna upon them to eat, and had given them of the corn of heaven, thus uniting into one the idea of manna as food with the corn of heaven. But the corn of heaven ἄρτος ἐκ τοῦ οὐρανοῦ has an entirely different meaning from what is meant by carnal food. The meaning of ἄρτος is expressed in Hebrew in the following verses of the Book of Sirach and of the Proverbs of Solomon:

Sirach xv. 3. Gives him the bread of reason to eat, and the water of wisdom to drink.

xxiv. 19. I have spread my branches, like a terebinth, and my branches are the branches of glory and of grace.

20. I am like a grapevine which bringeth forth grace; and my flowers are the fruit of glory and of riches.

21. Approach unto me, ye who want me, and still your hunger with my fruit.

Prov. ix. 5. Come, eat of my bread, and drink of the wine which I have mingled.

32. Εἶπεν οὖν αὐτοῖς ὁ Ἰησοῦς, Ἀμὴν ἀμὴν λέγω ὑμῖν, Οὐ Μωσῆς δέδωκεν ὑμῖν τὸν ἄρτον ἐκ τοῦ οὐρανοῦ· ἀλλ' ὁ πατήρ μου δίδωσιν ὑμῖν τὸν ἄρτον ἐκ τοῦ οὐρανοῦ τὸν ἀληθινόν.

33. Ὁ γὰρ ἄρτος τοῦ Θεοῦ ἐστιν ὁ καταβαίνων ἐκ τοῦ οὐρανοῦ, καὶ ζωὴν διδοὺς τῷ κόσμῳ.

John vi. 32. Then Jesus said unto them, Verily, verily, I say unto you, Moses gave you not that bread from heaven; but my Father giveth you the true bread from heaven.

33. For the bread of God is he which cometh down from heaven, and giveth life unto the world.

32. And Jesus said to them, You know yourselves that it was not Moses who gave you this bread from heaven, but my Father gives you true bread from heaven.

33. For the bread of God is that which comes down from heaven, and gives life to the world.

Jesus at once corrects the misunderstanding which may arise from mixing up the two kinds of food, the manna from heaven with the bread of heaven, that is, with the law received by Moses from God in heaven. He says, the bread from heaven is not bread from heaven, that is, the law of God, because Moses gave it, but because it is from God and gives life to the world. If the manna were under discussion, there would not in Verse 32 be a perfect, which designates that God has given and gives the true bread, that is, the comprehension to the world, and there would not be a present tense in Verse 32.

34. Εἶπον οὖν πρὸς αὐτὸν, Κύριε, πάντοτε δὸς ἡμῖν τὸν ἄρτον τοῦτον.

35. Εἶπε δὲ αὐτοῖς ὁ Ἰησοῦς, Ἐγώ εἰμι ὁ ἄρτος τῆς ζωῆς· ὁ ἐρχόμενος πρός με οὐ μὴ πεινάσῃ, καὶ ὁ πιστεύων εἰς ἐμὲ οὐ μὴ διψήσῃ πώποτε.

36. Ἀλλ᾽ εἶπον ὑμῖν ὅτι καὶ ἑωράκατέ με, καὶ οὐ πιστεύετε.

John vi. 34. Then said they unto him, Lord, evermore give us this bread.

35. And Jesus said unto them, I am the bread of life :[b] he that cometh[d] to me shall never hunger ;[c] and he that believeth on me shall never thirst.

36. But I said unto you, That ye also have seen me,[a] and believe not.

34. And they said to him, Then give us that bread.

35. And Jesus said to them, I am the bread of life : he who gives himself to me will never be hungry ; and he who will believe me, will never thirst.

36. But I have told you already, and you have seen and do not believe.

(*a*) I, — my teaching.

(*b*) The bread of life, — the law of life.

(*c*) πεινάω means *to hunger, to be unsatisfied, suffer with a desire.* The same is meant by διψάω.

(*d*) Again the verb ἔρχομαι, which is with incredible stubbornness translated by *to go.* What can *to go to me* mean here ? It cannot mean *to walk,* so what does it mean ?

Luke vi. 47. Whosoever cometh to me, and heareth my sayings, and doeth them, I will shew you to whom he is like.

John iii. 20. For every one that doeth evil hateth the light, neither cometh to the light, lest his deeds should be reproved.

21. But he that doeth truth cometh to the light, that his deeds may be made manifest, that they are wrought in God.

John v. 40. And ye will not come to me, that ye might have life.

John xiv. 6. Jesus saith unto him, I am the way, the truth, and the life : no one cometh unto the Father, but by me.

Acts xix. 18. And many came, and confessed, and shewed their deeds.

'Εξομολογούμενοι, according to the dictionary, means *having united with some one.*

(e) In many texts με, which destroys the sense, is wanting. Without this με it is clear that Jesus is referring to what he said about the men who hear and do not understand, and who look and do not see.

87. Πᾶν ὃ δίδωσί μοι ὁ πατήρ, πρὸς ἐμὲ ἥξει· καὶ τὸν ἐρχόμενον πρὸς με οὐ μὴ ἐκβάλω ἔξω.	*John vi.* 37. All that the Father giveth me shall come to me; and him that cometh to me I will in no wise cast out.	37. Everything which the Father gives me will come to me; and him who gives himself to me I will not cause to perish.

Everything which my Father has given in my charge, as the king gave the talents, will come back to me, as the talents given for increase came back, and he who follows me, my example, will not be cast into the outer darkness, will not be destroyed. In this verse, as also in the following one, two ideas are expressed side by side : one, as to what the teaching of Jesus consists in ; the other, what the consequences of his teaching will be. Πᾶν is of the neuter gender (and so it is translated by *all*) and refers to the principle of life which is received from the Father. Τόν (translated by who) refers to him who follows the teaching. In the same way, all in Verse 39 designates the comprehension which the Father has given me, and πᾶς in Verse 40 designates every man who follows the teaching.

38. Ὅτι καταβέβηκα ἐκ τοῦ οὐρανοῦ, οὐχ ἵνα ποιῶ τὸ θέλημα τὸ ἐμόν, ἀλλὰ τὸ θέλημα τοῦ πέμψαντός με.	*John vi.* 38. For I came down from heaven, not to do mine own will, but the will of him that sent me.	38. Because I have come down from heaven, not to do my will, but the will of the Father who sent me.
39. Τοῦτο δέ ἐστι τὸ θέλημα τοῦ πέμψαντός με πατρός, ἵνα πᾶν ὃ δέδωκέ μοι, μὴ ἀπολέσω ἐξ αὐτοῦ, ἀλλὰ ἀναστήσω αὐτὸ ἐν τῇ ἐσχάτῃ ἡμέρᾳ.	39. And this is the Father's will which hath sent me, that of all which he hath given me I should lose nothing, but should raise it up again at the last day.	39. And the will of my Father who has sent me is this, that I should not cause to perish anything of what he has given me, but should keep it alive to the last day.

40. Τοῦτο δέ ἐστι τὸ θέλημα τοῦ πέμψαντός με, ἵνα πᾶς ὁ θεωρῶν τὸν υἱὸν καὶ πιστεύων εἰς αὐτὸν ἔχῃ ζωὴν αἰώνιον, καὶ ἀναστήσω αὐτὸν ἐγὼ τῇ ἐσχάτῃ ἡμέρᾳ.

40. And this is the will of him that sent me, that every one which seeth the Son, and believeth on him, may have everlasting life: and I will raise him up at the last day.

40. For this is the will of him who has sent me. So that every one who has come to know the son of man and believes in him has life. And I will keep him awake until the last day.

(a) Here ought to be a period. The ἵνα which follows has to be translated as though it were ὥστε, for which it is frequently used in John.

The Jews ask, Show us what kind of food it is which gives life. He replies, That you may see in me. I live on this food alone, and this food is the execution of the Father's will. My life is the comprehension of God, and so I do his will. But the will of the Father is this, that every man should comprehend the Father within him, and should to his last day live by this comprehension alone.

41. Ἐγόγγυζον οὖν οἱ Ἰουδαῖοι περὶ αὐτοῦ, ὅτι εἶπεν, Ἐγώ εἰμι ὁ ἄρτος ὁ καταβὰς ἐκ τοῦ οὐρανοῦ.
42. Καὶ ἔλεγον, Οὐχ οὗτός ἐστιν Ἰησοῦς ὁ υἱὸς Ἰωσήφ, οὗ ἡμεῖς οἴδαμεν τὸν πατέρα καὶ τὴν μητέρα; πῶς οὖν λέγει οὗτος, Ὅτι ἐκ τοῦ οὐρανοῦ καταβέβηκα;

John vi. 41. The Jews then murmured at him, because he said, I am the bread which came down from heaven.
42. And they said, Is not this Jesus, the son of Joseph, whose father and mother we know? how is it then that he saith, I came down from heaven?

41. And the Jews began to dispute, because he said, I am the bread who came down from heaven.
42. And said, Is not this Jesus, the son of Joseph? We know his father and his mother. How then does he say that he came down from heaven?

Reuss says that the character of the discourses of John consists in letting the interlocutors intentionally understand the words of Jesus in their coarsest sense. This remark is not always just, and in the present case the Jews know well what he is speaking about. The words, The bread from heaven, they understand precisely in the sense of the law of God. Their remark that he is the son of Joseph and that they know his relatives is the same which is made in Luke after his preaching in Nazareth. Otherwise their words have no meaning. The fact that he is the son of Joseph or not, and their acquaintance with his relatives, do not elucidate or obscure the statement that he is a piece of bread that has come down from heaven. The surprise that he, the son · of a carpenter, should give them the law of God is only natural.

	John vi.	
43. Ἀπεκρίθη οὖν ὁ Ἰησοῦς καὶ εἶπεν αὐτοῖς, Μὴ γογγύζετε μετ' ἀλλήλων.	43. Jesus therefore answered and said unto them, Murmur not among yourselves.	43. And Jesus answered and said to them, Do not dispute among yourselves.
44. Οὐδεὶς δύναται ἐλθεῖν πρός με, ἐὰν μὴ ὁ πατὴρ ὁ πέμψας με ἑλκύσῃ αὐτόν, καὶ ἐγὼ ἀναστήσω αὐτὸν τῇ ἐσχάτῃ ἡμέρᾳ.	44. No man can come to me, except the Father which hath sent me draw him: and I will raise him up at the last day.[a]	44. No man can believe me, if the Father who has sent me does not draw him. And I will keep him awake to the last day.
45. Ἔστι γεγραμμένον ἐν τοῖς προφήταις, 'Καὶ ἔσονται πάντες διδακτοὶ τοῦ Θεοῦ.' πᾶς οὖν ὁ ἀκούσας παρὰ,τοῦ πατρὸς καὶ μαθὼν, ἔρχεται πρός με·	45. It is written in the prophets, And they shall be all taught of God. Every man therefore that hath heard, and hath learned[b] of the Father, cometh unto me.	45. It is written in the prophets, And you will be all taught by God. He who knows about the Father and has learned the truth will give himself to me.
46. Οὐχ ὅτι τὸν πατέρα τις ἑώρακεν, εἰ μὴ ὁ ὢν παρὰ τοῦ Θεοῦ, οὗτος ἑώρακε τὸν πατέρα.	46. Not that any man hath seen the Father, save he which is of God, he hath seen the Father.[c]	46. Not that any man has seen the Father; but he who is in God has seen the Father.

(*a*) The words, I will wake him at the last day, seem to me to be interpolated here. These words are a repetition of what was said before and introduce here an irrelevant thought about the consequences of following the teaching, and break the connection between Verses 44 and 45. These words are not clever and make no sense, and may be left out.

(*b*) Many texts have μαθὼν τὴν ἀλήθειαν *having learned the truth*.

(*c*) This verse is almost a repetition of a verse of the first chapter. This verse answers directly the doubts of the Jews and their objections.

Their objections may be expressed as follows: What law of God canst thou, a simple carpenter, reveal to us? The law of God was revealed by Moses, who saw God himself.

To this Jesus replies and speaks of God the spirit who is revealed in the souls of all men through the comprehension. Not man in the flesh and blood sees the Father, but the comprehension knows the Father.

	John vi.	
47. Ἀμὴν ἀμὴν λέγω ὑμῖν, Ὁ πιστεύων εἰς ἐμὲ ἔχει ζωὴν αἰώνιον.	47. Verily, verily, I say unto you, He that believeth on me hath everlasting life.	47. Verily I tell you, He who believes has non-temporal life.
48. Ἐγώ εἰμι ὁ ἄρτος τῆς ζωῆς.	48. I am that bread of life.	48. I am the bread of life.
49. Οἱ πατέρες ὑμῶν ἔφαγον τὸ μάννα ἐν τῇ ἐρήμῳ, καὶ ἀπέθανον·	49. Your fathers did eat manna in the wilderness, and are dead.	49. Your fathers ate manna in the wilderness and died.
50. Οὗτός ἐστιν ὁ ἄρτος ὁ ἐκ τοῦ οὐρανοῦ καταβαίνων, ἵνα τις ἐξ αὐτοῦ φάγῃ καὶ μὴ ἀποθάνῃ.	50. This is the bread which cometh down from heaven, that a man may eat thereof, and not die.ᵃ	50. I am the bread from heaven, and he who eats of it does not die.
51. Ἐγώ εἰμι ὁ ἄρτος ὁ ζῶν, ὁ ἐκ τοῦ οὐρανοῦ καταβάς· ἐάν τις φάγῃ ἐκ τούτου τοῦ ἄρτου, ζήσεται εἰς τὸν αἰῶνα. καὶ ὁ ἄρτος δὲ ὃν ἐγὼ δώσω ἡ σάρξ μου ἐστίν, ἣν ἐγὼ δώσω ὑπὲρ τῆς τοῦ κόσμου ζωῆς.	51. I am the living bread which came down from heaven: if any man eat of this bread, he shall live for ever: and the bread that I will give is my flesh,ᵇ which I will give for the lifeᶜ of the world.	51. I am the bread of life which came down from heaven. If any man eats of this bread, he will live for ever: and the bread which I will give is my carnal life; I have given it in place of the life of the world.

(a) Jesus again corrects the mistake which the Jews made in the beginning of the discussion, when they called the manna the bread of heaven. The bread of heaven is a spiritual food, which gives life that is not subject to death.

(b) σάρξ means *carnal man.*

(c) ζωή at times means *the spiritual life,* and at others *the carnal life;* but in John always, without exception, means the temporal, carnal world, as opposed to the life of the spirit, and so must be translated by *life of the world.*

The sentence is obscure, and cannot help being obscure, since in the sentence Jesus by the accepted comparison of the bread with the teaching expresses a new idea, which is, that his teaching consists in this, that we must live by the spirit and neglect the carnal life, which has several times been said in a different form, He who does not renounce his life, does not take the cross, and so forth; but even from the idea of the author of the gospel the sentence must be obscure. The Jews do not understand a thing, and Jesus proceeds to make the idea clear. And on this obscure sentence whole dogmas have been reared. Leaving out of consideration the absurdity and abomination of the dogmas, we cannot help but observe that this sentence, on which the dogmas are based, is translated quite incorrectly in the sense of a dogma. Ὑπέρ cannot mean *for*; τοῦ κόσμου ζωῆς cannot mean *the life of men*; if we forget the incorrectness of the translation, it is, as translated, a conglomerate of words without any meaning.

This is what the church has to say about it (Interpretation of the Gospel of John, p. 135, and addition to this interpretation):

The bread is my flesh, etc.: Such is the essential complement of the previous discourse about the bread by a new elucidatory feature. The Lord suddenly solves his enigmatic discourse with this feature, which absolutely startles his hearers.

Heretofore he spoke under the image of the bread of his own person in general, as of a subject of faith, but now he speaks clearly, precisely, and definitely: the bread of which I speak is my flesh. "He speaks here clearly of the mysterious communion of his body." (Theoph.) The flesh, the same as the body, the bodily composition of the God-man, is a word which must be understood here strictly in its literal sense, as there is no reason for taking it in a transferred meaning. The word bread has in this whole discourse apparently a metaphorical, or improper, meaning, since by it is expressed Christ's person in general, and by the word flesh a definite, concrete meaning is given to him; as the word manna, which concretely defines the general meaning

of the bread which anciently gave sustenance to the Jews in the
desert, here has obviously a literal meaning, so also the word
flesh defines the general meaning of bread. Consequently, the
bread which we partake of in the communion is not a representation of the Lord's body, but the Lord's flesh itself; for he did
not say, The bread which I give you is a representation of my
flesh, but, It is my flesh (Theoph.).

Which I will give for the life of the world: An allegorical expression about the Messiah's sacrifice on the cross. The Lord's flesh
was offered up by him on the cross, as a true sacrifice to God for
the redemption of the sins of this world, as a transforming sacrifice for the sin of him who brought it. Since this sacrifice on
the cross on Golgotha is still ahead, the Lord speaks of it in the
future. I will give for the life of the world, that is, that
the world may be spiritually alive in union with God who is
reconciled through this sacrifice. A means for attaining this
life is the faith in the redeeming death of Messiah, the God-man;
by dint of this faith the whole world would receive this life, if
the whole world believed in it, since the redeeming sacrifice was
brought by Christ for all men, for the whole world, for the life
of the whole world, which heretofore was estranged from God
and consequently abided in spiritual death on account of the sin
for which the conciliating sacrifice had not yet been brought by
the son of God. Here we already see clearly an indication by the
Lord of the paschal lamb, which his hearers were soon to eat on
the approaching feast of the passover; in the next division this
indication is even clearer and more determined. The Lord
teaches about himself as the paschal lamb which has taken upon
itself the sins of the whole world; the paschal lamb was only an
emblem of this lamb. The Lord now, before the passover, explains to his hearers that the time of figures has passed, that
truth itself is at hand; the partaking of the paschal lamb would
give way to the partaking of the body of Christ, which was
offered as a sacrifice for the sins of the whole world. In view of
this contention, the Lord confirms the discourse, defining it much
more clearly by private features, and pointing to the necessity of
what he has been speaking, but without replying to their question how, for with the carnal tendency of their spirit it would be
impossible for them to understand it.

Except you eat, etc.: The answer, by its external composition,
resembles the answer to Nicodemus about the regeneration (iii.
3–5). As there the expression, Born again, in response to the
question how? is explained by a complement, Born of water and
of the Spirit; so here the expression, The bread is my flesh, is

explained by the complement, Eat my flesh, and drink my blood, and in neither case is the indication of the necessity of the action explained by how it is to be. The connection of the answer with the question is this: You do not comprehend how I will give you my flesh to eat? You will not understand it now; but I tell you an incontestable truth (verily, verily), that the eating of my flesh and the drinking of my blood are absolutely necessary for the attaining of the eternal life; he who will not do so will not have eternal life.

The expression, To eat my flesh, with the complementary, To drink my blood, more clearly still than before points to his death, as a sacrifice for the sin of the world, and at the same time to the paschal lamb, which was shortly to be eaten. It is true, the blood of the paschal lamb was not a part of the paschal supper, but in the event which was memorized by the paschal supper, and in that which was transformed by it, the blood had an essential significance. Upon leaving Egypt the door-posts and thresholds of the Jewish habitations were smeared with it as a sign that their first-born were saved from the hand of the destroying angel, and at the killing of the paschal lamb in the temple, the horns of the altar, which reminded men of the door-posts and thresholds of the Jewish houses, were sprinkled with its blood. At the paschal supper the blood was symbolically represented by the wine. Since the paschal lamb was emblematic of Christ, as the liberation of the Jews from Egypt was an emblem of the redemption of the world, we must see in the words of Christ, Is meat, and, Drink his blood, a substitution of Christ's flesh for the allegorical paschal lamb, and of the blood of Christ for the symbolical wine at the paschal supper. It is a new passover which the Lord prophetically foreshows in the present discourse. The blood, as protecting against death, as a symbol of which was the preservation by the blood of the paschal lamb of the first-born of the Jews from the hand of the destroying angel; the flesh, as sustaining life, the symbol of which was the partaking of the flesh of the paschal lamb, consequently, in general, the preservation from death and the communication of life, — in these two facts is the whole idea of the redemption realized. Consequently, he who wants to apply to himself the redemption, which was accomplished by Christ in his death on the cross, must eat his flesh and drink his blood, or else he will not be a participant of this redemption, or, in other words, he will not have life, that is, eternal life, and will remain unredeemed, that is, will abide in eternal death, in estrangement from communion with God.

He that eateth my flesh, etc. : The same idea as in the preceding verse is expressed, only in a positive sense, as a promise.

And I will raise him: The Lord turns the vision of the believers to the last aim, to which this promise of giving the eternal life through the eating of his flesh and blood is to extend, — to the resurrection, after which there will be the eternal, that is, the blessed life. The relation of these words, I will raise, etc., to what precedes is as follows : He who eats my flesh and drinks my blood has in him eternal life, by dint of which I will not cause him to perish, but will raise him in the last day.

For my flesh, etc. : A foundation both of a negative and a positive assurance of the necessity of eating the flesh of the son of man, and of drinking his blood. This is necessary, because this, and this alone, is the true meat and the true drink, that is, communicates true life to men, eternal life. He who eats every other meat, and drinks every other drink is subject to death; the Lord's body and blood give immortality. With these words he wants to assure them of what he has said, so that they may not regard his words as a riddle or parable, but shall know that it is absolutely necessary to eat his body.

This is what Reuss says (Vol. VI., pp. 190–192):

Comme il y est question de manger la chair et de boire le sang de Christ, il s'est trouvé de tout temps des commentateurs qui y ont vu une allusion directe à la sainte-Cène. Les théologiens réformés surtout insistaient sur ce rapprochement parce qu'ils y voyaient la confirmation directe (v. 63) de leur conception du sacrement. Nous ne saurions cependant admettre qu'il puisse y avoir dans notre texte une allusion directe à la sainte-Cène, parce que celle-ci n'était pas encore instituée et que Jésus parle d'une condition du salut qu'il s'agissait de remplir dès ce moment-là; les deux phrases : celui qui *croit* a la vie éternelle (v. 47), et : celui qui *mange* de ce pain (qui est ma chair) vivra éternellement, sont absolument identiques pour le sens, malgré la diversité de la forme; *manger la chair* de Christ, est la formule figurée et symbolique pour *croire* en lui, par la raison que croire, c'est s'unir, s'assimilier intimement, entièrement. Entre la simple *chair* (v. 51) et la *chair* et le *sang* (v. 53), il n'y a pas la moindre différence. La seconde phrase est plus complète; c'est une locution usuelle pour désigner l'homme, soit d'après sa nature physique seule (1 Cor. xv. 50), soit comme personne (Matth. xvi. 17. Gal. i. 16), mais ici elle n'introduit aucun élément nouveau; toutes les deux équivalent au seul mot *pain*, au commencement (v. 51) comme à la fin (v. 58) du morceau. Du reste, l'évangéliste ne parlant nulle part de la Cène dans son livre, aurait été volontairement inintelligible pour ses lecteurs, pour ne pas dire que Jésus l'aurait été bien davantage si telle avait été son arrière pensée. Il peut être permis à la théologie de se servir de notre texte pour l'appliquer, par *analogie*, au sacrement, et pour jeter, par ce rapprochement, quelque lumière sur une institution au sujet de laquelle les textes scripturaires sont extrêmement peu explicites. Mais l'exégèse ne peut que constater que le nôtre n'est pas écrit dans ce but spécial. (A l'occasion de la Cène, il est parlé du *corps* de Christ et non de sa *chair*.)

Une opinion plus généralement répandue parmi les commentateurs, est celle qui voit dans notre 51e verset une allusion à la mort de Christ considérée comme base, cause ou moyen du salut. On trouve la preuve directe de cette interprétation, d'abord dans la mention expresse du *sang*, ensuite dans la phrase : *que je donnerai* (au futur). Que le Nouveau Testament, d'un bout à l'autre, considère la mort sanglante du Christ comme la condition du salut des hommes, cela ne saurait être l'objet d'un doute, et s'il en était question ici, il n'y aurait là rien qui dût nous surprendre. Nous pensons même qu'avec le texte vulgaire, qui dit : le pain que je donnerai, c'est ma chair *que je donnerai* pour la vie du monde, l'allusion à la mort serait trop directe pour pouvoir être contestée. Mais ce second : *que je donnerai*, manque dans d'anciens témoins et pourrait bien avoir été ajouté pour compléter une phrase en apparence défectueuse. Or, le reste donne un sens parfait sans cette allusion spéciale, qui est étrangère à tout le discours. Nous avons déjà dit que *chair et sang* ne disent pas plus ici que *chair* tout court ; cette dernière locution n'est jamais employée pour parler de la mort de Christ ; le futur du v. 51 (le pain que je donnerai) ne se rapporte pas à l'événement unique de sa mort, mais à la communion de foi qui se reproduira pour chaque individu en son temps. Les phrases : manger la chair du Fils (v. 53), *me* manger (v. 57), manger ce pain (v. 58), sont évidemment synonymes, et signifient: demeurer en lui, et le faire demeurer en soi (v. 58), c'est-à-dire croire, et avoir ainsi la vie en soi (v. 53), une vie désormais permanente, qui implique la résurrection (v. 54). Dans tout cela il n'y a pas un mot de la mort de Christ. Et s'il était vrai que le *sang* doit être spécialement rapporté à cette mort, il s'en suivrait que les phrases des v. 57 et 58 seraient incomplètes et insuffisantes.

This discussion is correct in its analysis of the church teaching, but is faulty in that it recognizes the translation, I will give for the life of the world, as having no meaning whatsoever, and still more, in that it ascribes to these words the meaning of the redemption, that is, in assuming that Jesus is talking nonsense.

52. Ἐμάχοντο οὖν πρὸς ἀλλήλους οἱ Ἰουδαῖοι, λέγοντες, Πῶς δύναται οὗτος ἡμῖν δοῦναι τὴν σάρκα φαγεῖν;

John vi. 52. The Jews therefore strove among themselves, saying, How can this man give us his flesh to eat?

52. And the Jews began to murmur among themselves, and said, How can he give us meat to eat?

53. Εἶπεν οὖν αὐτοῖς ὁ Ἰησοῦς, Ἀμὴν ἀμὴν λέγω ὑμῖν, Ἐὰν μὴ φάγητε τὴν σάρκα τοῦ υἱοῦ τοῦ ἀνθρώπου, καὶ πίητε αὐτοῦ τὸ αἷμα, οὐκ ἔχετε ζωὴν ἐν ἑαυτοῖς.

53. Then Jesus said unto them, Verily, verily, I say unto you, Except ye eat the flesh of the Son of man, and drink his blood, ye have no life in you.⁰

53. And Jesus said to them, Verily, I tell you, If you do not eat the flesh of the son of man, and drink his blood, there will be no life in you.

54. Ὁ τρώγων μου τὴν σάρκα, καὶ πίνων μου τὸ αἷμα, ἔχει ζωὴν αἰώνιον, καὶ ἐγὼ ἀναστήσω αὐτὸν τῇ ἐσχάτῃ ἡμέρᾳ.

54. Whoso eateth⁰ my⁰ flesh and drinketh my blood, hath eternal life; and I will raise him up at the last day.⁰

54. He who eats his flesh and drinks his blood has non-temporal life.

55. Ἡ γὰρ σάρξ μου ἀληθῶς ἐστι βρῶσις, καὶ τὸ αἷμά μου ἀληθῶς ἐστι πόσις.

55. For my flesh is meat indeed, and my blood is drink indeed.⁰

55. For my flesh is food indeed, and my blood is true drink.

56. Ὁ τρώγων μου τὴν σάρκα, καὶ πίνων μου τὸ αἷμα, ἐν ἐμοὶ μένει, κἀγὼ ἐν αὐτῷ.

56. He that eateth my flesh, and drinketh my blood, dwelleth in me, and I in him.ᶠ

56. He who eats my flesh and drinks my blood is in me, and I am in him.

57. Καθὼς ἀπέστειλέ με ὁ ζῶν πατήρ, κἀγὼ ζῶ διὰ τὸν πατέρα· καὶ ὁ τρώγων με, κἀκεῖνος ζήσεται δι' ἐμέ.

57. As the living Father hath sent me, and I live by the Father; so he that eateth me, even he shall live by me.

57. And as the living Father has sent me, and I live by the Father; so he who eats me is spirit, and he will live only by my will.

58. Οὗτός ἐστιν ὁ ἄρτος ὁ ἐκ τοῦ οὐρανοῦ καταβάς· οὐ καθὼς ἔφαγον οἱ πατέρες ὑμῶν τὸ μάννα, καὶ ἀπέθανον· ὁ τρώγων τοῦτον τὸν ἄρτον ζήσεται εἰς τὸν αἰῶνα.

58. This is that bread which came down from heaven: not as your fathers did eat manna, and are dead: he that eateth of this bread shall live for ever.ᶠ

58. Such is the bread which came down from heaven; not as your fathers ate the manna, and died. He who will chew this bread, will live a non-temporal life.

(a) Before this Jesus said that the bread which comes from heaven, that is, the law of God, is for him this, that he gives his carnal life for the life of the spirit, — this is the heavenly bread which he teaches. Flour bread is the food of the life of the world; the bread, the carnal life itself, is the food of the spirit. And now he says that the flesh and the blood, in which, according to the conceptions of the Jews, life was, must serve as food for the spirit. Food, bread, is needed for the carnal life, but the whole carnal life is only food for the non-temporal life.

(b) τρώγω, to gnaw, chew.

(c) An interpolation.

(d) Many texts read αὐτοῦ, and not μου.

(e) My body and blood are indeed only food and drink of the spirit.

This comprehension is the consciousness of my life.

Every one who lives, lives only by expending his bodily life, whether he wishes, thinks, or works; every action of life is the eating up of his flesh and blood, a movement in the direction of annihilating the flesh.

(f) He who eats my flesh, that which wears out my body, — what is it? this is the source of everything, this is God. This is the comprehension, the beginning of everything, and I myself. I am in it, and it is in me.

(g) And as I live in the flesh by the will of somebody, — of the Father of life, as he calls the source of everything, — even so this comprehension will live by my will, by my comprehension. This idea is expressed in the following:

24. Ἀμὴν ἀμὴν λέγω ὑμῖν, Ἐὰν μὴ ὁ κόκκος τοῦ σίτου πεσὼν εἰς τὴν γῆν ἀποθάνῃ, αὐτὸς μόνος μένει· ἐὰν δὲ ἀποθάνῃ, πολὺν καρπὸν φέρει.

25. Ὁ φιλῶν τὴν ψυχὴν αὐτοῦ ἀπολέσει αὐτήν· καὶ ὁ μισῶν τὴν ψυχὴν αὐτοῦ ἐν τῷ κόσμῳ τούτῳ, εἰς ζωὴν αἰώνιον φυλάξει αὐτήν.

John xii. 24. Verily, verily, I say unto you, Except a corn of wheat fall into the ground and die, it abideth alone: but if it die, it bringeth forth much fruit.

25. He that loveth his life shall lose it; and he that hateth his life in this world shall keep it unto life eternal.

24. You know yourselves that if a kernel of wheat falls into the ground and does not die, it remains. But if it dies, it brings forth a great increase.

25. He who loves his soul will cause it to perish; and he who does not love his soul in this world will keep it for ever.

(*a*) These verses from the farewell discourse directly explain the idea of what precedes, and so I place them here.

59. Ταῦτα εἶπεν ἐν συναγωγῇ διδάσκων ἐν Καπερναούμ.

60. Πολλοὶ οὖν ἀκούσαντες ἐκ τῶν μαθητῶν αὐτοῦ εἶπον, Σκληρός ἐστιν οὗτος ὁ λόγος· τίς δύναται αὐτοῦ ἀκούειν;

61. Εἰδὼς δὲ ὁ Ἰησοῦς ἐν ἑαυτῷ, ὅτι γογγύζουσι περὶ τούτου οἱ μαθηταὶ αὐτοῦ, εἶπεν αὐτοῖς, Τοῦτο ὑμᾶς σκανδαλίζει;

62. Ἐὰν οὖν θεωρῆτε τὸν υἱὸν τοῦ ἀνθρώπου ἀναβαίνοντα ὅπου ἦν τὸ πρότερον;

63. Τὸ πνεῦμά ἐστι τὸ ζωοποιοῦν, ἡ σὰρξ οὐκ ὠφελεῖ οὐδέν· τὰ ῥήματα ἃ ἐγὼ λαλῶ ὑμῖν, πνεῦμά ἐστι καὶ ζωή ἐστιν.

John vi. 59. These things said he in the synagogue, as he taught in Capernaum.

60. Many therefore of his disciples, when they had heard this, said, This is a hard saying; who can hear it?

61. When Jesus knew in himself that his disciples murmured at it, he said unto them, Doth this offend you?

62. What and if ye shall see the Son of man ascend up where he was before?

63. It is the Spirit that quickeneth; the flesh profiteth nothing: the words that I speak unto you, they are spirit, and they are life.

59. He spoke these things, as he taught in an assembly in Capernaum.

60. Many of his disciples heard it, and said, This is a hard saying. Who can understand it?

61. And Jesus divined that his disciples were murmuring about it, and he said to them, You are disturbed,

62. Because you see that the son of man is becoming what he was before.

63. The spirit lives, but the body is not good for anything. The words which I told you are that there is spirit, and there is life.

(*a*) There ought to be no punctuation-mark here. Ἐὰν is used by John in the sense of *when, that*. Jesus says, What offends you is that you see that the son of man is God.

THE EXECUTION OF THE LAW GIVES TRUE LIFE

And Jesus was sorry for men, because they perished not knowing wherein the true life was, and suffered and were harassed, themselves not knowing why, like abandoned sheep without a shepherd. And Jesus says to the people, You worry about the life of the flesh: you are hitched to a wagon which you cannot pull, and have put on a yoke which was not made for you. Comprehend my teaching and follow it, and you will know rest and joy in life. I give you another yoke and another wagon,

— spiritual life. Hitch yourselves to it, and you will learn of rest and bliss from me.

You must be meek and humble, and then you will find bliss in your life, for my teaching is a yoke which is made for you, and the execution of my teaching is a light wagon, made according to your strength.

And Jesus went through cities and villages, and taught all the blessedness of life according to the will of God. Then he chose seventy men from among those who were near to him, and sent them to those places where he wanted himself to be. He said to them, Many men do not know the good of the true life, — I am sorry for all of them and wish to teach all, but as the master is not able to attend to the harvest of the whole field, so I cannot attend to it. Go to different cities, and in all places announce the coming of God and the law of God. Say that to be blessed one must be a vagrant, and that the law is all in five rules against evil: (1) not to be angry; (2) not to commit debauchery; (3) not to swear, to make no promises whatever; (4) not to resist evil, not to go to court; and (5) not to make any distinction between men, and to disregard kings and kingdoms.

And so execute these rules yourselves. First of all, be mendicants, vagrants. Take nothing with you, neither scrip, nor bread, nor money. All you must have is raiment on your body, and footgear. Announce the blessedness of the mendicants, and so, above all, be an example of mendicancy. Choose no hosts to stop with, but stay in whatever house you enter first. When you come into the house, greet the hosts. If they receive you, all is well; and if not, go to another house. You will be hated for what you will say, and they will attack and drive you away. And if they drive you away, go to another village; and if they drive you from it, go to another still. They will drive you, as wolves drive the sheep, but do not lose your courage and do not weaken to the last hour. And they will take you into court and will judge you, and flog you, and take you before the officers, that you may justify yourselves before them. And when they will take you to court, do not lose your courage, and do not think what you are going to say. The spirit of God will tell you what to say. Before you will have gone through all the cities, men will understand your teaching, and will turn to you.

Be not afraid. What is hidden in the souls of men will come out. What you will tell to two or three will be scattered among thousands. Above all, do not fear those who may kill your body. What of it if they kill your body? They can do nothing to your soul. So do not fear them. Fear this, that your body and soul may not perish, if you depart from the law. This is what you want to fear.

For one cent you can buy five sparrows, and even they do not die without the will of God. And a hair of the head will not fall without the will of God, so what are you to fear, if you are in the will of God? God will be with him who before men will be one with the will of God; but who before men will renounce the will of God, him God will renounce also. Not all will believe in my teaching, that it is necessary to be a mendicant, a vagrant, not to be angry, not to commit debauchery, not to swear, not to judge or go to court, not to wage war. And those who will not believe will hate it, because it deprives them of what they like, and there will be dissension.

My teaching will, like a fire, burn up the world. And so there must be dissension in the world. There will be dissension in every house. Father will be against son, mother against daughter, and the housefolk will be haters of those who will understand my teaching. And they will kill them. For he who will understand my teaching will see no meaning in his father, or mother, or wife, or children, or all his property. He who thinks more of his father or mother than of my teaching has not comprehended my teaching. He who is not at all times ready for all kinds of sufferings of the flesh is not my disciple. He who will care for this carnal life will cause the true life to perish, and he who will cause this carnal life to perish according to my teaching will save his life.

The seventy disciples went out over the cities and villages, and did what Jesus had commanded. When they returned, they told Jesus with joy, The devilish teaching about anger, adultery, oaths, judgments, and wars is everywhere giving way before us.

And Jesus said to them, Do not rejoice because the evil is yielding to you, but because you are in the will of God.

And then Jesus rejoiced on account of the power of the spirit, and said, From the fact that my disciples have understood me and that the evil is vanquished by them, I see that thou art the highest spirit, — the beginning of everything, truly the Father of men, — because what the wise and learned men could not understand with all their learning, the unreasoning have comprehended by recognizing themselves to be the children of the Father. And thou, as the Father, hast disclosed everything to them, through the love which is between a father and his son. Everything which a man needs to know is disclosed to him through the love of the Father for the son and of the son for the Father. Only him who recognizes himself as the son does the Father recognize.

And the people of his house came and wanted to bind him, for they thought that he was mad.

And the Pharisees and the lawyers came from Jerusalem, and said, He is mad: he wants to mend a lesser evil with a greater evil. That there may be no mendicants, he wants to make all men mendicants, and he wants nobody to be punished, and the robbers to kill everybody, and to have no wars, though then the enemies will kill everybody.

And he said, You say that my teaching is evil, and at the same time you say that I destroy the evil. That cannot be, for evil cannot be destroyed by evil. If I destroy evil, my teaching cannot be evil, for evil cannot go against itself. If evil went against itself, there would be no evil. You cast out the evil according to your law. How do you cast out the evil? By the law of Moses, and this law is from God. But I cast out the evil with the spirit of God, which has always been in you. It is only for this reason that I can expel the evil. And the fact that I expel evil is a proof to you that my teaching is true, and that the spirit of God is in men and is stronger than the carnal lusts. If that did not exist, it would not be possible to vanquish the lust of evil, as it is impossible to enter the house of a strong man and rob it. To rob the house of a strong man, it is necessary first to bind the man. And thus are men bound by the spirit of God.

He who is not with me is against me. He who does not harvest in the field only loses the corn, for he who is not with me is not with the spirit of God, — he is an adversary of the spirit.

And so I tell you that every human mistake and every false interpretation will be forgiven, but the false interpretation about the spirit of God will not be forgiven. If a man says a word against another, that will pass; but if he will say a word against what is holy in man, — against the spirit of God, that will not pass unnoticed; scold me as much as you please, but do not call evil the good which I am doing. Man will not be forgiven for calling the good evil, that is, the works which I do. One has to be with the spirit of God, or against it.

Either consider the tree good, and its fruit good, or consider it bad, and its fruit bad, for by its fruit is the tree esteemed. You see me expel evil, consequently my teaching is good. Every man who expels evil, no matter what his teaching may be, cannot be against us, but is with us, for one can expel evil only with the spirit of God.

After that Jesus came for the holiday to Jerusalem. And there was then a pool in Jerusalem. And they said about this pool that an angel stepped into it, and that caused the water of the pool to well up, and if one leaped into the water immediately after it began to well up, he was cured from whatever disease he may have had.

And there were porches built around this pool. And on these porches lay all kinds of sick people, waiting for the water in the pool to well up, in order to leap into it.

Jesus came to the pool, and saw a man lying on a porch. Jesus asked who he was. The man told him that he had been ailing for thirty-eight years, and that he had been waiting for a long time to be the first to leap into the pool, after the water had begun to well up, but that he could never succeed, for others got in before him.

Jesus looked at him, and said, In vain dost thou wait here for a miracle from the angel. There are no miracles. There is one miracle, and that is, that God has given life to men, and it is necessary to live with all one's powers. Do not wait for anything at this pool, but take thy bed, and live according to the divine law, according to the strength which God will give thee.

The sick man obeyed him, and got up and went away.

Jesus said to him, Thou seest thyself that thou hast the strength. See to it that thou wilt not believe again in all this deception. Do not make this error again, but live according to the power which God gives thee.

And the man went and told everybody what had happened to him. And all those who had been working the deception of the pool and were making a living thereby grew angry, and they did not know how to wreak their vengeance and to annoy the sick man and Jesus for having disclosed their deception. They found a pretext for doing so in its being a Sabbath, for on the Sabbath it

was not permitted, according to their law, to work. At
first they attacked the sick man, and said, How didst thou
dare take up thy bed on the Sabbath? It is not lawful
to work on the Sabbath.

The sick man said to them, He who raised me up told
me to take up the bed.

They said, Who ordered thee to do so?

He said, I do not know. A man came up to me and
went away again.

The Pharisees made their way to Jesus, and, finding
him, they said, How couldst thou order the man to rise
and take up his bed on a Sabbath?

To this Jesus said to them, My Father never stops
working, and so I will never stop working, whether it be
a week-day or a Sabbath. The Sabbath did not make
man, but man made the Sabbath.

Then the Jews grew angrier still, because he dared to
call God his Father. And they attacked him, and Jesus
replied to them, A man could not do anything of himself,
if God the Father — the spirit of God in man — did not
point out to him what to do. God, the Father of man,
lives and works always, and man lives and works always.
God the Father gave men reason for their own good, and
showed them what is good and what bad.

Just as God gives life, so also the spirit of God gives
life. God the Father does not choose and decide anything himself, but, having taught men what is good and
what bad, he leaves everything to man to do, so that men
may honour the spirit of God and obey it within themselves, as they honour and obey God. He who does not
honour the spirit of God in himself does not honour God.
You must understand that he who has completely abandoned himself to my teaching has exalted the spirit in
himself, and in it reposes his life, he has non-temporal
life and is already freed from death. It is clear that now
the dead, having comprehended the meaning of their life,

that they are the sons of God, will live. For as God is alive in himself, so is the son alive in himself. The freedom of the choice is the same as that the spirit of God is in man, — it is the whole man.

Do not marvel at this teaching; the time has come when all mortals will be divided. Some, who do good, will find life, and those who do evil will be destroyed.

I cannot choose anything of myself. What I have comprehended from the Father, that I choose. My choice is correct, if I do not hold to my own wish, but to the meaning which I have comprehended from the Father. If I were the only one to assure you that I am right, because I want it to be so, you might not have believed me. But there is another who gives the assurance about me, — that I am doing right. That is the spirit of God, and you know that this assurance is true.

You see by my works that the Father has sent me. God the Father has shown concerning me in your souls and in the Scriptures. You have not comprehended his voice, and you have not known him. You have not his firm comprehension within you, for you do not believe that which he has sent, — the spirit of God in your souls.

Try to comprehend it: you expect to find life in your souls, and you will find there within you the spirit of God.

But you will not believe me that you will have life.

I esteem little your praying in your temples, and your observing the fasts and the Sabbaths according to human laws; the true love of the true God is not in you.

I teach you in the name of my Father and of yours, but you do not understand me. If a man will teach you in his own name, you will believe him. What can you rely upon, since you receive your sayings from one another, and do not seek the teaching as to the Father of the son. I am not the only one who shows you that you are wrong before your Father. That same Moses, in whom you trust, shows you that you are wrong and do not understand him. If you relied on what Moses said, you would rely also on what I tell you. If you do not rely on his writings, you will not believe my teaching, either.

And that they might understand it, that they might understand that it is possible to enter into the will of God without an effort, he told them a parable: A king received an inheritance. In order to receive this inheritance, the king had for a time to depart from his kingdom. And so the king went away.

But before his departure he distributed his possessions among his subjects, giving to each according to his ability: to one five talents, to another two, to a third one, and he commanded them to work without him and to gain by these talents as much as each could.

When the king went away, each man did with his property whatever he could. Some worked, and he who had five talents earned other five talents; another with his one talent gained ten more; others with their two talents gained two, or with their one gained five more or only one more; and others again did not work with the money given to them by their master, but hid the money away in the ground. Those who had taken five talents had the five talents left; those who had taken two had two, and those who had taken one had one left. And others again, who did not work with the master's money, did not want to appear before the king, but sent word to him that they did not wish to be under his power.

When the time came, the king returned into his kingdom, and he called all his subjects to give accounts of themselves, what each had done with what had been given him.

And one servant came, the one to whom five talents had been given, and he said, With the five talents I have gained five more. And another came, to whom one talent had been given, and he said, Here, with the one talent

I have gained ten more. And then came he who had received two talents, and he brought two more, and the one who had received one brought five more. And still another to whom one talent had been given brought one more.

And the master praised them all alike and rewarded them alike. He said to all alike, I see that you are good and faithful servants: you have worked over my possessions, and so I receive you as equal participants in what is mine. We shall rule together.

After that came those subjects who had not worked over the master's possessions. And one of them said, Master, thou gavest me a talent at thy departure. I know that thou art a hard man and wantest to take from us what thou hast not given us, and so I was afraid of thee and from fear hid away thy talent. Here it is in full. What thou hast given me I return to thee. And others who had received five talents, and those who had received ten talents, brought back the master's talents, and they said the same to him.

Then the master said to them, Foolish people! You say that out of fear of me you hid your talents in the ground and did not work with them. If you knew that I was a hard man and will take what I have not given, why did you not try to do what I commanded?

If you had worked with my talent, your possessions would have been increased, and you would have done my will, and I might have had mercy on you, and you would not have fared worse. But now you have not got away from my power anyway.

And the master took the talents away from those who had not worked with them, and told his servants to give them to those who had gained more.

And the servants said, Master, they have enough as it is. But the king said, Give to those who have earned for me, for to him who looks after his own it shall be added, and from him who does not look after his own even the last shall be taken from him.

But drive away these foolish and lazy servants. Let them not be here. And drive away those also who sent word to me that they did not want to be in my power, and let them not be here.

This king is the beginning of life, — the spirit. The world is the kingdom, but he does not himself govern the kingdom, but, like a peasant, he casts out the seed and leaves it alone. And the field brings forth blades, ears, and kernels of its own accord. The talent is the comprehension in every man. God the spirit has put the comprehension in every man, and leaves men to live according to their will.

God himself decides nothing, but having instructed man in everything, leaves it to every man to decide for himself. Not all have the same talent, but each receives according to his ability. Not to all is the same comprehension given, but it is given, and for God there is no greater and no lesser. All God needs is work over the comprehension. Some work with the talent of their master; others do not work for their master; others again do not work and do not acknowledge the master. Some men live by the comprehension; others do not live by it; and others again do not acknowledge it. The master comes back and asks for an account. That is the temporal death and accounting of life. Some come and say that they have worked with the talent, and they enter into the life of the master. And the master does not count who has worked more, and who less. All become alike participants in the life of the master. He who accepts the comprehension has life.

He who has the comprehension and relies on him who has sent it has non-temporal life and knows no death: he has passed into life. Others come and say that they have not worked with the talent: they do not refuse the talent; they only say that there is no sense in working, for, whether they work or not, they will meet with punishment. They know the severity of the master. Other men have the comprehension, but do not rely on it. They say to themselves, Whether I work or not, I shall die, and nothing will be left, and so there is no sense doing anything with it. To this the king says, If thou knowest that I am severe, thou oughtest so much the more to have done my will. Why did you not try to do it? If men know that temporal death is inevitable, why should they not try to live by the doing of the will of God, — by the comprehension? And the king says, Take the talent from them, and give it to those who have. It makes no difference to the king where the talents are, so long as they are, just as it makes no difference to the peasant what kernel will bring forth ears, so long as he has a harvest. If the comprehension gives life to men according to their will, then those who do not hold it cannot live and stand outside of life. And after the temporal death nothing will be left of them. And of the men who do not acknowledge the king's power, the king says, Throw those men out. These other men not only fail to work with the comprehension and life, but even despise the Father of the spirit who has given it to them, — they, too, cannot live, and are also destroyed with death.

CHAPTER VI.

THE FOOD OF LIFE. MAN LIVES NOT BY BREAD ALONE.
OF THE CARNAL AND THE SPIRITUAL KINSHIP

46. Ἔτι δὲ αὐτοῦ λαλοῦντος τοῖς ὄχλοις, ἰδού, ἡ μήτηρ καὶ οἱ ἀδελφοὶ αὐτοῦ εἰστήκεισαν ἔξω, ζητοῦντες αὐτῷ λαλῆσαι.

47. Εἶπε δέ τις αὐτῷ, Ἰδού, ἡ μήτηρ σου καὶ οἱ ἀδελφοί σου ἔξω ἑστήκασι, ζητοῦντές σοι λαλῆσαι.

48. Ὁ δὲ ἀποκριθεὶς εἶπε τῷ εἰπόντι αὐτῷ, Τίς ἐστιν ἡ μήτηρ μου; καὶ τίνες εἰσὶν οἱ ἀδελφοί μου;

49. Καὶ ἐκτείνας τὴν χεῖρα αὐτοῦ ἐπὶ τοὺς μαθητὰς αὐτοῦ εἶπεν, Ἰδοὺ ἡ μήτηρ μου καὶ οἱ ἀδελφοί μου.

50. Ὅστις γὰρ ἂν ποιήσῃ τὸ θέλημα τοῦ πατρός μου τοῦ ἐν οὐρανοῖς, αὐτός μου ἀδελφὸς καὶ ἀδελφὴ καὶ μήτηρ ἐστίν.

Matt. xii. 46. While he yet talked to the people, behold, his mother and his brethren stood without, desiring to speak with him.

47. Then one said unto him, Behold, thy mother and thy brethren stand without, desiring to speak with thee.

48. But he answered and said unto him that told him, Who is my mother? and who are my brethren?

49. And he stretched forth his hand toward his disciples, and said, Behold my mother and my brethren!

50. For whosoever shall do the will of my Father which is in heaven, the same is my brother, and sister, and mother.

46. And while he talked, his mother and his brothers came up and stood at a distance, wishing to speak with him.

47. A man saw them, and said to him, Thy mother and thy brothers are standing a little way off: they want to speak with thee.

48. And he said, Who is my mother? and who are my brothers?

49. And he pointed with his hand to his disciples and said, Here are my mother and my brothers.

50. For he who does the will of God my Father is my brother, and my sister, and my mother.

Before this it said that for the true life there can be no place, no other care than life; there can be no considerations of what is done, of the past, of the temporal; now it says that there can be no other communion between men than the union in the will of God, which is one for all. The nearness of men to the kingdom of God depends only on the oneness in the will of God.

27. Ἐγένετο δὲ ἐν τῷ λέγειν αὐτὸν ταῦτα, ἐπάρασά τις γυνὴ φωνὴν ἐκ τοῦ ὄχλου εἶπεν αὐτῷ, Μακαρία ἡ κοιλία ἡ βαστάσασά σε, καὶ μαστοὶ οὓς ἐθήλασας.	*Luke xi.* 27. And it came to pass, as he spake these things, a certain woman of the company lifted up her voice, and said unto him, Blessed is the womb that bare thee, and the paps which thou hast sucked.	27. And it happened, as he said this, a woman from among the people lifted up her voice, and said to him, Blessed is the womb that bore thee, and the teats which thou hast sucked.
28. Αὐτὸς δὲ εἶπε, Μενοῦν μακάριοι οἱ ἀκούοντες τὸν λόγον τοῦ Θεοῦ καὶ φυλάσσοντες αὐτόν.	28. But he said, Yea, rather, blessed are they that hear the word of God, and keep it.[a]	28. But he said, Blessed is he, who understands the comprehension of God and keeps it.
57. Ἐγένετο δὲ πορευομένων αὐτῶν, ἐν τῇ ὁδῷ εἶπέ τις πρὸς αὐτόν, Ἀκολουθήσω σοι ὅπου ἂν ἀπέρχῃ, κύριε.	*Luke ix.* 57. And it came to pass, that, as they went in the way, a certain man said unto him, Lord, I will follow thee whithersoever thou goest.	57. And on the way a man said to Jesus, I will follow thee everywhere, my master.
58. Καὶ εἶπεν αὐτῷ ὁ Ἰησοῦς, Αἱ ἀλώπεκες φωλεοὺς ἔχουσι, καὶ τὰ πετεινὰ τοῦ οὐρανοῦ κατασκηνώσεις· ὁ δὲ υἱὸς τοῦ ἀνθρώπου οὐκ ἔχει ποῦ τὴν κεφαλὴν κλίνῃ.	58. And Jesus said unto him, Foxes have holes, and birds of the air have nests; but the Son of man hath not where to lay his head.[b]	58. And Jesus said to him, Foxes have holes, and birds have nests; but the son of man has no abiding place.

(a) The good of life cannot depend on anybody; nobody can transmit his good to another. The good is only the life of the comprehension.

(b) There is a double meaning to this verse: one, that the son of man, in the sense of man, must not trouble himself about the place where he is; it makes no difference where he is, provided he does not regard any particular place as peculiarly his own. He must be a vagrant.

The other, that the son of man — the spirit of God in man — is outside space, and that it is impossible to be where the son of man is, because it is everywhere and nowhere.

THE STORM ON THE LAKE

22. Καὶ ἐγένετο ἐν μιᾷ τῶν ἡμερῶν, καὶ αὐτὸς ἐνέβη εἰς πλοῖον καὶ οἱ μαθηταὶ αὐτοῦ· καὶ εἶπε πρὸς αὐτούς, Διέλθωμεν εἰς τὸ πέραν τῆς λίμνης· καὶ ἀνήχθησαν.

23. Πλεόντων δὲ αὐτῶν ἀφύπνωσε. καὶ κατέβη λαῖλαψ ἀνέμου εἰς τὴν λίμνην, καὶ συνεπληροῦντο, καὶ ἐκινδύνευον.

24. Προσελθόντες δὲ διήγειραν αὐτὸν, λέγοντες, Ἐπιστάτα, ἐπιστάτα, ἀπολλύμεθα. ὁ δὲ ἐγερθεὶς

25. Εἶπε δὲ αὐτοῖς, Ποῦ ἐστιν ἡ πίστις ὑμῶν;

26. Καὶ λέγει αὐτοῖς, Τί δειλοί ἐστε, ὀλιγόπιστοι; τότε ἐγερθεὶς ἐπετίμησε τοῖς ἀνέμοις καὶ τῇ θαλάσσῃ, καὶ ἐγένετο γαλήνη μεγάλη.

Luke viii. 22. Now it came to pass on a certain day, that he went into a ship with his disciples: and he said unto them, Let us go over unto the other side of the lake. And they launched forth.

23. But as they sailed, he fell asleep: and there came down a storm of wind on the lake; and they were filled with water, and were in jeopardy.

24. And they came to him, and awoke him, saying, Master, Master, we perish. Then he arose,

25. And he said unto them, Where is your faith?

Matt. viii. 26. And he saith unto them, Why are ye fearful, O ye of little faith? Then he arose, and rebuked the winds and the sea; and there was a great calm.

22. And one day he happened to go into a ship with his disciples, and he said to them, Let us sail to the other side of the lake, and they sailed away.

23. And as they sailed, there rose a great storm, and came over the lake; and they were drenched, and they were in danger; but he slept in the stern.

24. And his disciples came to him and awoke him, saying, Teacher, teacher, we perish. Then he rose,

25. And said to them, Where is your faith?

26. And he said to them, Why do you lose your courage, you of little faith? And he rebuked the wind and the sea; and the winds died down, and there was a calm.

Jesus expresses no fear before earthly dangers. He sleeps, while the storm strikes against the ship and the rain washes it. When he is wakened and told that they are perishing, he is surprised and rebukes them. They said that they believed in the true life outside of time and space, and at the first opportunity they showed by their timidity before earthly calamities that they did not believe in it. As the cares for the burial of the fathers and for the order of the house, as the ties of kinship, as the relations to other people cannot affect the life of the spirit, so also the danger of earthly death, and earthly death itself, cannot interfere with the life of the spirit. And Jesus sleeps and, on awakening, remains calm.

84. Μὴ οὖν μεριμνή-
σητε εἰς τὴν αὔριον· ἡ
γὰρ αὔριον μεριμνήσει
τὰ ἑαυτῆς. ἀρκετὸν τῇ
ἡμέρᾳ ἡ κακία αὐτῆς.

59. Εἶπε δὲ πρὸς
ἕτερον, Ἀκολούθει μοι.
ὁ δὲ εἶπε, Κύριε, ἐπίτρε-
ψόν μοι ἀπελθόντι πρῶ-
τον θάψαι τὸν πατέρα
μου.

60. Εἶπε δὲ αὐτῷ ὁ
Ἰησοῦς, Ἄφες τοὺς νε-
κροὺς θάψαι τοὺς ἑαυτῶν
νεκρούς· σὺ δὲ ἀπελθὼν
διάγγελλε τὴν βασιλείαν
τοῦ Θεοῦ.

61. Εἶπε καὶ ἕτερος,
Ἀκολουθήσω σοι, κύριε·
πρῶτον δὲ ἐπίτρεψόν μοι
ἀποτάξασθαι τοῖς εἰς τὸν
οἶκόν μου.

62. Εἶπε δὲ πρὸς
αὐτὸν ὁ Ἰησοῦς, Οὐδεὶς
ἐπιβαλὼν τὴν χεῖρα
αὐτοῦ ἐπ' ἄροτρον, καὶ
βλέπων εἰς τὰ ὀπίσω,
εὔθετός ἐστιν εἰς τὴν
βασιλείαν τοῦ Θεοῦ.

Matt. vi. 84. Take therefore no thought for the morrow:[a] for the morrow shall take thought for the things of itself. Sufficient unto the day is the evil thereof.

Luke ix. 59. And he said unto another, Follow me. But he said, Lord, suffer me first to go and bury my father.[b]

60. Jesus said unto him, Let the dead bury their dead: but go thou and preach the kingdom of God.

61. And another also said, Lord, I will follow thee; but let me first go bid them farewell, which are at home at my house.

62. And Jesus said unto him, No man, having put his hand to the plough, and looking back, is fit for the kingdom of God.

84. Do not trouble yourselves about the future. Sufficient is the evil for the present.

59. And to another Jesus said, Follow me. And that man said, Allow me first to go and bury my father.

60. And Jesus said to him, Let the dead bury the dead, but you follow me, and announce the gospel of the Lord.

61. And another man said, I will follow thee, but let me first attend to my house.

62. And Jesus said to him, He who has taken hold of the plough and looks back is not fit for the kingdom of God.

(*a*) In many texts, Take no thought for the morrow, is omitted. This verse is mentioned for the second time. It was given in Chapter IV. (The sermon on the mount.)

(*b*) Again two meanings: one, that all worldly cares, even the most important, such as burial seems to be, are works of death and of darkness. The one work of life is life, the dissemination of life.

The other, the main meaning is: for him who lives by life there is no death.

The last utterance includes the meaning of the first two, and in it lies the chief thought of this passage. The meaning of it is, that he who has come to know the kingdom of God, the life of the spirit, and yet cares for anything carnal, by this care for the carnal life acknowledges that he does not live by the life of the spirit. If a man, living by the life of the spirit, has a care for the carnal life, he will succeed as little in the life of the spirit, as he who ploughs and looks behind him, instead of looking before him.

This comparison has also another meaning. A man who imagines that he lives by the spirit and who at the same time reflects on the consequences which that which he is doing in life might have, is like the ploughman who, in his desire to make a furrow, looks, not forward at what he is doing, but backwards, at what he has done already.

JESUS AT THE HOUSE OF MARTHA AND MARY

81. Πλὴν ζητεῖτε τὴν βασιλείαν τοῦ Θεοῦ, καὶ ταῦτα πάντα προστεθήσεται ὑμῖν.

88. Ἐγένετο δὲ ἐν τῷ πορεύεσθαι αὐτούς, καὶ αὐτὸς εἰσῆλθεν εἰς κώμην τινά· γυνὴ δέ τις ὀνόματι Μάρθα ὑπεδέξατο αὐτὸν εἰς τὸν οἶκον αὐτῆς.

39. Καὶ τῇδε ἦν ἀδελφὴ καλουμένη Μαρία, ἣ καὶ παρακαθίσασα παρὰ τοὺς πόδας τοῦ Ἰησοῦ ἤκουε τὸν λόγον αὐτοῦ.

40. Ἡ δὲ Μάρθα περιεσπᾶτο περὶ πολλὴν διακονίαν· ἐπιστᾶσα δὲ εἶπε, Κύριε, οὐ μέλει σοι ὅτι ἡ ἀδελφή μου μόνην με κατέλιπε διακονεῖν; εἰπὲ οὖν αὐτῇ ἵνα μοι συναντιλάβηται.

41. Ἀποκριθεὶς δὲ εἶπεν αὐτῇ ὁ Ἰησοῦς, Μάρ-

Luke xii. 81. But rather seek ye the kingdom of God; and all these things shall be added unto you.*

Luke x. 38. Now it came to pass, as they went, that he entered into a certain village: and a certain woman named Martha received him into her house.

39. And she had a sister called Mary, which also sat at Jesus' feet, and heard his word.*

40. But Martha was cumbered about much serving, and came to him, and said, Lord, dost thou not care that my sister hath left me to serve alone? bid her therefore that she help me.

41. And Jesus answered and said unto her, Martha, Martha,

81. Seek only to be in the will of God, and everything else will be given you.

38. Jesus happened one day to be walking with his disciples, and they entered a village. A woman named Martha invited them to their house.

39. And she had a sister named Mary. Mary sat down at Jesus' feet, and listened to his teaching.

40. But Martha was busy preparing a good reception for them, and she went up to Jesus, and said, Evidently thou dost not care that my sister has left me to serve alone. Tell her to help me.

41. But Jesus said to her in reply, Oh, Martha, Martha, thou art troub-

θα, Μάρθα, μεριμνᾷς καὶ τυρβάζῃ περὶ πολλά·

42. Ἑνὸς δέ ἐστι χρεία. Μαρία δὲ τὴν ἀγαθὴν μερίδα ἐξελέξατο, ἥτις οὐκ ἀφαιρεθήσεται ἀπ᾽ αὐτῆς.

23. Ἔλεγε δὲ πρὸς πάντας, Εἴ τις θέλει ὀπίσω μου ἐλθεῖν, ἀπαρνησάσθω ἑαυτὸν, καὶ ἀράτω τὸν σταυρὸν αὐτοῦ καθ᾽ ἡμέραν, καὶ ἀκολουθείτω μοι.

24. Ὃς γὰρ ἂν θέλῃ τὴν ψυχὴν αὐτοῦ σῶσαι, ἀπολέσει αὐτήν· ὃς δ᾽ ἂν ἀπολέσῃ τὴν ψυχὴν αὐτοῦ ἕνεκεν ἐμοῦ, οὗτος σώσει αὐτήν.

25. Τί γὰρ ὠφελεῖται ἄνθρωπος, κερδήσας τὸν κόσμον ὅλον, ἑαυτὸν δὲ ἀπολέσας ἢ ζημιωθείς;

26. Ὃς γὰρ ἂν ἐπαισχυνθῇ με καὶ τοὺς ἐμοὺς λόγους, τοῦτον ὁ υἱὸς τοῦ ἀνθρώπου ἐπαισχυνθήσεται, ὅταν ἔλθῃ ἐν τῇ δόξῃ αὐτοῦ καὶ τοῦ πατρὸς καὶ τῶν ἁγίων ἀγγέλων.

---

thou art careful and troubled about many things:

42. But one thing is needful; and Mary hath chosen that good part, which shall not be taken away from her.

Luke ix. 23. And he said to them all, If any man will come after me, let him deny himself, and take up his cross daily, and follow me.

24. For whosoever will save his life shall lose it: but whosoever will lose his life for my sake, the same shall save it.

25. For what is a man advantaged, if he gain the whole world, and lose himself, or be cast away?

26. For whosoever shall be ashamed of me and of my words, of him shall the Son of man be ashamed, when he shall come in his own glory, and in his Father's, and of the holy angels.

---

ling thyself about many things,

42. But one thing is needed, and Mary has chosen what is best. What she has chosen will not be taken from her.

23. And he said to them all, If you wish to follow me, renounce yourselves and be prepared for everything at any time, and then follow me.

24. He who wants to save his life, will lose it. And he who causes his life to perish for my sake, will save it.

25. What profit is it to a man, if he should gain the whole world, and cause his ruin or his harm?

26. He who is ashamed of my words, of him the son of man will be ashamed, when he appears in the sense of the Father and the powers of God.

(*a*) This verse was given in Chapter IV.

(*b*) λόγος means *teaching*, as generally in Luke.

(*c*) The word *cross* I translate in the sense which is ascribed to it by all the interpreters. I do not use the word *cross* itself, because historically it has no meaning in the mouth of Jesus. Even if he knew that he was going to be crucified, his disciples could not have known it, and so the word had no meaning for them.

PARABLE OF THE RICH MAN

15. Εἶπε δὲ πρὸς αὐτούς, Ὁρᾶτε καὶ φυλάσ-

Luke. xii. 15. And he said unto them, Take

15. And he said to them, Take care, and be-

σεσθε ἀπὸ τῆς πλεονε-
ξίας· ὅτι οὐκ ἐν τῷ πε-
ρισσεύειν τινὶ ἡ ζωὴ
αὐτοῦ ἐστιν ἐκ τῶν ὑπαρ-
χόντων αὐτοῦ.

16. Εἶπε δὲ παραβο-
λὴν πρὸς αὐτούς, λέγων,
Ἀνθρώπου τινὸς πλου-
σίου εὐφόρησεν ἡ χώρα·

17. Καὶ διελογίζετο
ἐν ἑαυτῷ, λέγων, Τί
ποιήσω, ὅτι οὐκ ἔχω ποῦ
συνάξω τοὺς καρπούς μου;

18. Καὶ εἶπε, Τοῦτο
ποιήσω· καθελῶ μου τὰς
ἀποθήκας, καὶ μείζονας
οἰκοδομήσω, καὶ συνάξω
ἐκεῖ πάντα τὰ γεννήματά
μου καὶ τὰ ἀγαθά μου,

19. Καὶ ἐρῶ τῇ ψυχῇ
μου, Ψυχή, ἔχεις πολλὰ
ἀγαθὰ κείμενα εἰς ἔτη
πολλά· ἀναπαύου, φάγε,
πίε, εὐφραίνου.

20. Εἶπε δὲ αὐτῷ ὁ
Θεός, Ἄφρων, ταύτῃ τῇ
νυκτὶ τὴν ψυχήν σου
ἀπαιτοῦσιν ἀπὸ σοῦ· ἃ
δὲ ἡτοίμασας, τίνι ἔσται;

21. Οὕτως ὁ θησαυ-
ρίζων ἑαυτῷ, καὶ μὴ εἰς
Θεὸν πλουτῶν.

---

heed, and beware of covetousness: for a man's life consisteth not in the abundance of the things which he possesseth.

16. And he spake a parable unto them, saying, The ground of a certain rich man brought forth plentifully:

17. And he thought within himself, saying, What shall I do, because I have no room where to bestow my fruits?

18. And he said, This will I do : I will pull down my barns, and build greater; and there will I bestow all my fruits and my goods.

19. And I will say to my soul, Soul, thou hast much goods laid up for many years; take thine ease, eat drink, and be merry.

20. But God said unto him, Thou fool, this night thy soul shall be required of thee: then whose shall those things be, which thou hast provided?

21. So is he that layeth up treasure for himself, and is not rich toward God.

---

ware of every abundance, for there can be no life in what he possesses.

16. And he told them a parable, There was a rich man, whose land brought forth good harvests,

17. And he thought, What shall I do? I have no room to put my fruits away.

18. And he said, This is what I will do : I will pull down my barns, and build new ones; and I will take all my corn and all my possessions there.

19. And I will say to my soul, Soul, thou hast large possessions to last for many years. Sleep, eat, drink, and be merry.

20. And God said to him, Thou fool, this night thy soul will be taken from thee, so of what good are thy provisions?

21. So it happens with him who lays up for himself, and does not grow rich in God.

THE PARABLE OF THE FIG-TREE

1. Παρῆσαν δέ τινες
ἐν αὐτῷ τῷ καιρῷ ἀπαγ-
γέλλοντες αὐτῷ περὶ
τῶν Γαλιλαίων, ὧν τὸ
αἷμα Πιλάτος ἔμιξε μετὰ
τῶν θυσιῶν αὐτῶν.

2. Καὶ ἀποκριθεὶς ὁ
Ἰησοῦς εἶπεν αὐτοῖς,
Δοκεῖτε ὅτι οἱ Γαλιλαῖοι
οὗτοι ἁμαρτωλοὶ παρὰ
πάντας τοὺς Γαλιλαίους
ἐγένοντο, ὅτι τοιαῦτα
πεπόνθασιν;

Luke xiii. 1. There were present at that season some that told him of the Galileans, whose blood Pilate had mingled with their sacrifices.

2. And Jesus answering said unto them, Suppose ye that these Galileans were sinners above all the Galileans, because they suffered such things?

---

1. There were some present, and they told him of the Galileans, whom Pilate had killed.

2. And Jesus said to them in reply, Do you imagine that these Galileans were more sinful than the rest, that this happened to them?

3. Οὐχί, λέγω ὑμῖν· ἀλλ' ἐὰν μὴ μετανοῆτε, πάντες ὡσαύτως ἀπολεῖσθε.

4. Ἢ ἐκεῖνοι οἱ δέκα καὶ ὀκτώ, ἐφ' οὓς ἔπεσεν ὁ πύργος ἐν τῷ Σιλωάμ, καὶ ἀπέκτεινεν αὐτούς, δοκεῖτε ὅτι οὗτοι ὀφειλέται ἐγένοντο παρὰ πάντας ἀνθρώπους τοὺς κατοικοῦντας ἐν Ἰερουσαλήμ;

5. Οὐχί, λέγω ὑμῖν· ἀλλ' ἐὰν μὴ μετανοῆτε, πάντες ὁμοίως ἀπολεῖσθε.

6. Ἔλεγε δὲ ταύτην τὴν παραβολήν· Συκῆν εἶχέ τις ἐν τῷ ἀμπελῶνι αὐτοῦ πεφυτευμένην· καὶ ἦλθε καρπὸν ζητῶν ἐν αὐτῇ, καὶ οὐχ εὗρεν.

7. Εἶπε δὲ πρὸς τὸν ἀμπελουργόν, Ἰδού, τρία ἔτη ἔρχομαι ζητῶν καρπὸν ἐν τῇ συκῇ ταύτῃ, καὶ οὐχ εὑρίσκω· ἔκκοψον αὐτήν· ἱνατί καὶ τὴν γῆν καταργεῖ;

8. Ὁ δὲ ἀποκριθεὶς λέγει αὐτῷ, Κύριε, ἄφες αὐτὴν καὶ τοῦτο τὸ ἔτος, ἕως ὅτου σκάψω περὶ αὐτήν, καὶ βάλω κοπρίαν·

9. Κἂν μὲν ποιήσῃ καρπόν· εἰ δὲ μήγε, εἰς τὸ μέλλον ἐκκόψεις αὐτήν.

---

3. I tell you, Nay: but, except ye repent,* ye shall all likewise perish.

4. Or those eighteen, upon whom the tower in Siloam fell, and slew them, think ye that they were sinners above all men that dwelt in Jerusalem?

5. I tell you, Nay: but, except ye repent, ye shall all likewise perish.

6. He spake also this parable; A certain man had a fig tree planted in his vineyard; and he came and sought fruit thereon, and found none.

7. Then said he unto the dresser of his vineyard, Behold, these three years I come seeking fruit on this fig tree, and find none: cut it down; why cumbereth it the ground?

8. And he answering said unto him, Lord, let it alone this year also, till I shall dig about it, and dung it:

9. And if it bear fruit, well: and if not, then after that thou shalt cut it down.

---

3. Not at all. But if you do not come to your senses, you will all perish in the same way.

4. Or those eighteen, who were killed by the tower falling upon them, do you think that they deserved that more than all the other inhabitants of Jerusalem?

5. Not at all. But if you do not come to your senses, you will all perish in the same way.

6. And he told them this parable: A man had an apple-tree growing in his garden, and he came to see whether there was any fruit on it, and he found none.

7. And he said to the gardener, Three years I have been coming here and looking for fruit on this apple-tree, and there is none. Cut it down; why should it spoil the ground?

8. But the gardener said, Master, let it alone for another summer, and I will dig about it, and manure it,

9. Perhaps it will bear fruit; and if it does not bear then, cut it down.

(a) ἐὰν μὴ μετανοῆτε *if you do not change your ideas about what life is.*

Death, the loss of the possibility of living a true life, by the comprehension of God, is before us at any moment, as it came to the rich man in the night, when he was getting ready to live more; as it came to the men who were killed by Pilate, and to those who were killed by the tower. Every moment of our life is a happy accident, as the gardener's prayer to wait cutting down the tree, as it might bring forth fruit.

Verse 9 John the Baptist had said before, calling men to change their life.

54. Ἔλεγε δὲ καὶ τοῖς ὄχλοις, Ὅταν ἴδητε τὴν νεφέλην ἀνατέλλουσαν ἀπὸ δυσμῶν, εὐθέως λέγετε, Ὄμβρος ἔρχεται· καὶ γίνεται οὕτω·	Luke xii. 54. And he said also to the people, When ye see a cloud rise out of the west, straightway ye say, There cometh a shower; and so it is.	54. And he said to the people, When you see a cloud from the west, you say at once, There comes a shower, and so it is.
55. Καὶ ὅταν νότον πνέοντα, λέγετε, Ὅτι καύσων ἔσται· καὶ γίνεται.	55. And when ye see the south wind blow, ye say, There will be heat; and it cometh to pass.	55. And when it blows from the south, you say, It will be hot; and so it happens.
56. Ὑποκριταί, τὸ πρόσωπον τῆς γῆς καὶ τοῦ οὐρανοῦ οἴδατε δοκιμάζειν· τὸν δὲ καιρὸν τοῦτον πῶς οὐ δοκιμάζετε;	56. Ye hypocrites, ye can discern the face of the sky and of the earth; but how is it that ye do not discern this time?	56. You can guess by the looks of the earth and the sky; how then do you not guess in regard to your present condition?
57. Τί δὲ καὶ ἀφ᾿ ἑαυτῶν οὐ κρίνετε τὸ δίκαιον;	57. Yea, and why even of yourselves judge ye not what is right?	57. Why do you not see in yourselves what is right?

This place is repeated here in another significance. In Matthew it answered the question of the Pharisees about proofs. Here it points to this, that the destruction through death is as evident to men as the coming of the storm is by certain signs. How is it that you know and remember that there will be a storm, and you do not know and remember that there will be death?

25. Συνεπορεύοντο δὲ αὐτῷ ὄχλοι πολλοί· καὶ στραφεὶς εἶπε πρὸς αὐτούς,	Luke xiv. 25. And there went great multitudes with him: and he turned, and said unto them,	25. And a great multitude went with him; and he turned, and said to them,
26. Εἴ τις ἔρχεται πρός με, καὶ οὐ μισεῖ τὸν πατέρα ἑαυτοῦ καὶ τὴν μητέρα, καὶ τὴν γυναῖκα καὶ τὰ τέκνα, καὶ τοὺς	26. If any man come to me, and hate not his father, and mother, and wife, and children, and brethren, and sisters, yea, and his own life	26. He who comes to me, and does not esteem little his father, and mother, and wife, and children, and brothers, and sisters, and his car-

ἀδελφοὺς καὶ τὰς ἀδελφάς, ἔτι δὲ καὶ τὴν ἑαυτοῦ ψυχήν, οὐ δύναταί μου μαθητὴς εἶναι.

27. Καὶ ὅστις οὐ βαστάζει τὸν σταυρὸν αὐτοῦ, καὶ ἔρχεται ὀπίσω μου, οὐ δύναταί μου εἶναι μαθητής.

28. Τίς γὰρ ἐξ ὑμῶν, θέλων πύργον οἰκοδομῆσαι, οὐχὶ πρῶτον καθίσας ψηφίζει τὴν δαπάνην, εἰ ἔχει τὰ πρὸς ἀπαρτισμόν;

29. Ἵνα μήποτε θέντος αὐτοῦ θεμέλιον, καὶ μὴ ἰσχύοντος ἐκτελέσαι, πάντες οἱ θεωροῦντες ἄρξωνται ἐμπαίζειν αὐτῷ,

30. Λέγοντες, Ὅτι οὗτος ὁ ἄνθρωπος ἤρξατο οἰκοδομεῖν, καὶ οὐκ ἴσχυσεν ἐκτελέσαι.

31. Ἢ τίς βασιλεύς, πορευόμενος συμβαλεῖν ἑτέρῳ βασιλεῖ εἰς πόλεμον, οὐχὶ καθίσας πρῶτον βουλεύεται εἰ δυνατός ἐστιν ἐν δέκα χιλιάσιν ἀπαντῆσαι τῷ μετὰ εἴκοσι χιλιάδων ἐρχομένῳ ἐπ᾽ αὐτόν;

32. Εἰ δὲ μήγε, ἔτι αὐτοῦ πόρρω ὄντος, πρεσβείαν ἀποστείλας ἐρωτᾷ τὰ πρὸς εἰρήνην.

33. Οὕτως οὖν πᾶς ἐξ ὑμῶν, ὃς οὐκ ἀποτάσσεται πᾶσι τοῖς ἑαυτοῦ ὑπάρχουσιν, οὐ δύναταί μου εἶναι μαθητής.

34. Καλὸν τὸ ἅλας· ἐὰν δὲ τὸ ἅλας μωρανθῇ, ἐν τίνι ἀρτυθήσεται;

35. Οὔτε εἰς γῆν οὔτε εἰς κοπρίαν εὔθετόν ἐστιν· ἔξω βάλλουσιν αὐτό. ὁ ἔχων ὦτα ἀκούειν ἀκουέτω.

---

also, he cannot be my disciple.

27. And whosoever doth not bear his cross, and come after me, cannot be my disciple.

28. For which of you, intending to build a tower, sitteth not down first, and counteth the cost, whether he have sufficient to finish it?

29. Lest haply, after he hath laid the foundation, and is not able to finish it, all that behold it begin to mock him,

30. Saying, This man began to build, and was not able to finish.

31. Or what king, going to make war against another king, sitteth not down first, and consulteth whether he be able with ten thousand to meet him that cometh against him with twenty thousand?

32. Or else, while the other is yet a great way off, he sendeth an ambassage, and desireth conditions of peace.

33. So likewise, whosoever he be of you that forsaketh not all that he hath, he cannot be my disciple.

34. Salt is good: but if the salt have lost his savour, wherewith shall it be seasoned?

35. It is neither fit for the land, nor yet for the dunghill; but men cast it out. He that hath ears to hear, let him hear.

---

nal life also, cannot be instructed by me.

27. And he who does not drag his cross and do the same as I do, cannot be instructed.

28. For each of you, wishing to build a house, will first sit down and figure out his expenses, to see whether he can finish it.

29. Lest, having begun without finishing it, men might mock him,

30. Here is a man who has begun to build and was not able to finish.

31. Or a king, going to wage war against another king, sits down first and thinks whether he is able with ten thousand to fight against twenty thousand.

32. Or else, he will send ambassadors from a distance, to make peace.

33. So none of you can be taught by me, unless you have first made your accounts.

34. Salt is good; but if it is not salted, it cannot be corrected.

35. It is neither dirt, nor dung, and has to be thrown out. He who has sense will understand.

(a) ἀποτάσσομαι I translate by *to make an account.*

Jesus says, To be taught by me the true life, which saves from death, it is necessary to renounce everything. And that a man may not be sorry for the renunciation, he needs only figure out the advantages and disadvantages of the carnal and the spiritual life. Consider your condition here, in this world, as he who builds a house and a king getting ready to wage war consider theirs.

Very well, thou lovest thy father, mother, children, thy life. Very well, if thou canst finish this life as thou finishest building a house; if thou canst stave off death, which goes against thee with all its host; if thou canst, or thinkest thou canst, then build thy life. But if thou seest that thou canst not, that thy house will remain unfinished, that thou canst not conquer the king who is going against thee, then stop building, make peace, and follow me to that life which I am showing you. There can be no middle. If thou believest that only that life which gives the comprehension is life, then live by that comprehension, and then thou wilt not be sorry for anything, but wilt gladly give up thy carnal life; but if thou dost not believe and art sorry for the carnal life, thou hadst better not follow me. The meaning of my teaching is the renunciation of the carnal life. If thou wishest to be my disciple, and hast not renounced everything, and art sorry for something, thou art like unsalted salt, which is not fit for anything.

THE PARABLE OF THE SUPPER

15. Ἀκούσας δέ τις τῶν συνανακειμένων ταῦτα εἶπεν αὐτῷ, Μακάριος, ὃς φάγεται ἄρτον ἐν τῇ βασιλείᾳ τοῦ Θεοῦ.

Luke xiv. 15. And when one of them that sat at meat with him heard these things, he said unto him, Blessed is he that shall eat bread in the kingdom of God.

15. When one of those who were with him heard it, he said to him, Blessed is he who eats bread in the kingdom of God.

16. Ὁ δὲ εἶπεν αὐτῷ, Ἄνθρωπός τις ἐποίησε δεῖπνον μέγα, καὶ ἐκάλεσε πολλούς·	16. Then said he unto him, A certain man made a great supper, and bade many:	16. And Jesus said, A man prepared a great feast, and invited many.
17. Καὶ ἀπέστειλε τὸν δοῦλον αὐτοῦ τῇ ὥρᾳ τοῦ δείπνου εἰπεῖν τοῖς κεκλημένοις, Ἔρχεσθε, ὅτι ἤδη ἕτοιμά ἐστι πάντα.	17. And sent his servant at supper time to say to them that were bidden, Come; for all things are now ready.	17. And sent his servant to tell the guests, It is time for the supper. Go, it is ready now.
18. Καὶ ἤρξαντο ἀπὸ μιᾶς παραιτεῖσθαι πάντες. ὁ πρῶτος εἶπεν αὐτῷ, Ἀγρὸν ἠγόρασα, καὶ ἔχω ἀνάγκην ἐξελθεῖν καὶ ἰδεῖν αὐτόν· ἐρωτῶ σε, ἔχε με παρῃτημένον.	18. And they all with one consent began to make excuse. The first said unto him, I have bought a piece of ground, and I must needs go and see it: I pray thee have me excused.	18. And they began one after another to excuse themselves. The first said, I have bought a piece of ground, and I must go and see it.

(a) The meaning of this verse is a doubt in the very kingdom of God. This man says, Very well, we shall divide everything up, but how if there is no kingdom of God?

This parable resembles the parable in Matthew, but has a different meaning. In order not to make a mistake in its significance, we must clearly understand the occasion on which it was said. Doubt is expressed whether there will be the kingdom of God, for which the carnal life is to be given up. The parable expresses an answer to the doubt. Jesus says, There can be no doubt. You are called, and you know that there is a feast, but you do not come, not because you are in doubt, but because you are busy with your false wealth.

19. Καὶ ἕτερος εἶπε, Ζεύγη βοῶν ἠγόρασα πέντε, καὶ πορεύομαι δοκιμάσαι αὐτά· ἐρωτῶ σε, ἔχε με παρῃτημένον.	*Luke xiv.* 19. And another said, I have bought five yoke of oxen, and I go to prove them: I pray thee have me excused.	19. Another said, I have bought five yoke of oxen, and I go to try them: pray, have me excused.
20. Καὶ ἕτερος εἶπε, Γυναῖκα ἔγημα, καὶ διὰ τοῦτο οὐ δύναμαι ἐλθεῖν.	20. And another said, I have married a wife, and therefore I cannot come.	20. A third said, I have just married, and therefore I cannot come.

21. Καὶ παραγενόμε-νος ὁ δοῦλος ἐκεῖνος ἀπήγ-γειλε τῷ κυρίῳ αὐτοῦ ταῦτα. Τότε ὀργισθεὶς ὁ οἰκοδεσπότης εἶπε τῷ δούλῳ αὐτοῦ, Ἔξελθε ταχέως εἰς τὰς πλατείας καὶ ῥύμας τῆς πόλεως, καὶ τοὺς πτωχοὺς καὶ ἀναπήρους καὶ χωλοὺς καὶ τυφλοὺς εἰσάγαγε ὧδε.

22. Καὶ εἶπεν ὁ δοῦ-λος, Κύριε, γέγονεν ὡς ἐπέταξας, καὶ ἔτι τόπος ἐστί.

23. Καὶ εἶπεν ὁ κύριος πρὸς τὸν δοῦλον, Ἔξελθε εἰς τὰς ὁδοὺς καὶ φραγ-μοὺς, καὶ ἀνάγκασον εἰσ-ελθεῖν, ἵνα γεμισθῇ ὁ οἶκός μου.

24. Λέγω γὰρ ὑμῖν, ὅτι οὐδεὶς τῶν ἀνδρῶν ἐκείνων τῶν κεκλημένων γεύσεταί μου τοῦ δεί-πνου.

21. So that servant came, and shewed his lord these things. Then the master of the house being angry said to his servant, Go out quickly into the streets and lanes of the city, and bring in hither the poor, and the maimed, and the halt, and the blind.

22. And the servant said, Lord, it is done as thou hast commanded, and yet there is room.

23. And the lord said unto the servant, Go out into the highways and hedges, and compel them to come in, that my house may be filled.

24. For I say unto you, That none of those men which were bidden shall taste of my supper.

21. And the servant came and told every-thing to his master. The master grew angry, and said to his servants, Go out at once into the streets and into the square, and bring in the poor, and the needy, and the lame, and the blind.

22. And the servant said, Master, I have done everything as thou hast commanded, and yet there is room left.

23. And the master said to the servant, Go out into the streets and squares, and persuade all to come, that my house may be filled.

24. For I tell you, None of those who were in-vited will eat my sup-per.

The meaning of the parable is transparent and clear. In the sermon on the mount it said, Blessed are the poor, woe to the rich. And now we get the explanation why the poor are called, and they are glad, and come: they have nothing else to think of. But the rich are detained by their cares: one has to attend to his field, another to his oxen, a third to a wedding. All the poor come, and there is still room left for any one who wants to come. And it says what a man has to do, in order that he may be able to come: he has to leave behind worldly cares about his wealth; there is always room left for those who want to come, that is, to give up their wealth; but those who do not want to do so, who are busy with their oxen, their field, and their wives, cannot come, and they will not see the supper.

2. Ὡμοιώθη ἡ βασιλεία τῶν οὐρανῶν ἀνθρώπῳ βασιλεῖ, ὅστις ἐποίησε γάμους τῷ υἱῷ αὐτοῦ·

3. Καὶ ἀπέστειλε τοὺς δούλους αὐτοῦ καλέσαι τοὺς κεκλημένους εἰς τοὺς γάμους· καὶ οὐκ ἤθελον ἐλθεῖν.

4. Πάλιν ἀπέστειλεν ἄλλους δούλους, λέγων, Εἴπατε τοῖς κεκλημένοις, Ἰδού, τὸ ἄριστόν μου ἡτοίμασα, οἱ ταῦροί μου καὶ τὰ σιτιστὰ τεθυμένα, καὶ πάντα ἕτοιμα· δεῦτε εἰς τοὺς γάμους.

5. Οἱ δὲ ἀμελήσαντες ἀπῆλθον, ὁ μὲν εἰς τὸν ἴδιον ἀγρόν, ὁ δὲ εἰς τὴν ἐμπορίαν αὐτοῦ·

6. Οἱ δὲ λοιποὶ κρατήσαντες τοὺς δούλους αὐτοῦ ὕβρισαν καὶ ἀπέκτειναν.

7. Ἀκούσας δὲ ὁ βασιλεὺς ὠργίσθη, καὶ πέμψας τὰ στρατεύματα αὐτοῦ ἀπώλεσε τοὺς φονεῖς ἐκείνους, καὶ τὴν πόλιν αὐτῶν ἐνέπρησε.

8. Τότε λέγει τοῖς δούλοις αὐτοῦ, Ὁ μὲν γάμος ἕτοιμός ἐστιν, οἱ δὲ κεκλημένοι οὐκ ἦσαν ἄξιοι.

9. Πορεύεσθε οὖν ἐπὶ τὰς διεξόδους τῶν ὁδῶν, καὶ ὅσους ἂν εὕρητε καλέσατε εἰς τοὺς γάμους.

10. Καὶ ἐξελθόντες οἱ δοῦλοι ἐκεῖνοι εἰς τὰς ὁδοὺς, συνήγαγον πάντας ὅσους εὗρον, πονηρούς τε καὶ ἀγαθούς· καὶ ἐπλήσθη ὁ γάμος ἀνακειμένων.

11. Εἰσελθὼν δὲ ὁ βασιλεὺς θεάσασθαι τοὺς

Matt. xxii. 2. The kingdom of heaven is like unto a certain king, which made a marriage for his son,

3. And sent forth his servants to call them that were bidden to the wedding: and they would not come.

4. Again, he sent forth other servants, saying, Tell them which are bidden, Behold, I have prepared my dinner: my oxen and my fatlings are killed, and all things are ready: come unto the marriage.

5. But they made light of it, and went their ways, one to his farm, another to his merchandise:

6. And the remnant took his servants, and entreated them spitefully, and slew them.

7. But when the king heard thereof, he was wroth: and he sent forth his armies, and destroyed those murderers, and burned up their city.

8. Then saith he to his servants, The wedding is ready, but they which were bidden were not worthy.

9. Go ye therefore into the highways, and as many as ye shall find, bid to the marriage.

10. So those servants went out into the highways, and gathered together all as many as they found, both bad and good: and the wedding was furnished with guests.

11. And when the king came in to see the guests, he saw there a man

2. The kingdom of God is like this: a certain king made a marriage for his son,

3. And sent out his servants to invite the guests to the feast, and they would not come.

4. Again he sent other servants, saying, Tell the guests that the dinner is prepared; all the fatted oxen are killed. Everything is ready, come to the feast.

5. But the guests did not accept the call: one went to the field, and another to the market;

6. And others again seized the servants, treated them badly, and beat them.

7. The king was offended, and he sent his soldiers against them, and destroyed them, and burned their city.

8. Then the king said to his servants, The dinner is ready, but the guests did not agree.

9. Go now to the lanes, and whomsoever you find invite to the feast.

10. And the servants went along the roads and gathered as many as they found, both bad and good, and the rooms were full of guests.

11. And the king came out to see the feast, and he saw a man who had

ἀνακειμένους, εἶδεν ἐκεῖ ἄνθρωπον οὐκ ἐνδεδυμένον ἔνδυμα γάμου·

which had not on a wedding garment:

not on a wedding garment.

12. Καὶ λέγει αὐτῷ, Ἑταῖρε, πῶς εἰσῆλθες ὧδε μὴ ἔχων ἔνδυμα γάμου ; ὁ δὲ ἐφιμώθη.

12. And he saith unto him, Friend, how camest thou in hither not having a wedding garment? And he was speechless.

12. And he said to him, Friend, how didst thou come here without a wedding garment? The guest was silent.

13. Τότε εἶπεν ὁ βασιλεὺς τοῖς διακόνοις, Δήσαντες αὐτοῦ πόδας καὶ χεῖρας, ἄρατε αὐτὸν καὶ ἐκβάλετε εἰς τὸ σκότος τὸ ἐξώτερον· ἐκεῖ ἔσται ὁ κλαυθμὸς καὶ ὁ βρυγμὸς τῶν ὀδόντων.

13. Then said the king to the servants, Bind him hand and foot, and take him away, and cast him into outer darkness; there shall be weeping and gnashing of teeth.

13. Then the king said to the servants, Bind him hand and foot, and take him and throw him into the darkness away from here.

14. Πολλοὶ γάρ εἰσι κλητοί, ὀλίγοι δὲ ἐκλεκτοί.

14. For many are called, but few are chosen.

14. For many are called, but few are chosen.

(a) He who came to a wedding had to put on a garment furnished by the host. He who did not put it on showed his contempt for the master and did not do his will.

John vi. 44. No man can unite with me, if the Father who has sent me did not draw him to himself. And I will raise him by the last day.

Matt. vii. 21. Not every one who says to me, Lord, Lord, will receive the kingdom of God, but he who does the will of the Father in heaven, who has sent me.

The parable of the wedding of the king is only an explanation of these thoughts. The parable of the wedding and of the feast is repeated in Luke. In spite of the close resemblance of the parables themselves, their application is different. Both the idolatrous and the free churches acknowledge this fact. But both see in these two parables only an indication that the Jews will not be saved, while the Gentiles will.

It seems to me that that idea is so simple and so poor that, if Jesus really had such a thought, he would not have given himself the trouble to elucidate it by parables.

Reuss (Vol. I., p. 486):

Le maître de la maison, c'est Dieu; le festin, c'est la félicité du royaume de Dieu; l'invitation a été faite, il y a longtemps déjà; enfin le moment du festin arrive, tout est prêt: cela se rapporte à l'Evangile, à la bonne nouvelle que le royaume est proche, et qu'avec le repentir et la foi on y entrera directement; le serviteur qui va prendre les invités, c'est Jésus s'adressant aux Juifs, à ceux qui connaissent la loi et les prophètes, aux gens d'école, aux riches.

For him who reads the Gospel straight, as it is written, these parables are an elucidation of one and the same thought, as expressed in the parable of the talents, in the whole teaching, and in all the other parables, but with new shades. These parables most closely resemble the parable of the talents. What is new here is that, while the parable of the talents elucidates the verse which says that the Father's will is that I should not waste anything he has given me, this one explains the idea that no one can come to me, if the Father did not draw him. The Father draws to him, as the king calls all to supper and wishes to have as many guests as possible. The Father calls and draws all to him. If some will not come, others will. If some seeds fall by the wayside, on the stones, and into the thorns, others will fall on good ground, and there will be fruit. The Father does more than sow the field and wait: he has prepared the good and calls to him. But to some people it seems that the affairs which occupy them are more important, and some simply fail to come, while others, like the inhabitants of the city, in the parable of the talents, who do not at all wish to acknowledge the king, offend the servants and kill them.

The king destroys these and fills his rooms for the supper with those who want to come.

The comprehension calls all. Some hear and understand it, but do not wish to abandon themselves to it, — and they remain, such as they were, with the possibility of life; others simply do not acknowledge the comprehension and are hostile to it, and so they are destroyed; others again unite with the comprehension.

One part of the thought is expressed, but another is still left, namely, about those who acknowledge the comprehension. Some guests do the master's will and receive the good which he gives to them, — the wedding garment. The comparison of the doing of the master's will with the garment given by the master shows that the execution of the master's will is not difficult, and that, independently of the doing of the master's will, it is a good in itself.

Matt. xi. 28. Come unto me, all ye that labour, and are heavy laden, and I will give you rest. 29. Take my yoke upon you, and learn of me: for I am meek and lowly in heart; and ye shall find rest unto your souls. 30. For my yoke is easy, and my burden is light.

Others did not do the master's will, did not accept the garment, and these the master had thrown out. With them happened what had happened with those who beat the servants. Some unite with the comprehension and fulfil it, others do not. Those who do not are destroyed, like those who are hostile to it.

This is the way the church interprets Matthew's parable. One gets horrified as one reads these careless interpretations. It is as though the whole matter concerned some pope. They write anything that passes through their head. To John Chrysostom it occurred that it means that the Jews received it, and the Gentiles did not, and he writes at haphazard, not noticing that it says, Some refused, and some killed. He writes, They did more than that, — they killed. And this nonsense and incorrect deviation from the meaning has been repeated a thousand years.

Here is the interpretation of the church (pp. 400–402):

This parable evidently represents the rejection of the Jews and the calling of the Gentiles. The Gospel was first of all intended for and preached to the Jews as a chosen people; but

in their blindness they rejected it; then it was turned to the
Gentiles, and they accepted it, — such is the idea which is lying
at the foundation of the parable. As regards the details and
particular points, — many of them serve only as an adornment
of figurative language and do not contain any mysterious significance.

To call them that were bidden: Consequently, these bidden
guests were called before, that is, they had been informed that
there would be a feast at the house of the king at a given time,
and they were invited to be present; the calling by the servants
is merely an invitation to come to the feast which was ready.
The Jews had indeed been prepared by the law and the prophets
about the kingdom of Messias which was to be opened, and had
been called by them to take part in it. ·Then, when this kingdom of Messias was opened, the Jews had been called by John
to take part in it, and he sent them to Christ, saying, To him it
will be added, but from me it will be taken; then by the Son
himself, for he says, Come unto me, all ye that labour, and are
heavy laden, and I will give you rest (Matt. xi. 28), and again,
If any man thirst, let him come unto me, and drink (John
vii. 35). He called them not only with words, but also with
works.

And they would not come: Of course, not all refused; many believed John and believed in Christ. But here reference is had
to the majority of people in general, for it says in general that
the Jews denied Christ, though many believed in him.

Sent forth other servants: From the context these other servants might be the apostles who, filled with the Holy Ghost,
were witnesses of the Gospel in Jerusalem and in the whole of
Judea according to the promise of the Lord (Acts i. 8). They
again solemnly called the formerly bidden Jews into the opened
kingdom of Christ, when, according to the previous expression,
the dinner was fully prepared.

Made light of it: By disregarding the invitation of the king,
the guests expressed their contempt for the king who bade them
come.

To his farm, to his merchandise: They were so buried in their
selfish affairs, that for their sake they neglected the king's invitation. Thus the attachment for worldly goods deflects us from
the gratification of the higher spiritual needs. The worldly,
selfish considerations kept the Jews, in the persons of their representatives, from entering into the kingdom of Christ. And
not only the fact that they did not come is bad, but what is
most senseless and terrible is this: they received very badly

those who came, and killed ... they killed Stephen, put to death James, and offended the apostles.

PARABLE OF THE RICH MAN AND THE STEWARD

1. Ἄνθρωπός τις ἦν πλούσιος, ὃς εἶχεν οἰκονόμον· καὶ οὗτος διεβλήθη αὐτῷ ὡς διασκορπίζων τὰ ὑπάρχοντα αὐτοῦ.

2. Καὶ φωνήσας αὐτὸν εἶπεν αὐτῷ, Τί τοῦτο ἀκούω περὶ σοῦ; ἀπόδος τὸν λόγον τῆς οἰκονομίας σου· οὐ γὰρ δυνήσῃ ἔτι οἰκονομεῖν.

3. Εἶπε δὲ ἐν ἑαυτῷ ὁ οἰκονόμος, Τί ποιήσω, ὅτι ὁ κύριός μου ἀφαιρεῖται τὴν οἰκονομίαν ἀπ' ἐμοῦ; σκάπτειν οὐκ ἰσχύω, ἐπαιτεῖν αἰσχύνομαι.

4. Ἔγνων τί ποιήσω, ἵνα, ὅταν μετασταθῶ τῆς οἰκονομίας, δέξωνταί με εἰς τοὺς οἴκους αὐτῶν.

5. Καὶ προσκαλεσάμενος ἕνα ἕκαστον τῶν χρεωφειλετῶν τοῦ κυρίου ἑαυτοῦ, ἔλεγε τῷ πρώτῳ, Πόσον ὀφείλεις τῷ κυρίῳ μου;

6. Ὁ δὲ εἶπεν, Ἑκατὸν βάτους ἐλαίου. καὶ εἶπεν αὐτῷ, Δέξαι σου τὸ γράμμα, καὶ καθίσας ταχέως γράψον πεντήκοντα.

7. Ἔπειτα ἑτέρῳ εἶπε, Σὺ δὲ πόσον ὀφείλεις; ὁ δὲ εἶπεν, Ἑκατὸν κόρους σίτου. καὶ λέγει αὐτῷ, Δέξαι σου τὸ γράμμα, καὶ γράψον ὀγδοήκοντα.

8. Καὶ ἐπῄνεσεν ὁ κύριος τὸν οἰκονόμον τῆς ἀδικίας, ὅτι φρονίμως

Luke xvi. 1. There was a certain rich man, which had a steward; and the same was accused unto him that he had wasted his goods.

2. And he called him, and said unto him, How is it that I hear this of thee? Give an account of thy stewardship; for thou mayest be no longer steward.

3. Then the steward said within himself, What shall I do? for my lord taketh away from me the stewardship: I cannot dig; to beg I am ashamed.

4. I am resolved what to do, that, when I am put out of the stewardship, they may receive me into their houses.

5. So he called every one of his lord's debtors unto him, and said unto the first, How much owest thou unto my lord?

6. And he said, A hundred measures of oil. And he said unto him, Take thy bill, and sit down quickly, and write fifty.

7. Then said he to another, And how much owest thou? And he said, A hundred measures of wheat. And he said unto him, Take thy bill, and write fourscore.

8. And the lord commended the unjust steward, because he had done wisely: for the

1. There was a rich man, who had a steward; and the steward was accused of wasting the master's goods.

2. And he called him, and said, There are rumours about thee. Give me an account of thy stewardship, for thou canst no longer be a steward.

3. And the steward said to himself, What shall I do when the master takes away from me the stewardship? I have no strength to plough; to beg I am ashamed.

4. I know what to do that, when I am put out of the stewardship, good people may receive me in their houses.

5. So he called every one of his master's debtors, and said, How much dost thou owe my master?

6. And he said, A hundred pails of oil. And he said to him, Take thy bill, and sit down and write quickly fifty.

7. Then he said to another, How much dost thou owe? A hundred measures of bread. And he said to him, Take thy bill, and write eighty.

8. And the master commended the steward of the irregular wealth, because he had

ἐποίησεν· ὅτι οἱ υἱοὶ τοῦ αἰῶνος τούτου φρονιμώτεροι ὑπὲρ τοὺς υἱοὺς τοῦ φωτὸς εἰς τὴν γενεὰν τὴν ἑαυτῶν εἰσι.

9. Κἀγὼ ὑμῖν λέγω, Ποιήσατε ἑαυτοῖς φίλους ἐκ τοῦ μαμωνᾶ τῆς ἀδικίας, ἵνα, ὅταν ἐκλίπητε, δέξωνται ὑμᾶς εἰς τὰς αἰωνίους σκηνάς.

10. Ὁ πιστὸς ἐν ἐλαχίστῳ καὶ ἐν πολλῷ πιστός ἐστι· καὶ ὁ ἐν ἐλαχίστῳ ἄδικος καὶ ἐν πολλῷ ἄδικός ἐστιν.

11. Εἰ οὖν ἐν τῷ ἀδίκῳ μαμωνᾷ πιστοὶ οὐκ ἐγένεσθε, τὸ ἀληθινὸν τίς ὑμῖν πιστεύσει;

12. Καὶ εἰ ἐν τῷ ἀλλοτρίῳ πιστοὶ οὐκ ἐγένεσθε, τὸ ὑμέτερον τίς ὑμῖν δώσει;

18. Οὐδεὶς οἰκέτης δύναται δυσὶ κυρίοις δουλεύειν· ἢ γὰρ τὸν ἕνα μισήσει. καὶ τὸν ἕτερον ἀγαπήσει· ἢ ἑνὸς ἀνθέξεται, καὶ τοῦ ἑτέρου καταφρονήσει· οὐ δύνασθε Θεῷ δουλεύειν καὶ μαμωνᾷ.

9. And I say unto you, Make to yourselves friends of the mammon of unrighteousness; that, when ye fail, they may receive you into everlasting habitations.

10. He that is faithful in that which is least is faithful also in much: and he that is unjust in the least is unjust also in much.

11. If therefore ye have not been faithful in the unrighteous mammon, who will commit to your trust the true riches?

12. And if ye have not been faithful in that which is another man's, who shall give you that which is your own?

13. No servant can serve two masters: for either he will hate the one, and love the other: or else he will hold to the one, and despise the other. Ye cannot serve God and mammon.

9. And I tell you, Make for yourselves friends of the wealth of unrighteousness, that, when it will fail you, you may be received under the everlasting roofs.

10. He who does right in little things will do right in great things. And he who does wrong in little things will do wrong in great things.

11. If therefore you do wrong in the unrighteous wealth, who will commit to your trust the real wealth?

12. And if you do not right in what is another's, who will give you what is your own?

13. No servant can serve two masters: either he will esteem the one little, and will please the other, or he will work well for the one, and will neglect the other. You cannot work for God and for wealth.

children of this world are in their generation wiser than the children of light.

(a) Τὸν οἰκονόμον τῆς ἀδικίας is translated by *the unjust steward.* This translation is incorrect, for then it would say ἄδικον, and not τῆς ἀδικίας, as indeed it says in Verse 10; since τῆς ἀδικίας refers in the next verse to τοῦ μαμωνᾶ, and the meaning is here the same, that is, that the steward was a steward over ill-gotten wealth, I put in the word *wealth.*

(b) More correctly *of his kind.*

(c) πιστός has here the meaning of *believing,* as in:

John xx. 27. Then saith he to Thomas, Reach hither thy finger, and behold my hands; and reach hither thy hand, and thrust it into my side; and be not faithless, but believing.

Acts xvi. 15. And when she was baptized, and her household, she besought us, saying, If ye have judged me to be faithful to the Lord, come into my house, and abide there. And she constrained us.

1 Tim. iv. 3. Forbidding to marry, and commanding to abstain from meats, which God hath created to be received with thanksgiving of them which believe and know the truth.

This parable is regarded as the most incomprehensible and offensive parable. It has been explained in every imaginable way, without getting anything out of it. But we need only refrain from giving any interpretation to this, that only the mendicant vagrants are in the kingdom of God; that he who has possessions will not be admitted, will not even be able to enter through the gates of the kingdom of God; that the first condition for entering into the kingdom of God consists in rejecting possessions; that it is impossible to serve God and mammon, as it is impossible with one eye to look upon the sky, and with the other upon the earth, — we need only refrain from interpreting all that, which has been said so many times before from all sides, and the parable is so clear and simple that there is no need for any interpretations.

This is the way our churchmen interpreted it (Interpretation of the Gospel of Luke, pp. 473–475):

I say unto you: Of course, this is said to all hearers and followers of the Lord without exception; but in the present case the discourse is more particularly directed to the publicans, for the parable is especially adapted to them, to the correction and proper direction of their manner of acting. It is as though the Lord said, You publicans can in some way make use of the example of the unjust steward; with the property of his master he gained friends for himself, who will receive him into their houses, when he has lost his place. And so will you, if you are guided in business by selfish ends, if you make dishonest use of everything which the Lord has entrusted to you, be compelled sooner or later to give an account of your misdeeds, which could not be unknown to the Omniscient One. Ought you not to have a thought for this, that you should not be left without a roof in misfortune, and, while the wealth is in your hands, use it for the advantage of your souls, for the acquisition of an eternal home? Here is the means for it: use it for the advantage of your neighbours, the poor, the needy. The discharged steward by his inventiveness, though it was connected with the deception of his master, acquired for himself friends and a home in misfortune.

Emulate this inventiveness of the children of this life (of course, without the use of deception), succour your neighbours with your wealth, and these poor will prepare for you an everlasting habitation, as the friends prepared a temporary abode for the unjust steward.

Unrighteous mammon: Mammon is the same as wealth; the wealth is called unrighteous in the same sense in which the steward is called above an unjust steward, and as farther down it is opposed to righteous mammon, that is, in the sense of its unrighteousness and deception. Wealth furnishes causes and pretexts and means for an unjust, unscrupulous, and dishonest manner of actions, as is shown by the example of the allegorical steward; in that sense it is unrighteous, in that it leads to an unrighteous, incorrect, and unjust manner of acting. On the other hand, it is unrighteous even because it is false, deceptive, transitory, in contradistinction to true, spiritual wealth, the wealth of the virtues, the everlasting, incorruptible wealth. With this unrighteous wealth it is none the less possible, by using it correctly, to make friends of the poor, the needy, in general of those who demand aid and succour here on earth, and they will get for us everlasting habitations in heaven, since such a use of wealth is a virtue, for which will follow the reward in the kingdom of heaven.

Reuss interprets it much better. His whole interpretation would be quite correct, if only he did not misinterpret the chief teaching of the Gospel about possessions being incompatible with the kingdom of God (Reuss, Vol. I., pp. 496–501):

Cet homme administrait mal; les intérêts de son patron souffraient entre ses mains, il détournait l'argent à son profit, ou ne le faisait pas valoir (sect. 105), etc. Le maître apprend cela et lui enjoint de rendre ses comptes. L'économe sait qu'il perdra sa place, parce qu'il ne pourra pas se justifier; il va se trouver sans moyens d'existence, et ne se sent pas disposé à gagner sa vie par le travail manuel. Il imagine donc de se créer des resources en faisant des arrangements avec les débiteurs (fermiers?) de son maître. Comme toutes les affaires ont été entre ses mains, cette intrigue peut réussir; le maître ne pourra pas faire intervenir les tribunaux, les billets (contrats, obligations) qui lui seront remis, seront les seuls qui existent, les seuls qui puissent obliger les débiteurs, lesquels, déchargés (frauduleusement, il est vrai, au point de vue du créancier; mais de gré à gré et valablement, en tant que l'économe avait procuration) d'une bonne partie de leur dette (fermage?), devaient se trouver disposés à accorder des avantages à l'homme qui leur avait fait cette gracieuseté. Toute l'histoire revient donc à dire que l'homme de la parabole s'assura ce qu'on appelle aujourd'hui des pots de vin; seulement ces pots de vin, d'après le but de la parabole, devaient se payer en nature, par d'autres services à rendre. Le maître pouvait en être fâché comme propriétaire; mais ici, où il s'agit de l'appré-ciation d'un acte, *considéré au point de vue de celui qui en est l'auteur*, et non d'une réalité historique, le maître ne peut s'em-pêcher de reconnaître que c'était un moyen *ingénieux* de parer aux éventualités. Si cet individu, dit-il, n'a pas soigné mes intérêts à moi, il a du moins pourvu aux siens propres. Et la manière dont il a été trompé lui arrache, malgré lui, sans doute, un aveu que le narrateur peut très-convenablement appeler un éloge.

2° *L'application* (v. 8, 9). Ici il faut avant tout bien se pénétrer de deux choses: du sens du mot de *prudence*, et de la portée du comparatif et de la comparaison, contenus dans le v. 8. La prudence n'est pas une qualité morale (Matth. x. 16, sect. 40); c'est l'aptitude de l'esprit à trouver et à disposer les moyens de manière à atteindre le but et à éviter ainsi les chances contraires. Cette qualité, est-il dit, les *enfants du siècle* la possèdent générale-ment à un plus haut degré que les *enfants de la lumière*. Le terme d'*enfants* (fils), d'après un trope hébreu bien connu et souvent employé dans le Nouveau Testament (Luc x. 6, Marc iii. 17, Eph. ii. 2, etc.), sert à circonscrire l'adjectif de qualité; les enfants du siècle, du monde, sont donc les mondains, ceux qui se préoccupent avant tout ou exclusivement des intérêts matériels; les enfants de la lumière (Jean xii. 36, 1 Thess. v. 5, Eph. v. 8) sont ceux qui, éclairés par l'esprit de Dieu, dirigent leurs regards et leur activité vers le ciel et les biens qu'il nous réserve. Or, l'expérience prouve que les premiers ont plus de *savoir faire* que les seconds, nous voulons dire qu'ils montrent une plus grande intelligence des conditions de la réussite dans ce qu'ils se proposent. Dans l'application spéciale à l'argent, cela veut donc dire que les premiers savent très-bien s'en servir pour arriver à leurs fins, qu'ils savent faire *leurs* affaires, tandis que les seconds ne font pas aussi bien les leurs, et ne tirent pas des moyens dont ils disposent tous les avantages qu'il serait possible de réaliser, dans leur intérêt tel qu'ils le conçoivent. (La phrase accessoire : *dans leurs rapports avec leurs semblables*, applicable dans la pensée de l'orateur aux enfants du siècle seuls, et non pas également aux enfants de la lumière, découle directement de la parabole, l'économe ayant su faire ses affaires avec des gens qui le valaient, qui étaient de sa trempe, qui savaient trouver leur avantage à lui faire trouver le sien.)

Il est donc entendu que si Jésus à son tour, prenant la parole après le maître de la parabole (v. 9 : *Et moi je vous dis.* . . .), présente l'économe comme une espèce de modèle, il n'est pas question d'un jugement moral à porter sur cet homme, tout aussi peu qu'il sera question d'approuver moralement la conduite du juge qui fait son devoir pour ne pas être importuné (sect. 80), ou celle de l'individu qui oblige son ami à contre cœur (sect. 62). On peut apprendre quelque chose, et même beaucoup, de ceux qui, à bien des égards, ne suivent pas le bon chemin ; si eux, par exemple, songent à l'avenir et se ménagent, avec les moyens dont ils disposent aujourd'hui, une position sûre pour des éventualités difficiles, pourquoi vous, *à plus forte raison*, n'agiriez-vous pas d'une manière analogue, et cela avec des intentions plus pures, dans un but plus noble et plus élevé ?

Or, cet avenir était, pour l'économe, le jour où il pouvait trouver un asile dans les maisons des débiteurs de son maître ; pour les disciples, enfants de la lumière, c'est la perspective des demeures éternelles. Il reste donc à examiner les deux autres points de la comparaison, les amis et le mammon.

Par les *amis*, la plupart des commentateurs entendent assez naturellement les hommes pour le bien desquels on aura employé sa fortune. Mais cette interprétation n'est pourtant pas à l'abri de toute objection. Comment Jésus peut-il dire, comme si cela allait de soi, que les hommes auxquels on aura fait du bien seront morts avant leurs bienfaiteurs, de manière à *recevoir* ceux-ci dans le séjour des bienheureux, quand ils y arriveront à leur tour ? Et puis, sont-ce donc les hommes qui assurent une place à leurs semblables dans ce séjour-là, comme les débiteurs de la parabole le font à l'égard de l'économe ? Nous croyons donc plutôt que les *amis* sont des personnes ou puissances qui disposent de ces places ; le pluriel, qui a engagé quelques interprètes à songer de préférence aux anges, ne nous gênera pas ici,

parce qu'il est tout simplement emprunté au récit parabolique.
L'amitié qu'on doit songer à gagner par un bon emploi des biens
de la terre, c'est celle de Dieu (Luc xix. 17, sect. 90), et s'il
fallait absolument aller plus loin pour justifier le pluriel, le
Christ se présenterait immédiatement à notre esprit pour
l'expliquer (Matth. xxv. 34 suiv., sect. 106).

Cette question s'est compliquée par suite d'une variante fort
curieuse dans notre texte. La leçon vulgaire est traduite assez
convenablement : *lorsque* vous *viendrez à mourir* (litt.: *à manquer*) ; mais des témoins anciens et respectables ont une leçon
beaucoup moins facile et par conséquent très-digne d'attention :
quand IL (le mammon) *viendra à manquer*, quand vous n'en aurez
plus. Cette leçon convient très-bien à la parabole : l'économe se
fit des amis pour le moment où ses ressources antérieures lui
feraient défaut ; le disciple de Christ doit en faire autant pour le
moment où les biens matériels n'y peuvent plus rien (Matth. vi.
20, sect. 14, Luc xii. 33, sect. 66).

Nous arrivons à une dernière expression du v. 9, qui est bien
la plus difficile de toutes et qui a le plus dérouté l'exégèse. L'objet avec lequel on doit se faire des amis est appelé (littéralement)
le mammon de l'injustice. Que le mot hébreu, que nous avons conservé avec l'évangéliste, signifie la *richesse, l'argent,* l'avoir pécu-
niaire qu'on amasse, cela n'a plus besoin d'être démontré (Matth.
vi. 24, sect. 14). Que le génitif (*de l'injustice*) provienne d'un
idiotisme de la langue hébraïque et doive être rendu par l'adjectif, cela ne souffre pas de difficulté. *Le juge de l'injustice* (Luc
xviii. 6, sect. 80) est certainement un juge injuste ; dans notre
texte même, deux lignes plus haut, il était question de l'*économe
de l'injustice ;* et deux lignes plus bas (v. 11), l'adjectif remplace
le génitif dans la phrase dont nous nous occupons. Mais qu'est-ce
donc que la *richesse injuste ?* S'arrêtant à la signification ordi-
naire de l'adjectif, on a souvent pensé à un bien mal acquis,
quoique, à vrai dire, le mot *injuste* qualifie celui qui *agit* con-
trairement à la justice, ce qui est autre chose. Mais enfin,
devons-nous donc croire que Jésus supposait à ses disciples des
biens mal acquis ? Et si cela peut avoir été le cas pour quelques-uns, pourquoi ne leur dit-il pas de rendre à qui de droit ce
qu'ils ont mal acquis ? Ou bien, si cela n'était pas toujours possible, les aumônes faites avec de l'argent mal acquis effacent-elles
le premier tort, de sorte que les *amis* au ciel n'y regarderont plus ?
Et puis, l'économe de la parabole était-il donc *injuste* (comme
l'appelle la bible allemande) ? Il manquait à son devoir, il
trompait, il était *infidèle,* comme l'appelle très-bien la bible
française. Enfin, on remarquera qu'au v. 11, l'opposé de la

richesse prétendue *injuste*, est la richesse *véritable*, le *vrai* trésor, ce qui nous fait voir clairement que le premier adjectif est mal traduit. Et au v. 10, le contraire d'*injuste* est *fidèle*, ce qui semble devoir de nouveau nous recommander de remplacer le mot *injuste* par *infidèle*.

Par ces diverses raisons, on a été amené à donner au mot grec du texte le sens d'*infidèle*. Pour l'économe, cela allait de soi ; la richesse infidèle devait être celle qui trompe son possesseur, parce qu'elle n'est pas assurée ; elle peut être enlevée, perdue de diverses manières, et en tout cas elle ne nous suit pas dans l'autre vie, elle est passagère. On a même signalé cet emploi du terme dans la littérature rabbinique. En apparence, cette seconde interprétation est de beaucoup préférable à la première ; à y regarder de près, elle donne également prise à la critique. L'économe et l'argent peuvent être appelés infidèles tous les deux, mais chacun dans un autre sens. L'un a positivement et méchamment *trompé* son maître, l'autre peut *manquer* accidentellement au sien. La différence nous semble assez grande pour rendre douteux l'expédient exégétique tout entier.

Mais ce qui nous détermine surtout à abandonner cette explication, c'est qu'elle ôte à l'adjectif, dans l'un des deux cas, toute valeur *morale*, tandis qu'elle la lui conserve dans l'autre cas. Jamais, dans le Nouveau Testament, cet adjectif, d'un usage d'ailleurs si fréquent, n'est dépouillé de toute portée morale ; il indique toujours un vice, c'est-à-dire une qualité positivement mauvaise, et non pas seulement un défaut, c'est-à-dire l'absence d'un avantage matériel. Voilà pourquoi nous avons hardiment mis dans notre traduction, à la place du terme impossible d'*injuste*, et du terme insuffisant de *trompeur*, le mot *mauvais*, et si l'on veut passer en revue tous les passages de l'évangile où Jésus parle de l'argent, on verra bien que nous n'avons pas eu tort. La parabole de l'économe prouvait une fois de plus que l'argent peut être une cause de péché. Et comme malheureusement il exerce sur l'homme une puissance d'attraction telle, que celui-ci y résiste bien difficilement, Jésus était autorisé à le qualifier comme il le fait, lors même que nous voudrions pas faire valoir ici sa coutume d'employer partout les termes les plus absolus, quand il s'agit de juger soit les hommes, soit les choses.

D'après cela, nous ramènerons sa pensée à cette thèse, que personne ne contestera : L'argent est un mal, tant qu'il est un but ; il *peut* devenir un bien, quand il est employé comme moyen pour arriver à un but élevé et salutaire. Ce résultat sera confirmé par les maximes que Luc ajoute après la parabole.

38 *Maximes détachées* (v. 10–18). Nous ne tenons pas trop à

cette désignation. Si l'on insistait pour les faire regarder comme partie intégrante de la morale de la fable, nous ne ferions pas opposition. En tout cas, Luc a été très-bien inspiré en les plaçant ici. Seulement le passage parallèle de Matthieu fait avoir qu'avec les moyens fournis par la tradition, ce n'était pas la seule combinaison possible.

Ces maximes sont, quand on y regarde bien, au nombre de deux : l'une (v. 13), que nous avons déjà rencontrée ailleurs, ne nous arrêtera pas ici ; l'autre reproduit une seule et même pensée sous trois formes différentes (v. 10, 11, 12) ; celle-ci, en effet, est dans un rapport plus intime avec la parabole. Le disciple de · Christ est aussi une espèce d'économe, l'administrateur d'un bien qui ne lui appartient pas en propre, qu'il doit faire valoir dans l'intérêt de son maître (comp. la parabole des talents). Or, la qualité essentielle, unique même, qu'on est en droit d'exiger dans l'économe (outre l'intelligence des affaires dont il n'est pas question ici), c'est la *fidélité* (1 Cor. iv. 1). C'est de cette qualité que parle notre texte : Celui qui n'est pas fidèle à l'égard de la chose *moindre*, ne le sera pas à l'égard de *beaucoup* ; celui qui ne l'est pas à l'égard de la richesse *mauvaise* (fausse, prétendue, corruptrice), ne le sera pas à l'égard de la *vraie* richesse ; celui qui ne l'est pas à l'égard de ce qui *ne lui appartient pas*, ne recevra pas ce qui (autrement) lui était réservé. Ces sentences n'ont pas besoin de commentaire. L'une des séries d'épithètes s'applique aux biens de la terre, l'autre aux biens spirituels. La première sentence, toute figurée, se borne à présenter leur valeur respective sous forme d'un simple rapport de quantité ; la seconde énonce ce rapport d'une manière propre et directe ; la troisième, enfin, fait ressortir cet élément important, que les biens célestes sont destinés à devenir une véritable propriété, tandis que les biens de la terre, même dans le cas le plus favorable, ne sont jamais qu'un prêt.

One can see that only the opposition to the teaching by not recognizing property as an evil, is keeping the parable from being entirely clear. From this follow such circumlocutions as : *L'argent est un mal, tant qu'il est un but ; il peut devenir un bien, quand il est employé comme moyen ;* and to be *fidèle à l'argent de la richesse mauvaise.* Nowhere does it say that money can be a good ; everywhere and at all time the opposite is said, and here wealth is called the wealth of unrighteousness, and to be true in relation to unrighteousness is not to have unrighteousness. From this conventional comprehension of the parable, from these circumlocutions there follows, besides the obscurity, the low and fragmentary comprehension of the parable, which has a profound significance and is connected with the whole teaching.

The meaning of the parable, if we are to believe the words of the Gospel, is very simple: to secure his life, a man gives to others his false possessions, which do not belong to him. This man has secured himself through the false possessions which are not his own, that is, he has given what is false and not his own, and receives in return what is real. Jesus says, And you do the same: Give up your imaginary property, your carnal life with everything which is supposed to belong to it. But if you do not give up this false property, which is not in your power, how are you going to get the real life? The carnal life is expressed by property, and the word living even has the meaning both of possessions and of life. Give up your property that you may receive life.

This parable is only an elucidation from another side of the feast of Chapter XIV. Chapter XV. speaks of something else. Chapter XVI, the parable of the steward, is only an elucidation of the parable of the supper and is in its thought directly connected with it.

PARABLE OF THE RICH MAN AND OF LAZARUS

14. Ἤκουον δὲ ταῦτα πάντα καὶ οἱ Φαρισαῖοι φιλάργυροι ὑπάρχοντες, καὶ ἐξεμυκτήριζον αὐτόν.

15. Καὶ εἶπεν αὐτοῖς, Ὑμεῖς ἐστε οἱ δικαιοῦντες ἑαυτοὺς ἐνώπιον τῶν ἀνθρώπων, ὁ δὲ Θεὸς γινώσκει τὰς καρδίας ὑμῶν· ὅτι τὸ ἐν ἀνθρώποις ὑψηλὸν, βδέλυγμα ἐνώπιον τοῦ Θεοῦ ἐστιν.

Luke xvi. 14. And the Pharisees also, who were covetous, heard all these things: and they derided him.

15. And he said unto them, Ye are they which justify yourselves before men; but God knoweth your hearts: for that which is highly esteemed among men is abomination in the sight of God.

14. And the Pharisees, who are fond of money, heard this, and began to deride him.

15. And he said to them, You justify yourselves before men; but God knows your hearts: what is highly esteemed among men is abomination in the sight of God.

16. Ὁ νόμος καὶ οἱ προφῆται ἕως Ἰωάννου· ἀπὸ τότε ἡ βασιλεία τοῦ Θεοῦ εὐαγγελίζεται, καὶ πᾶς εἰς αὐτὴν βιάζεται.

19. Ἄνθρωπος δέ τις ἦν πλούσιος, καὶ ἐνεδιδύσκετο πορφύραν καὶ βύσσον, εὐφραινόμενος καθ᾽ ἡμέραν λαμπρῶς.

20. Πτωχὸς δέ τις ἦν ὀνόματι Λάζαρος, ὃς ἐβέβλητο πρὸς τὸν πυλῶνα αὐτοῦ ἡλκωμένος,

21. Καὶ ἐπιθυμῶν χορτασθῆναι ἀπὸ τῶν ψιχίων τῶν πιπτόντων ἀπὸ τῆς τραπέζης τοῦ πλουσίου· ἀλλὰ καὶ οἱ κύνες ἐρχόμενοι ἀπέλειχον τὰ ἕλκη αὐτοῦ.

22. Ἐγένετο δὲ ἀποθανεῖν τὸν πτωχόν, καὶ ἀπενεχθῆναι αὐτὸν ὑπὸ τῶν ἀγγέλων εἰς τὸν κόλπον τοῦ Ἀβραάμ· ἀπέθανε δὲ καὶ ὁ πλούσιος, καὶ ἐτάφη.

23. Καὶ ἐν τῷ ᾅδῃ ἐπάρας τοὺς ὀφθαλμοὺς αὐτοῦ, ὑπάρχων ἐν βασάνοις, ὁρᾷ τὸν Ἀβραὰμ ἀπὸ μακρόθεν, καὶ Λάζαρον ἐν τοῖς κόλποις αὐτοῦ·

24. Καὶ αὐτὸς φωνήσας εἶπε, Πάτερ Ἀβραάμ, ἐλέησόν με, καὶ πέμψον Λάζαρον, ἵνα βάψῃ τὸ ἄκρον τοῦ δακτύλου αὐτοῦ ὕδατος, καὶ καταψύξῃ τὴν γλῶσσάν μου· ὅτι ὀδυνῶμαι ἐν τῇ φλογὶ ταύτῃ.

25. Εἶπε δὲ Ἀβραάμ, Τέκνον, μνήσθητι ὅτι ἀπέλαβες σὺ τὰ ἀγαθά σου ἐν τῇ ζωῇ σου, καὶ Λάζαρος ὁμοίως τὰ κακά·

---

16. The law and the prophets were until John: since that time the kingdom of God is preached, and every man presseth into it.

19. There was a certain rich man, which was clothed in purple and fine linen, and fared sumptuously every day:

20. And there was a certain beggar named Lazarus, which was laid at his gate, full of sores,

21. And desiring to be fed with the crumbs which fell from the rich man's table: moreover the dogs came and licked his sores.

22. And it came to pass, that the beggar died, and was carried by the angels into Abraham's bosom: the rich man also died, and was buried;

23. And in hell he lifted up his eyes, being in torments, and seeth Abraham afar off, and Lazarus in his bosom.

24. And he cried and said, Father Abraham, have mercy on me, and send Lazarus, that he may dip the tip of his finger in water, and cool my tongue; for I am tormented in this flame.

25. But Abraham said, Son, remember that thou in thy lifetime receivedst thy good things, and likewise Lazarus evil things: but now he

---

16. The law and the prophets were until John; since then the kingdom of God is announced, and every man goes into it by force.

19. There was a rich man, who was clothed in silk and velvet, and he made merry every day.

20. And there was a poor vagrant named Lazarus. And Lazarus was full of sores and lay at the gate of the rich man.

21. Lazarus wanted to live on the remnants from the rich man's table; but the dogs came and even licked his sores.

22. And the poor vagrant died, and the angels carried him to Abraham; the rich man also died, and he was buried.

23. And in hell he lifted up his eyes, and saw Abraham afar off, and Lazarus with him.

24. And the rich man spoke, and said, Father Abraham, have pity on me, and send Lazarus to me, that he may dip his finger in water, and cool my throat; for it is hot in this fire.

25. And Abraham said, Remember, my son, that thou receivedst in thy lifetime as many good things as Lazarus received evil things: he

νῦν δὲ ὅδε παρακαλεῖται, σὺ δὲ ὀδυνᾶσαι.	is comforted, and thou art tormented.	has been called here, but thou art tormented.
26. Καὶ ἐπὶ πᾶσι τούτοις, μεταξὺ ἡμῶν καὶ ὑμῶν χάσμα μέγα ἐστήρικται, ὅπως οἱ θέλοντες διαβῆναι ἐντεῦθεν πρὸς ὑμᾶς μὴ δύνωνται, μηδὲ οἱ ἐκεῖθεν πρὸς ἡμᾶς διαπερῶσιν.	26. And beside all this, between us and you there is a great gulf fixed: so that they which would pass from hence to you cannot; neither can they pass to us, that would come from thence.	26. And more than all that, between us and you there is a great gulf. Even if one wanted to pass from us to you, he could not do so.
27. Εἶπε δέ, Ἐρωτῶ οὖν σε, πάτερ, ἵνα πέμψῃς αὐτὸν εἰς τὸν οἶκον τοῦ πατρός μου,	27. Then he said, I pray thee therefore, father, that thou wouldest send him to my father's house:	27. And the rich man said, I pray thee, father, send Lazarus to my house:
28. Ἔχω γὰρ πέντε ἀδελφούς· ὅπως διαμαρτύρηται αὐτοῖς, ἵνα μὴ καὶ αὐτοὶ ἔλθωσιν εἰς τὸν τόπον τοῦτον τῆς βασάνου.	28. For I have five brethren; that he may testify unto them, lest they also come into this place of torment.	28. I have five brothers. Let him explain things to them, lest they come to this place of torment.
29. Λέγει αὐτῷ Ἀβραάμ, Ἔχουσι Μωσέα καὶ τοὺς προφήτας· ἀκουσάτωσαν αὐτῶν.	29. Abraham saith unto him, They have Moses and the prophets; let them hear them.	29. And Abraham said to him, They have Moses and the teachers: let them hear them.
30. Ὁ δὲ εἶπεν, Οὐχί, πάτερ Ἀβραάμ· ἀλλ' ἐάν τις ἀπὸ νεκρῶν πορευθῇ πρὸς αὐτούς, μετανοήσουσιν.	30. And he said, Nay, father Abraham: but if one went unto them from the dead, they will repent.	30. But he said, No, father Abraham: if one went to them from the dead, they would come to their senses.
31. Εἶπε δὲ αὐτῷ, Εἰ Μωσέως καὶ τῶν προφητῶν οὐκ ἀκούουσιν, οὐδὲ ἐάν τις ἐκ νεκρῶν ἀναστῇ πεισθήσονται.	31. And he said unto him, If they hear not Moses and the prophets, neither will they be persuaded, though one rose from the dead.	31. And Abraham said to him, They have not heard Moses and the prophets; neither will they obey, though one rose from the dead and went to them.

(a) *Moreover* has here the meaning that Lazarus did not have a chance to eat the remnants, for the dogs ate them; they ate them up so clean that they even licked the sores of Lazarus.

(b) Is wanting in many texts.

The parable, or rather fable, which stands directly after the parable of the steward explains the same simple idea that the poor are blessed, for they receive blessedness, and woe to the rich, for they have received everything which they wanted, and since this gospel truth is avoided by the church, this fable, like the parable of the steward, represents itself as very difficult.

This is what the church babbles about it (pp. 481–484):

By all these features are designated the luxury of the rich man and the poverty of Lazarus, and we must assume that this rich man was not compassionate toward the poor man and did not wish to console him and lighten his sufferings, but lived for his own pleasure. It does not appear from the parable that the rich man was stingy, but only that he was pitiless and heartless toward the poor man.

Was carried by the angels: That is, his soul was carried by the angels. It was the belief of the Jews that the souls of the righteous are carried to heaven by angels, and the Lord affirms this belief. There is no need of seeing here a figurative expression, but we must accept it in a literal sense. If the angels are ministering spirits, who are sent out to serve those who wish to inherit salvation, they, serving man as guardian spirits, during his lifetime, naturally cannot leave him in the most important moments after death.

Into Abraham's bosom: That is, to the kingdom of heaven. The figure of speech is taken from the accumbent attitude at feasts, when to recline on the breast was a sign of the particular nearness of the accumbent persons. Since the Jews had no doubt but that Abraham was God's friend and lived in bliss in heaven, the statement that Lazarus reclined on Abraham's bosom is the same as though it said that Lazarus was deemed worthy of bliss in the kingdom of heaven.

And was buried: This is not said of the beggar; it is to be assumed that the beggar's funeral was poor and there is nothing to be said about it; but the burial of the rich man was magnificent and so it is mentioned, in order to show that in life and at death the rich man received all the goods of this earth. But the rich man's and the beggar's condition after death are represented in a reverse relation: the beggar is in the bosom of Abraham, while the rich man is in hell in torments. Hell is represented in the parable with the following features: (1) it is a place removed from the blessedness of the righteous; (2) a place of torments; (3) separated by a great gulf from the abode of the holy souls; (4) the torments in it are great.

Seeth Abraham afar off, etc.: This, of course, increases his torments, but at the same time gives the unfortunate man some hope of getting an alleviation of them. Thus the spiritual contemplation of the bliss of the righteous no doubt increases the sufferings of the sinners in hell and can rouse in them hope of alleviation, however vain such hope might be.

Have mercy on me: Have mercy on my sufferings and lighten them. Send Lazarus, that same beggar who in his lifetime lay on the ground before his gate, in the hope of getting something to eat from the crumbs of his table. What a striking contrast, especially for the rich Pharisees, who heard the Lord and derided his teaching about the proper use of wealth.

That he may dip the tip of his finger, etc.: This shows that with a glutton the organ of gluttony, the mouth, suffers most; his tongue is parched from the strong thirst produced by the heat, and he asks Abraham to command Lazarus to lighten his torments at least a little. The flame, the fire, is a symbol of the greatest torments; the figure is taken, no doubt, from the punishment of burning, so common with the ancients.

Son: A hint at the prejudice of the Jews in regard to their supposed rights, as the descendants of Abraham, to the kingdom of Messias, a hint which still more increased the sufferings of the rich sinner.

Receivedest thy good things: All the good, all the pleasures and joys of the world, which only riches can give.

And likewise Lazarus evil things: Poverty, contempt, vital sufferings.

He is comforted, and thou art tormented: It is represented that Lazarus is in bliss only because he suffered on earth and that the rich man suffers torment only because he lived in comfort on earth. But, no doubt, the answer has to be complemented here by the idea that Lazarus with his calamities was righteous, while the rich man with his riches was unrighteous, as he did not know how in a proper way to make use of his wealth.

There is a great gulf fixed, etc.: No doubt, in the literal sense the place of torment of the sinners is separated from the place of bliss of the righteous; but also a moral gulf is meant, a moral condition of both, by which those who have been confirmed in evil cannot become righteous and vice versa. This does not deny the teaching of the church, according to which those who die in repentance, but have not become perfect in the struggle, may, by the prayers of the church, pass from the condition of torments into a condition of bliss. Sinners and righteous are taken here in an unconditional sense.

This is what Reuss says (pp. 505, 506):

2° La forme de la parabole laisse beaucoup à désirer au point de vue éthique. En effet, le v. 25 dit simplement et froidement : Toi, tu es tourmenté, *parce que* tu as reçu ta part de bien sur la terre ; lui, il a eu sa part de maux, *donc* il est consolé. La rémunération future est ainsi présentée comme une simple compensation matérielle, et le mérite moral n'y entre pour rien. On peut dire, à la rigueur, et l'on ne manque jamais de dire dans l'usage homilétique qu'on fait de la parabole, que le riche a été un homme sans pitié, parce qu'il a laissé le pauvre mourir de misère à sa porte même ; on peut ajouter que le v. 30 parle, après coup, de conversion. Mais on ne peut pas nier que d'après le texte, tel que nous l'avons, l'unique vertu de Lazare a été d'être pauvre autant qu'on peut l'être. Il n'est pas dit le moindre mot pour expliquer que cette pauvreté n'était pas l'effet naturel et mérité de sa propre conduite, comme c'est le cas, neuf fois sur dix, dans le monde des réalités ; il n'est rien dit des qualités morales qu'il aurait eues dans sa pauvreté. Son entrée au paradis n'est motivée en aucune façon, et au point de vue de la morale, l'exégèse est forcée d'amplifier le récit pour tourner cette difficulté. On est ainsi amené à penser qu'au gré de Jésus la pauvreté par elle-même est un avantage et la richesse un désavantage, en vue du but final de la vie terrestre, et l'on ne manquera pas de passages parallèles à citer en faveur de cette thèse. Cependant cela ne nous paraît pas suffire pour expliquer le texte.

3° La difficulté est précisément celle que nous avons dû chercher à écarter dans le récit précédent. Il faut donc insister sur ce fait que Jésus, pas plus ici que la première fois, n'a voulu inculquer la vérité que nous avons l'habitude d'y chercher de préférence, celle de la rémunération ; mais une autre, que nous n'y cherchons point ordinairement, savoir celle de la nécessité de *songer à temps* à l'avenir au-delà de la tombe, en face des biens terrestres. C'est l'homme riche seul qui est en vue ; Lazare appartient uniquement au cadre ; ou bien il sert à mettre en relief le portrait principal. Sa personne n'est pas plus importante dans le tableau que celle des cinq frères. Or, pour songer à l'avenir, l'homme est suffisamment instruit : il a Moïse et les prophètes. S'il ne veut pas les écouter, il n'écoutera pas non plus les ressuscités. Jésus savait par expérience que les miracles mêmes n'arrivent pas à vaincre la mauvaise volonté (sect. 28, 63). Vous êtes riches ; usez de vos richesses, non pour votre plaisir seul, mais pour le bien commun ; les nécessiteux sont à vos portes. Qu'ils soient toujours méritants au même degré c'est là une question secondaire. De nos jours, un pareil principe est bien plus important et plus fécond qu'autrefois, l'aumône individuelle est le plus souvent stérile, n'étant plus le seul moyen d'exercer la charité.

C'est d'ailleurs la seule parabole dans laquelle un personnage fictif soit désigné par un nom propre. Cela a fait penser à quelques-uns qu'il s'agit ici d'une histoire véritable.

Reuss's conscientiousness and stupidity in this place throw a peculiar light on the matter. He says naïvely: "*La difficulté est —*" He might have added that he tries to find the same *difficulté* in the sermon on the mount and in many other passages. He is surprised to read "*parce que tu as reçu la part de bien sur la terre,*" etc. Yes, the same is said in the sermon on the mount; the same makes us recognize that poverty is regarded as a good according to the Gospel. "*Mais on ne peut pas nier que d'après le texte, tel que nous l'avons, l'unique vertu de Lazare a été d'être pauvre autant qu'on peut l'être,*" and, "*On est ammené à penser qu'au gré de Jésus la pauvreté par elle même est un avantage et la richesse un désavantage.*" It is laughable and pitiful.

The whole teaching of Jesus consists in this alone, that indeed man cannot otherwise express his faith in his teaching than by the renunciation of property, and that is all the teaching consists in, while the interpreters find in surprise that he regarded poverty as an advantage, and wealth as a disadvantage.

The theoretical meaning of the parable is this, that the lifetime is given to exalt the son of man, to give up the carnal life, in order to receive the true life. Death will come, and man will be deprived of this possibility. Christ expresses in a most material, derisive manner the thought, on the one hand, that when life comes to an end and death comes, all worldly affairs will be useless, and, on the other, that it is impossible to turn back the possibility of life. And he adds that it is not necessary to look anywhere for the proofs of the insufficiency of the mere earthly life, and that it is clear to everybody that a dead man cannot come back to tell what has happened to him, after he is dead, as the rich man is suggesting.

The practical meaning of the parable is the same, but it says directly what has to be done in order that one may attain the true life. It is possible to give up the carnal life, not in words merely, by not retaining riches, so long as there are men who are poor and suffer cold. And so the retention of possessions, as long as there are poor people, is incompatible with life. To give up life, it is necessary first to give up property, and he who does not give it up cannot receive life.

This whole parable is remarkable for its ironical tone. The last remark, that if the dead rose they would not be believed, hints at the fable of the resurrection of Jesus.

THE CHIEF COMMANDMENTS

85. Καὶ ἐπηρώτησεν εἷς ἐξ αὐτῶν νομικὸς, πειράζων αὐτὸν, καὶ λέγων,	*Matt.* xxii. 35. Then one of them, which was a lawyer, asked him a question, tempting him, and saying,	35. And one of the lawyers, tempting him, asked him,
36. Διδάσκαλε, ποία ἐντολὴ μεγάλη ἐν τῷ νόμῳ;	36. Master, which is the great commandment in the law?	36. Teacher, which is the great commandment in the law?

This discourse with the lawyer must be placed before the discourse with the rich youth. We must remember that according to the law of Moses, as the lawyers understood it and as we understand it, it is by no means possible to say that to love God and your neighbour is a great commandment.

Deut. vi. 5. And thou shalt love the Lord thy God with all thine heart, and with all thy soul, and with all thy might.

Lev. xix. 18. Thou shalt not avenge, nor bear any grudge against the children of thy people, but thou shalt love thy neighbour as thyself: I am the Lord.

In the law there are many rules, and it is possible to select any two rules, that is, to say a thousand different things by the aid of the law. Consequently, Love God and thy neighbour, as the chief commandment, is not Moses' thought, but that of Jesus, and the lawyer, in agreeing with him and repeating these commandments, repeats only what Jesus has said before. In the discourse with the youth, Jesus, counting out the commandments, at the end of the most common commandments mentions as the completion of them all the commandment to love the neighbour, and repeats only what is already known; consequently this discourse (the rules which Jesus gave) ought to stand first.

37. Ὁ δὲ Ἰησοῦς εἶπεν αὐτῷ, 'Ἀγαπήσεις Κύριον τὸν Θεόν σου, ἐν ὅλῃ τῇ καρδίᾳ σου, καὶ ἐν ὅλῃ τῇ ψυχῇ σου, καὶ ἐν ὅλῃ τῇ διανοίᾳ σου.'	37. Jesus said unto him, Thou shalt love the Lord thy God with all thy heart, and with all thy soul, and with all thy mind.[b]	37. Jesus said to him, Thou shalt love the Lord thy God with all thy heart, with all thy soul, and with all thy power.
38. Αὕτη ἐστὶ πρώτη καὶ μεγάλη ἐντολή.	38. This is the first and great commandment.	38. This is the first great commandment.
39. Δευτέρα δὲ ὁμοία αὐτῇ, 'Ἀγαπήσεις τὸν πλησίον σου ὡς σεαυτόν.'	39. And the second is like unto it, Thou shalt love thy neighbour as thyself.	39. The second is like it: Thou shalt love thy neighbour as thyself.
40. Ἐν ταύταις ταῖς δυσὶν ἐντολαῖς ὅλος ὁ νόμος καὶ οἱ προφῆται κρέμανται.	40. On these two commandments hang all the law and the prophets.	40. In these two commandments is all the law and the prophets.
32. Καὶ εἶπεν αὐτῷ ὁ γραμματεύς, Καλῶς, διδάσκαλε, ἐπ' ἀληθείας εἶπας, ὅτι εἷς ἐστι Θεός, καὶ οὐκ ἔστιν ἄλλος πλὴν αὐτοῦ.	32. And the scribe said unto him, Well, Master, thou hast said the truth: for there is one God; and there is none other but he:	32. And the lawyer said again, Well hast thou said, teacher, that he is one, and that there is no other but he.
33. Καὶ τὸ ἀγαπᾷν αὐτὸν ἐξ ὅλης τῆς καρδίας, καὶ ἐξ ὅλης τῆς συνέσεως, καὶ ἐξ ὅλης τῆς ψυχῆς, καὶ ἐξ ὅλης τῆς ἰσχύος, καὶ τὸ ἀγαπᾷν τὸν πλησίον ὡς ἑαυτόν, πλεῖόν ἐστι πάντων τῶν ὁλοκαυτωμάτων καὶ τῶν θυσιῶν.	33. And to love him with all the heart, and with all the understanding,[b] and with all the soul, and with all the strength, and to love his neighbour as himself, is more than all whole burnt offerings and sacrifices.[c]	33. And to love him with all thy heart, with all thy understanding, with all thy life, and with all thy strength, and to love thy neighbour as thyself, is more important than all the services.
34. Καὶ ὁ Ἰησοῦς, ἰδὼν αὐτὸν ὅτι νουνεχῶς	34. And when Jesus saw that he answered	34. And Jesus, looking at him, said to him,

ἀπεκρίθη, εἶπεν αὐτῷ, Οὐ μακρὰν εἶ ἀπὸ τῆς βασιλείας τοῦ Θεοῦ.

discreetly, he said unto him, Thou art not far from the kingdom of God.

Thou art not far from the kingdom of God.

(*a*) καὶ τῶν θυσιῶν is wanting in many texts and is superfluous.

(*b*) In Deuteronomy the words *and with all thy mind* are wanting, and so I omit them.

The continuation of the verse in Deuteronomy says, And these words which I command thee this day, shall be in thine heart: And thou shalt teach them diligently unto thy children, and shalt talk of them when thou sittest in thine house, and when thou walkest by the way, and when thou liest down, and when thou risest up. And bind them to thine hand to be a deed for thee, and bind them to thine eyes, to look through them.

And so the idea is that it is not enough to love God with words, but we must love him in such a way as to do his will. His will is expressed in the following, Love thy neighbour, and so Jesus answers directly the lawyer's question as to which is the greatest commandment, Honour God so as to love thy neighbour as thyself.

OF THE RICH MAN AND OF RICHES

17. Καὶ ἐκπορευομένου αὐτοῦ εἰς ὁδὸν, προσδραμὼν εἷς καὶ γονυπετήσας αὐτὸν ἐπηρώτα αὐτόν, Διδάσκαλε ἀγαθέ, τί ποιήσω ἵνα ζωὴν αἰώνιον κληρονομήσω;

18. Ὁ δὲ Ἰησοῦς εἶπεν αὐτῷ, Τί με λέγεις ἀγαθόν; οὐδεὶς ἀγαθός, εἰ μὴ εἷς, ὁ Θεός.

17. Εἰ δὲ θέλεις εἰσελθεῖν εἰς τὴν ζωὴν, τήρησον τὰς ἐντολάς.

18. Λέγει αὐτῷ, Ποίας; ὁ δὲ Ἰησοῦς εἶπε,

Mark x. 17. And when he was gone forth into the way, there came one running, and kneeled to him, and asked him, Good[a] Master, what shall I do that I may inherit eternal life?

18. And Jesus said unto him, Why callest thou me good? there is none good but one, that is, God.[b]

Matt. xix. 17. But if thou wilt enter into life,[c] keep the commandments.

18. He saith unto him, Which? Jesus said,

17. One day a commander came running up to Jesus, and kneeled before him, and asked him, Good teacher, tell me what good I must do that I may inherit eternal life?

18. And Jesus said to him, What is the use of talking about the good? There is none good, but God.

17. If thou wilt have life, keep the commandments.

18. He said to him, Which? Jesus said,

Τό, οὐ φονεύσεις· οὐ μοιχεύσεις· οὐ κλέψεις.

19. Οὐ ψευδομαρτυρήσεις· τίμα τὸν πατέρα σου καὶ τὴν μητέρα· καὶ, ἀγαπήσεις τὸν πλησίον σου ὡς σεαυτόν.

20. Λέγει αὐτῷ ὁ νεανίσκος, Πάντα ταῦτα ἐφυλαξάμην ἐκ νεότητός μου· τί ἔτι ὑστερῶ;

21. Ὁ δὲ Ἰησοῦς ἐμβλέψας αὐτῷ ἠγάπησεν αὐτὸν, καὶ εἶπεν αὐτῷ, Ἕν σοι ὑστερεῖ·

21. Εἰ θέλεις τέλειος εἶναι, ὕπαγε, πώλησόν σου τὰ ὑπάρχοντα, καὶ δὸς πτωχοῖς· καὶ ἕξεις θησαυρὸν ἐν οὐρανῷ· καὶ δεῦρο, ἀκολούθει μοι.

22. Ὁ δὲ στυγνάσας ἐπὶ τῷ λόγῳ ἀπῆλθε λυπούμενος· ἦν γὰρ ἔχων κτήματα πολλά.

23. Καὶ περιβλεψάμενος ὁ Ἰησοῦς λέγει τοῖς μαθηταῖς αὐτοῦ, Πῶς δυσκόλως οἱ τὰ χρήματα ἔχοντες εἰς τὴν βασιλείαν τοῦ Θεοῦ εἰσελεύσονται.

24. Οἱ δὲ μαθηταὶ ἐθαμβοῦντο ἐπὶ τοῖς λόγοις αὐτοῦ. ὁ δὲ Ἰησοῦς πάλιν ἀποκριθεὶς λέγει αὐτοῖς, Τέκνα, πῶς δύσκολόν ἐστι τοὺς πεποιθότας ἐπὶ τοῖς χρήμασιν εἰς τὴν βασιλείαν τοῦ Θεοῦ εἰσελθεῖν.

25. Εὐκοπώτερόν ἐστι κάμηλον διὰ τῆς τρυμαλιᾶς τῆς ῥαφίδος διελθεῖν, ἢ πλούσιον εἰς τὴν βασιλείαν τοῦ Θεοῦ εἰσελθεῖν.

26. Οἱ δὲ περισσῶς

Thou shalt do no murder, Thou shalt not commit adultery, Thou shalt not steal, Thou shalt not bear false witness,

19. Honour thy father and thy mother: and, Thou shalt love thy neighbour as thyself. (Ex. xx. 13-16; Lev. xix. 18.)

20. The young man saith unto him, All these things have I kept from my youth up: what lack I yet?

Mark x. 21. Then Jesus beholding him loved him, and said unto him, One thing thou lackest.·

Matt. xix. 21. If thou wilt be perfect, go and sell that thou hast, and give to the poor, and thou shalt have treasure in heaven: and come and follow me.

Mark x. 22. And he was sad at that saying, and went away grieved: for he had great possessions.

23. And Jesus looked round about, and saith unto his disciples, How hardly shall they that have riches enter into the kingdom of God!

24. And the disciples were astonished at his words. But Jesus answereth again, and saith unto them, Children, how hard is it for them that trust in riches to enter into the kingdom of God!

25. It is easier for a camel to go through the eye of a needle, than for a rich man to enter into the kingdom of God.

26. And they were as-

Thou shalt not kill, Thou shalt not commit adultery, Thou shalt not steal, Thou shalt not bear false witness.

19. Honour thy father and love thy neighbour as thyself.

20. And the commander said to him, All that I have kept from my youth. What do I lack?

21. Jesus looked at him and smiled, and said, One thing thou lackest:

21. If thou wilt fulfil everything, go and sell everything which thou hast, and give to the poor, and thou shalt have treasure in God: then come and follow me.

22. The man was sad at these words, and went away: for he had great possessions.

23. And seeing how he was saddened, Jesus looked round and said to his disciples, Now you see how incompatible it is for those who have possessions to enter into the kingdom of God!

24. The disciples were frightened at these words. But Jesus turned to them and said, Yes, children, I tell you again, it is incompatible for those who have possessions to enter into the kingdom of God!

25. It is more possible for a camel to go through the eye of a needle, than for a rich man to enter into the kingdom of God.

26. They were even

ἐξεπλήσσοντο λέγοντες πρὸς ἑαυτούς, Καὶ τίς δύναται σωθῆναι;

27. Ἐμβλέψας δὲ αὐτοῖς ὁ Ἰησοῦς λέγει, Παρὰ ἀνθρώποις ἀδύνατον, ἀλλ᾽ οὐ παρὰ τῷ Θεῷ· πάντα γὰρ δυνατά ἐστι παρὰ τῷ Θεῷ.

tonished out of measure, saying among themselves, Who then can be saved?

27. And Jesus looking upon them saith, With men it is impossible, but not with God: for with God all things are possible.

more frightened, and said to one another, Who then can preserve his life?

27. And Jesus looking at them said, According to the human understanding it seems impossible, but according to God it is possible.

(a) ἀγαθός cannot have here the meaning of *good*, nor *virtuous*, for from the context it appears that Jesus does not deny these qualities in himself, but points out to the young man that he and his disciples are not blessed, that they do not experience and do not give earthly happiness, but, on the contrary, are subject to even greater discomforts than other people. The meaning of ἀγαθός in the sense of *happy*, *blessed* occurs in 1 Peter iii. 10 : For he that will love life, and see good days, let him refrain his tongue from evil, and his lips that they speak no guile.

Ἀγαθός has the meaning of *good*, without the distinction of whether it is communicated by another, or experienced by oneself, that is, *beneficent* and *good*. The young man asks in general about the good, about happiness, how he may obtain the good, happiness, comfort. And Jesus says, good, that is, satisfied, is God only. We cannot attain the good, meaning by it what is agreeable for us, but we can acquire life.

(b) In many texts we find πατήρ or πατὴρ ἐν τοῖς οὐρανοῖς instead of *God*, and this seems to me to be better, because, in my opinion, the last words, Honour thy father, refer to God the Father.

(c) Jesus is not talking of eternal life, but of life in general.

(d) In many texts *and mother* is omitted. I take *and mother* to be an interpolation, and that the father is here God, and that with the last words are repeated the commandments which were said to the lawyer, Honour God and love thy neighbour.

What confirms us in this supposition is this, that the commandments, Thou shalt not kill, commit adultery, steal, and lie, are given in the order in which they are given in Moses. But the commandment, Honour thy father and thy mother, is mentioned last, though it stands before. I assume that Jesus counts out the four commandments in order to say that he does not reject the commandments of Moses, but at the end adds his own, of which it was said before that it contains the whole law and the prophets. He says, Dost thou acknowledge the commandments, those of Moses and the last, in which everything is contained, Love God and thy neighbour?

(e) One thing thou lackest, is apparently said in derision. Jesus repeats his words, and says, Thou lackest one little thing, and that is, to fulfil these commandments.

(f) δυσκόλως really means *uncomfortably passed ;* it is generally used in the sense of *uncomfortably, improperly, incompatibly.* These words express the same as what was said in the sermon on the mount about it being impossible to serve two masters, God and mammon.

(g) παρά with the dative has here the meaning of what depends on anybody's judgment. 1 Peter ii. 20, Rom. ii. 13, Gal. iii. 11, and elsewhere. This meaning is especially clear with Θεῷ, where it signifies *to have power, the possibility.* It seemed to the disciples that it was impossible, and so he said, According to human judgment it is indeed impossible, but according to God it is possible.

The sense of the discourse is this, that a rich and important personage comes to Jesus and says, Thou art a teacher of the good and of happiness, so tell me what good and happiness dost thou teach?

Jesus says, I do not teach any good or happiness, for God alone is good and happy, but I teach life, how to attain life. And to attain life, it is necessary to do the commandments, and the commandments are these, In addition to the old ones about not killing, not committing adultery, also these, Honour God in such a way as to love thy neighbour as thyself.

The rich man replied, I have fulfilled all these commandments. Jesus says, If thou hadst fulfilled the last two commandments, or even one of them, thou wouldst not have any possessions.

If thou didst really fulfil this commandment about loving thy neighbour as thyself, thou wouldst not have anything of thy own; thou wouldst have distributed everything to those who have not; if thou wishest to fulfil the commandments, go and distribute thy possessions.

The important personage frowned and went away. Then Jesus said to the disciples, You see that it is true, as I have said, that the kingdom of God belongs to the poor, that you cannot serve God and mammon. It is utterly impossible for him who has possessions to enter into the kingdom of God.

The disciples were frightened. But he said to them, It is impossible for him who has possessions to enter into the kingdom of God; it is easier for a camel to go through an eye of a needle, than for him who has possessions to enter into the kingdom of God. They were frightened more than ever, and they said, How is this possible? But he said, Judging in human fashion it is impossible, but judging according to the spirit, according to God, it is not only possible, but you cannot even think differently.

No parable, it seems, has given its interpreters more trouble than this one.

This is what the church says (pp. 352 and 355):

If thou wilt be perfect: Such a man as for the acquisition of the eternal life has nothing unfinished, nothing lacking, for whom there are no obstacles to overcome in order to obtain eternal life.

Go and sell that thou hast, etc.: The young man boasts of having kept the commandments of the law. Now the law demanded that he should love his neighbour as himself, and that he should love the Lord his God more than all. The Lord says to the young man that if he really has gained such love or wishes to gain it, if he loves and wants to love God and his neighbour as the law demands, he must devote to God and to his neighbour both himself and everything which he has, consequently also his wealth. Sell your possessions, distribute them to the poor, and follow me.

Follow me : Be my disciple.

Thou shalt have treasure in heaven : Such is the reward for this exploit. Jesus commands the youth to leave his wealth, showing him that he not only does not deprive him of his wealth, but even adds more to it, which surpasses that which he commands him to distribute, which surpasses it as much as heaven surpasses earth, and even more. At the same time he calls this treasure an ample reward, singular, and such as no one can take away, offering this to the young man as much as is in the power of man. And so it is not enough to contemn riches, they must also be used for the good of the poor, and one must, in particular, follow Christ, that is, do everything which he may command, be prepared for suffering, even for death. (Chrys.) This commandment about distributing one's possessions to the poor is given conditionally : if thou wilt be perfect. We may say of it what was said above of celibacy : All men cannot receive this saying.

How hardly shall they that have riches, etc. : Christ with all his power rebukes, not the riches, but him who is addicted to the riches.

The danger of riches in the matter of salvation or of the moral perfection does not lie in them, but in this, that to the sinful nature of man they present many temptations and obstacles in observing the commandments of the law and of the will of God, when man loves them inordinately.

It is easier for a camel, etc. : This was a popular Jewish proverb, which is still current among the Arabs. To show that a certain thing was impossible or exceedingly difficult of execution, they used to say, that it was easier for a camel or an elephant to pass through an eye of a needle than for the thing to happen. However, some people do not understand an animal by the camel, but a thick rope which is used by boatmen in throwing out the anchors with which to steady the ships. In neither sense can the words be taken in their literal sense; all that is intended is to show the impossibility or unusual difficulty. But why did Jesus tell his disciples that it is difficult for a rich man to enter into the kingdom of heaven, since they were poor and had nothing? Of course, in order to teach them not to be ashamed of their poverty, and, as it were, in order to justify himself for having advised them before not to have anything.

Who then can be saved? If it is so difficult for a rich man to be saved, who has the power and the means to do so much good, who can after that be saved? the conclusion of the disciples is from the greater to the lesser.

Or: if it is so difficult for the rich to be saved, who of them will be saved?

Beheld them: This is noticed also in St. Mark, as a peculiarity during this answer of the Lord. With his meek and calm glance he soothed their agitated thoughts and destroyed the doubt, for this is meant by the evangelist's remark, He beheld.

With men this is impossible, etc.: It is impossible for men, with their human means, to have a rich man saved; men are powerless to do so, but God is all-powerful, and for him nothing is impossible. His loving and saving grace is able to do that which man is absolutely unable to do with all his strength and means. But in what manner will the impossible be made possible? If thou renouncest thy possessions, distributest them among the poor, and abandonest thy evil lusts; for the words of Jesus Christ do not ascribe the works of salvation exclusively to God, but at the same time express the difficulty of this exploit for us, as can be seen from what follows.

This is what Reuss says (pp. 527–530):

Dans cette péricope, le fond de la narration est le même chez les trois évangélistes et les différences ne portent que sur des détails peu importants. Néanmoins ces différences sont de nature à nous faire reconnaître des rédactions plus ou moins libres ou indépendantes l'une de l'autre.

Le personnage qui est mis en scène est désigné par Matthieu comme un *jeune homme,* par Luc comme un *chef* (de synagogue ou magistrat?); les deux versions peuvent s'accorder à la rigueur. La question qu'il pose à Jésus paraît avoir été inspirée par un sentiment louable, à moins qu'on ne veuille supposer gratuitement qu'il était venu pour entendre dire qu'il ne lui restait plus rien à faire. Il ne se connaissait ni vices, ni péchés graves; mais il pensait qu'il fallait quelque chose de plus que la *justice* vulgaire pour aspirer à la félicité éternelle ; et se représentant les conditions de l'entrée au royaume de Dieu comme une certaine quantité de choses à faire, il demandait à connaître ce qui pouvait encore lui manquer.. Il aborde Jésus fort poliment avec une formule caressante : Mon *bon* maître !

C'est à cette formule, prononcée sans aucune arrière-pensée, que Jésus l'arrête pour lui faire comprendre que la chose dont il s'enquiert est infiniment plus sérieuse qu'il ne pense : *Pourquoi m'appelles-tu bon ? Il n'y a de bon que Dieu seul.* Le Seigneur a parfaitement compris que cet homme ne doutait pas le moins du monde qu'il ne fût bon lui-même ; qu'il ne se faisait pas de souci au sujet de la portée idéale de ce terme ou de cette notion, qu'il n'avait aucune idée de la grandeur des devoirs, mesurés d'après la sainteté absolue de Dieu et les besoins infinis de l'humanité. Eh bien, il doit apprendre avant tout à mesurer la distance qui le sépare du but, ou plutôt, à entrevoir un but sur lequel il n'avait jamais jeté un regard. Le grand prophète auquel il parle, qu'il a cru devoir consulter, de préférence à tout autre mortel, au sujet des conditions du salut, décline lui-même l'honneur d'être appelé *bon ;* à plus forte raison, tout autre se gardera d'être trop présomptueux à cet égard. Dieu seul *est* bon, parfaitement, invariablement. L'homme ne doit pas être appelé bon, ni surtout s'estimer tel, non pas seulement parce qu'il a réellement des défauts et qu'il peut faire une chute, mais par une raison dont on parle moins souvent : le meilleur peut et doit toujours progresser, il lui reste toujours quelque chose à faire, chaque jour amène pour lui de nouveaux devoirs. Il n'y a pour lui jamais de sabbat réservé à la contemplation joyeuse d'une œuvre parfaitement achevée (Jean v. 17 ; ix. 4). Dans ce sens-là, nous pouvons reconnaître, sans que notre sentiment en soit blessé, sans que nous ayons à reprocher à Jésus une affectation de fausse modestie, qu'il a pu et dû refuser la qualification que cet homme lui donnait, pour l'éclairer en même temps sur sa propre valeur morale et pour détruire les illusions qu'il se faisait. On comprend que certains lecteurs aient été offusqués d'une phrase qui paraissait contredire la thèse de l'impeccabilité de Jésus. Aussi voyons-nous dans le texte de Matthieu, tel que la critique l'a rétabli, un essai de faire disparaître cette difficulté. Mais il n'en est que plus sûr que les deux autres textes nous ont conservé la forme authentique du discours.

Après cela, Jésus, répondant au fond de la question, commence par renvoyer son interlocuteur à la loi (comp. Luc x. 25, sect. 60). Il n'a pas pu vouloir dire qu'une observation plus ou moins rigoureuse et littérale de certains préceptes, pour la plupart négatifs, suffisait pour gagner le ciel et mériter le titre de bon. Le sermon de la montagne nous préserverait au besoin d'une pareille erreur. Mais il pouvait vouloir faire faire à son présomptueux interlocuteur un retour sur lui-même, l'amener à sonder sa conscience, et en général le préparer, par cette caté- chisation basée sur la loi, à des instructions plus spécialement évangéliques. Le *bon* Israélite est à toute épreuve, il subit l'exa- men avec une entière assurance et à sa grande satisfaction. Il a tout fait, tout observé, et depuis sa jeunesse. Ne faudrait-il rien de plus ?

Il fait parade de ses illusions avec tant de candeur, que Jésus le *prend en affection.* Evidemment, comme Juif, il était ce qu'il pouvait et devait être. La loi, la règle traditionnelle, ne lui demandait rien de plus. Jésus va donc élargir le cercle du devoir, et se sert à ce propos d'une formule très-énergique, étonnante et même, si l'on veut, absurde, au point de vue du bon sens pratique (Luc xii. 33, sect. 60), mais parfaitement propre à rendre palpable l'idée qu'elle devait représenter. La pierre de touche qu'il applique à l'or de cette vertu légale, c'est tout simple- ment la question de savoir si elle irait jusqu'à l'abnégation des intérêts terrestres *légitimes,* en vue de biens supérieurs, mais pure- ment spirituels. S'il pouvait rester le moindre doute à cet égard, le fait que Marc explique lui-même l'invitation de Jésus par cette autre formule : *se charger de sa croix* (sect. 40, Matth. x. 38 ; comp. xvi. 24, sect. 50), et puis l'interprétation donnée plus bas par le v. 29 des trois textes, prouvent que nous aurions bien tort de ne voir dans la phrase que nous avons sous les yeux, que le conseil positif et direct de jeter l'argent par la fenêtre. La vertu chrétienne ne doit pas se tracer des limites. L'*amour* de l'argent est une des mille pierres d'achoppement contre lesquelles la fai- blesse morale vient se heurter, un des écueils qui en révèlent la fragilité. Il n'est signalé ici qu'à titre d'exemple, et l'on aurait tort de croire que cette histoire ne doit pas avoir une portée plus générale, ou qu'elle doit signaler la *richesse* elle-même, objective- ment, comme un mal. (Voyez surtout l'explication donnée par Marc, v. 24, et qui est incontestablement juste, bien qu'elle puisse avoir été ajoutée par le rédacteur, de son propre chef.)

Cette seconde épreuve, le jeune homme ne la soutient pas. Le royaume de Dieu, la vie éternelle, telle qu'il l'a conçue, ne vaut pas ce prix, à son gré. Jésus le voit partir à regret, et il proclame avec douleur devant ses disciples une vérité qu'il a bien souvent déjà répétée sous des formes diverses [Matth. vi. 19 ss. (sect. 14) ; xii. 49 (sect. 29) ; xiii. 44 ss. (sect. 34) ; x. 9 ss., 37

ss. (sect. 40) ; xvi. 24 ss. (sect. 50). Luc ix. 62 (sect. 58) ; xii.
22 ss. (sect. 66) ; xiv. 26 ss. (sect. 73), etc.], mais qu'il trouvait
bien difficile à inculquer aux hommes, celle, qu'il n'y a de sauvé
que celui qui sait au besoin renoncer ; qu'en vue du ciel, il faut
savoir sacrifier les biens de la terre ; qu'il y a des moments décisifs où il faut choisir entre l'un et l'autre. Les hommes sont
si peu disposés à faire ce choix dans le sens qui leur serait salutaire, que Jésus hasarde le mot *impossible*, qu'il semble désespérer
de trouver chez eux l'héroïsme moral qu'il réclame. L'image
du *chameau* et du *trou de l'aiguille* a le même sens que celle de la
montagne transportée par la simple parole ; c'est l'expression figurée de l'impossibilité. On n'a pas besoin pour cela de substituer (comme on l'a proposé) au chameau un câble, ou au trou
de l'aiguille une étroite poterne, au risque d'amoindrir la force du
dicton proverbial. Les talmudistes et les Arabes l'ont aussi et
renchérissent même sur le chameau en le remplaçant par l'élé-
phant.

Les disciples comprennent si bien la portée des paroles de leur
Maître qu'ils s'écrient tout consternés : *Qui donc peut être sauvé !*
Cela ne veut pas dire : Si les riches risquent de manquer le ciel,
eux qui ont tant de moyens de bien faire, à plus forte raison les
pauvres, qui n'ont rien à donner, n'y arriveront pas. Ils veulent
dire : Si ce que tous les hommes désirent le plus, est un empêche-
ment dans la voie du salut, comment espérer que quelqu'un
arrive jusqu'au bout ? Nous ajouterons dans le même sens :
Riche et pauvre sont des termes extrêmement vagues et purement relatifs ; la quotité matérielle de la fortune terrestre ne
détermine pas le degré d'attachement du cœur aux choses
d'ici-bas, ni les chances plus ou moins grandes que peut avoir
un homme de réussir dans ses efforts à le vaincre. Seulement
le cas particulier, qui donne ici lieu à la réflexion du Seigneur,
présentait cette vérité sous la forme la plus palpable et la plus
populaire. Voilà pourquoi cette forme est acceptée et employée
par lui.

Aussi ajoute-t-il un autre mot qui fait voir clairement que la
portée du premier s'étendait bien au-delà de ce que l'on appelle
vulgairement l'aisance et la richesse. Si le salut, la certitude
de la vie éternelle, l'entrée du royaume de Dieu, était le fait des
hommes seuls, de leurs efforts constants et infatigables, de leurs
forces et de leur volonté, aucun n'y arriverait. Il leur faut à
tous l'appoint des forces divines, l'assistance du saint esprit,
l'appui de la grâce. *Pour* Dieu et *par* Dieu tout est possible.
Ce passage est l'un de ceux qui prouvent de la manière la plus
directe que la théologie évangélique, telle qu'elle a été dévelop-

pée par Paul, a ses racines dans l'enseignement de Jésus lui-
même. Plus haut (Luc xvii. 10, sect. 77), nous lisions que
l'homme n'a point de récompense à réclamer, lors même qu'il
aurait fait tout son devoir ; ici nous apprenons qu'il ne peut pas
même le faire sans que Dieu lui vienne en aide. Ces deux textes
se complètent l'un l'autre.

They have to interpret everything in such a way as to
prove that one may be rich, knowing that the poor are
starving, and yet be a Christian. And they distort the
teaching, and misinterpret what has so clearly and with
such insistency been said so often.

The Gospel begins by saying that John runs into the
wilderness, becomes a mendicant, preaches that he who
has two garments should give one to the poor, and he
who has food should also give it, and reproaches the rich
for their riches and their cruelty.

According to the interpretation of the church it means
only that John the Baptist smeared people for the kingdom of Jesus, but that what is said about wealth and
poverty is only for an adornment of speech.

Jesus goes into the wilderness as a mendicant and
struggles against the temptation of wealth, — this means
nothing, — it is only the devil who is tempting God.

Jesus returns into the world, renounces his home, his
family, his property, and keeps the company of mendicants, and preaches to mendicants, — all that means
nothing. All that shows only the meekness of God.

Jesus says that God is displeased with rich sacrifices,
that he rejoices only in the love and compassion toward
one another, — that is only a quotation from the prophets.

Jesus explains that the kingdom of God consists in
renouncing the life of the flesh and in living by the
spirit, — that is only an explanation of the relations of
the persons of the Trinity, and has no other significance.

Jesus, replying to the disciples of John, says that the
mendicants will know of his good, — that is again an

adornment of speech. Finally, Jesus delivers his sermon in clear words, which are accessible to everybody, saying directly what men have to do that they may fulfil his teaching. This sermon is regarded both by the learned and by the unlearned as the brightest and clearest place in the Gospel. And this sermon Jesus begins with the words, Blessed are you vagrants, for yours is the kingdom of God, and unfortunate are you rich men, for you esteem the reward of the flesh. To these words is added the little word τῷ πνεύματι, which has no connection with anything, and these words are interpreted as sentimental phrases, which have reference to meekness; of the fact that riches and possessions are the source of evil, are cruel, Jesus does not say a word. Not Jesus said that, but Proudhon; and Proudhon is a liar, — he is a socialist and an infidel. In the whole sermon nothing but this teaching about disinterestedness is elucidated and confirmed. In Chapter V. the rules are given which lead to the impossibility of possessions. If all offences are to be forgiven, and one is not to defend his own, nor to go to court, nor to resist the enemy, then all property is unthinkable. All these rules are rejected and are taken to be nothing but sentimental phrases.

In Chapter VI. it says, Collect nothing, do not lay up treasure, that is, have nothing, and, If you lay by, you will not be the children of God. It is impossible, it says so outright, it is impossible to connect the service of God and of mammon. It is clear that if thou hast collected and laid by, thou wilt not give to the poor from what thou hast laid by. But the poor always exist; and so it is impossible to lay by, for thou art in the power of God. If thou layest by, thou wilt die. Have no care for the morrow. This seems precise and clear.

But Jesus seems to foresee that men will try to conceal this, and will misinterpret it, so he adds a few parables: about the feast to which only the poor come; about the unjust steward; about the rich man and Lazarus; he expresses from every side the idea that it is impossible to enter into the kingdom of God with possessions.   No, he is speaking of everything but of my money-bags, and wealth does no harm; on the contrary, it is very nice.

More than that.   In the discourse with the young man the same thing is expressed with such simplicity and clearness that it is impossible to discover any new interpretation for it.   But they interpret and invent for Jesus such rules as will allow the money-bags to remain untouched.   Terrible efforts of glibness of mind and tongue are directed toward the proof of this possibility.   They invent an Ebion, who has never existed, and who is supposed to have founded a sect which recognized the necessity of poverty as a condition for entering into the kingdom of God.   Ebion means $\pi\tau\omega\chi\acute{o}s$, that is, precisely what Jesus commanded, and the disciples called themselves *ebions*.   The Ebionites, that is, those who executed his teaching, are a sect, and those who invented the Trinity and the sacraments and admit riches, courts, wars, are the true followers.   But the first disciples of Jesus, the apostles, did not understand the teaching of Christ.

Acts ii. 44. And all that believed were together, and had all things common;

45. And sold their possessions and goods, and parted them to all men, as every man had need.

46. And they, continuing daily with one accord in the temple, and breaking bread from house to house, did eat their meat with gladness and singleness of heart,

47. Praising God, and having favour with all the people. And the Lord added to the church daily such as should be saved.

Acts iv. 32. And the multitude of them that believed were of one heart and of one soul: neither said any of them that aught of the things which he possessed was his own; but they had all things common.

33. And with great power gave the apostles witness of the resurrection of the Lord Jesus: and great grace was upon them all.

84. Neither was there any among them that lacked: for as many as were possessors of lands or houses sold them, and brought the prices of the things that were sold,

85. And laid them down at the apostles' feet: and distribution was made unto every man according as he had need.

But no, they want to retain the money-bags and yet be regarded as children of the kingdom.

God be with them and with their money-bags. Let them keep them, if they will only leave the teaching of Christ in peace. This teaching cannot be followed just a little: they say themselves that it is the truth. If it is the truth, there can be no little truth,— it is either the truth or a lie. In order to understand a truth just a little, one has to become mad, as the men of the so-called science have gone mad, such as Renan, Strauss, Baur, Reuss, and all those who consider religion from the rhetorical standpoint.

Thus Renan says (*Les Apôtres*, p. 381):

La foi absolue est pour nous un fait complètement étranger. En dehors des sciences positives, d'une certitude en quelque sorte matérielle, toute opinion n'est à nos yeux qu'un à peu près, impliquant une part de vérité et une part d'erreur. La part d'erreur peut être aussi petite que l'on voudra; elle ne se réduit jamais à zéro, quand il s'agit de choses morales, impliquant une question d'art, de langage, de forme littéraire, de personnes. Telle n'est pas la manière de voir des esprits étroits et obstinés, des Orientaux par exemple. L'œil de ces gens n'est pas comme le nôtre; c'est l'œil d'émail des personnages de mosaïque, terne fixe. Ils ne savent voir qu' . . . etc., etc.

That is, he says, We do not believe in anything, and we judge about everything. We are right, and we judge those who believe. We are so much used to this learned rigmarole that we are even not struck by such utterance, but if we were to analyze it, we should find it to be the delirium of an insane man, who says, I am the king, and all those who do not accept my rule are mistaken.

A man who does not believe in anything does not

know anything,—he is a spiritual patient. But the learned man shows and proves it throughout the book. In all his books he frequently speaks sympathetically of Christ's teaching, and then he suddenly condemns Christ's teaching from the height of some unuttered principle. If a man says something, he must know something, so what does he know? In vain will you look for an answer: *La critique et la science.* But what is this *la critique et la science?* Expressing myself in elevated style,—as they would speak of their own business,—science, history, and historical criticism are one of the sides of the universal, traditional human knowledge, which is constantly growing and illuminating humanity. The branch with which we busy ourselves is the history of the life of humanity, of the formation of its popular, governmental, social, cultural relations. The division to which we devote ourselves is the history of the evolution of the religions. The special case to which we devote ourselves is the evolution of Christianity. Very well. The first question: Is the tradition of human knowledge one or several? The Hindoo, the Chinese knowledge does not seem to have entered into our tradition, and it denies our own. I shall be told: Ours includes or will include everything, for it is free and seeks only for light. The Chinese say differently; but, all right, I shall agree with you.

Second question: Is not the life of humanity too great a subject for knowledge? Since the labours of one thousand men will not be enough to describe the life of one man, how can the life of all humanity be described? I shall be told: There are generalizations of the form of the life of humanity; we find these, and then we classify under them the phenomena of life, compare, find new laws, verify them by facts, and such a doctrine forms the science of history.

I ask: Are these generalizations of form, in which

human life appears, always one and the same, unchangeable, absolute?

I am told: Yes, these forms are the evolution of nationalities, states, their institutions, laws, culture, religion.

Very well. I understand these forms, but do not see why these forms interest you so much. I know other forms also: agriculture, industry, commerce.

I am told: We include these too, so far as we have material for them.

All right. I know still other forms: education, domestic life.

We include them, too.

I know also entertainments, attires.

We include them, too.

I know also the relation to animals, to the home folk, to savages; I know also the building of houses, the preparation of food; I know also the relation to space, whether people live in one spot, or whether they move about, and whether much or little; I know also how labour is distributed; I know also about relations in friendship and enmity, and an endless number of other things.

If only the known forms have been chosen and up to the present only the forms of the existence of the state have been chosen and successfully studied, this is not due to the fact that these forms interest us so much, but because we consider them important, and because we consider certain forms of the state better and others worse, so that the historical investigations in this sense are made on the basis of an ideal which we had concerning the life of the state.

The investigation of the others consists in the verification of this, to what extent the phenomena under discussion agree with those which we have regarded as good, and all that is possible in relation to all the phenomena of human life as long as we have the naïve conviction that in the given case we know what is best. But here the historians met with a little unpleasantness. In the heat of their game they began, like a child throwing all its toys into a basket, to throw into theirs everything which came their way: commerce, and culture, and customs, and the historical evolution of life (they are very fond of this expression): though it did not all go into their basket, it in no way interfered with their game. If these men are convinced that the Paris of the year 1880 is an ideal of the historical evolution of life, they find it possible to take this as an ideal and describe every other historical evolution of life, by comparing it with this ideal; but in the heat of the game they have also snapped up religion. Why, there are all kinds of religions and they act differently on the lives of the nations, and they are a toy, so pick it up. But this game was a hot coal. It burned all the toys, and nothing was left.

Indeed, take any phenomenon of human life! If I know for certain how to view this phenomenon in the best manner possible, I am able to describe it in all cases and to follow its development and decay; but what is to be done with religion (in Russian — faith)? Faith is not a relation of man to country, market, or the franchise, but something which he knows well, and on which his whole life is based, from which flows his relation to all the manifestations of life, — to the state, to the family, to property, to amusements, to the arts, to the sciences, to everything. And so it is, in the first place, impossible to gobble up faith and chuck it into the basket, and if you do, you cannot do anything with it, for the structure of the state may be judged by what I consider to be the best state, and of culture and the laws I can judge only by those which I consider to be the best, and so I can say something about religion, because I know the best, but nobody knows such.

And suddenly it turns out that the historian says that there is no faith now though there was before; but faith is the foundation of life, that is, the historian acknowledges that he really does not know wherein the meaning of life consists, and so the meaning of what he said before of other things disappears, and all the toys burn up.

But the historians do not see that. Without knowing any real religion, they most naïvely judge of religion, of that from which flows the life of men, on the basis of small manifestations of public life, that is, on the basis of governmental, economic, and other manifestations.

Thus Strauss criticizes the whole teaching of Christ, because the German life would be destroyed, whereas he is used to it.

Strauss (p. 622):

Es ist nicht zu verkennen, dass in dem Muster, wie es Jesus in Lehre und Leben darstellte, neben der vollen Ausgestaltung einiger Seiten, andere nur schwach umrissen, oder auch gar nicht angedeutet sind. Voll entwickelt findet sich Alles, was sich auf Gottes- und Nächsten-liebe, auf Reinheit des Herzens und Lebens des Einzelnen bezieht; aber schon das Leben des Menschen in der Familie tritt bei dem selbst familienlosen Lehrer in den Hintergrund; dem Staate gegenüber erscheint sein Verhältniss als ein lediglich passives; dem Erwerb ist er nicht blos für sich, seines Berufs wegen, abgewendet, sondern auch sichtbar abgeneigt, und Alles vollends, was Kunst und schönen Lebensgenuss betrifft, bleibt völlig ausserhalb seines Gesichtskreises. Dass dies wesentliche Lücken sind, dass hier eine Einseitigkeit vorliegt, die theils in den besonderen Lebensverhältnissen Jesu ihren Grund hat, sollte man nicht läugnen wollen, da man es nicht läugnen kann. Und die Lücken sind nicht etwa der Art, dass nur die vollständige Durchführung fehlte, während der regelnden Grundsatz gegeben wäre, sondern für den Staat ins besondere, den Erwerb und die Kunst, fehlt von vornherein der rechte Begriff, und es ist ein vergebliches Unternehmen, die Thätigkeit des Menschen als Staatsbürger, das Bemühen um Bereicherung und Verschönerung des Lebens durch Gewerbe und Kunst nach den Vorschriften oder dem Vorbilde Jesu bestimmen zu wollen. Sondern hier war eine Ergänzung, sowohl aus anderen Volksthümlichkeiten, als anderer Zeit und Bildungsverhältnissen heraus, erforderlich, wie sie zum Theil schon rückwarts in demjenigen lag, was Griechen und Römer in dieser Hinsicht vor sich gebracht hatten, zum Theil aber der weiteren Entwicklung der Menschheit und ihrer Geschichte vorbehalten blieb.

Renan (*Vie de Jésus,* Chapitre XI., Le Royaume de Dieu, p. 178):

Ces maximes, bonnes pour un pays où la vie se nourrit d'air et de jour, ce communisme délicat d'une troupe d'enfants de Dieu, vivant en conscience sur le sein de leur père, pouvaient convenir à une secte naïve, persuadée à chaque instant que son utopie allait se réaliser.

And this stupidity is so enticing that the moment a man has not his own ideas, and knows nothing, since he does not believe in anything, and wants to philosophize, he begins to write a history of religion. In all the novels wise men are all the time writing histories of religion, that is, that which one cannot even think about, that is, that which makes me out to be insane.

JESUS AND ZACCHEUS

1. Καὶ εἰσελθὼν διήρχετο τὴν Ἰεριχώ.

2. Καὶ ἰδοὺ ἀνὴρ ὀνόματι καλούμενος Ζακχαῖος, καὶ αὐτὸς ἦν ἀρχιτελώνης, καὶ οὗτος ἦν πλούσιος·

3. Καὶ ἐζήτει ἰδεῖν τὸν Ἰησοῦν τίς ἐστι, καὶ οὐκ ἠδύνατο ἀπὸ τοῦ ὄχλου, ὅτι τῇ ἡλικίᾳ μικρὸς ἦν.

4. Καὶ προδραμὼν ἔμπροσθεν ἀνέβη ἐπὶ συκομορέαν, ἵνα ἴδῃ αὐτόν· ὅτι δι᾽ ἐκείνης ἤμελλε διέρχεσθαι.

5. Καὶ ὡς ἦλθεν ἐπὶ τὸν τόπον, ἀναβλέψας ὁ

Luke xix. 1. And Jesus entered and passed through Jericho.
2. And, behold, there was a man named Zaccheus, which was the chief among the publicans, and he was rich.
3. And he sought to see Jesus who he was; and could not for the press, because he was little of stature.
4. And he ran before, and climbed up into a sycamore tree to see him; for he was to pass that way.
5. And when Jesus came to the place, he looked up, and saw him,

1. And entering Jericho, Jesus walked through the city.
2. And there was a man named Zaccheus, who was the chief of the tax-collectors, and he was rich.
3. And he wanted to see Jesus, what kind of a man he was; and he could not make his way through the crowd, because he was little of stature.
4. So he ran ahead and climbed up a tree to see him when he passed that way.
5. When Jesus passed by, he looked at him, and said, Zaccheus,

'Ιησοῦς εἶδεν αὐτὸν, καὶ εἶπε πρὸς αὐτὸν, Ζακχαῖε, σπεύσας κατάβηθι· σήμερον γὰρ ἐν τῷ οἴκῳ σου δεῖ με μεῖναι.

6. Καὶ σπεύσας κατέβη, καὶ ὑπεδέξατο αὐτὸν χαίρων.

7. Καὶ ἰδόντες ἅπαντες διεγόγγυζον, λέγοντες. Ὅτι παρὰ ἁμαρτωλῷ ἀνδρὶ εἰσῆλθε καταλῦσαι.

8. Σταθεὶς δὲ Ζακχαῖος εἶπε πρὸς τὸν Κύριον, Ἰδοὺ, τὰ ἡμίση τῶν ὑπαρχόντων μου, κύριε, δίδωμι τοῖς πτωχοῖς· καὶ εἴ τινός τι ἐσυκοφάντησα, ἀποδίδωμι τετραπλοῦν.

9. Εἶπε δὲ πρὸς αὐτὸν ὁ Ἰησοῦς. Ὅτι σήμερον σωτηρία τῷ οἴκῳ τούτῳ ἐγένετο, καθότι καὶ αὐτὸς υἱὸς Ἀβραάμ ἐστιν.

10. Ἦλθε γὰρ ὁ υἱὸς τοῦ ἀνθρώπου ζητῆσαι καὶ σῶσαι τὸ ἀπολωλός.

---

and said unto him, Zaccheus, make haste, and come down; for to-day I must abide at thy house.

6. And he made haste, and came down, and received him joyfully.

7. And when they saw it, they all murmured, saying, That he was gone to be guest with a man that is a sinner.

8. And Zaccheus stood, and said unto the Lord; Behold, Lord, the half of my goods I give to the poor; and if I have taken anything from any man by false accusation, I restore him fourfold.

9. And Jesus said unto him, This day is salvation come to this house,* forasmuch as he also is a son of Abraham.[b]

10. For the Son of man is come to seek and to save that which was lost.

---

make haste, and climb down; for to-day I want to stay at thy house.

6. Zaccheus climbed down at once, and joyfully received him in his house.

7. And they saw it, and began to grumble, saying, Why did he stop at the house of a sinner?

8. And Zaccheus went up to Jesus, and said to him, Sir, half of my goods I will give to the beggars, and if I have wronged any one, I will give him fourfold.

9. And Jesus said in reply, Now the child of this house will be saved, for he is a son of Abraham.

10. For the work of the son of man consists in finding and saving what has perished and is perishing.

(a) οἶκος means *kind, generation*. Here by the word οἶκος, the person spoken of is meant, namely, Zaccheus. Jesus calls him the *species of this house*, and I translate it by *the child of this house*.

(b) *Son of Abraham* has a special meaning. This meaning is clearly expressed in Gal. iii. 7: Know ye therefore that they which are of faith, the same are the children of Abraham. In the same sense we have here the son of Abraham, that is, he who believes in the same way as Abraham, who does as Abraham, who by the sacrifice of his son showed his faith.

Evidently Zaccheus knew Christ's teaching and was fond of it or else he would not have made such an effort to see Jesus, and evidently Jesus, seeing him in such a perilous position, and noticing the expression of his face, and maybe hearing the words which expressed this love for his teaching, addressed him. Just so we must assume that Jesus spoke with him in his house, and that Zaccheus' words as to giving away half his property were an answer to Jesus' teaching.

41. Καὶ καθίσας ὁ᾿Ιησοῦς κατέναντι τοῦ γαζοφυλακίου, ἐθεώρει πῶς ὁ ὄχλος βάλλει χαλκὸν εἰς τὸ γαζοφυλάκιον. καὶ πολλοὶ πλούσιοι ἔβαλλον πολλά·

42. Καὶ ἐλθοῦσα μία χήρα πτωχὴ ἔβαλε λεπτὰ δύο, ὅ ἐστι κοδράντης.

43. Καὶ προσκαλεσάμενος τοὺς μαθητὰς αὐτοῦ, λέγει αὐτοῖς, ᾿Αμὴν λέγω ὑμῖν, ὅτι ἡ χήρα αὕτη ἡ πτωχὴ πλεῖον πάντων βέβληκε τῶν βαλόντων εἰς τὸ γαζοφυλάκιον.

44. Πάντες γὰρ ἐκ τοῦ περισσεύοντος αὐτοῖς ἔβαλον· αὕτη δὲ ἐκ τῆς ὑστερήσεως αὐτῆς πάντα ὅσα εἶχεν ἔβαλεν, ὅλον τὸν βίον αὐτῆς.

Mark xii. 41. And Jesus sat over against the treasury, and beheld how the people cast money into the treasury: and many that were rich cast in much.

42. And there came a certain poor widow, and she threw in two mites, which make a farthing.

43. And he called unto him his disciples, and saith unto them, Verily I say unto you, That this poor widow hath cast more in, than all they which have cast into the treasury:

44. For all they did cast in of their abundance; but she of her want did cast in all that she had, even all her living.

41. And Jesus sat down opposite the money-box and watched the people put the money into the box; and many rich people passed by and threw in much money.

42. And there came a certain poor widow and she put into the box two mites, which make a farthing.

43. And he called his disciples, and said to them, Verily, I tell you, This poor widow has put more than the rest into the box.

44. For they threw in of their abundance; but she of her want threw in everything she had, — all her living.

Men are in the habit of measuring by the use which the sacrifice brings, and so Jesus, pointing to the two mites of the widow, said that she who gave up everything which she had, her whole life, was the only one who really gave; but the rest gave nothing, for they gave what to them was superfluous.

This little parable is very important. It simply confirms from another side the statement that in order to be able to do the will of God, it is absolutely necessary to be poor. In order to give something, it is first necessary to give up everything, to have nothing. To give up three-fourths of one's property and yet not to deprive oneself of anything in life means not to give up anything.

As a rule people who do not like this demand and interpretation of Jesus, and no rich men like it, say, We are commanded to give up everything, and this no one does, or can do, consequently it is untrue; and yet it is better to give up at least a little of one's abundance, — at least the poor will be filled and the naked clothed.

But such a reflection is based on a want of comprehension of the teaching. Jesus Christ nowhere commands men to give to the poor, so that the poor may be filled and satisfied; he says that a man must give everything to the poor, in order that he himself may be happy. He does not command or say what each must give, but announces the true good to men and says that a man who has attained the true good and who is seeking the true life will by all means give up all his possessions and thus find happiness. It is impossible to serve God and mammon, is not a rule, it is a reality: not that it is not fit to do so, but it is impossible.

He who will not leave his house, possessions, and family, and will not follow me, cannot be my disciple, that is, has not comprehended me: he who has comprehended me will do so for the very reason that he has comprehended.

The young man who boasted of observing the commandments, even the commandment about loving his neighbour as himself, was convicted by this very fact. He had not yet entered into the possibility of keeping the commandments, if he had not got rid of his riches. Riches are an obstacle to entering into the kingdom of God. Consequently those who assure us that, if it is impossible to do what Jesus Christ commands, it is better at least to give something for the benefit of the poor, are speaking of something different from what Jesus says. Jesus not only fails to speak of the material use, he does not even know it. He commands us to give away our possessions that they may not be an obstacle to life; after a man has given away his possessions, he teaches us that a man's happiness consists in pitying and loving men.

Consequently, in order to obtain the possibility of giving up his life, a man must first of all give up his unrighteous wealth, and so those who give or establish a mite for the poor must leave Jesus Christ and his teaching in peace. He does not command it. If they do so, they do it for their amusement; and let them say so. But giving of one's abundance Jesus Christ considers as a matter of indifference, that is, he says nothing about it, though he distinctly forbids giving in such a way that others should see it.

THE MEASURE OF GOOD

3. Καὶ ὄντος αὐτοῦ ἐν Βηθανίᾳ, ἐν τῇ οἰκίᾳ Σίμωνος τοῦ λεπροῦ, κατακειμένου αὐτοῦ, ἦλθε γυνὴ ἔχουσα ἀλάβαστρον μύρου νάρδου πιστικῆς πολυτελοῦς· καὶ συντρίψασα τὸ ἀλάβαστρον, κατέχεεν αὐτοῦ κατὰ τῆς κεφαλῆς.	*Mark* xiv. 3. And being in Bethany, in the house of Simon the leper, as he sat at meat, there came a woman having an alabaster box of ointment of spikenard very precious; and she brake the box, and poured it on his head.	3. Jesus happened to be in the house of Simon the leper. A woman came up to him: she was rich in the possession of a pitcher of precious oil. She broke the pitcher, and poured the oil on Jesus' head.

(*a*) In Matthew and in Mark we find the same expression, ἔχουσα ἀλάβαστρον μύρου, which ought to be translated by *had in her possession a pitcher of oil*, and which I translate by *she was rich in the possession of a pitcher of oil.* From the meaning of what follows, especially from the words ἔχουσα μύρου, *she had in her possession*, we must understand that she was a vender of oil, and that that was everything she had, at least at that moment. If the woman did not always carry that oil, then she would have to go with the set purpose of fetching the oil, and then the chief significance of the passage would be lost; besides, if it had not been so, it would have said so. Instead of ἔχουσα, *having the oil*, it would have said *bringing the oil*. But it says ἔχουσα, and so we must inevitably assume that this woman always carried the precious oil with her. And if she carried it, she did so for the purpose of selling it, or transferring it from one place to another. In any case, the woman was carrying a precious thing and not only did not have in mind wasting it, but carried and watched it as a precious thing. This we must keep in mind, in order that what follows may be clear. The word precious is given in all three gospels, in order to accentuate it.

(*b*) The fact that she broke the pitcher shows that she could not open it quickly, and, above all else, that she esteemed little the preciousness of the oil.

The detail about wiping it off with her hair is out of place and evidently mixed up with the incident with the harlot.

3. Ἡ δὲ οἰκία ἐπληρώθη ἐκ τῆς ὀσμῆς τοῦ μύρου.	*John* xii. 3. And the house was filled with the odour of the ointment.	3. And the whole room was filled with the pleasant odour of the oil.
8. Ἰδόντες δὲ οἱ μαθηταὶ αὐτοῦ ἠγανάκτησαν, λέγοντες, Εἰς τί ἡ ἀπώλεια αὕτη;	*Matt.* xxvi. 8. But when his disciples saw it, they had indignation, saying, To what purpose is this waste?	8. And the disciples were displeased, and they said to one another, To what purpose is this waste of the precious oil?
9. Ἠδύνατο γὰρ τοῦτο τὸ μύρον πραθῆναι πολλοῦ, καὶ δοθῆναι τοῖς πτωχοῖς.	9. For this ointment might have been sold for much, and given to the poor.	9. This oil might have been sold for much, and given to the poor.
4. Λέγει οὖν εἷς ἐκ τῶν μαθητῶν αὐτοῦ, Ἰούδας Σίμωνος Ἰσκαριώτης, ὁ μέλλων αὐτὸν παραδιδόναι,	*John* xii. 4. Then saith one of his disciples, Judas Iscariot, Simon's son, which should betray him,	4. Then one of his disciples, Judas Iscariot, the one who betrayed him, said,
5. Διατί τοῦτο τὸ μύρον οὐκ ἐπράθη τριακοσίων δηναρίων, καὶ ἐδόθη πτωχοῖς;	5. Why was not this ointment sold for three hundred pence, and given to the poor?	5. It ought to have been sold: the oil is worth three hundred pence, and it ought to be given to the poor.

6. Εἶτε δὲ τοῦτο, οὐχ ὅτι περὶ τῶν πτωχῶν ἔμελεν αὐτῷ, ἀλλ' ὅτι κλέπτης ἦν, καὶ τὸ γλωσσόκομον εἶχε, καὶ τὰ βαλλόμενα ἐβάσταζεν.

10. Γνοὺς δὲ ὁ Ἰησοῦς εἶπεν αὐτοῖς, Τί κόπους παρέχετε τῇ γυναικί; ἔργον γὰρ καλὸν εἰργάσατο εἰς ἐμέ.

7. Πάντοτε γὰρ τοὺς πτωχοὺς ἔχετε μεθ' ἑαυτῶν, καὶ ὅταν θέλητε δύνασθε αὐτοὺς εὖ ποιῆσαι· ἐμὲ δὲ οὐ πάντοτε ἔχετε.

8. Ὃ εἶχεν αὕτη, ἐποίησε· προέλαβε μυρίσαι μου τὸ σῶμα εἰς τὸν ἐνταφιασμόν.

9. Ἀμὴν λέγω ὑμῖν, Ὅπου ἂν κηρυχθῇ τὸ εὐαγγέλιον τοῦτο εἰς ὅλον τὸν κόσμον, καὶ ὃ ἐποίησεν αὕτη λαληθήσεται εἰς μνημόσυνον αὐτῆς.

6. This he said, not that he cared for the poor; but because he was a thief, and had the bag, and bare what was put therein.

Matt. xxvi. 10. When Jesus understood it, he said unto them, Why trouble ye the woman? for she hath wrought a good work upon me.

Mark xiv. 7. For ye have the poor with you always, and whensoever ye will ye may do them good; but me ye have not always.[a]

8. She hath done what she could: she is come aforehand to anoint my body to the burying.

9. Verily I say unto you, Wheresoever this gospel shall be preached throughout the whole world, this also that she hath done shall be spoken of for a memorial of her.

6. He said this, not that he cared for the poor; but because he was a thief, and had the box for the poor upon him.

10. Jesus understood it, and said, Why do you trouble this woman? Leave her alone, for she has done a good act on me.

7. You always have the poor among you, and you can do them good whenever you please; but I am not always with you.

8. What she had she gave away: she has beforehand anointed my body for the burial.

9. Verily I tell you, Wherever in the world the true good will be told, a word will be said of what she has done.

(a) If to the words, Ye have the poor with you always, there were not added, But me ye have not always, the meaning of Jesus would be this, Do not rebuke the woman for not having given to the poor whom you do not see, but having given to me; the poor are always before you; whomever you pity is poor. I am poor and she has pitied me, and has done well. But the words, Me ye have not always, and the next verse about her having done it as a preparation for the burial, shows that he is hinting at his death. In my opinion, Jesus, replying to Judas' reflection in regard to the profit, says, There is no profit in a good deed, and every deed may be interpreted as being useful or useless, as you may wish. It is impossible to do a more reckless act than what this woman has done, but even this act may be interpreted in the sense of profitableness.

She has poured the oil over my body. You say, In vain has she done so. How do you know? I shall die soon, and then it will appear that she did well, — she has prepared my body for the burial.

Oil is poured over Jesus as it is poured over a dead body, and he jestingly expresses his thought that no one can know what is useful, and what not.

But after the jest in response to the expression of the usefulness of the act, Jesus speaks of the significance of the deed in the sense of the good, and here says that this act is the best expression of the good which he teaches.

The disciples measure the good by its use, and so condemn the woman and trouble her, and she does not know whether she has done well or not in taking pity on Christ and in having given him everything of value which she had. Judas in particular is dissatisfied.

Christ says, Do not trouble her, — she has done the greatest good which she could do. Do not speak of the poor, whom you do not see, nor pity, nor love. She saw me, and she pitied me and gave me everything she had.

Nothing better can be done. The woman wasted three hundred pence, because she pitied Christ and wanted to do him some good. Is it a good act, or not? We are so accustomed to live according to the law of Judas Iscariot, that there is not a single man who, seeing such a deed, would not say that it is a senseless and even bad act. The example is exceedingly striking. The vessel with the precious oil is wasted. For what? Who profits by it?

There, in the street, there are hundreds of the poor. Would it not be better to give it to them? It could not have caused Jesus Christ any pleasure. He himself pities the poor, so how can he help condemning the foolish woman? Judas condemned her, and all the disciples after him. And the reflection, why the woman is foolish and has done a foolish act, is so simple and so clear, that nothing can be said. But Jesus Christ did not condemn her; on the contrary, he praised her, and said, Everywhere, in the whole world, where the true good will be announced, they will tell of what she did. She rejected her riches in the name of pity. She did something senseless as far as the children of this world are concerned, for the sake of pity. In her act she united both foundations of Jesus' teaching, Give up everything which thou hast, and pity and love thy neighbour. With one act she gave away and showed pity: she broke the vessel with the oil, lost everything which she had, and anointed Jesus' head, because she pitied him. What would come of it, Judas thought and knew. He said that the oil was wasted. But we, who are among those to whom the true good has been announced according to the foolish act of this woman, understand the meaning of the Gospel. It is easy to condemn, not only this act, but any other act of love and compassion. It is always possible to do something more useful, but every act of love and compassion calls forth, not in Judas, but in the sons of God, a desire to imitate such an act, to do something greater or even the same; only in Judas it produces a reflection about usefulness.

But John the Divine has explained the meaning of Judas' reflection. He said, It was not because he had any care for the poor, but because he was a thief and carried the box for the poor. It is incomprehensible how after these simple, clear, apposite words there can be any charitable institutions in Christian societies. They are directly based on the reflection of Judas, and directly contradict the words of Jesus Christ, You have always the poor with you. The explanations of John the Divine leave no doubt as to the significance of the men who establish such institutions : They do it, not because they care for the poor, but because they carry the money-boxes, and because they are thieves.

The thieves are unfortunately too often to be taken in the direct sense, and always in the transferred sense : not the care of the poor, but the care for worldly advantages and combinations, and vanity make them judge like Judas, and do the same as he did.

	Mark ix.	
31. Ἐδίδασκε γὰρ τοὺς μαθητὰς αὐτοῦ, καὶ ἔλεγεν αὐτοῖς, Ὅτι ὁ υἱὸς τοῦ ἀνθρώπου παραδίδοται εἰς χεῖρας ἀνθρώπων, καὶ ἀποκτενοῦσιν αὐτόν· καὶ ἀποκτανθείς, τῇ τρίτῃ ἡμέρᾳ ἀναστήσεται.	31. For he taught his disciples, and said unto them, The Son of man is delivered into the hands of men, and they shall kill him; and after that he is killed, he shall rise the third day.	31. And he taught his disciples, and said to them, The son of man is delivered into the power of men, and he will be killed, and he will rise on the third day after he is killed.
32. Οἱ δὲ ἠγνόουν τὸ ῥῆμα, καὶ ἐφοβοῦντο αὐτὸν ἐπερωτῆσαι.	32. But they understood not that saying, and were afraid to ask him.	32. But they did not understand his saying, and were afraid to ask him.

Jesus tells his disciples and the people that, although his whole teaching is an announcement of the true good, which gives life to all men, one must be prepared for all earthly sufferings, in order to follow this teaching ; that the elders, priests, and learned men will not accept this teaching about the son of man and will reject him ; that the son of man, that is, all men, who will confess the consciousness of God, will have to experience many persecutions and torments. The words about the son of man rising on the third day either has this sense, that, in spite of all persecutions, the son of man cannot be destroyed and will soon rise again, or they have no sense. The first meaning must be the correct one, for immediately after this Jesus says that soon, so soon that many who were present would not yet have died, the teaching of the son of man will take possession of men, and will appear not in persecution, but in force.

But why suffer? Why should men who profess the teaching of love suffer? Is it not possible to avoid suffering, to obviate what causes suffering? Is it not possible to conceal that which will agitate and infuriate people? says Simon Peter. And Jesus angrily replies to him, Away from me, tempter! Thou thinkest of human, and not of divine things. For divine things there are no sufferings, no torments. He who wants to follow me, he who has comprehended the teaching must renounce this earthly life and must not be ashamed and afraid to show the truth before men.

Verse 31. The son of man, the consciousness of God, is given into the power of men. Men have oppressed it and will oppress it, but it will rise up again.

---

33. Πωλήσατε τὰ ὑπάρχοντα ὑμῶν, καὶ δότε ἐλεημοσύνην. ποιήσατε ἑαυτοῖς βαλάντια μὴ παλαιούμενα, θησαυρὸν ἀνέκλειπτον, ἐν τοῖς οὐρανοῖς, ὅπου κλέπτης οὐκ ἐγγίζει, οὐδὲ σὴς διαφθείρει.

12. Ἔλεγε δὲ καὶ τῷ κεκληκότι αὐτόν, Ὅταν ποιῇς ἄριστον ἢ δεῖπνον, μὴ φώνει τοὺς φίλους σου, μηδὲ τοὺς ἀδελφούς σου, μηδὲ τοὺς συγγενεῖς σου, μηδὲ γείτονας πλουσίους· μήποτε καὶ αὐτοί σε ἀντικαλέσωσι, καὶ γένηταί σοι ἀνταπόδομα.

13. Ἀλλ' ὅταν ποιῇς δοχήν, κάλει πτωχούς, ἀναπήρους, χωλούς, τυφλούς·

14. Καὶ μακάριος ἔσῃ· ὅτι οὐκ ἔχουσιν ἀνταποδοῦναί σοι· ἀνταποδοθήσεται γάρ σοι ἐν τῇ ἀναστάσει τῶν δικαίων.

Luke xii. 33. Sell that ye have, and give alms; provide yourselves bags which wax not old, a treasure in the heavens that faileth not, where no thief approacheth, neither moth corrupteth.

Luke xiv. 12. Then said he also to him that bade him, When thou makest a dinner or a supper, call not thy friends, nor thy brethren, neither thy kinsmen, nor thy rich neighbours; lest they also bid thee again, and a recompense be made thee.

13. But when thou makest a feast, call the poor, the maimed, the lame, the blind:

14. And thou shalt be blessed; for they cannot recompense thee: for thou shalt be recompensed at the resurrection of the just.

33. Sell your estates, and give alms. Provide yourselves with bags which do not grow old, an inexhaustible treasure with God, where no thief can approach and no moth can fly.

12. And if thou wishest to give a dinner or a supper, do not call thy friends, brothers, relatives, or rich neighbours, for the purpose that they may call you also and pay you back.

13. But when thou makest a feast, call the poor, the maimed, the lame, the blind:

14. And thou wilt be happy; for they cannot pay you back, but thou wilt be recompensed at the reëstablishment of the just.

Life consists in doing the will of God.

In order to do the will of God it is necessary to give up the carnal life as a food for the life of the spirit. He who does the will of God gives the carnal life for the life of the spirit. The fulfilment of the will of God is possible only by giving the carnal life as a food for the life of the spirit. In this consists the complement and the fulfilment of the worship which Jesus has given; in this lies the new divine worship, as compared with the old. Such is the difference between the law as given by Moses and the worship by deeds as given by Jesus Christ; in this does the serving of God in the spirit and with works consist.

Jesus said, In the kingdom of God will be the vagrants, the mendicants, and not the rich and mighty, because the will of God consists in fulfilling the law. But the whole law is in five rules, Not to offend, not to commit debauchery, not to swear, not to judge, not to wage war. He who fulfils this law will not be rich and mighty: he will be what men call a vagrant, a mendicant; he will give up his carnal life and will be in the power of God. To be in the kingdom of God and to fulfil the law of God, one must do so in fact, by giving the carnal life for the life of the spirit. In this consists the peculiarity of the teaching of Jesus,—in this is the revelation of the comprehension.

28. Τί δὲ ὑμῖν δοκεῖ; ἄνθρωπος εἶχε τέκνα δύο, καὶ προσελθὼν τῷ πρώτῳ εἶπε, Τέκνον, ὕπαγε, σήμερον ἐργάζου ἐν τῷ ἀμπελῶνί μου.

29. Ὁ δὲ ἀποκριθεὶς εἶπεν, Οὐ θέλω· ὕστερον δὲ μεταμεληθεὶς, ἀπῆλθε.

30. Καὶ προσελθὼν τῷ δευτέρῳ εἶπεν ὡσαύτως. ὁ δὲ ἀποκριθεὶς εἶπεν, Ἐγώ, κύριε· καὶ οὐκ ἀπῆλθε.

Matt. xxi. 28. But what think ye? A certain man had two sons; and he came to the first, and said, Son, go work to-day in my vineyard.

29. He answered and said, I will not; but afterward he repented, and went.

30. And he came to the second, and said likewise. And he answered and said, I go, sir; and went not.

28. What do you think? A man had two sons; and he came to the first, and said, Go work to-day in the garden.

29. He replied, and said, I will not; but afterward he thought it over, and went.

30. And the father came to the second, and said the same. But he said in reply, Yes, father; and he did not go.

| 31. Τίς ἐκ τῶν δύο ἐποίησε τὸ θέλημα τοῦ πατρός; Λέγουσιν αὐτῷ, Ὁ πρῶτος. | 31. Whether of them twain did the will of his father? They say unto him, the first. | 31. Which of the two did his father's will? They say to him, The first. |

This parable is only in Matthew, and is introduced into the discussion of John's meaning. Its significance is there very obscure, and it adds nothing to what has been said without the parable. However, the meaning of this parable refers to Verse 21 of Chapter VII. and to what follows, and elucidates the idea which is expressed in those verses.

| 21. Οὐ πᾶς ὁ λέγων μοι, Κύριε, Κύριε, εἰσελεύσεται εἰς τὴν βασιλείαν τῶν οὐρανῶν· ἀλλ' ὁ ποιῶν τὸ θέλημα τοῦ πατρός μου τοῦ ἐν οὐρανοῖς. | *Matt. xxi.* 21. Not every one that saith unto me, Lord, Lord, shall enter into the kingdom of heaven; but he that doeth the will of my Father which is in heaven. | 21. Not every one who says to me, Lord, Lord, will enter the kingdom of God, but he who does the will of my Father in heaven. |

TO RECEIVE THE TRUE LIFE MAN MUST RENOUNCE THE FALSE LIFE OF THE FLESH

For the life of the spirit there can be no difference between relatives and strangers. Jesus says that his mother and brothers signify nothing to him as mother and brothers: close to him are only those who do the will of the common Father.

Man's blessedness and life do not depend on his domestic relations, but on the life of the spirit. Jesus says that blessed are those who keep the comprehension of the Father. For a man living by the spirit there is no home. Animals have homes, but man lives by the spirit, and so cannot have a home. Jesus says that he has no definite place for himself. To do the will of the Father one does not need any definite place, — it is everywhere and at all times possible. Carnal death cannot be terrible to men who give themselves to the will of the Father, for the life of the spirit does not depend on the death of the flesh. Jesus says that he who believes in the life of the spirit cannot be afraid of anything. No cares can keep a man from living by the spirit. To the words of the man, that he will later fulfil the teaching of Jesus, but that first he wants to bury his father, Jesus replies, Only the dead can trouble themselves about burying the dead, but the living always live in the fulfilment of the will of the Father.

The cares about family and domestic matters cannot interfere with the life of the spirit. He who troubles himself to find out what his carnal life will profit from doing the will of the Father, is doing the same that the ploughman does, when he ploughs and looks backward, and not forward. The cares for the joys of the carnal life, which seem so important to people, are a dream. The only real work of life is the announcement of the will of the Father, the attention paid to it, and the fulfilment of it. To Martha's rebuke that she is attending herself to the supper, while her sister Mary is not helping her, but is listening to his teaching, Jesus says, Why dost thou rebuke her? Look after thy cares, if thou needest that which thy cares give thee, but let those who do not need carnal pleasures do that one thing which is necessary for life. Jesus says, He who wants to attain the true life, which consists in doing the will of the Father, must first of all renounce his personal wishes: he must not only keep from arranging his life as he wishes, but must also be prepared for all privations and sufferings. He who wants to arrange his carnal life as he wishes will lose the true life of the fulfilment of the will of the Father.

There is no advantage in acquiring for the carnal life, if this acquisition causes the life of the spirit to perish. Nothing causes the life of the spirit to perish so much as selfishness, the acquisition of wealth. Men forget that, no matter how much wealth and how much property they

may acquire, they are liable to die at any moment, and
their possessions are not needed for their life. Death
hangs over every one of us : sickness, murder, unfortunate accidents, may at any second cut our life short.
Carnal death is an inevitable condition of every second
of life. If a man lives, he must look at every hour of
his life as at an hour of grace, given to him by somebody's favour. We must remember this, and not say that
we do not know it. We know and foresee what happens
in heaven and on earth, but we forget the death which,
we know, is lying in wait for us at any second.

If we do not forget this, we cannot abandon ourselves
to the life of the flesh,—we cannot count on it. In
order to follow my teaching, a man must count up the
advantages from serving the carnal life of his will and
the advantages from doing the will of the Father. Only
he who has clearly figured that out can be my disciple.
He who has made the correct account will not be sorry
to give up the seeming good and the seeming life in
order to obtain the true good and the true life.

The true life has been given to men, and men know
and hear its call, but deprive themselves of it, as they are
distracted by momentary cares. The true life is like a
feast, which a rich man gave, when he invited the guests.
He called the guests, just as the voice of the spirit of God
calls all men to him. But some of the guests were busy
with commerce, others with their farms, and others again
with domestic matters, — and they did not come to the
feast. But the poor, who have no carnal cares, came to
the feast and were made happy. Even so men, being
distracted by the cares of the carnal life, deprive themselves of the true life. He who will not completely
renounce all cares and terrors of carnal life cannot do the
will of the Father, for it is impossible to serve oneself
a little and God a little. It is necessary to figure out
whether it is advantageous to serve one's flesh, whether

it is possible to arrange life as one wants to arrange it.
We must do the same that a man does who wants to
build a house or go to war. He will make his account,
to see whether he can finish building, or whether he will
obtain a victory. When he sees that he cannot, he does
not waste his labours, nor his army. Or else he will
waste it and will become a laughing-stock of people. If
it were possible to arrange the carnal life as one wants
to arrange it, one ought to serve his flesh; but, since it
is impossible to do so, it is better to abandon everything
carnal, and to serve the spirit, or else it will be neither
this nor that. You cannot arrange your carnal life, and
the life of the spirit you will lose, and so, to do the will
of the Father, it is necessary completely to renounce the
carnal life.

The carnal life is that seeming wealth which is
entrusted to us by others, and which we must use in such
a way as to obtain the true wealth. If a steward is
living with a rich man, and knows that, no matter how
much he may serve his master, the master will discharge
him and leave him without anything, the steward acts
wisely if, as long as he is still in charge of the wealth,
which is not his own, he will do good to people. If then
the master will abandon him, those to whom he has done
good will receive him and will feed him.

The same ought men to do with their carnal life. The
carnal life is that foreign wealth of which they are in
charge for but a short time. If they make good use of
this wealth, they will receive their own true wealth. If
we do not give up our false possessions, we shall not
receive the true possessions. It is impossible to serve
the false life of the flesh and the spirit, — one has to
serve the one or the other. One cannot serve wealth and
God. What is great before men is an abomination before
God. Before God wealth is evil. The rich man is guilty
for the very reason that he eats much and luxuriously,

while the poor starve at his door. Everybody knows that the property which thou dost not give up to others is a non-fulfilment of the will of the Father.

An Orthodox rich chief once came to Jesus, and began to boast of keeping the commandments of the law. Jesus reminded him that there was a commandment to love all men as oneself, and that in this consisted the will of the Father. The chief said that he kept also this commandment. Then Jesus told him, That is not true. If thou wantest to do the will of the Father, thou wouldst not have any possessions. It is impossible for thee to do the will of the Father, if thou hast any property which thou hast not distributed to others. And Jesus said to the disciples, People think that it is impossible to live without possessions, but I tell you, The true life consists in giving to others what belongs to one.

A man named Zaccheus heard the teaching of Christ and believed him. He invited him to his house, and said to him, I give half of my possessions to the pocr, and I will give fourfold to whomsoever I have offended. And Jesus said, Here is a man who does the will of the Father, for there is not any one position in which a man does the will of God, but our whole life is its fulfilment, and this man fulfils it.

The will of the Father is that all men should return to it.

The good cannot be measured: it cannot be said who has done more, who less. The widow who gives away her last mite gives more than the rich man who gives away thousands. Nor can the good be measured by its being useful or useless. As an example of how the good ought to be done may serve the woman who pitied Jesus and senselessly poured three hundred pence' worth of oil on his feet. Judas said that she acted foolishly, that with that money the poor could have been fed. But Judas was a thief: he lied and, speaking of the carnal profit, was not thinking of the poor. What is needed is not profit, not quantity, but the doing of the will of the Father: to love and to live for others.

One day Jesus' mother and brothers came to him, and could not see him, for there was a great multitude about him. And a man, seeing them, went up to Jesus and said:

Thy family, thy mother and thy brothers, are standing outside: they want to see thee.

My mother and brothers are those who understand the will of the Father and do it.

And a woman said, Blessed is the womb that bore thee, and the teats which thou hast sucked. To this Jesus said, Blessed are always those who have comprehended the comprehension of the Father, and who keep it.

And a man said to Jesus, I will follow thee, wherever thou mayest go. And Jesus said to him, There is no place for thee to go to, for I have no home, no place, where I live. Only animals have lairs and dens, but man is spirit, and he is everywhere at home, if he lives by the spirit.

One day Jesus was sailing in a ship with his disciples. He said, Let us sail to the other side.

A storm rose on the sea and began to drench them, and they were almost drowned. But he was lying at the stern, and sleeping. They awakened him, and said, Teacher, does it not make any difference to thee that we are drowning? And when the storm subsided, he said, Why are you so timid, and have no faith in the life of the spirit?

Jesus said to a man, Follow me. And the man said, My old father has died. Let me first bury him, and then I will follow thee. And Jesus said to him, Let the dead bury the dead: and if thou wishest to be alive, do the will of the Father and proclaim it.

And another man said, I will be thy disciple, and will

do the will of the Father, as thou commandest, but allow me first to arrange matters at home. And Jesus said to him, If a ploughman looks back, he cannot plough. No matter how much you may look back, you cannot plough. A man must forget everything but the furrow which he is making, and then only will he be able to plough. If thou discussest what it will profit the life of the flesh, thou hast not comprehended the real life, and thou canst not live by it.

After this it once happened that Jesus and his disciples entered a village. And a woman named Martha invited them to her house.

And Martha had a sister Mary, and she sat down at the feet of Jesus and listened to his teaching. And Martha was trying to give them a good entertainment. And Martha went up to Jesus, and said, Thou dost not even care that my sister has left me alone to serve. Tell her to work with me.

And Jesus replied to her, Martha, Martha, thou carest and troublest thyself about many things, but there is only one thing necessary, and Mary has chosen the one thing which she needs and which no one will take from her. For life nothing but the food of the spirit is needed.

And Jesus said to all, He who wants to follow me must renounce his will and must be prepared at all times for all privations and for all sufferings of the flesh, and then only can he follow me.

For he who wants to care for his carnal life will lose the true life. But he who loses the carnal life, doing the will of the Father, will save the true life; for what profit is it to a man if he has the whole world, and loses or injures his life?

And hearing this, a man said, It is well, if there is a life of the spirit; but how if we give up everything, and there is not that life?

To this Jesus said, You know that the doing of the

will of the Father gives life to all; but you are drawn away from this life by false cares, and you reject it. You do like this: a man prepared a dinner, and sent out the servants to call the guests, but the guests excused themselves.

One said, I have bought a piece of land, and I must go and see it. Another said, I have bought some oxen, and I must go and try them. The third said, I have married, and I am going to have a wedding.

And the servants came, and told their master that no one was coming. Then the master sent the servants out to call in the beggars. The beggars did not excuse themselves, but came. And when they came, there was still room left.

And the master sent the servants to invite more men, saying, Go and tell them all to come to my dinner. Let there be as many as possible at the dinner; but those who have refused on the ground of being busy will miss it.

Everybody knows that the doing of the will of God gives life, but they do not come, because they are distracted by the deception of wealth.

And Jesus said, Beware of riches, for thy life does not depend on having more than others have.

There was a rich man, and he had a good harvest of corn. And he said to himself, I will build new barns, I will make them large, and will gather all my wealth in them. And I will say to my soul, Here, soul, is everything in abundance for thee: eat, drink, and live for thy pleasure.

And God said to him, Fool! This very night will thy soul be taken, and everything which thou hast gathered will be left for others. Thus is done to all who prepare for the carnal life, and do not live in God.

And Jesus said to them, You say that Pilate killed the Galileans. Were these Galileans worse than other men, that this has happened with them? Not at all. We are all such men, and all of us will perish in the same way, if we do not find salvation from death. And those eighteen men who were killed by the tower, when it fell in, were they some special men, worse than the rest of the inhabitants of Jerusalem? Not at all. If we do not save ourselves from death, we shall die in the same way, if not one day, then another.

If we have not yet perished like them, we ought to think in this manner: a man has an apple-tree growing in his garden. The master comes into the garden to look at the tree, and sees that it has no fruit on it. So the master says to the gardener, I have been coming here these three years, and the apple-tree is still barren. It has to be cut down, for it wastes the ground. And the gardener says, Let us wait awhile, master. I will dig it round, and will put manure all about it, and we shall see whether it will give fruit next summer. If it does not, we shall cut it down then.

Even so we are a barren apple-tree, as long as we live in the flesh and do not bear the fruit of the life of the spirit. Only through somebody's favour are we left until the next summer. If we do not bear fruit, we shall perish like the one who built the barns, like the Galileans, like the eighteen men killed by the tower, and like all who do not bear fruit, dying an everlasting death.

In order to understand this, no wisdom is needed, for anybody can see it. Not only in domestic matters, but in everything which is going on in the world we are able to reflect and guess in advance. If the wind is from the west, we say, It is going to rain, and so it happens. How is this? The weather we can predict, and yet we cannot foresee that we shall all die and perish, and that the only salvation for us is the life of the spirit, the doing of its will.

And a great multitude went with Jesus, and he once

more said to all, He who wants to be my disciple must esteem little his father, mother, wife, children, brothers, sisters, and all his property, and must at all times be prepared for everything. Only he who does what I am doing follows my teaching, and only that man will be saved from death.

For each man will figure out, before he begins anything, whether what he is doing is profitable, and if it is, he will do it; and if not, he gives it up. Every man who builds a house first sits down and figures out how much money he needs, how much he has, and whether he will have enough with which to finish building it, lest he begin and do not finish it, and men laugh at him.

Even so he who wants to live the carnal life must first figure out whether he can finish what he has begun.

Every king, who wants to wage war, first considers whether he can go with ten thousand against twenty thousand. If he figures out that he cannot, he will send messengers to make peace, and will give up the idea of fighting. So let each man, before giving himself up to the carnal life, consider whether he can wage war against death, or whether death is stronger than he. And if it is, let him make peace with it in advance.

Thus every one of you must first settle with what he considers to be his own, his family, his money, his possessions, and when he figures out what advantage he will derive from them, and understands that there is none, he will be able to be my disciple, and not before.

The kingdom of heaven does not come in an external manner. Of the kingdom of heaven, which saves from death, we cannot say that it has come, or that it will come; that it is here, or there; it is within you, in your souls.

For, if the time comes and you want to find salvation in life and you look for it in a certain time, you will not find it. And if they will tell you, Salvation is here, salvation is there, do not look for it anywhere, but within yourselves, for salvation is sudden, like lightning, and everywhere; there is no time and space for it, — it is in your souls.

And as salvation was for Noah and for Lot, so it is always for the son of man. Life remains the same for all men: all eat and drink and get married, but some perish, and others are saved.

There was an evil judge, who feared neither God nor man, and a poor widow begged him; but the judge did not decide in her favour. The widow begged the judge day and night. The unjust judge said, What shall I do? I will decide as the widow wishes, for she gives me no rest.

You must understand that even the unjust judge did what the widow asked him to do. How, then, will the Father refuse to do what men ask him for day and night without cessation?

But besides the Father there is the son of man who is seeking the truth, and we cannot fail to believe in him.

He who will give up the false, temporal wealth for the true life according to the will of the Father will do the same as did the wise steward.

A man was a steward of a rich master; he saw that his master would discharge him, and that he would be left without bread and without a home.

And the steward said to himself, This is what I will do: I will quietly distribute the master's goods to the peasants and will cut down their debts; then, if the master sends me away, the peasants will remember the good I have done to them, and will not abandon me.

And so the steward did. He called up the peasants, those who were in debt to the master, and rewrote their bills. Instead of one hundred he wrote fifty, and instead of sixty he wrote twenty, and so he did to all.

And the master heard of it, and said to himself, Indeed, he has done wisely, for else he would have to go a-begging. He has caused me a loss, but he has calculated well, for in the carnal life we all understand how to calculate correctly, but in the life of the spirit we do not wish to comprehend.

Even so we must do with the unjust wealth: we must give it away in order to receive the life of the spirit. If we shall regret giving up such trifles as wealth for the life of the spirit, it will not be given to us. If we do not give up the false wealth, our own life will not be given to us. It is impossible to serve at once two masters, God and wealth,— the will of God and our own will. Either the one, or the other.

When the Orthodox heard that, they laughed at Jesus, for they love wealth.

And he said to them, You think that because men respect you for your riches, you are really respected. No, God does not look without, but within, into the heart. What is high before men is insignificant before God. The kingdom of God is now on earth, and great are they who enter into it; but it is not the rich, but the poor, who enter. That has always been so according to your law, and according to Moses and the prophets. Hear what the rich and the poor are according to your faith.

There was a rich man. He dressed himself in costly garments and made merry every day. And there was a vagrant named Lazarus, who was scurfy. And Lazarus came into the yard of the rich man, thinking that he might get the remnants from the rich man's table, but he did not get even those; for the rich man's dogs ate the remnants clean and even licked the wounds of Lazarus.

And both Lazarus and the rich man died. In hell the rich man saw Abraham a long way off, and Lazarus the scurfy was sitting with him.

The rich man said, Father Abraham, Lazarus the scurfy

is sitting with thee: he used to wallow at the gate of my house. I dare not trouble thee. Send Lazarus the scurfy to me: let him dip his finger in water and refresh my throat, for I am burning in fire. But Abraham said, Why should I send Lazarus to thee, in hell? Thou hadst everything thou wantedst in the other world, while Lazarus saw nothing but sorrow there. It is time for him to have pleasure now. Even if he wanted to do it for thee, he cannot, for between you and us there is a great gulf, and it is impossible to cross it. We are living, but you are dead.

Then the rich man said, Father Abraham, at least send Lazarus the scurfy to my house: I have five brothers, and I am sorry for them: let him tell them how dangerous wealth is, or else they will have to suffer torment themselves. But Abraham said, They know, as it is, that wealth is dangerous, for Moses and all the prophets have told them that.

But the rich man said, Still it would be better if one risen from the dead came to them, for that would bring them to their senses. And Abraham said, If they do not listen to Moses and the prophets, they will not listen to one risen from the dead.

All know that we should divide with our brother and do good to men, and the whole law of Moses and all the prophets say nothing else. You know it, but do not wish to do it, because you love wealth.

And a rich Orthodox chief went up to Jesus, and said to him, Thou art a good teacher! Tell me what I must do that I may receive eternal life.

Jesus said, Why dost thou call me good? Good is only the Father. If thou wishest to receive life, do the commandments.

The chief said, There are many commandments; which must I keep? Jesus said, Do not kill, do not commit debauchery, do not steal, do not lie, and also honour thy Father and do his will, and love thy neighbour as thyself.

And the Orthodox chief said, All these commandments I have been keeping from childhood; but I ask what else I must do according to thy teaching.

Jesus looked at him, at his rich garments, and he smiled and said, Thou lackest one little thing: thou hast not fulfilled what thou sayest. If thou wishest to do these commandments, Do not kill, do not commit debauchery, do not steal, do not lie, and, above all, the commandment, Love thy neighbour as thyself, go and sell thy estate and give it to the poor, and then thou wilt do the will of the Father.

When the chief heard this, he frowned and went away, for he was sorry to part from his possessions.

And Jesus said to his disciples, You see that it is absolutely impossible to be rich and do the will of the Father.

The disciples were frightened at these words. But Jesus repeated, and said, Yes, children, he who has wealth cannot be in the will of God. Much easier it is for a camel to pass through the eye of a needle than for a rich man to do the will of the Father.

And they were frightened more than before, and said, If so, it is impossible to save one's life.

And he said, To a man it seems impossible to save one's life without possessions, but God will save a man without possessions.

One day Jesus happened to pass through the town of Jericho. In this city there was a rich farmer of taxes named Zaccheus. This Zaccheus had heard of Jesus' teaching and believed in it. When he heard that Jesus was in Jericho, he wanted to see him. There were so many people all about him, that it was not possible to make one's way through them.

Then he ran forward and climbed a tree, that he might see Jesus as he passed by.

And indeed, as Jesus went by, he saw Zaccheus, and, having learned that Zaccheus believed in his teaching, he said, Climb down from the tree and go home, and I will go to thy house. Zaccheus climbed down, ran home, and prepared a reception for Jesus.

The people began to judge and to say about Jesus, He has gone into the house of a tax-collector, a rascal.

In the meantime Zaccheus said to Jesus, Sir, this is what I will do: I will give half of my possessions to the poor, and from the rest I will pay all whom I have injured.

And Jesus said, Now thou art saved. Thou wert dead, and art alive; thou wert lost, and hast found thyself, for thou hast done like Abraham, when he wished to sacrifice his son, in order to show his faith. For the whole life of man consists in finding and saving what is perishing in one's soul.

It is impossible to measure a sacrifice by its size. One day Jesus and his disciples happened to sit opposite a money-box. Men were placing what they had into the box for God. And rich men walked up to the box, and placed a great deal in it. And then a poor widow came up and placed two mites in it.

And Jesus pointed to her, and said to his disciples, You saw the poor widow put in two mites: she has put in more than the rest, for the others put in what they did not need for life, while she put in everything she had, her whole life.

Jesus happened to be in the house of Simon the leper. And a woman entered the house. This woman had a pitcher with precious oil worth three hundred pence.

Jesus said to his disciples that his death was near. When the woman heard this, she took pity on Jesus, and wanted to show him her love and anoint his head with oil. And she forgot everything, how much her oil cost, and broke the pitcher, and anointed his head and feet, and spilled all the oil.

And the disciples began to judge her, saying that she had done badly. And Judas, the one who later betrayed Jesus, said, How much has been wasted!

The oil could have been sold for three hundred pence, and so many poor might have profited by it. And the disciples began to rebuke the woman, and she was troubled and did not know whether she had done right or wrong.

Then Jesus said to them, In vain do you trouble the woman, for she has truly done well. Why do you mention the poor? If you wish to do good to the poor, do it: they are always present, so there is no need of speaking of them. If you pity the poor, go and pity them and do good to them. She has pitied me and has done me a real good, for she has given me everything which she had. Who of you can tell what is needed, and what not? How do you know that it was not necessary to pour the oil over me? She has at least poured oil over me, so as to prepare my body for burial, and so it is necessary. She has truly done the will of the Father: she forgot herself and pitied another; she forgot the carnal calculation and gave away everything which she had.

CPSIA information can be obtained at www.ICGtesting.com
Printed in the USA
LVOW051844281011

252554LV00017B/198/P

9 781142 179168